THE MAHABI

THE MAHABHARATA

Volume 5
(Sections 60 to 66)

Translated by
BIBEK DEBROY

PENGUIN BOOKS

An imprint of Penguin Random House

PENGUIN BOOKS

USA | Canada | UK | Ireland | Australia
New Zealand | India | South Africa | China

Penguin Books is part of the Penguin Random House group of companies
whose addresses can be found at global.penguinrandomhouse.com

Published by Penguin Random House India Pvt. Ltd.
4th Floor, Capital Tower 1, MG Road,
Gurugram 122 002, Haryana, India

First published by Penguin Books India 2012
This edition published 2015

Translation copyright © Bibek Debroy 2012

10 9 8 7 6 5 4 3 2

ISBN 9780143425182

Typeset in Sabon by Eleven Arts, New Delhi
Printed at Replika Press Pvt. Ltd, India

www.penguin.co.in

For my wife, Suparna Banerjee (Debroy),
who has walked this path of dharma with me

Ardha bhāryā manuṣyasya bhāryā śreṣṭhatamaḥ sakhā
Bhāryā mulam trivargasya bhāryā mitram mariṣyataḥ
Mahabharata (1/68/40)

Nāsti bhāryāsamo bandhurnāsti bhāryasamā gatiḥ
Nāsti bhāryasamo loke sahāyo dharmasādhanaḥ
Mahabharata (12/142/10)

Contents

FAMILY TREE
Bharata/Puru Lineage

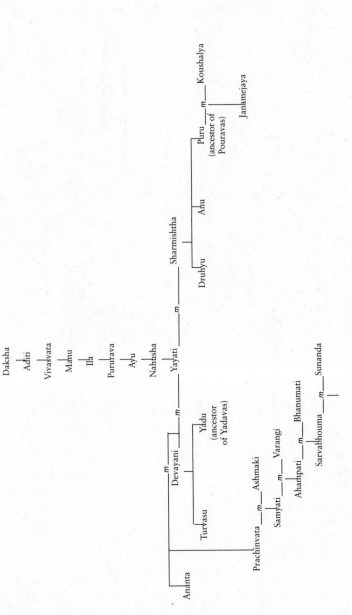

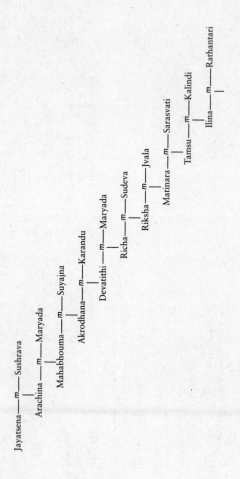

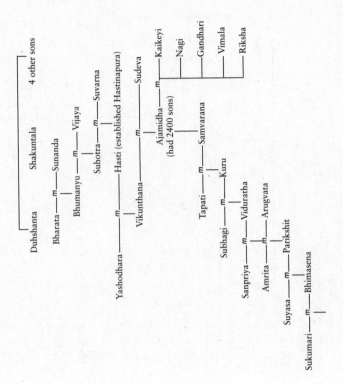

Duhshanta — Shakuntala — 4 other sons

Bharata — *m* — Sunanda

Bhumanyu — *m* — Vijaya

Suhotra — *m* — Suvarna

Hasti (established Hastinapura)

Yashodhara — *m* — Vikunthana

Sudeva

Ajamidha — *m* — Kaikeyi
(had 2400 sons)

Nagi

Gandhari

Vimala

Riksha

Samvarana

Tapati — *m* — Kuru

Subhagi — *m* — Viduratha

Sanpriya — *m* — Aruvyata

Amrita — *m* — Parikshit

Suyasa — *m* — Bhimasena

Sukumari — *m*

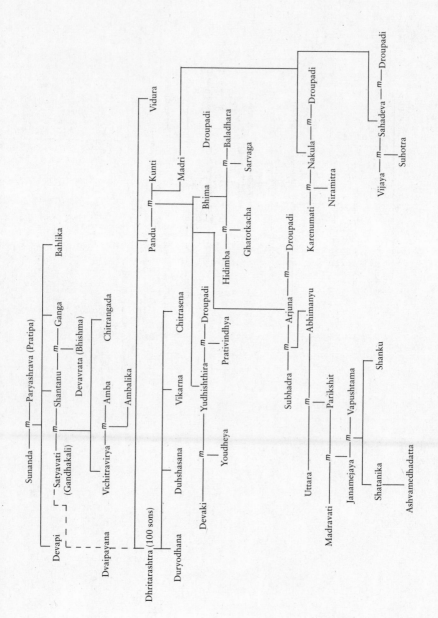

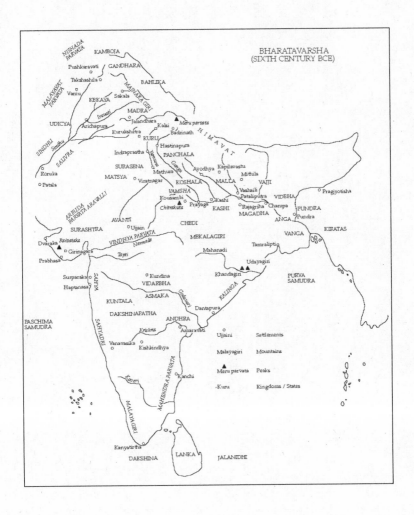

BHARATAVARSHA
(SIXTH CENTURY BCE)

Acknowledgements

Carving time out from one's regular schedule and work engagements to embark on such a mammoth work of translation has been difficult. It has been a journey of six years, ten volumes and something like 2.25 million words. Sometimes, I wish I had been born in nineteenth-century Bengal, with a benefactor funding me for doing nothing but this. But alas, the days of gentlemen of leisure are long over. The time could not be carved out from professional engagements, barring of course assorted television channels, who must have wondered why I have been so reluctant to head for their studios in the evenings. It was ascribed to health, interpreted as adverse health. It was certainly health, but not in an adverse sense. Reading the Mahabharata is good for one's mental health and is an activity to be recommended, without any statutory warnings. When I embarked on the hazardous journey, a friend, an author interested in Sanskrit and the Mahabharata, sent me an email. She asked me to be careful, since the track record of those who embarked on unabridged translations of the Mahabharata hasn't always been desirable. Thankfully, I survived, to finish telling the tale.

The time was stolen in the evenings and over weekends. The cost was therefore borne by one's immediate family, and to a lesser extent by friends. Socializing was reduced, since every dinner meant one less chapter done. The family has first claim on the debt, though I am sure it also has claim on whatever merits are due. At least my wife, Suparna Banerjee (Debroy) does, and these volumes are therefore dedicated to her. For six long years, she has walked this path of dharma along with me, providing the conducive home cum family environment that made undistracted work possible. I suspect Sirius has no claim on the merits, though he has been remarkably patient at the times when he has been curled up near my feet and I have been translating away. There is some allegory there about a dog keeping company when the Mahabharata is being read and translated.

Most people have thought I was mad, even if they never quite said that. Among those who believed and thought it was worthwhile, beyond immediate family, are M. Veerappa Moily, Pratap Bhanu Mehta and Laveesh Bhandari. And my sons, Nihshanka and Vidroha. The various reviewers of different volumes have also been extremely kind and many readers have communicated kind words through email and Twitter, enquiring about progress.

Penguin also believed. My initial hesitation about being able to deliver was brushed aside by R. Sivapriya, who pushed me after the series had been commissioned by V. Karthika. And then Sumitra Srinivasan became the editor, followed by Paloma Dutta. The enthusiasm of these ladies was so infectious that everything just snowballed and Paloma ensured that the final product of the volumes was much more readable than what I had initially produced.

When I first embarked on what was also a personal voyage of sorts, the end was never in sight and seemed to stretch to infinity. There were moments of self-doubt and frustration. Now that it is all done, it leaves a vacuum, a hole. That's not simply because you haven't figured out what the new project is. It is also because characters who have been part of your life for several years are dead and gone. I don't mean the ones who died in the course of the actual war, but the others. Most of them faced rather tragic and unenviable ends. Along that personal voyage, the Mahabharata changes you, or so my wife tells me. I am no longer the person I was when I started it, as an individual. That sounds cryptic, deliberately so. Anyone who reads the Mahabharata carefully is bound to change, discount the temporary and place a premium on the permanent.

To all those who have been part of that journey, including the readers, thank you.

The original ten volumes were published sequentially, as they were completed, between 2010 and 2014.

Introduction

The Hindu tradition has an amazingly large corpus of religious texts, spanning Vedas, Vedanta (*brahmanas*,[1] *aranyakas*,[2] Upanishads,), Vedangas,[3] *smritis*, Puranas, dharmashastras and *itihasa*. For most of these texts, especially if one excludes classical Sanskrit literature, we don't quite know when they were composed and by whom, not that one is looking for single authors. Some of the minor Puranas (Upa Purana) are of later vintage. For instance, the Bhavishya Purana (which is often listed as a major Purana or Maha Purana) mentions Queen Victoria.

In the listing of the corpus above figures itihasa, translated into English as history. History doesn't entirely capture the nuance of itihasa, which is better translated as 'this is indeed what happened'. Itihasa isn't myth or fiction. It is a chronicle of what happened; it is fact. Or so runs the belief. And itihasa consists of India's two major epics, the Ramayana and the Mahabharata. The former is believed to have been composed as poetry and the latter as prose. This isn't quite correct. The Ramayana has segments in prose and the Mahabharata has segments in poetry. Itihasa doesn't quite belong to the category of religious texts in a way that the Vedas and Vedanta are religious. However, the dividing line between what is religious and what is not is fuzzy. After all, itihasa is also about attaining the objectives of *dharma*,[4]

---

[1] Brahmana is a text and also the word used for the highest caste.

[2] A class of religious and philosophical texts that are composed in the forest, or are meant to be studied when one retires to the forest.

[3] The six Vedangas are *shiksha* (articulation and pronunciation), *chhanda* (prosody), *vyakarana* (grammar), *nirukta* (etymology), *jyotisha* (astronomy) and *kalpa* (rituals).

[4] Religion, duty.

artha,[5] *kama*[6] and *moksha*[7] and the Mahabharata includes Hinduism's most important spiritual text—the Bhagavad Gita.

The epics are not part of the *shruti* tradition. That tradition is like revelation, without any composer. The epics are part of the *smriti* tradition. At the time they were composed, there was no question of texts being written down. They were recited, heard, memorized and passed down through the generations. But the smriti tradition had composers. The Ramayana was composed by Valmiki, regarded as the first poet or *kavi*. The word kavi has a secondary meaning as poet or rhymer. The primary meaning of kavi is someone who is wise.

And in that sense, the composer of the Mahabharata was no less wise. This was Vedavyasa or Vyasadeva. He was so named because he classified (*vyasa*) the Vedas. Vedavyasa or Vyasadeva isn't a proper name. It is a title. Once in a while, in accordance with the needs of the era, the Vedas need to be classified. Each such person obtains the title and there have been twenty-eight Vyasadevas so far.

At one level, the question about who composed the Mahabharata is pointless. According to popular belief and according to what the Mahabharata itself states, it was composed by Krishna Dvaipayana Vedavyasa (Vyasadeva). But the text was not composed and cast in stone at a single point in time. Multiple authors kept adding layers and embellishing it. Sections just kept getting added and it is no one's suggestion that Krishna Dvaipayana Vedavyasa composed the text of the Mahabharata as it stands today.

Consequently, the Mahabharata is far more unstructured than the Ramayana. The major sections of the Ramayana are known as *kanda*s and one meaning of the word kanda is the stem or trunk of a tree, suggesting solidity. The major sections of the Mahabharata are known as *parva*s and while one meaning of the word parva is limb or member or joint, in its nuance there is greater fluidity in the word parva than in kanda.

The Vyasadeva we are concerned with had a proper name of Krishna

---

[5] Wealth. But in general, any object of the senses.
[6] Desire.
[7] Release from the cycle of rebirth.

Dvaipayana. He was born on an island (*dvipa*). That explains the
Dvaipayana part of the name. He was dark. That explains the Krishna
part of the name. (It wasn't only the incarnation of Vishnu who
had the name of Krishna.) Krishna Dvaipayana Vedavyasa was also
related to the protagonists of the Mahabharata story. To go back
to the origins, the Ramayana is about the solar dynasty, while the
Mahabharata is about the lunar dynasty. As is to be expected, the
lunar dynasty begins with Soma (the moon) and goes down through
Pururava (who married the famous apsara Urvashi), Nahusha and
Yayati. Yayati became old, but wasn't ready to give up the pleasures
of life. He asked his sons to temporarily loan him their youth. All
but one refused. The ones who refused were cursed that they would
never be kings, and this includes the Yadavas (descended from Yadu).
The one who agreed was Puru and the lunar dynasty continued
through him. Puru's son Duhshanta was made famous by Kalidasa
in the Duhshanta–Shakuntala story and their son was Bharata,
contributing to the name of Bharatavarsha. Bharata's grandson was
Kuru. We often tend to think of the Kouravas as the evil protagonists
in the Mahabharata story and the Pandavas as the good protagonists.
Since Kuru was a common ancestor, the appellation Kourava applies
equally to Yudhishthira and his brothers and Duryodhana and
his brothers. Kuru's grandson was Shantanu. Through Satyavati,
Shantanu fathered Chitrangada and Vichitravirya. However, the
sage Parashara had already fathered Krishna Dvaipayana through
Satyavati. And Shantanu had already fathered Bhishma through
Ganga. Dhritarasthra and Pandu were fathered on Vichitravirya's
wives by Krishna Dvaipayana.

The story of the epic is also about these antecedents and
consequents. The core Mahabharata story is known to every Indian
and is normally understood as a dispute between the Kouravas
(descended from Dhritarashtra) and the Pandavas (descended from
Pandu). However, this is a distilled version, which really begins
with Shantanu. The non-distilled version takes us to the roots of the
genealogical tree and at several points along this tree we confront a
problem with impotence/sterility/death, resulting in offspring through
a surrogate father. Such sons were accepted in that day and age. Nor

was this a lunar dynasty problem alone. In the Ramayana, Dasharatha of the solar dynasty also had an infertility problem, corrected through a sacrifice. To return to the genealogical tree, the Pandavas won the Kurukshetra war. However, their five sons through Droupadi were killed. So was Bhima's son Ghatotkacha, fathered on Hidimba. As was Arjuna's son Abhimanyu, fathered on Subhadra. Abhimanyu's son Parikshit inherited the throne in Hastinapura, but was killed by a serpent. Parikshit's son was Janamejaya.

Krishna Dvaipayana Vedavyasa's powers of composition were remarkable. Having classified the Vedas, he composed the Mahabharata in 100,000 shlokas or couplets. Today's Mahabharata text doesn't have that many shlokas, even if the Hari Vamsha (regarded as the epilogue to the Mahabharata) is included. One reaches around 90,000 shlokas. That too, is a gigantic number. (The Mahabharata is almost four times the size of the Ramayana and is longer than any other epic anywhere in the world.) For a count of 90,000 Sanskrit shlokas, we are talking about something in the neighbourhood of two million words. The text of the Mahabharata tells us that Krishna Dvaipayana finished this composition in three years. This doesn't necessarily mean that he composed 90,000 shlokas. The text also tells us that there are three versions to the Mahabharata. The original version was called Jaya and had 8,800 shlokas. This was expanded to 24,000 shlokas and called Bharata. Finally, it was expanded to 90,000 (or 100,000) shlokas and called Mahabharata.

Krishna Dvaipayana didn't rest even after that. He composed the eighteen Maha Puranas, adding another 400,000 shlokas. Having composed the Mahabharata, he taught it to his disciple Vaishampayana. When Parikshit was killed by a serpent, Janamejaya organized a snake-sacrifice to destroy the serpents. With all the sages assembled there, Vaishampayana turned up and the assembled sages wanted to know the story of the Mahabharata, as composed by Krishna Dvaipayana. Janamejaya also wanted to know why Parikshit had been killed by the serpent. That's the background against which the epic is recited. However, there is another round of recounting too. Much later, the sages assembled for a sacrifice in Naimisharanya and asked Lomaharshana (alternatively, Romaharshana) to recite what he had heard at Janamejaya's snake-sacrifice. Lomaharshana was a *suta*, the sutas being charioteers and bards or raconteurs. As the son of a suta, Lomaharshana is also referred to as Souti. But Souti or Lomaharshana aren't quite his proper names. His proper name is Ugrashrava. Souti refers to his birth. He owes the name Lomaharshana to the fact that the body-hair (*loma* or *roma*) stood up (*harshana*) on hearing his tales. Within the text therefore, two people are telling the tale. Sometimes it is Vaishampayana and sometimes it is Lomaharshana. Incidentally, the stories of the Puranas are recounted by Lomaharshana, without Vaishampayana intruding. Having composed the Puranas, Krishna Dvaipayana taught them to his disciple Lomaharshana. For what it is worth, there are scholars who have used statistical tests to try and identify the multiple authors of the Mahabharata.

As we are certain there were multiple authors rather than a single one, the question of when the Mahabharata was composed is somewhat pointless. It wasn't composed on a single date. It was composed over a span of more than 1000 years, perhaps between 800 BCE and 400 ACE. It is impossible to be more accurate than that. There is a difference between dating the composition and dating the incidents, such as the date of the Kurukshetra war. Dating the incidents is both subjective and controversial and irrelevant for the purposes of this translation. A timeline of 1000 years isn't short. But even then, the size of the corpus is nothing short of amazing.

* * *

Familiarity with Sanskrit is dying out. The first decades of the twenty-first century are quite unlike the first decades of the twentieth. Lamentation over what is inevitable serves no purpose. English is increasingly becoming the global language, courtesy colonies (North America, South Asia, East Asia, Australia, New Zealand, Africa) rather than the former colonizer. If familiarity with the corpus is not to die out, it needs to be accessible in English.

There are many different versions or recensions of the Mahabharata. However, between 1919 and 1966, the Bhandarkar Oriental Research Institute (BORI) in Pune produced what has come to be known as the critical edition. This is an authenticated text produced by a board of scholars and seeks to eliminate later interpolations, unifying the text across the various regional versions. This is the text followed in this translation. One should also mention that the critical edition's text is not invariably smooth. Sometimes, the transition from one shloka to another is abrupt, because the intervening shloka has been weeded out. With the intervening shloka included, a non-critical version of the text sometimes makes better sense. On a few occasions, I have had the temerity to point this out in the notes which I have included in my translation. On a slightly different note, the quality of the text in something like Dana Dharma Parva is clearly inferior. It couldn't have been 'composed' by the same person.

It took a long time for this critical edition to be put together. The exercise began in 1919. Without the Hari Vamsha, the complete critical edition became available in 1966. And with the Hari Vamsha, the complete critical edition became available in 1970. Before this, there were regional variations in the text and the main versions were available from Bengal, Bombay and the south. However, now, one should stick to the critical edition, though there are occasional instances where there are reasons for dissatisfaction with what the scholars of the Bhandarkar Oriental Research Institute have accomplished. But in all fairness, there are two published versions of the critical edition. The first one has the bare bones of the critical edition's text. The second has all the regional versions collated, with copious notes. The former is for the ordinary reader, assuming he/she knows Sanskrit. And the latter is for the scholar. Consequently, some popular beliefs no longer find a place in the critical edition's text. For example, it is believed that Vedavyasa dictated the text to Ganesha, who wrote it down. But Ganesha had a condition before accepting. Vedavyasa would have to dictate continuously, without stopping. Vedavyasa threw in a counter-condition. Ganesha would have to understand each couplet before he wrote it down. To flummox Ganesha and give himself time to think, Vedavyasa threw in some cryptic verses. This attractive anecdote has been excised from the critical edition's text. Barring material that is completely religious (specific hymns or the Bhagavad Gita), the Sanskrit text is reasonably easy to understand. Oddly, I have had the most difficulty with things that Vidura has sometimes said, other than parts of Anushasana Parva. Arya has today come to connote ethnicity. Originally, it meant language. That is, those who spoke Sanskrit were Aryas. Those who did not speak Sanskrit were mlecchas. Vidura is supposed to have been skilled in the mlechha language. Is that the reason why some of Vidura's statements seem obscure? In similar vein, in popular renderings, when Droupadi is being disrobed, she prays to Krishna. Krishna provides the never-ending stream of garments that stump Duhshasana. The critical edition has excised the prayer to Krishna. The never-ending stream of garments is given as an extraordinary event. However, there is no intervention from Krishna.

How is the Mahabharata classified? The core component is the couplet or shloka. Several such shlokas form a chapter or *adhyaya*. Several adhyayas form a parva. Most people probably think that the Mahabharata has eighteen parvas. This is true, but there is another 100-parva classification that is indicated in the text itself. That is, the adhyayas can be classified either according to eighteen parvas or according to 100 parvas. The table (given on pp. xxiii–xxvi), based on the critical edition, should make this clear. As the table shows, the present critical edition only has ninety-eight parvas of the 100-parva classification, though the 100 parvas are named in the text.

Eighteen-parva classification	100-parva classification	Number of adhyayas	Number of shlokas
(1) Adi	1) Anukramanika[8]	1	210
	2) Parvasamgraha	1	243
	3) Poushya	1	195
	4) Pouloma	9	153
	5) Astika	41	1025
	6) Adi-vamshavatarana	5	257
	7) Sambhava	65	2394
	8) Jatugriha-daha	15	373
	9) Hidimba-vadha	6	169
	10) Baka-vadha	8	206
	11) Chaitraratha	21	557
	12) Droupadi-svayamvara	12	263
	13) Vaivahika	6	155

[8] Anukramanika is sometimes called anukramani.

Eighteen-parva classification	100-parva classification	Number of adhyayas	Number of shlokas
	14) Viduragamana	7	174
	15) Rajya-labha	1	50
	16) Arjuna-vanavasa	11	298
	17) Subhadra-harana	2	57
	18) Harana harika	1	82
	19) Khandava-daha	12	344
		Total = 225	Total = 7205
(2) Sabha	20) Sabha	11	429
	21) Mantra	6	222
	22) Jarasandha-vadha	5	195
	23) Digvijaya	7	191
	24) Rajasuya	3	97
	25) Arghabhiharana	4	99
	26) Shishupala-vadha	6	191
	27) Dyuta	23	734
	28) Anudyuta	7	232
		Total = 72	Total = 2387
(3) Aranyaka	29) Aranyaka	11	327
	30) Kirmira-vadha	1	75
	31) Kairata	30	1158
	32) Indralokabhigamana	37	1175
	33) Tirtha-yatra	74	2293
	34) Jatasura-vadha	1	61
	35) Yaksha-yuddha	18	727
	36) Ajagara	6	201
	37) Markandeya-samasya	43	1694
	38) Droupadi-Satyabhama-sambada	3	88
	39) Ghosha-yatra	19	519
	40) Mriga-svapna-bhaya	1	16
	41) Vrihi-drounika	3	117
	42) Droupadi-harana	36	1247
	43) Kundala-harana	11	294
	44) Araneya	5	191
		Total = 299	Total = 10239
(4) Virata	45) Vairata	12	282
	46) Kichaka-vadha	11	353
	47) Go-grahana	39	1009
	48) Vaivahika	5	179

Eighteen-parva classification	100-parva classification	Number of adhyayas	Number of shlokas
		Total = 67	Total = 1736
(5) Udyoga	49) Udyoga	21	575
	50) Sanjaya-yana	11	311
	51) Prajagara	9	541
	52) Sanatsujata	4	121
	53) Yana-sandhi	24	726
	54) Bhagavat-yana	65	2055
	55) Karna-upanivada	14	351
	56) Abhiniryana	4	169
	57) Bhishma-abhishechana	4	122
	58) Uluka-yana	4	101
	59) Ratha-atiratha-samkhya	9	231
	60) Amba-upakhyana	28	755
		Total = 197	Total = 6001
(6) Bhishma	61) Jambukhanda-vinirmana	11	378
	62) Bhumi	2	87
	63) Bhagavad Gita	27	994
	64) Bhishma vadha	77	3947
		Total = 117	Total = 5381
(7) Drona	65) Dronabhisheka	15	634
	66) Samshaptaka-vadha	16	717
	67) Abhimanyu-vadha	20	643
	68) Pratijna	9	365
	69) Jayadratha-vadha	61	2914
	70) Ghatotkacha-vadha	33	1642
	71) Drona-vadha	11	692
	72) Narayanastra-moksha	8	538
		Total = 173	Total = 8069
(8) Karna	73) Karna-vadha	69	3870
(9) Shalya	74) Shalya-vadha	16	844
	75) Hrada pravesha	12	664
	76) Tirtha yatra	25	1261
	77) Gada yuddha	11	546
		Total = 64	Total = 3315
(10) Souptika	78) Souptika	9	515
	79) Aishika	9	257
		Total = 18	Total = 771

Eighteen-parva classification	100-parva classification	Number of adhyayas	Number of shlokas
(11) Stri	80) Vishoka	8	194
	81) Stri	17	468
	82) Shraddha	1	44
	83) Jala-pradanika	1	24
		Total = 27	Total = 713
(12) Shanti	84) Raja-dharma	128	4509
	85) Apad-dharma	39	1560
	86) Moksha Dharma	186	6935
		Total = 353	Total = 13006
(13) Anushasana	87) Dana Dharma	152	6450
	88) Bhishma-svargarohana	2	84
		Total = 154	T otal = 6493
(14) Ashva-medhika	89) Ashvamedhika	96	2743
(15) Ashra-mavasika	90) Ashrama-vasa	35	737
	91) Putra Darshana	9	234
	92) Naradagamana	3	91
		Total = 47	Total = 1061
(16) Mousala	93) Mousala	9	273
(17) Mahapra-sthanika	94) Maha-Prasthanika	3	106
(18) Svargarohana	95) Svargarohana	5	194
Hari Vamsha	96) Hari-vamsha	45	2442
	97) Vishnu	68	3426
	98) Bhavishya	5	205
		Total = 118	Total = 6073
Grand total = 19	Grand total = 98 (95 + 3)	Grand total = 2113 (1995 + 118)	Grand total = 79,860 (73787 + 6073)

Thus, interpreted in terms of BORI's critical edition, the Mahabharata no longer possesses the 100,000 shlokas it is supposed to have. The figure is a little short of 75,000 (73,787 to be precise). Should the Hari Vamsha be included in a translation of the Mahabharata? It doesn't quite belong. Yet, it is described as a *khila* or supplement to the Mahabharata and BORI includes it as part of the critical edition, though in a separate volume. In this case also, the translation of the Hari Vamsha will be published in a separate and independent volume. With the Hari Vamsha, the number of shlokas increases to a shade less than 80,000 (79,860 to be precise). However, in some of the regional versions the text of the Mahabharata proper is closer to 85,000 shlokas and with the Hari Vamsha included, one approaches 95,000, though one doesn't quite touch 100,000.

Why should there be another translation of the Mahabharata? Surely, it must have been translated innumerable times. Contrary to popular impression, unabridged translations of the Mahabharata in English are extremely rare. One should not confuse abridged translations with unabridged versions. There are only five unabridged translations—by Kisori Mohan Ganguly (1883–96), by Manmatha Nath Dutt (1895–1905), by the University of Chicago and J.A.B. van Buitenen (1973 onwards), by P. Lal and Writers Workshop (2005 onwards) and the Clay Sanskrit Library edition (2005 onwards). Of these, P. Lal is more a poetic trans-creation than a translation. The Clay Sanskrit Library edition is not based on the critical edition, deliberately so. In the days of Ganguly and Dutt, the critical edition didn't exist. The language in these two versions is now archaic and there are some shlokas that these two translators decided not to include, believing them to be untranslatable in that day and age. Almost three decades later, the Chicago version is still not complete, and the Clay edition, not being translated in sequence, is still in progress. However, the primary reason for venturing into yet another translation is not just the vacuum that exists, but also reason for dissatisfaction with other attempts. Stated more explicitly, this translation, I believe, is better and more authentic—but I leave it to the reader to be the final judge. (While translating 80,000 shlokas is a hazardous venture, since Ganguly and Dutt were Bengalis, and P. Lal was one for many purposes, though not by birth, surely a fourth Bengali must also be pre-eminently qualified to embark on this venture!)

A few comments on the translation are now in order. First, there is the vexed question of diacritical marks—should they be used or not? Diacritical marks make the translation and pronunciation

more accurate, but often put readers off. Sacrificing academic
purity, there is thus a conscious decision to avoid diacritical marks.
Second, since diacritical marks are not being used, Sanskrit words
and proper names are written in what seems to be phonetically
natural and the closest—such as, Droupadi rather than Draupadi.
There are rare instances where avoidance of diacritical marks can
cause minor confusion, for example, between Krishna (Krishnaa)
as in Droupadi[8] and Krishna as in Vaasudeva. However, such
instances are extremely rare and the context should make these
differences, which are mostly of the gender kind, clear. Third, there
are some words that simply cannot be translated. One such word is
dharma. More accurately, such words are translated the first time
they occur. But on subsequent occasions, they are romanized in the
text. Fourth, the translation sticks to the Sanskrit text as closely as
possible. If the text uses the word Kounteya, this translation will
leave it as Kounteya or Kunti's son and not attempt to replace it
with Arjuna. Instead, there will be a note explaining that in that
specific context Kounteya refers to Arjuna or, somewhat more
rarely, Yudhishthira or Bhima. This is also the case in the structure
of the English sentences. To cite an instance, if a metaphor occurs
towards the beginning of the Sanskrit shloka, the English sentence
attempts to retain it at the beginning too. Had this not been done,
the English might have read smoother. But to the extent there is
a trade-off, one has stuck to what is most accurate, rather than
attempting to make the English smooth and less stilted.

As the table shows, the parvas (in the eighteen-parva classification)
vary widely in length. The gigantic Aranyaka or Shanti Parva can be
contrasted with the slim Mousala Parva. Breaking up the translation
into separate volumes based on this eighteen-parva classification
therefore doesn't work. The volumes will not be remotely similar in
size. Most translators seem to keep a target of ten to twelve volumes
when translating all the parvas. Assuming ten volumes, 10 per cent
means roughly 200 chapters and 7000 shlokas. This works rather
well for Adi Parva, but collapses thereafter. Most translators therefore
have Adi Parva as the first volume and then handle the heterogeneity

[9] Krishna or Krishnaa is another name for Droupadi.

across the eighteen parvas in subsequent volumes. This translation approaches the break-up of volumes somewhat differently, in the sense that roughly 10 per cent of the text is covered in each volume. The complete text, as explained earlier, is roughly 200 chapters and 7,000 shlokas per volume. For example, then, this first volume has been cut off at 199 chapters and a little less than 6,500 shlokas. It includes 90 per cent of Adi Parva, but not all of it and covers the first fifteen parvas of the 100- (or 98-) parva classification.

* * *

The Mahabharata is one of the greatest stories ever told. It has plots and subplots and meanderings and digressions. It is much more than the core story of a war between the Kouravas and the Pandavas, which everyone is familiar with, the culmination of which was the battle in Kurukshetra. In the Adi Parva, there is a lot more which happens before the Kouravas and the Pandavas actually arrive on the scene. In the 100-parva classification, the Kouravas and the Pandavas don't arrive on the scene until Section 6.

From the Vedas and Vedanta literature, we know that Janamejaya and Parikshit were historical persons. From Patanjali's grammar and other contemporary texts, we know that the Mahabharata text existed by around 400 BCE. This need not of course be the final text of Mahabharata, but could have been the original text of Jaya. The Hindu eras or *yuga*s are four in number—Satya (or Krita) Yuga, Treta Yuga, Dvapara Yuga and Kali Yuga. This cycle then repeats itself, with another Satya Yuga following Kali Yuga. The events of the Ramayana occurred in Treta Yuga. The events of the Mahabharata occurred in Dvapara Yuga. This is in line with Rama being Vishnu's seventh incarnation and Krishna being the eighth. (The ninth is Buddha and the tenth is Kalki.) We are now in Kali Yuga. Kali Yuga didn't begin with the Kurukshetra war. It began with Krishna's death, an event that occurred thirty-six years after the Kurukshetra war. Astronomical data do exist in the epic. These can be used to date the Kurukshetra war, or the advent of Kali Yuga. However, if the text was composed at different points in time, with additions and interpolations, internal consistency in astronomical data is unlikely. In popular belief, following two alternative astronomers, the Kurukshetra war has been dated to 3102 BCE (following Aryabhatta) and 2449 BCE (following Varahamihira). This doesn't mesh with the timelines of Indian history. Mahapadma Nanda ascended the throne in 382 BCE, a historical fact on which there is no dispute. The Puranas have genealogical lists. Some of these state that 1050 years elapsed between Parikshit's birth and Mahapadma Nanda's ascension. Others state that 1015 years elapsed. (When numerals are written in words, it is easy to confuse 15 with 50.) This takes Parikshit's birth and the Kurukshetra war to around 1400 BCE. This is probably the best we can do, since we also know that the Kuru kingdom flourished between 1200 BCE and 800 BCE. To keep the record straight, archaeological material has been used to bring forward the date of the Kurukshetra war to around 900 BCE, the period of the Iron Age.

As was mentioned, in popular belief, the incidents of the Ramayana took place before the incidents of the Mahabharata. The Ramayana story also figures in the Mahabharata. However, there is no reference to any significant Mahabharata detail in the Ramayana. Nevertheless, from reading the text, one gets the sense that the Mahabharata represents a more primitive society than the Ramayana. The fighting in the Ramayana is more genteel and civilized. You don't have people hurling rocks and stones at each other, or fighting with trees and bare arms. Nor do people rip apart the enemy's chest and drink blood. The geographical knowledge in the Mahabharata is also more limited than in the Ramayana, both towards the east and towards the south. In popular belief, the Kurukshetra war occurred as a result of a dispute over land and the kingdom. That is true, in so far as the present text is concerned. However, another fight over cattle took place in the Virata Parva and the Pandavas were victorious in that too. This is not the place to expand on the argument. But it is possible to construct a plausible hypothesis that this was the core dispute. Everything else was added as later embellishments. The property dispute was over cattle and not land. In human evolution, cattle represents a more primitive form of property than land. In that stage, humankind is still partly nomadic and not completely settled. If this hypothesis is true, the Mahabharata again represents an earlier period compared to the Ramayana. This leads to the following kind of proposition. In its final form, the Mahabharata was indeed composed after the Ramayana. But the earliest version of the Mahabharata was composed before the earliest version of the Ramayana. And the events of the Mahabharata occurred before the events of the Ramayana, despite popular belief. The proposition about the feud ending with Virata Parva illustrates the endless speculation that is possible with the Mahabharata material. Did Arjuna, Nakula and Sahadeva ever exist? Nakula and Sahadeva have limited roles to play in the story. Arjuna's induction could have been an attempt to assert Indra's supremacy. Arjuna represents such an integral strand in the story (and of the Bhagavad Gita), that such a suggestion is likely to be dismissed out of hand. But consider the following. Droupadi loved Arjuna a little bit more than the others. That's the reason she was denied admission to heaven. Throughout the text, there are innumerable instances where Droupadi faces difficulties. Does she ever summon Arjuna for help on such occasions? No, she does not. She summons Bhima. Therefore, did Arjuna exist at all? Or were there simply two original Pandava brothers—one powerful and strong, and the other weak and useless in physical terms. Incidentally, the eighteen-parva classification is clearly something that was done much later. The 100-parva classification seems to be older.

The Mahabharata is much more real than the Ramayana. And, therefore, much more fascinating. Every conceivable human emotion figures in it, which is the reason why it is possible to identify with it even today. The text itself states that what is not found in the Mahabharata, will not be found anywhere else. Unlike the Ramayana, India is littered with real places that have identifications with the Mahabharata. (Ayodhya or Lanka or Chitrakuta are identifications that are less certain.) Kurukshetra, Hastinapura, Indraprastha, Karnal, Mathura, Dvaraka, Gurgaon, Girivraja are real places: the list is endless. In all kinds of unlikely places, one comes across temples erected by the Pandavas when they were exiled to the forest. In some of these places, archaeological excavations have substantiated the stories. The war for regional supremacy in the Ganga–Yamuna belt is also a plausible one. The Vrishnis and the

Shurasenas (the Yadavas) are isolated, they have no clear alliance (before the Pandavas) with the powerful Kurus. There is the powerful Magadha kingdom under Jarasandha and Jarasandha had made life difficult for the Yadavas. He chased them away from Mathura to Dvaraka. Shishupala of the Chedi kingdom doesn't like Krishna and the Yadavas either. Through Kunti, Krishna has a matrimonial alliance with the Pandavas. Through Subhadra, the Yadavas have another matrimonial alliance with the Pandavas. Through another matrimonial alliance, the Pandavas obtain Drupada of Panchala as an ally. In the course of the royal sacrifice, Shishupala and Jarasandha are eliminated. Finally, there is yet another matrimonial alliance with Virata of the Matsya kingdom, through Abhimanyu. When the two sides face each other on the field of battle, they are more than evenly matched. Other than the Yadavas, the Pandavas have Panchala, Kashi, Magadha, Matsya and Chedi on their side. The Kouravas have Pragjyotisha, Anga, Kekaya, Sindhu, Avanti, Gandhara, Shalva, Bahlika and Kamboja as allies. At the end of the war, all these kings are slain and the entire geographical expanse comes under the control of the Pandavas and the Yadavas. Only Kripacharya, Ashvatthama and Kritavarma survive on the Kourava side.

Reading the Mahabharata, one forms the impression that it is based on some real incidents. That does not mean that a war on the scale that is described took place. Or that miraculous weapons and chariots were the norm. But there is such a lot of trivia, unconnected with the main story, that their inclusion seems to serve no purpose unless they were true depictions. For instance, what does the physical description of Kripa's sister and Drona's wife, Kripi, have to do with the main story? It is also more real than the Ramayana because nothing, especially the treatment of human emotions and behaviour, exists in black and white. Everything is in shades of grey. The Uttara Kanda of the Ramayana is believed to have been a later interpolation. If one excludes the Uttara Kanda, we generally know what is good. We know who is good. We know what is bad. We know who is bad. This is never the case with the Mahabharata. However, a qualification is necessary. Most of us are aware of the Mahabharata story because we have read some version or the other, typically an abridged one. Every abridged version simplifies and condenses, distills out the core story. And in doing that, it tends to paint things in black and white, fitting everything into the mould of good and bad. The Kouravas are bad. The Pandavas are good. And good eventually triumphs. The unabridged Mahabharata is anything but that. It is much more nuanced. Duryodhana isn't invariably bad. He is referred to as Suyodhana as well, and not just by his father. History is always written from the point of view of the victors. While the Mahabharata is generally laudatory towards the Pandavas, there are several places where the text has a pro-Kourava stance. There are several places where the text has an anti-Krishna stance. That's yet another reason why one should read an unabridged version, so as not to miss out on these nuances. Take the simple point about inheritance of the kingdom. Dhritarashtra was blind. Consequently, the king was Pandu. On Pandu's death, who should inherit the kingdom? Yudhishthira was the eldest among the brothers. (Actually, Karna was, though it didn't become known until later.) We thus tend to assume that the kingdom was Yudhishthira's by right, because he was the eldest. (The division of the kingdom into two, Hastinapura and Indraprastha, is a separate matter.) But such primogeniture was not universally clear. A case can also be established for Duryodhana, because he was Dhritarashtra's son. If primogeniture was the rule, the eldest son of the Pandavas was Ghatotkacha, not Abhimanyu. Before both were killed, Ghatotkacha should have had a claim to the throne. However, there is no such suggestion anywhere. The argument that Ghatotkacha was the son of a rakshasa or demon will not wash. He never exhibited any demonic qualities and was a dutiful and loving son. Karna saved up a weapon for Arjuna and this was eventually used to kill Ghatotkacha. At that time, we have the unseemly sight of Krishna dancing around in glee at Ghatotkacha being killed.

In the Mahabharata, because it is nuanced, we never quite know what is good and what is bad, who is good and who is bad. Yes, there are degrees along a continuum. But there are no watertight and neat compartments. The four objectives of human existence are dharma, artha, kama and moksha. Etymologically, dharma is that which upholds. If one goes by the Bhagavad Gita, pursuit of these four are also transient diversions. Because the fundamental objective is to transcend these four, even moksha. Within these four, the Mahabharata is about a conflict of dharma. Dharma has been reduced to *varnashrama* dharma, according to the four classes (*varna*s) and four stages of life (*ashrama*s). However, these are collective interpretations of dharma, in the sense that a Kshatriya in the *garhasthya* (householder) stage has certain duties. Dharma in the Mahabharata is individual too. Given an identical situation, a Kshatriya in the garhasthya stage might adopt a course of action that is different from that adopted by another Kshatriya in the garhasthya stage, and who is to judge what is wrong and what is right? Bhishma adopted a life of celibacy. So did Arjuna, for a limited period. In that stage of celibacy, both were approached by women who had fallen in love with them. And if those desires were not satisfied, the respective women would face difficulties, even death. Bhishma spurned the advance, but Arjuna accepted it. The conflict over dharma is not only the law versus morality conflict made famous by Krishna and Arjuna in the Bhagavad Gita. It pervades the Mahabharata, in terms of a conflict over two different notions of dharma. Having collectively married Droupadi, the Pandavas have agreed that when one of them is closeted with Droupadi, the other four will not intrude. And if there is such an instance of intrusion, they will go into self-exile. Along comes a Brahmana whose cattle have been stolen by thieves. Arjuna's weapons are in the room where Droupadi and Yudhishthira are. Which is the higher dharma? Providing succour to the Brahmana or adhering to the oath? Throughout the Mahabharata, we have such conflicts, with no clear normative indications of what is wrong and what is right, because there are indeed no absolute answers. Depending on one's decisions, one faces the consequences and this brings in the unsolvable riddle of the tension between free will and determinism, the so-called karma concept. The boundaries of philosophy and religion blur.

These conflicts over dharma are easy to identify with. It is easy to empathize with the protagonists, because we face such conflicts every day. That is precisely the reason why the Mahabharata is read even today. And the reason one says every conceivable human emotion figures in the story. Everyone familiar with the Mahabharata has thought about the decisions taken and about the characters. Why was life so unfair to Karna? Why was Krishna partial to the Pandavas? Why didn't he prevent the war? Why was Abhimanyu killed so unfairly? Why did the spirited and dark Droupadi, so unlike the Sita of the Ramayana, have to be humiliated publicly?

* * *

It is impossible to pinpoint when and how my interest in the Mahabharata started. As a mere toddler, my maternal grandmother used to tell me stories from *Chandi*, part of the Markandeya Purana. I still vividly recollect pictures from her copy of *Chandi*: Kali licking the demon Raktavija's blood. Much later, in my early teens, at school in Ramakrishna Mission, Narendrapur, I first read the Bhagavad Gita, without understanding much of what I read. The alliteration and poetry in the first chapter was attractive enough for me to learn it by heart. Perhaps the seeds were sown there. In my late teens, I stumbled upon Bankimchandra Chattopadhyay's *Krishna Charitra*, written in 1886. Bankimchandra was not only a famous novelist, he was a brilliant essayist. For a long time, *Krishna Charitra* was not available other than in Bengali. It has now been translated into English, but deserves better dissemination. A little later, when in college, I encountered Buddhadeb Bose's *Mahabharater Katha*. That was another brilliant collection of essays, first serialized in a magazine and then published as a book in 1974. This too was originally in Bengali, but is now available in English. Unlike my sons, my first exposure to the Mahabharata story came not through television serials but comic books. Upendrakishore Raychowdhury's Mahabharata (and Ramayana) for children was staple diet, later supplanted by Rajshekhar Basu's abridged versions of both epics, written for adults. Both were in Bengali. In English, there was Chakravarti Rajagopalachari's abridged translation, still a perennial favourite. Later, Chakravarthi Narasimhan's selective unabridged translation gave a flavour of what the Mahabharata actually contained. In Bengal, the Kashiram Das version of the Mahabharata, written in the seventeenth century, was quite popular. I never found this appealing. But in the late 1970s, I stumbled upon a treasure. Kolkata's famous College Street was a storehouse of old and second-hand books in those days. You never knew what you would discover when browsing. In the nineteenth century, an unabridged translation of the Mahabharata had been done in Bengali under the editorship of Kaliprasanna Singha (1840–70). I picked this up for the princely sum of Rs 5. The year may have been 1979, but Rs 5 was still amazing. This was my first complete reading of the unabridged version of the Mahabharata. This particular copy probably had antiquarian value. The pages would crumble in my hands and I soon replaced my treasured possession with a republished reprint. Not longer after, I acquired the Aryashastra version of the Mahabharata, with both the Sanskrit and the Bengali together. In the early 1980s, I was also exposed to three Marathi writers writing on the Mahabharata. There was Iravati Karve's *Yuganta*. This was available in both English and in Marathi. I read the English one first, followed by the Marathi. The English version isn't an exact translation of the Marathi and the Marathi version is far superior. Then there was Durga Bhagwat's *Vyas Parva*. This was in Marathi and I am not aware of an English translation. Finally, there was Shivaji Sawant's *Mritunjaya*, a kind of autobiography for Karna. This was available both in English and in Marathi. Incidentally, one should mention John Smith's excellent abridged translation, based on the Critical Edition, and published while this unabridged translation was going on.

In the early 1980s, quite by chance, I encountered two shlokas, one from Valmiki's Ramayana, the other from Kalidasa's *Meghadutam*. These were two poets separated by anything between 500 to 1,000 years, the exact period being an uncertain one. The shloka in *Meghadutam* is right towards the beginning, the second shloka to be precise. It is the first day in the month of Ashada. The yaksha has been cursed and has been separated from his beloved. The mountains are covered with clouds. These clouds are like elephants, bent down as if in play. The shloka in the Valmiki Ramayana occurs in Sundara Kanda. Rama now knows that Sita is in Lanka. But the monsoon stands in the way of the invasion. The clouds are streaked with flags of lightning and garlanded with geese. They are like mountain peaks and are thundering, like elephants fighting. At that time, I did not know that elephants were a standard metaphor for clouds in Sanskrit literature. I found it amazing that two different poets separated by time had thought of elephants. And because the yaksha was pining for his beloved, the elephants were playing. But because Rama was impatient to fight, the elephants were fighting. I resolved that I must read all this in the original. It was a resolution I have never regretted. I think that anyone who has not read *Meghadutam* in Sanskrit has missed out on a thing of beauty that will continue to be a joy for generations to come.

In the early 1980s, Professor Ashok Rudra was a professor of economics in Visva-Bharati, Santiniketan. I used to teach in Presidency College, Kolkata, and we sometimes met. Professor Rudra was a left-wing economist and didn't think much of my economics. I dare say the feeling was reciprocated. By tacit agreement, we never discussed economics. Instead, we discussed Indological subjects. At that point, Professor Rudra used to write essays on such subjects in Bengali. I casually remarked, 'I want to do a statistical test on the frequency with which the five Pandavas used various weapons in the Kurukshetra war.' Most sensible men would have dismissed the thought as crazy. But Professor Rudra wasn't sensible by usual norms of behaviour and he was also a trained statistician. He encouraged me to do the paper, written and published in Bengali, using the Aryashastra edition. Several similar papers followed, written in Bengali. In 1983, I moved to Pune, to the Gokhale Institute of Politics and Economics, a stone's throw away from BORI. *Annals of the Bhandarkar Oriental Research Institute (ABORI)* is one of the most respected journals in Indology. Professor G.B. Palsule was then the editor of ABORI and later went on to become Director of BORI. I translated one of the Bengali essays into English and went and met Professor Palsule, hoping to get it published in ABORI. To Professor Palsule's eternal credit, he didn't throw the dilettante out. Instead, he said he would get the paper refereed. The referee's substantive criticism was that the paper should have been based on the critical edition, which is how I came to know about it. Eventually, this paper (and a few more) were published in ABORI. In 1989, these became a book titled *Essays on the Ramayana and the Mahabharata*, published when the Mahabharata frenzy had reached a peak on television. The book got excellent reviews, but hardly sold. It is now out of print. As an aside, the book was jointly dedicated to Professor Rudra and Professor Palsule, a famous economist and a famous Indologist respectively. Both were flattered. However, when I gave him a copy, Professor Rudra said, 'Thank you very much. But who is Professor Palsule?' And Professor Palsule remarked, 'Thank you very much. But who is Professor Rudra?'

While the research interest in the Mahabharata remained, I got sidetracked into translating. Through the 1990s, there were abridged translations of the Maha Puranas, the Vedas and the eleven major Upanishads. I found that I enjoyed translating from the Sanskrit to English and since these volumes were well received, perhaps I did do a good job. With Penguin as publisher, I did a translation of the Bhagavad Gita, something I had always wanted to do. *Sarama and Her Children*, a book on attitudes towards dogs in India, also with Penguin, followed. I kept thinking about doing an unabridged translation of the Mahabharata and waited to muster up the courage. That courage now exists, though the task is daunting. With something like two million words and ten volumes expected, the exercise seems open-ended. But why translate the Mahabharata? In 1924, George Mallory, with his fellow climber Andrew Irvine, may or may not have climbed Mount Everest. They were last seen a few hundred metres from the summit, before they died. Mallory was once asked why he wanted to climb Everest and he answered, 'Because it's there.' Taken out of context, there is no better reason for wanting to translate the Mahabharata. There is a steep mountain to climb. And I would not have dared had I not been able to stand on the shoulders of the three intellectual giants who have preceded me—Kisori Mohan Ganguli, Manmatha Nath Dutt and J.A.B. van Buitenen.

Bibek Debroy

SECTION SIXTY
Amba-Upakhyana Parva

This parva has 755 shlokas and twenty-eight chapters.

Upakhyana *is a short tale or episode and this section is so named because it has the short account of Amba, who was reborn as Shikhandi. This section ends Udyoga Parva and everything is set for the war.*

Chapter 833(170)

'Duryodhana asked, "O foremost among the Bharata lineage! When you see Shikhandi in the field of battle, with arrows raised and ready to slay you, what is the reason for you not to kill him? O mighty-armed one! You said earlier that you would kill the Panchalas and the Somakas. O Gangeya! O grandfather! Tell me the reason for this."[1]

'Bhishma replied, "O Duryodhana! Together with the lords of the earth, listen to the reason why I will not kill Shikhandi when I see him in the field of battle. My father, King Shantanu, was a bull among the Bharata lineage and had dharma in his soul. O bull among men! In course of time, he met his destiny. O foremost among the Bharata lineage! I then fulfilled my promise. I consecrated my brother Chitrangada as the great king. When he died, abiding by the instructions of Satyavati and in accordance with the decreed rites, I instated Vichitravirya as the king. O Indra among kings! Though he was young, he was consecrated by me in accordance with dharma. Vichitravirya had dharma in his soul and glanced towards me for everything. O son![2] I desired to obtain brides for him and reflected on those who would be equal in beauty and lineage. O mighty-armed one! At that time, I heard that the three daughters of the king of Kashi would be given away in a *svayamvara*.[3] All of them were unrivalled in beauty and their names were Amba, Ambika and Ambalika. O bull among the Bharata lineage! All the kings of the earth had been summoned there. O Indra among kings! Amba was the eldest and Ambika was the one in the middle, while Ambalika was the youngest princess. On a single chariot, I went to the capital of the lord of Kashi. O mighty-armed one! O lord of the earth! I saw the three ornamented maidens there and the kings, the lords of the earth, who had assembled there. Established in battle, I challenged

---

[1]Shikhandi also belongs to the lineage of the Panchalas.

[2]The word used is *tata*. This means son, but is affectionately used towards anyone who is younger or junior.

[3]Ceremony where a lady chooses her own husband from assembled suitors.

all those kings. O bull among the Bharata lineage! I raised those maidens onto my chariot. Knowing that they were being offered as *viryashulka*,[4] I raised them onto my chariot and told all the lords of the earth who had assembled there, 'Bhishma, Shantanu's son, is taking these maidens away by force.' I repeated the challenge. 'O kings! Use the limits of your strength to set them free. O lords of men! I am forcibly abducting them, in front of your eyes.' At this, all those lords of the earth arose, with weapons upraised. Enraged, they instructed their charioteers to yoke the chariots. Some were on chariots that were like the clouds. Others were on elephants and were warriors who fought on elephants. Other lords of the earth were on the backs of horses. They arose, with weapons upraised. O lord of the earth! Those lords of the earth surrounded me from all directions. With a great mass of chariots, they attacked me from all sides. I repulsed them with a great shower of arrows. I vanquished all those kings, like the king of the gods against the *danava*s. I brought down their colourful and gold-embellished standards. With a single arrow each, I brought them down on the ground. O bull among men! I laughed and used my flaming arrows to bring down their horses, elephants and chariots in that battle. On seeing the dexterity of my palms, they were shattered and retreated. After vanquishing those lords of the earth, I returned to Hastinapura. O descendant of the Bharata lineage! O mighty-armed one! I recounted my deed to Satyavati and handed over the maidens for my brother.'"

Chapter 834(171)

'Bhisma said, "O best of the Bharata lineage! I approached my mother, the mother of brave ones and saluting her, told the

---

[4]However, viryashulka is not the same as a svayamvara. Svayamvara is a ceremony where the maiden herself (*svayam*) chooses her husband (*vara*) from assembled suitors. Viryashulka is when the maiden is offered to the suitor who shows the most valour (*virya*), *shulka* meaning price.

daughter of the Dasha lineage,[5] 'I have vanquished the kings and have
obtained these daughters of the lord of Kashi for Vichitravirya. I have
abducted them in accordance with the norms of viryashulka.' O king!
She inhaled the fragrance of my head. With her eyes filled with tears,
Satyavati told me, 'O son! It is through good fortune that you have
obtained victory.' With Satyavati's permission, a date was fixed for
the marriage. The eldest daughter of the lord of Kashi spoke these
bashful words. 'O Bhishma! You are knowledgeable about dharma
and you are skilled in all the sacred texts. You should listen to my
words and then act towards me in accordance with dharma. In my
mind, I had earlier chosen the lord of Shalva as my groom. Without
this being known to my father, he had also chosen me in secret. I
desire someone else. O king! O Bhishma! Especially because you are
a Kourava, how can you, who have studied the sacred texts, make
someone like that live in this household? O bull among the Bharata
lineage! Now that you know this, make up your mind about what
should be done. O mighty-armed one! You should do that which
is appropriate. O lord of the earth! It is evident that King Shalva
is waiting for me. O mighty-armed one! O supreme among those
who uphold dharma! You should take pity on me. O brave one! We
have heard that you are famous in this world for being truthful to
your vows.'"

Chapter 835(172)

'Bhishma said, "O lord of men! I then informed Kali[6] Satyavati,
the advisers, the brahmanas and the priests and allowed the
eldest maiden, Amba, to leave. On obtaining the permission, the
maiden went to the capital of the lord of Shalva. She was protected
by aged brahmanas and accompanied by her nurse. Travelling the

[5]*Dasha* is a slave or a servant and is a term used for shudras. However, dasha
is also used for fishermen and Satyavati was the daughter of a fisherman.
[6]Because she was dark, Satyavati was also known as Kali.

entire distance, she went to that lord of men and told King Shalva
these words. 'O mighty-armed one! O immensely radiant one! I have
arrived here, before you.' O lord of the earth! But the lord of Shalva
smiled and told her, 'O one with the beautiful complexion! You have
belonged to another one before this and I do not wish you as my wife.
O fortunate one! Therefore, return again to the descendant of the
Bharata lineage! After you have been forcibly abducted by Bhishma,
I do not desire you. You were won by Bhishma and seemed to be
delighted then. He defeated all the lords of the earth in a great battle.
O one with the beautiful complexion! You have gone to another one
before. I am a king who is instructed by dharma and am skilled in
knowledge. How can I accept as my wife a lady who has gone to
someone else before? O fortunate one! Go wherever you wish. Do
not waste your time here.' O king! Amba was struck by the arrows
of the god of love and told him, 'O lord of the earth! Do not speak
in this fashion. I wasn't happy when I was abducted by Bhishma, the
destroyer of enemies. After driving away the lords of the earth, he
used force on me and I was weeping. O lord of Shalva! I love you.
Love me back in return. I am an innocent maiden. Dharma does not
approve of the abandoning of those who love you. I have come here
after obtaining the permission of Gangeya, who never retreats from
the field of battle. I have obtained his permission and have come here
before you. O lord of the earth! The mighty-armed Bhishma does
not want me. I have heard that all Bhishma's exertions were for the
sake of his brother. O king! Gangeya has given my sisters, Ambika
and Ambalika, whom he had also abducted, to his younger brother
Vichitravirya. O lord of Shalva! I have never desired any man other
than you. O tiger among men! I swear on my head that I have not
thought of anyone but you. O Indra among kings! I have come before
you and I have not gone to any other man earlier. O Shalva! I am
telling you the truth. I swear on my own self that this is the truth.
O one with the large eyes! Love me. A maiden has come to you of
her own accord. I have not been to any other man earlier. O Indra
among kings! I desire your favours.' O foremost among the Bharata
lineage! But though she spoke in this way, Shalva abandoned the
daughter of the king of Kashi, the way a snake discards its old skin.

She sought his favours with these and many other words. O bull
among the Bharata lineage! But the king who was the lord of Shalva
did not show her his favours. Then the eldest daughter of the king
of Kashi was overcome by anger. With tears in her eyes and with her
voice choking with tears, she said, 'O lord of the earth! Having been
discarded by you, I will go wherever I wish. I will go to the virtuous.
It has been rightly said that where there is virtue, there is truth.' O
Kouravya! The maiden spoke in this way and lamented piteously.
But the lord of Shalva abandoned her and Shalva repeatedly said,
'O one with the beautiful hips. Go. Go from here. I am frightened
of Bhishma. You are Bhishma's property.' She was thus addressed
by Shalva, who was not far-sighted. She departed wretchedly from
the city, weeping like a female osprey.'"

Chapter 836(173)

'Bhishma said, "O descendant of the Bharata lineage! As she
departed from the city, she thought to herself. 'There is no
young woman on earth who faces such a difficult situation as me.
I have been separated from my relatives. I have been treated badly
by Shalva. I am incapable of returning to the city of Varanasahrya.[7]
Bhishma granted me permission because I wished to go to Shalva.
Will I blame myself or the unassailable Bhishma? Or should it be
my foolish father who arranged for the svayamvara? Is it my own
fault that I did not jump down from Bhishma's chariot? When that
terrible war raged on earlier, should I have descended and run away to
Shalva? The consequences are that I have to endure the fruits of this
conduct, like a foolish person. Shame on Bhishma. Shame on my evil
father, whose intelligence is foolish. He offered me as viryashulka, as
if I am a woman who can be offered at a price. Shame on me. Shame

[7] Varana means elephant and Varanasahrya is another name for Hastinapura.

on King Shalva. Shame on the creator. It is because of everyone's
bad sentiments that I now confront this calamity. In every way, a
man must endure what destiny has determined. But Shantanu's son,
Bhishma, is the chief reason for my hardship. I see that I now have
to exact vengeance on Bhishma, through austerities and fighting. It
is my view that he is the reason behind my misery. But which lord
of the earth is capable of withstanding Bhishma in battle?' Having
reflected in this way, she left the city.

'"She went to the hermitages of great-souled ascetics who were
sacred in their conduct. Surrounded by those ascetics, she spent
a night there. O mighty-armed one! O descendant of the Bharata
lineage! The one with the sweet smiles told them everything about
herself and the details of what had happened, the abduction, the
release and the abandonment by Shalva. A great brahmana named
Shaikhavatya lived there. He was rigid in his vows and aged in
his austerities. He was a preceptor in the sacred texts and in the
*aranyaka*s.[8] Shaikhavatya, the great ascetic and sage, spoke to the
distressed maiden, who was sighing and was overcome by grief
and misery. 'O fortunate one! Now that this has happened, what
can ascetics do for you? We are immensely fortunate ones who live
in hermitages. We are great souls engaged in austerities.' O king!
But she told him, 'Show me a favour. I wish to wander around and
perform extremely difficult austerities. Because of my stupidity, I
must have performed deeds in earlier bodies. I have must acted in
evil ways and this must certainly be the fruit. O ascetics! I am not
interested in returning to my relatives. I have been rejected. I am
unhappy. I have been wronged by Shalva. O ascetics! O those who
are devoid of sin! I wish to be instructed here. You are the equals
of the gods. Be compassionate towards me.' He then consoled the
maiden with examples, sacred knowledge and reasons. Together
with the other brahmanas, he comforted her and promised that he
would act accordingly.'"

[8]The aranyakas are specific sacred texts, composed in the forest (*aranya*)
and meant to be studied there.

Chapter 837(174)

'Bhishma said, "Then all the ascetics engaged themselves in their respective tasks. The ones who followed dharma wondered about the maiden and thought, 'What will we do?' A few among those ascetics said, 'We should take her back to her father's residence.' Others thought that I[9] should be censured. Some others thought of going to the lord of Shalva and asking him to take her back. Others said no to this, because she had been rejected by him. All the ascetics, rigid in their vows, again said, 'O fortunate one! This having occurred, what can we learned ones do? O fortunate one! Listen to these beneficial words. There is no need for you to wander around. O fortunate one! Depart from here and go to your father's residence. The king, your father, will know what should be done next. You possess all the qualities. O fortunate one! Go and dwell there happily. O fortunate one! You have no refuge other than your father. O one with the beautiful complexion! For any *arya* lady, the husband or the father is the refuge. A husband is the refuge when things are smooth. A father is the refuge when things are rough. Roaming around is extremely difficult, especially for someone who is delicate. O beautiful one! Being a princess, you are naturally delicate. O fortunate one! O one with the beautiful complexion! There are many taints associated with dwelling in a hermitage. There will be none in your father's residence.' The brahmanas spoke these words to the ascetic lady. 'On seeing you alone in this deserted and dense forest, kings will solicit you. Therefore, do not set your mind on this.'

'"Amba replied, 'I cannot go again to my father's residence in the city of Kashi. There is no doubt that I will be disrespected by my relatives. O ascetics! It was different when I dwelt in my father's residence as a child. O fortunate ones! I will not go where my father is now. O foremost among brahmanas! I wish to practise austerities under the protection of ascetics, so that I do not confront great ill fortune, in this world or the next.'"

[9]Meaning Bhishma.

'Bhishma said, "When those brahmanas were reflecting on this, the ascetic *rajarshi* Hotravahana arrived in that forest. All the ascetics honoured the king. They worshipped and welcomed him and offered him a seat and water. After he had seated himself and had rested, in his hearing, those residents of the forest again spoke to the maiden. O descendant of the Bharata lineage! On hearing the story of Amba, the daughter of the king of Kashi, her mother's father[10] trembled and arose. O lord! He placed the maiden on his lap and comforted her. He asked her about the entire story of the reasons behind her hardships. In detail, she told him exactly what had happened. Then the rajarshi was overcome by great grief and misery. The extremely great ascetic thought in his mind about what should be done next. He trembled and in great grief, told the distressed maiden, 'O fortunate one! Do not go to your father's residence. I am your mother's father. O daughter! Depend on me. I will dispel your sorrows. O daughter! You have become desiccated. I think you have had enough. Listen to my words and go to the ascetic Rama,[11] Jamadagni's son. Rama will remove your extremely great unhappiness and sorrow. If he does not listen to his words,[12] he will kill Bhishma in battle. Go to the foremost among the Bhargavas, whose energy is like that of the fire of destruction. That great ascetic will establish you on a smooth path.' She repeatedly shed many tears. She lowered her head before Hotravahana, her mother's father, and said, 'I will follow your instructions and will go. But will I be able to see that arya, famous in the world? How will Bhargava destroy my terrible misery? I wish to learn about this and I will go there after that.'"'

Chapter 838(175)

"Hotravahana said, 'O child! You will see Rama, Jamadagni's son, in the great forest. He is engaged in terrible austerities.

---

[10]Hotravahana was Amba's maternal grandfather.

[11]Parashurama.

[12]If Bhishma does not listen to Parashurama that he should take Amba back.

He is devoted to the truth. He is extremely strong. The rishis,[13] those
who are learned in the Vedas, the gandharvas[14] and the apsaras[15]
always worship Rama on Mahendra, the foremost among mountains.
O fortunate one! Go there. He is aged in austerities and is firm in
his vows. After saluting him by lowering your head, tell him these
words of mine. O fortunate one! Tell him once again about what you
desire. On hearing my name, Rama will do everything that you wish
for. O child! Rama is my friend. He is affectionate towards me and
is my well-wisher. The brave one is Jamadagni's son. He is supreme
among those who wield all weapons.'

'"While King Hotravahana was speaking to the maiden in this
way, Akritavrana, Rama's devoted follower, appeared.[16] All the
sages arose in their thousands and so did King Hotravahana from
Srinjaya, aged in years. O foremost among the Bharata lineage! As
is appropriate, those residents of the forest asked about each other's
welfare. Then they seated themselves around him[17] and conversed
about delightful subjects, beautiful and celestial ones. O Indra among
kings! They were happy and delighted. When they had finished, the
great-souled rajarashi Hotravahana asked Akritavrana about Rama,
foremost among maharshis. 'O Akritavrana! Where is it possible to
see Jamadagni's powerful and mighty-armed son, foremost among
those who have knowledge of the Vedas?'

'"Akritavrana said, 'O lord! O king! Rama always speaks about
you. "Rajarshi Srinjaya is my beloved friend." It is my belief that
Rama will be here tomorrow morning. You will see him when he
comes here, desiring to meet you. O rajarshi! Why has this
maiden come to the forest? Who does she belong to and what is her
relationship to you? I wish to know this.'

'"Hotravahana replied, 'O lord! She is my daughter's daughter.
She is the beautiful daughter of the king of Kashi. O unblemished

[13]Sages.

[14]Gandharvas are celestial musicians and semi-divine.

[15]Apsaras are celestial dancers who serve Indra, sometimes regarded as
wives of gandharvas.

[16]Though not explicitly stated, this is clearly Bhishma speaking again.

[17]Akritavrana.

one! She is the eldest and, with her sisters, was at the svayamvara.
She is famous by the name of Amba and she is the eldest daughter of
the lord of Kashi. O one rich in austerities! Ambika and Ambalika
are younger to her. O *brahmarshi*! For the sake of these maidens,
all the kshatriya kings gathered in the city of Kashi and there was
a great festival. Then the immensely valorous and greatly energetic
Bhishma, Shantanu's son, slighted the kings and abducted the three
maidens. O descendant of the Bharata lineage![18] The pure-souled
Bhishma vanquished the lords of the earth and went to Gajasahrya[19]
with the maidens. The lord then handed them over to Satyavati,
for the sake of a marriage with his brother Vichitravirya. O bull
among brahmanas! On seeing that arrangements had been made
for a marriage, in the midst of the ministers, this maiden told
Gangeya, "In my mind, I have chosen the brave lord of Shalva as my
husband. O one who is learned about dharma! When I have thought
of someone, you should not give me to someone else." When he
heard these words, Bhishma consulted with his ministers. Bhishma
made up his mind to give her up and with Satyavati's permission,
gave her leave to go to Shalva, the lord of Soubha. O brahmana!
The maiden was delighted at that time and went and told him, "I
have been given up by Bhishma. Act towards me in accordance with
dharma. O bull among kings! In my mind, I have chosen you earlier."
However, suspicious of her conduct, Shalva rejected her. Deciding
to undertake austerities, she came to this hermitage. I recognized
her when she recounted her lineage. She thinks that Bhishma alone
is responsible for her unhappiness.'

'"Amba said, 'O illustrious one! It is just as Srinjaya King
Hotravahana, the creator of my mother's body, has said. O one rich
in austerities! I do not wish to go back to my own city. O great sage! I
will be insulted there and am ashamed. O supreme among brahmanas!
I will do what the illustrious Rama asks me to. O illustrious one! It
is my view that this is what I should do.'"'

---

[18]There is a minor inconsistency, since Akritavrana is being addressed.
However, Bhishma is repeating the conversation to Duryodhana.

[19]Another name for Hastinapura, *gaja* meaning elephant.

Chapter 839(176)

' " A kritavrana said, 'O fortunate one! O woman! O child!
There are two hardships. Which of these do you actually
wish to redress? O fortunate one! If it is your view that the lord of
Soubha should be urged, then, desirous of your welfare, the great-
souled Rama will ask him accordingly. Or if you wish to see Bhishma,
the son of the river, vanquished in battle by the intelligent Bhargava
Rama, he will do that also. O one with the beautiful smiles! We will
think about what should be done after hearing your words, and
those of Srinjaya.'

'"Amba replied, 'O illustrious one! When he abducted me, Bhisma
acted out of ignorance. O brahmana! Bhishma did not know that
my mind was set on Shalva. Before deciding, you should bear this
in mind too. Having decided in accordance with what is right, then
determine what should be done. O brahmana! Decide what needs
to be done about both Bhishma, tiger among the Kurus, and the
king of Shalva. I have told you exactly about the reasons for my
unhappiness. O illustrious one! In accordance with the reasons,
decide on a course of action.'

'"Akritavrana said, 'O fortunate one! O one with the beautiful
complexion! What you have said about dharma is correct. Now listen
to these words of mine. O timid one! If the son of the river had not
taken you to Gajasahrya, on the instructions of Rama, Shalva would
have bowed down his head and accepted you. O fortunate one! O
beautiful one! But you have been won over and abducted. O one
with the beautiful waist! Therefore, King Shalva has a doubt about
you. Bhishma is insolent about his manliness and victory. I think it
is appropriate that action should be taken against Bhishma.'

'"Amba replied, 'O brahmana! That has always been the great
desire in my heart, if only I could kill Bhishma in battle. O mighty-
armed one! Whether you think that the fault lies with Bhishma or
King Shalva, chastise the one because of whom I have faced this
extreme misery.'"

'Bhishma said, "While they were conversing in this way, the day
passed. O best of the Bharata lineage! It was night and a pleasant

and cool breeze blew. Then Rama appeared, like the blazing fire in his energy. O king! He was surrounded by his disciples. The sage had matted hair and was clad in bark. The unblemished one with an indomitable soul held a bow in his hand and a sword and a battle axe. O tiger among kings! He approached King Srinjaya. On seeing him, all the ascetics and the immensely ascetic king arose, hands joined in salutation. So did the ascetic maiden. They eagerly honoured Bhargava with *madhuparka*.[20] Having been shown homage, he seated himself among them. O descendant of the Bharata lineage! Jamadagni's son and rajarshi Srinjaya conversed about earlier times. When this conversation was over, in due course of time, the rajarshi spoke these sweet words, full of meaning, to the immensely strong Rama, foremost among the Bhrigus. 'O Rama! This is my daughter's daughter. O lord! She is the daughter of the king of Kashi. O one who knows what should be done! Listen to her and decide on an appropriate course of action.' Rama replied, 'Tell me your supreme account.' She approached Rama, who was like a blazing fire. The beautiful one lowered her head at Rama's feet. She touched them with hands that were like the petals of lotuses and stood before him. Her eyes were filled with tears and she wept in grief. She sought refuge with the descendant of the Bhrigu lineage, the one who is everyone's refuge.

'"Rama said, 'O daughter of a king! You are like Srinjaya to me. Tell me about the grief in your mind and I will act in accordance with your words.'

'"Amba replied, 'O illustrious one! O one who is great in his vows! I have sought refuge with you. I am immersed in this ocean and mud of sorrow. O lord! Save me.'"

'Bhishma said, "Rama saw her beauty, her youthful age and her extremely delicate form and began to think. 'What is she going to say?' Flooded by compassion, Rama, supreme among those of the Bhrigu lineage, thought in this fashion for a long time. Rama spoke to the one with the beautiful smiles. 'Tell me.' She told Bhargava everything, exactly as it had happened. After having heard the words of the princess, Jamadagni's son made up his mind and told the one with the beautiful thighs, 'O beautiful one! I will send word to

[20]A respectful offering made to guests, consisting of honey and curd.

Bhishma, foremost among the Kurus. When he has heard my words, in conformity with dharma, that lord of men will act accordingly. O fortunate one! If Jahnavi's son[21] does not act in accordance with my words, I will use the energy of my weapons to burn him down in battle, together with his advisers. O princess! Or if you are so inclined, I will force the brave lord of Shalva to a course of action.'

'"Amba replied, 'O descendant of the Bhrigu lineage! When Bhishma heard that my mind had earlier turned towards King Shalva, he discarded me. I went to the king of Soubha and spoke words that were difficult to speak.[22] But doubting my character, he did not accept me. O descendant of the Bhrigu lineage! You should think about all this and then use your own intelligence to decide on the right course of action. Bhishma, the one who is mighty in his vows, is the root cause of my hardship. He used force to overcome and abduct me. O mighty-armed one! Bhishma is the reason behind this unhappiness. Kill him. O tiger among the Bhrigu lineage! It is because of him that I am wandering around in this supreme misery. O Bhargava! He is greedy and insolent because of his victory. O unblemished one! It is appropriate that you should take revenge against him. O lord! When the descendant of the Bharata lineage was abducting me, I thought of this resolution in my mind, that the one who is great in his vows should be killed. O Rama! O unblemished one! Therefore, fulfil this desire of mine. O mighty-armed one! Kill Bhishma, like Purandara[23] slew Vritra.'"'

Chapter 840(177)

'Bhishma said, "O lord! Having been thus asked to kill Bhishma, Rama spoke to the weeping maiden, who kept urging him

---

[21]Bhisma. Jahnavi is another name for Ganga.
[22]As a woman.
[23]Indra.

repeatedly. 'O descendant of Kashi! O one who is beautiful in complexion! I do not voluntarily take up weapons, except for the sake of those who are learned about the *brahman*.[24] What else can I do for you? O princess! Both Bhishma and Shalva will listen to my words and obey my instructions. O one with the unblemished limbs! I can do that. Do not grieve. O beautiful one! But I cannot take up weapons in any way, unless I am instructed to do so by brahmanas. That is my resolution.'

'"Amba replied, 'O illustrious one! Dispel the grief that Bhishma has unleashed on me. O lord! Without any delay, kill him.'

'"Rama said, 'O daughter of Kashi! If you speak the word, no matter how revered he is, Bhishma will follow my instructions and lower his head at your feet.'

'"Amba replied, 'O Rama! If you wish to do that which brings me pleasure, kill Bhishma in battle. Since you have made your promise, it is proper that you should make that pledge come true.'"

'Bhisma said, "O king! While Rama and Amba were arguing in this way, Akritavrana spoke these words to Jamadagni's son. 'O mighty-armed one! You should not give up the maiden who has sought refuge with you. O Rama! Kill Bhishma, who roars like an *asura*, in battle. O Rama! O mighty sage! If Bhishma challenges you in battle, he will either be vanquished, or he will act in accordance with your words. O descendant of the Bhrigu lineage! The task of this maiden will then be done. O brave one! O lord! The words that you have spoken will come true. O Rama! O great sage! Once upon a time, you took a pledge. O Bhargava! You promised the brahmanas that if a brahmana, a kshatriya, a vaishya or a shudra came to hate brahmanas, you would kill him in battle. O one who provides refuge! Even for the sake of your own life, you said you were incapable of forsaking a terrified person who seeks refuge with you, even if all the kshatriyas assemble against you in battle. O Bhargava! You said you would slay such insolent ones. O Rama! Bhishma, the extender of the Kuru lineage, is triumphant. O descendant of the Bhrigu lineage! Confront him in a battle and fight with him.'"

[24]The supreme soul, brahman or *paramatman*.

'"Rama replied, 'O supreme among rishis! I remember the promise
I made in earlier times. I will do what can be achieved through
conciliation. O brahmana! The task that this maiden from Kashi
has set her mind on is great. I will take this maiden and myself go to
Bhishma. Insolent in war, if he does not act in accordance with my
words, it is my certain resolution that I will kill that insolent person.
The arrows that I unleash do not remain in bodies.[25] You learnt that
earlier, in the battle with the kshatriyas.'"

'Bhishma said, "Having spoken in this way, the immensely
intelligent Rama arose, together with those who knew about the
brahman, having made up his mind to leave. The ascetics spent
the night there. They offered oblations into the fire. They prayed
and meditated. Then they departed, desiring to kill me. O great
king! O descendant of the Bharata lineage! With those bulls among
brahmanas and with the maiden, Rama went to Kurukshetra. Having
reached the Sarasvati, those great-souled ascetics, with the foremost
among the Bhrigus at the forefront, began to dwell there."'

Chapter 841(178)

'Bhishma said, "O king! On the third day after he had established
himself on that level terrain, the one who is great in his vows
sent word to me, saying that he had arrived. On learning that the
immensely strong lord, the store of energy, had arrived on the outskirts
of my kingdom, I was delighted. O Indra among kings! With a cow
in front of me and surrounded by brahmanas, sacrificial priests who
were the equals of the gods and other priests, I went there. On seeing
me arrive, Jamadagni's powerful son received the homage and spoke
these words to me. 'O Bhishma! What were your thoughts when you
abducted the daughter of the king of Kashi against her wishes? You
then abandoned her later. You have dislodged her from both inferior

---

[25]They are so powerful that they pass through the bodies.

and superior dharma.[26] Who can now go to someone who has been touched by you? O descendant of the Bharata lineage! Because she has been abducted by you, she has been refused by Shalva. O descendant of the Bharata lineage! O tiger among men! Therefore, following my counsel, take her back and let the princess abide by her own dharma. O king! O unblemished one! You do not deserve to treat her with such neglect.' On seeing that his mind wasn't that agitated,[27] I spoke to him. 'O brahmana! There is no way that I can give her to my brother again. O Bhargava! She has told me that she has given herself to Shalva earlier. Having obtained my permission, she went to the city of Soubha. Because of fear, compassion, avarice or gain, I cannot abandon the dharma of kshatriyas. That is the vow that I follow.'

"'Rama's eyes dilated with anger and he said, 'O bull among the Kurus! If you refuse to act in accordance with my words, I will kill you today, together with your advisers.' In great rage, Rama spoke these words repeatedly. His eyes were wide with anger. I repeatedly tried to pacify that scorcher of enemies with sweet words. But I was incapable of pacifying that tiger of the Bhrigu lineage. I then bowed my head down before that supreme among brahmanas and asked, 'What is the reason behind your desire to fight with me? When I was a child, you yourself taught me the four kinds of weapons.[28] O mighty-armed one! O Bhargava! You have instructed me and I am your student.' His eyes red with anger, Rama told me, 'O Bhishma! You know that I am your preceptor. O Kouravya! O lord of the earth! Yet, to bring about my pleasure, you are refusing to take back the daughter of Kashi. O descendant of the Kuru lineage! I am not

---

[26]The inferior dharma of remaining with Bhishma against her wishes and the superior dharma of going to Shalva.

[27]Parashurama's tone was conciliatory.

[28]The five types of weapons are *mukta* (those that are released from the hand, like a *chakra*), *amukta* (those that are never released, like a sword), *muktamukta* (those that can be released or not released, like a spear), *yantramukta* (those that are released from an implement, like an arrow) and *mantramukta* (magical weapons unleashed with incantations). When four types of weapons are mentioned, the mantramukta category is excluded.

interested in peace with you. O mighty-armed one! Take her back and save yourself and your lineage. Since you have tainted her, she will not find a husband.'

'"When he spoke in this way, I told Rama, the destroyer of enemy cities, 'O brahmarshi! Since this cannot be done, what is the point of striving towards it? I see my earlier teacher, Jamadagni's son. O illustrious one! I seek your favours, like in earlier times. Who will allow a woman to dwell in his house, established like a snake, knowing that she desires another? This is the great taint associated with women. O immensely radiant one! Even the fear of Vasava will not make me give up dharma. Without any delay, show me your favours, or do whatever you must do. O pure-souled one! O lord! An ancient shloka has been heard, chanted by the great-souled and immensely intelligent Marutta. "If a preceptor does not know what should be done and what should not be done, if he deviates from the right path and if he is arrogant, it is one's duty to abandon him." Because you are my preceptor, I have been affectionate and have greatly honoured you. But you are not acquainted with the conduct of a preceptor and I will therefore, fight with you. However, I cannot kill a preceptor in battle, especially one who is a brahmana, especially one who is rich in austerities. I am at peace with you. If one sees a brahmana with an upraised weapon, as if he is the kin of a kshatriya, and angrily kills him in the field of battle, without running away from the fight, dharma is clear that no sin is committed from killing a brahmana. O one rich in austerities! I am a kshatriya. I am established in the dharma of kshatriyas. A man does not commit adharma if he reacts in response to what another person has done. Instead, his welfare is ensured. If a person knows about artha and dharma and about the time and the place, even if he has doubts about what ensures artha, there is no doubt that he should do that which ensures welfare. In this case, there is doubt about where artha lies. But you are acting as if you know what is right. O Rama! Therefore, I will fight with you in a great battle. You will witness the valour of my arms and my superhuman bravery. O descendant of the Bhrigu lineage! Given this, I will do whatever I can. O brahmana! I will fight with you in Kurukshetra. O Rama! O great sage! Prepare yourself for the duel.

O Rama! You will be killed by hundreds of my arrows. Sanctified by my weapons in that great battle, you will obtain the worlds that you have earned for yourself. O one who is in love with war! Return from here and go to Kurukshetra. O mighty-armed one! O one rich in austerities! I will fight with you there. O Rama! That is the place where you had once sanctified your father.[29] O Bhargava! I will kill you there and sanctify you there. O Rama! O one who is unassailable in war! Go there swiftly. You have boasted in the past, saying that you are a brahmana. O Rama! You have often boasted in assemblies that you have exterminated kshatriyas from the world. But listen to my words. At that time, Bhishma had not been born and there were no kshatriyas like me, who could dispel your insolence about war and your love for fighting. O mighty-armed one! But Bhishma, the destroyer of enemy cities, has been born now. O Rama! There is no doubt that I will destroy your insolence in war.'"'

Chapter 842(179)

'Bhishma said, "O descendant of the Bharata lineage! Then Rama began to laugh and spoke to me. 'O Bhishma! It is your good fortune that you wish to fight with me in battle. O Kouravya! Together with you, I will go to Kurukshetra. O scorcher of enemies! I will do what you have asked me to and you should also go there. O Bhishma! Let your mother Jahnavi watch me kill you with hundreds of arrows, so that you become the food of vultures, crows and cranes. O king! Let the goddess,[30] worshipped by siddhas[31] and

---

[29]Parashurama was the son of Jamadagni. Jamadagni was killed by King Kartavirya Arjuna. In consequence, Parashurama exterminated kshatriyas from the earth twenty-one times. This blood created a lake in Kurukshetra and Parashurama offered oblations to his father there.

[30]Ganga.

[31]Siddhi means accomplishment. Siddhas are semi-divine species who have attained these superhuman accomplishments or faculties.

*charana*s,[32] be miserable when she sees you slain by me today and weep. The immensely fortunate river, the daughter of Bhagiratha, does not deserve to see this.[33] But she has given birth to an evil and diseased one like you, who cherishes war. O Bhishma! Come with me and let us go together. Let there be a battle today. O Kouravya! O bull among the Bharata lineage! Take everything, chariots and other things.' Rama, the vanquisher of enemy cities, spoke these words to me. O king! I bowed my head before him and said that it would be this way.

'"After speaking these words, desirous of fighting, Rama went to Kurukshetra. I entered the city[34] and told Satyavati everything. I performed the propitiatory rites and was blessed by my mother. O immensely radiant one! The brahmanas pronounced sacred words of benediction. I mounted a beautiful and silver chariot, yoked to white horses. It had been constructed well and had been prepared well. It was strewn with the hides of tigers. It was loaded with great weapons and every kind of implement. O king! It was driven by a brave charioteer born in a noble lineage, skilled in the knowledge of horses. He had often witnessed my deeds. I was covered in beautiful and white armour. O supreme among the Bharata lineage! I grasped a white bow. O lord of men! A white umbrella was held aloft my head and white whisks were brandished. I was attired in white. My headgear was white. All my ornaments were white. Applauded with benedictions of victory, I left Gajasahrya. O bull among the Bharata lineage! I arrived in Kurukshetra, the field where the battle would be fought. O king! Goaded by the charioteer, the horses, with the speed of the mind and the wind, swiftly bore me to the supreme field of battle. Like me, the powerful Rama also swiftly reached Kurukshetra. O king! In battle, we wished to show our valour to each other. I stood before the supreme ascetic Rama, so that he could see me. I grasped my supreme conch shell and began to blow on it. O king! All the brahmanas, the ascetics who lived in the forest, the gods and the masses of rishis assembled to witness the divine battle. Celestial

[32]Celestial singers.

[33]Ganga was brought down from heaven by Bhagiratha and is called Bhagiratha's daughter, Bhagirathi.

[34]Hastinapura.

garlands manifested themselves repeatedly. Divine musical instruments sounded. There was the rumbling of masses of clouds. All the ascetics who followed Bhargava surrounded the field of battle as witnesses.

'"The goddess who is my mother desires the welfare of all beings. O king! She manifested herself before me and said, 'What is it that you wish to do? O extender of the Kuru lineage! I will go to Jamadagni's son and plead with him. I will repeatedly tell him, "Do not fight with Bhishma, your student." O son! O king! And you should not behave so obstinately towards a brahmana. Why do you wish to fight with Jamadagni's son in a battle?' She censured me. 'O son! Do you not know that Rama, the destroyer of kshatriyas, is equal to Hara[35] in valour? Why do you wish to fight with him?' I joined my hands in salutation before the goddess. O foremost among the Bharata lineage! I accurately told her everything that had transpired at the svayamvara. O Indra among kings! I told her how I had tried to obtain Rama's favours earlier and about the ancient love of the daughter of the king of Kashi. My mother, the great river, then went to Rama. For my sake, the goddess sought to pacify the rishi Bhargava. She said, 'Do not fight with Bhishma, your student.' He replied to her, 'It is Bhishma that you should restrain. I am here because he is not doing what I desire.'"

'Sanjaya[36] said, "Out of affection towards her son, Ganga then returned to Bhishma. But his eyes were red with anger and he did not pay heed to her words. The great ascetic, foremost among the Bhrigus, with dharma in his soul, then appeared. The supreme among the brahmanas challenged him again to the battle."'

Chapter 843(180)

'Bhishma said, "I laughed and spoke to the one who stood ready for battle. 'You are standing on the ground and I do not wish

---

[35]Shiva.

[36]There is a conversation within a conversation, because Sanjaya is recounting the story to Dhritarashtra.

to fight with you while I am established on my chariot. O brave one! O mighty-armed one! O Rama! Mount a chariot and armour yourself, if you wish to fight with me in battle.' In that field of battle, Rama smiled and told me, 'The earth is my chariot. O Bhishma! The Vedas bear me, like well-trained horses. The wind is my charioteer. The mother of the Vedas is my armour.[37] O descendant of the Kuru lineage! I am protected well by these and will fight in the battle.' O son of Gandhari! Rama's truth is his valour and while speaking in this way, he covered me on all sides with a great shower of arrows. I then saw Jamadagni's son stationed on a celestial chariot. It was stocked with all kinds of radiant weapons that were extraordinary to look at. It was created from his mind and was sacred. It was as expansive as a city. It was yoked to celestial horses that were ready. It was decorated with gold. O mighty-armed one! It was adorned with a banner that had the sign of the moon embellished on it. He held a bow and his quivers were fastened. He had guards on his arms and fingers. His friend Akritavrana, learned in the Vedas and beloved of Bhargava, acted as his charioteer. Wishing to fight, Bhargava delighted my heart by repeatedly saying, 'Attack' and challenging me to do battle. He was unassailable and extremely strong and was like the rising sun. Alone, I approached Rama, the destroyer of kshatriyas. When I was at a distance of three shots of an arrow,[38] I restrained my mounts. I descended. Putting aside my bow, I advanced towards that supreme of rishis. I showed homage to Rama, supreme among brahmanas, in the prescribed fashion and offered him worship, speaking these supreme words. 'O Rama! I will fight with you in battle, though you are better than me and superior. You are my preceptor. You follow dharma. O lord! Bless me so that I may be victorious.'

"'Rama replied, 'O foremost among the Kurus! This is what should be done by those who desire prosperity. O mighty-armed one! This is dharma for those who fight with their superiors. O lord of the earth! Had you not approached me like this, I would have

---

[37]The mother of the Vedas is a reference to the metres Gayatri, Savitri and Sarasvati.

[38]That is, thrice the distance an arrow can travel.

cursed you. O Kourava! Make every effort to fight in this battle and resort to fortitude. I cannot bless you for your victory, because I am standing here, wishing to defeat you. Go and fight in accordance with dharma. I am pleased with your conduct.'"

'Bhishma said, "I bowed before him and swiftly ascended my chariot. Desiring battle, I once again blew on my conch shell, which was decorated with gold. O descendant of the Bharata lineage! A battle then ensued between him and me. As we sought to defeat each other, it lasted for many days. He was the first one to strike me, with nine hundred and sixty-nine arrows that were shafted with the feathers of cranes. They were like the fire in their energy. O lord of the earth! My four mounts and my charioteer were restrained in that battle. But since I was armoured, I remained firm. O descendant of the Bharata lineage! I bowed to the gods and brahmanas. While he stood established on that field of battle, I smiled and replied to him. 'Though you have behaved harshly towards me, I have honoured you as a preceptor. O brahmana! Listen again to what must be done if one wishes to accumulate a store of dharma. I will not strike the Vedas that are there in your body, your great brahmana characteristics, or the extremely great austerities that you have collected. O Rama! I will strike the dharma of kshatriyas that you have resorted to. When a brahmana raises his weapons, he becomes like a kshatriya. Behold the valour of my bow. Behold the strength of my arms. O brave one! I will slice your bow and arrows into two.' O bull among the Bharata lineage! I shot a sharp arrow[39] at him. The ends of his bow were shattered and it fell down on the ground. I shot nine hundred arrows towards Jamadagni's son. They had lowered tufts and were shafted with the feathers of cranes. They were directed towards his body and were spurred on by the wind. Those arrows sped on, seeming to spout blood, like serpents. All the limbs in his body were wounded and blood flowed out from those wounds. O king! At that time, Rama looked like Meru spouting out its minerals, or an *ashoka* tree at the end of the winter, covered with red blossoms, or like a *kimshuka* tree.[40]

[39]A specific type of arrow named *bhalla*, with a broad head.
[40]Tree with red blossoms.

'"At this, Rama was overcome by anger and took up another bow. He showered down sharp arrows, with golden shafts, on me. There were many terrible arrows, capable of piercing the heart. They were extremely fast and made me tremble. They were like flames, or the poison of snakes. I again summoned my patience in that battle. Enraged in that battle, I unleashed one hundred arrows at Rama. They were sharp and were like the fire or the sun, or like the venom of snakes. Struck by these, Rama seemed to lose his consciousness. O bull among the Bharata lineage! I was overcome by compassion and censured myself. 'Shame on battles and on kshatriyas!' O king! I was overcome by sorrow and repeatedly said, 'I am evil. I have committed a sin by acting like a kshatriya. My preceptor is a brahmana. He has dharma in his soul. He has been oppressed by my arrows.' O descendant of the Bharata lineage! I did not strike Jamadagni's son any more. Having heated the earth, once the day was over, the one with the thousand rays[41] departed and the fight was over."'

Chapter 844(181)

'Bhishma said, "O lord of the earth! My charioteer was revered for his skill in these matters. He removed the shafts from himself, from the horses and from me. The horses were bathed and rolled around on the ground. They obtained water and were refreshed. When the sun arose in the morning, the battle resumed. On seeing me swiftly approach, stationed and armoured on my chariot, the powerful Rama ensured that his chariot was also completely ready. When I saw that Rama was desirous of doing battle, I cast aside my excellent bow and swiftly descended from my chariot. O descendant of the Bharata lineage! As earlier, I showed him homage and then mounted my chariot again. Without any fear and ready to fight, I stood before Jamadagni's son. He enveloped

[41]The sun.

me with a great shower of arrows. I also covered him with a shower of arrows. O king! Enraged, Jamadagni's son again released arrows at me and they were like snakes with flaming mouths. O king! Swiftly, I repeatedly sliced them down in the sky with hundreds and thousands of sharp bhallas.

'"O mighty-armed one! At this, Jamadagni's powerful son released divine weapons at me and I repulsed them with my weapons. I wished to perform the superior deeds. In every direction, a great roar could be heard in the firmament. I used the *vayavya*[42] weapon against Jamadagni's son. O descendant of the Bharata lineage! Rama countered this with his *guhyaka* weapon.[43] I invoked the mantra and released the *agneya* weapon.[44] The lord Rama countered this with a *varuna* weapon.[45] In this fashion, I countered Rama's celestial weapons and Rama, the destroyer of enemies and knowledgeable in divine weapons, repulsed mine. O king! Rama, supreme among brahmanas and Jamadagni's immensely strong son, then suddenly turned to the left and enraged, struck me in the chest. O foremost among the Bharata lineage! I fainted and fell down on that supreme chariot. O foremost among the Bharata lineage! On seeing me in that miserable state and oppressed by Rama's arrows, my charioteer quickly carried me away to the distance of one *goruta*.[46] All of Rama's followers, Akritavrana and the others, were extremely delighted when they saw that I had fallen down pierced, having lost my consciousness. O descendant of the Bharata lineage! They cheered, and so did the maiden from Kashi.

'"When I had regained consciousness and got to know what had happened, I told my charioteer, 'O charioteer! Go where Rama is. I have regained my senses and my pain has gone.' O Kouravya! The

---

[42]Divine weapon named after Vayu, the wind god.

[43]Divine weapon named after guhyakas, semi-divine species who were companions of Kubera.

[44]Divine weapon named after Agni, the fire god.

[45]Divine weapon named after Varuna, the god of the ocean.

[46]Goruta is a measure of distance equal to two *kroshas*. It is so named because it is the distance from which a cow's (*go*) bellow can be heard.

extremely beautiful horses seemed to be dancing. They were as fleet as the wind. The charioteer bore me back on them. O Kourava! On having reached Rama, wishing to vanquish him, I was angry and covered the raging one with a net of arrows. Those arrows flew straight. But in that battle, Rama sliced them down with his own arrows, shooting three arrows for each one that I did. All my arrows were extremely sharp. However, in that great battle, all of them were sliced into two by hundreds of Rama's arrows. Wishing to kill Rama, Jamadagni's son, I again unleashed a flaming arrow that was extremely radiant and was like time itself. He was struck deeply and pierced by that arrow. Rama swiftly lost consciousness and fell down on the ground. When Rama fell down on the ground, a lamentation arose everywhere. O descendant of the Bharata lineage! The world was anxious, as if the sun had fallen down. Extremely anxious and overcome by grief, all the ascetics and the maiden from Kashi rushed towards the descendant of the Bhrigu lineage. They embraced him and comforted him gently, with cool water in their hands. O Kourava! They pronounced benedictions for his victory.

'"Rama arose. Though he was confused, he spoke these words to me. 'O Bhishma! Stand there. You are dead.' He affixed an arrow to his bow and released it. In that great battle, the swift arrow struck me on my left side. I was extremely agitated, like a tree whirled by the wind. O king! In that great battle, he killed my horses with swift weapons. His dexterity with arrows was such that he could carry away a single one of my body hair. To counter him in that battle, I also used swift weapons. O mighty-armed one! I unleashed an arrow that could not be countered and all those arrows, Rama's and mine, remained in the air[47] and swiftly covered the sky in every direction. The sun was covered in this net of arrows and no longer provided any heat. The wind could not pass through them, as if it had been restrained by clouds. The wind trembled and dashed against the sun's rays. From this friction, a fire was created in the sky. The arrows blazed, because of the colourful fire that had

[47]They did not fall down on the ground.

been created by them. O king! Everything on the ground was then reduced to ashes. O Kourava! Rama was angry and shot hundreds, thousands, millions,[48] one hundred millions, ten thousands, ten trillions and billions of swift arrows at me. But in that battle, I sliced them down with my own arrows, which were like the poison of snakes. O king! I shattered them and made them fall down on the ground, like serpents. O supreme among the Bharata lineage! Thus did the battle continue then. When twilight had passed, my preceptor withdrew."'

Chapter 845(182)

'Bhishma said, "O supreme among the Bharata lineage! When I encountered Rama the next day, there was again a terrible and tumultuous battle. From one day to the next, the brave lord, who has dharma in his soul and knows about the use of divine weapons, released many celestial weapons. O descendant of the Bharata lineage! But, in that terrible battle where one is ready to give up one's precious life, I repulsed them with weapons that could be used for countering. When many weapons were thus destroyed, the immensely energetic Bhargava became wrathful. He fought, ready to give up his own life. Having been restrained by weapons, Jamadagni's great-souled son grasped a spear that was terrible in form. It was like a flaming meteor that had been created by time itself. It blazed at the tip and covered the world with its energy. It flamed towards me, like the sun at the time of destruction. With my fiery arrows, I sliced it into three and it fell down on the ground. At that, a breeze with a sacred fragrance began to blow. When this was sliced down, Rama's anger was ignited. He hurled twelve

[48]*Prayuta* (million), *arbuda* (one hundred million), *ayuta* (ten thousand), *kharva* (ten trillion, or a very large number) and *nikharva* (billion).

other terrible spears at me. O descendant of the Bharata lineage!
I am incapable of describing their forms, their energy and their
speed. But I watched them in confusion. They advanced from all
the directions, like giant meteors, or the fire. They had many forms
and energy and flamed at the tips. They were like twelve suns, at the
time of the destruction of the world. O king! When I saw that net
of arrows[49] extending, I sliced them down with my net of arrows.
In that battle, I shot twelve arrows and countered those spears,
terrible in form. Jamadagni's great-souled son then hurled another
terrible spear at me. It possessed a golden shaft and was colourful,
with a golden tassel. It was like a giant meteor and was flaming. O
Indra among men! I repulsed it with my sword and shield and it fell
down. In that battle, I used divine arrows against Jamadagni's son
and showered his celestial horses and his charioteer. On seeing that
his colourful spear, which had the form of an unleashed snake, had
been repelled, the great-souled one, the oppressor of the Haihaya,[50]
was overcome by anger and grasped a divine weapon. A mass of
flaming arrows, without tufts,[51] manifested itself, like a terrible
swarm of locusts. They pierced and completely overwhelmed my
body, my horses, my chariot and my charioteer. My chariot was
covered everywhere with those arrows. O king! And so were my
mounts and my charioteer. The yoke of the chariot, the wheels and
the axle were shattered through those arrows. When that shower
of arrows was exhausted, I also showered arrows on my preceptor
in return. Bhargava's body, and his mass of brahmana energy, were
pierced by those arrows and began to discharge a lot of blood.
Rama was tormented by my net of arrows. I was also suffering
from many deep wounds. When the sun headed for the mountain
behind which it sets, the fighting ended in the afternoon."'

[49]The text says arrows, though Parashurama actually hurled twelve
spears.

[50]Kartavirya Arjuna was the king of Haihaya.

[51]The word used is *vishikha*, a special type of arrow. Vishikhas were minute
arrows, without feathered tufts.

Chapter 846(183)

'Bhishma said, "O Indra among kings! The unblemished sun arose in the morning and Bhargava's battle with me resumed again. Rama, supreme among those who wield weapons, stationed on a fast-moving chariot, showered a net of arrows on me, like Shakra at a mountain. My charioteer, my well-wisher, was hurt by that shower of arrows and fell down from the chariot. I was dejected. Being greatly struck by the force of those arrows, my charioteer became deeply unconscious and fell down on the ground. Oppressed by Rama's arrows, my charioteer gave up his life. O Indra among kings! For an instant, I was also overcome by fear. O king! When my charioteer was killed and my mind was agitated, Rama hurled deadly arrows at me. While I was still overwhelmed on account of the charioteer, Bhargava powerfully drew his firm bow and pierced me with an arrow. O king! It was an arrow that drank blood. It struck me on the clavicle. O Indra among kings! When I fell down, it fell down with me on the ground. O bull among the Bharata lineage! Rama then thought that I was dead. He repeatedly roared in delight, thundering like a cloud. O king! When I fell down, Rama rejoiced. Together with his followers, he emitted a loud roar. The Kurus were at my side and there were others who had come to witness the fight. When I fell down, they were supremely distressed.

'"O lion among kings! When I fell down, I saw eight brahmanas. They possessed the radiance of the sun and the fire. They surrounded me from every direction and in that field of battle, supported me with their arms. Supported by those brahmanas, I did not actually touch the ground. I was held up in the air by them, as if they were relatives. It was as if I was asleep in the air and they sprinkled drops of water on me. O king! The brahmanas who were supporting me spoke to me. 'Do not be scared. Everything will be fine.' Sustained by those words, I suddenly arose and saw my mother, foremost among rivers, stationed on my chariot. O Indra among Kouravas!

I saw that the great river was controlling and steering my horses. I touched my mother's feet and those of Arshtishena[52] and ascended my chariot. She had protected my chariots, my horses and my implements. I joined my hands in salutation and asked her to leave. I then myself controlled those horses, which were as fleet as the wind. O descendant of the Bharata lineage! I fought with Jamadagni's son, until the day was over. O foremost among the Bharata lineage! In that battle, I shot an arrow at Rama. It was fast and extremely powerful. It pierced him in the heart. Oppressed by that arrow, Rama lost his senses. He let go of his bow and sank down on the ground on his knees. When Rama, the one who gave away thousands,[53] fell down, clouds covered the sky and showered copious quantities of blood. Meteors fell down in hundreds. There were storms and earthquakes. Suddenly, Svarbhanu[54] swallowed up the blazing sun. Harsh winds began to blow. The earth trembled. Vultures, crows and cranes were delighted and circled around. The directions blazed. A jackal repeatedly howled in a terrible voice. Drums sounded in horrible tones, though they had not been struck. When the great-souled Rama became unconscious and fell down on the ground, there were all these terrible and fearful portents. The soft rays of the sun were covered. Enveloped in dust, it prepared to set. Night arrived, with a cool and pleasant breeze. Both of us withdrew from the fight. O king! In this way, there was a ceasefire then. When day dawned, it started again. From one day to another, it thus went on for twenty-three days."'

[52]Arshtishena is a sage (rajarshi) whom the Pandavas visited, such as in Section 35 (Volume 3). While he could have also arrived to witness the battle, there is no obvious reason for Arshtishena to be mentioned here. Though the Mahabharata never makes it clear, Arshtishena could have been Shantanu's elder brother, Devapi, who resorted to the forest. But there is no connection between Arshtishena and Parashurama. Some non-critical editions do not mention Arshtishena, but ancestors. It does make sense for Bhishma to show obeisance to his ancestors.

[53]Thousands of gifts and stipends.

[54]Rahu.

Chapter 847(184)

'Bhishma said, "O Indra among kings! O lord of the earth! That night, I bowed my head before the brahmanas, the ancestors, all the gods, the beings who roam in the night and to night itself. I retreated to my bed and in private, reflected about this in my mind. 'This extremely terrible and great battle between Jamadagni's son and me has been going on for many days. I cannot defeat the immensely valiant brahmana in the field of battle. He is immensely strong. If I am capable of vanquishing Jamadagni's powerful son, let the gods be favourable and show me the way tonight.' O Indra among kings! Wounded by arrows, I fell asleep that night. The foremost among brahmanas had raised me when I had fallen down from the chariot. They had held me and comforted me, asking me not to be afraid. O great king! When it was almost dawn, on my right side, they appeared in a dream. O extender of the Kuru linage! Listen. They surrounded me and spoke these words. 'O Gangeya! Arise and do not be frightened. You have nothing to be scared of. O tiger among men! We are protecting you, because you have sprung from our own bodies. There is no way in which Rama, Jamadagni's son, can defeat you in battle. O bull among the Bharata lineage! But you will vanquish Rama in battle. You will recognize this beloved weapon of yours. When you were in an earlier body, you used to be familiar with it. O descendant of the Bharata lineage! This was created by Vishvakarma. It is Prajapatya and is known by the name of *prasvapan*.[55] Rama does not know about this, nor does any other man on earth. O mighty-armed one! O Indra among kings! Remember it and use it with force. O lord of men! Rama will not be killed with this weapon. O one who shows honours! Therefore, there will be no sin if you use it. Oppressed by the force of your arrow, Jamadagni's son will fall asleep. O Bhishma! Having thus defeated him, you will

---

[55]Vishvakarma is the architect of the gods. Prajapatya can be interpreted as another name for the weapon, or as a weapon that is associated with (or used) by Prajapati (Brahma). Prasvapan means something that puts one to sleep.

then make him rise up again, with this beloved weapon of yours, named *sambodhana*.[56] O Kouravya! When you are stationed on your chariot in the morning, act as we have asked you to. Whether one is asleep, or whether one is dead, we regard the two as equal. O king! Rama will never become mortal. Therefore, when it arrives before you,[57] use prasvapan.' O king! Having said this, all those supreme among brahmanas disappeared. All those eight were similar in form. All of them were radiant, like the sun personified."'

Chapter 848(185)

'Bhishma said, "O descendant of the Bharata lineage! When night was over, I woke up. I thought about my dream and was extremely delighted. O descendant of the Bharata lineage! Then a tumultuous battle started between him and me. It was extraordinary for all beings and made the body hair stand up. Bhargava showered arrows down on me. O descendant of the Bharata lineage! I countered them with a net of arrows. Thereupon, the greatly ascetic was again supremely enraged. Like it had happened the day before, he angrily hurled a spear at me. It was like Indra's *vajra* to the touch. It was as resplendent as Yama's staff. It flamed like the fire and licked all directions of that field of battle. O tiger among the Bharata lineage! With great force, it struck me on the shoulder. It was like the altar of a sacrificial fire in the sky.[58] Thus wounded by the mighty-armed Rama, whose eyes were red, terrible streams of blood began to flow, like minerals streaming from mountains.

"'I was extremely angry at Jamadagni's son. I hurled an arrow at him. It was like death, like the poison of serpents. O great king!

---

[56]Sambodhana means calling or addressing. In this context, it thus means a weapon that awakens someone by calling him up.

[57]When it is summoned mentally.

[58]Suggesting that it was large.

The brave one, supreme among brahmanas, was struck on the forehead and shone like a mountain, with a peak at the top. He was extremely angry and turned towards me. Powerfully, he drew his bow and shot an arrow at me. It was like time and death. It was terrible and was capable of destroying enemies. Like a hissing serpent, the terrible arrow struck me on the chest. O king! Covered with blood, I fell down on the ground. When I regained my senses, I hurled an unblemished spear at Jamadagni's intelligent son. It flamed like lightning. It struck that foremost among brahmanas between the arms. O king! He lost his senses and began to tremble. His friend Akritavrana, the great ascetic and brahmana, embraced him and repeatedly comforted him with auspicious words. Thus comforted, Rama, the one with the great vows, became angry and was overcome with intolerance. He manifested the supreme weapon known as *brahma*. To counter it, I also used the supreme brahma weapon. It blazed, appearing like something at the end of an era.[59] O supreme among the Bharata lineage! The two brahma weapons encountered each other in mid-air, without reaching either Rama or me. O lord of the earth! The sky became only a great mass of energy and all the beings were distressed. O descendant of the Bharata lineage! Because of the energy of those weapons, the rishis, the gandharvas and the gods were extremely tormented and oppressed. The earth, with its mountains, forests and trees, trembled. The tormented beings were supremely afflicted. O king! The sky blazed. The ten directions were full of smoke. Those that were in the sky were no longer capable of remaining in the firmament. There was a great lamentation in the world, with the gods, the asuras and the *rakshasas*. O descendant of the Bharata lineage! I decided that this was the time and prepared to release my beloved prasvapan weapon, as those who knew about the brahman had asked me to. As soon as I thought about the weapon in my mind, it appeared before me.'"

---

[59]There is destruction at the end of an era, with an all-encompassing fire. The weapon is being compared to something at the time of destruction, such as the fire.

Chapter 849(186)

'Bhishma said, "O king! At this, there was the sound of a great tumult in the sky. 'O Bhishma! O descendant of the Kuru lineage! Do not release prasvapan.' But I aimed that weapon at the descendant of the Bhrigu lineage. While I was aiming prasvapan, Narada spoke these words to me. 'O Kourvaya! The masses of gods are established in the firmament. They are restraining you now. Do not use prasvapan. Rama is an ascetic with brahmana qualities. He is a brahmana and your preceptor. O Kouravya! You should never show him disrespect in any way.' Then I saw those eight, who knew about the brahman, stationed in the sky. O Indra among kings! They smiled and spoke softly to me. 'O foremost among the Bharata lineage! Do as Narada has asked you to. O bull among the Bharata lineage! That will be supremely beneficial for the world.' In that field of battle, I then withdrew the weapon prasvapan. In that battle, in accordance with the prescription, I readied the blazing *brahmastra*.[60] O prince! On seeing that the weapon had been withdrawn, Rama was enraged. He suddenly raised his voice and spoke these words. 'I have been defeated by the extremely evil-minded Bhishma.'[61] Then Jamadagni's son saw his father, and his father, and his father also.[62]

'"They surrounded him and in a comforting voice, spoke these words. 'O son! Never act in such a rash way again, especially fighting with a kshatriya like Bhishma. O descendant of the Bhrigu lineage! It is the dharma of kshatriyas to fight. The supreme riches of brahmanas are studying and observing vows. Earlier, we asked you to do this for a specific purpose[63] and you took up arms and performed a fierce

[60]Divine weapon named after Brahma.

[61]Because Bhishma had voluntarily withdrawn the weapon and in a way, Parashurama had been defeated.

[62]Ourva's son was Richika, Richika's son was Jamadagni and Jamadagni's son was Parashurama. So Ourva, Richika and Jamadagni had arrived. They were descended from Bhrigu. Bhrigu's son was Chyavana and Chyavana's son was Ourva.

[63]When Jamadagni was killed by Kartavirya Arjuna.

deed. O son! You have fought enough with Bhishma. You have been defeated. O mighty-armed one! Withdraw from the field of battle. O fortunate one! Let there be an end to wielding the bow. O unassailable one! O Bhargava! Give it up and practise austerities. Bhishma is Shantanu's son and he has been restrained by all the gods. They have asked him to withdraw from the battle. They have repeatedly told him, "Do not fight with Rama, your preceptor. O extender of the Kuru lineage! It is not proper for you to defeat Rama in battle. O Gangeya! In the field of battle, show respect to this brahmana. We are your seniors and therefore, we are restraining you." Bhishma is foremost among the Vasus. O son! It is fortunate that you are still alive. Shantanu's son, Gangeya, is an immensely famous Vasu. How can he be defeated by you? O Rama! Refrain. Arjuna is foremost among the Pandavas. He is Purandara's powerful son. He is the brave Nara Prajapati, the ancient and eternal god.[64] He is famous in the three worlds as the valiant Savyasachi. At the right time, it has been ordained by the self-creating one[65] that he will be the cause of Bhishma's death.' Thus addressed by his ancestors, Rama replied to his ancestors. 'I will not refrain from this battle. That is the vow that I observe. I have never withdrawn from the forefront of battle earlier. O grandfathers! If it so pleases you, let the son of the river withdraw from the fight. There is no way that I will withdraw from this fight.' O king! Then those sages, with Richika at the forefront and with Narada, approached me and said, 'O son![66] Honour the supreme brahmana and withdraw from the battle.' I told them, 'No, because of my respect for the dharma of kshatriyas, my vow in this world is that I will never withdraw from a fight. I will not withdraw and retreat. I will not be pierced by arrows on my back. Greed, misery, fear or the possibility of gain cannot make me abandon this eternal dharma. This is my firm resolution.' O king! Then all the sages, with Narada at the forefront and Bhagirathi, my mother, stood in the midst

---

[64]Nara and Narayana are ancient rishis, Nara is identified with Arjuna and Narayana with Krishna.

[65]Brahma.

[66]The word used is tata.

of that field of battle. Firm in my resolution to continue fighting, I stood in that field of battle, with an arrow fixed to my bow.

'"In that field of battle, they again spoke collectively to the descendant of the Bhrigu lineage. 'O Bhargava! Be pacified. The heart of brahmanas is like butter. O Rama! O Rama! O supreme among brahmanas! Refrain from fighting. O Bhargava! Bhishma is incapable of being killed by you and you by Bhishma.' All of them addressed him in this way and obstructed him in the field of battle. His ancestors made the descendant of the Bhrigu lineage lay down his weapons. Then I again saw those eight, who were knowledgeable about the brahman. They were as resplendent as eight rising planets. While I stood on the field of battle, they spoke these affectionate words to me. 'Go to the mighty-armed Rama, your preceptor. Do what is beneficial for the world.' On seeing that Rama had withdrawn because of the words of his well-wishers and for the welfare of the world, I acted in accordance with the words that had been spoken to me. I was severely wounded. But I went up to Rama and honoured him. Rama, the great ascetic, smiled affectionately at me and said, 'O Bhishma! In this world, there is no kshatriya like you who roams the earth. Go. In this fight, I have been extremely satisfied with you.' In my presence, Bhargava summoned the maiden. In the midst of those ascetics, he spoke these miserable words."'

Chapter 850(187)

'"Rama said, 'O beautiful one! In the sight of all the worlds, to the supreme extent of my capacity, I have shown great manliness. But in battle, I have not been able to establish my superiority over Bhishma, supreme among those who wield weapons, even though I exhibited my supreme weapons. This is the ultimate of my power. This is the ultimate of my strength. O fortunate one! Go wherever you wish. What else can I do for you? Seek refuge with Bhishma. There is no other recourse for you. Unleashing his great weapons, Bhishma has vanquished me.'"

'Bhishma said, "Having spoken in this way, the great-minded Rama sighed and was silent. The maiden then spoke to the descendant of the Bhrigu lineage. 'O illustrious one! It is just as your illustrious self has said. The intelligent Bhishma is invincible in battle, even to the gods. You have performed my task to the best of your capacity and the best of your endeavours. In this battle, you have been unrestrained in valour and have used many weapons. But in the end, he could not be surpassed in battle. Under no circumstances, will I go back to Bhishma again. O one rich in austerities! O extender of the Bhrigu lineage! Instead, I will go where I can myself bring Bhishma down in battle.' Her eyes red with anger, the maiden spoke in this way. Thinking about my death, she made up her mind to engage in austerities. O descendant of the Bharata lineage! After taking leave from me, Rama, supreme among the Bhrigu lineage, went with the sages to Mahendra, from where he had come. Praised by the brahmanas, I ascended my chariot and having entered the city, told my mother, Satyavati, everything that had transpired. O great king! She congratulated me. I instructed wise men to watch over the maiden's doings and from one day to another, they reported to me her goings, words and deeds. Every day, they were engaged in ensuring my welfare. From the moment the maiden left for the forest to perform austerities, I was miserable and wretched. It was as if I had lost my senses. O son![67] No kshatriya can vanquish me in battle with valour, except one who knows about the brahman, has performed austerities and is rigid in his vows.

'"O king! Because of my fear, I informed Narada and Vyasa about her deeds. Both of them told me, 'O Bhishma! You should not be despondent about the deeds of the daughter of Kashi. Through human efforts, who can counteract destiny?' O great king! The maiden resorted to a circle of hermitages that was on the banks of the Yamuna and engaged in superhuman austerities. She gave up food. She became thin and coarse. She had matted hair. She became covered with dirt and mud. Rich in austerities, she lived on air for

[67]The word used is tata.

six months and was like a pillar. Later, the beautiful one went to the banks of the Yamuna and stood in the water for one year, without taking any food. After that, for another year, she survived on a single leaf every day. She was terrible in her anger and stood on the tips of her toes. She continued in this way for twelve years and heated up heaven. None of her relatives were capable of restraining her. She went to Vatsabhumi,[68] frequented by siddhas and charanas. This was the hermitage of great-souled ascetics whose deeds were sacred. In that sacred region, she bathed day and night. O king! O Kouravya! The maiden from Kashi roamed around, as she willed, in the hermitage of Nanda, in the sacred hermitage of Uluka, the hermitage of Chyavana, the region of the brahman, Prayaga, the sacrificial region of the gods, the forests of the gods, Bhogavati, the hermitage of Koushika, the hermitage of Mandavya, the hermitage of Dilipa, Rama's lake[69] and the hermitage of Pailagargya. O king! O lord of the earth! The maiden from Kashi bathed at these *tirtha*s and performed terrible austerities.

'"O Kouraveya! My mother arose from the water and asked her, 'O fortunate one! Why are you undergoing this pain? Tell me truthfully.' O king! The unblemished one joined her hands in salutation and replied, 'O one with the beautiful eyes! Bhishma has not been defeated by Rama in battle. When he raises his arrows, who else can strive against that lord of the earth? I will myself observe extremely difficult austerities for Bhishma's destruction. O goddess! I will roam around the earth in order to kill that king. May this be the fruit that I obtain in another body.' The river that goes to the ocean then said, 'O beautiful one! You are following a crooked path. O one with the unblemished limbs! O lady! This desire of yours is impossible to accomplish. O maiden from Kashi! O beautiful one! If you observe a vow for Bhishma's destruction, if you indeed give up your body in this vow, you will only become a crooked river that

---

[68]This has been translated as the name of a hermitage. But it could also be a reference to the Vatsa kingdom, located at the confluence of the Ganga and the Yamuna.

[69]Meaning Parashurama and the lake in Kurukshetra.

has water during the rainy season. You will have terrible tirthas that no one will recognize. You will only flow during the rains and will remain dry for eight months. You will have terrible and fearful crocodiles and will be horrible to all beings.' O king! Having spoken thus, my immensely fortunate and beautiful mother smiled and tried to restrain the maiden from Kashi.

'"The one with the beautiful complexion did not eat or drink water, sometimes for eight months, sometimes for ten months. O Kourvaya! In her desire for more tirthas, the daughter of the king of Kashi again roamed around and fell into[70] Vatsabhumi. O descendant of the Bharata lineage! She became a river in Vatsabhumi, known as Amba.[71] She only flows in the rainy season. She has many crocodiles and terrible tirthas. She is crooked. O king! Through her austerities, half of the maiden became a river in Vatsa. The other half remained a maiden."'

Chapter 851(188)

'Bhishma said, "All the ascetics saw that she was firm in her resolution to perform austerities. O son![72] They tried to stop her and asked, 'What do you wish to accomplish?' The rishis were aged in their austerities and the maiden replied to them, 'I have been abandoned by Bhishma and have been dislodged from the dharma I would have obtained through a husband. O ones rich in austerities! I have consecrated myself for his death and not for the sake of any world.[73] I have resolved that I will achieve peace only through Bhishma's death. It is because of his deeds that I have obtained this eternal and infinite misery. I have been deprived of the world

[70]Because she became a river.
[71]There is an Amba River in Maharashtra, but that doesn't fit.
[72]The word used is tata.
[73]Obtained through austerities.

of a husband. I am neither a woman, nor a man. O ones rich in austerities! I will not desist until I have slain Gangeya in battle. This is the resolution in my heart and I am engaged for this purpose. I am disgusted with my state as a woman and I have made up my mind to become a man. I wish to exact vengeance on Bhishma. I should not be dissuaded again.' The god who wields the trident, Uma's consort, manifested himself. In the midst of the *maharshi*s, he showed his own form to the beautiful one. He satisfied her with a boon and she asked for my defeat. The god replied to the intelligent one, 'You will kill him.' At this, the maiden spoke to Rudra. 'O god! How can a woman like me be victorious in battle? O Uma's consort! Since I am a woman, my mind is deep.[74] O lord of beings! You have promised Bhishma's defeat. O one with the bull on the banner![75] Act so that your promise comes true, so that I can kill Bhishma, Shantanu's son, in battle.' The Mahadeva, with the bull on his banner, spoke truthfully to the maiden. 'O fortunate one! I do not utter false words. What I have said will come true. You will attain manhood and will kill Bhishma in battle. When you enter another body, you will remember everything. You will be born as a maharatha in Drupada's lineage. You will be an extremely honoured warrior who is swift in the use of weapons. O fortunate one! Everything will be exactly as I have said it will be. You will become a man after some time has passed.' Having thus spoken, Mahadeva Kapardi Vrishadhvaja[76] disappeared, while all the brahmanas looked on. In the sight of those maharshis, the unblemished one, the one with the beautiful complexion, gathered wood from the forest. She constructed an extremely large funeral pyre and set fire to it. O great king! When the fire was blazing, with rage igniting her senses, she said, 'This is for Bhishma's destruction.' O king! On the banks of the Yamuna, the eldest daughter of Kashi entered the fire.'"

[74]Probably signifying that the mind is calm and is not agitated or angry.

[75]Shiva has a bull on his banner.

[76]Mahadeva, Kapardi and Vrishadhvaja are Shiva's names. Mahadeva means the great god. Kapardi means the one with matted hair and Vrishadhvaja means the one with the bull on his banner.

Chapter 852(189)

'Duryodhana asked, "O Gangeya! How did the one who had been a maiden earlier become Shikhandi? O grandfather! O foremost among men in a battle! Tell me that."

'Bhishma said, "O Indra among kings! O lord of the earth! The beloved wife and queen of King Drupada did not have any sons. O great king! At that time, King Drupada satisfied Shankara for the sake of an offspring. Having determined to bring about our death, he resorted to terrible austerities.[77] He said, 'O illustrious one! I wish to have a son to exact vengeance on Bhishma.' But he obtained a daughter from Mahadeva, not a son. The god of gods replied, 'You will have a female child, who will be male. O lord of the earth! Return. It will not be otherwise.' He returned to the city and told his wife, 'O queen! I have made endeavours for a son and have performed great austerities. But Shambhu has said that we will have a daughter who will later become a man. When I repeatedly pleaded with him, Shambhu replied, "That is destiny and it cannot be otherwise. It is fated that way."' When her season arrived, King Drupada's spirited wife purified herself and united with Drupada. As had been decreed by destiny, she conceived at the right time, through Parshata.[78] O lord of the earth! This is what Narada told me. O descendant of the Kuru lineage! O descendant of the Kuru lineage! When the lotus-eyed queen conceived, out of hope for a son, the mighty-armed King Drupada happily tended to his beloved wife. King Drupada was childless. O lord of men! At the right time, Drupada's illustrious queen gave birth to a daughter who was supreme in her beauty. O Indra among kings! The king was without a son and had it proclaimed, 'A son has been born to me.' O lord of men! King Drupada concealed the facts and had all the rites performed for a son, as if he had a son. Drupada's

[77]This doesn't make sense. There was no enmity between Drupada and Bhishma. However, the plural 'our' is used in the text, not 'mine'. So this could be a reference to Drona and Drupada's enmity with Drona. However, Drupada had already obtained Dhrishtadyumna to ensure Drona's death.

[78]Parshata is Drupada's name.

queen protected the secret and made every effort to say that a son
had been born. Other than Parshata, no one else in the city knew. Out
of respect for the words of the god with extraordinary energy,[79] he
concealed that it was a daughter and said that it was a son. The king
performed all the rites connected with birth and everything else that
was decreed, as if it was a male child. He was known as Shikhandi.
I alone knew, through a spy, through Narada's words, through the
words of the god[80] and through Amba's austerities."'

Chapter 853(190)

'Bhishma said, "Drupada took great care about all his relatives.
O Indra among kings! Shikhandi[81] became supremely skilled
in painting and the arts. In the use of arrows and other weapons,
she became Drona's student. O great king! The beautiful[82] mother
asked the king to find a wife for the daughter, as if she were a son.
Parshata saw that his daughter had become mature. Knowing that
she was a woman, with his wife, he began to worry. Drupada said,
'My daughter has become mature and this increases my sorrows.
Following the words of the one who wields the trident, I have
concealed her. O great queen! That can never turn out to be false.
How can the creator of the three worlds utter a falsehood?' The wife
replied, 'O king! If it pleases you, listen to the words that I have to
say. O son of Prishata! Having heard, you should then carry out
your own tasks. O king! Let her take a wife in accordance with the
prescribed rites. It is my firm view that his[83] words will come true.'
Having thus decided on a course of action, the couple chose as a bride

[79]Meaning Shiva.

[80]Shiva.

[81]The text doesn't actually mention the name. It has been inserted here for
the sake of clarity.

[82]Literally, fair in complexion.

[83]Shiva's.

the daughter of the lord of Dasharna. King Drupada, lion among
men, asked about all the kings who had pure lineages. As Shikhandi's
wife, he chose the daughter of the king of Dasharna. The king of
Dasharna was known as Hiranyavarma. The lord of the earth gave
his daughter away to Shikhandi. King Hiranyavarma of Dasharna
was an extremely powerful king. He was unassailable and possessed
a large army. He was high-minded.

'"O supreme among kings! When the marriage had been
performed, the maiden attained maturity and so did the maiden
Shikhandi. Having obtained a wife, Shikhandi returned to Kampilya.[84]
For some time, the maiden did not know that she[85] was a woman.
When Hiranyavarma's daughter got to know this about Shikhandi, she
was ashamed and reported to her nurses and friends that Shikhandi,
the daughter of the king of Panchala, was a maiden. O tiger among
kings! The nurses from Dasharna were supremely distressed and
sent messengers[86] with the news. All the messengers told the lord
of Dasharna about the deception, exactly as it had happened and
the king was filled with anger. O great king! At that time, Shikhandi
conducted himself like a male in the royal household. Disregarding the
fact that he was a woman, he sported himself happily. O bull among
the Bharata lineage! O Indra among kings! When Hiranyavarma heard
about this a few days later, he was afflicted with anger. The king of
Dasharna was overcome with terrible rage. He sent a messenger to
Drupada's abode. Kanchanavarma's[87] messenger went to Drupada.
He took him aside and privately said, 'O king! The king of Dasharna
has spoken these words. O unblemished one! He is extremely enraged
at having been deceived by you. "O king! I have been insulted by you
and your bad counsel, that out of the delusion in your heart, you have
sought my daughter for your own daughter. O evil-minded one! You

[84]The capital of Panchala. Later known as Kampilgarh and Koil. Now
known as Aligarh.

[85]Shikhandi.

[86]To Hiranyavarma.

[87]Both *hiranya* and *kanchana* mean gold or golden. Hiranyavarma and
Kanchanavarma are synonyms.

will now reap the fruits of that deception. Be steady. I will uproot you, with your relatives and your advisers."'"'

Chapter 854(191)

'Bhishma said, "O king! Thus addressed by the messenger, Drupada was like a thief who had been caught in the act and could not utter a word. He made extreme efforts to pacify his in-law, through messengers who used sweet words to argue this wasn't the case. But the king[88] again ascertained the truth of the matter, that the daughter of Panchala was actually a maiden, and swiftly marched out. In accordance with the words of the nurses, he sent messengers to all his infinitely energetic friends about the deception that had been practised on his daughter. That supreme among kings assembled an army. O descendant of the Bharata lineage! He made up his mind to invade Drupada. O Indra among kings! King Hiranyavarma consulted with his friends about what should be done vis-a-vis the king of Panchala. All the great-souled kings decided, 'O king! If it is true that Shikhandi is a woman, we will bind the king of Panchala and take him home. We will instate another king as the king of Panchala. We will kill King Drupada, together with Shikhandi.' Having learnt about their resolution, the lord of men[89] again sent his *kshatta*[90] to Parshata with the words, 'Be steady. I am going to kill you.' King Drupada was timid by nature. In addition, the lord of men was guilty. He was overcome by dreadful fright. After having sent the messenger from Dasharna away, Drupada became extremely distressed. The lord of men, the king of Panchala, met his wife in private and spoke these words to Shikhandi's beloved mother. His heart was overcome by great fear and oppressed with grief. 'My extremely powerful in-law

---

[88]Hiranyavarma.

[89]Hiranyavarma.

[90]The word means the son of a shudra mother and a kshatriya father. It is applied for a steward or charioteer.

is full of anger. King Hiranyavarma will attack me with an army. I am a fool. What will I now do about our daughter? It is suspected that your son Shikhandi is actually a woman. Having determined that this is the truth and thinking that he has been deceived, with his friends, his forces and his followers, he wishes to destroy me. O one with the beautiful hips! O lovely one! Tell me what is true and what is false. O fortunate one! Having heard your words, I will act accordingly. I am in danger and so is the child Shikhandi. O queen! O one with the fair complexion! You also confront a great hardship. I am asking you to tell me everything. O one with the beautiful hips! O one with the beautiful smiles! Do not be frightened about Shikhandi. Knowing the truth, I will make arrangements. O one with the beautiful thighs! I was myself deceived because of the lawful rites that had been performed for a son. Thus I deceived the king of Dasharna, the lord of the earth. O immensely fortunate one! Tell me and I will act for our welfare.' The lord of men knew, but wished to establish his innocence before others.[91] Thus addressed, the queen replied to the lord of the earth in public.'"

Chapter 855(192)

'Bhishma said, "O lord of men! O mighty-armed one! Then Shikhandi's mother told her husband everything about the maiden Shikhandi. 'O king! I was without a son and was scared of my co-wives. Though Shikhandi was born as a girl, I reported that she was male. O best of men! O bull among kings! Out of affection towards me, you performed the rites for a son, though those for a daughter should have been performed. O king! Then you got the daughter of the lord of Dasharna as a wife. You remembered the purport of the words the god had spoken earlier. Though born as a girl, she would become a man later. So we overlooked it.' On hearing this, Drupada

[91]This part of the conversation was happening in public.

Yajnasena reported the entire truth to his advisers. O king! The king consulted with them, about what should be done to protect the subjects. O Indra among men! Though he had himself deceived the king of Dasharna, he was certain the matrimonial alliance was an appropriate one and was attentive to the consultations. O descendant of the Bharata lineage! The city was naturally protected for times of emergency. O Indra among kings! He fortified it more and adorned it everywhere. O bull among the Bharata lineage! Together with his wife, the king was extremely distressed at this enmity with the lord of Dasharna. Thinking about this great enmity with his in-law in his mind, he began to worship the gods. O king! On seeing him thus devoted to the gods and worshipping them, his wife, the queen, spoke these words. 'In times of prosperity, the worship of the gods is truly praised by the virtuous. Great worship is recommended for those who are immersed in an ocean of grief. Worship all the gods. Let there be large quantities of donations. Let oblations be offered into the fire, so that Dasharna can be countered. O lord! Think in your mind about how he can be restrained without a fight. Through the grace of the gods, all of this will happen. O one with the large eyes! Have consultations with your ministers, so that the city is not destroyed. O king! Act accordingly. O lord of the earth! Destiny, together with human endeavour, brings great success. But when they act against each other, neither succeeds. Therefore, together with your advisers, take appropriate measures for the city. O lord of the earth! Then worship the gods, as you please.' The spirited maiden, Shikhandi, was overcome with grief at seeing them converse in this fashion and was filled with shame. She thought, 'It is because of me that both of them are suffering.' She made up her mind to kill herself.

'"Having been overcome by terrible misery, she decided this and left the residence for the deep and deserted forest. O king! This happened to be ruled by a *yaksha*[92] named Sthunakarna. O lord! Because they were afraid of him, people avoided that forest. Sthuna's abode was constructed with bricks and was plastered white. It was

[92]Yakshas are semi-divine species and companions of Kubera, the god of treasure.

full of smoke from parched grain. It had high walls and a gate. O
king! Drupada's daughter, Shikhandi, entered there. She fasted for
many days and dried her body out. The yaksha Sthuna had eyes
like honey and showed himself to her. 'Why have you begun to do
this? Tell me and I will do it without any delay.' She replied to the
yaksha, 'This is impossible to accomplish.' However, the guhyaka[93]
told her, 'I will do it. O daughter of a king! I am the follower of the
lord of riches.[94] I am one who grants boons. I will even give what
cannot be granted. Tell me what you wish.' O descendant of the
Bharata lineage! Then Shikhandi told everything, in complete detail,
to the foremost of yakshas, Sthunarkarna. 'O yaksha! My father
faces a calamity and will soon be destroyed. In great anger, the lord
of Dasharna is invading him. The king with the golden armour[95] is
great in his strength and great in his energy. O yaksha! Therefore,
save me and my father and my mother. You have promised that you
will relieve my unhappiness. O yaksha! O unblemished one! Through
your favours, make me a man, before that king attacks my city. O
great yaksha! O guhyaka! Bestow your favours on me.'"

Chapter 856(193)

'Bhishma said, "O bull among the Bharata lineage! The yaksha
heard Shikhandi's words. Overpowered by destiny, he thought
about this in his mind. O Kourava! This was indeed destined for my
grief. He said, 'O fortunate one! Listen to me. I will do what you
desire, but there is a condition. For a limited period of time, I will
give you my male organ. But I tell you truthfully that when that time
is over, you must return to me. I am a lord whose wishes always

[93]Demi-gods similar to the yakshas, companions of Kubera.
[94]Kubera.
[95]The text uses the word Hemakavacha, translated as golden (*hema*) armour
(*kavacha*). This has the same meaning as Hiranyavarma, so Hemakavacha can
also be interpreted as a proper name.

come true. I can roam in the sky and can assume any form at will. Save your city and your relatives through my favours. O daughter of a king! I will bear your female organ. Promise me this and I will do what brings you pleasure.' Shikhandi replied, 'O illustrious one! I will return your male organ to you. O one who roams in the night! You will only bear my female organ for a limited period of time. When King Hemavarma[96] has returned to Dasharna, I will become a maiden again and you will become a man.' O king! Having said this, they made an agreement with each other. They transferred to each other their respective organs. O lord of men! The yaksha Sthunakarna wore the female organ and Shikhandi obtained the yaksha's blazing form. O king! Having become a man, Shikhandi from Panchala happily entered the city and went and met his father. He told Drupada everything, exactly as it had happened. On hearing this, Drupada was overcome with joy. Together with his wife, he remembered Maheshvara's words.

'"O king! He sent a message to the lord of Dasharna. 'My son is a man. You should have faith in me.' The king of Dasharna suddenly approached. Drupada, the king of Panchala, was full of grief and anger. When the lord of Dasharna approached Kampilya, he sent a messenger, supreme in the knowledge of the brahman, to him,[97] with the words, 'Honour him well and tell him this, on my instructions. "O evil-minded one! You chose my daughter for your daughter. There is no doubt that you will witness the fruits of that disrespect today."' O supreme among kings! Having been thus addressed, the brahmana messenger left for the city, under the instructions of the king of Dasharna. The foremost one approached Drupada in the city. O Indra among kings! Together with Shikhandi, the king of Panchala honoured him well and offered him a cow and the gift given to a guest.[98] He did not accept those honours and spoke these words in reply. 'The brave king Kanchanavarma has spoken thus. "O vile one! You have deceived me for the sake of your daughter. O evil-minded

---

[96]Hemavarma has the same meaning as Hiranyavarma.
[97]To Drupada.
[98]*Arghya.*

one! You will reap the fruits of that wicked deed. O lord of men!
Give me a fight. In the head of the battle today, I will uproot you,
together with your advisers, your sons and your relatives."' O best of
the Bharata lineage! In the midst of his ministers, the king heard all
these insulting words, spoken by the lord of Dasharna through that
foremost messenger. He bowed and said, 'O brahmana! You have
delivered the words that my in-law has spoken. My messenger will
carry the reply.' Drupada sent a brahmana messenger, knowledgeable
in the Vedas, to the great-souled Hiranyavarma. O king! He went
to the king who was the lord of Dasharna and repeated the words
spoken by Drupada. 'Let proper enquiries be made to show that my
son is a man. Someone has uttered a falsehood. What has been heard
should not be faithfully believed.' On hearing Drupada's words,
the king was distressed. He despatched supreme ladies, who were
extremely beautiful in form, to ascertain if Shikhandi was a woman
or a man. Having been sent, they learnt the truth. O Indra among
Kouravas! They reported everything to the immensely powerful king
of Dasharna—that Shikhandi was a man. Having done this, the king
was delighted. He approached his in-law and cheerfully dwelt with
him. That lord of men happily gave Shikhandi elephants, horses,
cows and many hundreds of servant-maids. Having been honoured
and having again conveyed his daughter,[99] King Hemavarma was
pacified that there had been no sin and returned happily. Shikhandi
was also delighted.

   "'After some time had passed, Naravahana Kubera[100] was touring
through the worlds and arrived in Sthuna's residence. The protector
of riches hovered over his house[101] and inspected it. He saw that
the yaksha Sthuna's abode was colourfully ornamented, with many
kinds of garlands. There was parched grain and fragrances and
beautiful canopies. It was delightful with the smoke of incense. It
was adorned with flags and pennants. There was food and drink,

---

[99]Back to the marital state.

[100]Kubera is described as Naravahana, because he has a man (*nara*) as his
mount or vehicle (*vahana*).

[101]Kubera was in the air, in his celestial vehicle or *vimana*.

grain and meat and a supply of liquor. When he saw that place, decorated in every direction, the lord of the yakshas spoke to the yakshas who were following him. 'O infinitely valiant ones! Sthuna's residence is decorated well. But why is the extremely evil-minded one not appearing before me now? The evil-souled one knows that I am here. But he does not appear before me. It is my view that a severe punishment should be levied on him.' The yakshas replied, 'O king! A daughter named Shikhandi was born to King Drupada. For her, and for some reason, he has given her his marks of a man. He has accepted the marks of a woman. Having become a woman, he remains in his house. That is the reason he has not appeared. He is ashamed that he now has the form of a woman. O king! That is the reason you have not seen Sthuna today. Having heard this, do what you think is proper. Let the vimana be stationed here.' The lord of yakshas replied, 'Let Sthuna be brought here.' And repeatedly said, 'I will punish him.' O lord of the earth! O great king! On being summoned by the Indra among the yakshas, he went and stood there, ashamed in his female form. O descendant of the Kuru lineage! The lord of riches was extremely wrathful and cursed him. 'O guhyaka! This female form of the sinful one will remain.' Thus did the great-souled lord of the yakshas speak. 'O one who has committed an evil act! Since you have insulted the yakshas in your wicked wisdom and have given your organ away to Shikhandi, accepting the organ of a woman, in your extremely vile intelligence, you have committed an act that has never been done before. Therefore, from now on, you will be a woman and not a man.' For the sake of Sthuna, the yakshas sought to appease Vaishravana.[102] They repeatedly asked him to set a time limit to the curse. O son![103] Then the great-souled Indra among the yakshas replied to his followers, all those masses of yakshas, wishing to set a limit to the curse. 'When Shikhandi has been killed in battle, the yaksha Sthuna will regain his old form. Let the great-spirited one not be anxious.' Having thus spoken, the illustrious

[102]The son of Vishrava, Kubera.

[103]The word used is tata.

god, worshipped by the yakshas and the rakshasas, departed with all his followers, who could travel in an instant.

'"Having been cursed, Sthuna lived there. At the appointed time, Shikhandi came to the one who travels in the night. He approached him and said, 'O lord! I have arrived before you.' Sthuna was delighted and repeatedly told him, 'I am pleased with you.' On seeing that the prince Shikhandi had arrived, without being deceitful about it, he told him everything that had transpired. The yaksha said, 'O son of a king! It is because of you that Vaishravana has cursed me. Go and happily travel the world, as you desire. I think that this, your coming here and the sight of Poulastya,[104] has been destined from earlier and cannot be countered.' O descendant of the Bharata lineage! Having been thus addressed by the yaksha Sthuna, Shikhandi was filled with great joy and returned to his city. He worshipped brahmanas, gods, sanctuaries and crossroads with many fragrances and garlands and a great deal of riches. Drupada of Panchala and his relatives found extreme delight in his son, Shikhandi, who had accomplished his objective. O bull among the Kurus! He gave Shikhandi to Drona as a student. O great king! This was a son who had been a woman earlier. Shikhandi, the son of a king, together with Parshata Dhrishtadyumna and all of you, learnt the four parts of *Dhanurveda*. O son![105] Through spies, who pretended to be stupid and were deaf and blind, appointed by me against Drupada, I got to know exactly what was going on. O great king! Thus, Drupada's offspring is both a woman and a man. O foremost among the Kouravas! He became a supreme *ratha*.[106] The eldest daughter of the king of Kashi was known by the name of Amba. O bull among the Bharata lineage! She was born in Drupada's lineage as Shikhandi. When he appears before me with a bow in his hand, desiring to fight, I will not glance at him even for an instant and will not strike. This

---

[104]Kubera. Kubera was the son of Vishrava and Vishrava was the son of Pulastya.

[105]The word used is tata.

[106]A ratha is a great warrior.

has always been my vow and it is renowned throughout the earth.
O descendant of the Kourava lineage! I will not shoot arrows at a
woman, one who has earlier been a woman, one who has the name
of a woman and one who has the form of a woman. Because of this
reason, I will not kill Shikhandi. O son![107] I know the truth about
Shikhandi's birth. Therefore, I will not kill him, when he seeks to
slay me. Bhishma would rather kill himself than kill a woman. When
I see him stationed in battle, I will not kill him."

'Sanjaya said, "On hearing this, King Kouravya Duryodhana
thought for some time, reflecting that this was worthy of Bhishma."'

Chapter 857(194)

'Sanjaya said, "When the night had passed and it was morning, in
the midst of the entire army, your son again asked the grandfather.
'O Gangeya! The supreme army of the Pandaveyas has many men,
elephants and horses and is full of many *maharatha*s. It is protected
by immensely strong and great archers, Bhima, Arjuna and the others,
with Dhrishtadyumna at the forefront. It is as if it is protected by
the guardians of the world themselves.[108] It is unassailable. It is as
unstoppable as a raging ocean. In a great battle, this ocean of soldiers
cannot be ruffled even by the gods. O Gangeya! O immensely radiant
one! By what time will you be able to destroy it, or the great archer
the preceptor, or the immensely strong Kripa? Or Karna, who prides
himself in war, or Drona's son,[109] supreme among brahmanas? All of
you in my army are knowledgeable about the use of divine weapons.
Therefore, I wish to know this. I have always had a supreme curiosity
in my heart about this. O mighty-armed one! Tell me about this.'"

[107]The word used is tata.
[108]*Lokapala*s. The guardians (*pala*) of the worlds (*loka*) are eight in
number—Indra, Vahni (Agni), Yama, Nairrita, Varuna, Maruta, Kubera and
Isha (Ishana). Sometimes, Vayu is listed instead of Indra.
[109]Ashvatthama.

'Bhishma replied, "O foremost among the Kurus! O lord of the earth! This is indeed worthy of you, that you should ask about the strengths and weaknesses of the enemy and about your own side. O king! O mighty-armed one! Hear about the limits of my strength in battle, the limits of my weapons and the valour of my arms in battle. In battle, an ordinary man must be fought without deceit. Those who know maya[110] must be fought with maya. That is the determination of dharma. Let me divide the days, taking the forenoon of each day as my share. O immensely radiant one! I think that I can take ten thousand warriors as my share. It is my view that I can take one thousand rathas as my share. O mighty-armed one! O descendant of the Bharata lineage! In this fashion, I can kill the soldiers of the Pandavas. In this way, always armoured and always ready, I can destroy this great army over a certain period of time. O descendant of the Bharata lineage! If I am stationed in battle and unleash my great weapons, which are capable of killing hundreds and thousands, I can kill them in one month."

'Sanjaya said, "O Indra among kings! On hearing Bhishma's words, King Duryodhana then asked Drona, supreme among the Angiras lineage. 'O preceptor! In how much time can you slay the soldiers of the sons of Pandu?' Drona smiled and replied, 'O best of the Kurus! I am aged. My energy and strength are weak. It is my view that with the fire of my weapons, I can consume the army of the Pandavas in one month, just like Bhishma, Shantanu's son. That is the limit of my power and strength.' Kripa Sharadvata said two months and Drona's son promised the destruction of the army in ten nights. But Karna, skilled in the use of great weapons, promised it in five nights. When the son of the one who heads to the ocean[111] heard the words of the suta's son, he laughed out aloud and spoke these words. 'O Radheya! As long as you have not encountered Partha in battle, wielding arrows, a sword and a bow, with Achyuta Vasudeva steering the chariot, till that time you can think in this way. You are capable of speaking a lot and saying anything that you want.'"'

---

[110]Illusion.
[111]Bhishma, the son of a river.

Chapter 858(195)

Vaishampayana said, 'O best of the Bharata lineage! Having heard this, Kounteya[112] summoned his brothers in private and spoke these words to them. "I have spies in the army of Dhritarashtra's son. When night had passed, they brought me this news. Duryodhana asked the son of the river, the one who is great in his vows. 'O lord! How long will you take to kill the soldiers of the Pandus?' He told the evil-minded son of Dhritarashtra that he would take a month. Drona promised the same period of time. Goutama[113] said double the time. We hear that Drona's son, skilled in the use of great weapons, promised ten nights. When Karna, skilled in the use of divine weapons, was asked in the assembly of the Kurus, he promised to kill the army in five days. O Arjuna! Therefore, I wish to hear your words. In how many days can you destroy the enemies in battle?" Thus addressed by the king, Gudakesha Dhananjaya looked towards Vasudeva and replied in these words. "All of them are great-souled and skilled in the use of weapons. They can fight in many ways. O great king! There is no doubt that they will kill your soldiers. But I speak the truth when I say that you should not be tortured in your mind. When I have Vasudeva as an aide, on a single chariot, I can slay the three worlds in an instant, with the immortals, with their mobile and immobile objects, and with everything that is the past, the present and the future. That is my view. I possess the terrible and great weapon that Pashupati gave me when there was a duel with the hunter.[114] At the end of a yuga, that is employed by Pashupati to destroy all the beings. O tiger among men! I know how to use that. Gangeya does not know this, nor do Drona and Goutama. O king! Neither do Drona's son and the son of the suta. One should not use such divine weapons to kill ordinary people in battle. Without resorting to deceit, we will vanquish our enemies in battle. O king! These tigers among men are your aides. All of them are skilled in

---

[112]Yudhishthira.

[113]Kripa.

[114]Shiva disguised as a hunter. This has been described in Section 31.

the use of divine weapons. All of them delight in war. All of them
have bathed themselves in *Vedanta*[115] and are invincible. O Pandava!
They will even kill the soldiers of the gods in battle. Shikhandi,
Yuyudhana,[116] Parshata Dhrishtadyumna, Bhimasena, the twins,
Yudhamanyu, Uttamouja, Virata and Drupada, who are the equals
of Bhishma and Drona in battle, and you yourself are capable of
annihilating the three worlds. You are like Vasava in your radiance.
If a man looks at you in anger, there is no doubt that he will soon
cease to exist. O Kourava![117] I know this.'''

Chapter 859(196)

Vaishampayana said, 'The sky was clear in the morning. On
the instructions of Dhritarashtra's son, Duryodhana, the
kings advanced towards the Pandavas. All of them had bathed and
purified themselves. They were garlanded and were dressed in white
garments. They wielded weapons and banners. Benedictions had
been pronounced on them and oblations offered into the fire. All of
them were learned in the Vedas. All of them were brave. They were
excellent in the observance of vows. All of them had performed deeds.
All of them possessed many auspicious signs. They were extremely
strong and wished to earn supreme worlds[118] in the field of battle.
All of them were focused in their minds and trusted each other. Vinda
and Anuvinda from Avanti, the Kekayas and the Bahlikas—all of
them marched out, with Bharadvaja[119] at the forefront. There were
Ashvatthama, Shantanu's son, Saindhava Jayadratha, rathas from

[115]Literally, Vedanta means the end of the Vedas and is identified with the
philosophy of the Upanishads.

[116]Satyaki.

[117]Since Kuru was a common ancestor, the Pandavas can also be referred
to as Kouravas.

[118]After death.

[119]Drona.

the south, the west and the mountainous regions, Shakuni, the king of Gandhara, everyone from the east and the north, Shakas, Kiratas, Yavanas, Shibis and Vasatis. Their own soldiers accompanied and surrounded the maharathas. All these maharathas marched out in the second division of the army—Kritavarma with his soldiers, the immensely strong Trigartas and King Duryodhana, surrounded by his brothers. Shala, Bhurishrava, Shalya and Brihadbala from Kosala followed at the rear, with Dhritarashtra's son at the forefront. These maharathas desired to fight and were armoured. They advanced over the plain ground to the western[120] side of Kurukshetra. O descendant of the Bharata lineage! Duryodhana set up a camp there and with its decorations, it looked like a second Hastinapura. O Indra among kings! Even skilled men who lived in the city, could not distinguish between the city and the camp. The Kouravya king constructed many other similar fortresses, in hundreds and thousands, for the kings. O king! The hundreds of dwellings of the troops stretched out on that field of battle in a circle and extended over five *yojanas*.[121] According to their energy and their strength, the lords of the earth entered their respective camps. There were thousands of these and they were opulent. For those great-souled ones and their soldiers, and also for those who would not fight, King Duryodhana apportioned out excellent food. There were elephants, horses, men, artisans, others who followed, bards, singers, minstrels, traders, courtesans and whores.[122] There were also those who had gathered as spectators. In the proper way, King Kourava attended to all of them.'

Chapter 860(197)

Vaishampayana said, 'O descendant of the Bharata lineage! In a similar way, Kounteya Yudhishthira, the son of Dharma, urged

---

[120]This can also be translated as towards the back of Kurukshetra.

[121]A yojana is a measure of distance and is between eight and nine miles.

[122]Two separate words are used in the text for courtesans, *ganika* and *vara*.

his warriors, with Dhrishtadyumna at the forefront. He instructed the leaders of the Chedis, the Kashis and the Karushas, who were firm in their valour, the general Dhrishtaketu, the destroyer of enemies and the slayer of foes, Virata, Drupada, Yuyudhana, Shikhandi and the two great archers from Panchala, Yudhamanyu and Uttamouja. The brave ones wore colourful armour and were adorned in golden earrings. They blazed like a fire in a sacrificial altar, when clarified butter is poured into it. The great archers were as resplendent as planets. The lord of the earth, bull among men, honoured the soldiers in the appropriate fashion and instructed the soldiers to advance. Pandu's son first sent Abhimanyu, Brihanta and all the sons of Droupadi, who were led by Dhrishtadyumna. Yudhishthira despatched Bhima, Yuyudhana and Pandava Dhananjaya in the second part of the army. As the delighted warriors collected their weapons of war and moved and dashed around, the sound seemed to touch heaven. With the other kings and with Virata and Drupada, the king himself marched at the rear. That army with terrible archers had Dhrishtadyumna at the forefront. It looked like the Ganga, overflowing, retreating and then flowing again. So as to confuse the intelligence of the sons of Dhritarashtra, the king again regrouped his army. Pandava ordered Droupadi's sons, great archers, Nakula, Sahadeva, all the Prabhadrakas, ten thousand horses, two thousand elephants, ten thousand infantry, five thousand chariots and the invincible Bhimasena to be the first division of the army. He placed Virata, Jayatsena from Magadha, the two maharathas from Panchala, Yudhamanyu and Uttamouja, both of whom were valiant and great-souled and wielded clubs and bows, in the middle. Vasudeva and Dhananjaya also followed them in the centre. These men wielded weapons and were consumed with rage. Those brave ones carried twenty thousand flags. There were five thousand elephants and chariots everywhere, with infantry and soldiers, brandishing bows, swords and clubs. There were thousands in the front and thousands at the rear. The other kings mainly surrounded the spot

---

These are synonyms. Some non-critical versions read *chara* (spy) instead of vara. Chara should probably be right.

where Yudhishthira himself was, with his soldiers and an ocean of troops. O descendant of the Bharata lineage! There were thousands of elephants, tens of thousands of horses and thousands of chariots and infantry. Depending on these, he marched against Dhritarashtra's son, Suyodhana. There were hundreds and thousands, and tens of thousands, of men at the rear. In thousands and tens of thousands, those delighted men sounded thousands of kettledrums and tens of thousands of conch shells.'

This ends Udyoga Parva.

Bhishma Parva

In the 18-parva classification of the Mahabharata, Bhishma Parva is sixth. This segment covers the first ten days of the war and is named after Bhishma, because Bhishma was the commander during this phase of the battle. Other than Bhishma, no major warriors are killed in this parva which also includes the Bhagavad Gita. This parva has 117 chapters. In the 100-parva classification of the Mahabharata, Sections 61 through 64 constitute Bhishma Parva. In the numbering of the chapters in Bhishma Parva, the first number is a consecutive one, starting with the beginning of the Mahabharata. And the second number, within brackets, is the numbering of the chapter within the parva.

Jambukhanda-Vinirmana Parva

This parva has 378 shlokas and eleven chapters.

Vinirmana *means creation, as well as measuring out,
the latter meaning being relevant here. Jambukhanda or
Jambudvipa is one of the continents on earth. It is the
central one. This section is about geography and is so
named because it gives the measure of Jambukhanda.*

Chapter 861(1)

Janamejaya asked, 'How did those brave ones, the Kurus, the
Pandavas, the Somakas and the extremely fortunate kings who
had assembled from many countries, fight?'

Vaishampayana said, 'O lord of the earth! Listen to how those
brave ones, the Kurus, the Pandavas and the Somakas, fought in

Kurukshetra, the region where austerities were performed. Arriving in Kurukshetra, the extremely powerful Pandavas, together with the Somakas, were desirous of victory and advanced against the Kouravas. All of them were accomplished in the study of the Vedas and rejoiced at the prospect of battle. They wished to be victorious in the fight and were ready to be slain in the field of battle. They advanced towards the invincible army of Dhritarashtra's son and, together with their soldiers, set up camp on the western side, facing the east. In the prescribed fashion, Kunti's son, Yudhishthira, instructed that thousands of camps should be set up in the region beyond Samantapanchaka.[1] The entire earth seemed to be devoid of horses, men, chariots and elephants, with only children and the aged remaining. O supreme among kings! That large army was as large as the entire spread of Jambudvipa,[2] over which the sun radiates heat. All the varnas were together and the expanse covered many yojanas, encompassing in due course, all the regions, rivers, mountains and forests. King Yudhishthira, bull among all men, instructed that the best of food, and every object of enjoyment, should be supplied to them and their mounts. Yudhishthira assigned diverse kinds of signs to them, so that in this fashion, they would know that they belonged to the Pandaveya side.[3] With the time for battle having arrived, Kouravya[4] instructed that all of them should have signs and emblems, so that they might be recognized. When Dhritarashtra's great-minded son saw the tops of the standards of the Parthas, he and all the kings arrayed themselves against the Pandavas. He was in the midst of one thousand elephants and was surrounded by his brothers, with a white umbrella held aloft his head. On seeing Duryodhana thus,

[1]Samantapanchaka is another name for Kurukshetra, usually explained because of the five (*pancha*) lakes created by Parashurama. Alternatively, it is said that the land was five yojanas in every direction.

[2]The earth is divided into different continents (*dvipa*). The number varies, but is usually stated to be seven. The central one is Jambudvipa, named after *jambu*, the *jamun* tree. Bharatavarsha is in the centre of Jambudvipa.

[3]That is, there were passwords and other signs that the Pandava army would use with each other.

[4]Yudhishthira.

all the Pandava soldiers were delighted. All of them blew on giant
conch shells and sounded thousands of kettledrums. The Pandavas
and the valiant Vasudeva were delighted to see that their soldiers were
rejoicing. To delight their warriors, Vasudeva and Dhananjaya, tigers
among men who were stationed on their chariot, blew their divine
conch shells. Both Panchajanya and Devadatta resounded.[5] At this,
like deer on hearing the sound of a roaring lion, the warriors and the
mounts released urine and excrement. At that time, Dhritarashtra's
army was frightened on hearing this. A terrible dust arose and nothing
could be seen. Enveloped in the dust raised by the soldiers, the sun
disappeared. Clouds rained down showers of flesh and blood and this
covered all the soldiers. It was extraordinary. Then, near the ground,
a wind arose, carrying small stones. The troops were afflicted with
this, but the dust was dispelled. O king! The two armies stood ready
and stationed in Kurukshetra, delighted at the prospect of battle, like
two turbulent oceans. The encounter between those two armies was
extraordinary, like two oceans when the end of a yuga has arrived.
When the Kouravas[6] assembled their armies, the entire earth became
empty, with the exception of the aged and children.

'O bull among the Bharata lineage! Then the Kurus, Pandavas
and Somakas had an agreement and established rules of dharma
that would be followed in the war. When hostilities ceased, there
would be friendliness towards each other, as was the appropriate
behaviour earlier. There would be no resort to deceit again. Those
engaged in a war of words would be countered with words. Those
who had withdrawn from the midst of battle should not be killed
under any circumstances. O descendant of the Bharata lineage! A
ratha should only fight with a ratha, one on an elephant with another
on an elephant, one on a horse with another on a horse and a foot
soldier with a foot soldier. Any striking should be in accordance with
appropriateness, valour, energy and age and after a challenge had
been issued. It should not be against one who was unsuspecting or
distressed, or was engaged in fighting with another, or was distracted

---

[5]Panchajanya is Krishna's conch shell and Devadatta is Arjuna's.
[6]Meaning both Yudhishthira and Duryodhana.

or retreating. One who was without a weapon or without armour should never be killed. One should never strike charioteers, those carrying burdens,[7] those carrying weapons and those who sound kettledrums or conch shells. Having concluded this agreement, the Kurus, the Pandavas and the Somakas looked at each other in supreme wonder. Those great-souled bulls among men stationed themselves and together with their soldiers, were extremely delighted in their minds.'

Chapter 862(2)

Vaishampayana said, 'When the terrible war was imminent, the illustrious rishi Vyasa, best among all those who knew all the Vedas and Satyavati's son, the grandfather of the Bharatas, watched, in the morning and the evening.[8] The illustrious one could see the past, the present and the future. He met the king, Vichitravirya's son,[9] in private, in distress and in sorrow over the evil conduct of his sons and spoke these words.

'Vyasa said, "O king! The time has arrived for you, your sons and the lords of the earth. They have assembled in battle and will kill each other. O descendant of the Bharata lineage! Their time is over and they will be destroyed. Remember that all this is due to destiny and do not sorrow in your mind. O lord of the earth! If you wish to witness the battle, I will give you sight, so that you can see the war."

[7]The word used in the text is *dhurya*. This means one who carries a burden and can be a beast or a man.

[8]The Critical edition may have got this wrong. It uses the word *sandhya*, which means both morning and dusk. Some non-critical versions use the word *sainya*. In that case, Vyasa would have seen the soldiers extending to the front and the rear (instead of morning and dusk) and that fits better.

[9]Dhritarashtra was Vichitravirya's son because his mother was Vichitravirya's wife. But Dhritarashtra was actually Vyasa's son. In that sense, Vyasa was a grandfather.

'Dhritarashtra replied, "O supreme among brahmarshis! I do not wish to see my relatives being killed. Through your energy, I wish to hear about the smallest details in this war."'

Vaishampayana said, 'Since he did not wish to see the war, but wished to hear about it, the lord of all boons granted a boon to Sanjaya.[10]

'Vyasa said, "O king! This Sanjaya will describe the war to you. Nothing in this entire battle will remain unseen to him. O king! Having obtained this divine eyesight, Sanjaya will know everything about the battle and will recount it to you. Whether it is evident or hidden, whether it is night or day, Sanjaya will know everything, even if it is thought of in the mind. Weapons will not pierce him. Nor will he be constrained by exhaustion. Gavalgana's son will emerge alive from the battle. O bull among the Bharata lineage! I will spread the deeds of the Kurus and all the Pandavas. Do not sorrow. This was destined a long time ago. Therefore, you should not sorrow. It could not have been averted. Where dharma exists, victory is there."'

Vaishampayana said, 'Having spoken in this way, the illustrious great-grandfather[11] again spoke to the mighty-armed Dhritarashtra. "O great king![12] There will be a great destruction in this battle. Many fearful portents can be seen. Hawks, vultures, crows, herons and wild crows are assembling in great numbers at the ends of the forests. These birds are extremely agitated at seeing the prospects of a war. These predators will feed on the flesh of elephants and horses. With the terrible sound of 'khatakhata', signifying a calamity, the herons are flying in the centre, towards the southern direction.[13] O

---

[10]In earlier sections, such as Section 60, there is a suggestion that Sanjaya knew what was going on, without being actually present. However, the boon of being able to see from afar, is bestowed here.

[11]The text uses the word *prapitamaha*, though Vyasa is actually the paternal grandfather.

[12]The text does not explicitly state that this is Vyasadeva speaking. It is left implicit. Hence, we have inserted these quotation marks.

[13]'Khatakhata' is a crackling sound. When meteors fall down, signifying a calamity, they make this sound. The south is the direction of death.

descendant of the Bharata lineage! I have always been observing, both at dawn and dusk. When it rises, the sun is covered by headless torsos.[14] They have three colours. They are white and red at the edges and are black in the neck. They are tinged with lightning. They look like clubs and envelope the sun. Irrespective of what time of the day it is, during the day and at night, I have seen the sun, the moon and the stars blazing. This signifies destruction. Even when it is the full moon night in Kartika, the moon is so bereft of radiance that it cannot be seen. It has the complexion of fire and the sky has the same complexion. Heroes, kings and brave princes, with arms like clubs, will be killed. Those brave kings will cover the earth. At night, I always hear a terrible sound in the sky, that of a boar and a cat fighting. The idols of the gods sometimes tremble and sometimes laugh. They vomit blood from their mouths, sweat and fall down. O lord of the earth! Kettledrums sound without being struck. The great chariots of the kshatriyas move, without being yoked. Cuckoos, woodpeckers, blue jays, watercocks, parrots, herons and peacocks utter terrible sounds. When the sun rises, hundreds of locusts can be seen. They are like ornamented warriors wielding arms, armoured and riding on horses. O descendant of the Bharata lineage! At both dawn and dusk, the directions blaze, as if on fire. There are showers of blood and bone. O king! Arundhati is famous and revered by virtuous ones in the three worlds. She moves Vasishtha to the back.[15] O king! Shanaishchara is based in Rohini and is oppressing it. The mark on the moon has disappeared, signifying a great danger.[16] Even when there are no clouds, a great and terrible roar can continuously be heard. The mounts weep and shed drops of tears."'

[14]That is, clouds in this shape. The headless torso can be an allusion to Rahu.

[15]Arundhati is the rishi Vasishtha's devoted wife. However, Vasishtha and Arundhati are also stars in Ursa Majoris or *saptarshi*, the constellation of the Great Bear. As a star, Vasishtha is prominent, while Arundhati is faint. As a sign of abnormal times, Arundhati is shining more than Vasishtha.

[16]Shanaishchara or Shani is the planet Saturn. Rohini is the fourth of the twenty-seven *nakshatra*s.

Chapter 863(3)

'Vyasa said, "Cows give birth to asses. Sons have intercourse with their mothers. When it is not the season, trees in the forest can be seen to produce flowers and fruit. Princes are pregnant and are giving birth to monsters. Predatory birds are feeding on other birds and jackals on other animals. Inauspicious animals with terrible teeth are born, with three horns, four eyes, five legs, two penises, two heads and two tails. They have wide open jaws and are emitting inauspicious sounds. There are horses with three feet, crests, four eyes and horns. In your city, the wives of those who are learned about the brahman are seen to give birth to birds and peacocks. O lord of the earth! Mares give birth to calves and she-dogs to jackals. Cocks, mynahs[17] and parrots are uttering inauspicious sounds. Women are giving birth to four and five daughters at the same time. As soon as they are born, they are dancing, singing and laughing. In their houses, inferior ones can be seen to be playing, suckling, dancing and singing. These are signs of a great calamity. Driven by destiny, other children are seen to paint armed men who are running around, with staffs in their hands. Desirous of fighting, they are laying siege to cities. Lotuses, blue lotuses and night-lotuses[18] are growing on trees. Strong winds are blowing and the dust is not abating. The earth is trembling and the sun seems to have been swallowed by Rahu.[19] The white planet has passed beyond Chitra and is established there.[20] In particular, all this shows harm for the Kurus. There is an

---

[17]*Sharika*, the bird *Turdus Salica*.

[18]*Padma* (a lotus in general), *utpala* (a blue lotus) and *kumuda* (a lotus that grows in the night or a water lily) respectively.

[19]Rahu is a demon. At the time of the churning of the ocean, he disguised himself as a god and began to drink *amrita*. This was noticed by the sun and the moon and they reported this to Vishnu, who sliced off Rahu's head with his *chakra*. Rahu is a head without a body. Seeking revenge against the sun and the moon, he swallows them at the time of an eclipse.

[20]The white planet is Shukra. Chitra is the fourteenth nakshatra, Spica. Shukra has passed beyond Chitra, towards the fifteenth nakshatra, Svati (Arcturus), whose lord is Rahu. The white planet might also be Ketu.

extremely terrible comet and it is based in Pushya and is oppressing it.[21] This great planet will be inauspicious for the armies. Angaraka is retrograde and is in Magha, while Brihaspati is in Shravana.[22] The son of the sun is in Bhaga nakshatra and is oppressing it.[23] O lord of the earth! Shukra is rising towards Purva Proshthapada. Having crossed it, it is glancing towards Uttara.[24] The dark planet is blazing, with smoke and fire. It is based in, and is attacking, Indra's energetic nakshatra, Jyeshtha.[25] Dhruva is flaming and is circling towards the left in a terrible way.[26] The harsh planet is established between Chitra and Svati.[27] The one with radiance like the fire is retrograde, having completed its regular course.[28] It is full of the energy of the brahman and is red in its body. It is established in Shravana. The earth that produces fruit is full of every kind of grain.[29] Every stalk of barley has five ears and every stalk of paddy a hundred ears. Cattle are the foremost in all the worlds and they sustain the entire universe. When they are milked after calving, they only yield blood.

'"The bows radiate rays of light. The swords are flaming terribly. The weapons are seen to be unsheathed. A battle is at hand. The weapons, the water, the armour and the standards are shining with

[21]Pushya is the eighth nakshatra.

[22]Angaraka is Mars, while Magha is the tenth nakshatra. Brihaspati is Jupiter, while Shravana is the twenty-second nakshatra.

[23]The son of the sun is Shani and Bhaga is the presiding deity for the eleventh nakshatra, Purva Phalguni. However, we have earlier been told that Saturn is in Rohini. There is a contradiction in the positions of the planets across these two chapters.

[24]Shukra is Venus and Purva Proshthapada is the same as Purva Bhadrapada, the twenty-fifth nakshatra. Uttara means Uttara Bhadrapada, the twenty-sixth nakshatra.

[25]The dark planet is Saturn, Jyeshtha is the eighteenth nakshatra and its presiding deity is Indra. However, we have earlier been told that Saturn is in Rohini.

[26]Dhruva is the pole star.

[27]The harsh planet is probably Rahu.

[28]Because of the energy of the brahman and Shravana, this seems to be Jupiter.

[29]Even if it is the wrong season for that kind of grain.

the complexion of the fire, foretelling great destruction. In every direction, animals and birds can be seen, emitting harsh noises and their mouths blazing. This signifies a great calamity. A bird with one wing, one eye and one leg is flying in the sky at night. It is screaming terribly, repeatedly vomiting blood. The blazing planets are stationed, with copper-red crests. But the radiance of saptarshi[30] has been dimmed. The two blazing planets, Brihaspati and Shani, are near Vishakha[31] and have become stationary for a year. The terrible planet is established like a comet and has robbed Krittika, the first among nakshatras in brilliance, of its radiance.[32] O lord of the earth! The nakshatras were earlier classified into three groups.[33] Budha's[34] glances are descending on them and this engenders great fear. Earlier, the night of the new moon used to be on the fourteenth, fifteenth or sixteenth lunar day. But like now, I do not know of it occurring on the thirteenth. On the thirteenth lunar day and in the same month, eclipses of the sun and the moon took place. These eclipses occurred at the wrong times, signifying a destruction of living beings. All the directions are covered in dust and dust is showering everywhere. There are terrible and ill portents in the clouds. Blood showers down in the night. There are also terrible showers of flesh

---

[30]Saptarshi means the seven (*sapta*) great sages (rishi). But here, it means the constellation Ursa Majoris (Great Bear).

[31]Vishakha is the sixteenth nakshatra.

[32]The identification of the terrible planet is not clear, but it could be Ketu, Rahu's headless torso. Krittika is the Pleiades, the third of the twenty-seven nakshatras. The reference to Krittika as the first might also mean that the ordering of the nakshatras used to be different earlier.

[33]There are different ways of classifying the twenty-seven nakshatras. The three-fold classification can be a reference to their categorization as upward looking, downward looking and ones that look straight or sideways. Alternatively, kings are divided into three categories, those who own elephants, those who own horses and those who own men. The nine nakshatras that begin with Ashvini signify danger to kings who own horses, if evil planets influence them. The nine nakshatras that begin with Magha have the same implication for kings who own elephants and the nine nakshatras that begin with Mula have that implication for kings who own men.

[34]Budha is Mercury.

on the fourteenth day of the dark lunar fortnight. The rakshasas are not satiated and utter terrible roars in the middle of the night. The great rivers are flowing in the opposite direction and water has turned into blood. The wells are foaming and roaring like bulls. Meteors are descending with roars, inter-mingled with dry thunder.[35] It is now night and the impaired sun will arise at dawn. Giant and fiery meteors have covered everything in the four directions. Maharshis have said that when the sun is thus afflicted, the earth will drink the blood of thousands of kings. From Kailasa and Mandara and also from the Himalaya mountains, thousands of sounds are heard, as the summits fall down. There are giant tremors in the ground and because of this, the four oceans are repeatedly overflowing their shores. Fierce winds that are full of pebbles are blowing, crushing the trees. In villages, towns and sanctuaries, trees are falling down. When brahmanas pour oblations into the fire, it becomes yellow, red or blue. The flames bend to the left and have a bad smell. They are generally full of smoke and make harsh sounds. O lord of the earth! Touch, smell and taste have become contrary. The standards of kings tremble repeatedly and emit smoke. Kettledrums and war drums release showers of coal dust. From the tops of palaces and the gates of cities, vultures form circles and fly to the left, uttering terrible cries. They are uttering terrible cries of 'paka, paka'[36] and so are the crows. They are perching on the tops of standards and this forebodes the destruction of the kings. Distressed and weeping horses and thousands of elephants are trembling and are running here and there, releasing urine and dung. O descendant of the Bharata lineage! Having heard this and the time having arrived, do what is necessary, so that the world does not head towards destruction."'

Vaishampayana said, 'Having heard the words of his father, Dhritarashtra said, "I think that all of this has been ordained earlier and there is no doubt that it will happen. If there is a battle and kshatriyas kill, in accordance with the dharma of kshatriyas, they will attain the world of heroes and only obtain happiness. These

---

[35]That is, without rain.

[36]This doesn't mean anything. It is just the sound being uttered by the birds.

tigers among men will give up their lives in this great battle and will obtain fame in this world and great happiness for a long time in the other world."'

Chapter 864(4)

Vaishampayana said, 'O supreme among kings! Having been thus addressed by his son Dhritarashtra, the sage who is an Indra among wise ones, engaged in supreme meditation. The greatly ascetic one, who knew about time, then again spoke these words. 'O Indra among kings! There is no doubt that time destroys the universe. It again creates the worlds. There is nothing that is eternal. Show the path of dharma to your relatives, the Kurus, your kin and your well-wishers. You are capable of restraining them. It has been said that the slaughter of relatives is inferior. Do what brings me pleasure. O lord of the earth! Death himself has been born in the form of your son. Slaughter has not been praised in the Vedas. It can never be beneficial. He who kills, kills the dharma of his lineage, and it is like killing one's own body. Destiny has brought you to this path, though you are capable of following the path of virtue. In the form of the kingdom, calamity looms and makes you give up what brings happiness, for the destruction of the lineage and the earth. Your wisdom has suffered greatly. Show your sons dharma. O unassailable one! What is there in a kingdom, if one obtains sin with it? Preserve your fame, dharma and deeds and go to heaven. Let the Pandavas obtain their kingdom and the Kouravas obtain peace." Thus, the Indra among brahmanas sorrowfully spoke these words to Ambika's son, Dhritarashtra, and the one who was skilled in speech again spoke these words.

'Dhritarashtra said, "My knowledge of what exists and what does not exist is like yours. I know the exact truth. O father! But people are deluded because of selfishness. Know me to be such an ordinary person. O one whose power is unmatched! Through your favours, show me the firm direction. O maharshi! They are not under my control. I do not desire to commit a sin. You represent sacred dharma, fame, deeds, fortitude and learning. You are the revered grandfather of the Kurus and the Pandavas."

'Vyasa replied, "O Vichitravirya's son! O king! Openly tell me what is in your mind. As you wish, I will dispel your doubts."

'Dhritarashtra said, "There are signs that portent victory in a battle. O illustrious one! I wish to hear exactly about these."

'Vyasa replied, "The fire[37] has a cheerful radiance and its flames rise up straight. It circles to the right and the crest is devoid of smoke. The oblations offered have a sacred fragrance. These are said to be the signs of victory. When the conch shells and drums are sounded, there is a great and deep sound. The sun and the moon have pure rays. These are said to be the signs of victory. Whether they are seated or flying, the crows utter beneficial cries. O king! Those who are at the back urge an advance, while those at the front urge restraint.[38] When vultures, swans, parrots, cranes and woodpeckers utter beneficial cries and circle to the right, the brahmanas say that victory in a battle is certain. When the ornaments, armour and flags are golden in complexion and radiant, incapable of being looked at, such men obtain the favours of happiness and defeat the soldiers of the enemies. O descendant of the Bharata lineage! When spirited warriors utter happy shouts and when their garlands do not fade, they overcome their enemies in battle. Those who utter kind words before penetrating enemy formations and those who warn before striking are victorious. When hearing, sight, taste, touch and smell are undistorted and auspicious and the warriors are always happy, victory is certain. Winds that blow, clouds, crows become favourable and so are the showers from clouds and rainbows. O lord of the earth! These are the signs of victory. O lord of men! But if these are contrary, that is a sign of death. Whether the army is small or large, the cheerfulness of the masses of warriors is said to be a certain sign

[37]The sacrificial fire.

[38]It is not clear what this refers to. Nor is the meaning clear. If it refers to crows, crows at the back of an army are auspicious, while those in front of the army are inauspicious.

of victory. If a single warrior is frightened, he can cause an extremely large army to be alarmed and flee, even those who are brave warriors. If a large army is broken up, it is incapable of being rallied. It is like a herd of deer frightened by the mighty force of the water. Once a great army is routed, it is incapable of being rallied. O descendant of the Bharata lineage! On seeing it shattered, even brave warriors become dejected. On seeing the fright and the flight, the fear increases in every direction. O king! The army is suddenly scattered and is destroyed by the enemy. O lord of the earth! Even a brave one, a leader of many soldiers of the four types,[39] is incapable of rallying such a giant army. An intelligent person always endeavours and always looks for ways. It is said that success through negotiations is the best, and that through dissension[40] is medium. O lord of the earth! Victory obtained through battle is the worst. There are many great evils associated with fighting and slaughter is said to be the first. Even fifty brave ones who know each other, are cheerful, are not bound by family ties and are firm in their resolution, can crush a large army. Even five, six or seven can ensure victory, as long as they do not retreat. O descendant of the Bharata lineage! Vinata's son, Garuda, does not seek a large number of followers for assistance, when he sees a large number of birds.[41] O descendant of the Bharata lineage! The number of soldiers does not ensure victory. Victory is uncertain. That depends on destiny. Even those who are victorious in battle, have to suffer losses."'

Chapter 865(5)

Vaishampayana said, 'O intelligent one! Having spoken these words to Dhritarashtra, Vyasa departed. On hearing these

---

[39]Elephants, horses, chariots and infantry.

[40]Among the enemy.

[41]The assumption is that there is going to be a fight between Garuda and the birds.

words, Dhritarashtra meditated on them. Having thought about them
for some time, he sighed repeatedly. O bull among the Bharata lineage!
He asked Sanjaya, the one whose soul was controlled. "O Sanjaya!
Those brave lords of the earth are delighted at the prospect of battle.
They wish to strike each other with different kinds of weapons. For
the sake of the earth, those lords of the earth are prepared to give up
their lives. They will not be pacified. They will strike each other to
increase the numbers in Yama's abode. Desiring earthly prosperity,
they will not tolerate each other. O Sanjaya! Therefore, I think that
the earth must possess many qualities. Tell me about them. Many
thousands, millions, tens of millions and hundreds of millions of
brave people have gathered in Kurujangala.[42] O Sanjaya! I wish
to hear the exact details of the expanse of the countries and cities
from which they have come. Through the favours of the brahmana
rishi Vyasa, whose energy is infinite, you possess the lamp of divine
intelligence and the eyesight of knowledge."

'Sanjaya replied, "O immensely wise one! According to my
wisdom, I will tell you about the qualities of the earth. Behold them
with the eyesight of the sacred texts. O bull among the Bharata
lineage! I bow down before you. There are two kinds of beings in
this world, mobile and immobile. Depending on birth, mobile beings
are of three kinds—those born from eggs, those from sweat[43] and
those from wombs. O king! Out of all mobile beings, those born
from wombs are the best. Of those born from wombs, humans and
animals are supreme. O king! They[44] have diverse forms and are
divided into fourteen groups. Seven dwell in the forest and seven live
in villages.[45] O king! Lions, tigers, boars, buffaloes, elephants, bears
and monkeys—these seven are said to be forest dwellers. Cattle, goats,
men, sheep, horses, mules and donkeys—these seven are considered to
be village dwellers by righteous ones. O king! These are the fourteen
kinds of animals, domestic and wild. O lord of the earth! These have

[42]Literally, the forest of the Kurus. Another name for Kurukshetra.
[43]Like insects.
[44]Animals.
[45]That is, they are domestic.

been mentioned in the Vedas and sacrifices are established on them. Out of domestic ones, men are the best and lions among wild ones. All beings sustain their lives by living on each other. Those that are immobile are said to be *udbhija*s and these have five species—trees, shrubs, creepers, plants and those without stems, of the species of grass.[46] There are thus nineteen kinds.[47] They have five universal constituents.[48] There are twenty-four all together. These are described as *gayatri* and this is known to the world.[49] He who truly knows all these to be the sacred gayatri, possesses all the qualities. O foremost among the Bharata lineage! He will not be destroyed. Everything is born from the earth. When destroyed, everything goes into the earth. All beings are established in the earth. The earth is eternal. He who possesses the earth, possesses all the mobile and immobile objects in the universe. That is why the kings desire it and are prepared to kill each other.'"

Chapter 866(6)

'Dhritarashtra said, "O Sanjaya! O one who knows about the measure of different things! Tell me about the names and the

---

[46]Trees are *vriksha*. Shrubs are *gulma*, they grow from a clump. Creepers are *lata*, they require a support. Plants are *valli*, these are also creepers of a sort, but they creep along the earth (like pumpkins). These plants only survive for a year. Grass is *trina*.

[47]Fourteen mobile and five immobile.

[48]The five constituents of matter—*kshiti* or *prithivi* or *bhumi* (earth), *apa* (water*)*, *tejas* or *agni* (fire or energy), *marut* or *vayu* (wind or air) and *vyoma* or *akasha* (the sky or ether). These are known as *bhuta*s and pancha (five) bhuta collectively.

[49]Gayatri has several nuances. It is a mantra in the Vedas and is described as the mother of the Vedas. It is equated with the brahman or paramatman. In personified form, Gayatri is a goddess and Brahma's consort. She is equated with Brahma and is the source of all creation.

measures of rivers, mountains, places inhabited by people, everything else on earth and forests. O Sanjaya! Tell me everything."

'Sanjaya replied, "O great king! Because everything in the earth is based on the five universal constituents, the learned regard all of them as equal. These are bhumi, apa, vayu, agni and akasha. Each of them does not possess a quality from the preceding one. Therefore, bhumi is the foremost, as has been said by the rishis who know the truth about the qualities. These are sound, touch, sight and taste, with smell as the fifth.[50] O king! There are four qualities in apa, it does not possess smell. There are three qualities in tejas—sound, touch and sight. Vayu has sound and touch, while akasha has only sound. O king! These five qualities exist in the five constituents of matter, and beings in all the worlds are established on them. When there is homogeneity, they exist separately and independently.[51] When they do not exist in their natural state, they depend on each other and embodied beings are created. There is no exception to this. They are destroyed, with the one that succeeds merging into the one that precedes it. They are created in that way too, with each resulting from the one that precedes it.[52] All of them cannot be measured. Their forms are those of the lord himself.[53] Beings consisting of the five bhutas are seen in the universe. Men use reason to try and identify their measure.[54] But these are things that cannot be thought of. They cannot be fathomed through reason. They are beyond nature and this is a sign that they are inconceivable. O descendant of the Kuru lineage! I will now tell you about the island named Sudarshana.[55] O great king! This island

[50]Bhumi possesses all the five qualities.

[51]Before creation. This is a reference to the five constituents of matter, not the qualities.

[52]At the time of destruction, earth merges into water, water merges into fire, fire merges into air and air merges into ether. At the time of creation, air is created from ether, fire is created from air, water is created from fire and the earth is created from water.

[53]Brahma.

[54]The bhutas, constituents of matter or elements.

[55]These shlokas about Sudarshana are difficult to understand. Perhaps some allegory is intended and the text is not meant to be taken literally.

is circular and in the form of a wheel. It is full of rivers and other waterbodies. It has mountains that look like masses of clouds. It has cities of different types and beautiful countries. It has trees laden with flowers and fruits and is prosperous, with riches and crops. It is surrounded in every direction by the salty ocean. Just as a man can see his own face in a mirror, the island Sudarshana can be seen in the disc of the moon. Two of its parts look like the *pippala*[56] and two others look like a large hare. It is surrounded on all sides with every kind of medicinal plants. Besides this, everything else is water, and listen as I briefly describe this to you.'"

Chapter 867(7)

'Dhritarashtra said, "O Sanjaya! You have briefly described that island. Now tell me about it in detail. Tell me about that part of the land that looks like a hare. Then tell me about the measure of the part that looks like a pippala."'

Vaishampayana said, 'Thus addressed by the king, Sanjaya spoke these words.

'"O great king![57] From the east to the west, there are six mountains that are full of jewels. In both directions, they are immersed in the eastern and western ocean. They are named Himavan; Hemakuta; Nishadha, supreme among mountains; Nila, full of lapis lazuli; Shveta, with the complexion of silver; and the mountains known as Shringavan, made up of every kind of mineral. O king! These are mountains frequented by siddhas and charanas. The distance from one to the other is one thousand yojanas. O descendant of the Bharata lineage! There are many sacred countries or *varsha*s. In all of these, dwell many different kinds of beings. This is the varsha known as Bharata and the one known as Himavat comes after that. The region

[56]Sacred fig tree, kind of banyan. Also known as *plaksha* and pipal.
[57]These words are spoken by Sanjaya.

known as Harivarsha is beyond Hemakuta. O great king! To the south of Nila and to the north of Nishadha, is a mountain named Malyavan that stretches from the east to the west. Beyond Malyavan is the mountain known as Gandhamadana. Between these two,[58] there is the circular and golden mountain of Meru. It is as radiant as the rising sun, or a fire without smoke. O lord of the earth! It is said to be 84,000 yojanas high and 84,000 yojanas deep.[59] The worlds are established on it, above and diagonally. O lord! There are four islands along its sides. O descendant of the Bharata lineage! These are Bhadrashva, Ketumala, Jambudvipa and Uttara Kuru, the abode of those who have performed virtuous deeds. The bird Sumukha, Suparna's[60] son, saw that all the birds on Meru had golden feathers and thought that there was no difference there between superior, average and inferior birds. He therefore decided to leave the place. The supreme among stellar bodies, the sun, always revolves around it.[61] So do the moon, all the nakshatras and Vayu.[62] O great king! That mountain is full of divine flowers and fruit. It is full of mansions that are made out of polished gold. O king! The masses of gods, gandharvas, asuras, rakshasas and masses of apsaras always go to that mountain to sport there. Brahma, Rudra and Shakra, the lord of the gods, assemble there, to perform different kinds of sacrifices, with a lot of donations. Tumburu, Narada, Vishvavasu, Haha and Huhu[63] went there and satisfied the foremost among immortals with different kinds of hymns. O fortunate one! The seven sages, and the great-souled Kashyapa Prajapati, always go there on the day of the new moon and the full moon. O lord of the earth! Kavya Ushanas[64] also goes to the summit, with the *daitya*s. The jewels that exist in all the mountains come from the jewels there. A fourth part of those is

[58]Malyavan and Gandhamadana.
[59]Meru extends both above the earth and inside the earth.
[60]Garuda's.
[61]Meru.
[62]The wind or the wind god.
[63]Tumburu, Vishvavasu, Haha and Huhu are the names of gandharvas.
[64]Shukracharya, the preceptor of the demons.

enjoyed by the illustrious Kubera. He gives only a sixteenth part of those riches to men.

'"On its northern side is the divine, auspicious and beautiful forest of Karnikara. It is full of flowers everywhere and extends across several mountains. The illustrious Pashupati[65] himself, the creator of beings, sports there, surrounded by divine beings and accompanied by Uma. He wears a radiant garland of *karnikara* flowers[66] that extends down to his feet. His three eyes blaze, like three rising suns. The Siddhas are extremely terrible in their austerities. They are excellent in their vows and truthful and can see him. Those who are evil in conduct are incapable of seeing Maheshvara. O lord of men! A stream of milk issues from the summit of that mountain. This is the sacred and auspicious Ganga, the beautiful Bhagirathi. She has three flows[67] and is worshipped by the virtuous. She flows with a terrible roar. With great force, she descends into the beautiful lake Chandramas. That sacred lake is like an ocean and has been created from her. Even the mountains are incapable of bearing her. But in earlier times, Maheshvara bore her on his head for a hundred thousand years.

'"O lord of the earth! Ketumala is on the western side of Meru. Jambukhanda is also there and is extremely large.[68] It is like Nandana.[69] O descendant of the Bharata lineage! The lifespan there is ten thousand years. The men have golden complexions and the women are like apsaras. Everyone is without disease and devoid of sorrow. They are always delighted in their minds. Humans born there have the complexion of molten gold. On the summit of

[65]Shiva. Shiva's consort is Uma.

[66]Karnikara is also the name of a flower. It is colourful, but has no fragrance.

[67]Ganga flows in the sky, the earth and the nether world. She is called Mandakini in the sky, Ganga on earth and Bhogavati in the nether world.

[68]Jambukhanda or Jambudvipa is at the centre of the seven dvipas (islands), which are spread out in a concentric circle. Meru is at the centre of Jambukhanda. Jambukhanda is named after the jamun (the Indian blackberry). Bharatavarsha is in Jambukhanda.

[69]The name of Indra's pleasure garden.

Gandhamadana, Kubera, lord of the guhyakas, spends his time in delight, with the rakshasas and surrounded by masses of apsaras. There are smaller mountains and hills at the feet of Gandhamadana. The maximum lifespan there is eleven thousand years. O king! The men there are dark, energetic and extremely strong. All the women have the complexion of lotuses and are extremely beautiful to look at. Shveta is beyond Nila and Hiranyaka is beyond Nila.[70] The varsha named Airavata is bounded by Shringavat.[71] O great king! The two varshas to the south and the north are in the form of a bow. Ilavrita is in the middle of the five varshas.[72] A varsha that is towards the north surpasses one to its south in qualities like lifespan, stature, health, dharma, kama and artha. O descendant of the Bharata lineage! Beings live together in these varshas. O great king! The earth is thus covered with mountains. The large mountain Hemakuta also has the name of Kailasa. O king! Vaishravana[73] sports there with the guhyakas. To the north of Kailasa and near Mount Mainaka, there is the large and divine Mount Manimaya, with a golden peak. To its side,[74] there is the large, divine, auspicious and beautiful Vindusara,[75] with golden sand. After having seen Ganga Bhagirathi, King Bhagiratha lived there for many years. There are many sacrificial stakes made out of gems there and sanctuaries made out of gold. The immensely famous one with a thousand eyes[76] attained salvation there. The creator Bhutapati,[77] the eternal lord of

[70]Varsha is a continent and usually nine such continents are mentioned—Kuru, Hiranmaya, Ramyaka, Ilavrita, Hari, Ketumala, Bhadrashva, Kinnara and Bharata. Hiranyaka is the same as Hiranmaya and Airavata is the same as Ilavrita. Shveta and Nila are the names of mountains.

[71]The name of a mountain.

[72]Probably referring to Hiranyaka, Ramyaka, Ilavrita, Hari and Ketumala.

[73]Vishrava's son, Kubera.

[74]There is a typo in the Critical edition's text here. It should read *parshva* (side) instead of Partha.

[75]A lake.

[76]Indra.

[77]Literally the lord of all beings, Shiva.

all beings, supreme in his energy, is worshipped there, surrounded by his followers. Nara, Narayana, Brahma, Manu and Sthanu,[78] as the fifth, are always present there. The goddess with the three flows[79] first showed herself there. She emerged from Brahma's world and divided herself into seven streams—Vasvokasara, Nalini, the sin-cleansing Sarasvati, Jambunadi,[80] Sita, Ganga and Sindhu as the seventh. She is inconceivable and divine and the lord himself[81]thought of ways of dividing her. At the end of a yuga, it is there that sacrifices have been performed on a thousand occasions. The Sarasvati can be seen sometimes and sometimes she is invisible. Ganga, with the seven flows, is thus famous in the three worlds.

'"The rakshasas live on Himavat, the guhyakas on Hemakuta. The *sarpas*, the *nagas*,[82] the *nishadas* and those rich in austerities live on Gokarna. Shveta mountain is said to be the abode of gods and asuras. O king! The gandharvas live on Mount Nishadha and brahmarshis on Nila. O great king! Shringavat is where the ancestors wander around. O great king! These are the divisions into seven varshas. Diverse types of mobile and immobile beings are placed in them. Different types of prosperity, divine and human, can be seen in them. This is incapable of being described. But those who desire their own welfare, have faith in them. O king! You asked me about the divine region that is in the form of a hare and I have told you. On two sides of the hare, to the north and to the south, there are two varshas. The ears[83] are Nagadvipa and Kashyapadvipa. O king! The head is the beautiful Mount Malaya, with the hue of copper. This is the second part of the dvipa that has the shape of a hare."

[78]Shiva.

[79]Ganga.

[80]*Nadi* means river.

[81]Probably meaning Shiva.

[82]Sarpas are snakes, nagas are serpents. Unlike sarpas, nagas have semi-divine qualities. They can assume any form at will and dwell in a separate nether world.

[83]Of the hare.

Chapter 868(8)

'Dhritarashtra said, "O Sanjaya! What is to the north and on the eastern side of Meru? O immensely intelligent one! Tell me everything about Mount Malyavan."

'Sanjaya replied, "O king! To the south of Nila and on the northern side of Meru is Uttara Kuru, inhabited by the siddhas. The trees there yield sweet fruit and are always full of flowers and fruit. The flowers have excellent fragrance and the fruits are succulent. O lord of men! Some of the trees there yield fruit that satisfy every desire. O lord of men! Other trees there are known as those that yield milk. They yield milk that is like amrita, with the six different kinds of taste.[84] They also yield garments[85] and the fruits are also ornaments. The entire ground is strewn with jewels and fine golden sand. O lord of men! Everything is pleasant to the touch and there is no mud. The men who are born there are those who have been dislodged from the world of the gods. Whether on plain or uneven terrain, everyone is similar in beauty and qualities. Twins are born there and the women are the equals of apsaras. They drink the milk there and the milk is like amrita. When the twins are born, they grow up equally. They are similar in beauty and qualities and wear similar garments. O lord! Like *chakravakas*,[86] they are devoted to each other. They are without disease, devoid of sorrow and always delighted in their minds. O great king! They live for eleven thousand years and never abandon each other. There is a bird named Bharunda. It has sharp beaks and is extremely strong. When they die, this picks up the dead and hurls them into mountainous caverns. O king! I have briefly described Uttara Kuru to you.

'"I will now describe the eastern side of Meru to you exactly. O lord of the earth! Bhadrashva is the first. There is a forest of *bhadrasala*[87]

[84]Sweet, sour, salty, pungent, bitter and acidic.

[85]As bark.

[86]The ruddy goose.

[87]Either the *kadamba* or the *devadaru* (deodar) tree.

there and a large tree named Kalamra. O great king! Kalamra is beautiful and always has flowers and fruit. This dvipa is one yojana in expanse and is frequented by siddhas and charanas. The men there are white and possess energy and great strength. The women there are lovely. They are beautiful to look at and have the complexion of the moon. They have the radiance of the moon. They have the complexion of the moon. Their faces are like the full moon. Their bodies are as cool as the moon and they are skilled in dancing and singing. O bull among the Bharata lineage! The lifespan there is ten thousand years. They always remain young by drinking the juice of Kalamra. To the south of Nila and to the north of Nishadha, there is a large and eternal jambu tree by the name of Sudarshana. It has fruits that provide every object of desire. It is sacred and is worshipped by the siddhas and charanas. The eternal Jambudvipa owes its naming to this. O bull among the Bharata lineage! That king of trees rises up to heaven. O lord of men! It is one thousand and one hundred yojanas tall. When measured by hand, the fruit of that is two thousand and five hundred cubits in circumference. When ripe, it bursts and falls down on the ground with a loud noise. O king! It releases a juice that is silvery in colour. O lord of men! The juice of the jambu fruit becomes a river. Having circled Meru, this goes to Uttara Kuru. O lord of men! People are always delighted at having drunk this juice. Having drunk the juice of this fruit, they do not suffer from old age. There is a gold named Jambunada there and it is used for divine ornaments. Men who are born there have the complexion of the rising sun. O bull among the Bharata lineage! The fire known as Samvartaka blazes on the summit of Malyavan. This is the fire of destruction. On the summit of Malyavan, towards the east, are smaller mountains. Malyavan extends for one thousand and fifty yojanas. Men who are born there have the complexion of gold.[88] They have all been dislodged from Brahma's world and are knowledgeable about the brahman. They torment themselves through austerities and hold up their semen. For

---

[88]The word used is *maharajata*, which also means turmeric.

the sake of protecting beings, they enter the sun. There are sixty-six thousand of them.[89] They surround the sun and travel ahead of the sun. Having been heated by the sun for sixty-six thousand years, they enter the lunar circle."'

Chapter 869(9)

'Dhritarashtra said, "O Sanjaya! Tell me the names of the varshas and the mountains. And tell me accurately about those who dwell in the mountains."

'Sanjaya said, "To the south of Shveta and to the north of Nila, is the varsha named Ramanaka.[90] Men who are born there are white in complexion. All of them are extremely handsome to look at. The people born there are fond of sexual pleasures. O great king! Happy in their minds, they live for eleven thousand and five hundred years. To the south and to the north of Mount Shveta, is the varsha named Hairanyavat[91] and the river Hairanvati. O great king! Everyone there is rich, handsome and a follower of the yakshas. O king! They are extremely strong and are always delighted in their minds. O lord of men! The lifespan there is eleven thousand and five hundred years. O lord of men! Shringavat has three peaks. One is made of jewels and another is extraordinary and is made of gold. Another has jewels everywhere and is adorned with beautiful mansions. The goddess Shandili,[92] who illuminates herself, always resides there. O lord of men! To the north of that peak and on the frontiers of the ocean, is the varsha named Airavata,[93] which

[89]These are the *valakhilya* sages, usually stated to be sixty thousand in number. They are as long as a thumb and were created from Brahma's body. They precede the sun's chariot.

[90]The same as Ramyaka.

[91]The same as Hiranmaya.

[92]Shandili was a female ascetic who lived on Mount Rishabha. The story of Garuda's encounter with her has been described in Section 54 (Volume 4).

[93]The same as Ilavrita. This varsha is supreme because Mount Shringavan is there.

is supreme because of Shringavan. The sun does not heat there. Men do not decay there. The moon and the nakshatras cover[94] and are the only source of illumination there. Humans who are born there have the radiance of lotuses, the complexion of lotuses, eyes that are like the petals of lotuses and fragrance like the petals of lotuses. They do not blink their eyes. Extremely fragrant, they do not partake of food and are in control of their senses. O king! All of them have been dislodged from the world of the gods and are without sin. O lord of men! O supreme among Bharatas! Men have a lifespan of thirteen thousand years there. The lord Hari dwells to the north of the milky ocean, in Vaikuntha. His chariot is made out of gold and has eight wheels. It is yoked to beings and has the speed of the mind. It has the complexion of fire and is extremely swift. It is embellished with gold. O bull among the Bharata lineage! He is the lord of all beings and all prosperity. He is finite and infinite. He is the one who acts. He is the one who makes everyone act. O king! He is earth, water, sky, wind and energy. He is the sacrifice for all beings. The fire is his mouth.'"

Vaishampayana said, 'O lord of men! Having been thus addressed by Sanjaya, the high-minded king, Dhritarashtra, meditated about his sons. O great king! Having thought, he again spoke these words. "O son of a suta! There is no doubt that time destroys the universe and creates everything again. There is nothing that is eternal. Nara and Narayana know everything and hold up all beings. The gods call him Vaikuntha and he is known as Lord Vishnu.[95]"'

Chapter 870(10)

'Dhritarashtra said, "Tell me about Bharatavarsha, where this senseless army has gathered, and for which, my son Duryodhana is so avaricious. The sons of Pandu desire it and my

[94]The sky.
[95]Nara and Narayana are both manifestations of Vishnu. Vaikuntha means immeasurable and is the name of Vishnu's abode, as well as Vishnu's name.

mind is immersed in it. O Sanjaya! I am asking you, because you
are skilled."

'Sanjaya said, "O king! Listen to my words. The Pandavas are
not covetous about this. It is Duryodhana who covets it, and so does
Shakuni Soubala. There are other kshatriyas, who are the kings of
many countries, who are greedy about Bharatavarsha and cannot
tolerate each other. O descendant of the Bharata lineage! I will now
describe to you the land that is named after Bharata.[96] O king! This
is loved by the god Indra, Vaivasvata Manu,[97] Prithu Vainya,[98] the
great-souled Ikshvaku,[99] Yayati,[100] Ambarisha,[101] Mandhata,[102]
Nahusha,[103] Muchukunda,[104] Shibi Oushinara,[105] Rishabha,[106]
Aila,[107] King Nriga[108] and other powerful kshatriyas. O great king!
O Indra among kings! O descendant of the Bharata lineage! O

[96]Though written as Bharata, the country is actually Bhaarata and is named
after Bharata.

[97]Each *manvantara* (era) is presided over by a sovereign known as Manu. It
is because humans are descended from Manu that they are known as *manava*.
There are fourteen manvantaras and fourteen Manus to preside over them. The
present manvantara is the seventh and the Manu who presides over this is known
as Vaivasvata, because he was born from the sun (Vivasvat).

[98]Vainya means Vena's son. King Prithu was a virtuous king who was Vena's
son. Prithivi or *prithvi*, the earth, is named after Prithu.

[99]The founder of the solar dynasty.

[100]The son of Nahusha. Both the Pandavas and the Yadavas are descended
from Yayati. Yayati's story has been recounted in Section 7 (Volume 1).

[101]King of the solar dynasty, the son of Nabhaga.

[102]King of the solar dynasty, the son of Yuvanashva. Mandhata's story has
been recounted in Section 33 (Volume 3).

[103]King of the lunar dynasty. Nahusha's story has been recounted in Section
49 (Volume 4).

[104]Mandhata's son.

[105]Oushinara means the son of Ushinara. Shibi was the son of King Ushinara
of the lunar dynasty and was famous for his generosity.

[106]King mentioned in the *Bhagavata Purana* as the father of Bharata.

[107]Aila means the son of Ila. Ila was the daughter of Vaivasvata Manu and
gave birth to Pururava. Aila means Pururava.

[108]King Nriga inadvertently donated the same cow to two brahmanas. He was
cursed and became a lizard that lived in a well. Krishna rescued him from this curse.

scorcher of enemies! All of them loved Bharata and I will describe this varsha as I have heard it.

"'O king! Listen as I tell you what you have asked. Mahendra, Malaya, Shuktiman, Rikshavan, Vindhya, Pariyatra—these are the seven noble mountains.[109] O king! Near them, there are thousands of other mountains that are unknown. They are full of substance and large, with beautiful foothills. There are other unknown and inferior mountains, inhabited by those who have inferior means of subsistence. O Kouravya! O lord! There are aryas and *mlecchas*[110] and men from mixed lineage. O lord of men! O Kourava! They drink water from the rivers—the great Ganga, Sindhu, Sarasvati, Godavari, Narmada, the great river Bahuda,[111] Shatadru,[112] Chandrabhaga,[113] the great river Yamuna, Drishadvati,[114] Vipasha,[115] Vipapa, Sthulavaluka, the river Vetravati,[116] the downward-flowing Krishnavena,[117] Iravati,[118] Vitasta,[119] Payoshni,[120] Devika,[121] Vedasmriti, Vetasini, Trideva, Ikshumalini, Karishini, Chitravaha, the downward-flowing Chitrasena, Gomati, Dhutapapa, the great river Vandana, Koushiki,[122] Trideva,[123] Kritya, Vichitra, Lohatarini, Rathastha, Shatakumbha, Sarayu,[124] Charmanvati,[125]

---

[109]That is, in Bharatavarsha.

[110]Barbarians, those who do not speak Sanskrit.

[111]There is a Bahuda river in Andhra Pradesh.

[112]Sutlej.

[113]Chenab.

[114]Identified with the Chautang River in Haryana. Drishadvati means a river with many stones in it.

[115]Beas.

[116]Betwa River in Madhya Pradesh and Uttar Pradesh.

[117]Krishnavena is the river Krishna and the tributary Venna.

[118]Ravi.

[119]Jhelum.

[120]Probably the Tapti.

[121]In Udhampur district of Jammu and Kashmir.

[122]The Koshi river.

[123]Trideva is mentioned twice.

[124]In Uttar Pradesh.

[125]Chambal.

Vetravati,[126] Hastisoma, Disha, Shatavari, Payoshni,[127] Bhaimarathi, Kaveri, Chuluka, Vapi, Shatabala, Nichira, Mahita, Suproyaga, Pavitra, Kundala, Sindhu,[128] Vajini, Puramalini, Purvabhirama, Vira, Bhima,[129] Oghavati,[130] Palashini, Papahara, Mahendra, Pippalavati, Parishena, Asikni,[131] Sarala, Bharamardini, Puruhi, Pravara, Mena, Mogha, Ghritavati, Dhumatyamati, Krishna, Suchi, Chhavi, Sadanira, Adhrishya, the great river Kushadhara, Shashikanta, Shiva, Viravati, Vastu, Suvastu, Gouri, Kampana, Hiranvati, Hiranvati,[132] Chitravati, the downward-flowing Chitrasena,[133] Rathachitra, Jyotiratha, Vishvamitra, Kapinjala, Upendra, Bahula, Kuchara, Ambuvahini, Vainandi, Pinjala, Venna,[134] the great river Tungavena, Vidisha, Krishnavenna,[135] Tamra, Kapila, Shalu, Suvama, Vedashva, the great river Harisrava, Shighra, Picchila, the downward-flowing Bharadvaji, the downward-flowing Koushiki,[136] Shona,[137] Bahuda,[138] Chandana,[139] Durgamanta, Shila, Brahmamedhya, Brihadvati, Charaksha, Mahirohi, Jambunadi, Sunasa, Tamasa,[140] Dasi, Trasamanya, Varanasi,[141] Lola, Adhritakara, the great river Purnasha, Manavi and the great river Purnasha. O lord of men! O descendant of the

[126]Vetravati is mentioned twice.

[127]Payoshni is mentioned twice.

[128]Sindhu is mentioned twice.

[129]Originates in Maharashtra, tributary of the Krishna.

[130]This could mean the Apaga river in Haryana.

[131]Another name for Chandrabhaga, so this has already been mentioned.

[132]Hiranvati is mentioned twice.

[133]Chitrasena is mentioned twice.

[134]Venna has already been mentioned, in conjunction with Krishna.

[135]This has already been mentioned, though the earlier mention said Krishnavena.

[136]Koushiki is mentioned twice.

[137]The Shon River.

[138]Bahuda has already been mentioned.

[139]Tributary of the Padma.

[140]The river Tons, tributary of the Ganga that flows through Madhya Pradesh and Uttar Pradesh.

[141]Varuna and Asi Rivers in Varanasi.

Bharata lineage! There are others—Sadaniramaya, Vritya, Mandaga, Mandavahini, Brahmani, Mahagouri, Durga, Chitropala, Chitrabarha, Manju, Makaravahini, Mandakini,[142] Vaitarani,[143] the great river Koka, Shuktimati, Maranya, Pushpaveni, Utpalavati, Lohitya,[144] Karatoya,[145] Vrishabhangini, Kumari, Rishikulya, Brahmakulya, Sarasvati, Supunya, Sarva and the revered Ganga. O lord of men! All of these are mothers of the universe. All of them are extremely strong.[146] Other than these, there are hundreds and thousands of other rivers. O king! To the extent I remember, I have described these rivers to you.

'"After this, listen to me as I recount the names of countries. O descendant of the Bharata lineage! They are Kuru, Panchala, Shalva, Madreya, Jangala, Shurasena, Kalinga, Bodha, Mouka, Matsya, Sukuta, Soubala, Kuntala, Kashi, Koshala, Chedi, Vatsa, Karusha, Bhoja, Sindhu, Pulinda, Uttamouja, Dasharna, Mekala, Utkala, Panchala, Koushija, Ekaprishtha, Yugandhara, Soudha, Madra, Bhujinga, Kashi,[147] Parakashi, Jathara, Kukkusha, Sudasharna, Kunti, Avanti, Parakunti, Govinda, Mandaka, Shanda, Vidarbha, Upavasika, Ashmaka, Pamsurashtra, Goparashtra, Panitaka, Adirashtra, Sukutta, Balirashtra, Kerala,[148] Vanarasya, Pravaha, Vakra, Vakrabhaya, Shaka, Videha, Magadha, Suhma, Vijaya, Anga, Vanga, Kalinga, Yakrillomana, Malla, Sudeshna, Prahuta, Mahisha, Karshika, Vahika, Vatadhana, Abhira, Kalatoya, Aparandhra, Shudra, Pahlava, Charmakhandika, Atavi, Shabara, Marubhouma, Marisha, Upavrisha, Anupavrisha, Surashtra, Kekaya, Kuttaparanta,

---

[142]Tributary of the Alakananda.

[143]In Orissa.

[144]Tributary of the Brahmaputra.

[145]In Rajshahi division in Bangladesh.

[146]This doesn't sound right and there may be a typo in the Critical edition. As in some non-critical versions, it should read *phala*, not *bala*. In that case, the rivers produce great merit.

[147]Kashi has already been mentioned.

[148]We haven't followed the Critical edition here, which uses the word *kevala*. Kerala fits better.

Dvaidheya, Kaksha, Samudranishkuta and Andhra. O king! O lord
of men! There are other mountainous regions and regions on the
outside of the mountains—Angamalada, Magadha, Manavarjaka,
Mahyuttara, Pravrisheya, Bhargama, Pundra, Bharga, Kirata,
Sudoshna, Pramuda, Shaka, Nishada, Nishadha, Anarta, Nairrita,
Dugula, Pratimatsya, Kushala, Kunata, Tiragraha, Taratoya,
Rajika, Ramyakagana, Tilaka, Parasika, Madhumanta, Prakutsaka,
Kashmira, Sindhu, Souvira, Gandhara, Darshaka, Abhisara, Kuluta,
Shaibala, Bahlika, Darvika, Sakacha, Darva, Vataja, Amaratha,
Uraga, Bahuvadya, Kouravya, Sudamana, Sumallika, Vaghra, Karisha,
Kashi,[149] Kulinda, Upatyaka, Vanayu, Dashaparshva, Romana,
Kushabindu, Kaccha, Gopalakaccha, Langala, Paravallaka, Kirata,
Barbara, Siddha, Videha,[150] Tamralingaka, Oushtra, Pundra,
Sairandhra, Parvatiya and Marisha. O bull among the Bharata lineage!
There are other countries to the south—Dravida, Kerala,[151] Prachya,
Bhushika, Vanavasina, Unnatyaka, Mahishaka, Vikalpa, Bhushaka,
Karnika, Kuntika, Soudrida, Nalakalaka, Koukuttaka, Chola,
Konkana, Malavana, Samanga, Kopana, Kukura, Angadamarisha,
Dhvajini, Utsava, Sanketa, Trigarta, Sarvaseni, Tryanga, Kekaraka,
Proshtha, Parasancharaka, Vindhya, Pulaka, Pulinda, Kalkala,
Malaka, Mallaka, Paravartaka, Kulinda, Kulika, Karantha, Kuraka,
Mushaka, Stanavala, Satiya, Pattipanjaka, Adidaya, Sirala, Stuvaka,
Stanapa, Hrishividharbha, Kantika, Tangana and Paratangana.
O supreme among the Bharata lineage! There are other mleccha
people to the north—Yavana, Kamboja, Daruna, other mleccha
people, Sakshadruha, Kuntala, Huna, Parataka, Maradha, China
and Dashamalika. These are inhabited by others born from kshatriya,
vaishya and shudra lineages. There are *shudra-abhira*s, Daradas,
Kashmiras, Pashus, Svashikas, Tukharas, Pallavas, Girigahvaras,
Atreyas, Bharadvajas, Stanayoshikas, Oupakas, Kalingas, different
races of *kirata*s,[152] Tamaras, Hamsamargas and Karabhanjakas.

[149]Kashi has already been mentioned.
[150]Videha has already been mentioned.
[151]In our translation, we have already mentioned Kerala.
[152]Hunters.

'"O lord! I have only given brief indications about these countries. If the earth and its qualities and strengths are properly used, it becomes like a milch cow that yields objects of desires and leads to the great fruit of the three objectives.[153] The brave kings who know about dharma and artha are covetous of these. Because of greed for these riches, they have readily agreed to give up their lives in battle. The earth is the refuge and is desired by those who have the bodies of gods and men. O foremost among the Bharata lineage! The kings desire to enjoy the earth and have become like dogs that are trying to snatch meat from each other. Their desires will never be satisfied. O king! It is for this reason that the Kurus and the Pandavas have tried to obtain the possession of the earth through conciliation, gifts, dissension and chastisement.[154] O bull among men! If the earth is looked after well, she becomes the father, the mother, the son and heaven for all beings."'

871(11)

'Dhritarashtra said, "O suta! O Sanjaya! Tell me about the dimensions, the lifespan, the good and evil fruits and the past, present and future of Bharatavarsha, Haimavat and Harivarsha. Tell me in detail."

'Sanjaya said, "O bull among the Bharata lineage! O extender of the Kuru lineage! There are four yugas in Bharatavarsha—*krita, treta, dvapara* and *pushya*.[155] O lord! The first is krita yuga and after that treta yuga follows. Dvapara comes after that and pushya follows thereafter. O supreme among Kurus! O supreme among kings! The measure of the lifespan in krita yuga is said to be four thousand years. O lord of men! That of treta is three thousand years.

[153]Dharma, artha and kama.
[154]Sama, dana, bheda and danda respectively.
[155]Kali.

In the present one of dvapara, it is two thousand. O bull among the Bharata lineage! No fixed lifespan has been prescribed for pushya. People will die in the womb, or once they are born. O king! Men are born in krita and have offspring who are immensely strong, great in spirit and possess all the qualities. There are sages and those rich in austerities. O king! They are great in their endeavour, great-souled, devoted to dharma and truthful. O king! Those born in krita yuga are rich and handsome, with long lifespans. Kshatriyas born in treta yuga are extremely brave warriors, supreme among those who wield bows. Those brave ones are emperors.[156] O great king! When dvapara begins, all the varnas have great endeavour and great valour. But they seek to kill each other. O king! O descendant of the Bharata lineage! Those who are born in pushya are limited in their energy and men are wrathful. They are greedy and untruthful. They suffer from jealousy, vanity, anger, deception and malice. O descendant of the Bharata lineage! There is wrath and greed on earth in pushya. O king! O lord of men! The part that remains of dvapara is very small.[157] Haimavat is superior to Harivarsha in all qualities and so on."'[158]

---

[156]*Chakravarti.*
[157]The rest of it has already passed.
[158]That is, Harivarsha is superior to Bharatavarsha.

Bhumi Parva

This parva has eighty-seven shlokas and two chapters.

Chapter 872(12): 37 shlokas   Chapter 873(13): 50 shlokas

Bhumi means land or the earth and this section is so named because it has a description of the earth.

Chapter 872(12)

'Dhritarashtra said, "O Sanjaya! You have described Jambukhanda exactly to me. Now tell me exactly about its expanse and dimensions. O Sanjaya! Without leaving any gaps, also tell me exactly and accurately about the dimensions of the oceans, Shakadvipa, Kushadvipa, Shalmalidvipa and Krounchadvipa. O son of Gavalgana! Tell me everything about Rahu, the moon and the sun."

'Sanjaya said, "O king! There are many dvipas spread throughout the earth. But I will tell you about seven of them and about the moon, the sun and the planet.[1] O lord of the earth! The mountain of Jambu extends, in its entirety, over eighteen thousand and six hundred

---

[1]The word planet is in the singular. So Sanjaya will only tell Dhritarashtra about Rahu.

yojanas. It is said that the salty ocean is double this in expanse. It[2] has many countries and is decorated with jewels and coral. It is decorated with many beautiful mountains that have diverse kinds of minerals. Inhabited by siddhas and charanas, the ocean is circular. O king! I will tell you exactly about Shakadvipa. O descendant of the Kuru lineage! Listen to me, as I describe it to you appropriately. O lord of men! In dimensions, it is double the size of Jambudvipa. O great king! The ocean is double this in expanse. O foremost among Bharatas! It[3] is surrounded on all sides by the milky ocean. There are many sacred countries there. People who are there, do not die. How can there be famine there? They[4] are endowed with forgiveness and energy. O bull among the Bharata lineage! I have briefly and exactly told you about Shakadvipa. O great king! What else do you desire to hear?"

'Dhritarashtra said, "O Sanjaya! You have, briefly and exactly, told me about Shakadvipa. O immensely wise one! Now accurately, tell me everything in detail."

'Sanjaya said, "O king! There are seven mountains there and they are adorned with gems. They are stores of jewels. Listen to the names of the rivers that are there. O lord of men! Everything there is supreme in qualities and sacred. The supreme one is known as Meru and is the abode of gods, rishis and gandharvas. O great king! The mountain named Malaya extends towards the east. The clouds are generated there and spread out in all the directions. O Kouravya! Next is the large mountain Jaladhara. Vasava always extracts supreme water from there. O lord of men! It is from this that we obtain showers during the monsoon. The tall mountain of Raivataka is always established there. The grandfather has decreed that Revati nakshatra should be above it in the sky.[5] O Indra among kings! To the north, is the large mountain named Shyama. O lord of countries! All the people there are dark in complexion."

---

[2]The ocean.
[3]Shakadvipa.
[4]The people who live there.
[5]The grandfather is Brahma. Revati is the twenty-seventh nakshatra.

'Dhritarashtra asked, "O Sanjaya! A great doubt has arisen in my mind now, because of what you have said. O son of a suta! Why are the people there dark in complexion?"

'Sanjaya said, "O immensely wise one! O descendant of the Kuru lineage! In all the dvipas, there are those who are fair and those who are dark in complexion. O king! There is also a mixture of the two complexions. O descendant of the Bharata lineage! But because it is full of such people, it is known as Shyama.[6] O illustrious one! Because the people there are dark, this mountain is called Shyama. O Indra among Kouravas! Beyond this, there is the great mountain Durgashaila. Then there is Kesara. The wind that blows there has the fragrance of saffron.[7] Measured in yojanas, each[8] is twice the height of the one that has preceded it. O Kouravya! The learned have said that there are seven varshas there. O great king! That of the great Meru is Mahakasha, that of Jalada is Kumudottara, that of Jaladhara is said to be Sukumara, that of Raivata is Koumara, that of Shyama is Manichaka and that of Kesara is Modaki.[9] Beyond that, is Mahapuman,[10] in the middle of Shakadvipa. O Kouravya! O great king! In length, breadth and circumference, this is as large as the famous and large tree that is in the midst of Jambudvipa. There are many sacred countries there, where Shankara[11] is worshipped. The siddhas, the charanas and the gods go there. O king! O descendant of the Bharata lineage! All the people follow dharma there, and so do the four varnas. They are engaged in their own tasks and no instances of theft can be seen. O great king! They have long lives and are free from old age and death. The people there prosper, like rivers during the monsoon. The rivers there are full of pure water. O Kouravya!

---

[6]*Shyama* means dark.

[7]*Kesara* means saffron, which is why the mountain is so named.

[8]Each mountain.

[9]There is a varsha corresponding to each of the seven mountains. Raivata is the same as Raivataka. Malaya is being referred to as Jalada, *jalada* meaning something that provides water, such as a cloud. The clouds strike against mountains and provide water.

[10]The name of another mountain.

[11]Shiva.

O supreme among the Bharata lineage! Ganga divides herself into several flows—Sukumari, Kumari, Sita, Kaveraka, Mahanadi, the river Manijala and Ikshuvardhanika. O extender of the Kuru lineage! There are many other sacred rivers there, in hundreds and thousands, and Vasava draws water from them to shower down. It is impossible to enumerate the names, lengths and dimensions of these. All these rivers are holy. As the worlds know, there are four sacred countries there—Maga, Mashaka, Manasa and Mandaga. O king! Magas are usually brahmanas and are devoted to their own tasks. The kings of Mashaka are devoted to dharma and tend to every desire.[12] O great king! The vaishyas of Manasa earn their living through deeds. With all their desires gratified, they are brave and are firmly devoted to dharma and artha. The shudra men of Mandaga always follow the conduct of dharma. O Indra among kings! There is no king there, no punishment, and no one to be punished. They are devoted to their own dharma and protect dharma and each other. One is capable of saying this much about that dvipa. Only this much can be heard about the immensely energetic Shakadvipa.”'

Chapter 873(13)

'Sanjaya said, “O Kouravya! O great king! I will tell you about what is heard about the dvipa to the north. Listen to me. There is an ocean there, with waters made out of clarified butter.[13] Beyond that, there is an ocean with waters made of curd.[14] Next is an ocean with waters made out of liquor.[15] And there is another ocean with water made out of sweat.[16] O lord of men! Each of these dvipas is double the size of the one that has preceded it. O great king! They

[12]Of the brahmanas.
[13]*Ghrita.*
[14]*Dadhi.*
[15]*Sura.*
[16]*Gharma.* Alternatively, where the waters are heated.

are surrounded by mountains on all sides. In the dvipa that is in the centre, there is a great mountain named Goura, made out of red arsenic. O king! To the west is a mountain named Krishna, which resembles Narayana. Keshava himself protects the divine jewels there. Prajapati is seated there and bestows happiness on beings. Other than the countries, *kusha* grass grows in the midst of Kushadvipa. O king! The *shalmali*[17] tree is worshipped in Shalmalidvipa. There is the mountain of Mahakrouncha in Krounchadvipa. It is a store of gems. O great king! It is always worshipped by the four varnas. O king! There is the extremely large mountain of Gomanta, which is a store of every kind of mineral. The handsome and lotus-eyed lord, Narayana Hari, always resides there, praised by those who have obtained salvation. O Indra among kings! There is another mountain in Kushadvipa and it is marked with coral. There is a second golden and inaccessible mountain named Sudhama. O Kouravya! There is the third radiant mountain, Kumuda. The fourth has the name of Pushpavan and the fifth is Kushoshaya. The sixth has the name of Harigiri and these six are the foremost among mountains. As one progresses, the space between two mountains is double that between the preceding two.

'"The first varsha is Oudbhida and the second is Venumandala. The third is Rathakara and the fourth is known as Palana. The fifth varsha is Dhritimat and the sixth varsha is Prabhakara. The seventh varsha is Kampila and this is the collection of seven varshas. O lord of the universe. Gods, gandharvas and other beings roam and sport there. People do not die there. O king! There are no bandits there and no mleccha tribes. O king! Everyone there is usually fair and delicate. O lord of men! I will tell you about the remaining varshas, as it has been heard. O great king! Listen with an attentive mind. In Krounchadvipa, there is a large mountain named Krouncha. Beyond Krouncha is Vamanaka and after Vamanaka is Andhakaraka. O king! Beyond Andhakara[18] is Mainaka, supreme among mountains. O king! Beyond Mainaka is Govinda, best among mountains. O

[17]The silk-cotton tree.
[18]Andhakara is the same as Andhakaraka.

king! Beyond Govinda is the mountain named Nibida. O extender of the lineage! The range between successive mountains is double.[19] Listen. I will tell you about the countries that are located there. The country near Krouncha is Kushala, while that near Vamana[20] is Manonuga. O extender of the Kuru lineage! The country beyond Manonuga is Ushna. Pravaraka is beyond Ushna, Andhakaraka beyond Pravara.[21] The country beyond Andhakaraka is said to be Munidesha. Dundubhisvana is said to be beyond Munidesha. O lord of men! This is frequented by siddhas and charanas and people are generally fair. O great king! These countries are frequented by gods and gandharvas. There is a mountain named Pushkara in Pushkara and it is full of gems and jewels. The god Prajapati himself, always resides there. O lord of men! All the gods, accompanied by the maharshis, always worship him with eloquent words and reverent homage. Different kinds of jewels from Jambudvipa are used in this. O descendant of the Kuru lineage! In all these dvipas, people and brahmanas observe *brahmacharya*[22] and self-control and are truthful. Health and life expectancy progressively becomes double.[23] O king! O descendant of the Bharata lineage! The land in each of these dvipas constitutes a single country. In each of these countries, only a single dharma is seen. The lord Prajapati himself raises his staff of chastisement there. O great king! He always resides in those dvipas and protects them. O king! He is the king. He is the one who provides bliss.[24] He is the father. He is the grandfather. O foremost among men! He protects all the mobile and immobile beings. O Kouravya! O great king! Cooked food manifests itself before the beings there and they always eat it. Beyond this is seen the world

[19]Progressively, the distance between the second and the third is double that between the first and the second and so on.

[20]Vamana is the same as Vamanaka.

[21]Pravara is the same as Pravaraka.

[22]Usually the stage of celibacy, when one is studying. However, brahmacharya also means worship of the brahman or following the path of the brahman.

[23]It is left implicit that this occurs as one progressively moves northwards, from one varsha to the next.

[24]The word used is *shiva*, which means the benign one who ensures bliss.

named Sama. O great king! This has four corners and thirty-three circles. O Kouravya! O foremost among the Bharata lineage! The four elephants, revered by the worlds, reside there.[25] O king! They are Vamana, Airavata, Supratika who has rent temples and mouth, and another one.[26] I cannot enumerate the dimensions of these elephants. That has always remained unknown—upwards, downwards and diagonally. O great king! The wind freely blows there from all the directions and the elephants seize it with trunks that are extremely radiant, designed to draw up, and with tips like lotuses. As soon as the elephants have seized the wind, they release it with their breath. O great king! It arrives here and sustains all beings."

'Dhritarashtra said, "O Sanjaya! You have told me in detail about the first.[27] You have also described the dvipas. O Sanjaya! Now tell me what is left."

'Sanjaya said, "O great king! O foremost among the Kouravas! I have spoken about the dvipas. Now listen as I exactly tell you about the planets and Svarbhanu[28] and about their dimensions. O great king! It has been heard that the planet Svarbhanu is spherical. Its diameter is twelve thousand yojanas. O unblemished one! Because it is large, its circumference is forty-two thousand yojanas.[29] That is what the ancient and learned ones have said. O king! The diameter of the moon is said to be eleven thousand yojanas. O foremost among the Kuru lineage! The circumference of this great-souled one, who provides cool rays, is thirty-eight thousand and nine hundred yojanas.[30] O descendant of the Kuru lineage! O king! The diameter of the sun is ten thousand yojanas and its circumference is thirty-five

[25]There are four elephants that dwell in the four directions. These are known as *diggaja*, the elephant (gaja) for a direction (*dik*).

[26]The temples and mouth are rent because of rutting when an elephant is in musth. The name of the fourth elephant is not mentioned. Sometimes, eight or ten elephants are said to dwell in the respective eight or ten directions.

[27]The first subject, the geography. However, Dhritarashtra had also asked about Rahu and about the sun and the moon.

[28]Another name for Rahu.

[29]This gives a value of Pi of 3.5.

[30]This gives a value of Pi of 3.45.

thousand and eight hundred. O unblemished one! This is because it is so large. Thus it has been heard about the extremely benevolent and fast-moving giver of light. O descendant of the Bharata lineage! These are the dimensions indicated for the sun. O great king! Because of its large size, at the appropriate time, Rahu envelopes both the moon and the sun. I have briefly recounted this to you. O great king! With the sight of the sacred texts, I have told you everything that you had asked, exactly. Be at peace. As instructed there,[31] I have told you about the creation of the universe. O Kouravya! Therefore, pacify your son Duryodhana.[32] O foremost among the Bharata lineage! Having heard the delightful account of Bhumi Parva, a king obtains prosperity and success and is honoured by virtuous ones. The life expectancy, strength, deeds and energy of such a lord of the earth increase, if he follows the vows and listens to it on the day of the new moon or the full moon. His ancestors and grandfathers are gratified. You have now heard everything about the merits that have earlier flowed from Bharata Varsha, where we now are.'''

[31]In the sacred texts.

[32]The connection between a geographical description and Duryodhana's pacification is not obvious.

Bhagavad Gita Parva

This parva has 994 shlokas and twenty-seven chapters.

This section is so named because it includes the Song Celestial or the Bhagavad Gita, the teachings of Krishna to Arjuna. The section begins with the dramatic news that Bhishma has been killed. When Sanjaya tells Dhritarashtra this, Dhritarashtra (and the reader) is astounded, wishing to know how this came to be. After a description of the

arrangements for war, the rest of this section is
the Bhagavad Gita.

Chapter 874(14)

Vaishampayana said, 'Sanjaya, Gavalgana's son, was wise. He
could see everything, the past, the present and the future. In
great distress, he suddenly rushed from the field of battle to where
Dhritarashtra was immersed in thought and told him that Bhishma,
the intermediate one of the Bharata lineage, had been killed.[1] "O bull
among the Bharata lineage! I am Sanjaya and I bow down before
you. Shantanu's son, Bhishma, the grandfather of the Bharatas, has
been slain. He was foremost among all warriors. He was the resort
of all archers. That grandfather of the Kurus is now lying down on a
bed of arrows. Depending on his valour, your son embarked on that
game of dice. O king! That Bhishma is now lying down, having been
killed on the field of battle by Shikhandi. On a single chariot, that
maharatha had earlier defeated all the lords of the earth in a great
battle in Kashi.[2] Descended from the Vasus, he fought with Rama,
Jamadagni's son, in a battle. Jamadagni's son could not kill him. But
he has now been slain by Shikhandi. He was like the great Indra in
his valour and like the Himalayas in his steadfastness. He was like the
ocean in his gravity and like the earth in his patience. Arrows were
like his teeth. The bow was his mouth. The sword was his tongue.
He was invincible. He was a lion among men. Today, your father[3]

[1]Sanjaya need not of course have gone to the field of battle. He could see
what was happening without being physically present. The Critical edition has
the word *madhyamam* as a description of Bhishma. This means an intermediate
one, someone in the middle. Bhishma was an intermediate one between the earlier
generation of the Bharatas and the newer one. However, this sounds contrived.
Since non-critical versions have the standard word *pitamaham* (grandfather),
the Critical version may have erred.

[2]These incidents have been recounted in Section 60.

[3]The word father is being used in a loose sense.

has been brought down by the one from Panchala.[4] On seeing him ready for battle, the large army of the Pandavas trembled in fear, like a herd of cattle on seeing a lion. He protected your army and formations for ten nights. He performed extremely difficult deeds and has now departed, like the setting sun. Like Shakra,[5] he calmly showered thousands of arrows. For ten days, every day, he killed ten thousand warriors in battle. Like a tree struck by the wind, he has been killed and is lying down on the ground. O king! O descendant of the Bharata lineage! He did not deserve this and this is because of your evil counsel."'

Chapter 875(15)

'Dhritarashtra asked, "How has Bhishma, bull among the Kurus, been killed by Shikhandi? My father was the equal of Vasava. How has he been brought down from his chariot? O Sanjaya! What happened to my sons when they were deprived of Bhishma? He was powerful and was like the gods. He observed brahmacharya for the sake of his superior.[6] He was great in spirit and great in strength, a great archer. When that maharatha, a tiger among men, was killed, what was the state of their[7] minds then? My mind is pierced with great grief on hearing that he has been killed. He was a bull among the Kuru lineage. He was a brave one who did not waver. He was a bull among men. When he advanced, who followed him? Who were the ones who preceded him? O Sanjaya! Who was at his side and who advanced with him? He was a bull among kshatriyas who could not be dislodged. Which brave ones were with that bull among rathas when he suddenly penetrated the formation of chariots? Who were

---

[4]Shikhandi.

[5]Indra.

[6]That is, Bhishma's father Shantanu. Bhishma adopted a life of celibacy so that Shantanu could marry Satyavati.

[7]Referring to Duryodhana and his brothers.

at the rear?[8] That destroyer of enemies, who was like the sun and an equal of the one with the thousand rays, suddenly attacked the enemy soldiers and spread terror amidst the enemy. On the instructions of Kourava,[9] he performed difficult deeds in battle. He devoured their ranks. Who tried to repulse him? O Sanjaya! He was accomplished and unassailable. When Shantanu's son advanced against them in battle, how did the Pandavas counter him? He slaughtered the soldiers. He possessed arrows for his teeth. He was swift. The bow was his gaping mouth. The terrible sword was his tongue. He was invincible. He was the ultimate of tigers among men. He was modest. He had never been vanquished. How could Kounteya bring down such an unvanquished one in battle? He was a terrible and fierce archer. He was stationed on his supreme chariot. With his sharp arrows, he sliced off the heads of enemies. On seeing him ready in battle, like the invincible fire of destruction, the great army of the Pandavas always trembled. That destroyer of troops destroyed the soldiers for ten nights. After having accomplished extremely difficult deeds, he has now departed like the setting sun. Like Shakra, he created a shower of inexhaustible arrows. In ten days, he slaughtered a hundred million warriors in battle. He is lying down on the bare ground, like a tree destroyed by the wind. This is because of my evil counsel. That descendant of the Bharata lineage did not deserve this. On witnessing the terrible valour of Bhishma, Shantanu's son, how was the army of the Pandavas capable of striking him down? How did the sons of Pandu engage with Bhishma in battle? O Sanjaya! While Drona was still alive, how could Bhishma not be victorious? When Kripa was near him, and so was Bharadvaja's son,[10] how could Bhishma, supreme among warriors, be killed? Bhishma was an *atiratha*.[11] Even the gods were incapable of withstanding him. How

[8]Guarding him.

[9]Duryodhana.

[10]Bharadvaja's son is Drona. However, Drona has already been mentioned. Hence, if the word son is interpreted with some latitude, this could also mean Ashvatthama.

[11]An atiratha is a supreme warrior. The classification of rathas, maharathas and atirathas has been given in Section 59 (Volume 4).

could Shikhandi of Panchala kill him in battle? He always rivalled
Jamadagni's extremely powerful son[12] in battle. Jamadagni's son,
who was Shakra's equal in valour, could not defeat him. How could
Bhishma, with the strength of a maharatha, be killed in battle? O
Sanjaya! Without knowing about that brave one, I cannot obtain
any peace. O Sanjaya! Which of my great archers did not desert
that undecaying one? On Duryodhana's instructions, which brave
ones surrounded him? When all the Pandavas advanced against
the undecaying Bhishma, with Shikhandi at the forefront, were the
Kurus frightened? Did they abandon him? The roar of his bow, with
its shower of arrows, was like a giant cloud. The great twang of
his bow was like a tall and mighty cloud. He showered arrows on
the Kounteyas, together with the Panchalas and the Srinjayas. He
slaughtered the brave warriors of the enemy, like the wielder of the
vajra against the danavas.

'"He was like a terrible and surging ocean, with his invincible
arrows like crocodiles. The bows were like waves. That interminable
ocean was without boats and without islands. The clubs and swords
were like whirling sharks.[13] The masses of horses and elephants were
like crocodiles. There were many spirited horses, elephants, infantry
and chariots. All those warriors of the enemy were immersed in
that battle. Through his energy and anger, that scorcher of enemies
consumed them. Which brave one could repulse him, like the shore
against the abode of sharks?[14] O Sanjaya! For Duryodhana's sake,
Bhishma, the destroyer of enemies, performed deeds in battle. Who
were in front of him then? Bhishma was infinitely energetic. Who
protected his right axle? With devotion and care, who guarded him
at the back from enemy warriors? So as to protect him, who were
immediately in front of Bhishma? When that brave one fought in
battle, which brave ones protected his front axle? O Sanjaya! Who
were stationed at his left axle and attacked the Srinjayas? Who
protected his unassailable advance guard? Who protected his sides?

[12]Parashurama.
[13]*Makara*, mythical aquatic creature, translated here as shark.
[14]The way the shore drives back the ocean.

He has traversed along the difficult path.[15] O Sanjaya! Who were the
ones who fought with the enemy warriors in general? If our brave
ones protected him and were protected by him, how did he not swiftly
vanquish that invincible army[16] in battle? He was like the lord of all
the worlds, the supreme god Prajapati. O Sanjaya! How were the
Pandavas capable of striking him? He was our refuge and the Kurus
resorted to him when fighting with the enemy. O Sanjaya! You have
told me that Bhishma, tiger among men, has fallen. My son resorted
to the great strength of that valiant one and ignored the Pandavas.
How could he have been slain by the enemy? My father was great
in his vows. He was unassailable in battle. In earlier times, desiring
to slay the danavas, all the gods sought his help. When he was born,
the immensely valiant Shantanu, the protector of the world, gave up
sorrow, grief and dejection. He possessed the qualities of a son. He
was wise. He was devoted. He was a refuge. He was devoted to his
own dharma. He was pure. He knew the truth about the Vedas and
the Vedangas.[17] How could he have been killed? He was skilled in
all weapons. He was modest. He was self-controlled. He was calm.
He was spirited. On hearing that Shantanu's son has been killed, I
think that the rest of my army has already been slain. It is my view
that adharma has become stronger than dharma. The Pandavas
desire the kingdom and have killed their aged senior. Jamadagni's
son, Rama, is supreme among those who know all weapons. In
earlier times, when he raised his weapons for the sake of Amba,
he was defeated by Bhishma in battle.[18] He was the equal of Indra
in deeds. He was foremost among all archers. You have said that
Bhishma has been killed. What can be a greater misery than this?
Jamadagni's valiant son, Rama, the destroyer of enemy warriors, who
made it a vow to kill kshatriyas, could not defeat him in battle. That

[15]Referring to Bhishma's death.

[16]Referring to the army of the Pandavas.

[17]There are six Vedangas—*shiksha* (articulation and pronunciation), *chhanda*
(prosody), *vyakarana* (grammar), *nirukta* (etymology), *jyotisha* (astronomy)
and *kalpa* (rituals).

[18]The story has been told in Section 60.

extremely intelligent one has now been killed by Shikhandi. It is thus evident that Drupada's son, Shikhandi, is superior in energy, valour and strength to the immensely valorous Bhargava,[19] invincible in battle. That brave one[20] was accomplished in battle. He was skilled in the use of all weapons. He was knowledgeable about supreme weapons. That bull among the Bharata lineage has been killed. In that assembly of enemies, who were the brave ones who followed that destroyer of foes? Tell me how the battle between Bhishma and the Pandavas proceeded.

'"O Sanjaya! With that brave one killed, my army is like a woman without a son. My soldiers are like a demented herd of cattle, without a protector. In a great battle, his manliness was supreme in the worlds. When he fell, what was the state of my army then? O Sanjaya! Despite being alive, what strength remains in us now? We have caused our greatly valorous father to be killed, chief among virtuous ones in the world. We are immersed in fathomless water, without seeing a boat that we can use to cross. I think that my sons must be grief-stricken, extremely miserable at Bhishma's death. My heart must be made out of extremely hard stone. On hearing about the death of Bhishma, tiger among men, it is not being rent asunder. He was a bull among the Bharata lineage and possessed weapons, intelligence and policy. He was immeasurable and unassailable. How was he killed in battle? One cannot be freed from death through weapons, valour, austerities, intelligence, steadfastness or giving up. Destiny is extremely powerful and cannot be transgressed by anyone in the world. O Sanjaya! You have told me that Bhishma, Shantanu's son, has been killed. Tormented by grief on account of my sons, I thought of the great misery and sought salvation from Shantanu's son, Bhishma. O Sanjaya! When he saw Shantanu's son lying down on the ground like a sun, to whom did Duryodhana resort? O Sanjaya! When I reflect with my intelligence on the lords of the earth who are on my side and those of the enemy, I do not see what remnants

[19]Parashurama belonged to the Bhargava lineage.
[20]Bhishma.

will be left in either army. The dharma of kshatriyas, as instructed
by the rishis, is terrible, since, desiring the kingdom, the Pandavas
have killed Shantanu's son. We also desired the kingdom and have
killed our grandfather. The Parthas, and my sons, are established in
the dharma of kshatriyas and no crime attaches to them. O Sanjaya!
When there is a great calamity, even a virtuous person should perform
this task. One should exhibit ultimate valour, to the best of one's
capacity. This has been laid down. He was modest and unvanquished.
O son![21] When he was engaged in slaughtering soldiers, how did
the sons of Pandu counter Shantanu's son? How were the soldiers
arrayed and how did he fight with the great-souled ones?

'"O Sanjaya! How was my father, Bhishma, killed by the enemies?
When Bhishma was killed, what did Duryodhana, Karna, Shakuni
Soubala and Duhshasana say? This gambling board is strewn with
the bodies of men, elephants and horses. There are terrible arrows,
lances, clubs, swords and spikes as dice. Those evil ones have entered
the assembly hall of this difficult war. Those bulls among men are
gambling and have offered their lives as stakes. Who was won?
Who won? O Sanjaya! Who was successful in his objective? Other
than Bhishma, Shantanu's son, who else has been brought down?
Tell me. After hearing that Devavrata[22] has been slain, I cannot
obtain peace. My father[23] was the performer of terrible deeds. On
hearing this, I am grief-stricken. Thinking about the great injury
that will befall my sons, my heart was anguished. O Sanjaya! You
have made that fire blaze, by sprinkling clarified butter on it. On
seeing that Bhishma, famous in all the worlds, and the one who
had accepted a great burden, has been slain, I think that my sons
must be grieving. I wish to hear about the misery that has arisen
from Duryodhana's deeds. O Sanjaya! Therefore, tell me everything
exactly as it has happened in that war that will destroy the earth,
brought about by the evil intelligence of my son. O Sanjaya! Tell
me everything, whether it is good or bad. In his desire for victory,

[21]The word used is tata.
[22]Bhishma's name.
[23]Bhishma.

what did Bhishma finally accomplish in the battle? He possessed energy. He was skilled in weapons. How was the battle between the soldiers of the Kurus and the Pandavas? Tell me exactly, in due order, with the time of occurrence.'"

Chapter 876(16)

'Sanjaya said, "O great king! You are a worthy person and the question that you have asked is fitting. However, you should not ascribe the fault to Duryodhana. One who suffers because of his own evil conduct, should not blame other men. This is not right and you should not do this. O great king! A man who is reprehensible in all his conduct deserves to be killed by everyone because of those censurable deeds. The Pandavas are not wise about deceitful ways. They waited, with their followers and advisers. They looked towards you and bore it. They forgave and dwelt for a long time in the forest. O lord of the earth! Hear about this gathering of horses, elephants and infinitely energetic kings, which I have seen through sight obtained through the strength of yoga. Do not sorrow in your mind. O lord of men! All this has been preordained earlier. I bow down before your father, Parashara's wise son.[24] Through his favours, I have obtained divine and supreme wisdom. O king! I have sight beyond the senses and can hear from a great distance. I know the minds of others and am acquainted with the past and the future. I always know about rising and travelling through the sky. The great-souled one has granted me the boon of not being touched by weapons in battle. Listen in detail to the wonderful and extraordinary account. The great battle between the Bharatas makes the body hair stand up.

'"O great king! When the soldiers were arrayed in accordance with the prescribed battle formations, Duryodhana spoke to

[24]Krishna Dvaipayana Vedavyasa was Dhritrashtra's biological father and was the son of the sage Parashara.

Duhshasana. 'O Duhshasana! Let the chariots be yoked immediately for Bhishma's protection. Instruct all our soldiers to advance swiftly. What I have thought about for many years, has now come to pass. With their soldiers, the Pandavas and the Kurus have met. I do not think that there is anything in this battle more important than Bhishma's protection. If he is protected, he will kill the Parthas and the Somakas, together with the Srinjayas. That pure-souled one has said, "I will not kill Shikhandi. I have heard that he was a woman earlier. Therefore, I will avoid him in battle." It is my view that because of this, Bhishma must be specially protected. Let all my soldiers station themselves, resolving to kill Shikhandi. Let all the soldiers from the east and the west, the south and the north, skilled in weapons, protect the grandfather. If unprotected, an extremely strong lion can be killed by a wolf. Let a lion not be killed by the jackal Shikhandi. Yudhamanyu protects Phalguna's[25] left and Uttamouja protects the right. Phalguna protects Shikhandi. Partha protects the one whom Bhishma will avoid. O Duhshasana! Act so that Gangeya is not slain.'

'"When night had passed, a great roar arose from all the lords of the earth. 'Yoke! Yoke!' O descendant of the Bharata lineage! The sound of conch shells and drums was like the roar of lions. There was the neighing of horses and the clatter of the wheels of chariots. Elephants trumpeted. Warriors roared. They slapped their arms and there was a tumultuous sound everywhere. O great king! When the sun arose, all the soldiers in the large armies of the Kurus and the Pandavas arose and completed all the arrangements. O Indra among kings! Your sons and the Pandavas possessed elephants and chariots decorated with gold. They could be seen in their radiance, like clouds streaked with lightning. An array of many chariots could be seen, like cities. Your father was extremely resplendent, like the full moon. The warriors were stationed in their battle formations, with bows, scimitars, swords,[26] clubs, javelins, spears and other shining weapons.

[25]Arjuna's.

[26]Both *rishti* and *khadga* are types of swords and both are mentioned. Hence, we have translated rishti as scimitar.

O lord of the earth! There were elephants, chariots, infantry and horses. There were hundreds and thousands of them, spread like a net. Resplendent standards of many different kinds could be seen. They were brilliant and there were thousands of them, belonging to us and to the enemy. They were golden and were adorned with jewels. They blazed like the fire. The kings possessed thousands of radiant standards. They shone like the great Indra's standard and resembled the great Indra's abode. The brave ones who desired to fight, glanced at them. Indras among men were at the forefront of their troops. Their weapons were raised. They had colourful guards on their palms and possessed quivers. Their eyes were like those of bulls. Shakuni Soubala, Shalya, Jayadratha from Sindhu, Vinda and Anuvinda from Avanti, Sudakshina from Kamboja, Shrutayudha from Kalinga, King Jayatsena, Brihadbala from Koshala and Satvata Kritavarma—these ten tigers among men were brave and possessed arms like clubs. They were performers of sacrifices at which a lot of gifts were donated. Each of them headed one *akshouhini*.[27] Other than this, there were many others who followed Duryodhana. There were immensely strong kings and princes, knowledgeable about policy. They could be seen armoured, heading their armies. All of them were attired in black deerskin. They had standards and wore garlands of *munja* grass.[28] They prepared themselves for Duryodhana's sake and were ready to go to Brahma's world.[29] They stationed themselves, heading the ten large armies. The eleventh large army of Kourava, Dhritarashtra's son, stood in front of all the soldiers, with Shantanu's son at the head. The undecaying one was in a white headdress. He had white horses and was clad in white armour. O great king! Bhishma could be seen like the rising moon. Stationed on his silver chariot, Bhishma had a standard with a golden palm tree. He could be seen by the Kurus

---

[27]An akshouhini is a large army and consists of 21,870 chariots, 21,870 elephants, 65,610 horses and 109,350 soldiers on foot.

[28]The Critical edition has got this wrong. The text says *munjamalina*, garlanded with munja grass. This does not fit. Some other versions say *yuddhashalina*, skilled in war. That fits much better.

[29]After death.

and the Pandavas like the one with the sharp rays,[30] enveloped by white clouds. Dhrishtadyumna, the great Srinjaya archer, was at the forefront[31] and they looked like small animals, glancing at a large and yawning lion. With Dhrishtadyumna at the forefront, all of them trembled repeatedly. O descendant of the Bharata lineage! These are the eleven large divisions of your army. The seven divisions of the Pandavas were also protected by great men. They were like two oceans meeting at the end of an era, infested with crazy sharks[32] and giant crocodiles. O king! We have not seen or heard of anything like this earlier, like those armies encountering each other in the prescribed manner.'"

Chapter 877(17)

'Sanjaya said, "Just as the illustrious Krishna Dvaipayana Vyasa had said, in that fashion, all the lords of the earth assembled for the encounter. On that day, the moon approached Magha.[33] The seven large and blazing planets[34] appeared in the sky. When the sun

[30]This may mean either the sun or the moon. However, Bhishma has already been compared to a moon, though sharp rays typically signify the sun, not the moon.

[31]Of the Pandavas.

[32]Makara.

[33]The tenth of the twenty-seven nakshatras. There is a problem of inconsistency, since other places don't say that the moon was in Magha on that day. A somewhat more complicated interpretation is also possible. The ancestors are the deity associated with Magha. After death, one goes to the world of the ancestors and spends some time there, before proceeding elsewhere. In the complicated interpretation, this shloka means that the moon approached the world of the ancestors. Consequently, if one died in the battle, one would not have to spend time in the world of the ancestors, but would proceed to heaven immediately, after traversing the world of the moon.

[34]Excluding Rahu and Ketu.

arose, it seemed to be divided into two parts. When the blazing sun arose in the sky, it had a flaming crest. The directions blazed. Desiring to feed on bodies, flesh and blood, jackals and crows cried out. Each day, the aged grandfather of the Kurus and Bharadvaja's son arose and with concentration, wished that the Parthas might not be killed and that the sons of Pandu might be victorious. Those undecaying scorchers of enemies fought for your sake only because they had taken a pledge. Your father, Devavrata, was knowledgeable about every aspect of dharma. He summoned all the lords of the earth and spoke these words to them. 'O kshatriyas! This great door that leads to heaven has been opened up. Pass through it and go the worlds of Shakra and Brahma.[35] This is the eternal path, indicated by the ancient ones, and those who have preceded them. Honour yourselves by fighting with great attention. Through such deeds, Nabhaga, Yayati, Mandhata, Nahusha and Nriga have been successful and have reached the supreme goal. It is adharma for a kshatriya to die from disease in his home. The eternal dharma is to die in the field of battle.' O bull among the Bharata lineage! Having been thus addressed by Bhishma, all the lords of the earth went to the heads of their armies and were resplendent in their supreme chariots. O bull among the Bharata lineage! But because of Bhishma, Vaikartana Karna, together with his advisers and relatives, cast aside his weapons in that battle. Without Karna, your sons and all the kings on your side marched out. They roared like lions and this resounded in the ten directions. There were white umbrellas and flags and pennants, elephants and horses. With charioteers, chariots and infantry, the army was splendid. There was the sound of drums and cymbals and also the noise of kettledrums. The earth trembled because of the roar of the wheels of chariots. The maharathas had golden armlets and bracelets and bows. They were as radiant as mobile mountains.

'"Bhishma's standard had a large palm tree with five stars. The general of the Kuru army was like the clear sun. O bull among the Bharata lineage! O king! As instructed by Shantanu's son,

[35]The text says brahman.

all the kings and great archers who were on your side stationed
themselves. With all the kings, Shaibya Govasana[36] advanced on a
king among elephants that was bedecked with flags and deserved
to carry kings. Ashvatthama, whose complexion was like the lotus,
was at the head of all the soldiers. He was ready and his standard
was adorned with a lion's tail. Shrutayudha, Chitrasena, Purumitra,
Vivimshati, Shalya, Bhurishrava, maharatha Vikarna—these seven
great archers were adorned in excellent armour. They rode their
chariots and followed Drona's son, ahead of Bhishma. Their great
standards were resplendent on their supreme chariots. The golden
flags were seen to be blazing. Drona, foremost among preceptors,
had a golden altar on his standard, adorned with a water pot and
the sign of a bow. Duryodhana's large standard had a bejewelled
elephant and led hundreds and thousands of soldiers. Pourava,
Kalinga, Sudakshina from Kamboja, Kshemadhanva, Sumitra and
other rathas were in front of him.[37] The king of Magadha guided
the forces from the front, on an extremely expensive chariot that
bore the standard of a bull. He was protected by the lord of Anga[38]
and the great-souled Kripa. That extremely large army from the
east looked like scattered autumn clouds. The immensely famous
Jayadratha stationed himself at the forefront of the soldiers.[39] He
had a beautiful silver standard, marked with the sign of a boar. A
hundred thousand chariots, eight thousand elephants and sixty
thousand horses were under his command. O king! Commanded by
the lord of Sindhu, foremost among standard bearers, that large army
was resplendent with chariots, elephants and horses. Together with
Ketumat, the lord of all the Kalingas advanced with sixty thousand
chariots and ten thousand elephants. His large elephants were like

[36]Govasana was his name. He was known as Shaibya because he was the
king of the Shibis.

[37]Duryodhana.

[38]Since Karna (the lord of Anga) had refused to fight, this mean's Karna's
son Vrishaketu.

[39]In all such instances, what is meant is that the individual concerned placed
himself at the head of the division of the army he was commanding, not at the
head of the overall army.

mountains. They were adorned with implements of war,[40] spears, quivers and standards and were beautiful. Kalinga was resplendent with a standard that bore the sign of a tree. He had a white umbrella and golden whisks. O king! Ketumat was also on an elephant, with a colourful and supreme goad.[41] He was stationed in that battle, like the sun amidst clouds. King Bhagadatta was stationed on a supreme elephant and was radiant in his energy. He was like the wielder of the vajra. Vinda and Anuvinda from Avanti were regarded as Bhagadatta's equal. They rode on the shoulders of elephants and followed Ketumat. O king! Instructed by Drona, the king who was Shantanu's son, the son of the preceptor,[42] Bahlika and Kripa, the arrays of chariots were arranged in *vyuhas*[43] with excellent heads. The elephants were the body. The horses were the sides. That fierce formation was ready to descend and attack on all sides."'

Chapter 878(18)

'Sanjaya said, "O great king! After some time, a tumultuous sound could be heard, when the warriors prepared to fight, and it made the heart tremble. There were the sounds of conch shells and drums. Elephants trumpeted. The wheels of the chariots thundered and the earth seemed to be torn apart. The horses neighed. The warriors roared. O unassailable one! The armies of your sons and those of the Pandavas encountered each other and trembled. The elephants and the chariots were decorated with gold and were seen to be radiant, like clouds with lightning. O lord of men! Those on your side had many different kinds of standards. They were adorned with golden rings and shone like the fire. O descendant of

---

[40]*Yantras* or machines.

[41]*Ankusha*, for driving the elephant.

[42]Ashvatthama.

[43]A vyuha is an arrangement of troops in battle formation and there were different types of vyuhas.

the Bharata lineage! Those on your side[44] and those on the side of
the enemy were seen to be as pure as the great Indra's standard, in
the great Indra's abode. The brave ones were clad in golden armour.
They blazed like the fiery sun. Armoured, they seemed to be like the
blazing planets. They held upraised weapons and wore guards on
their palms. They possessed standards. They had eyes like bulls. They
were great archers and placed themselves at the forefront. O lord
of men! Among your sons, there were those who protected Bhisma
from the rear—Duhshasana, Durvisaha, Durmukha, Duhsaha,
Vivimshati, Chitrasena and maharatha Vikarna. There were also
Satyavrata, Purumitra, Jaya, Bhurishrava and Shala. They were
followed by twenty thousand chariots. Abhishaha, Shurasena, Shibi,
Vasati, Shalva, Matysa, Ambashtha, Trigarta, Kekaya, Souvira,
Kitava and those from the east, west and the north Malava—all the
brave ones from these twelve regions[45] advanced, ready to give up
their lives. They protected the grandfather with an array of large
chariots. With an army that consisted of ten thousand swift elephants,
the king of Magadha followed that array of chariots. Those who
protected the wheels of chariots and the feet of the elephants in the
midst of that army numbered six million. The infantry marched in
advance, with bows, shields and swords in their hands. There were
many hundreds and thousands of them and they fought with nails
and lances. O descendant of the Bharata lineage! O great king! The
eleven akshouhinis of your sons looked like the Ganga separated
from the Yamuna.'"

Chapter 879(19)

'Dhritarashtra asked, "On seeing the eleven akshouhinis
arranged in battle formation, how did Pandava Yudhishthira,

---

[44]The standards.
[45]The Malavas being counted as one.

possessing fewer soldiers, arrange his counter-formations? Bhishma knew about all vyuhas—those of men, gods, gandharvas and asuras. How did Kounteya Pandava counter them?"

'Sanjaya said, "On seeing the soldiers of Dhritarashtra's sons arranged in battle formation, Dharmaraja Pandava, with dharma in his soul, spoke to Dhananjaya. 'O son![46] We know from the words of maharshi Brihaspati that a small number of soldiers must be arranged in condensed form, while a larger number can be extended at will. When a small number has to fight with a larger one, the arrangement should be *suchimukha*.[47] Compared to those of the enemy, our soldiers are few. O Pandava! Following the words and instructions of the maharshi, arrange the vyuha.' On hearing the words of Dharmaraja, Phalguna replied, 'O king! I will arrange a vyuha that is extremely invincible. This immovable vyuha is known by the name of Vajra and has been designed by the wielder of the vajra. Bhima is supreme among wielders of weapons. He is like a turbulent storm. No enemy can withstand him in battle. He will fight at the forefront. That supreme of men will pacify the energy of the enemy's soldiers. He is skilled in all the techniques used in war. He will lead us and fight from the front. On seeing him, all the kings, with Duryodhana at the forefront, will be confused and will retreat, like small animals at the sight of a lion. With him as a wall, all of us will resort to him, like all the immortals resort to the wielder of the vajra, and our fear will be dispelled. Bhima is foremost among the wielders of weapons. Vrikodara is a bull among men and is the performer of terrible deeds. Especially when he is enraged, there is no man in the world who can glance at him. Bhimasena wields a firm club, with substance like the vajra. When he roams around with great force, he can dry up the ocean. O lord of men! Kekaya, Dhrishtaketu and the valiant Chekitana—these advisers also look towards him. So do Dhritarashtra's sons.' This is what Bibhatsu said. O venerable one! When Partha spoke in this way, all the soldiers applauded the eloquent one in that field of battle. Having spoken in this way, the

---

[46]The word used is tata.
[47]In the shape of the mouth (*mukha*) of a needle (*suchi*).

mighty-armed Dhananjaya did what he had said. Phalguna arranged
the forces in the form of the vyuha and advanced.

'"On seeing the advancing army of the Kurus, the mighty army of
the Pandavas seemed to be like the overflowing, surging and moving
Ganga. Bhimasena, Parshata Dhrishtadyumna, Nakula, Sahadeva
and valiant Dhrishtaketu were in the vanguard. Surrounded by one
akshouhini, the king[48] was at the rear, protecting them from the
back with his brothers and sons. Madri's immensely radiant sons
protected Bhima's wheels. The swift sons of Droupadi and Subhadra
protected the rear. They were protected from the rear by maharatha
Dhrishtadyumna of Panchala, together with the brave Prabhadrakas,
foremost among rathas. Shikhandi was behind them, protected by
Arjuna. O bull among the Bharata lineage! He[49] advanced, determined
to bring about Bhishma's destruction. Maharatha Yuyudhana[50]
guarded Arjuna's rear and the two from Panchala, Yudhamanyu and
Uttamouja, guarded his wheels. Kunti's son, King Yudhishthira, was
in the centre of the army, surrounded by large and crazy elephants
that were like moving mountains. For the sake of the Pandavas, the
valorous Panchala Yajnasena[51] placed himself behind Virata, with
one akshouhini. O king! The chariots and great standards bore many
signs. They were adorned with the best of gold and looked like the sun
and the moon. Asking them to advance, maharatha Dhrishtadyumna,
together with his brothers and sons, protected Yudhishthira from
the rear. Surpassing all the chariots and many standards on your
side and those of the enemy, a giant ape was stationed on Arjuna's
standard. Many hundreds and thousands of infantry advanced in
front, protecting Bhimasena. They had swords, lances and scimitars in
their hands. There were ten thousand elephants, with musth trickling
from their temples and mouths. They were brave and were adorned
with glittering nets of gold. They were like moving mountains. They
flowed like clouds.[52] They were like mad mountains. They possessed

[48]Virata.
[49]Shikhandi.
[50]Satyaki.
[51]Drupada.
[52]Because of the musth.

the fragrance of lotuses. They followed the king at the rear, like moving mountains. Bhimasena whirled his terrible club, which was like a *parigha*.[53] The invincible and great-minded one was capable of crushing a large army. He was incapable of being looked at, like the sun, and was scorching, like the one with the rays. From a close distance, none of the warriors was capable of looking at him. The vyuha named Vajra was difficult to penetrate and faced every direction.[54] The bows were like streaks of lightning[55] and this terrible formation was protected by the wielder of the Gandiva. Arranging the army in this counter formation, the Pandavas waited. Protected by the Pandavas, it was invincible in the world of men.

'"At dawn, both sets of soldiers waited for the sun to rise. A wind, with drops of water, began to blow. Though there were no clouds, thunder could be heard. Dry winds began to blow from all directions and carried sharp stones from the ground below. Dust arose and covered the earth in darkness. O bull among the Bharata lineage! Large meteors fell down in an eastern direction. They struck the rising sun and were shattered, with a loud noise. O bull among the Bharata lineage! When the armies were arranged in this way, the sun lost its luminescence and the earth roared and trembled. O supreme among the Bharata lineage! The roar of thunder was repeatedly heard from all the directions. O king! A thick dust arose and nothing could be seen. The giant standards, adorned with nets of bells, golden ornaments and flags, and like the sun in their resplendence, were suddenly struck by the wind. All of them made a jingling sound, like a forest of palm trees. Thus those Pandavas, tigers among men, were stationed, delighted at the prospect of battle. They were in a counter-formation against the army of your sons. O bull among the Bharata lineage! They seemed to suck the marrow out from the warriors.[56] Bhimasena could be seen at the forefront, with a club in his hand."'

[53]An ordinary club is *gada*, parigha is an iron club. Bhima's gada is being compared to a parigha, which is stronger than an ordinary club.

[54]Indra's vajra was symmetrical on all sides.

[55]Vajra also means thunder. Hence the image of lightning.

[56]Of the Kouravas.

Chapter 880(20)

'Dhritarashtra asked, "O Sanjaya! My army, with Bhishma as the leader, and that of the Pandavas, with Bhima as the leader, desired to fight. When the sun arose, which of these was cheerful when it approached the other? To which side were the moon, the sun and the wind adverse? Against which army did predators utter inauspicious sounds? Which were the young ones who had cheerful complexions on their faces? Tell me all this, exactly and in detail."

'Sanjaya said, "O Indra among kings! When the two armies were equally arranged in vyuhas, they were equally cheerful. They were equally beautiful, as resplendent as forests. They were full of elephants, chariots and horses. Both the armies were large and terrible in form. O descendant of the Bharata lineage! Each one was incapable of withstanding the other. It was as if both had been created for conquering heaven. Both were protected by virtuous men. Dhritarashtra's sons, the Kurus, faced the west. The Parthas were stationed facing the east, ready to fight. The Kouravas were like the army of the Indra of the daityas, the Pandavas were like the army of the Indra of the gods. The wind blew from behind the Pandavas. The predators howled from behind the sons of Dhritarashtra. The elephants of your son could not bear the sharp smell from the musth of those Indras among elephants.[57] Duryodhana was on an elephant with the complexion of a lotus. It was armoured and had rent temples. It possessed a golden girdle. He was stationed in the midst of the Kurus and the bards and the minstrels praised him. A white umbrella with a golden chain, as brilliant as the moon, was held aloft his head. Shakuni, the king of Gandhara, followed him, surrounded in every direction by mountainous people from the region of Gandhara. The aged Bhishma was in front of all the soldiers. He had a white umbrella, a white bow, a conch shell, a white headdress, a white flag and white horses, and looked like a white mountain. All the sons of Dhritarashtra were in his army and also Shala, who came

---

[57]Belonging to the Pandavas.

from the country named Bahlika. The kshatriyas from Ambashtha, those from Sindhu and Souvira and the brave ones from the land of the five rivers[58] were also there.

'"The great-souled Drona was on a golden chariot with red horses. He was mighty-armed and his spirit never waned. He was the preceptor of almost all the kings. He was like an Indra on earth, protecting from the rear. Vardhakshatri, Bhurishrava, Purumitra, Jaya, Shalva, Matsya and all the Kekayas, with their brothers, were in the midst of all the soldiers. They possessed an army of elephants and wished to fight. Sharadvat's great-souled son[59] always fought in the front. He was the great archer Goutama, wonderful in fighting. With Shakas, Kiratas,[60] Yavanas[61] and Pahlavas, he stationed himself in the forefront of the army. That large army was protected by maharathas from Andhaka, Vrishni and Bhoja and also those from Sourashtra and the south-west, skilled in the use of weapons. There was also Kritavarma, who advanced behind your army. There were ten thousand *samshaptaka* rathas,[62] who had been created for death or for triumphing over Arjuna. O king! They were skilled in the use of weapons. They advanced with the brave Trigartas, resolved to follow Arjuna at every step. O descendant of the Bharata lineage! There were ten thousand fierce elephants on your side. A hundred chariots were assigned to each elephant, a hundred horses were assigned to each chariot, ten archers were assigned to each horse and ten shield-bearers were assigned to each archer. O descendant of the Bharata lineage! Thus did Bhishma arrange your troops in battle formation. From one day to another, Bhishma, the general and Shantanu's son, arranged it in human vyuhas, or vyuhas of gods, gandharvas and asuras. With a large number of maharathas, it was like the ocean on the night of the full moon. Arranged in a vyuha by Bhishma, the army

[58]Punjab.
[59]Kripa, also known as Goutama.
[60]Hunters.
[61]Greeks.
[62]These warriors took an oath that they would not retreat alive from the field of battle.

of Dhritarashtra's son was stationed facing the west, ready to fight. O Indra among kings! Your side was innumerable with standards. It was terrible. But though it was not like yours,[63] it seemed to me that the one of the Pandavas was larger and invincible, with leaders like Keshava and Arjuna.'"

Chapter 881(21)

'Sanjaya said, "On seeing the large army of Dhritarashtra's sons, ready to fight, Kunti's son, King Yudhishthira, was overcome by grief. Pandava saw the impenetrable vyuha that Bhishma had crafted. Having seen that it was impenetrable, he was distressed and spoke to Arjuna. 'O Dhananjaya! O mighty-armed one! When the grandfather fights on the side of the sons of Dhritarashtra, how will we be able to fight with them in this battle? Bhishma, the destroyer of enemies, whose energy is manifold, has crafted this immovable and impenetrable formation, in accordance with the decrees of the sacred texts. O destroyer of enemies! Together with our soldiers, we now have doubts. How can we be successful against this great vyuha?' O king! Thus addressed by Partha Yudhishthira, the destroyer of enemies, who was overcome by grief at the sight of your army, Arjuna replied, 'O lord of the earth! Listen. Those who are few can vanquish many brave ones who are superior in wisdom and possess qualities. O king! You do not suffer from malice and I will tell you the means. O Pandava! The rishi Narada, and Bhishma and Drona, know this. On an earlier occasion, at the time of the battle between the gods and the asuras, the grandfather himself said this to the great Indra and the denizens of heaven. "Those who desire victory, do not triumph through strength and valour, but through truth, non-violence, devotion to dharma and endeavour. One must give up adharma, avarice and delusion and resort to endeavour.

[63]Because it was smaller.

One must fight without pride. Where there is dharma, there will be victory." O king! Know that it is for this reason that our victory in this battle is certain. Narada has said that where there is Krishna, victory is there. Victory is Krishna's quality, it follows Madhava. Victory is one of his qualities and humility is another. Govinda is infinite in his energy. He is without pain even amidst a multitude of enemies. He is the eternal being. Where there is Krishna, victory is there. In earlier times, Hari manifested himself. He is Vaikuntha.[64] He has no weakness before weapons. In a loud tone, he spoke to the gods and the asuras, "Who among you wishes for victory?" The vanquished ones[65] replied, "We will follow Krishna and thereby obtain victory." Through his favours, Shakra and the other gods obtained the three worlds. O descendant of the Bharata lineage! Therefore, I do not see any reason for despondency. You have the lord of the universe and the lord of the thirty gods and because of this, you are assured of victory.'"

Chapter 882(22)

'Sanjaya said, "O bull among the Bharata lineage! Then King Yudhishthira arranged his soldiers in a counter-formation against Bhishma's and said, 'O extenders of the Kuru lineage! The Pandavas are arrayed in a counter-formation, in accordance with the injunctions. Desiring to attain supreme heaven, fight well.' Protected by Savyasachi, Shikhandi stood in the middle of the army. Protected by Bhima, Dhrishtadyumna was in the front. O king! The southern segment was protected by the handsome Yuyudhana,[66] foremost archer among the Satvatas and Shakra's equal. Yudhishthira was on

[64]Without weakness or lassitude. Vaikuntha is both the name of Vishnu's abode and a name for Vishnu. Here, it is being used in the latter sense.
[65]Before Krishna appeared, the gods had been vanquished by the demons.
[66]Satyaki.

a chariot that was like the great Indra's vehicle. It bore an excellent standard with gold and jewels and had a golden harness. He was stationed in the midst of his array of elephants. An extremely white and beautiful umbrella, with a handle made of tusks, was held aloft his head. Maharshis circumambulated him and sung his praises. Priests, maharshis and aged ones chanted his praises so that his enemies would be destroyed. They used meditation, mantras and herbs and pronounced words of benediction. The supreme among Kurus gave the great-souled brahmanas garments, cows, fruits, flowers and gold. He advanced like Shakra of the immortals. Arjuna's chariot possessed one hundred bells. It was embellished with the best of gold and was as resplendent as the fire, blazing like a thousand suns. It was yoked to white steeds and possessed excellent wheels. It had an ape on its banner. It was driven by Keshava and he[67] was stationed on it, with the Gandiva and arrows in his hands. There was no archer who was equal to him on earth. Nor will there ever be such a one. Bhimasena assumes a terrible form for the destruction of your sons. Without any weapons and with his bare hands, in a battle, he can reduce to ashes men, horses and elephants. The twins were with Vrikodara and they protected the brave charioteers. In this world, he[68] is like the great Indra himself. He was like an angry lion that was playing. Vrikodara was as insolent as a king of elephants. On seeing him in the vanguard of the army, the spirit of your soldiers was overcome by fear and anxiety and they trembled, like elephants caught in the mud.

'"O foremost among the Bharata lineage! Janardana then spoke to Gudakesha,[69] the invincible prince who was stationed in the midst of the army. Vasudeva said, 'Bhishma will attack our soldiers like a lion. He will protect with his power and strength. He is the flag of the Kuru lineage. That performer of three hundred horse sacrifices is there. Other soldiers surround the illustrious one, like clouds enveloping the one with the virtuous rays. O foremost among brave ones! Slay those troops, wishing to fight with the bull among the Bharata lineage.'"

[67]Arjuna.
[68]Bhima.
[69]Arjuna.

'Dhritarashtra asked, "O Sanjaya! Which warriors from which side were delighted and advanced to fight first? Who were confident in their minds and who were dejected and dispirited? Who struck first in the battle that makes the heart tremble? Was it from my side or that of the Pandavas? O Sanjaya! Tell me all this. Amidst whose soldiers were garlands and pastes fragrant?[70] Whose warriors roared and uttered auspicious words?"

'Sanjaya said, "At that time, the soldiers from both sides were cheerful. The garlands and pastes of both sides were equally fragrant. O bull among the Bharata lineage! The soldiers were arrayed in battle formation and when they met each other, there was an extremely terrible encounter. There was the tumultuous sound of musical instruments, intermingled with that of conch shells and drums. There was the trumpeting of elephants and the soldiers were filled with joy.'"

Chapter 883(23)

'Dhritarashtra asked, "O Sanjaya! Having gathered on the holy plains of Kurukshetra, wanting to fight, what did my sons and the sons of Pandu do?"

'Sanjaya said, "At that time, on seeing the Pandava soldiers assembled in battle formation, King Duryodhana went to the preceptor[71] and spoke the following words. 'O preceptor! Look at this great army of the Pandavas, assembled in battle formation by the son of Drupada,[72] your talented student. Here there are courageous warriors with mighty bows, the equals of Bhima and Arjuna in battle—Yuyudhana,[73] Virata, Drupada and other maharathas, Dhristaketu[74] and Chekitana,[75] the valiant king of Kashi, Purujit from the Kuntibhoja clan and

[70]As an auspicious sign.
[71]Dronacharya.
[72]Drupada's son was Dhrishtadyumna and he was also Dronacharya's student.
[73]Another name for Satyaki.
[74]The son of Shishupala, from Chedi.
[75]Of the Yadava clan.

Shaibya, greatest among men, the powerful Yudhamanyu,[76] the brave Uttamouja,[77] the son of Subhadra,[78] the sons of Droupadi—all of them are maharathas. O best among brahmanas! Now you should know the main warriors and leaders in my army. For your knowledge, I am naming them. You yourself, and Bhishma, and Karna, and Kripa, who wins battles, Ashvatthama, and Vikarna[79] and the son of Somadatta.[80] There are many other brave warriors, ready to give up their lives for my sake. All of them are skilled in battle and they are armed with various weapons of attack.[81] That army of ours, protected by Bhishma, is unlimited. But this army of theirs, protected by Bhima, is limited.[82] All of you occupy your respective positions at all the entry points to the army formations. It is Bhishma who must be protected.'

'"Creating happiness in his[83] heart, the powerful eldest of the Kuru clan and the grandfather roared loudly like a lion and blew his conch shell. Then, suddenly, conch shells and kettledrums, other kinds of drums and trumpets began to blare. That sound became tremendous. Then, seated in a great chariot to which white horses were harnessed, Madhava[84] and Pandava[85] blew their divine conch

[76]Of the Panchala clan.

[77]King Drupada's son.

[78]Abhimanyu.

[79]One of the Kourava brothers.

[80]Bhurishrava.

[81]*Shastra* is a weapon and so is a *praharana*. These words can be used synonymously. But etymologically, there is a difference between the two. Shastra is something that is used to kill. Praharana is something that is used to beat someone up. And *astra* is something that is thrown. The text uses both shastra and praharana.

[82]This is the obvious meaning. *Paryapta* means that which can be measured and is therefore limited. *Aparyapta* is that which is unlimited, such as the Kourava army is. This is the straightforward interpretation, the Kourava army being larger than the Pandava one by a considerable magnitude. There were eleven akshouhinis on the Kourava side and seven on the Pandava side. However, a more convoluted interpretation is also possible, since paryapta also means adequate. Thus, the Kourava army is inadequate, but the Pandava army is adequate.

[83]His means Duryodhana's. Duryodhana's statement having ended, we are back with Sanjaya.

[84]Krishna.

[85]Arjuna.

shells. Hrishikesha[86] blew the conch shell named Panchajanya and Dhananjaya[87] blew the conch shell named Devadatta. Vrikodara,[88] whose deeds give rise to fear, blew the giant conch shell named Poundra. King Yudhishthira, the son of Kunti, blew the conch shell named Anantavijaya. Nakula blew the conch shell named Sughosha and Sahadeva blew the conch shell named Manipushpaka. The king of Kashi, with the great bow, and maharatha Shikhandi, Dhristadyumna, Virata and Satyaki, who is never defeated, Drupada, the sons of Droupadi, and the mighty-armed son of Subhadra, all of them blew their separate conch shells, O lord of the earth! That tremendous sound echoed in the sky and on earth and pierced the hearts of those who were on the side of the sons of Dhritarashtra. Then, the son of Pandu,[89] with the monkey on his banner, saw the friends of Dhritarashtra thus arranged in battle formation and got ready to use his weapons. O lord of the earth! He raised his bow and told Hrishikesha the following words. 'O Achyuta![90] Place my chariot in between the two armies, while I look at those who are desirous of battle and are assembled here. Let me see with whom I will have to fight in this war-related business. In a desire to do good to the evil-hearted son of Dhritarashtra, they have gathered here, desirous of fighting. I want to see them.' O, descendant of the Bharata lineage! Thus spoken to by Gudakesha,[91] Hrishikesha placed that magnificent chariot between the two armies, in front of Bhishma, Drona and all the other rulers of the earth and said, 'O Partha! Look at those of the Kuru clan who are assembled here.' There, Partha saw fathers and grandfathers, teachers and maternal uncles, brothers, sons, grandsons and friends,[92] fathers-in-law and well-wishers in those two assembled armies.

[86]Krishna. Hrishikesha means lord of the senses.

[87]Arjuna.

[88]Bhima. *Vrikodara* means someone with the belly of a wolf.

[89]Arjuna.

[90]Krishna. *Achyuta* can be translated as someone who is firm and has not fallen.

[91]Another name for Arjuna. *Gudakesha* means someone who has conquered sleep.

[92]*Sakha* has been translated by us as a friend and *suhrida* as a well-wisher. All these terms can be translated as friend, but in the Sanskrit, there are differences

'"Seeing them, all the friends and relatives assembled there, the son of Kunti was overcome with great pity.[93] And in sadness, uttered the following words. 'O Krishna! Having seen these relatives here, assembled with a desire to fight, my body is going numb and my mouth is going dry. My body is quivering and my body hair is standing up. My skin is burning and the Gandiva is slipping from my hands. O Keshava! I cannot stand and my mind is in a whirl. The omens that I see are ill ones. I don't see any good that can come from killing one's relatives in a war. O Krishna! I don't want victory. Nor do I want the kingdom or happiness. O Govinda! What will we do with the kingdom or with pleasures or with life itself? Those for whose sake we want the kingdom and pleasures and happiness, they are gathered here in war, ready to give up their lives and their riches—preceptors, fathers, sons and grandfathers, maternal uncles, fathers-in-law, grandsons, brothers-in-law and other relatives. O Madhusudana! I don't want to kill them, even if they kill me. Forget this earth, even for the kingdoms of the three worlds. O Janardana! What pleasure will we derive from killing the sons of Dhritarashtra? Although they are assassins,[94] sin alone will be our lot if we kill them. Therefore, we cannot kill the sons of Dhritarashtra, with their friends. O Madhava! How can we be happy after killing our relatives? Although their minds are befuddled with greed and they do not see the sin that comes from opposing friends or from destroying the family line. O Janardana! We can see the sin that comes from destroying the family line. Why should we not have the

---

of nuance. A *mitra* is someone with whom one works together. A sakha is a kindred soul. A *bandhu* is someone from whom one cannot bear to be separated, a relative. A suhrida is someone who is always devoted and a *bandhava* is someone who accompanies you to palaces and cremation grounds, a kin.

[93]*Kripa* has been translated as pity. *Daya* is also pity. But there is a difference between the two and this will be explained in the next chapter.

[94]According to the sacred texts, there are six types of assassins (*atatayi*)— arsonists, poisoners, those who bear arms to kill you, those who steal wealth, those who steal land and those who steal other people's wives. The sacred texts sanction the killing of these types of criminals. Hence, killing the Kouravas is sanctioned by law. However, Arjuna faces a conflict between law and morality.

knowledge to refrain from committing this sin? When the lineage is destroyed, the traditional family dharma is also destroyed. When dharma is destroyed, evil overwhelms the entire lineage. O Krishna! When evil arises, the women of the family become corrupted. O descendant of the Vrishnis! When the women are corrupted, hybrid castes are born.[95] Hybrid castes ensure that the lineage, and those who destroyed the lineage, both go to hell. Because their ancestors fall[96] and are deprived of offerings of funereal cakes and drink. From those sins of those who destroy the lineage and from hybrid castes being generated, the ancient dharma of the castes and the dharma of the family are both destroyed. O Janardana! If the family dharma is destroyed, those men are doomed to spend an eternity in hell. So we have heard. Alas! Because of our greed for the kingdom and for happiness, we have got ready to kill our relatives. We are certain to commit a great sin. With me unarmed and unresisting, if the sons of Dhritarashtra, with weapons in their hands, kill me in battle, that will be better for me.' Saying this, in that battlefield, Arjuna sat down in his chariot. He threw away his bow and arrows, his mind overwhelmed with grief."'

Chapter 884(24)

'Sanjaya said, "Seeing him[97] thus overcome with pity,[98] his eyes filled with tears and struck thus with grief, Madhusudana spoke the following words.

[95]Because the men have been killed in war.
[96]Fall from heaven.
[97]Arjuna.
[98]The word used is kripa, which means pity or compassion. Daya also translates as pity or compassion, but there is a difference between kripa and daya. If daya is the passion, one tries to do something actively to remove the reason for pity or compassion. That is, daya is the path of the strong. Kripa is passive, without the necessary action and is the path of the weak.

'"The lord said, 'O Arjuna! From where, when we have this emergency, has this kind of weakness overcome you? This does not lead to heaven or fame, and characterizes those who are not aryas. O Partha! Give up this weakness, this is not deserving of you. O one who scorches the foes! Give up this petty weakness of heart.'

'"Arjuna said, 'O Madhusudana! How will I use arrows to fight in this war against Bhishma and Drona? O slayer of enemies! They are deserving of worship. In this world, it is better to beg for alms than to kill one's respected preceptors. If I kill my elders, the wealth and other objects of desire that I enjoy, will be drenched in their blood. I don't know which is better for us, they defeat us or we defeat them. The sons of Dhritarashtra are in front of me. Those are the people we don't want to kill in order to live. My normal nature has been overtaken by a sense of helplessness.[99] Confused about what is dharma, I am asking you. Tell me that which is decidedly best for me. I am your disciple. I have sought refuge in you. Instruct me. This grief is exploiting my senses and I don't see what will remedy that, even if I win lordship over the gods, or this earth, without any enemies and prosperous.'"

'Sanjaya said, "Having said this to Hrishikesha, Gudakesha, the scorcher of foes, told Govinda, 'I will not fight,' and fell silent. O descendant of the Bharata lineage! To the person who was immersed in grief between the two armies, as if with a smile, Hrishikesha spoke the following words.

'"The lord said, 'You speak as if you are wise, but you are grieving over those that one should not sorrow over. The wise don't sorrow over those who are dead or those who are alive. It is not the case that I, or you, or these kings, did not exist before this. Nor is it the case that we won't exist in the future, all of us will be there. The soul passes through childhood, youth and age in this body, and likewise, attains another body. The wise don't get bewildered by this. O Kounteya! Because of contact between senses and objects, feelings of warmth and cold, pleasure and pain result. But these are temporary

---

[99]The word *karpanya* can be translated in ways other than helplessness also, such as wretchedness, a pitiable state, or even ignorance.

and are created and disappear. O descendant of the Bharata lineage!
Therefore, tolerate these. O best among men! The wise person who is
not affected by these and who looks upon happiness and unhappiness
equally, attains the right to immortality. That which is untrue doesn't
have an existence. That which is true has no destruction. But those
who know the truth realize the ends of both these.[100] But know that
which pervades all of this is never destroyed. No one can destroy
that which is without change.[101] It has been said that all these bodies
inhabited by the soul are capable of destruction. But the soul is
eternal, incapable of destruction and incapable of being established
through proof. Therefore, O descendant of the Bharata lineage!
Fight. He who knows this[102] as a slayer and he who thinks of this
as something that is slain, both of them do not know. This is not a
slayer, nor can it be slain. This is never born, nor does it ever die.
This does not come into existence because it has been born. This has
no birth, it is eternal and without destruction. It has no end. When
the body is killed, this is not killed.[103] O Partha! He who knows
this to be without destruction, eternal, without birth and incapable
of change, how can that person cause anyone to be slain? Or how
can he slay anyone? Like a person discards worn-out clothes and
accepts others that are new, like that, the soul discards worn-out

[100]This is a complicated shloka and is subject to diverse interpretations. At
one level, the soul is eternal. This is the truth or the reality. The body, the senses
and the world are untrue and unreal. They have no existence, in the sense of
being illusory.

[101]This shloka also gets into complicated issues of interpretation. 'That'
means the brahman, or paramatman. This is eternal and pervades everything.
The body and the world are transitory. But the human soul (*jivatman*) is also
eternal. Are the body and the world illusions, or are they real? What is the
relationship between the paramatman and the jivatman? Such questions have
led to intense philosophical speculation. The Gita uses the word atman for both
the paramatman and the jivatman.

[102]Atman.

[103]The sacred texts speak of six types of transformations or maladies
(*vikara*)—birth, existence, increase, end, decrease and destruction. The atman
is thus not subject to any of these.

bodies and attains others that are new. Weapons cannot cut this.[104]
Fire cannot burn this. Nor can water wet this. And the wind cannot
dry this. This cannot be cut. This cannot be burnt. This cannot be
wetted. And this cannot be dried. This is eternal and is everywhere.
This is stable and does not move. This has no beginning. It has been
said that this has no manifestation, that this cannot be thought of
and that this has no transformation.[105] Therefore, knowing this to
be like that, you should not grieve.

   ""'O mighty-armed warrior! But if you think this to be subject
to continual birth and continual death, even then, you should not
grieve for this. Because death is inevitable for anyone who is born
and birth is inevitable for anyone who is dead. Therefore, because
this is inevitable, you should not grieve. O descendant of the Bharata
lineage! Beings are not manifest in the beginning. They are manifest
in the middle and are not manifest again after death. What is there to
sorrow over?[106] Some people see this[107] as a wonder. Like that, some
others speak of this as a wonder. And some others hear of this as a
wonder. But having heard, they are unable to understand this.[108] O
descendant of the Bharata lineage! In everyone's body, the atman is
indestructible. Therefore, you should not mourn about any being.[109]

   ""'Also considering your natural dharma, you should not waver.
Because there is nothing better for a kshatriya than a war fought for

[104]Atman.

[105]Transformation or vikara has been mentioned in an earlier footnote.

[106]This is the straightforward translation. Not being manifest (*avyakta*) means
not recognizable by the senses. Hence, apart from the period of life, beings are
part of the infinite, both before birth and after death. In a more complicated
interpretation, the reference is not to beings, but to the world itself, avyakta
standing for primeval matter or *prakriti*. In this interpretation, the world is part
of this primeval matter before creation and after destruction, and in between,
has a separate existence.

[107]The atman.

[108]That is, it is impossible to comprehend the nature of the atman.

[109]This concludes one segment, the *jnana* yoga section, so to speak. In
case this has not been enough to convince Arjuna, Krishna now moves on to a
karma yoga argument. However, this is not just any action, but action without
attachment.

the sake of dharma. O Partha! This war has arrived on its own, like an open door to heaven. Happy are the kshatriyas who obtain a war like this. But if you do not take part in this war in the cause of dharma, then you will forsake your natural dharma and fame, and sin will accrue to you. And all people will forever talk about your ill fame. For someone who is honoured, dishonour is worse than death. These great warriors will think that you have withdrawn from the war because of your fear. And those who have so far respected you will lighten their opinion of you. Your enemies will say many things that should not be said and will criticize your prowess. Is anything more painful than that? If you are slain, you will attain heaven. If you win, you will enjoy the earth. O Kounteya! Therefore, arise, deciding certainly to fight. Therefore, get ready to fight, looking upon happiness and unhappiness, gain and loss and victory and defeat equally. And sin will not touch you. O Partha! You have just been told the wisdom that comes from knowledge of the self.[110] Now listen to the knowledge about yoga.[111] When united with this knowledge, you will be able to discard the bonds of action. In this,[112] the possibility of effort coming to waste does not exist. Nor is there the chance of committing a sin. Even a little bit of this dharma protects from great fear. O descendant of the Kuru lineage! This certain knowledge is unwavering.[113] But for those who cannot focus, their wisdom is many-branched and like the infinite. O Partha! Those who are ignorant say these flowery words, praising the Vedas[114] and claiming there is nothing else. They are addicted to desire, think of heaven as the supreme objective and

[110]This is known as *sankhya*. The word *buddhi* has many nuances or meanings, depending on the context. Here, we have translated it as wisdom.

[111]Meaning karma yoga.

[112]Karma yoga without attachment.

[113]That is, karma yoga without attachment is focused. But action with attachment becomes diffused.

[114]That is, rites and rituals of the Vedas, without the knowledge. The Vedas have four parts—Samhita, Brahmana, Aranyaka and Upanishad. The Samhita and Brahmana sections are known as karma *kanda*, they prescribe rites and rituals. The Aranyaka and Upanishad sections are known as *jnana* kanda, they are the paths of knowledge.

are enamoured of the fruits of birth and action.[115] They praise many
rites and rituals that lead to pleasure and wealth. They are addicted
to pleasure and wealth and because of those words, their minds are
deluded. They cannot focus on one object—the intellect that allows
one to discriminate. The Vedas deal with the three *guna*s.[116] O
Arjuna! Rise above the three gunas. Without doubt,[117] always resort
to sattva. Do not be bothered about that which is yet to be attained
or preserving what has already been attained.[118] Realize the atman.
Whatever purpose is achieved by many small bodies of water is also
achieved by one large body of water. Like that, whatever all the Vedas
achieve is achieved by a person who knows the brahman. You have
the right to action alone. You never have the right to the fruit. Do
not be motivated to act because of the fruit. But don't be motivated
to not acting either. O Dhananjaya! Perform action by resorting to
yoga.[119] Give up attachment. Look upon success and failure equally.
This equal attitude is known as yoga. O Dhananjaya! Action is far
inferior to the yoga of wisdom.[120] Seek refuge in this wisdom. Pitiable

[115]The cycle of action (karma) leading to birth (*janma*), birth leading to action,
action leading to fruit (*phala*) and fruit leading to further rebirth.

[116]*Sattva*, *rajas* and *tamas*. The world, and everything in it, is a mixture of
these three qualities or gunas and this shloka asks Arjuna to rise above these
three gunas. But the shloka also asks Arjuna to be always under the quality of
sattva. Depending on one's point of view, there may or may not be an issue of
interpretation here. In one interpretation, rising above the three gunas means
suppressing rajas and tamas and therefore, sattva is needed to rise above the three
gunas. In an alternative interpretation, rising above the three gunas is interpreted
as being without attachment.

[117]The word used is *dvandva*, meaning doubt. But it also means opposite
sensations, like pleasure and pain or happiness and unhappiness. Therefore,
dvandva is the outcome of the senses and to be without dvandva means to rise
above the senses and look on everything equally.

[118]Yoga means what is yet to be attained, while *kshema* means what has
already been attained.

[119]As the second part of the shloka makes clear, the word yoga is used here
in the very specific sense of treating success and failure equally.

[120]Buddhi yoga. The sense is that the motivation behind the action is superior
to the outwardly effect of the action.

are those who crave after the fruit. He who has this wisdom, discards good action and evil action in this life itself. Therefore, use yoga in what you do. Yoga is the skill of action. The learned who have this wisdom abandon the fruit of action and are freed from the fetters of birth. They certainly attain that place which is bereft of all blemishes. When your intellect transcends this maze of delusion, then you will attain indifference between that which has already been heard and that which is yet to be heard.[121] Your mind is distracted at what you have heard. But when your intellect is unwavering and focused on samadhi, then you will attain yoga.'[122]

'"Arjuna asked, 'O Keshava! What are the signs of a person who has attained samadhi and whose intellect doesn't waver? How does he speak, how does he sit and how does he walk?'

'"The lord said, 'O Partha! A person is said to be unwavering in intellect when he banishes all desires from his mind. He is content within his own atman. He is not disturbed by unhappiness and he is beyond desiring happiness. He has overcome attachment, fear and anger and he is known as a sage who is unwavering in his intellect. In everything, he has no emotion, regardless of whether something pleasant or something unpleasant has been attained. He is not pleased, nor is he dissatisfied and in him, wisdom is established. Like a tortoise withdraws its limbs, such a person withdraws his senses, in every way, from sensual objects. In him is wisdom established. Sensual objects are withdrawn from the body of a person who is starving himself;[123]

[121]Meaning, praise of fruits and of heaven. The word *shruti* can mean that which is heard, or the Vedas. In this shloka and the next, if shruti is interpreted as the Vedas, one means the ritualistic aspects of the Vedas, which speak of fruits like heaven.

[122]In a general sense, yoga means union between jivatman and the paramatman. That is also samadhi, union between the human and the divine. There are two words in this shloka, *nishchala* and *achala* and the meanings differ marginally. Nischala has a negative nuance in the sense that the mind is not attracted towards irrelevant distractions. Achala has a positive nuance in the sense that the mind is focused on whatever one is meditating on and doesn't waver from that.

[123]Starving himself is the straightforward interpretation. However, a more general interpretation is also possible, that is, the reference is to a person who restrains his senses from addiction to sensual objects.

but not desire. In him,[124] who has seen the paramatman, even desire is restrained. O Kounteya! Even if a learned man takes care, the turbulent senses violently steal his mind. He who is devoted to me, controls all those[125] and focuses his mind on me. If a person can so control his senses, in him is wisdom established. If a man thinks about sensual objects, this gives birth to attachment about those.[126] From attachment is created desire and desire gives birth to anger. Anger gives birth to delusion and delusion leads to confusion of memory.[127] From confusion of memory comes loss of intellect and loss of intellect results in destruction. But he who has controlled his mind is freed from attachment and hatred.[128] Having used himself to control his senses, he uses these to enjoy objects and satisfy himself. When there is such serenity, in him is eliminated all unhappiness. Because in the mind of someone at peace, wisdom is quickly established. He who has no control, has no intellect. He who has no control, has no thought.[129] Without thought, there is no peace. How can there be happiness for someone who has no peace? The wind rocks a boat on the water. Like that, the mind follows a sense[130] devoted to objects and even a single sense robs him of wisdom. O, mighty-armed one! Therefore, he whose senses have been withdrawn from objects in every way, in him has wisdom been steadily established. When it is night to ordinary beings, the controlled person is awake then. When ordinary beings are awake, the sage perceives that as night. Just as the waters enter an ocean and leave the full ocean undisturbed, like that, all sensual objects enter that person, but leave him at peace, unlike those attached to desire. A man who gives up all desire and exists without longing, without ego and without a sense of ownership, he attains peace. O Partha! This is the state of being established in the brahman. If one

[124]In a person in whom wisdom is established.

[125]The senses.

[126]Objects.

[127]Confusion of memory about what is right.

[128]Attachment to sensual objects and hatred when desired outcomes don't result.

[129]Intellect and thought about the paramatman.

[130]There are five senses—sight, hearing, smell, taste and touch.

attains this, one is not deluded. Even at the end,[131] established in this state, one attains union with the brahman.'"'

Chapter 885(25)[132]

" " Arjuna said, 'O Janardana! If in your opinion knowledge is superior to action, then why are you engaging me in this terrible action? These mixed words seem to be confounding my intellect. Tell me definitely that one thing that is best for me.'

"'The lord said, 'O pure of heart! I have said it before that in this world, there are two paths. There is jnana yoga for those who follow sankhya and there is karma yoga for *yogis*.[133] Without performing action, man is not freed from the bondage of action. And resorting to *sannyasa*[134] does not result in liberation. No one can ever exist, even for a short while, without performing action. Because the qualities of nature[135] force everyone to perform action. The ignorant person who exists by controlling his organs of action,[136] while his mind remembers the senses, is said to be deluded and is a hypocrite.[137]

---

[131]That is, at the time of death.

[132]In the earlier chapter, two paths are mentioned—jnana yoga and karma yoga, though the expression karma yoga is never directly used. Arjuna infers a suggestion that jnana yoga or the path of knowledge is superior to karma yoga or the path of action. This chapter explains that this suggestion is incorrect and that avoidance of action is not the answer. Instead, detached action is the key.

[133]Followers of sankhya are those who tread the path of knowledge and the word yogi is being used for those who tread the path of action.

[134]That is, giving up action.

[135]Prakriti has been translated as nature. And the qualities are the three gunas of sattva, rajas and tamas.

[136]That is, limbs and the like. The five organs of action are the mouth, hands, feet, the anus and sexual organs. The five senses of knowledge are sight, hearing, smell, taste and touch.

[137]Instead of being a hypocrite, one can use the stronger translation of being a liar.

O Arjuna! But he who restrains the senses through his mind and
starts the yoga of action with the organs of action, while remaining
unattached, he is superior. Therefore, do the prescribed action.[138]
Because action is superior to not performing action. And without
action, even survival of the body is not possible. O Kounteya! All
action other than that for sacrifices shackles people to the bondage of
action.[139] Therefore, do action for that purpose, without attachment.
Earlier,[140] Prajapati[141] created beings, accompanied by a sacrifice[142]
and said—with this,[143] may you increase, and may this grant you
all objects you desire. Through this,[144] cherish the gods and those
gods will cherish you. By cherishing each other, you will obtain
that which is most desired. Because, cherished by the sacrifice, the
gods will give you all desired objects. He who enjoys these without
giving them[145] their share, is certainly a thief. Righteous people who
enjoy the leftovers[146] of sacrifices are freed from all sins. But those
sinners who cook only for themselves live on sin. Beings are created
from food and food is created from rain clouds. Rain clouds are
created from sacrifices and sacrifices are created from action. Know
that action is created from the Vedas and the Vedas are created

[138]There is scope for interpreting what prescribed action (*niyatam* karma)
is. Is it rites and rituals? In that case, it doesn't quite apply to Arjuna, because
he is not a brahmana. Is it duty? Is it action without attachment?

[139]This translation is problematic. Traditionally, yajna means a sacrifice, but
the Gita is against such rituals. The word yajna has also been equated with God
in the sense of Vishnu, but that's not terribly convincing either. It is also possible
that these sections may have been interpolated into the Gita later. They don't
quite fit. However, later, the Gita uses the word yajna in a broader sense.

[140]Meaning, before creation.

[141]Brahma.

[142]The word sacrifice (yajna) causes a problem again. As opposed to the
creation itself, sacrifice may mean laying down prescribed duties for these
created beings.

[143]The yajna.

[144]The yajna again.

[145]The gods.

[146]Leftovers after gods and guests have had their shares.

from the brahman. Therefore, the omnipresent brahman is always present in sacrifices.[147] In this way, the cycle goes on and he who does not follow this, is addicted to his senses and lives a sinner's life. O Partha! He lives in vain. But the man who takes pleasure in the atman, is content with the atman and is satiated with the atman, has no duties. In this world, he has no need for action, nor anything to lose from inaction. He doesn't need the refuge of any being for anything. Therefore, be unattached and always perform prescribed action. Because a man who performs action when unattached attains the highest liberation.

'"'Janaka[148] and others attained liberation through action. One should perform action with an eye to preserving the worlds. Whatever a great man does, ordinary people also do that. Whatever he accepts as duty, others also follow that. O Partha! In the three worlds, I have no duties. There is nothing I haven't attained, there is nothing yet to be attained. Yet, I am engaged in action. O Partha! If I ever relax and stop performing action, then men will follow my path in every way. If I don't perform action, then all these worlds will be destroyed. I will be the lord of hybrids[149] and responsible for the destruction of these beings. O descendant of the Bharata lineage! Ignorant people perform action by being attached to that action. But the wise perform similar action unattached, for the welfare and preservation of the worlds. The wise will not befuddle the minds of the ignorant who are attached to action. Being knowledgeable, they will themselves perform all action and keep

[147]This requires explanation, since there are three 'brahmas' in the shloka. The first two have conventionally been identified with the Vedas and the third with the brahman, although in a few rare cases, the third has also been identified with Vedas. That leaves the word *akshara*, meaning something that is indestructible. This too, is the brahman.

[148]Righteous king. However, there was more than one king named Janaka and this reference is to the first Janaka, the son of Mithi, from whom Mithila obtained its name. This Janaka, also mentioned in the Ramayana, is different from the Janaka who was Sita's father.

[149]The sense is to convey a broader message of mixture and confusion.

them[150] engaged. All action is completed, in every way, through the qualities of nature.[151] He who is deluded by the ego, thinks that he is the doer. O mighty-armed one! But he who truly knows the division of the qualities[152] and different types of action[153] knows that qualities manifest themselves in senses and does not get attached.[154] Those who are deluded by nature's qualities are attached to action by senses and organs. The omniscient should not disturb[155] those ignorant and misguided people. Focusing your mind on the supreme being, vest all action in me. Be without desire, without ownership and without fever[156] and fight. People who, faithfully and without finding fault, always follow this view of mine, they too are freed from the bondage of action.[157] But know that those who in an attempt to find fault don't follow this view of mine, they have no sense and all their knowledge will be deluded and destroyed. Even a wise person acts according to his own nature. Nature drives all beings. Why should one use restraint?[158] For each sense, in its respective area, attachment and aversion are certain.[159] But don't be overcome by

[150]The ignorant ones. The Gita doesn't favour renunciation and withdrawal from action.

[151]Nature is prakriti and the qualities are the three gunas mentioned earlier.

[152]The gunas.

[153]Different in the sense of being performed by different senses or organs.

[154]Another difficult shloka to translate. Nature's (prakriti) qualities work on each other and get action done through the senses and the organs. This realization means that one ceases to think of oneself as the doer.

[155]In the sense of distracting them from action. That is, learned people shouldn't ask ignorant ones to desist from action.

[156]Mental fever of suffering and sorrow.

[157]The expression without finding fault is significant. There must therefore have been opposition to this view or teaching. For instance, there was the school of sannyasa or renunciation, which advocated the giving up of all action.

[158]From this shloka alone, it is not clear what restraint is meant. The next shloka suggests it is restraint of the senses. Because nature has its own way, forcible restraint of the senses is pointless. The point is not to restrain the senses, but rise above them.

[159]If taste is the sense in question, a sweet taste can lead to attachment. But as its opposite, a bitter taste can lead to aversion.

those. They are obstacles. One's own dharma,[160] even if followed imperfectly, is superior to someone else's dharma, even if followed perfectly. It is better to be slain while following one's own dharma. Someone else's dharma is tinged with fear.'

'"Arjuna said, 'O descendant of the Vrishni lineage! By whom are these men compelled? Despite being unwilling, it is almost as if they are forced into evil action.'[161]

'"The lord said, 'This is desire. This is anger. These are born from the rajas quality. These are insatiable and great sins.[162] Here,[163] know them to be enemies. Like smoke covers the fire, like dust covers the mirror, like the womb covers the foetus, in that way, this[164] is covered by that.[165] O Kounteya! This is the perennial enemy of the wise. Knowledge is covered by this desire that is insatiable like the fire. All senses, the mind and intellect, are its[166] seat. This[167] uses these[168] to veil knowledge and delude beings. O bull among the Bharata lineage! Therefore, you should first control your senses. Destroy this[169] that is like sin and is the destroyer of knowledge.[170] It is said the senses are

[160]One's own dharma is *svadharma*. Most English translations translate this is as one's own duty. That of course begs the question of what one's own duty is. In the context of the Gita, this meant *varnashrama* dharma, which meant that a person's duty depended on his varna (caste) and his *ashrama* (stage of life). A kshatriya's duty was to fight. Even when the rigidity of varnashrama dharma is relaxed, one's duty continues to be a function of one's chosen profession.

[161]Deviation from svadharma or falling prey to the senses.

[162]There are six vices or sins—*kama* (desire), *krodha* (anger), *lobha* (avarice), *moha* (delusion), *mada* (vanity) and *matsarya* (envy). But here, desire and anger have been singled out.

[163]In this world.

[164]Meaning either this world, or knowledge.

[165]The sins, specifically desire. Alternatively, ignorance can also be meant.

[166]Desire's.

[167]Desire.

[168]The senses.

[169]Desire.

[170]We have used the word knowledge, but the shloka has two words signifying knowledge—jnana and *vijnana*. Jnana is knowledge one learns from one's teachers or from the sacred texts. Vijnana is a special type of jnana and is knowledge one picks up through introspection, meditation and self-realization.

superior.[171] The mind is superior to the senses. Intellect is superior to the mind. That[172] is superior to intellect. O mighty-armed one! In this way, use intellect to realize that which is superior to the intellect. Use your inner strength to calm the atman[173] and destroy the enemy that is difficult to defeat, in the form of desire.'"'

Chapter 886(26)

'"The lord said, 'I instructed this eternal yoga[174] to Vivasvat[175] and Vivasvat told it to Manu. Manu told it to Ikshaku. In this way, handed down by tradition, the royal sages[176] knew this.[177] O scorcher of foes! In this world, because of the long passage of time,

[171]Superior to objects, because senses are subtle. Or perhaps even superior to the body.

[172]The atman.

[173]There is scope for interpretation here, because there are two atmans in the shloka. Use the atman to calm the atman. That's the literal translation, but what does it mean? We have translated the first atman as inner strength. Or the first atman may be the intellect and the second atman may mean the mind.

[174]Eternal, immutable or indestructible. The yoga is eternal or immutable in the sense that following it leads to imperishability. This yoga is a splicing of karma yoga, jnana yoga and bhakti yoga, because one spills over into another and differences between the three are artificial. The expression 'this' yoga is used because the yoga has already been described in earlier chapters.

[175]One of the twelve *aditya*s born to the sage Kashyapa and Aditi. Vivasvat is thus a manifestation of the sun god and his dynasty is the solar dynasty (*surya vamsha*). Vivasvat's son is Manu, known as Vaivasvata Manu. Manu is actually a title and there are fourteen Manus. Vaivasvata Manu, or the present Manu, is the seventh in this line of fourteen and the reference is to the beginning of treta yuga in the present manvantara (cycle of creation and destruction). Vaivasvata Manu's son was Ikshaku.

[176]The expression is rajarshi, which means a king (*raja*) who is a sage (rishi), despite being a king. Janaka is an example.

[177]The yoga.

this yoga has been destroyed.[178] You are my follower and friend.[179] Therefore, today, I will tell you that old yoga, because this is excellent and secret knowledge.'

'"Arjuna said, 'Your birth was later and Vivasvat's birth was earlier. How will I understand that you instructed this earlier?'

'"The lord said, 'O Arjuna! Many are the births that you and I have been through. I know them all. O scorcher of foes! You know not. I have no birth. I am indestructible. I am the lord of all beings. But even then, though existing in my own nature, I come into existence through my own resolution.[180] O descendant of the Bharata lineage! Whenever dharma goes into a decline and adharma is on the ascendance, then I create myself. To protect the righteous and to destroy the sinners and to establish dharma, I manifest myself from yuga to yuga.[181] O Arjuna! He who thus knows the nature of my divine[182] birth and action, he is not born again when he dies, but attains me. Many, purified through the meditation of knowledge, have immersed themselves in me and sought refuge in me, discarding attachment, fear and anger. O Partha! Whoever worships me, in whatever way, I entertain them in that way. Everywhere, men follow along my path. In this world, people who desire success in their action, worship gods. Because in the world of men, success through action occurs quickly.[183] In accordance with gunas and action, the

[178]That is, knowledge of the yoga has been destroyed.

[179]The word used is sakha, which as mentioned earlier, means kindred soul.

[180]The word used in the Sanskrit is maya, translated often as illusion. Resolution is a better translation in this context. This, and the next two shlokas, brings in the idea of *avatara* (incarnation). Usually, Vishnu is believed to have had ten incarnations. But twenty-two or twenty-four incarnations are also known.

[181]Yuga is an era or epoch. Each of Brahma's days consists of four yugas—satya, treta, dvapara and kali.

[182]The birth is divine because it is not the outcome of normal laws of birth and death, but results from Krishna's own will.

[183]The sense is that karma yoga without attachment does lead to results, but that path is difficult and takes time. In contrast, pursuit of pleasure and wealth is easier and faster. Because people want quick results, they worship other gods, who help them achieve pleasure and wealth, even though these are transient.

four varnas were created by me.[184] But despite being the creator of
these, know me to be constant[185] and not the agent.[186] Actions do
not touch me, nor do I desire the fruits of action. He who knows
me in this fashion, is not tied down by action. Knowing this, those
who sought liberation in the past, performed action. Therefore, you
perform action alone, the path followed by predecessors in earlier
times. Even the wise are confused about what is action and what
is inaction.[187] Therefore, I will tell you what action[188] is. Knowing
this, you will be freed from evil. Action itself has to be understood
and prohibited action must also be understood. Inaction must also
be understood. Because the path of action is difficult to comprehend.
He who perceives inaction in action and perceives action in inaction,
he is wise among men, has yoga and has the right to all action.[189] He

[184]In the translation, we have left the word as varna instead of caste, because
the equation of varna with caste, and more importantly, when the caste system
developed historically and when caste became hereditary, are questions subject
to debate. The three gunas or qualities are sattva, rajas and tamas. The sattva
quality predominates in brahmanas and their prescribed action is studying and
priestly duties. The rajas quality, with some sattva quality, predominates in
kshatriyas and their prescribed action is fighting and ruling. The rajas quality,
with some tamas quality, predominates in vaishyas and their prescribed action
is agriculture and trade. The tamas quality predominates in shudras and their
prescribed action is serving the other three castes.

[185]Without change and immutable.

[186]The paramatman is both *nirguna* (without qualities) and *saguna* (with
qualities). In the saguna or active form, the paramatman is the creator and the
agent. But in the nirguna form, the paramatman is inactive or passive and not
the agent.

[187]The word used is *akarma*. Etymologically, this can mean action or
inaction, the non-performance of action, the sense in which it has been
translated. However, akarma can also mean the performance of action that is
undesirable. But the next shloka indicates that performance of undesirable or
prohibited action is *vikarma*.

[188]And by implication, what is inaction.

[189]This sounds confusing. Action is performed by the organs and the senses,
not the atman. The wise or intelligent person thus sees inaction in action, and the
vanity of action and attachment to its fruits are given up. There are those who
indulge in inaction or renunciation, giving up action. But the wise or intelligent

whose efforts are always devoid of desire for fruit and ego,[190] he whose actions have been burnt by the fire of knowledge, the learned call him wise. He who has given up attachment to action and its fruit is always content and without refuge.[191] Even when he is immersed in action, he does nothing. Without attachment, controlled in mind and senses, having discarded all ownership[192] and performing action only through the body,[193] he does not attain the bondage of sin. Satisfied with unsought gains,[194] beyond opposites,[195] bereft of envy and regarding success and failure equally, even if he performs action, he is not bound down. Beyond attachment, free[196] and with a mind established in knowledge, when he performs action for a yajna alone,[197] everything is destroyed.[198] The receptacles used for offerings[199] are the brahman.

---

person realizes that not only does action continue to be performed even when ostensibly inaction is resorted to, there is vanity in this idea of giving up action. Because the person who has resolved to give up action, is not the atman either. Therefore, there is action in inaction. Wisdom is in yoga or union with the paramatman. And because one gives up the right to all action and inaction, one has the right to all action.

[190]The expression used is devoid of *kamasankalpa*. Kama is desire, implying desire for the fruits of action. *Sankalpa* is will or resolution, implying the will or ego of performing action or inaction. Discarding sankalpa means discarding this ego.

[191]Without refuge in action or its fruits, attained or unattained.

[192]*Parigraha* is giving or taking of possessions, such as giving alms or receiving them. Since that has been given up, all ownership has been discarded.

[193]Realizing that the body is not the same as the atman. An alternative interpretation of performing action only for the sake of preserving the body is possible. But that is the path of renunciation, a path the Gita doesn't approve of.

[194]Unsought in the sense of these being gains one hasn't made an effort to obtain. Nor has one craved for these gains.

[195]Opposite feelings of happiness and unhappiness or heat and cold.

[196]Free from all emotions and sense of ownership.

[197]In this context, yajna should not be translated as a sacrifice. Yajna doesn't mean a ritualistic sacrifice. It means action performed for union (yoga) with the paramatman.

[198]The action and the fruits of the action are destroyed and don't lead to bondage, because this is inaction.

[199]In a yajna.

The oblations are the brahman. In the fire that is the brahman, the offerer, who is the brahman, performs the sacrifice. He who sees thus and is immersed in the brahman in all action attains the brahman alone as a destination.

""'Other yogis perform divine yajnas.[200] Others use the yajna as an offering to the fire that is the brahman.[201] Others offer senses like hearing as offerings to the fire that is self-control.[202] Others offer sounds and other objects to the fire that is the senses.[203] Others offer all action of the senses[204] and action of the breath of life[205] as offerings to the fire of self-control,[206] lit up through knowledge. Some use the yajna of offering gifts, others use the yajna of penance. Some use the yajna of yoga and still others, firm in their resolve and careful, use the yajna of knowledge.[207] Others offer the prana breath in the apana breath[208] and the apana breath in the prana breath.[209]

[200]Divine yajnas are ritualistic yajnas performed for various gods.

[201]That is, everything is offered to the brahman. This may mean all action and its fruit. It may also mean the symbolic offering of the jivatman to the paramatman.

[202]They control their senses.

[203]They remain unattached to the senses.

[204]Senses mean the five senses or organs of action (the mouth, hands, feet, the anus and sexual organs) as well as the five senses of knowledge (sight, hearing, smell, taste and touch).

[205]The breath of life is *prana* and this has five actions—prana (exhalation), *apana* (downward inhalation), *vyana* (diffusion through the body), *udana* (upward inhalation) and *samana* (digestive breath).

[206]The yoga of *atmasanyama* or focusing the atman in the intellect.

[207]The word used is *svadhaya*, meaning studying on one's own. This is interpreted as studying the Vedas.

[208]This shloka brings in pranayama. Prana is a general expression for the breath of life, as well as a specific term for the act of exhalation. *Ayama* means control or restraint, so pranayama is control of the breath of life. Pranayama has three components—*puraka*, *rechaka* and *kumbhaka*. Puraka is when the inhaled apana air fills up the exhaled prana air and temporarily stops its exit. Rechaka is when the exhaled prana air stops the entry of the inhaled apana air. Kumbhaka is when prana and apana are both controlled and the air is restrained inside the body. Offering the prana breath in the apana breath is therefore puraka.

[209]Rechaka.

Others restrain the flow of the prana and apana breath and practise pranayama.[210] Others control their food and offer the senses to the breath of life.[211] All these, learned in the yajnas, become sinless through yajnas. The leftovers[212] of sacrifices are like amrita and those who partake of these attain the eternal brahman. O best of the Kuru lineage! Those who don't perform yajnas have no existence in this world, forget other worlds. Many yajnas of this type are prescribed in the brahman's mouth.[213] Know them all to be the outcome of action. Knowing this, you will attain liberation. O scorcher of foes! A yajna performed with knowledge is superior to a yajna full of objects.[214] O Partha! All actions and their fruit end in knowledge. Attain that knowledge by prostrating, questioning and serving. The wise, those who are versed with the truth, will instruct you in wisdom. O Pandava! Knowing that, you will never fall prey to this kind of delusion again. Through this, you will see all the beings in your atman and then in me. Even if you are a greater sinner than all the other sinners, you will cross all oceans of sin with the boat of knowledge alone. O Arjuna! Like a raging fire burns to ashes pieces of wood, like that, the fire of knowledge burns all action to ashes. In this world, there is nothing as pure as knowledge. With the passage of time, he who is accomplished in yoga, himself attains that[215] within his heart. Knowledge is attained by the faithful, the unwavering and those who control their senses. Having attained knowledge, they quickly achieve supreme peace.

[210]Kumbhaka.

[211]The Sanskrit says offer prana to prana. The first prana, in the plural, has traditionally been interpreted as the senses. The second prana can either be the senses or the breath of life.

[212]After gods have had their share.

[213]The Sanskrit states brahman. This is important because most translations and interpretations interpret this brahman as the Vedas and therefore suggest sacrifices prescribed by the Vedas. Not only is this interpretation forced, the Gita doesn't generally assign such supremacy to the Vedas. Most ritual yajnas involve offerings made to the fire and Agni is therefore thought of as the mouth of the gods. In this broader definition of yajnas, probably no more than that extended metaphor is meant, when thinking of the brahman's mouth.

[214]That is, a yajna where offerings of objects have the main focus.

[215]The knowledge.

The ignorant, the faithless and the doubting are destroyed. For the doubting person, this world, other worlds and happiness don't exist. O Dhananjaya! He who has offered up all action through yoga and he who has used knowledge to slice away doubt, actions cannot bind such a person—who is focused on the atman. O descendant of the Bharata lineage! Therefore, use the sword of knowledge to slice away this doubt in your heart, resulting from your own ignorance. Follow yoga! Arise!"'"

Chapter 887(27)[216]

"'"Arjuna said, 'O Krishna! You are asking me to give up all action and you are also asking me to practise yoga.[217] Between these two, tell me decidedly which one is better.'[218]

"'"The lord said, 'Renunciation and action both lead to liberation. But of these two, karma yoga is superior to renunciation of action. O mighty-armed one! He who does not desire and he who does not hate, know him to be a perpetual sannyasi.[219] Freed from opposites,[220] he is happily freed from bondage. The ignorant,[221] not the wise, speak of renunciation and action as distinct.[222] If one of

[216]Sannyasa is sometimes interpreted as renunciation or the giving up of action and jnana yoga or the path of knowledge is therefore interpreted as this path of inaction. This chapter compares sannyasa yoga and karma yoga and argues against such a narrow interpretation of sannyasa and jnana.

[217]That is, karma yoga. Hence, practice of action.

[218]The issue arises because pursuit of knowledge (jnana yoga) has been stated to be better and this suggests renunciation (sannyasa) of action. Yet, there is an emphasis on karma yoga.

[219]That is, one doesn't have to renounce the world or renounce action to become a sannyasi.

[220]Opposite sentiments of happiness and unhappiness, love and aversion and so on.

[221]More literally, children.

[222]In the Sanskrit, the word sankhya stands for knowledge or renunciation and the word yoga for action or karma yoga.

these is followed properly, the fruits of both result. Whatever place is attained by the followers of knowledge is also attained by those who practise action. He truly sees, who sees renunciation and action as identical. O mighty-armed one! Without action, renunciation is only the cause of unhappiness.[223] The sage who uses yoga attains the brahman quickly. He who practises yoga, he who is pure of heart, he who has controlled his body, he who has controlled his senses, he who sees his own atman in the atman of all beings, he is not tied down, even if he performs action. The wise who follow yoga know that they are not doing anything even when they see, hear, touch, smell, eat, go, dream[224] or breathe, speak, discard, accept, open and close.[225] They think of the senses circulating among the senses.[226] He who establishes himself in the brahman[227] and giving up attachment, performs action, is not touched by sin, like water on the leaf of a lotus. To purify their hearts, yogis give up attachment[228] and perform action only with their bodies, minds, intellect and senses. Attached to yoga and discarding attachment to fruits of action, they attain perpetual peace.[229] Those who do not follow yoga and are attached to fruits because of desire remain in bondage. Discarding all action through his mind,[230] the person who controls his body, the city with the nine gates,[231] remains in happiness. He doesn't do anything himself. Nor does he cause anyone to do anything. The atman[232] doesn't create

[223]Alternatively, renunciation can only be attained with difficulty.

[224]That is, sleep.

[225]Open and close refers to the action of the eyelids.

[226]The atman doesn't get involved in senses, action or objects.

[227]This amounts to transcending the personal ego of thinking oneself to be the performer of action.

[228]Attachment to fruits of action, as well as to egos. Yogis means *karmayogis*.

[229]Alternatively, peace that results from steadfastness.

[230]Recognizing that action is performed by the senses and the organs. That is, action is mentally discarded, not physically.

[231]The nine gates of the body are two eyes, two ears, two nostrils, the mouth, the anus and the genital organ.

[232]The word used in the Sanskrit is *prabhu*, meaning lord. Depending on how lord is interpreted, the meaning can change. For instance, lord can be interpreted as the lord of all the worlds, instead of lord of the body, as we have

ownership in the body, nor action. Nor does it create a relation with
the fruits of action. Nature[233] acts. The omnipresent lord doesn't
accept the sins or the good deeds of anybody. Knowledge is shrouded
in ignorance. That is why beings are deluded. But in those in whom
that ignorance has been destroyed by the knowledge of the atman,
in them that knowledge expresses the great truth,[234] like the sun.
Those whose intellect is focused on that,[235] egos are focused on that,
devotion is focused on that and adherence is focused on that, those
in whom sins have been destroyed through knowledge, those beings
are not reborn.[236] The wise look equally upon a brahmana who is
learned and humble, a cow, an elephant, a dog and an outcaste.[237]
Those whose minds are established in equality overcome the earth
in this world.[238] Because the brahman is equal and without fault,
therefore, they[239] remain established in the brahman. Established
in the brahman, such a person learned in the brahman, is poised in
intellect and without delusion, not delighted at receiving something
pleasant, or agitated at receiving something unpleasant. Unattached
to external objects, his mind focused on the brahman, he obtains the
happiness that vests in the atman. He enjoys eternal bliss. Pleasures
from touch[240] have a beginning and an end and are the reason for
unhappiness. O Kounteya! The wise person does not obtain pleasure
from these. In this,[241] before giving up the body, he who can tolerate

---

interpreted it. For instance, in the next shloka, the paramatman or lord of the
worlds is meant and the word used is *vibhu*, meaning supreme lord. Therefore,
prabhu probably means the atman.

[233] The word used is *svabhava*, meaning one's own nature.

[234] The great truth can also be interpreted as the paramatman.

[235] Throughout this shloka, that means the paramatman.

[236] More literally, those beings do not return.

[237] The word used is *shvapaka*, which means dog-eater or someone who cooks
food for dogs. This is usually equated with *chandala* or outcaste.

[238] This is not very clear. We have translated *sarga*, which can also mean
creation, as the earth. The sense probably is that one can win or overcome this
earth, with its birth and death, in this world itself, without waiting for future worlds.

[239] Those whose minds are established in equality.

[240] That is, pleasure through the senses.

[241] This world or this body.

the forces of desire and anger is a yogi and such a man is happy. He whose happiness is inside,[242] he whose pleasure is inside and he whose light is inside, that yogi alone has realized the brahman and obtains liberation in the brahman. Those who are without sin, without doubt, controlled in mind and engaged in the welfare of all beings, such rishis attain liberation in the brahman. Freed from desire and anger, controlled in mind and knowing the atman, such sages attain liberation in the brahman all around them.[243] Banishing external objects of touch from the mind, focusing the eyes between the two eyebrows, controlling the prana and the apana breath equally within the nose,[244] poised in the senses, mind and intellect, beyond desire, fear and anger, wishing liberation, such a sage is always free. Knowing[245] me to be the enjoyer of all yajnas and penance, the lord of all the worlds and the well-wisher of all beings, attains peace.'"

Chapter 888(28)[246]

" "The lord said, 'An ascetic[247] and a yogi is he who performs prescribed action without attachment to the fruits of the action, not someone who gives up sacrifices[248] and action. O descendant of the Pandu lineage! What is known as asceticism, know that to be yoga. Because without giving up desire, no one can become a yogi. For a sage desirous of ascending to yoga, action is said to be

[242]Inside means in the atman.

[243]Because the brahman exists all around.

[244]This is kumbhaka.

[245]The free sage is doing the knowing. In this shloka, the subject is not explicitly stated. And it is also the free sage who attains peace.

[246]There was a reference to dhyana or meditation earlier and this takes the discussion forward.

[247]The word used is sannyasi.

[248]The word used is *niragni*. Agni (the fire) is associated with prescribed rites and sacrifices and niragni is someone who has given up the sacred fire, that is, these rites and rituals. Such a person is a mendicant who lives by alms.

the means. For a person who has ascended to yoga, tranquillity[249]
is said to be the means. When a person who gives up desire loses
addiction to sensual outcomes and is also not attached to action,
then he is said to have ascended to yoga. Use the atman to raise the
atman. Do not lower the atman. The atman is the atman's friend
and the atman is the atman's enemy.[250] The atman which has been
used to conquer the atman is the atman's friend. For someone who
has failed to control the atman, the atman harms like an enemy.
For someone who has controlled the atman[251] and is tranquil,[252]
the paramatman[253] is undisturbed with cold, warmth, happiness,
unhappiness and respect and disrespect. He whose atman is satiated
with knowledge,[254] who is undisturbed and has conquered his senses,
and he who looks upon a lump of earth, stone and gold equally, is
said to be yogi who has achieved union. Equal in treatment towards
well-wisher, colleague,[255] enemy, neutral,[256] arbiter, a hateful person,
friend[257] and a righteous person or a sinner, he[258] is superior.

[249]Tranquillity in the sense of self-possession. The word used is *shama* and
this has also been translated as inaction. In that case, inaction is the means for
a person who has ascended to yoga.

[250]Realizing the essence of the atman is the core of yoga. One should use one's
own self or atman to understand the true nature of the atman. Then the self or
atman becomes the true atman's friend. Otherwise, it is the true atman's enemy.

[251]Specifically, controlled the senses.

[252]Transcending emotions like attachment and aversion.

[253]Union between the paramatman and the jivatman is the core of yoga. But
here, the word paramatman is used in the sense of the jivatman.

[254]The words jnana and vijnana are both used. Both mean knowledge. But as
mentioned earlier, jnana is knowledge obtained through instruction and vijnana
is knowledge obtained through self-realization and introspection.

[255]The words suhrida and mitra are both used. As mentioned earlier, suhrida
is a well-wisher and a mitra is someone with whom one works together.

[256]*Udasin* and *madhyastha* both refer to disputes. Udasin is someone who is
neutral to the dispute and madhyastha is someone who tries to arbitrate.

[257]We have translated bandhu as friend. As mentioned earlier, a bandhu is
someone from whom one cannot bear to be separated and generally means a
relative.

[258]Such a person.

'"'Seated in a secluded place, alone, controlled in mind and body, without desire, without receiving and giving,[259] a yogi should always try to pacify his atman. In a pure place that is not too high and not too low, unmoving, he will place his seat, cloth and hide on kusha grass.[260] There, focusing the intellect, controlling the action of the mind and the senses, seated on that seat, he will practise yoga to purify the atman. Still, body, head and neck erect and unmoving, gazing at the tip of one's nose[261] and not looking in any other direction. Tranquil in the atman, without fear, established in the rite of brahmacharya, controlling the mind and uniting the intellect with me, immerse yourself in me. In this way, the yogi will always pacify the atman and be unwavering in his mind, and established in me, will attain supreme and peaceful liberation. O Arjuna! He who eats too much cannot achieve yoga. Nor he who doesn't eat at all. Nor he who sleeps too much or stays awake too much. He who is measured in food and movement, measured in effort towards action, measured in sleep and awakening. For him, yoga destroys unhappiness. When the intellect is specially controlled and established in the atman, in that situation, indifferent towards all desire, yoga is said to have been achieved. For a yogi whose intellect is controlled and the atman is united, know the simile to be a lamp that doesn't flicker in a place where there is no wind. When the mind is controlled and rendered inactive through the practice of yoga, when the atman sees the atman in the atman and is satiated.[262] When he[263] feels the extreme bliss that is beyond the senses and realized through the intellect, undisturbed from truth.[264]

[259]Without receiving and giving objects.

[260]Kusha is sacred grass. On a bed of kusha grass, will first be placed the hide (*ajina*) of an animal (like a tiger) and then on top of that, a piece of cloth (*chaila*) to get the seat.

[261]Tip of one's nose is the literal translation. Some say, tip or top of the nose is to be interpreted from the bottom up, so it means the middle of the eyebrows. Others say the tip means the sky ahead of the tip of the nose.

[262]The sentence sounds incomplete in the English rendering. But the description is of a state when yoga is achieved.

[263]The yogi.

[264]The sentence sounds incomplete in the English rendering. Again, that is when yoga is achieved.

Obtaining that, not[265] thinking other gains to be superior to this. Established in that, not disturbed even by great unhappiness. Know this, without any contact with unhappiness, to be yoga. Without hopelessness,[266] one must practise that yoga with perseverance. Forsaking in entirety all desire that results from wishes,[267] using the mind itself to restrain the senses from everything, using concentrated intellect to gradually withdraw, establishing the mind in the atman and thinking about nothing,[268] withdrawing from whatever the fickle and restless mind veers towards, withdrawing it from that, bring it under the control of the atman. Tranquil in mind, having pacified the rajas quality, without sin,[269] having attained the brahman, the yogi achieves supreme happiness. Like that, always concentrating on the atman, the pure yogi easily obtains intense bliss from proximity to the brahman. The person immersed in yoga looks on everything equally and sees the atman in all beings and all beings in the atman. He sees me everywhere and everything in me. I am never invisible to him. Nor is he invisible to me. He is based in equality and worships me, I who am present in everything. Wherever that yogi is, he is established in me. O Arjuna! He who compares[270] with his own self and regards happiness and unhappiness in everything[271] equally, that yogi is supreme, according to me.'

[265]The subject is suppressed in the Sanskrit. It is the yogi, practising yoga.

[266]The word hopelessness requires clarification. Hopelessness can result because one may practise yoga for a long time without getting close to liberation.

[267]The two words sankalpa (wish) and kama (desire) are almost synonymous and the Gita often uses them interchangeably. However, this shloka draws a difference between the two, suggesting that desire results from wishes.

[268]That is, thinking about nothing else. What has been described is also called raja yoga or *samadhi* yoga. This has eight components—*yama* (the practice of moral virtues), *niyama* (purity in habits, study and practice of austerities), *asana* (posture), pranayama (the control of breath), *pratyahara* (withdrawal of the mind), *dharana* (concentration), dhyana (meditation) and samadhi (merging with the paramatman).

[269]This can also be translated as without ignorance.

[270]Because of the realization that there is no difference between one's own self and someone else.

[271]In every being.

'"Arjuna said, 'O Madhusudana! Because of restlessness,[272] I don't see the yoga based on equality that you have propounded as permanent. O Krishna! The mind is restless and the senses strong and firm. Therefore, I think restraining it is as difficult as the wind.'[273]

'"The lord said, 'O mighty-armed one! There is no doubt that the mind is restless and difficult to control. But O Kounteya! Through practice and detachment, it can be restrained. My view is that yoga is difficult for someone whose mind is uncontrolled. But it is possible to achieve for someone whose mind is controlled and who makes special effort.'

'"Arjuna said, 'O Krishna! A person who has faithfully practised yoga, but later becomes careless and his mind deviates from yoga, cannot achieve liberation through yoga. What happens to him? O mighty-armed one! Distracted from the path of attaining the brahman, such a wavering person is dislodged from both,[274] like a torn cloud. Doesn't he perish? O Krishna! I have this doubt that only you can completely eliminate. Because there is no one other than you who can remove this doubt.'

'"The lord said, 'O Partha! In this world, nor in the other world, is there any destruction. Because, O son,[275] a person who acts well[276] never comes to grief. He who has deviated from the path of yoga attains the worlds of the righteous[277] and dwells there for many years. Thereafter, he is born in a righteous and wealthy household. Or he is born in the family of wise yogis. But such birth is very rare in this world. O descendant of the Kuru lineage! In that birth, obtains[278]

---

[272]Of the mind.

[273]Restraining the mind is as difficult as restraining the wind.

[274]The word both needs explanation. Such a person is denied liberation because he has deviated from yoga. At the same time, he is deprived heavenly pleasures because he hasn't followed that path either.

[275]The word used is tata.

[276]Even if this falls short of the complete yoga of liberation or deviates from the path.

[277]There are many such worlds (lokas) and it will be incorrect to think of this only as heaven (svarga). The Gita will have more details later.

[278]The subject is suppressed in the Sanskrit.

that intelligence[279] about liberation from an earlier birth and thereafter, strives again for liberation. Because of that earlier practice, is almost involuntarily, attracted.[280] A person who seeks yoga transcends the Vedas.[281] Striving harder than on that earlier occasion, pure in heart, the yogi obtains liberation after many lives and later, achieves the supreme objective. The yogi is superior to those who practise austerities, superior to the learned[282] and superior to those who perform action.[283] That is my view. O Arjuna! Therefore, become a yogi. My view is that he who is devoted and worships me, with his self immersed in me, is the most accomplished among all yogis.'"

Chapter 889(29)[284]

‘ " The lord said, 'O Partha! Listen to how you will know, without any doubt, the complete truth about me—mind attached to me, seeking refuge in me and immersed in yoga. I will completely tell you about the knowledge with self-realization.[285] Knowing that, there is nothing more remaining to know. Among thousands of men, rarely one tries for liberation. Among those who try for liberation, perhaps one[286] gets to know my true nature. Earth,

---

[279]About liberation.

[280]To the path of yoga.

[281]The word used in the Sanskrit is *shabdabrahma*, as opposed to the paramatman, brahman or *parabrahma*. Shabdabrahma is the ritualistic elements of the Vedas, the karma kanda. A person who wishes to know about yoga does better than someone who practises rituals alone.

[282]Those who are learned in the sacred texts alone.

[283]Those who perform action like sacrifices for the purpose of attaining heaven.

[284]The first six chapters constitute almost a distinct sub-component of the Gita. Although this first sub-component also has a mix of jnana yoga and even bhakti yoga, the emphasis is on karma yoga. With the seventh chapter, we move to the second sub-component and there is a switch in emphasis to bhakti yoga.

[285]This is knowledge through self-realization (vijnana), as opposed to knowledge through instruction or texts (jnana).

[286]By implication, among thousands.

water, fire,[287] air, sky, mind, intellect and ego—these are the eight parts of my nature. These are inferior nature.[288] O mighty-armed one! Besides this, know my superior and other nature[289] that is the essence of living beings. The universe is held up by this. Know all matter[290] to be born from these.[291] I am the reason for the creation of the entire universe and its destruction. O Dhananjaya! There is nothing superior to me. Like jewels on a string, all this is threaded in me. O Kounteya! In the water, I am the sap. In the sun and the moon, I am the radiance. In all the Vedas, I am the Om syllable.[292] In the sky, I am the sound. In humans, I am manifest as prowess,[293] and as pure fragrance in the earth. I become energy in the fire, life in all living beings. I become austerity in ascetics. O Partha! Know me to be the eternal seed of all beings. I am intellect in the intelligent. I become energy in those who are energetic. O bull among the Bharata lineage! I am strength, without desire and without attachment,[294] in those who are strong. In all living beings, I become desire that is sanctioned by dharma.[295] And know all the three conditions, with

[287]More generally, energy.

[288]The Gita uses the expression *apara* prakriti. This corresponds to what is called prakriti in sankhya philosophy, the original source of the material world. And the Gita uses the expression *para* prakriti for what is called purusha in sankhya philosophy. Apara prakriti is inert or inactive and insensate. Para prakriti is active and sensate.

[289]Para prakriti.

[290]Sensate and insensate.

[291]Para prakriti.

[292]The word used in the text is *pranava*.

[293]The word used is *paurusha* and in stating that the brahman is present in human prowess, there are two related nuances. First, prowess has a divine origin and therefore, one shouldn't be vain about it. Second, if the brahman is present in humans as prowess, there is no reason for weakness and one should attempt to awaken this innate prowess.

[294]Desire is kama and is an emotion that concerns objects that haven't been obtained. Attachment is *raga* and is an emotion that concerns objects that have already been obtained and are in one's possession.

[295]Everyone is not able to transcend desire. For ordinary people, some desire that concerns householder's duties or the physical act of existence is sanctioned by dharma.

sattva, rajas and tamas predominating,[296] to be derived from me. I am not in them. They are in me. This entire universe is deluded by these three gunas and the resultant conditions. And is not able to know me, who is above these and without change. It is indeed difficult to overcome this divine aspect[297] of mine, immersed in gunas. Those who seek refuge in me alone, they are able to overcome this maya. The evildoers, ignorant and worst among men, lose their knowledge because of maya and resort to demonic states. They do not worship me. O bull among the Bharata lineage! O Arjuna! There are four types of people, pure of heart, who worship me—those who are suffering, those who want satisfaction,[298] those who want self-knowledge and those who know. Of these, those who know, always united and worshipping only one,[299] are the best. I am extremely beloved by one who knows. And he is also my beloved. All these[300] are righteous. But the man who knows is like my atman. That is my view. Therefore, the united man who knows seeks refuge in me, the supreme of objectives. After many births are over, he attains the knowledge that Vasudeva is everything and attains me. Such great souls are extremely rare. Those whose knowledge has been robbed by those desires, according to their own nature, follow prescribed rites to worship other gods. Whatever form a devotee wishes to worship faithfully, in whatever way, in that[301] and that,[302] I make the faith firm and unwavering. With that faith, whatever form is worshipped and whatever fruits are obtained

[296]*Bhava* has been translated as condition. When sattva dominates, the condition is characterized by thirst for knowledge, lack of attachment and the like. When rajas dominates, the condition is characterized by delight, pride, lust and the like. When tamas dominates, the condition is characterized by sorrow, illusion, sloth and the like.

[297]The word used is maya and is commonly translated as illusion. For present purposes, maya seems to mean apara prakriti or prakriti of sankhya philosophy, created from the three gunas and therefore, constituting ignorance.

[298]In this world or in heaven. The first three categories are driven by desire, of one form or another.

[299]Always united with me and worshipping me alone.

[300]These four.

[301]That form of god or idol.

[302]That rite or method.

as a result, are actually bestowed by me alone. The fruits of those[303] who have little intellect come to an end.[304] Worshippers of gods attain the gods. My devotees attain me. Those who are ignorant don't realize my supreme and unchanging nature and think of me, the one who is unmanifest, as manifest. Shrouded in my powers of yoga and maya, I am not evident to everyone. I am not born and am without change. But the ignorant world does not know me. O Arjuna! I know all beings in the past, the present and the future. But no one knows me. O descendant of the Bharata lineage! O scorcher of foes! All beings are deluded at birth from opposite sensations,[305] resulting from desire and aversion. But those whose sins have been overcome and those who are virtuous in action, they are freed from the delusion of opposite sensations and worship me, firm in their vows. Those who want to free themselves from decay and death and seek refuge in me, they know about the brahman, about the individual atman[306] and about action in its entirety. Those who know me as the one who underlies all beings, all gods and all yajnas, right till the time of death, their mind is fixed on me and they know me.'"

Chapter 890(30)[307]

" " Arjuna asked, 'O supreme among men! What is that brahman, what is the individual atman[308] and what is action? What

---

[303]Those worshippers.

[304]Are temporary.

[305]Dvanda, mentioned earlier. Opposite sensations like pleasure and pain or happiness and unhappiness.

[306]The jivatman.

[307]This takes off from the last shloka of the last chapter, where there is a reference to the one who underlies all beings (adhibhuta), underlies all gods (adhidaiva) and underlies all yajnas (adhiyajna). This chapter is an answer to Arjuna's questions about these and reiterates the road to unification with the supreme spirit.

[308]The Sanskrit uses the expression adhyatma. This is usually, but not

is said to underlie all beings and what is said to underlie all gods?[309] O Madhusudana! Who underlies all yajnas[310] in this body and how? By those who can control their atmans, how are you known at the time of death?'

'"The lord said, 'The indestructible brahman is the supreme spirit and its inhabitation of individual beings is called adhyatma. Action is the offering[311] that leads to the creation and sustenance of all beings. O supreme among those who possess bodies! Perishable elements are adhibhuta and the *purusha* is adhidaiva. In this body, I myself am adhiyajna. At the time of death, he who remembers me, gives up his body and leaves, he attains my essence. There is no doubt about this. O Kounteya! Whatever essence is remembered at the time of death, giving up the body, a person immersed in that essence is the essence that he attains. Therefore, always think of me. And fight. With mind and intellect offered to me, you will without doubt attain me alone. O Partha! United in the practice that is like yoga, without following anyone else, thinking of the divine supreme spirit with the mind, attains that.[312] He who thinks of the omniscient, without beginning,

---

always, interpreted as the individual atman or jivatman. Adhyatma has also been interpreted as the natural trait of any object.

[309]These expressions occur in the last verse of the preceding chapter. We have translated adhibhuta as that which underlies all beings and adhidaiva as that which underlies all gods. Adhibhuta is the temporary element that occupies all beings, such as that object's nature or the body. Adhidaiva is the creator, Hiranyagarbha or Brahma. That last verse of the preceding chapter also has reference to that which underlies all yajnas, that is, adhiyajna. Adhiyajna is Vishnu. However, as we have said earlier, adhyatma has also been interpreted as the natural trait of any object. In that interpretation, adhibhuta is the temporary trait of any object and adhidaiva is its permanent counterpart. Paraphrased, the brahman is without qualities. But the brahman is manifested in a form with qualities for purposes of creating the universe and the elements and that is adhyatma. However, the universe and all action are temporary, they are adhibhuta. Nevertheless, the universe and all action retain a permanent quality and that is adhidaiva.

[310]Adhiyajna.

[311]In sacrifices.

[312]The subject is suppressed in the Sanskrit. The subject is the yogi and he attains the supreme spirit.

the controller of everything, finer than the minutest, the upholder of everything, with a form that is beyond thought, self-resplendent like the sun and beyond darkness,[313] at the time of death,[314] with devotion, with the mind fixed, with the strength of yoga used to hold the breath of life between the brows, he attains the resplendent supreme spirit. He is the one whom those who know the Vedas speak of as indestructible, he is the one into whom unattached yogis enter, he is the one to attain when brahmacharya is practised, I will briefly tell you about reaching that goal of supreme liberation.

""Using all the senses and organs[315] to control the mind and restrain it in the heart, bearing the breath of life between the brows, establishing one's atman in yoga, uttering the single syllable Om that is the brahman and remembering me, he who gives up his body and leaves, he attains the goal of supreme liberation. O Partha! He who does not think of other things and remembers me every day and all the time, I am easily attainable to that yogi who is always focused.[316] Great souls who attain me, because they have achieved supreme liberation, are freed from rebirth, which is transient and the abode of sorrow. O Arjuna! From all the worlds up to *brahmaloka*, beings have to return.[317] But O Kounteya! There is no rebirth for those who have attained me.[318] Those who know that a thousand yugas are Brahma's day and a thousand yugas are Brahma's night know

[313]Beyond darkness can be interpreted in the metaphorical sense of being beyond transient nature. This description of the supreme spirit draws on the Upanishads.

[314]The thinking is taking place at the time of death.

[315]The Sanskrit says all the gates, and we have translated this as all the senses and organs. As mentioned earlier, the nine gates of the body are the two eyes, two ears, two nostrils, the mouth, the anus and the genital organ.

[316]Through rebirth.

[317]Through rebirth.

[318]There are seven lokas or worlds and in ascending order, these are *bhuh* (the earth), *bhuvah*, *svah*, *mahah*, *janah*, *tapah* and *satya* or *brahma*. Depending on one's action, one may attain one of these lokas. But that residence there is temporary and is only for the duration that one's righteous action entitles one to. Thereafter, one is reborn on earth unless one attains the brahman, when one is freed from the cycle.

the truth about day and night.[319] When Brahma's day arrives, every manifest object is created from the unmanifest. When Brahma's night arrives, like that, everything dissolves into the unmanifest. These[320] are the beings who are born again and again and destroyed when night arrives. O Partha! When day arrives, they are involuntarily created again. But superior to that unmanifest is the other supreme and eternal unmanifest being that is not destroyed when all beings are destroyed.[321] What is spoken of as the unmanifest and indestructible, what is said to be the supreme liberation, attaining which beings do not have to return, that is my supreme abode. O Partha! All beings are established in that. And by that is everything pervaded. That supreme purusha can only be attained through unwavering devotion. O bull among the Bharata lineage! I will now tell you about the road[322] which, if traversed, doesn't lead to yogis being reborn and about the road which, if traversed, leads to rebirth. The resplendence of the fire, the day, the bright half of the lunar month,[323] the six months

---

[319]Yuga is an era or epoch. Each of Brahma's days consists of four yugas—satya, treta, dvapara and kali. But before that, time is not the same for the gods and humans. Six human months correspond to a divine day and six human months correspond to a divine night. Therefore, 360 human years are equivalent to one divine year. Measured in divine years, satya yuga is 4,000 years, treta yuga is 3,000 years, dvapara yuga is 2,000 years and kali yuga is 1,000 years, giving a total of 10,000 years. But there are also 500 years as transition periods from one yuga to another, so a four yuga cycle actually consists of 12,000 divine years. A four yuga cycle, known as mahayuga, is therefore 4,320,000 human years, satya yuga contributing 1,728,000, treta yuga 1,296,000, dvapara yuga 864,000 and kali yuga 432,000 years. One thousand mahayugas are Brahma's day and another 1,000 mahayugas are Brahma's night. Each of Brahma's days is called a kalpa. The beginning of a kalpa is when creation occurs and at the end of the kalpa, there is destruction.

[320]There is an emphasis that it is the same beings that are born again and again.

[321]The first unmanifest is Brahma when he is sleeping, or nature (prakriti). The second unmanifest is the brahman or paramatman.

[322]*Kala* should actually be translated as time or period. But, in what follows, the enumeration is of path or road. Broadly, there are two roads to liberation—*devayana* and *pitriyana*. Devayana is the path of austerities, penance and knowledge, leading to the attainment of brahmaloka (Brahma's world). Pitriyana is the path of action, righteous householder duties and action, leading to the attainment of chandraloka (the world of the moon).

[323]*Shuklapaksha.*

when the sun heads north,[324] along that path those who worship the brahman attain the brahman.[325] Smoke, night, the dark half of the lunar month[326] and the six months when the sun heads south,[327] along that path, the yogi attains the energy of the moon and returns again.[328] In this world, these two paths of light and darkness are said to be eternal. One leads to non-return and the other leads to return. O Partha! Knowing these two paths, a yogi is never deluded. O Arjuna! Therefore, at all times, resort to yoga. Knowing the prescribed good fruit that accrues from knowledge of the Vedas, yajnas, practice of austerities and donation of alms, the yogi transcends all these and attains the supreme and original abode.'"'

Chapter 891(31)[329]

' ''The lord said, 'You are not a detractor.[330] I will tell you this extremely secret knowledge with self-realization.[331] Knowing this, you will be freed from all evil. This is extremely secret

[324]*Uttarayana*, when the sun is in the northern *solstice*.

[325]This is descriptive of devayana. Those who follow devayana are said to first attain energy and then, in ascending order, day, shuklapaksha, six months of uttarayana, the year, the sun, the moon, lightning, ending with brahmaloka.

[326]*Krishnapaksha*.

[327]*Dakshinayana*, when the sun is in the southern solstice.

[328]Is subject to rebirth. This is descriptive of pitriyana. Those who follow pitriyana are said to first attain smoke and then, in ascending order, night, krishnapaksha, six months of dakshinayana, *pitriloka* (the world of the ancestors), and the sky, ending with chandraloka.

[329]The nature of the paramatman has been discussed in the preceding chapter and that chapter also explained bhakti yoga. This chapter extends those arguments and it is argued that compared to jnana yoga, the path of bhakti yoga is easier. In addition, the path of bhakti yoga is one that is available to everyone.

[330]The Sanskrit can be translated as someone who is not envious or not a detractor who finds fault. Had Arjuna been such a person, secret knowledge shouldn't have been divulged to him.

[331]As mentioned earlier, knowledge is jnana and self-realization is vijnana.

and the king of knowledge.[332] It is the best, pure, leads to direct
and eternal results, is sanctioned by dharma and is easy to practise.
O scorcher of foes! People who show disrespect to this dharma
don't attain me and traverse the path of death and this world. This
entire universe is pervaded by me in my unmanifest form. All beings
are established in me. But I am not established in them. Witness
my divine yoga. Again, the beings are not established in me.[333]
My atman holds up the beings and sustains the beings, but I am
not established in the beings. Know that like the great wind, which
goes everywhere, and is always established in the sky, all beings
are established in me. O Kounteya! At the time of destruction,[334]
all beings are dissolved in my nature and at the time of creation, I
create them. I keep my nature under control and repeatedly create
these many beings, helpless according to their own nature.[335] O
Dhananjaya! But I am unattached to those acts and am established
in indifference. Those acts cannot tie me down. O Kounteya! Because
of my lordship, nature gives birth to this universe with its moveable
and immovable objects. Because of this, the universe is repeatedly
created.[336] The ignorant do not know my supreme nature as the
great lord of all beings. They show disrespect to me as someone who
has adopted a human form. Their desire is fruitless, their action is
fruitless, their knowledge is fruitless, their minds waver and their
deluded nature is ruled by demonic qualities.[337] O Partha! But those

[332]Both for secret and knowledge, the qualifying word raja is used. This can
also be translated as royal. That explains the title of the chapter.

[333]This apparent contradiction is the reason why the word yoga is used in this
shloka. The paramatman is both with qualities (saguna) and nirguna (without
qualities). In saguna form, beings are established in the paramatman, but not
in nirguna form. Also, the paramatman is not established in beings because it is
more than beings and the universe taken together.

[334]At the end of a kalpa, destruction takes place and creation occurs when
a new kalpa starts.

[335]The beings are helpless because their rebirth and nature is preordained
by their earlier action.

[336]Alternatively, because of this, the universe goes round and round.

[337]That is, those who are ignorant and show disrespect. Actually, the words
asura and rakshasa are both used in the Sanskrit and we have captured both

great souls who seek refuge in divine qualities are unwavering in their minds and worship me, knowing me to be the indestructible origin of all beings. Careful and firm in their rites, they[338] faithfully offer obeisance and always sing my praise, always focused on worshipping me. Some worship me through the yajna that is the path of knowledge. Some worship me as one, others as separate.[339] I, who pervade the universe, am worshipped in many forms. I am *kratu*, I am yajna, I am *svadha*,[340] I am the herbs, I am the mantra, I indeed am the clarified butter, I am the fire, I am the offering. I am the father, mother, grandfather and sustainer of this universe. I am all that is pure and is to be known. I am the Om syllable. I am also the *Rik, Saman* and *Yajus*.[341] I am the goal, the sustainer, the controller, the witness, the abode, the sanctuary, the well-doer, the creator, the destroyer, the preserver, the repository and the indestructible seed.[342] O Arjuna! I provide heat. I attract the water and rain it down again. I am immortality and death. I am the eternal and the transient.[343]

---

as demons. However, asura is the antithesis of gods (sura) and rakshasa is a separate species.

[338]The subject is actually suppressed in the Sanskrit.

[339]Worshipping as one means regarding the worshipper and the worshipped as identical. This can be called the *advaitva* attitude. Worshipping as separate is the *dvaitva* attitude, where the worshipper and the worshipper are regarded as distinct.

[340]Kratu, yajna and svadha are all words for sacrifices, but they have been listed separately in the shloka. Svadha is a sacrifice performed specifically for dead ancestors, like *shraddha* ceremonies. Kratu is a ritualistic yajna, with prescribed rites. The word yajna can be used in the broader and non-ritualistic sense.

[341]The respective hymns that collectively constitute the Rig, the Sama and the Yajur Veda.

[342]The repository of everything after destruction, and the seed of creation.

[343]I provide heat as the sun and attract water up in the sky as clouds. The Sanskrit uses the words *sat* and *asat* and we have translated these as eternal and the transient, meaning the indestructible brahman and the transient universe. However, sat can also be translated as unmanifest nature and asat as its manifest counterpart. Indeed, in some Upanishads, sat is taken to mean what can be seen, that is, the universe and asat is taken to mean what cannot be seen, that is, the brahman. This will then be exactly the opposite of what we have translated. However, our translation is in conformity with usage elsewhere in the Gita.

Those who know the three arts[344] worship me through yajnas, drink
the soma juice and purified of sins, wish to attain heaven. They
attain sanctified heaven[345] and in heaven, enjoy the celestial objects
enjoyed by the gods. Having enjoyed the greatness of heaven, when
their good deeds are exhausted, they enter the mortal earth. In this
way, the practitioners of the three dharmas,[346] followers of desire,
go back and forth. Those who worship me, minds focused on me
alone and always immersed in me, I preserve for them what has been
attained and what is yet to be attained.[347] O Kounteya! Those with
devotion who faithfully worship other gods, they too, worship me
alone. But not in the indicated way. Because I alone am the receiver
of offerings and the granter of fruits at all yajnas. But they do not
know my true nature and therefore, are cast down.[348] Those who
worship the gods attain the gods. Those who worship the ancestors
attain the ancestors.[349] Those who worship the elements[350] attain
the elements. And mine[351] attain me. He who faithfully worships me
with a leaf, a flower, a fruit or water, from that pure-hearted person,
I gladly accept those faithful offerings. O Kounteya! Whatever you
do, whatever you partake, whatever you offer, whatever you donate,
whatever you meditate, offer that to me. In this way, you will be freed
from the bondage of the fruits of righteous and evil action. With
your self in the yoga of sannyasa,[352] freed, you will attain me. I am
the same to all beings. I have no one I hate, nor anyone I love. But

---

[344]The three Vedas—the Rig Veda, the Sama Veda and the Yajur Veda. The
Atharva Veda came later.

[345]Here, heaven can also be translated as the abode of Indra.

[346]The three Vedas again.

[347]What is yet to be attained is yoga and what has been attained is kshema.

[348]To rebirth on earth.

[349]*Pitris* or manes.

[350]Alternatively, the spirits. The worshippers of yakshas or *raksha*s are
examples.

[351]My worshippers.

[352]As has been said earlier, sannyasa doesn't mean asceticism and the
abjuring of action. It means detachment and offering all action and its fruit to
the paramatman.

those who worship me with devotion, they are established in me. And I am established in them. Even if the most evil of persons worships me single-mindedly, he should be thought of as a righteous person. Because his resolve is correct. Swiftly, he[353] becomes a righteous person and attains eternal peace. O Kounteya! My worshippers are never destroyed. This you can vouch for. O Partha! Even those who are of evil birth, women, vaishyas and shudras,[354] having sought refuge in me, they will certainly attain supreme liberation. There is no need to repeat[355] about pure brahmanas and devoted rajarshis. This earth is temporary and leads to unhappiness. Therefore, having attained,[356] worship me. With mind immersed in me, become my devotee, my worshipper and one who offers obeisance to me. In this way, with your atman united in me as the refuge, you will attain me alone.'"'

Chapter 892(32)[357]

" " The lord said, 'O mighty-armed one! Listen once more to my supreme words. These are pleasing you and for

---

[353]The most evil of persons.

[354]The idea is that the shastras are prohibited to women, vaishyas and shudras. But bhakti yoga is available to everyone. Those of evil birth means people whose evil actions in earlier lives have led to their present lowly stations. The construction doesn't suggest 'those who are of evil birth' as an adjective for women, vaishyas or shudras. Instead, a separate category seems to be meant, perhaps those who were outside the fourfold caste system.

[355]That they will attain supreme liberation.

[356]This shloka causes a translation problem because the sentence is incomplete. Having attained what? One possibility is—having attained the status of pure brahmanas and royal sages. Another possibility is to link it to the clause about the earth being temporary and the source of unhappiness. Hence, having attained a status that is permanent and the source of happiness and so on. Either way, the translation, or the interpretation, doesn't seem very convincing.

[357]This is a continuation of the topics covered in the immediately preceding chapters. The nature of the paramatman is described. Thereafter, there is a listing

your welfare, I am saying this. The host of gods does not know of my origin.[358] Nor do the maharshis. Because, in every way, I am the original cause of the gods and the great sages. He who knows me as without origin and without birth and as the greatest lord of the worlds, is freed from delusion among men[359] and freed from all sins. Intellect, knowledge, freedom from delusion, forgiveness, truthfulness, control over the senses, control over thoughts, happiness, unhappiness, creation, destruction, fear and freedom from fear, non-violence, equality,[360] satisfaction, austerity, donations, fame and lack of fame—all these states of beings indeed owe their origin to me. The seven great sages,[361] the four who came before them[362] and the Manus[363] owe their origin to me and were created from my resolution. In this world, everything is descended from them. There is no doubt that he who truly knows my divine yoga[364] is united with unwavering

---

of the paramatman's *vibhuti* (divinity or strength), as manifested in different objects and beings.

[358]The word *prabhava* can also be translated as strength, instead of origin.

[359]Alternatively, on earth.

[360]Equality across all beings and across all sentiments.

[361]There are two listings of the seven great sages (saptarshis), with a large degree of overlap. The first list is Marichi, Angirasa, Atri, Pulastya, Pulaha, Kratu and Vashishtha. The second list is Bhrigu, Marichi, Atri, Angira, Pulaha, Pulastya and Kratu.

[362]Who are the four who came before the seven great sages? This causes problems of interpretation. Usually, commentators take this to mean the four great sages Sanaka, Sananda, Sanatana and Sanatkumara, who preceded the saptarshis. However, these sages never married and talk of their descendants doesn't quite make sense. Therefore, this is sometimes interpreted in a metaphorical sense. That is, these four are the four manifestations (*murti* or *vyuha*) of Vasudeva—Vasudeva as the soul, Sankarshana as a living being, Pradyumna as the mind and Aniruddha as the ego.

[363]As was mentioned earlier, there are fourteen Manus in a kalpa. The list of names varies. But the most common list of the present fourteen Manus is Svayambhuva, Svarochisha, Uttama, Tamasa, Raivata, Chakshusha, Vaivasvata or Satyavrata, Savarni, Dakshasavarni, Brahmasavarni, Dharmasavarni, Rudrasavarni, Devasavarni and Indrasavarni. The present Manu is Vaivasvata.

[364]The word yoga is twice used in this shloka, with different senses. We have translated vibhuti as divine, but it can also be translated in the sense of might or

yoga.[365] I am the origin of everything. From me is everything instituted. Knowing this, the wise, immersed in devotion, worship me. Minds on me, lives in me, explaining my nature to each other, and always conversing,[366] they[367] attain satisfaction and happiness. I provide that kind of yoga of intellect to those who are always immersed in me and lovingly worship me. Using that, they attain me. With compassion towards them, I am always established inside them as the bright lamp of knowledge, destroying the darkness born out of ignorance.'

"'Arjuna said, 'You are the supreme brahman, the supreme abode and supreme sacredness. You are the eternal purusha, self-resplendent, the predecessor of the gods, without birth and omnipresent. All the sages and Devarshi Narada[368] and Asita-Devala[369] and Vyasa[370] describe you thus. You have yourself also told me this. O Keshava! I accept all that you are telling me as true. Because, O Lord, even the gods and the demons do not know your manifestations.[371] O

---

strength. Given the use of the word vibhuti, yoga (the first usage) simply means divine power and glory.

[365]Now yoga means union with the paramatman and the required meditation and self-realization.

[366]About me.

[367]The subject is actually suppressed.

[368]Narada is a divine sage (devarshi). He was created mentally (rather than physically) by Brahma.

[369]Many translations translate Asita and Devala as separate sages. That's not true. The same sage, who lived on the banks of the Sarasvati River, is sometimes called Asita, sometimes Devala and sometimes Asita-Devala.

[370]Vyasa means Vedavyasa or Vyasadeva. He is the collator of the four Vedas, hence the title of Vedavyasa or Vyasadeva. However, in the task of collating and dividing the Vedas, Vedavyasa or Vyasadeva is a title and there has been more than one Vedavyasa. Twenty-eight to be precise. Alternatively, the same Vedavyasa was reborn twenty-eight times. This particular Vedavyasa is the son of the sage Parashara, his mother's name being Satyavati. His actual name is Krishna Dvaipayana, Krishna because he was dark and Dvaipayana because he was born on an island. Krishna Dvaipayana Vedavyasa also authored the Mahabharata and the Puranas.

[371]If the gods and the demons do not know, an ordinary mortal is hardly expected to do so.

supreme being! O creator of beings! O lord of beings! O lord of
the gods! O lord of the universe! You alone know your own self
through your own self. Whatever divine powers you use to pervade
these worlds, you alone are capable of relating to me in detail those
self-resplendent divine powers. O yogi! How can I always think of
you and know you? O illustrious one! In what objects can you be
thought of by me? O Janardana! Tell me once again, in detail, about
the power of your yoga. Because, hearing your immortal words, I
am not satisfied.'

"'The lord said, 'O foremost among the Kuru lineage! All right.
I will tell you about my main divine manifestations. Because there is
no end to the detail of my powers.[372] O Gudakesha! I am the atman
established in the heart of all beings. It is I who am the origin, the
middle and also the end of all beings.[373] I am Vishnu among the
adityas.[374] I am the radiant sun among the shining bodies. I am
Marichi among the maruts.[375] I am the moon among the stars.[376] I am
the Sama Veda among the Vedas.[377] Among the gods, I am Vasava. I
am the mind among the senses. And in beings, I am the consciousness.
I am Shankara among the *rudra*s.[378] I am Kubera among the yakshas

[372]So the telling will be selective.

[373]The three stages of creation, preservation and destruction.

[374]The word aditya means born of Aditi and can refer to all gods in general.
However, in this context, it means the twelve manifestations of the sun. These
are Dhata, Mitra, Aryama, Rudra, Varuna, Surya, Bhaga, Vivasvan, Pusha,
Savita, Tvasta and Vishnu. According to some accounts, one of these shines in
each month.

[375]The maruts are gods of the wind. The number of the maruts varies from
place to place, but in most cases, it is forty-nine.

[376]Nakshatra can also be translated as constellation.

[377]This is slightly strange, because the Rig Veda is usually regarded as chief
among the Vedas. The Sama Veda has hymns that are sung. So perhaps the
rationale is that in bhakti yoga, or the path of devotion, songs have greater
appeal than mantras that are merely recited.

[378]As a god, Rudra is both one and many. As a single god, Rudra occurs in
the Vedas and in the Upanishads. However, there are also descriptions of eleven
rudras—Aja, Ekapada, Ahivradhna, Virupaksha, Sureshvara, Jayanta, Bahurupa,
Tryambaka, Aparajita, Vivasvata and Haya. Sometimes, one has Raivata, Savitra,

and the rakshas.[379] I am fire among the *vasus*.[380] Among the mountains, I am Meru.[381] O Partha! Know me to be Brihaspati,[382] foremost among the priests. Among generals, I am Skanda.[383] Among waterbodies, I am the ocean. Among great sages, I am Bhrigu.[384] Among words, I am the single syllable.[385] Among yajnas, I am *japa* yajna.[386] Among immovable objects, I am the Himalayas. Among all trees, I am the fig tree.[387] And among divine sages, I am Narada.

Pinaki and Ajaikapada replacing Aja, Ekapada, Aparajita and Vivasvata in the list. However, in no list of the eleven rudras does Shankara figure as a name. So this probably means Shankara as the lord of the rudras, rather than the chief one in a list.

[379]Accounts of creation differ. According to one account, Brahma created some creatures in the night. At that time, Brahma was hungry and the resultant creatures also turned out to be hungry. Some tried to eat Brahma and these became the yakshas. Others tried to prevent these devourers and these came to be known as the rakshas. According to other accounts, Brahma created water and then created beings. Some of these wanted to worship and these came to be known as yakshas. Others wanted to protect the water and came to be known as rakshas. The Sanskrit doesn't use the word Kubera. The Sanskrit expression is literally translated as lord of wealth, which of course, is Kubera. Kubera is also the lord of the yakshas, though not quite of the rakshas.

[380]The word used for fire is *pavaka*. The fire god is Agni and his companions are the vasus, who are eight in number—Apa, Dhruva, Soma, Dhara, Anila, Anala, Pratyusha and Prabhasa. Sometimes, Dyu is mentioned instead of Apa.

[381]A mountain at the centre of the earth.

[382]The concept of Brihaspati has evolved over time. Beyond a point, Brihaspati became the priest and the preceptor of the gods.

[383]That is, Kartikeya, the general of the gods.

[384]One of the seven great sages. According to one account, Bhrigu kicked Vishnu and thereby left his footprint on Vishnu's chest.

[385]Om.

[386]There are different kinds of yajnas and the Gita has already mentioned them. Yajnas are usually associated with ritualistic sacrifices and the Gita has already said that these are inferior to yajnas that involve karma yoga and bhakti yoga. There is thus a broader interpretation of the word yajna. The word japa means uttering prayers in an undertone and continuously. Hence, japa yajna means invoking Krishna's name (*nama*) and is thus also called nama yajna.

[387]*Ashvattha*, a holy tree.

Among gandharvas I am Chitraratha.[388] And among those who have attained liberation, I am the sage Kapila.[389] Among horses, know me to be Ucchaishrava, arising from the immortal nectar.[390] Among great elephants Airavata and among men, the king. Among weapons I am vajra.[391] Among cows I become *kamadhenu*.[392] I become Kandarpa for procreation.[393] And among snakes I am Vasuki.[394] Among serpents I am Ananta. Among those who inhabit the water, I am Varuna.[395] Among the ancestors I am Aryama.[396] Among those who control,[397] I am Yama. Among demons I am Prahlada.[398] Among those who

[388]Gandharvas are a semi-divine species and they were celestial singers and musicians. Chitraratha is the king of the gandharvas.

[389]The great sage Kapila, son of Kardama and Devahuti and proponent of sankhya philosophy.

[390]The immortal nectar is amrita and the gods and the demons collectively churned the ocean to raise amrita. Together with the amrita, the horse Ucchaishrava and the elephant Airavata arose from the ocean and were accepted by Indra.

[391]Indra's thunderbolt.

[392]The cow that yields all objects of desire, sometimes known as Surabhi. The word used in the shloka is actually *kamadhuk*, which means a granter of wishes.

[393]Kandarpa is the god of love, also known as Kama or Madana. The suggestion probably is that desire for procreation is superior to desire for desire's sake alone.

[394]We have translated the sarpa of shloka 28 as serpent and the naga of shloka 29 as snake. This is unsatisfactory. Ananta is the king of nagas and Vasuki is the king of sarpas. What is the difference between sarpas and nagas? Some people translate sarpa as a poisonous snake and naga as a non-poisonous snake. But that's not quite true. Both Ananta and Vasuki are the sons of Kadru and are brothers. However, here, they are quite clearly mentioned as distinct species. Sarpas and nagas seem to be differentiated in two ways. First, unlike sarpas, nagas can assume human form. Second, unlike sarpas, nagas have separate geographical areas of habitation. Sarpas live on earth.

[395]The lord of the ocean.

[396]Aryama is a manifestation of the sun and is the ruler of the pitris, ancestors or manes.

[397]Those who control the fruits of righteous and evil conduct.

[398]We have translated daityas as demons. Daityas are a specific category of demons, the progeny of Diti. Although born into this clan, Prahlada, the son of

devour,[399] I am time. And I am the lion[400] among animals. Among birds, I am the son of Vinata.[401] Among those that purify, I am the wind. Among those who bear weapons, I am Rama. Among fish, I am the shark.[402] And among rivers, I am Jahnavi.[403] O Arjuna! I alone am the beginning, the end and the middle of all created objects. Among all forms of knowledge, I am knowledge of the self. Among debaters, *vada*.[404] Among letters, I am the letter 'A'. Among different forms of *samasa*, I am dvanda.[405] Indeed I am indestructible time. My face is in every direction. I am the controller of destiny. I am death that robs everything. And I am the origin of the future. Among women, I am fame, prosperity, speech, memory, intellect, fortitude and forgiveness. In the Sama Veda, I am *brihat sama*.[406] Among metres, I am gayatri. Among months, I am Margashirsha.[407] Among seasons, I am *kusumakara*.[408] I am gambling among those who wish

---

Hiranyakashipu, was a devotee of Vishnu's. Eventually, Prahlada became the king of the daityas.

[399]There is a slight problem of translation, because the word *kalayatam* can mean those things that overcome us or those things that devour us.

[400]Actually, the Sanskrit text doesn't use the expression lion. Instead, it uses the expression king of animals.

[401]The son of Vinata is Garuda, king of the birds.

[402]The word used is makara and a makara is not quite a crocodile. It is part mythical and is sometimes also translated as a crocodile.

[403]The river Ganga. Ganga is also known as Jahnavi because she was the daughter of the king Jahnu.

[404]There are three kinds of arguments used in debating. *Jalpa* represents arguments to establish one's own point of view. *Vitanda* represents arguments advanced to neutralize the opponent's point of view. Vada is delinked from the objective of winning and is simply an impartial and objective attempt to deduce the truth.

[405]Samasa is part of grammar and the samasa rules are used for compounding words. Dvanda is one type of rule.

[406]Type of mantra where the lord is worshipped as the lord of everything.

[407]The month of Agrahayana. The month of Agrahayana or Margashirsha is the foremost month because at that time, this used to be the first month of the year.

[408]A collection of flowers, that is, spring.

to cheat.[409] I am energy in the energetic. I am victory, perseverance, I am the sattva quality in the righteous. I am Vasudeva among the Vrishnis. I am Dhananjaya among those of the Pandu clan. I am Vyasa among the sages. Among the wise, I am the wise Ushanasa.[410] I am *danda* among those who rule.[411] I am strategy for those who wish to win. Among secret subjects, I am silence. I am knowledge among the wise. O Arjuna! Whatever is the seed of origin of every being, that is me alone. There is nothing moveable or immovable that can come into being without me. O scorcher of foes! There is no end to my divine glory. Whatever I have stated of this expanse of glory is only a brief indication. Know that whatever object is glorious, prosperous or indeed extremely powerful, that has originated from a part of my energy. O Arjuna! But what is the need to know all these details? I am established, holding up this entire universe with only a part of me.'"'

Chapter 893(33)[412]

' "Arjuna said, 'Out of compassion for me, the extremely secret adhyatma knowledge that you have stated has destroyed this delusion of mine. O one with eyes like lotus leaves! From you I have heard in detail about the creation and destruction of all beings, and also your eternal greatness. O supreme lord! What you have said about yourself is indeed like that. O supreme being! I wish to see your divine form. O lord! If you think that I am worthy of seeing that, then, O lord of yoga, show me your indestructible self.'

[409]Gambling representing the best form of cheating.

[410]Ushanasa is another name for Shukracharya, son of Bhrigu, and preceptor of the demons. Shukracharya is also a writer on the law. The word *kavi* doesn't mean a poet. It means someone who is wise, a seer.

[411]Those who ruled had four methods or stratagems—danda (punishment), *sama* (appeasement), *dana* (bribery) and *bheda* (sowing dissension).

[412]This chapter is about the vision of the universal form.

'"The lord said, 'O Partha! Behold my divine multi-dimensioned, multi-hued, multi-shaped hundreds and thousands of forms. O descendant of the Bharata lineage! See the adityas, the vasus, the rudras, the *ashvinis* and the maruts.[413] See the many wonderful things you have never seen before. O Gudakesha! In my body, in one place, see the entire universe, with all that is moveable and immovable. Also see today, whatever else you want to see. You will not be able to see me with your own eyes. Therefore, I am giving you divine sight. Witness my divine glory.'"

'Sanjaya said, "O king! Having said this, Hari, the great lord of yoga, then showed Partha the divine and supreme form—with many mouths and eyes, with many miraculous things to see, adorned in many resplendent ornaments, with many divine weapons raised, with divine garlands and clothing, anointed with divine fragrances, extremely wonderful everywhere, resplendent, infinite, with faces in every direction. If the brilliance of a thousand suns simultaneously rises in the sky, then that brilliance can rival the brilliance of that great soul. Then Pandava saw the entire universe in one place, divided into many parts, in that great god of gods' body. Then, amazed and with his body hair standing up, Dhananjaya bowed down before the god with his head lowered and, with joined palms, said . . .

'"Arjuna said, 'O lord! In your body I see all the gods and all the different types of beings, the divine sages and all the serpents and the creator Brahma, seated on a lotus. O lord of the universe! O universal form! I see you, with many arms, many stomachs, many faces and many eyes, everywhere. And I don't see an end, a middle or a beginning to you. With a crown, with a mace, with the chakra, resplendent everywhere, like a mass of energy, impossible to see,[414] brilliant like the burning fire and the sun, impossible to measure, I see you in every direction. I have no doubt that you are eternal and

---

[413]The twelve adityas, eight vasus, the eleven rudras and the forty-nine maruts mentioned earlier. The two ashvinis are physicians of the gods, named thus because their mother (Samjna) was then (at the time of conception) in the form of a mare (*ashva*). Their names are actually Ashvini and Revanta.

[414]With ordinary eyes.

supreme and the only thing worth knowing. You are the supreme
refuge of this universe. You are the indestructible and original being,
the upholder of ancient dharma. I behold you without beginning,
middle and end, infinite in strength, with uncountable arms, the sun
and moon in your eyes, face like ignited fire, scorching this universe
with your energy. O great soul! This space between the sky and the
earth is pervaded only by you. The directions are also pervaded.
Witnessing this miraculous and terrible form, the three worlds are
suffering.[415] That array of gods is entering you alone. Some are
frightened and, with joined palms, are craving protection. The array
of great sages and pure souls are uttering words of pacification and
are worshipping you, with pure and profound prayers. The rudras,
the adityas, the vasus and the *saddhyas*,[416] the *vishvadevas*,[417] the
ashvinis and the maruts, those who partake warm food,[418] the
gandharvas, the yakshas, the asuras and arrays of the siddhas[419]
are all gazing at you with amazement. O mighty-armed one! The
worlds are terrified, and so am I, at witnessing your great form, with
many faces and eyes, many stomachs, many arms, thighs and feet,
fearsome with many teeth. O Vishnu! Touching the sky, resplendent,
multi-hued, mouths stretched out, eyes large and fiery—seeing you, I
am frightened and I cannot maintain my fortitude and peace. Seeing
your several faces, fearsome with teeth and blazing like the fire of
destruction, I have lost my sense of direction. I cannot find happiness.
O lord of the gods! O refuge of the universe! Have mercy. All those
sons of Dhritarashtra, with the collected kings, and Bhishma, Drona
and that son of a suta[420] and the chief warriors on our side are

[415]There is a minor contradiction in what Arjuna has said. No one other
than Arjuna has seen, or can see, this universal form.

[416]The saddhyas are gods, twelve or thirteen in number.

[417]The vishvadevas is a collective word for gods and divine energy taken
together, originally believed to be thirty-three in number (eleven on earth, eleven
in the sky and eleven in heaven). This later became 330 million.

[418]These are the pitris, ancestors or manes, to whom warm food is served.

[419]The siddhas are a semi-divine species, inhabiting the area between the sun
and the earth and 88,000 in number.

[420]As was mentioned earlier, sutas were charioteers and raconteurs. Although

dashing into your fearsome mouth with the terrible teeth. Some of them can be seen, heads smashed and attached to the joints of the teeth. Truly, like many currents in rivers head towards and enter the ocean, thus, those warriors of this earth are entering your mouths, flaming in all directions. As moths driven to destruction speedily enter a blazing fire, like that, these people are also swiftly entering your mouths, for destruction. O Vishnu! In all directions, you are repeatedly licking, having swallowed all the worlds[421] with your flaming mouths. Your fierce resplendence is scorching, having filled the universe with energy. Who are you? Tell me, you of the fierce form! I bow down before you. O great god! Be merciful. I wish to know you, you who are the beginning. Because I do not understand your inclination.'

'"The lord said, 'I am the terrible destroyer[422] of people. I am now about to destroy these people. Even without you,[423] all the warriors in the opposing army formations will not exist. O Savyasachi! Therefore, arise! Attain fame. Triumph over enemies and enjoy the undisputed kingdom. These have already been slain by me. You will only be the instrument. Kill Drona and Bhishma and Jayadratha and Karna and the other brave warriors also, already killed by me. Don't be apprehensive. You will be able to triumph over enemies in battle. Fight.'"

'Sanjaya said, "Hearing these words of Keshava's, the trembling Kiriti[424] joined his palms and saluting Krishna, again said in a faltering tone, bowing down in fear . . .

---

born into a royal family, Karna was raised by a suta and was therefore known as the son of a suta.

[421]Or having swallowed all the people. The word loka can be translated in either way.

[422]The word kala can also be translated as time. But kala also means destroyer or fate or Yama. In this context, destroyer seems to be a better translation. Similarly, loka has been translated as people, but also means world.

[423]That is, even if Arjuna does not fight.

[424]Arjuna was also known as Kiriti. Kiriti means someone who wears a crown and Arjuna was so named because he received a crown from Indra.

'"Arjuna said, 'O Hrishikesha! It is natural that the universe is extremely delighted to hear of your glory and is attracted to you, the rakshas are scared and flee in all directions and all the arrays of siddhas bow down. O great soul! O infinite! O lord of the gods! O refuge of the universe! You are greater than Brahma and the original agent. Why should you not be saluted? The manifest and the unmanifest and the indestructible[425] that is beyond, is also you. You come before the gods. You are the eternal being. You are the abode of the universe after destruction. You are the knower, that which is to be known and the supreme abode. By you is the universe pervaded and you are infinite in form. You are Vayu,[426] Yama,[427] Agni,[428] Varuna,[429] Shashanka,[430] Prajapati[431] and the great-grandfather.[432] I salute you a thousand times. And again salute you. And yet again salute you. I salute you in front and from the back. I salute you everywhere, in every direction. O possessor of infinite energy and unlimited strength! You pervade everything. Therefore, you are everything. Without knowing your glory and also this,[433] inadvertently and in affection, thinking of you as a friend, expressions like O Krishna, O Yadava, O friend, have been rudely used by me. O Achyuta![434] At times of sport, sleeping, sitting or eating, alone

[425]The brahman or the paramatman.

[426]The god of the wind.

[427]The god of death.

[428]The god of fire.

[429]The god of the ocean.

[430]The moon or the moon god.

[431]Meaning, in this context, Brahma. The word *prajapati* literally means lord or creator of beings. Brahma mentally created ten sages who later created other beings. These ten sages, who were also known as prajapatis, were Marichi, Atri, Angira, Pulastya, Pulaha, Kratu, Vasishtha, Daksha, Bhrigu and Narada. Other beings were descended from them and Brahma is therefore the grandfather (*pitamaha*). Since the word prajapati is used in the shloka in the singular rather than the plural, it clearly means Brahma.

[432]If Brahma is the grandfather (pitamaha), great-grandfather (prapitamaha) is Brahma's creator, that is, the brahman or the paramatman.

[433]The universal form.

[434]Krishna, meaning the one without decay.

or in front of other equals, in jest, you have faced irreverence, and for that, I crave forgiveness from you, whose power is beyond thought. O infinite power! You are the father, worshipped, teacher and also the greatest of all movable and immovable objects in the worlds. In the three worlds, there is no one equal to you. Where can there be someone greater than you? O god! For that reason, I prostrate my body and bow before this revered god, craving your blessings. Like a son's by the father, a friend's by a friend and a lover's by the beloved, forgive.[435] O god! Having seen that which has not been witnessed before, I am delighted. But again, my mind is disturbed by fear. Therefore, show me your earlier form. O lord of the gods! O abode of the universe! Be merciful. I wish to see your earlier form, crowned, with a mace and chakra[436] in hand. O thousand-armed one! O universal form! Become manifest in your four-armed form.'[437]

'"The lord said, 'O Arjuna! Having been pleased, with my powers of yoga, I have shown this resplendent, infinite, primeval and supreme universal form. Apart from you, this has not been seen by anyone before. O great hero of the Kuru lineage! Not through the Vedas, yajnas, study, nor through donations, nor even action or severe austerities, can this form of mine be witnessed by anyone other than you in this human world. Be not fearful at witnessing this fierce form of mine. Be not bewildered. Overcoming fear, with a happy mind, may you behold that, my earlier form.'"

'Sanjaya said, "Having said this, Vasudeva again showed Arjuna his natural form. Having again assumed his peaceful form, the great soul assured the scared Arjuna.

'"Arjuna said, 'O Janardana! Having seen your peaceful and

[435]This sentence sounds incomplete in the English rendering. Like a father, a friend or a beloved forgives, the son's, friend's or lover's errors or transgressions, forgive mine.

[436]If chakra has to be translated, it can only be translated as disc or discus. The chakra is Vishnu and Krishna's weapon.

[437]This requires explanation. Krishna has two arms, but Vishnu has four. The explanation therefore is that Arjuna knew Krishna to be a manifestation of Vishnu. Alternatively, Krishna could have adopted Vishnu's form temporarily.

human form, my mind is now calmed and I am in control of my
senses. I have become normal.'

"The lord said, 'The form of mine that you have seen is difficult
to witness. The gods themselves are always desirous of seeing this
form. Not through the Vedas, nor austerities, nor donations, nor even
yajnas, is it possible to see me in the form that you have seen me in. O
scorcher of foes! O Arjuna! It is only through single-minded devotion
that this form of mine can be truly known or seen, or it becomes
possible to get immersed in me. O Pandava! He who undertakes
action for my sake, is attached to me, is devoted to me, is detached
and without enmity towards all beings, attains me.'"

Chapter 894(34)[438]

"Arjuna said, 'In this way, there are devotees who are always
immersed in you and worship you and there are those
who think of the unmanifest and the indestructible.[439] Who among
these is the best yogi?'[440]

"The lord said, 'Those who worship me, with minds fixed on
me and always united in me with supreme devotion, in my view,
they are the best yogis. But those who worship the indestructible,
indescribable, unmanifest, omnipresent, unthinkable, original,[441]

---

[438]This concludes the bhakti yoga segment. The issue is simple. Is it better to
worship the nirguna form of the paramatman or the saguna form? The former
is the path of knowledge (jnana) and the latter is the path of devotion (bhakti).
For most people, the latter is easier.

[439]The brahman or the paramatman.

[440]Paraphrased, is bhakti yoga superior or is jnana yoga superior? The word
yogi is being used for someone who achieves union with God.

[441]The word *kutastha* can be translated in various ways. We have translated
it in the sense of being the original cause of everything. But it can also mean
unchanging or the refuge of this illusory world. There can even be a metaphorical
interpretation of being immovable like the peak of a mountain.

immovable and constant, controlling properly the senses and looking upon everything equally, acting for the welfare of all beings, they only attain me. Those who wish to immerse their minds in the unmanifest, find it more difficult. Because those who possess bodies[442] attain the goal of the unmanifest with great perseverance.[443] O Partha! Those who offer all action to me, are devoted to me and with single-minded yoga, meditate on me and worship me with minds rendered unto me, I become swiftly their rescuer from this mortal world that is like an ocean. Establish your mind in me alone.[444] Fix your intellect on me. After that,[445] there is no doubt that you will live with me alone. O Dhananjaya! If you cannot steady your mind and fix it on me, then practise yoga[446] and wish to attain me. If you don't succeed in the practice, then do only my deeds.[447] Even if you do acts for my pleasure, you attain liberation. If however, you are unable to perform these deeds also, then control your mind, give up attachment to the fruits of all action and seek refuge in the yoga that is mine.[448] Knowledge is superior to practice. Meditation is superior to knowledge. Giving up attachment to the fruits of

[442]And therefore possess a sense of the individual self and the individual ego.

[443]That is, the path of jnana yoga is difficult. The path of bhakti yoga is easier.

[444]In some interpretations, there is an emphasis on the 'alone' clause, arguing that this is superior to establishing one's mind on the brahman and therefore, this shloka demonstrates the superiority of bhakti yoga to jnana yoga. This interpretation seems to be both contrived and unnecessary.

[445]After death.

[446]Practise yoga, with practise used as a verb, makes for better English. But a literally more accurate translation is, through the yoga of practice. The word yoga is used in many different senses in the Gita. Later shlokas suggest that the yoga of practice means pranayama.

[447]This is not the same as performing action without attachment. That comes in the next shloka. Here, deeds mean rites or acts associated with bhakti yoga, such as listening to or singing devotional songs, ceremonies of worship and the like.

[448]That is, karma yoga, where action and fruits of all action are offered up to the brahman.

action is superior to meditation. After renunciation, tranquillity is attained.[449] He who has no hatred for all beings, is friendly and also displays compassion, is without sense of ego, without pride, regards happiness and unhappiness in the same way and is forgiving, is always satisfied, a yogi and controlled in mind, firm in resolution[450] and with mind and intellect immersed in me, such a devotee of mine is dear to me. He from whom other people are not disturbed and he who is not disturbed by other people and he who is free from delight, dissatisfaction,[451] fear and concern, is dear to me. Without desire,[452] pure, enterprising, neutral, without pain and one who has renounced all fruit,[453] such a devotee is dear to me. He who is not delighted,

[449]Historically, this shloka has caused several problems of interpretation. By practice, one means the practice of yoga, or pranayama. Since this can be purely mechanical, knowledge (jnana) must be superior to this. But in what sense is dhyana (meditation) superior to knowledge? The answer certainly lies in the distinction drawn between jnana (knowledge) and vijnana (self-realization). Jnana is knowledge learnt from one's teachers or from the sacred texts. Vijnana is a special type of jnana and is knowledge picked up through introspection, meditation and self-realization. So the knowledge of this shloka is specific knowledge picked up from elsewhere and is not knowledge in a general sense. And vijnana or knowledge through meditation and self-realization is superior to jnana. Most historical commentators preferred renunciation of action to karma yoga. The preference was for sannyasa. Therefore, there were problems in interpreting the superiority of action to meditation. And by linking up this shloka with the preceding one, it was argued that karma yoga was for those who couldn't perform meditation and follow the path of jnana, jnana being interpreted generally, rather than in the specific sense of knowledge picked up from teachers or sacred texts.

[450]This firmness of conviction or resolution is interpreted as firmness of faith in Krishna.

[451]The word used is *amarsha*. This can be translated as dissatisfaction from not having attained one's desires. But it can also be translated as envy, because others have got what they want.

[452]Or, without expectation.

[453]Renouncing all fruit is not a literal translation. A literal translation is renouncing all attempts, beginnings or endeavours (*arambha*). However, attempts, beginnings or endeavours are for specific gains, in this world or the next. Hence, someone who has renounced these is someone who has renounced all fruits.

nor hates, he who does not sorrow, nor desires, he who has given up good and evil,[454] such a devotee is dear to me. Equal between friend and enemy, and respect and insult, equal between cold and warmth, happiness and unhappiness and without all attachment, like between criticism and praise, restrained in speech,[455] satisfied with whatever is obtained, without habitation[456] and controlled in mind, such a devoted man is dear to me. Those who are devoted and look upon me as the supreme goal and worship according to this immortal dharma mentioned earlier, such devotees are extremely dear to me.'"'

Chapter 895(35)[457]

'"The lord said, 'O Kounteya! This body is known as the kshetra.[458] He who knows this is called the kshetrajna by those who have the knowledge.[459] O descendant of the Bharata lineage! In every field, know me to be the kshetrajna. My view is that knowledge about kshetra and kshetrajna is knowledge.[460] Briefly, hear from me what is that kshetra, its nature and its transformation, and cause and effect within it. Also that[461] and its power. The rishis have sung this[462] in different metres in several diverse ways.

[454]The interpretation of giving up good and evil is that one has given up the good and evil fruits or results of action.

[455]A literal translation of *mouni* is someone who is silent or doesn't speak.

[456]Without habitation or without a home presumably means someone who is not attached to the home or habitation.

[457]With this chapter, there is a switch in emphasis to jnana yoga.

[458]Field or repository.

[459]The body is the kshetra. The person who knows the body is someone who has a sense of ownership of the body and this is the kshetrajna, that is, the jivatman or the individual soul. Those who know about kshetra and kshetrajna call the individual soul kshetrajna.

[460]That is true knowledge.

[461]The kshetrajna.

[462]The theory of kshetra and kshetrajna.

The definite logical arguments are also there in the Brahmasutra passages.[463] The great elements,[464] the ego, the intellect and the unmanifest,[465] the ten organs of sense[466] and the single one[467] and the objects of the five senses,[468] desire, hatred, happiness, unhappiness, combination,[469] consciousness, patience, these together are said to be the kshetra and its transformations. Lack of ego, lack of arrogance, lack of injury,[470] forgiveness, humility, servitude towards teachers, purity, single-mindedness[471] and control over the self, detachment towards gratification of the senses and lack of vanity, indifference towards unhappy travails like birth, death, aging and disease, non-attachment,[472] no sense of belonging in wife, son and home, always equality in mind whether good or evil results, faithfulness in devotion to me, fixedness and non-deviation in yoga, habitation in secluded

---

[463]The reference to the sages (rishis) singing is to the Vedas. The Brahmanas, the Aranyakas and the Upanishads followed the Vedas and are collectively known as Vedanta. One interpretation is that this shloka refers to the Vedas and the Vedanta, and in the latter case, especially to the Upanishads, because it is there that the nature of the brahman is particularly discussed. However, there is also a collection of aphorisms (sutras) known as Brahmasutra. This is ascribed to Badarayana, Badarayana being identified as Vedavyasa. If the Brahmasutra was compiled before the Gita, the second part of this shloka could also be a reference to this specific text.

[464]The five core elements of prithvi or kshiti (the earth), apa (water), tejas (energy), vayu or marut (the wind) and akasha or vyoma (the sky).

[465]As mentioned earlier, the unmanifest (avyakta) means primeval matter or prakriti.

[466]The ten organs of sense are the five organs of action (the mouth, hands, feet, the anus and sexual organs) and the five senses (sight, hearing, smelling, tasting and touching).

[467]By the single one, is meant the mind.

[468]The objects of the five senses are rupa (form), shabda (sound), gandha (smell), rasa (flavour) and sparsha (touch).

[469]The word samghata means union, combination or collection. Because the senses are united in the body, combination refers to the body.

[470]Towards others.

[471]In righteous action.

[472]Towards objects.

spots, aversion to crowds, devotion to knowledge about the atman and search for true knowledge—these are known as knowledge. Anything opposed is ignorance. I will state that which is to be known. Knowing that, attains immortality.[473] That brahman, without origin, is my form. It is said, both eternal and transient.[474] That[475] has hands and feet everywhere, eyes, heads and mouths everywhere, and ears everywhere, is established in everything in this world. Manifest in the qualities of all the senses, but without any senses, alone, like the abode of everything, without qualities and the preserver of all qualities.[476] That is outside all beings and yet inside them, moving and unmoving, beyond knowledge because of subtleness, far and yet near. That is indivisible, but exists in every being in divided form. Know[477] as the preserver, destroyer and creator of all beings. That is the light of all bright bodies. Said to be beyond darkness. Knowledge, that which is to be known and attainable through knowledge, is established in the heart of everything.[478] Briefly, kshetra and that which is knowledge, and to be known, have been stated. Knowing this, my devotee attains my nature.[479] Know both prakriti and purusha to be without origin. And know transformations and the qualities[480] to result from prakriti.[481] Prakriti is said to be the reason behind cause

[473]The subject is suppressed. With that knowledge, the seeker attains immortality.

[474]The subject is again suppressed and is a reference to the brahman. We have translated sat and asat as the eternal and the transient, meaning the indestructible brahman and the transient universe. However, sat can also be translated as unmanifest nature and asat as its manifest counterpart.

[475]The brahman.

[476]The brahman is both nirguna (without qualities) and saguna (with qualities).

[477]Know the brahman, the object is suppressed in the shloka.

[478]The brahman is established.

[479]The word used is bhava, which can be translated in different ways. The devotee attains or realizes the brahman's nature. Alternatively, the devotee gains Krishna's love and affection.

[480]The qualities (gunas) of sattva, rajas and tamas.

[481]In sankhya philosophy, prakriti is the original source of the material world and is active. The Gita has earlier used the expression apara prakriti for

and effect,[482] purusha said to be[483] for happiness and unhappiness in enjoyment, because purusha is established in prakriti and enjoys prakriti's qualities.[484] And its[485] good and evil birth is because of its association with these qualities. The supreme being in this body is known as one who witnesses, one who allows, one who sustains, one who enjoys, the supreme lord and the paramatman. He who knows the nature of purusha, and of prakriti, with the qualities, whatever be the position he is in, will not be reborn. Some, through meditation, see the atman in the atman with the atman.[486] Others use sankhya yoga[487] and still others use karma yoga. And others, failing to know,[488] hear from others and worship. Even they, who are devoted to hearing, transcend death. O best of the Bharata lineage! Whatever movable and immovable objects are created, know them to result from the link between kshetra and kshetrajna. He truly sees who beholds the indestructible supreme lord equally in all beings, while everything else is destructible. He who sees the great lord equally established in everything, he doesn't kill the atman with the atman,[489] and therefore, attains supreme liberation. He who perceives

---

prakriti. Purusha (the soul) is inert or inactive and the Gita has earlier used the expression para prakriti for purusha.

[482]This is the straightforward translation. But in interpretations, the senses are the cause and the body is the effect.

[483]The reason.

[484]Otherwise, the inactive purusha shouldn't have a sense of happiness or unhappiness.

[485]Of the purusha.

[486]Because the word atman can mean different things, there is a problem of interpretation. The simplest meaning is the following. Some people themselves (with the atman) use meditation to see the atman (the paramatman) in themselves (in the atman). But atman can also mean body, mind or intellect. Hence, an alternative translation is to use the mind to see the paramatman in the intellect or to use the mind to see the paramatman in the body.

[487]Here, sankhya yoga probably means jnana yoga, or the path of knowledge. But it can also mean sannyasa yoga or the path of renunciation.

[488]Failing to know through their own efforts.

[489]What does killing the atman with the atman mean? Incidentally, instead of a strong translation of killing, a weaker translation of doing violence to is also possible. The traditional interpretation of killing the atman with the atman

all action as being performed by prakriti and the atman as a non-agent, he truly beholds. When he sees the different aspects of beings as established in one[490] and also everything manifested from there, he attains the brahman. O Kounteya! Because it is without origin and without qualities, this paramatman is unchanging and although based in the body, does nothing. It is not attached.[491] As the sky that is everywhere is not attached because of its subtlety, like that, the atman is not attached, though it is in every body. O descendant of the Bharata lineage! Just as a single sun lights up the entire world, like that, a single *kshetri* lights up all kshetras.[492] Those who, through their eyes of knowledge, know the difference between kshetra and kshetrajna in this way and freedom from beings and prakriti,[493] they attain the supreme goal.'''

Chapter 896(36)[494]

' '' The lord said, 'I am again stating the excellent and supreme out of all types of knowledge. Knowing that, all the sages

---

is the following. Uplifting one's self (atman) is possible. Not attempting to do this is tantamount to killing oneself. If the weaker translation of doing violence is used, another interpretation is possible. He who has attained true knowledge sees the same paramatman in everything and knows that there is no difference between doing harm to one's own self and to someone else. He avoids doing violence to the atman (someone else) with the atman (one's own self).

[490]The paramatman.

[491]Specifically, not attached to the fruit of action.

[492]Kshetra is of course bodies. And the word kshetrajna has been used for the jivatman. Here, the word kshetri obviously stands for the paramatman and kshetri and kshetrajna are effectively synonymous.

[493]What does freedom from beings and prakriti mean? Prakriti is the root cause of being and beings and prakriti therefore stands for ignorance. Knowledge brings freedom from this ignorance. Therefore, one could also have said—'freedom of beings from prakriti'. Indeed, some translations state it thus. But our translation is a more correct rendering of the Sanskrit.

[494]This chapter is about the three gunas (qualities) of sattva, rajas and tamas.

are freed from this[495] and attain supreme liberation. Seeking refuge in this knowledge and attaining my true nature, they are not born at the time of creation, nor suffer at the time of destruction. O descendant of the Bharata lineage! The great brahman[496] is my womb. Into that, I place the seed.[497] And from that, all the beings are created. O Kounteya! The different forms that are created in all wombs, the great brahman[498] is like their mother[499] and I am the father who provides the seed. O mighty-armed one! The qualities sattva, rajas and tamas, generated from nature, bind the indestructible atman in the body. O sinless one! Among these,[500] sattva is shining because it is pure and is without sin, but ties down the atman because of attachment to happiness and knowledge.[501] O Kounteya! Know rajas to be based on desire and the origin of thirst and attachment.[502] That[503] binds the atman[504] firmly because of attachment to action. O descendant of the Bharata lineage! Know tamas to be born from ignorance and the source of delusion in every being. That[505] binds firmly through

[495]The bondage of life.

[496]Meaning, prakriti or nature.

[497]We have translated *yoni* as womb and *garbha* as seed. Instead of seed, embryo would have been more accurate, but seed sounds better.

[498]Nature again.

[499]The word used is yoni, which can also be translated as womb.

[500]The three gunas or qualities.

[501]Because this knowledge is not knowledge of the paramatman, nor is it happiness that comes from such supreme knowledge. Hence, there is attachment and that binds the atman. Some commentators have argued that the pure sattva quality involves supreme bliss and supreme knowledge. However, ordinarily sattva is mixed with rajas and tamas and that gives rise to attachment to happiness and knowledge that is less than supreme.

[502]We have translated *trishna* as thirst, but it can also be translated as desire or greed. What is the difference between thirst or desire, and attachment? One is attached to what one already possesses. And one is thirsty for or desirous of what one does not already possess.

[503]The rajas quality.

[504]The expression used is 'occupier of the body', meaning the atman.

[505]The tamas quality.

error,[506] sloth and sleep.[507] O descendant of the Bharata lineage! Sattva attaches to happiness and rajas attaches to action. Tamas veils knowledge and attaches to errors. O descendant of the Bharata lineage! Sattva overcomes rajas and tamas and becomes strong, rajas, sattva and tamas, and tamas, sattva and rajas.[508] Know that when the light of knowledge is ignited in all the gates of this body,[509] it is only then that sattva becomes strong. O best of the Bharata lineage! Greed,[510] inclination, beginnings of action,[511] restlessness and desire—these are created when rajas becomes strong. O descendant of the Kuru lineage! Darkness, lack of enterprise, inadvertence and delusion—these are created when tamas becomes strong. If a being dies when sattva becomes strong, then he attains the shining[512] world reserved for those who have the supreme knowledge. Death when rajas become strong leads to rebirth as someone addicted to action. And death when tamas,[513] leads to rebirth as subhuman species.[514] It has been said that sattva-type action has the fruit of pure happiness, rajas-type has the fruit of unhappiness and tamas-type has the fruit of ignorance. From sattva, wisdom results, and from rajas, greed, and from tamas, only inadvertence, delusion and ignorance result. Those with a preponderance of sattva ascend above.[515] Those with

[506]Alternatively, inadvertence.

[507]What is bound is not specified. But clearly, the atman is meant.

[508]That is, rajas overcomes sattva and tamas and becomes strong. Similarly, tamas overcomes sattva and rajas and becomes strong. The point is that all three gunas are combined in every being. However, in every being, one of the gunas tends to dominate, compared to the other two.

[509]As stated earlier, the nine gates of the body are two eyes, two ears, two nostrils, the mouth, the anus and the genital organ.

[510]For other people's possessions.

[511]These beginnings of action are because of attachment to the fruits.

[512]Pure or unsullied instead of shining is also possible.

[513]That is, when tamas becomes strong.

[514]That is how this is invariably interpreted. However, the Sanskrit original should literally be translated as species that is confused and ignorant. That is not necessarily subhuman.

[515]That is, to heaven and among the gods.

rajas stay in the middle.[516] Those with despicable tamas qualities, descend below.[517] When the seer doesn't see any agent other than the qualities and knows that which is beyond the qualities, he attains my nature.[518] When the being transcends the three qualities that are the origin of the body, he attains immortality, free from birth, death, old age and unhappiness.'

'"Arjuna said, 'O lord! From what signs does one know one who has transcended? What is his conduct? And how does he transcend these three qualities?'

'"The lord said, 'O Pandava! He who is engaged in knowledge and inclination and delusion and yet does not hate, nor desire if these are withdrawn.[519] He is established in indifference and the qualities don't disturb him. Knowing the action of the qualities to be of this form, he is steady and doesn't waver. Equal between happiness and unhappiness, established in himself,[520] equal between earth, stone and gold, similar in treatment of the loved and the hated, tranquil, similar between praise and censure. He who treats respect and insult alike, friend and enemy alike and discards all beginnings of action,[521] he is said to have transcended

[516]The middle means the earth and among humans. Those with rajas, means those with a preponderance of rajas.

[517]Below may mean hell, among the demons. It may also mean a lowly rebirth.

[518]The realization that the atman is not an agent sinks in. Action is performed by the gunas or qualities of prakriti.

[519]The subject is suppressed in the shloka and is a reference to someone who has transcended the three qualities. If sattva predominates, there is engagement in knowledge. If rajas predominates, there is engagement in inclination (for action). And if tamas predominates, there is engagement in delusion. However, even if there is such engagement, the transcender doesn't hate the happiness or unhappiness that results. And even if there is withdrawal from such engagement, the transcender doesn't desire the engagement or its fruit. He is completely detached.

[520]That is, established in the atman.

[521]As has been said before, beginnings of action are for specific gains, in this world or the next. Hence, someone who has renounced these is someone who has renounced all fruits.

the qualities.' He who worships me single-mindedly and with unwavering devotion, he transcends these qualities and is worthy of attaining the state of the brahman. Because I am the embodiment of the brahman—indestructible, immortal,[522] and also of eternal dharma and absolute bliss.'"'[523]

Chapter 897(37)

" " The lord said, 'They say the ashvattha tree,[524] with a root above and branches below, is indestructible. He who knows that its leaves are the metres[525] knows the truth. Specially nurtured by the gunas, with objects[526] as its shoots, its branches extend upwards and downwards. In the world of men, its rootlings[527] stretch downwards, the cause of action. In this,[528] this form[529] is not felt, nor the end, nor the beginning. Nor even its establishment.

[522]There are two alternative interpretations, both of which are possible and make sense. First, the brahman is indestructible and immortal. Second, 'I' am indestructible and immortal.

[523]That is, I am the embodiment of eternal dharma and absolute bliss.

[524]The ashvattha tree is the holy fig tree. It has a root above, because the origin or root of the world is the brahman. This comparison of the ashvattha tree with the world also occurs in the Upanishads. The subject of the sentence is left implicit. That is, we don't know who is doing the saying. But obviously, 'they' stands for those who know the truth.

[525]Metres mean the Vedas.

[526]The interpretation is that these objects are those that gratify the five senses (sight, hearing, smelling, tasting and touching).

[527]This should also be translated as roots, but is liable to cause confusion. The main root, the brahman, has already been described as extending upwards. But this is a banyan tree, with additional rootlings descending to the ground. Since action and its fruits are secondary, rather than primary, there is a comparison with rootlings.

[528]This world.

[529]This tree's form.

Slicing the thick root of this ashvattha with the weapon of firm detachment, thereafter, one must seek that goal, the attainment of which means no return,[530] stating, "I seek refuge in that original being, from whom this eternal process is created," without pride and delusion, having conquered the fault of attachment, constant in the knowledge of the atman, having restrained desire, freed from the opposites of happiness and unhappiness, the wise go to that indestructible goal. Attaining that, there is no return. The sun cannot light that,[531] nor the moon, nor fire. That is my supreme abode. Indeed, part of my eternal form is established as beings in nature and attracts the mind and six[532] senses to the world of beings. Like the wind carries away fragrance from receptacles,[533] the lord,[534] when it discards one body and attains another one, takes these[535] with it and leaves. This[536] is established in the ears, the eyes, touch, the tongue, the nose and also the mind and enjoys objects. The deluded do not see the establishment and also the enjoyment and progress, with the qualities as attributes.[537] Those with eyes of wisdom, see this. Careful[538] yogis, established in the atman, see this. Despite care, those who are not established in the atman, and are without consciousness, don't see this. The energy in the sun that lights up the entire world, that in the moon and that too in the fire, know that energy to be mine. I enter the earth and hold

[530]No rebirth.

[531]The brahman.

[532]The five senses (sight, hearing, smelling, tasting and touching) plus the mind add up to six.

[533]Meaning flowers.

[534]The lord of the body or the jivatman.

[535]The word 'these' is a continued reference to the six senses, or the five senses and the mind.

[536]The jivatman.

[537]The establishment and enjoyment in the present body and the progress to another body is also by the jivatman. And it is also the jivatman that has the qualities (gunas) as attributes.

[538]Care or exertion in meditation.

up the beings with my energy. As the watery moon, I nourish all the herbs.[539] I am established in the bodies of beings as the fire of digestion. I mingle with the prana and apana breath[540] and digest the four types of food.[541] I am established in the hearts of all beings. I result in memory and knowledge and their lack. Indeed, it is I who am the knowledge of the Vedas and the origin of Vedanta. And I am the knower of the Vedas.[542] The destructible and the indestructible, these two purushas exist in the world. All these beings are destructible.[543] The fixed is known as the indestructible.[544] That apart, there is a supreme purusha known as the paramatman, who enters the three worlds and sustains them—the indestructible Lord. Because I am beyond destruction and superior even to the indestructible, therefore, I am known as the supreme being[545] in this world[546] and in the Vedas. O descendant of the Bharata lineage! Without delusion, he who knows me as the supreme being, he is omniscient and worships me in every way. O pure one! O descendant of the Bharata lineage! Thus, this extremely secret knowledge has been related by me. This understanding leads to knowledge and accomplishment.'"[547]

---

[539]The moon is believed to be watery and the source of all sap and juice, required to nourish plants and trees.

[540]Prana is the breath of exhalation and apana is the breath of downward inhalation.

[541]The four types of food are those that are chewed (*charvya*), sucked (*choshya* or *chushya*), licked (*lehya*) and drunk (*peya*).

[542]That is, I am established in the intellect that gets to know the Vedas.

[543]The destructible purusha.

[544]The fixed is the jivatman or the indestructible purusha.

[545]The word used for the supreme being is *purushottama*.

[546]The word used is loka, which can mean the world. But it can also mean among people. And in some interpretations, the word is taken to mean the Puranas, because these are popular among all people.

[547]Accomplishment of all that is prescribed. The implicit suggestion is that Arjuna should also become knowledgeable and accomplished.

Chapter 898(38)[548]

" "The lord said, 'O descendant of the Bharata lineage!
Absence of fear, pureness of heart,[549] steadiness in jnana
yoga,[550] donation, and control,[551] yajnas, self-study,[552] practice of
austerities and simplicity,[553] absence of injury to others, truthfulness,
lack of anger, renunciation, tranquility, lack of criticism of others,
compassion towards beings, lack of avarice, gentleness, sense
of shame,[554] steadfastness, energy, forgiveness, perseverance,
cleanliness, absence of hatred, absence of ego—these belong to
the person born towards divine wealth.[555] O Partha! Arrogance,
insolence, egoism, anger, cruelty and ignorance—these belong to birth
towards demonic wealth. Divine wealth is for liberation. Demonic
wealth is for bondage. O Pandava! Do not sorrow. You have been
born towards divine wealth. O Partha! In this world, two types of
beings are created, divine and demonic. The divine has been stated
in detail. Hear from me about the demonic. Demonic people do not
know about inclination and disinclination.[556] In them, there is no
purity nor righteousness, nor even truthfulness. They say the world

---

[548]This chapter explains the difference between divine and demonic tendencies.

[549]Alternatively, resorting to the sattva quality.

[550]Two possible interpretations are possible here. First, jnana yoga, or the path of knowledge. Second, jnana and yoga, that is the path of knowledge and the path of action or karma yoga, the word yoga being interpreted as karma yoga.

[551]Of the senses.

[552]Of the sacred texts like the Vedas. Or what has been called japa yajna earlier, that is, meditation.

[553]Or uprightness.

[554]Sense of shame because of evil action committed.

[555]The sense is that one's action in earlier lives determine birth so as to possess these divine attributes, characteristic of sattva qualities. Twenty-six attributes are listed in these three shlokas.

[556]Inclination towards righteous action and disinclination or restraint from evil action.

is full of falsehood,[557] without basis,[558] without a lord, created without continuity[559] and with no reason other than to satisfy desire. Resorting to such views, with distorted minds, little intelligence and cruel action, they perform evil deeds. They are born to destroy the world. Seeking refuge in insatiable desires, deluded with a sense of insolence, pride and arrogance, accepting search of the untrue[560] and performing impure rites, they act. Resorting to immeasurable thoughts till the time of destruction,[561] convinced certainly that the enjoyment of desire is supreme, tied down with the noose of a hundred hopes, prone to lust and anger and accepting evil means for the sake of desire gratification, they wish to accumulate wealth. Today I have gained this. I will get that desired object later. I have this and again that wealth will also be mine. This enemy has been killed by me. I will also kill the others. I am the lord, I am the enjoyer. I am the successful, strong and happy. I am wealthy and of noble descent. Who is there equal to me? I will perform yajnas, I will donate.[562] I will pleasure myself. Deluded by ignorance in this way,

[557]This falsehood has also been interpreted as falsehood of sacred texts like the Vedas and the Puranas.

[558]Without the basis of dharma and adharma. Dharma holds things up and is therefore the basis.

[559]There is a slight problem of interpretation here. Instead of translating as without continuity, one can also say that the world is created through mutual union between men and women. In that case, the subsequent clause about satisfying desire will mean lust. The world is created because of lust and there is no other purpose. In the broader interpretation, desire is more than narrow lust. And creation has a continuity from the paramatman to the sky, from the sky to the wind, from the wind to fire, from fire to water, from water to the earth and so on. By emphasizing mutual union as the source of creation, this continuity is being negated.

[560]Search of the untrue is interpreted as worship of various gods with different mantras. And some of these rites can be impure.

[561]Time of destruction means the time of death and there is the conviction that no other objective except the satisfaction of desire exists. The thoughts are about desirable objects and the senses and these are immeasurable or uncountable.

[562]These yajnas or donations are driven by the wrong motive of self-gratification and therefore, don't lead to liberation.

minds distracted by many thoughts, caught in the net of delusion, addicted to gratification of desires, they are hurled into impure hell. Self-glorifying, haughty, proud because of wealth, they insolently perform unsanctioned rites that are yajnas only in name. Resorting to vanity, strength, insolence, desire and anger, they hate me in their own bodies and in the bodies of others and are disfavoured. In this world, I hurl those hateful, cruel, evil and worst among men into demonic births,[563] several times. O Kounteya! From birth to birth, the deluded don't attain me and obtaining demonic births, go down even further.[564] Desire, anger and avarice—these are the three types of doors to hell and destroyers of the atman. Give up these three. O Kounteya! The man who is freed from these three dark doors and follows that which is good for the atman, thereafter attains the supreme goal. He who deviates from the prescription of the shastras[565] and acts as he desires like doing, that person doesn't attain liberation or happiness or the supreme goal. Therefore, in deciding what should be done and what should not be done, the shastras are your test. In this,[566] get ready to perform action knowing what the shastras prescribe.'"'

Chapter 899(39)

' " Arjuna said, 'Those who discard[567] the prescriptions of the shastras, but worship[568] with recourse to faith, what is their devotion like? Is it sattva, rajas or tamas?'

[563]Demonic birth means birth into a subhuman species.

[564]Because there is a hierarchy in subhuman species also. For example, insects will be lower than animals.

[565]The sacred texts.

[566]What 'this' means is not clear. It can certainly mean this world. It has also been interpreted as this arena of action. Finally, it has also been interpreted as this country of action, that is, India.

[567]Implicitly, this discarding of the shastras is being done inadvertently, perhaps through ignorance or sloth. The reference is not to those who discard the shastras deliberately and consciously, as a mark of disrespect.

[568]Or, those who sacrifice.

'"The lord said, 'According to their nature, people show three kinds of faith—sattva-type, rajas-type and tamas-type. Listen to this. O descendant of the Bharata lineage! Everyone's faith follows his inner nature. This being[569] is full of faith. The kind of faith one has makes the person. Those of the sattva-type worship the gods, those of the rajas-type, yakshas and rakshas.[570] The others, of the tamas-type, worship ghosts[571] and devils.[572] Those who perform terrible austerities, not sanctioned by the shastras, full of insolence and ego and deriving strength from desire and attachment,[573] devoid of consciousness, torture the elements in the body and also me, inside the body.[574] Know them to be driven by demonic resolution. The favoured food of all is of three types and so too, sacrifices, meditation and donations. Listen to the distinction between these. The sattva-type favour food that increases life expectancy, vitality,[575] strength, freedom from disease, happiness and joy—tasty, oily, nourishing and pleasant. The rajas-type favour food that is extremely spicy, acidic, salty, hot, pungent, dry and burning—increasing unhappiness, sorrow and disease. The tamas-type favour food cooked a long time

---

[569] Any human being, the word used in the Sanskrit is purusha. A convoluted interpretation is possible, with the word purusha being taken to mean the supreme being. So the supreme being is full of faith and is manifested to humans depending on the kind of faith that human being possesses.

[570] That is, worship yakshas and rakshas. The yakshas are semi-divine species, the rakshas can loosely be translated as demons. Accounts of creation vary. In some accounts, some created beings tried to eat Brahma and these became the yakshas. Others tried to prevent these devourers and these came to be known as the rakshas. According to other accounts, Brahma created water and then created beings. Some of these wanted to worship and these came to be known as yakshas. Others wanted to protect the water and came to be known as rakshas. But the general purport of the shloka is clear enough. Those of the rajas-type worship species that are less than divine.

[571] Or spirits, the Sanskrit is pretas.

[572] The class of devils or demons, bhutaganah.

[573] Alternatively, possessed of desire, attachment and strength.

[574] Inside the body as the atman.

[575] The word used is sattva, which can also be translated as strength or steadfastness, instead of vitality. Alternatively, one can also translate this as food that increases the sattva quality.

ago,[576] no longer succulent[577] and with a bad smell, stale[578] and tasted by others[579]—impure. The sacrifices performed according to prescribed rites, pacifying the mind, without attachment to fruits and only because such sacrifices ought to be performed, are of the sattva-type. O best of the Bharata lineage! But know sacrifices performed in search of fruits or indeed because of insolence,[580] to be of the rajas-type. Sacrifices without following prescribed rites, without donating food, without mantras, without donations and without faith, are said to be of the tamas-type. Worship of gods, brahmanas,[581] teachers and the wise, purity, simplicity, brahmacharya and non-violence[582]—these are known as physical austerities. Not uttering words that lead to anxiety, speaking the truth and that which is pleasant and leads to welfare,[583] and self-study[584]—these are known as verbal austerities. Tranquility of mind, lack of cruelty, reserve in speech, control of one's self, purity in attitude[585]—all these are known as mental austerities. These three

[576]Implying food that is cold.

[577]Alternatively, this can be translated as food that is burnt.

[578]Alternatively, food cooked the day before.

[579]Or simply, leftover food.

[580]The insolence results from a desire to establish one's wealth, greatness or righteousness.

[581]The word used is *dvija* and translating it as brahmana is indeed indicated. However, dvija means twice-born and thus applies to any of the first three castes.

[582]*Ahimsa* is invariably translated as non-violence. But it really means lack of injury towards others.

[583]In places like the *Manu Samhita*, a reference is made to three kinds of speech—that which is true (satya), that which is pleasant (*priya*) and that which leads to welfare (*hita*). The moral dilemma is obvious. Does one speak the truth even if it does not lead to overall welfare? Both in the *Manu Samhita* and in the Mahabharata, the suggestion is that the truth shouldn't be spoken if the truth doesn't lead to overall welfare. However, the truth should be spoken even if it is unpleasant to hear.

[584]The literal translation is only self-study. However, this is usually translated as study of the shastras or even more specifically, study of the Vedas.

[585]This is interpreted as purity in behaviour towards others. A translation as purity of heart is also possible.

types of austerities performed single-mindedly by men, without attachment to fruits and with supreme faith, are said to be of the sattva-type. Austerities performed with the objective of obtaining praise, respect or worship, and based on insolence, are said to be of the rajas-type and in this,[586] are temporary and uncertain. Austerities performed on the basis of delusion, resulting in the oppression of one's self or undertaken to destroy others, are said to be of the tamas-type. Alms donated for the sake of donation,[587] to those who have not benefited the donor,[588] and based on place, time and subject[589]—are said to be of the sattva-type. But donations for the sake of return favours or for the fruits or given unwillingly, are said to be of the rajas-type. Donations in the wrong place, at the wrong time and to the wrong subject, given without respect and disdainfully—are said to be of the tamas-type. "Om tat sat"—in these three ways, the brahman has been described in the sacred texts. From this, in the past, brahmanas and the Vedas and yajnas have been created. Therefore, according to prescribed rites, sacrifices, donations and austerities by those who are learned in the brahman, are always undertaken after uttering "Om". Those who desire liberation, give up desire for fruits and undertake sacrifices, donations and austerities after uttering "Tat". O Partha! "Sat" is used to signify existence and superiority. And the word "Sat" is also used for auspicious acts. Steadfastness in sacrifices, donations and austerities is known as "Sat" and action performed towards those ends is also indeed known as "Sat". O Partha! Sacrifices, donations and austerities and any other action, undertaken without faith, are known as the opposite of "Sat", with nothing[590] in this world or in the afterworld.'"

[586]This means this world. So the fruits are temporary and uncertain in this world.

[587]That is, without any ulterior motive.

[588]Or will not benefit the donor in the future. There is no quid pro quo.

[589]The sacred texts indicate appropriate place, time and subject for donations.

[590]That is, without fruits.

Chapter 900(40)

❝ ❝ A rjuna said, 'O mighty-armed one! O Hrishikesha! O slayer
of Keshi![591] I wish to separately understand the essence
of renunciation and relinquishing.'[592]

'"The lord said, 'The wise know the relinquishing of action that
satisfies desires as sannyasa. The discriminating call the relinquishing
of the fruits of all action *tyaga*. Some learned people say that all action
is associated with evil and should be relinquished. Some others say
that action like sacrifices, donations and austerities should not be
relinquished. O supreme among the Bharata lineage! Listen to my
decided views about that relinquishing. O tiger among men! It has
been said that relinquishing is of three types. Sacrifices, donations
and austerities are not to be relinquished. Those actions certainly
have to be performed, because sacrifices, donations and austerities
purify the hearts of the learned. O Partha! But even these actions
should be performed through relinquishing attachment and fruits.[593]
That is my decided and supreme view. It is not advisable to renounce
indicated action.[594] Discarding this through delusion is known as
tamas-type.[595] He who relinquishes action because action leads
to discomfort and requires physical exertion, performs rajas-type
relinquishing. He doesn't receive the fruits from relinquishing. O
Arjuna! Sattva-type relinquishing is known as that where attachment
and fruits are relinquished and action is performed only because it is
indicated action. Immersed in the sattva quality, steady in learning
and without doubt, the relinquisher doesn't hate disagreeable action

[591]Krishna, thus named because he killed the demon Keshi.

[592]Sannyasa (renunciation) and tyaga (relinquishing) may seem to have
identical meanings. However, sannyasa is also the fourth stage (ashrama) of life,
when one renounces action. But, earlier, the Gita hasn't used the word sannyasa in
this sense of asceticism and the word has been used more in the sense of tyaga.

[593]That is, fruits resulting from the action. By relinquishing attachment is
meant giving up a sense of ownership or ego in performing the action.

[594]By indicated action is meant one's own dharma or svadharma, which
varies from person to person.

[595]A tamas-type, that is, dark or evil kind of relinquishing.

or become addicted to agreeable action. He who possesses a body cannot give up action in its entirety. Because he relinquishes fruits of action, he is known as a true relinquisher. Those who don't relinquish face three types of fruits of their action in the afterworld—bad, good and mixed. But *sannyasis* don't.[596] O mighty-armed one! In the sacred texts,[597] five reasons are described in support of performing all action. Hear these from me. The abode and also the agent, different types of instruments and different and various types of endeavour—and the fifth is the divine.[598] Whatever action, appropriate or inappropriate, a man begins through the body, the mind and speech, is caused by these five. Although this is the state of affairs,[599] he who thinks of the absolute atman as the agent, his intelligence is unrefined and that ignorant person doesn't see.[600] He who has no sense of ego and whose intelligence is unattached, even if he slays all these people, doesn't really kill and is not tied down.[601] Knowledge, that which can be known and the knower, are the three impetuses behind action.[602]

[596]Sannyasis don't face such fruits of action. By a sannyasi is meant a person who relinquishes attachment and fruits, not one who relinquishes action.

[597]The word sankhya is used in the Sanskrit. This may either mean sankhya philosophy specifically, or it may mean sacred texts like the Vedas in general.

[598]This is a difficult shloka to understand. The abode of any action is the human body. The agent is the ego or the ownership of the action. The different types of instrument are the senses and various types of endeavour are pranayama. All four are required for any action to take place. That leaves the divine element and this has been interpreted in various ways. First, this can mean divinities who rule over different parts of the body and different types of senses. Second, it can be the influence of the paramatman, working through the body. Third, it can be the residual element as a determinant of action, after all the other four have been accounted for. Fifth, it can be the effect of action performed in earlier births.

[599]That is, action is due to these five determining causes.

[600]Doesn't see the truth.

[601]Such a person is not tied down by the fruits of the action. The mention of killing dramatizes the point. And after all, Arjuna is being addressed against the background of Arjuna refusing to kill his friends and relatives.

[602]Because action requires a resolution that the action should take place and this involves knowledge, that which can be known and the knower. Without these three, the resolution will not materialize.

The action, the instrument and the agent form the base for action. According to qualities, three types of differences in knowledge and action and the agent are described in sankhya.[603] Listen properly to that too. That which in all beings, in differentiated form, sees the undifferentiated and indestructible substance,[604] know that to be sattva-type knowledge. But the knowledge through which one sees in all beings, in differentiated form, differentiated and separate substances, know that to be rajas-type knowledge. But that which is attached to a single action,[605] is illogical, trivial and without true knowledge, that is known as tamas-type.[606] Action where fruits have been relinquished, without attachment, without love or hate, performed only because it is indicated, is known as sattva-type.[607] Again, action undertaken, with great difficulty, by those with desire for fruits or with a sense of ego, is known as rajas-type. Action begun under delusion, without consideration of consequences, destruction, injury[608] and one's own capabilities, is known as tamas-type. An agent who is without attachment, without sense of ego, patient and enthusiastic, equal in attitude towards success and failure, is known as sattva-type. An agent who is attached, desirous of fruits of action, avaricious, injurious,[609] impure and swayed by joy and sorrow, is known as rajas-type. An agent who is not steady, vulgar,[610] insolent,

---

[603]Meaning, sankhya philosophy. The three impetuses of knowledge, that which can be known and the knower have been cited. The action, the instrument and the agent have been cited as the base for action. Of these six, knowledge, action and the agent have been now singled out for detailed attention and the reason is clear. The knower is identified with the agent, that which can be known is identified with knowledge and the instrument isn't independent either. That leaves the other three.

[604]The brahman or the paramatman.

[605]Without appreciating the whole.

[606]Tamas-type knowledge.

[607]Sattva-type action.

[608]Injury to others and destruction of objects like wealth.

[609]Avaricious towards objects owned by others and injurious towards others.

[610]The word used is *prakrita*, which can also be translated as unrefined or illiterate.

fraudulent, disrespectful,[611] lazy, despondent and procrastinating is known as tamas-type. O Dhananjaya! According to quality of intellect and perseverance, there are three types of differences. Listen to what is being said, separately and comprehensively. O Partha! The intellect[612] that knows inclination and disinclination, right action and wrong, fear and freedom from fear, bondage and liberation, is sattva-type. O Partha! The intellect through which one does not correctly understand dharma and adharma and right action and wrong, is rajas-type. O Partha! The intellect through which one thinks evil action is righteous, and in every way thinks the opposite,[613] shrouded in ignorance, that is tamas-type. O Partha! The perseverance through which one uses unwavering yoga to focus the functions of the mind, the breath of life and the senses, that perseverance is sattva-type. O Partha! O Arjuna! The perseverance through which dharma, artha and kama are sought and according to the area, fruits desired, is known as rajas-type. O Partha! The perseverance through which the misguided person doesn't discard dreaming,[614] fear, sorrow, despondency and ego, is known as tamas-type. O bull among the Bharata lineage! Now hear from me about the three types of happiness. Where happiness comes from gradual practice and there is an end to unhappiness, that which is initially like poison but at the end like ambrosia, based on the tranquility of one's intellect focused on the atman, that is known as sattva-type. That which comes from association with objects and the senses and is initially like ambrosia but at the end like poison, that happiness is said to be rajas-type. The happiness that, at the beginning and at the end, binds and deludes the atman and that which is created from sleep, sloth and inadvertence,[615] is known as tamas-type. On earth, in heaven and even among the gods,

---

[611]This is interpretation rather than literal translation. Instead of disrespectful, it can also be a person who inhibits the actions of others.

[612]That is, the intellect that knows the difference between these.

[613]The opposite of what should actually be thought.

[614]Meaning sleep.

[615]Inadvertence about right action.

there doesn't exist anything that is free from these three qualities generated from nature.

'"'O scorcher of foes! The actions[616] of brahmanas, kshatriyas, vaishyas and also shudras are separately segregated in accordance with qualities that result from their natures. Control over the mind, control over the senses, meditation, purity, forgiveness, simplicity, knowledge, self-realization and indeed faith are natural actions for brahmanas. Valour, bravery, perseverance, dexterity, willingness to fight, generosity and capacity to rule[617] are natural actions for kshatriyas. Agriculture, preservation of cattle and trade are natural actions for vaishyas. Servitude is natural action for shudras. A man who faithfully follows his indicated course of action, attains liberation. Listen to how liberation is obtained by following one's indicated course of action. Through his own action, man obtains liberation by worshipping him who is the origin of beings and their endeavour, and him who pervades all this.[618] Even when performed imperfectly, svadharma[619] is superior to someone else's dharma, performed well. Sin does not result if one's natural action is undertaken. O Kounteya! Natural action should not be discarded, even if it is tainted. Because all action is tainted, just as fire is shrouded by smoke. He who is detached everywhere, has conquered his atman,[620] has overcome desire through sannyasa,[621] attains the supreme liberation of freedom from action. O Kounteya! Learn briefly from me how one who has attained liberation attains the brahman. That is the supreme form of knowledge. United with pure intellect, controlling the atman with perseverance, discarding objects like sound and renouncing love and

---

[616]Prescribed actions or duties.

[617]A more literal translation is lordliness or sovereignty.

[618]The world or the universe.

[619]One's own dharma is svadharma. This can be translated as one's own indicated course of action or duty. This meant varnashrama dharma, which meant that a person's duty depended on his varna (caste) and his ashrama (stage of life).

[620]Interpreted as controlling the senses or overcoming a sense of ego.

[621]Sannyasa doesn't mean giving up action. It means giving up attachment to action and fruits of action.

aversion, inhabiting a secluded place, eating little, restraining speech, body and the mind, constantly practising meditation, seeking refuge in renunciation, discarding ego, power, insolence, desire, anger and possessions,[622] tranquil and without ego, he is fit for merging with the brahman. Tranquil in merging with the brahman, such a person does not sorrow and does not desire. Looking upon every being equally, he attains supreme devotion towards me. Through devotion, he comprehends my true nature, who I am and my different forms. Then, after knowing my true nature, enters.[623] Seeking refuge in me, he always performs all action and, through my blessings, attains the eternal and indestructible abode. Through the mind, offering up all action to me, devoted to me and seeking refuge in buddhi yoga,[624] always immerse your mind in me. With mind immersed in me, with my blessings, you will overcome all difficulties. But if, through a sense of ego, you don't listen to me, you will be destroyed. Through a sense of ego, you are thinking that you will not fight. But this resolution is false. Nature[625] will compel you. O Kounteya! Whatever you don't wish to do because of delusion, you will have to undertake in spite of that, because you are tied down by your natural duty. O Arjuna! The lord is established in the hearts of all beings and through maya, makes all beings whirl, as if they are mounted on machines.[626] O descendant of the Bharata lineage! In every way, seek refuge in him alone. Through his blessings, you will attain supreme tranquility and the eternal abode. I have explained to you this knowledge, which is the most secret of all secrets. Having examined it completely, do what you wish to do. Listen yet again to my supreme words, the most secret of all secrets. You are my dearly beloved. Therefore, I am telling you what is good for you. Immerse your mind only in

[622]The word used is parigraha, which in this context, means the acceptance of possessions, such as in the form of donations from other people, to sustain physical life.

[623]That is, enters me.

[624]The Gita uses the words buddhi yoga and karma yoga synonymously. Sometimes, the word yoga is used instead.

[625]Arjuna's nature as a kshatriya.

[626]In interpretations, the imagery used is of puppets on a string.

me, be devoted to me, worship me, bow in obeisance before me. I am pledging that you will attain me, because you are my beloved. Discard all dharmas[627] and seek refuge only in me. I will free you from all sins. Do not sorrow. You should not state this[628] to those who do not meditate,[629] or are devoid of devotion or do not wish to hear. Nor to those who show me disrespect. There is no doubt that he who explains this most secret knowledge to my devotees, displays supreme devotion towards me and will attain me alone. Among men, there is no one who does greater service to me.[630] In the world, there is no one, and there will be no one, more dear to me. And he who will study this dialogue[631] of ours on dharma, my view is that he will worship me through jnana yoga. The man who only listens with faith and without disrespect, he too will be freed from sin and attain the worlds attained by those who are pure of deeds. O Partha! Have you listened to this with single-minded concentration? O Dhananjaya! Has your delusion of ignorance been destroyed?'

'"Arjuna said, 'O Achyuta! Through your blessings, my delusion has been destroyed. I have obtained knowledge about what should be done and what shouldn't be done.[632] I am steady. I no longer suffer from doubt. I will do what you instruct.'"

[627]There is scope for interpretation in deciding what this discarding of all dharmas means. At an obvious level, these various dharmas mean those duties laid down in the shastras (sacred texts) and the injunction is to give up these rites and duties and adopt bhakti yoga instead. In more complicated interpretations, it is suggested that prakriti is subject to notions of dharma and adharma and purusha is beyond these. Therefore, the injunction is to immerse oneself in the brahman.

[628]This knowledge and more generally, the knowledge of the Gita.

[629]Also interpreted as those who do not follow their svadharma.

[630]Than one who undertakes the task of explaining this knowledge.

[631]The Gita again. Alternatively, this sacred dialogue, instead of dialogue on dharma.

[632]The word used in Sanskrit is *smriti*, which we have translated as knowledge about that which should be done and that which shouldn't be done. In an even more literal way, smriti can be translated as Arjuna having obtained his memory back.

'Sanjaya said, "I have thus heard this wonderful and thrilling[633] dialogue between the great souls Vasudeva and Partha. Through the blessings of Vyasa, I have heard this supreme and secret yoga directly from Krishna, the lord of all yoga, when he stated it. O king! Remembering again and again this sacred and wonderful dialogue between Keshava and Arjuna, I have repeatedly been exhilarated. O king! Remembering that extremely wonderful universal form of Hari, I am greatly amazed and repeatedly exhilarated. Wherever[634] there is Krishna, the lord of yoga, and Arjuna, the wielder of the bow, exist prosperity, victory, increase in wealth and sound policy. That is my conviction."'

[633]Literally, a dialogue that makes one's hair stand up.
[634]On whichever side.

Bhishma Vadha Parva

This parva has 3947 shlokas and seventy-seven chapters.

Vadha *means the act of killing. This section is so named because it is about the killing of Bhishma. The first ten days of the battle have Bhishma as the commander-in-chief. This section thus describes the first ten days of the battle. On the first day, Virata's son, Uttara, is killed. The second day has the Pandavas victorious, the highlight being Bhima's destruction of the Kalingas. There is a ding-dong battle on the third day, with Bhishma triumphant initially (which is when Krishna decides to take up arms), followed by Arjuna's victory. The Pandavas triumph on the fourth day and fourteen of Duryodhana's brothers are killed by Bhima. While there is a lot of fighting on the fifth day, the highlight is Bhurishrava's killing of ten of Satyaki's sons. On balance, the Pandava side is more successful on the sixth day. While there is a great deal of fighting, there is nothing that merits a special mention on the seventh day.*

On the eighth day, Bhima kills eight of Duryodhana's brothers. Iravat, Arjuna's son, kills several of Shakuni's brothers and is himself killed by the rakshasa Alambusa. Bhima again kills nine of Duryodhana's brothers. On the ninth day, the Pandavas eventually get the worst of it. Krishna decides to kill Bhishma and is restrained by Arjuna. The Pandavas consult Bhishma about how he may be killed and are advised to use Shikhandi. The tenth day is marked by Bhishma's downfall.

Chapter 901(41)

'Sanjaya said, "At that, on seeing Dhananjaya take up Gandiva and his arrows again, the maharathas[1] let out a tremendous roar. The brave Pandavas and Somakas and their followers were delighted and blew on conch shells that had been generated from the ocean. Drums, *peshis*,[2] *krakachas*[3] and trumpets made from the horns of cows were sounded together and there was a tumultuous sound. O lord of men! Gods, together with gandharvas, ancestors, siddhas and masses of charanas came to witness. The immensely fortunate rishis arrived, with Shatakratu at the forefront, desiring to see that great slaughter. O king! On seeing that the two armies, resembling two oceans, were ready to fight and were repeatedly moving, the brave Yudhishthira removed his armour and cast aside his supreme weapons. He swiftly descended from his chariot. Dharmaraja Yudhishthira joined his hands in salutation and advanced on foot, glancing towards the grandfather.[4] Restrained in speech, he advanced

---

[1]That is, the maharathas on the Pandava side.

[2]Kind of drum.

[3]A krakacha is a saw. But it also means a teak tree and it is possible that here, it means some kind of musical instrument made from teak trees.

[4]Bhishma.

towards the east, where the enemy forces were stationed. On seeing him advance, Dhananjaya, Kunti's son, also swiftly descended from his chariot and followed him, together with his brothers. The illustrious Vasudeva also followed him at the rear. Extremely anxious, the foremost kings[5] also advanced.

'"Arjuna said, 'O king! What are you doing? Why have you abandoned your brothers and are advancing on foot towards the east, where the enemy forces are stationed?'

'"Bhimasena said, 'O Indra among kings! Where are you going, having thrown your armour and weapons away? O lord of the earth! You have abandoned your brothers and are going towards the armoured enemy soldiers.'

'"Nakula said, 'O descendant of the Bharata lineage! You are my eldest brother. On seeing you advance in this fashion, my heart is terrified. Tell us where you are going.'

'"Sahadeva said, 'O king! A terrible fear confronts us in this battle, in the form of those whom we have to fight. Why are you advancing towards the enemy?'"

'Sanjaya said, "O descendant of the Kuru lineage! Though he was addressed in this way by his brothers, Yudhishthira did not utter a single word, but continued to advance. The immensely wise and great-minded Vasudeva smiled and told them, 'I know his intentions. He will fight with the enemy kings only after he has shown his respects to Bhishma, Drona, Goutama,[6] Shalya and all the other seniors. It has been heard in the accounts of earlier eras, that he who shows his respects towards his seniors and revered relatives in accordance with the sacred texts, and then fights with them, is certain to be victorious in battle. That is my view.' While Krishna was speaking, a great sound of lamentation arose in the army of Dhritarashtra's son, but the other one[7] remained silent. On seeing Yudhishthira from a distance, Dhritarashtra's son's

[5]On the Pandava side.
[6]Kripa.
[7]The army of the Pandavas.

soldiers conversed among themselves. 'This one is a disgrace to his lineage. The king has been frightened and is advancing towards Bhishma. Yudhishthira, together with his brothers, will seek shelter. When Dhananjaya, Pandava Vrikodara, Nakula and Sahadeva are protectors, why is the Pandava[8] frightened? Though he is famous on earth, he cannot have been born in a lineage of kshatriyas. His heart is frightened and he is dispirited at the prospect of battle.' Then all the soldiers praised the Kouravas. They were delighted in their minds and waved their garments around. O lord of the earth! All the warriors censured Yudhishthira and his brothers, together with Keshava. The Kourava soldiers cried 'Shame!' to Yudhishthira. O lord of the earth! Then they again became completely silent. What would the king say? What would Bhishma speak in reply? What about Bhima, who prided himself in battle? What about Krishna and Arjuna? What would they say? O king! Both armies were extremely curious on account of Yudhishthira. Surrounded by his brothers, he[9] penetrated the enemy army, full of arrows and lances, and swiftly advanced towards Bhishma. Bhishma, Shantanu's son, was ready for battle. The Pandava king grasped his feet with both his hands and spoke these words.

'"Yudhishthira said, 'O invincible one! O father![10] We are inviting you to fight with us. O father! Grant us the permission. Give us the blessings.'

'"Bhishma replied, 'O lord of the earth! O great king! O descendant of the Bharata lineage! If you had not come to me before this battle, I would have cursed you so that you might be defeated. O son! O Pandava! I am pleased with you. Fight and be victorious. Whatever else you might desire, obtain all that in this battle. O Partha! Ask for a boon. What is it that you desire? May it be such that you do not face defeat. A man is the servant of wealth. But wealth is never anyone's servant. O great king! This is the truth. I am tied to

[8]Yudhishthira.
[9]Yudhishthira.
[10]The word used is tata.

the Kouravas because of wealth. O descendant of the Kuru lineage!
That is the reason the words spoken by me are those of a eunuch.[11]
The Kouravyas have robbed me through wealth. Other than battle,
what else do you wish for?'

'"Yudhishthira said, 'O immensely wise one! Your counsel has
always been directed towards my welfare. Fight on the side of the
Kouravas. That has always been the boon I have asked.'

'"Bhishma replied, 'O king! O descendant of the Kuru lineage!
How can I help you? What shall I do? I will fight on the side of the
enemy. What else do you have to say?'

'"Yudhishthira said, 'You are invincible. How will we be able
to vanquish you in battle? If you wish to provide counsel for our
welfare and you find this to be desirable, tell me this.'

'"Bhishma replied, 'O Kounteya! Even if it were to be Shatakratu
himself, as long as I fight in battle, I do not see any man who can
vanquish me.'

'"Yudhishthira said, 'O grandfather! I bow down before you.
I am asking you to tell me about a means of victory. How can an
enemy kill you in battle?'

'"Bhishma replied, 'O son! I do not see anyone who can defeat
me in battle. The time for my death has not arrived. Come to me
again later.'"[12]

'Sanjaya said, "O descendant of the Kuru lineage! With his head
lowered in homage, Yudhishthira accepted Bhishma's words and
again showed him homage. In the midst of his brothers and while
all the soldiers looked on, the mighty-armed one then advanced
towards the preceptor's chariot. Having honoured Drona, he
circumambulated him. The king spoke beneficial words to the
invincible one. 'O illustrious one![13] I am requesting you. How can I
fight without incurring a sin? O brahmana! With your permission,
how can I triumph over all the enemies?'

[11]Because Bhishma cannot grant what Yudhishthira wishes.
[12]When the time of death arrives.
[13]The Critical edition doesn't put this in quotes.

'"Drona replied, 'O great king! Having decided to fight, if you had not come to me, I would have cursed you for your complete defeat. O Yudhishthira! O unblemished one! I have now been honoured by you and am satisfied. I grant you permission. Fight and be victorious. I will also do what you desire. Tell me what your wishes are. O great king! This being the case, other than the battle, what else do you want? A man is the servant of wealth. But wealth is never anyone's servant. O great king! This is the truth. I am tied to the Kouravas because of wealth. That is the reason I am tied like a eunuch.[14] Other than battle, what else do you want? I will fight for the sake of the Kouravas. But my prayers will be for your triumph.'

'"Yudhishthira said, 'O brahmana! Pray for my victory and counsel me about what is good for me. Fight for the sake of the Kouravas. That is the boon I ask of you.'

'"Drona replied, 'O king! When you have Hari as an adviser, your victory is certain. I wish that you are able to vanquish your foes in battle. Where there is dharma, Krishna is there. Where there is Krishna, victory is there. O Kounteya! Go and fight. Ask me. What will I tell you?'

'"Yudhishthira said, 'O foremost among brahmanas! Listen to what I am asking and telling you. You have never been defeated. How can we vanquish you in battle?'

'"Drona replied, 'As long as I am fighting in battle, you cannot be victorious. O king! Together with your brothers, try to kill me quickly.'

'"Yudhishthira said, 'O mighty-armed one! Tell us the means whereby you can be killed. O preceptor! I am bowing down before you. I am showing you homage and asking you.'

'"Drona replied, 'O son![15] As long as I am stationed in battle, when I am angrily fighting and am incessantly showering arrows, I do not see the enemy who can kill me. O king! Except when I am ready for death and have withdrawn myself from weapons and my senses, no warrior can kill me in battle. I tell you that this is true.

[14]Because Drona cannot grant what Yudhishthira wishes.
[15]The word used is tata.

I also tell you truthfully that if I hear extremely unpleasant news from a man whose words should be respected, I will abandon my weapons in battle.'"

'Sanjaya said, "O great king! Having heard these words from Bharadvaja's wise son,[16] he took the preceptor's permission and went towards Sharadvat's son.[17] Having honoured Kripa and circumambulated him, the king, skilled in the use of words, spoke these words to the one who was foremost among unassailable ones. 'O preceptor![18] I seek your permission to fight with you, without incurring any sin. O unblemished one! If I obtain your permission, I will defeat all enemies.'

'"Kripa replied, 'O great king! Having decided to fight, if you had not come to me, I would have cursed you for your complete defeat. A man is the servant of wealth. But wealth is never anyone's servant. O great king! This is the truth. I am tied to the Kouravas because of wealth. O great king! It is my view that I must fight for their sake. That is the reason I am tied like a eunuch.[19] Other than battle, what else do you want?'

'"Yudhishthira said, 'O preceptor! Listen to my words. Alas! I have to ask you this.'"

'Sanjaya said, "Having spoken these words, the king was dejected, and bereft of his senses, fell silent. But having divined what he wished to say, Goutama replied.[20] 'O lord of the earth! I am incapable of being slain. Fight and be victorious. O lord of men! I am pleased that you have come. I will arise every day and pray for your victory. I am telling you this truthfully.' O great king! Having heard these words of Goutama, the king took Kripa's permission and went to where the king of Madra was. Having honoured Shalya, he circumambulated him. The king spoke these beneficial words to the invincible one. 'O revered one![21]

[16]Drona's father was the sage Bharadvaja.

[17]Kripa.

[18]The Critical edition doesn't explicitly have this within quotes. Before Drona's arrival, Kripa used to be the preceptor.

[19]Because Kripa cannot grant what Yudhishthira wishes.

[20]Goutama is Kripa. The Critical edition doesn't explicitly have this within quotes.

[21]The Critical edition doesn't explicitly have this within quotes.

I seek your permission to fight with you, without incurring any sin. O great king! If I obtain your permission, I will defeat the enemies.'

'"Shalya replied, 'O great king! Having decided to fight, if you had not come to me, I would have cursed you for your defeat in battle. I am pleased with the honour you have shown me. Let it be as you desire. I grant you permission. Fight and be victorious. O brave one! Tell me anything else that you want. What can I give you? A man is the servant of wealth. But wealth is never anyone's servant. O great king! This is the truth. I am tied to the Kouravas because of wealth. O nephew![22] I will do what you wish for and act according to your desires. I am speaking to you like a eunuch.[23] Other than battle, what else do you want?'

'"Yudhishthira said, 'O great king! Always counsel me about my supreme welfare. If you desire, fight for the enemy's cause. That is the boon I desire.'

'"Shalya replied, 'O supreme among kings! In the present case, tell me what I can do to help. I wish to fight in the enemy's cause. I am tied to the Kouravas because of wealth.'

'"Yudhishthira said, 'This was truly the boon I had asked for when the preparations were being made. When the son of the suta fights, you should act so as to diminish his energy.'

'"Shalya replied, 'O son of Kunti! This desire of yours will be satisfied. Go and fight as you please. I will try for your victory.'"

'Sanjaya said, "Having taken leave of his maternal uncle, the lord of Madra, Kounteya, surrounded by his brothers, emerged from that large army. In that field of battle, Vasudeva went to Radheya.[24] For the sake of the Pandavas, Gada's elder brother spoke to him.[25] 'O Karna! I have heard that out of enmity towards Bhishma, you will not fight. O Radheya! Until Bhishma has been killed, come over to our side. O Radheya! If you perceive both sides to be equal, after Bhishma has been killed, go and fight again and help Dhritarashtra's son.'

---

[22]Shalya's sister was Madri, Nakula and Sahadeva's mother.

[23]Because Shalya cannot grant what Yudhishthira wishes.

[24]Radha's son, Karna.

[25]Gada was Krishna's younger brother.

'"Karna replied, 'O Keshava! I will not do anything that causes displeasure to Dhritarashtra's son. Know that I am engaged in Duryodhana's welfare and have given up my life for him.'"

'Sanjaya said, "O descendant of the Bharata lineage! Having heard these words, Krishna refrained. He then returned to the Pandavas, who had Yudhishthira in the forefront. In the midst of the soldiers, the eldest Pandava loudly said, 'He who chooses us, will be regarded by us as an aide.' Yuyutsu[26] glanced towards them and with a delighted mind, spoke to Dharmaraja Yudhishthira, Kunti's son. 'O great king! O unblemished one! If you accept me, in this battle, I will fight for your cause and against the sons of Dhritarashtra.' Yudhishthira replied, 'Come. All of us will fight with your ignorant brothers. O Yuyutsu! O mighty-armed one! Vasudeva and all of us accept that you will fight in our cause. O prince! O immensely radiant one! It seems that you will be the sole strand and the only one to offer funeral cakes[27] in Dhritarashtra's lineage. Accept us. We accept you. Dhritarashtra's evil-minded and intolerant son will cease to exist.' Your son Yuyutsu then abandoned the Kouravyas. Accompanied by the sound of drums, he went to the army of the sons of Pandu. Together with his younger brothers, King Yudhishthira happily donned his armour again, as resplendent as gold. All those bulls among men ascended their chariots. They arranged themselves in battle formations, as they had earlier. They instructed that hundreds of drums and smaller drums[28] be played. In different ways, those bulls among men roared like lions. On seeing the Pandavas, tigers among men, stationed on their chariots, all the kings, together with Dhrishtadyumna, were delighted and roared again. They had witnessed the magnanimity of the sons of Pandu, who honoured those who should be shown honour. All the lords of the earth applauded this. The kings spoke about the friendship, compassion and kindness those great-souled ones displayed towards their relatives, on the appropriate occasions. 'Excellent', 'superb'—these words of praise

[26]Dhritarashtra's son through a vaishya woman.
[27]*Pinda*, to the ancestors.
[28]Two different types of drums are named—*dundubhi* and *pushkara*.

were heard everywhere. There were auspicious chants about their deeds, attracting the mind and the heart.[29] All the mlecchas and aryas who were there, and saw or heard about the conduct of the sons of Pandu, wept, their voices choking with tears. The spirited ones instructed hundreds of giant drums, pushkaras and conch shells, as white as milk, to be sounded.'"

Chapter 902(42)

'Dhritarashtra said, "My soldiers, and those of the others, were arranged in battle formations. Who was the first to strike, the Kurus or the Pandavas?"

'Sanjaya said, "O king! Your son Duryodhana advanced with his brothers,[30] placing Bhishma at the forefront of the army. Delighted in their minds and wishing to fight with Bhishma, so did the Pandavas, with Bhimasena at the forefront. There were clamorous sounds in both the armies, with krakachas, trumpets made out of the horns of cows, drums, kettledrums, tambourines and the roars of horses and elephants. O king! With a tumultuous sound, they rushed at us and we at them. In that great encounter and confrontation, the giant armies of the Pandavas and the sons of Dhritarashtra trembled, like a forest stirred by the wind. The loud roar of those masses of kings, elephants, horses and chariots, dashing against each other at that inauspicious hour, was like that of the ocean agitated by a storm. When that tumultuous sound arose and made the body hair stand up, the mighty-armed Bhimasena roared like a bull. Bhimasena's roars transcended the sounds of conch shells and drums, the trumpeting of elephants and the lion-like roars of the soldiers. Bhimasena's loud

---

[29]Towards the Pandavas.

[30]In the course of the war accounts, several of Duryodhana's brothers are mentioned by name. There is a listing of Duryodhana's brothers in Section 1 (Volume 1). However, the names of some of the minor brothers in the war accounts are at odds with that listing in Section 1 (Volume 1).

roar surpassed the neighing of thousands of horses in both the armies. On hearing the roar of that brave one, which was like the sound of the clouds or the sound of Shakra's thunder, your soldiers were frightened. All the animals excreted urine and dung, like animals do at the sound of a lion. He showed himself in a terrible form and roared like a giant cloud. He terrified the soldiers of your sons and attacked them. O king! When that mighty archer attacked them, he was surrounded by all the brothers who are your sons—Duryodhana, Durmukha, Duhsaha, Shala, atiratha Duhshasana, Durmarshana, Vivimshati, Chitrasena, maharatha Vikarna, Purumitra, Jaya, Bhoja and Somadatta's valorous son.[31] They showered him with arrows, like clouds enveloping the sun. They brandished their giant bows, which were like clouds tinged with lightning. They unleashed sharp arrows that were like virulent serpents.

"'At that, Droupadi's sons, Subhadra's maharatha son,[32] Nakula, Sahadeva and Parshata Dhrishtadyumna repulsed the sons of Dhritarashtra and pierced them with sharp arrows. They shattered them, like summits with the great force of thunder. In that first encounter, with the terrible sound of bows twanging against arm-guards, neither your side, nor that of the other, retreated. O bull among the Bharata lineage! I witnessed the dexterity of Drona's disciples. O king! They shot many arrows, which always found their mark. The roar of the bows did not cease, even for an instant. The flaming arrows were like stars in the sky. O descendant of the Bharata lineage! All the other kings were spectators, witnessing the spectacular encounter between relatives. O king! Remembering the injuries they had suffered from each other, the maharathas were enraged and challenged and strove. With elephants, horses and chariots, the armies of the Kurus and the Pandavas were extremely beautiful on the field of battle, like figures on a painting. Then all the kings grasped their bows. Instructed by your son, they advanced with their armies. Thousands of kings were instructed by Yudhishthira. They roared and attacked your son's army. The encounter between

[31]Bhurishrava.
[32]Abhimanyu.

the soldiers of both the armies was terrible. Because of the dust raised by the soldiers, the sun disappeared. They advanced. They retreated. They advanced again. One could not detect any difference between ours and those of the enemy. An extremely fearful and tumultuous battle raged. But your father[33] surpassed all the other soldiers."'

Chapter 903(43)

'Sanjaya said, "O lord of the earth! In the forenoon, there was an extremely fearful and terrible battle that destroyed the bodies of kings. Desiring victory in that battle, the Kurus and the Pandavas roared like lions, resounding in the sky and earth. There was a roar, the slapping of palms and the sound of conch shells. The brave ones roared at each other, like lions. O bull among the Bharata lineage! The bows twanged against arm-guards. There were the footfalls of the infantry and the loud roars of horses. Staffs and goads[34] descended. Weapons resounded. As the elephants dashed towards each other, bells jingled. There was a tremendous roar that made the body hair stand up. There was the roar of chariots, like the sound of the clouds. Cruel in their intentions and prepared to give up their lives, all of them[35] raised their standards and advanced against the Pandavas.

'"O king! Grasping a terrible bow, like the staff of death, Shantanu's son himself advanced against Dhananjaya. Arjuna grasped the bow Gandiva, famous in the world. In the forefront of that battle, the spirited one advanced against Ganga's son. Those two tigers of the Kuru lineage wished to kill each other. Ganga's son pierced Partha in that battle, but he did not waver. O king! Pandava did the same to Bhishma, but could not make him waver. The great archer Satyaki

---

[33]Bhishma.
[34]For elephants, ankusha.
[35]The Kurus.

dashed against Kritavarma. There was a tumultuous encounter between the two and it made the body hair stand up. Roaring and using sharp arrows, Satyaki pierced Kritavarma and Kritavarma Satyaki. They oppressed each other. With arrows in their bodies, those immensely strong ones were as resplendent as flowering kimshukas,[36] blossoming in the spring. The great archer Abhimanyu fought with Brihadbala.[37] O lord of the earth! In that battle, the king of Kosala sliced down the standard of Subhadra's son and brought down his charioteer. When his charioteer was brought down from the chariot, Subhadra's son was enraged. O great king! He pierced Brihadbala with nine arrows. With a sharp and yellow arrow, he sliced off his standard. With another he brought down his *parshni*.[38] With yet another, he brought down his charioteer. O king! They were angry and continued to weaken each other with sharp arrows. In that battle, Bhimasena fought with your proud maharatha son Duryodhana, who had been the cause of the enmity. Both of those tigers among men were immensely strong and were foremost among the Kurus. In that field of battle, they enveloped each other with showers of arrows. O descendant of the Bharata lineage! On seeing the wonderful ways those great-souled and skilled ones fought, all the beings were astounded. Duhshasana advanced against maharatha Nakula and pierced his innermost organs with many sharp arrows. O descendant of the Bharata lineage! Smiling, Madri's son used sharp arrows to slice down his[39] standard, bow and arrows. He then pierced him with twenty-five small arrows. Your son is unassailable. In that great battle, he pierced and brought down Nakula's horses, arrows and standard. Durmukha attacked the immensely strong Sahadeva. He fought him in that great battle and pierced him with a shower of arrows. In that great battle, the brave

[36]Tree with red blossoms.

[37]Brihadbala was the king of Kosala.

[38]Parshni has different meanings. When four horses are attached to a chariot, it means one of the outside horses. It can also mean one of the two charioteers who drive the outside horses, as opposed to the main charioteer (sarathi), or someone who guards the axles. The context suggests Abhimanyu brought down a person, not a horse.

[39]Duhshasana's.

Sahadeva used an extremely sharp arrow to bring down Durmukha's charioteer. Both of them were invincible in battle and attacked each other. Desiring to repulse each other, they used terrible arrows to create fright. King Yudhishthira himself advanced against the king of Madra. The king of Madra sliced the revered one's[40] bow into two. When his bow was sliced, Yudhishthira, Kunti's son, took up another bow that was stronger and more forceful. Angered, the king told the lord of Madra, 'Wait' and covered him with straight-tufted arrows.

'"O descendant of the Bharata lineage! In that battle, Dhrishtadyumna attacked Drona with a firm bow that was capable of destroying enemies. Thus angered, Drona sliced it into three and unleashed an extremely terrible arrow that was like the staff of death. Thus despatched in that battle, it penetrated his[41] body. Taking up another bow and fourteen arrows, Drupada's son pierced Drona in that encounter. O great king! In that battle, the violent Shankha[42] attacked Somadatta's son[43], who was also a violent warrior. Exclaiming 'Wait', 'Wait', the brave one pierced him[44] in the right arm in the battle. Somadatta's son then pierced Shankha in the shoulder. O lord of the earth! The bout between those two proud ones was as terrible as that between Vritra and Vasava. O lord of the earth! Enraged in that battle, maharatha Dhrishtaketu,[45] immeasurable in his soul, attacked Bahlika, who was also the embodiment of anger. O king! In that battle, Bahlika roared like a lion and oppressed the intolerant Dhrishtaketu with many arrows. The king of Chedi was angered and in that encounter, swiftly pierced Bahlika with nine arrows. It was like one mad elephant against another. They angrily attacked each other in that encounter and roared repeatedly. They fought in great rage, like Angaraka and Budha.[46] The rakshasa

---

[40]Yudhishthira.

[41]Dhrishtadyumna's body.

[42]Virata's eldest son.

[43]Bhurishrava.

[44]Shankha and Bhurishrava respectively.

[45]The king of Chedi.

[46]Angaraka is Mars and Budha is Mercury. Mars and Mercury are antagonistic planets.

Ghatotkacha was terrible in deeds. He attacked Alambusha, the performer of cruel deeds, like Shakra against Bala.[47] O descendant of the Bharata lineage! Ghatotkacha wounded the enraged and extremely strong rakshasa with ninety sharp arrows. In that encounter, Alambusha pierced Bhimasena's extremely strong son in many places with straight-tufted arrows. Wounded by arrows in that battle, they looked like the immensely strong Bala and Shakra in the battle between the gods and the asuras.

"'O king! In that battle, the powerful Shikhandi attacked Drona's son. Angered at this, Ashvatthama wounded Shikhandi with an extremely sharp iron arrow and made him tremble. O king! At this, Shikhandi struck Drona's son with a well-crafted, extremely sharp and extremely pointed arrow. In that bout, they struck each other with many other kinds of arrows. O king! Virata was the general of an army and in that battle, he quickly and impetuously attacked the brave Bhagadatta. Virata was extremely angry. He showered arrows on Bhagadatta, like clouds showering on a mountain. But in that encounter, Bhagadatta, lord of the earth, quickly enveloped Virata, like clouds around the rising sun. Sharadvat's son, Kripa, attacked Brihadkshatra from Kekaya. O descendant of the Bharata lineage! Kripa shrouded him with a shower of arrows. The angry Kekaya also showered arrows on Goutama. Having killed each other's horses and having sliced down each other's bows, both of them were bereft of their chariots. They wrathfully advanced against each other, intending to fight with swords. The battle that they fought was terrible in form and extremely fearful. King Drupada, the scorcher of enemies, intolerantly advanced against Jayadratha from Sindhu, who was cheerfully waiting. The king of Sindhu pierced Drupada with three tufted arrows and in that battle, was wounded in return. They fought a bout that was terrible in form and extremely fearful. It delighted the hearts of spectators and was like that between Angaraka and Shukra.[48]

---

[47]Ghatotkacha was Bhima and Hidimba's son and was a rakshasa. Alambusha was Rishyashringa's son and was also a rakshasa, fighting on the Kourava side.

[48]Shukra is Venus. Mars and Venus are antagonistic planets.

'"Your son Vikarna possessed swift horses. He advanced against the immensely strong Sutasoma[49] and a battle started. Though Vikarna pierced Sutasoma, he could not make him waver. Nor could Sutasoma make Vikarna waver and it was wonderful. In the cause of the Pandavas, maharatha Chekitana, tiger among men, angrily advanced against the valorous Susharma.[50] O great king! In that battle, Susharma repulsed maharatha Chekitana with a great shower of arrows. Chekitana was enraged in that great encounter and enveloped Susharma with arrows, like a great cloud on a mountain. O Indra among kings! The powerful Shakuni attacked the powerful Prativindhya, like a crazy elephant against another crazy one. Enraged, Yudhishthira's son pierced Soubala with sharp arrows in that battle, like Maghavan against a danava. In that battle, Shakuni also wounded the immensely wise Prativindhya with straight-tufted arrows. O Indra among kings! In that battle, Shrutakarma[51] attacked the valiant maharatha, Sudakshina from Kamboja. In that battle, Sudakshina pierced Sahadeva's maharatha son, but could not make him waver, like Mount Mainaka. At that, Shrutakarma was enraged and oppressed the maharatha from Kamboja with many arrows, wounding him all over his body. In that battle, the angry Iravan took great care and attacked the intolerant Shrutayusha.[52] In the encounter, Arjuna's maharatha son killed the horses of his opponent and roared loudly, being honoured by the soldiers. In that battle, the wrathful Shrutayusha used a supreme club to kill the horses of Phalguna's son and they continued to fight. In the battle, Vinda and Anuvinda from Avanti advanced against the valiant maharatha, Kuntibhoja, who was at the head of his army, together with his son. We witnessed the extraordinary valour of those

[49]Prativindhya, Sutasoma, Shrutakarma, Shatanika and Shrutasena were Droupadi's sons, respectively born from Yudhishthira, Bhima, Arjuna, Nakula and Sahadeva.

[50]Chekitana was the son of King Dhrishtaketu from Kekaya. Susharma was the king of Trigarta.

[51]There is an error. Since this is Sahadeva's son, this should actually read Shrutasena, not Shrutakarma.

[52]Iravan was Arjuna's son, through Ulupi. Shrutayusha was a rakshasa who fought on the Kourava side.

from Avanti there. They stationed themselves calmly, though they faced a large army. Anuvinda hurled a club at Kuntibhoja. But Kuntibhoja swiftly repulsed him with a torrent of arrows. Kuntibhoja's son pierced Vinda with an arrow. But he also pierced him in return and it was wonderful. O revered one! In that battle, together with their soldiers, the five brothers from Kekaya fought with the five from Gandhara, together with their soldiers. Your son Virabahu fought with Virata's son, Uttara, supreme among charioteers, and pierced him with sharp arrows. Uttara also pierced the steadfast one with sharp arrows. O king! In that battle, the king of Chedi attacked Uluka.[53] Uluka pierced him with sharp and feathered arrows. O lord of the earth! The battle that they fought was terrible in form. Unable to vanquish each other, they angrily wounded each other.

'"Thus, in that battle, there were thousands of duels between chariots, elephants, horses and infantry, on their side and on ours. For a short instant, the field of battle looked beautiful. O king! But it soon became maddening and nothing could be seen. In that battle, elephants were against elephants and chariots against chariots. Horses were against horses and infantry against infantry. The battle became extremely difficult and confusing. In that battle, large numbers of warriors attacked each other. The assembled devarshis, siddhas and charanas witnessed that terrible battle, equal to that between the gods and the asuras. O revered one! Thousands of elephants and chariots and masses of horses and foot soldiers behaved in a contrary way.[54] O tiger among men! It was repeatedly seen that chariots, elephants, cavalry and infantry fought with each other."'

Chapter 904(44)

'Sanjaya said, "O king! O descendant of the Bharata lineage! I will now tell you about the hundreds and thousands of bouts

[53]Uluka was Shakuni's son.

[54]Elephants should fight with elephants, horses with horses, chariots with chariots, etc. But this was not observed.

that took place there, without showing any considerations of respect.
The son did not recognize the father, or the father the son born
from his own loins. A brother did not recognize a brother there,
nor a sister's son his maternal uncle. The maternal uncle did not
recognize his sister's son, nor did a friend recognize his friend there.
The Pandavas and the Kurus fought as if they were possessed. O bull
among the Bharata lineage! Some tigers among men used chariots
to bring down and shatter chariots, destroying their yokes. Axles of
chariots clashed against axles of chariots. Seats clashed against seats
of chariots. Some united against others who were united. They all
wished to rob each other of their lives. Some chariots could not move,
because they were obstructed by other chariots. Gigantic elephants
had their temples shattered and fell down on other elephants. They
were angry and used their tusks to attack each other in many places.
Elephants adorned with decorations[55] and standards attacked the
elephants of the enemy. O great king! These were giant elephants
that encountered other powerful ones. Injured by the tusks, they
were greatly distressed and roared. But these were disciplined because
of their training. Urged by pikes and goads, elephants that were in
musth attacked others that were in musth. Attacked by those that
were in musth, giant elephants ran away everywhere, shrieking like
cranes. There were trained elephants, with shattered temples and
mouths. These supreme elephants were wounded by swords, lances
and iron arrows. Pierced in their innards, they fell down and lost
their lives. Others uttered terrible roars and ran away in different
directions. The foot soldiers who guarded the elephants were armed
and possessed broad chests. They had swords, bows, unblemished
battleaxes, clubs, maces, catapults,[56] lances, iron bludgeons and sharp
and polished cutlasses.[57] O great king! Grasping these, they could be
seen to run in every direction, desirous of taking each other's lives.
The resplendent cutlasses were steeped in the blood of brave men

[55]Actually, wooden structures on the elephants, howdahs.
[56]*Bhindipala.* Alternatively, short javelin.
[57]*Nistrimsha.* Rishti and nistrimsha are both swords. We have used cutlass
for nistrimsha only to distinguish it from rishti.

and seemed to shine brilliantly. The swords were whirled by the
arms of brave ones and made a whizzing sound. As they descended
on the inner organs of enemies, they generated a tremendous sound.
They were shattered by clubs and maces and by supreme swords.
They were gored by the tusks of the tusked ones and wounded by
the tusks. O descendant of the Bharata lineage! In every place, large
numbers of men were oppressed and let out sounds of lamentation,
like those of men who are about to die.

'"Those who were on extremely swift horses, with tails like those
of swans, attacked others on horses. They hurled giant spears that
were decorated with gold and were swift, sharp and polished. They
descended like snakes. There were some great rathas on swift horses.
They sliced off the heads of other brave rathas who were on horses.
A ratha on a horse approached many who were within the shooting
distance of an arrow and used straight-tufted iron arrows to kill them.
There were crazy elephants that were like mountains or clouds and
were adorned with gold. They brought down horses and crushed
them with their feet. The elephants were struck on their humps
and their flanks. They were pierced by spikes and some of them
roared in agony. There was terrible confusion there. Many supreme
elephants suddenly threw down horses and their riders and crushed
them. Using the tips of their tusks, elephants flung down horses and
their riders. They crushed chariots and their standards and roamed
around. There were some giant male elephants, extremely energetic
because of the musth strewing down their temples. They slew horses
and riders with their trunks and their feet. Some horses and chariots
were flung away by the elephants. All of them were thrown away
in all the directions, with a loud noise. Swift, polished and sharp
arrows were like serpents. They descended on the bodies of men and
riders and pierced their iron armour. Polished javelins were hurled
by the arms of brave ones. O lord of the earth! They were terrible,
like giant meteors, and descended. Blazing swords were taken out
from sheaths made out of the skins of tigers and leopards. Once
unsheathed, these polished swords were used to kill the enemies in
battle. There were soldiers who had their sides sliced open. Despite
this, they angrily attacked with swords, shields and battleaxes. Some

were pierced by javelins. Others were cut down by battleaxes. Some were destroyed by elephants. Others were oppressed by horses. Some were crushed by the wheels of chariots. Others were brought down by sharp arrows. O king! Thus oppressed, the men loudly called for their relatives, their sons, fathers, brothers and kin, their maternal uncles and nephews. In that field of battle, some others called for others.[58] O descendant of the Bharata lineage! A large number of combatants lost their weapons. Their thighs were broken and their hands and arms torn apart. Their sides were shattered. Some were still alive and could be seen to be screaming from thirst. O lord of the earth! They had only a little bit of strength left and were overcome by thirst. They had fallen down on the ground in that battle and asked for water. O descendant of the Bharata lineage! Others were weak and were covered in blood. Assembled there, they censured themselves and your son.

'"O venerable one! But there were other brave kshatriyas. Having acted in enmity towards each other, they did not cast away their weapons. Nor did they lament. They roared in delight towards each other. Lying there, they could be seen to bite their teeth with their own lips. Their bows were contracted and they glanced towards each other. There were others who suffered from wounds and had been oppressed by arrows. But even then, those extremely strong ones bore the pain silently and were firm in their hearts. There were other brave charioteers who had lost their chariots in battle. They had been thrown down and wounded by the supreme elephants. Having been brought down, they asked for the chariots of others. O great king! They were as beautiful as blossoming kimshuka trees. Many terrible cries were heard in every division of the armies. It was an extremely terrible encounter that destroyed heroes. In that battle, the father killed the son and the son killed the father. The sister's son killed the maternal uncle and the maternal uncle killed the sister's son. O king! A friend killed a friend and a relative killed a relative. Thus was the battle between the Kurus and the Pandavas. No mercy was shown in that fearful and terrible encounter. On encountering Bhishma, the

[58]That is, other relatives.

army of the Parthas trembled. O bull among the Bharata lineage!
The mighty-armed one's standard was adorned with five stars and a
palm tree. It was made out of silver. O king! When ascended on his
great chariot, Bhishma looked like the moon on Meru."'

Chapter 905(45)

'Sanjaya said, "O bull among the Bharata lineage! Most of that
terrible forenoon passed, an extremely terrible time that was
destructive of great warriors. Then, urged by your son, Durmukha,
Kritavarma, Kripa, Shalya and Vivimshati went to Bhishma and began
to protect him. Protected by those five atirathas, the maharatha[59]
penetrated the Pandava army. O descendant of the Bharata lineage!
Bhisma's palm standard was seen to slice through the Chedis, the
Kashis, the Karushas and the Panchalas in diverse ways. Bhishma's
bow and weapons then sliced off the heads[60] with extremely forceful,
straight-tufted and broad-headed arrows. O bull among the Bharata
lineage! As the chariot travelled along its path, Bhishma seemed to
be dancing. Some elephants were pierced by him in their vital parts
and screamed piteously.

'"Abhimanyu was extremely enraged and rushed towards
Bhishma's chariot, stationed on his own chariot, which was yoked to
supreme and tawny horses. His standard was embellished with pure
gold and looked like a karnikara.[61] He attacked Bhishma and those
supreme charioteers.[62] Striking the palm standard with sharp arrows,
the brave one fought with Bhishma and his followers. He pierced
Kritavarma with one and Shalya with five arrows and weakened his
great-grandfather with nine sharp arrows. He drew his bow back
fully and released an arrow that sliced down the standard embellished

[59]Bhishma.
[60]Of enemies.
[61]Tree, the Indian laburnum.
[62]The five who were protecting Bhishma.

with gold.[63] With a broad-headed and straight-tufted arrow that was capable of penetrating every kind of armour, he severed the head from the body of Durmukha's charioteer. With another broad-headed arrow, he sliced down Kripa's bow, decorated with gold. With many sharp and pointed arrows, he wounded all of them. The extremely angry maharatha seemed to be dancing around. On witnessing his dexterity, even the gods were satisfied. On seeing the success with which Krishna's son[64] hit the targets, all the charioteers, with Bhishma at the forefront, thought that he possessed the spirit of Dhananjaya himself. His bow twanged like Gandiva and when it was stretched and stretched again in every direction, it seemed to whirl like a circle of fire. Bhishma, the destroyer of enemy heroes, advanced towards him with great speed and in that battle, pierced Arjuna's son with nine arrows. He used three broad-headed arrows to slice down the standard of the immensely energetic one. Bhishma, rigid in his bows, used three broad-headed arrows to strike his charioteer. O venerable one! Kritavarma, Kripa and Shalya also pierced Krishna's son. But they could not make him tremble and he was as firm as Mount Mainaka. The brave one was surrounded by maharathas who were on the side of Dhritarashtra's son. Nevertheless, Krishna's son showered down arrows on those five charioteers. He repulsed their great weapons with showers of arrows. Releasing arrows towards Bhishma, Krishna's son roared loudly. O king! When he endeavoured thus in battle and released arrows towards Bhishma, his strength of arms was seen to be extremely great. Though he was valorous, Bhishma showered arrows at him. But in that battle, he sliced down all the arrows released from Bhishma's bow. In that encounter, the brave one used nine invincible arrows to slice down Bhishma's standard. At this, the people let out a loud shout. O descendant of the Bharata lineage! It[65] was made out of silver and was decorated with gold. It was extremely large and bore the mark of a palm. Sliced down by the arrows of Subhadra's son, it fell down on the ground. O bull

[63]Bhishma's standard.
[64]Krishna is also one of Arjuna's names and Abhimanyu was Arjuna's son.
[65]Bhishma's standard.

among the Bharata lineage! On seeing that the standard had been brought down by the arrows of Subhadra's son, Bhima roared loudly, so that Subhadra's son might be encouraged. Then, in that extremely terrible moment, the extremely strong Bhishma made many great and celestial weapons manifest themselves. The great-grandfather, immeasurable in his soul, enveloped Subhadra's son with hundreds and thousands of arrows with drooping tufts.

'"At this, ten great maharatha archers from the Pandava side swiftly advanced on their chariots, so as to protect Subhadra's son. O lord of the earth! They were Virata and his son, Parshata Dhrishtadyumna, Bhima, the five from Kekaya and Satyaki. When they advanced towards him in battle, Bhishma, Shantanu's son, pierced Panchala[66] with three and Satyaki with sharp arrows. He drew his bow completely back and used a sharp and tufted arrow, like a razor at the tip, to slice down Bhimasena's standard. O supreme among men! Bhima's standard was decorated with gold and bore the mark of a lion. Brought down by Bhisma, it fell down from the chariot. At this, in that battle, Bhima pierced Bhishma, Shantanu's son, with three arrows, Kripa with one and Kritavarma with eight. Riding on an elephant, Virata's son, Uttara, attacked the king who was the lord of Madra.[67] As that king of elephants advanced towards his chariot in that battle, irresistible in force, Shalya countered it. However, that king of elephants was enraged. It placed its leg on the yoke of the chariot and killed the four large and well-trained horses. Though the horses were killed, the lord of Madra remained on his chariot. So as to kill Uttara, he hurled a lance that was like a serpent. His[68] body and armour were pierced and he was submerged in great darkness.[69] With the grip on goad and lance loosened, he fell down from the shoulder of the elephant. Shalya grasped a sword and descended from his supreme chariot. With great valour, he sliced off the great trunk of that king among elephants. With its inner parts

[66]Dhrishtadyumna.
[67]Shalya.
[68]Uttara's.
[69]He lost his senses.

pierced by showers of arrows and with its trunk severed, the elephant let out a terrible roar. It fell down on the ground and died. Having performed this extraordinary deed, the maharatha lord of Madra swiftly ascended Kritavarma's radiant chariot.

"'On seeing that his brother Uttara had been slain and seeing that Shalya was stationed resplendently with Kritavarma, Shankha, Virata's son, blazed in anger, like a fire into which oblations have been poured. Wishing to kill Shalya, the lord of Madra, the powerful one extended his great bow, decorated with gold and bearing the mark of the sun, and attacked him. Surrounded on all sides by a large number of chariots, he advanced towards Shalya's chariot and enveloped him with a shower of arrows. On seeing him advance, with the valour of a crazy elephant, seven of your charioteers surrounded him from every direction,[70] wishing to protect the lord of Madra, who seemed to be advancing into the jaws of death. Roaring like thunder, the mighty-armed Bhishma grasped a bow that was as long as a palm tree and attacked Shankha in that battle. When they saw the immensely strong and great archer, the army of the Pandavas trembled, like a boat that is tossed around in a storm. Then Arjuna swiftly advanced and placed himself in front of Shankha, so as to protect him from Bhishma and a battle raged between the two. There were great cries and exclamations as the two warriors fought each other in that encounter. The energy of one seemed to merge into the energy of the other[71] and everyone was astounded. Then Shalya grasped a club in his hand and descended from his great chariot. O bull among the Bharata lineage! He killed Shankha's four horses. When his horses were slain, Shankha alighted from his chariot and grasping a sword, ran towards Bibhatsu's[72] chariot. Climbing onto it, he found peace again. Many shafted arrows were released from Bhishma's chariot and they covered everything on earth and in the

[70]The Critical edition abruptly excises some shlokas here, so that we never get to know who these seven were, or their subsequent bouts. They were Brihadbala, Jayatsena, Rukmaratha, Vinda, Anuvinda, Sudakshina and Jayadratha.

[71]The energies of Bhishma and Arjuna.

[72]Bibhatsu is Arjuna's name.

sky. Bhishma, foremost among the wielders of weapons, used his
arrows to kill large numbers of Panchalas, Matsyas, Kekayas and
Prabhadrakas. Abandoning the battle with Pandava Savyasachi, he[73]
rushed towards Panchala Drupada, surrounded by his soldiers. O
king! He enveloped his beloved relative with many arrows. Like a
forest consumed by a fire at the end of winter, Drupada's soldiers
were seen to be consumed by those arrows. Bhishma was stationed in
that battle, like a fire without smoke. He was like the sun at midday,
scorching with his energy. The Pandava warriors were incapable of
glancing at Bhishma. Oppressed by fear, the Pandavas looked in every
direction. But without seeing a protector, they were like cattle afflicted
by the cold. O descendant of the Bharata lineage! The soldiers were
slaughtered in large numbers and retreated in despondence. The
Pandava troops uttered great sounds of lamentation. Shantanu's
son, Bhishma, held a bow that was always drawn in the form of a
circle. He released flaming arrows that were like poisonous snakes.
Rigid in his vows, he created a continuous stream of arrows in every
direction. O descendant of the Bharata lineage! After indicating
which one he would target, he killed many Pandava rathas. When
the soldiers were crushed and shattered in every way, the sun set
and nothing could be seen. O bull among the Bharata lineage! On
seeing Bhishma stationed in that great battle, the Parthas withdrew
their soldiers."'

Chapter 906(46)

'Sanjaya said, "O bull among the Bharata lineage! When the
troops were withdrawn on the first day, Duryodhana was
delighted at having seen the enraged Bhishma in battle. With all
his brothers and all the lords of the earth who were on his side,
Dharmaraja swiftly went to Janardana. O king! Having witnessed

[73]Bhishma.

Bhishma's valour and overcome with great sorrow as he reflected
on his defeat, he spoke to Varshneya. 'O Krishna! Behold the great
archer Bhishma, whose valour is terrible. He consumes my soldiers
with his arrows, like a fire consumes dry grass. How can we possibly
glance at that great-souled one? He is licking up my soldiers, like a
fire fed with oblations. On seeing that immensely strong tiger among
men, armed with a bow, my soldiers are afflicted with arrows and
flee. The angry Yama, the wielder of the vajra, Varuna with the
noose and Kubera with the club can be vanquished in battle. But
the immensely energetic and greatly strong Bhishma is incapable of
being conquered. Without a boat, I am immersed in the fathomless
waters of Bhishma. O Keshava! Because of the weakness of my own
intelligence, I have encountered Bhishma. O Govinda! It is better
for me to retire to the forest and dwell there. I should not offer all
these lords of the earth to death, in Bhishma's form. O Krishna!
Bhishma is knowledgeable about great weapons and he will destroy
my soldiers. Like insects dash into a blazing fire and are destroyed,
my soldiers will advance towards their destruction. O Varshneya! I
have resorted to valour for the sake of a kingdom and am heading
towards destruction. My brave brothers are afflicted, oppressed
by arrows. Because of me and because of affection towards their
brother, they have been dislodged from their kingdom and from
happiness. We place a great value on life and now, life seems to be
extremely difficult to attain. For the remaining part of my life, I
will perform severe austerities. O Keshava! I will not bring about
the destruction of my friends in battle. With his divine weapons,
the immensely strong Bhishma incessantly kills many of my armed
rathas, who are themselves foremost among the wielders of arms.
O Madhava! Swiftly tell me what should be done for my own
welfare. I see Savyasachi stationed in battle, as if he was a neutral
spectator. Bhima alone remembers the dharma of kshatriyas. Using
the valour of his arms, the mighty-armed one fights to the best of
his capability. To the best of his capacity, this great-minded one kills
warriors with his club. He performs difficult deeds on elephants,
chariots, horses and infantry. O venerable one! But even if he were to
fight for a hundred years, in a fair fight, this brave one is incapable

of destroying the soldiers of the enemy. This friend of yours[74] is alone knowledgeable about all weapons. On seeing us consumed by Bhishma and the great-souled Drona, he looks on with indifference. Bhishma's divine weapons, and those of the great-souled Drona, are repeatedly consuming all the kshatriyas. O Krishna! Such is Bhishma's valour that, if he is enraged, together with all the kings on his side, he will certainly annihilate us. O lord of yoga! Look for a maharatha and great archer who can pacify Bhishma in battle, like clouds of rain against a conflagration. O Govinda! It is through your favours that the Pandavas will kill their enemies, regain their own kingdom and find delight with their relatives.' Having said this, the great-souled Partha remained silent for a long time, deep in reflection and with his senses robbed by misery.

'"On learning that Pandava was oppressed by sorrow, with his senses robbed by unhappiness, Govinda spoke, delighting all the Pandavas. 'O foremost among the Bharata lineage! Do not sorrow. You should not sorrow when all your brothers are brave and archers who are famous in all the worlds. O king! I am engaged in ensuring your welfare and so are maharatha Satyaki, the aged Virata and Drupada and Parshata Dhrishtadyumna. O supreme among kings! So are all these kings and their soldiers. O lord of the earth! They are waiting for your favours and are devoted to you. The immensely strong Parshata Dhrishtadyumna has always been engaged in your welfare and doing that which pleases you. He has been appointed as overall commander. The mighty-armed Shikhandi is certain to bring about Bhishma's death.' Having heard this, the king spoke to maharatha Dhrishtadyumna, in that assembly and in Vasudeva's hearing. 'O Dhrishtadyumna! O venerable one! Listen to what I am telling you. You should not transgress the words that I will speak. With Vasudeva's approval, you are our supreme commander. O bull among men! You are the commander of the soldiers of Pandu, just as in earlier times, Kartikeya always was that of the gods. O tiger among men! Display your valour and kill the Kouravas. O venerable one! O bull among men! I will follow you, Bhima and Krishna,

---

[74]Arjuna.

together with the sons of Madri and the armoured sons of Droupadi, and the foremost among all the other lords of the earth.' Delighting everyone, Dhrishtadyumna replied, 'O Partha! In earlier times, I have been ordained by Shambhu as the one who will kill Drona. O lord of the earth! I will now fight in battle with Bhishma, Drona, Shalya, Jayadratha and all the others intoxicated at the prospect of battle.' When that great archer, the Parshata who was unassailable in battle, the destroyer of brave ones and an Indra among kings, spoke in this way, everyone loudly applauded.

'"Partha told Parshata, the commander of the army, 'The vyuha[75] known by the name of Krouncharuna is the destroyer of all enemies.[76] When the gods and the asuras fought in earlier times, Brihaspati told this to Indra. Therefore, deploy this battle formation, which is destructive of enemy soldiers. This has not been seen before. Let the kings, together with the Kurus, now see it.' Having been thus addressed by that god among men, like Vishnu speaking to the wielder of the vajra, when it was morning, he placed Dhananjaya in the forefront of the entire army. His[77] standard had been constructed by Vishvakarma on Indra's[78] instruction and it was extremely beautiful as it fluttered in the path of the sun. It was decorated with flags and possessed the complexion of Indra's weapon.[79] It coursed through the sky like a traveller of the skies and was like a city of the gandharvas. O venerable one! It seemed to be dancing along, along the path that the chariot took. Partha, the wielder of Gandiva, was adorned with this jewel. He was adorned with it, like the self-creating one[80] is with the sun. King Drupada was at the head, surrounded by a large army. O lord of men! Kuntibhoja and Chedi were the two eyes.[81] O

---

[75]A vyuha is the arrangement of troops in battle formation.

[76]Krouncha is a curlew or osprey. So this vyuha was in the form of a bird.

[77]Arjuna's.

[78]The text uses the name Puruhuta. Puruhuta is one of Indra's names and means one who is worshipped by many.

[79]In this context, by Indra's weapon, one means Indra's bow. The rainbow is described as Indra's bow. Hence, the standard had the complexion of a rainbow.

[80]Brahma.

[81]Of the bird.

bull among the Bharata lineage! Dasharnas, Prayagas, together with masses of Dasherakas, Anupakas and Kiratas were the neck. O king! Together with Patachcharas, Hundas, Pouravakas and Nishadas, Yudhishthira was the back. Bhimasena, Parshata Dhrishtadyumna, Droupadi's sons, Abhimanyu and maharatha Satyaki were the wings. O descendant of the Bharata lineage! There were Pishachas, Daradas, Pundras, together with Kundivishas, Madakas, Ladakas, Tanganas, the further Tanganas, Bahlikas, Tittiras, Cholas and Pandyas. O king! These countries formed the right wing. O descendant of the Bharata lineage! Agniveshyas, Jagatundas, Paladashas, Shabaras, Tumbupas, Vatsas, together with the Nakulas,[82] Nakula and Sahadeva resorted to the left wing. There were ten thousand chariots on the joints of the wings, a hundred thousand on the head, a hundred million and twenty thousand on the back and one hundred and seventy thousand on the neck. O king! There were many elephants, like mobile mountains, on the joints of the wings, the wings and the tips of the wings. The rear was protected by Virata, together with Kekaya, the king of Kashi and Shaibya[83] and thirty thousand chariots. O descendant of the Bharata lineage! Thus did the Pandavas constitute a great vyuha and having clad themselves in armour and stationed themselves in battle, waited for the sun to rise. Their white umbrellas were radiant and had the hue of the sun. They were giant and unblemished and adorned their elephants and chariots.'"

Chapter 907(47)

'Sanjaya said, "O venerable one! O descendant of the Bharata lineage! The infinitely energetic Partha created that extremely terrible battle formation. On seeing that impenetrable and great Krouncha vyuha, your son went to the preceptor, Kripa, Shalya,

[82]This is Naakulas, not to be confused with the Pandava Nakula.
[83]The king of Chedi.

Somadatta's son, Vikarna and Ashvatthama, together with Duhshasana and all his brothers and the many brave warriors who were assembled there for the battle. At that time, he spoke these words, delighting all of them. 'All of you are armed with many weapons and are learned in the sacred texts and in arms. You are maharathas. Alone, each one of you is capable of slaying the sons of Pandu and their soldiers in battle, and you are united. Our forces are protected by Bhishma and are unlimited. O supreme among kings! Their forces are limited. Let the Samsthanas, Shurasenas, Venikas, Kukkuras, Arevakas, Trigartas and Yavanas remain with Shatrunjaya,[84] Duhshasana, the brave Vikarna, Nanda, Upanandaka[85] and Chitrasena,[86] together with the Panibhadrakas and with their respective troops at the forefront, protect Bhishma.' O venerable one! Then Drona, Bhishma and your sons created a giant vyuha to counter that of the Pandus. Like the lord of the gods, Bhishma advanced, leading a large army and surrounded by a large number of soldiers. O lord of the earth! The powerful and great archer, Bharadvaja's son,[87] followed him, with the Kuntalas, Dasharnas, Magadhas, Vidarbhas, Mekalas, Karnas[88] and Pravaranas. With all these soldiers, Bhishma was resplendent. The Gandharas, Sindhus, Souviras, Shibis and Vasatis and Shakuni and his own soldiers, protected Bharadvaja's son. With the Ashvatakas, Vikarnas,[89] Sharmilas, Kosalas, Daradas, Chuchupas, Kshudrakas and Malavas, Soubala and his soldiers and with all his brothers, King Duryodhana cheerfully advanced. O venerable one! Bhurishrava, Shala, Shalya, Bhagadatta and Vinda and Anuvinda from Avanti guarded the left flank. Somadatta's son, Susharma, Sudakshina from Kamboja, Shatayu and Shrutayu guarded the right flank. Ashvatthama, Kripa and Satvata Kritavarma guarded the rear, with a large number of soldiers. Their rear was protected

---

[84]One of Karna's sons.

[85]Vikarna, Nanda and Upanandaka are Duryodhana's brothers.

[86]Not to be confused with Chitrasena, the king of the gandharvas.

[87]Drona.

[88]Not to be confused with Karna.

[89]Not to be confused with Vikarna.

by kings from many countries and Ketuman, Vasumana and the powerful son of the king of Kashi.

'"O descendant of the Bharata lineage! All of your soldiers were delighted at the prospect of battle. They cheerfully blew on their conch shells and roared like lions. On hearing these sounds, the aged grandfather of the Kurus was delighted. The powerful one roared like a lion and blew on his conch shell. At this, conch shells, kettledrums, many different kinds of drums and battle-drums began to sound and there was a tumultuous uproar.[90] Hrishikesha and Dhananjaya were stationed on a giant chariot drawn by white horses and respectively blew on the excellent conch shells Panchajanya and Devadatta, decorated with gold and jewels. Vrikodara, terrible in deeds, blew on the giant conch shell Poundra. Kunti's son, King Yudhishthira, blew on Anantavijaya. Nakula blew on Sughosa and Sahadeva on Manipushpaka. The king of Kashi, Shaibya, maharatha Shikhandi, Dhrishtadyumna, Virata, maharatha Satyaki, the great archer from Panchala[91] and Droupadi's five sons—all of them blew on giant conch shells and roared like lions. The extremely loud and tumultuous roar created by those warriors echoed on earth and in the sky. O great king! Thus did the cheerful Kurus and Pandavas assemble again for battle, with a desire to torment each other in the encounter."'

Chapter 908(48)

'Dhritarashtra asked, "Having assembled in battle formation in this way, what did mine and those of the others do? How did those supreme among wielders of weapons strike?"

'Sanjaya replied, "All the troops were arranged in battle formation. The warriors were armoured and waited. The standards were raised up. On seeing his army, which was like the limitless ocean, your son,

---

[90]*Bheri*, peshi and *anaka* are the names of different kinds of drums.
[91]Meaning Drupada.

King Duryodhana, stationed himself in its midst and spoke to all the warriors on your side. 'You are armoured. Now fight.' Their minds were full of cruelty and they had given up the desire to live. With their standards raised, all of them rushed against the Pandavas. A terrible battle started and it made the body hair stand up. Your chariots and elephants were mixed up with that of the enemy. Charioteers released sharp arrows that were full of energy and shafted with gold. These descended on elephants and horses. When the battle commenced, the mighty-armed and armoured Bhishma, terrible in his valour, grasped a bow. The aged grandfather of the Kurus advanced and showered arrows on those brave men—Subhadra's son,[92] Bhimasena, Shini's maharatha son,[93] Kekaya, Virata, Parshata Dhrishtadyumna and the lords of Chedi and Matsya. At the encounter with that brave one, the great vyuha[94] wavered. The battle that was fought by all the soldiers was extremely great. Many horse-riders, charioteers and the foremost among elephants were slain. Masses of chariots on the Pandava side began to flee.

'"Arjuna, tiger among men, saw maharatha Bhishma. He angrily told Varshneya, 'Go where the grandfather is. O Varshneya! It is evident that when he is extremely enraged, engaged in Duryodhana's welfare, this Bhishma will destroy my army. O Janardana! Protected by the one who wields a firm bow, Drona, Kripa, Shalya, Vikarna and the sons of Dhritarashtra, with Duryodhana at the forefront, will slaughter the Panchalas. O Janardana! For the sake of our soldiers, I will go where Bhishma is.' Vasudeva replied, 'O Dhananjaya! O brave one! Be careful. I will take you towards the grandfather's chariot.' O lord of men! Having said this, Shouri[95] took the chariot, famous in the worlds, towards Bhishma's chariot. The horses had the complexion of cranes.[96] As it advanced, many flags fluttered. The standard was raised and the extremely terrible ape roared on

---

[92]Abhimanyu.
[93]Satyaki.
[94]Of the Pandavas.
[95]Krishna.
[96]This is a description of Arjuna's chariot.

it. The chariot was as radiant as the sun and it roared like a giant
cloud. Pandava slaughtered the soldiers of the Kouravas and the
Shurasenas and the one who dispelled the sorrow of his well-wishers
swiftly advanced to the battle. He descended with the force of an
intoxicated elephant, using his arrows to bring down warriors in that
battle. Shantanu's son, Bhishma, was protected by warriors who were
led by Saindhava[97] and those from the east, Souvira and Kekaya and
encountered him with force. Who other than the grandfather of the
Kurus and the two rathas Drona and Vaikartana[98] are capable of
withstanding the wielder of the Gandiva in battle?

"'O great king! Bhishma, the grandfather of the Kouravas, pierced
Arjuna with seventy-seven iron arrows. O king! Drona pierced him
with twenty-five arrows, Kripa with fifty, Duryodhana with sixty-
four, Shalya with nine arrows and Vikarna pierced Pandava with ten
broad-headed arrows. But though he was struck in every direction
with sharp arrows, the mighty-armed and great archer did not suffer
and was like a mountain that has been pierced. O bull among the
Bharata lineage! Kiriti's[99] soul is beyond measure. In return, he
struck Bhishma with twenty-five arrows, Kripa with nine, Drona,
tiger among men, with sixty arrows, Vikarna with three, Artayani[100]
with three and the king[101] with five arrows. Satyaki, Virata, Parshata
Dhrishtadyumna, Droupadi's sons and Abhimanyu surrounded
Dhananjaya. The great archer Drona was engaged in ensuring
Gangeya's[102] welfare. Panchala,[103] supported by the Somakas,
advanced against him. Bhishma, best among charioteers, swiftly
pierced Pandava with eighty sharp arrows. At this, your warriors
were extremely delighted. The powerful Dhananjaya was a lion
among charioteers. On hearing these roars of applause, he cheerfully

[97]Jayadratha.
[98]Karna.
[99]Kiriti is one of Arjuna's names.
[100]Another name for Shalya.
[101]Duryodhana.
[102]Gangeya is another name for Bhishma.
[103]Dhrishtadyumna.

penetrated their midst and having done that, sported with his bow and took aim at those maharathas. Dhananjaya reached the midst of those lions among charioteers. On seeing that his own soldiers were tormented by Partha in that battle, King Duryodhana, lord of men, spoke to Bhishma. 'O father![104] Pandu's powerful son is accompanied by Krishna. O Gangeya! He is destroying our soldiers and severing our roots, even though you and Drona, supreme among charioteers, are alive. It is because of you that maharatha Karna has discarded his weapons and does not fight in this battle with Partha, though he always has my welfare in mind. O Gangeya! Act so that Phalguna may be killed.' O king! Having been thus addressed, your father, Devavrata,[105] exclaimed, 'Shame on the dharma of kshatriyas,' and advanced towards Partha's chariot.

'"O king! All the kings saw that these two, both drawn by white horses, were ready to do battle. O descendant of the Bharata lineage! They roared like lions and blew on their conch shells. O venerable one! When Bhishma was stationed in battle, Drona's son,[106] Duryodhana and your son Vikarna surrounded him. All the Pandavas surrounded Dhananjaya. When they were stationed in battle, a great duel commenced. In that battle, Gangeya pierced Partha with nine arrows and Arjuna pierced him back with ten arrows that penetrated the inner organs. O Kourava! Arjuna prided himself on his skills in battle. With a thousand well-directed arrows, Pandava enveloped Bhishma in every direction. But Bhishma, Shantanu's son, repulsed Partha's net of arrows with his own net of arrows. Both of them were extremely cheerful. Both of them found delight in the battle. They fought against each other, each desiring to counter the other. But neither was superior to the other. The net of arrows released from Bhishma's bow were seen to be repulsed by Arjuna's arrows. In that fashion, the nets of arrows released from Arjuna's bow were all cut down by Gangeya's arrows and fell down on the ground. Arjuna pierced Bhishma with

---

[104]The word used is tata. While this means father, it is affectionately used for anyone who is senior.

[105]Bhishma.

[106]Ashvatthama.

twenty-five sharp arrows. And in that battle, Bhishma pierced Partha
with thirty arrows. Those extremely strong ones wounded each other's
horses, pierced the standards and struck the chariots and wheels of
the chariots. The destroyers of enemies seemed to be playing. O great
king! Bhishma, supreme among the wielders of weapons, was enraged.
With three arrows, he pierced Vasudeva between the breasts. O king!
Pierced by Bhishma's arrows, Achyuta Madhusudana was resplendent
in that battle, like a blossoming kimshuka. On seeing Madhava
thus pierced, Arjuna became extremely angry. In that encounter, he
pierced Gangeya's charioteer with three arrows. In that encounter,
the brave ones took aim against each other and endeavoured to kill
each other, but did not succeed. The chariots advanced and retreated,
traversing wonderful circles. Both charioteers displayed their skill
and dexterity in many ways. O king! In seeking their objective, the
maharathas repeatedly changed their positions and adopted different
paths, so that they could strike each other. Both of them roared like
lions and blew on their conch shells. Loud noises could be heard as
the maharathas twanged their bows. There was the sound of conch
shells and roars from the axles of the chariots. The earth began to
tremble, as if there was an earthquake underneath. O bull among the
Bharata lineage! No one could detect a weakness in either of them.
Both of them were powerful and valiant in battle. Each was equal
to the other. It was only through the signs that the Kouravas could
approach Bhishma and also through the signs that the sons of Pandu
could approach Partha.[107] O king! O descendant of the Bharata
lineage! On witnessing the valour displayed by these best of men in
the battle, all the beings were struck with wonder. O descendant of
the Bharata lineage! In that battle, no weakness was discernible in
either of the two, like those established in dharma. Nor could any
deceit be seen. In that battle, both became invisible because of the
nets of arrows and suddenly became visible again.

'"On witnessing the valour, the gods, together with the gandharvas,
the charanas and the rishis, spoke to each other. 'When they are

---

[107]The sense is that it was impossible to distinguish between Bhishma and
Arjuna, except through the signs on the respective standards.

enraged, neither of these maharathas is capable of being vanquished in battle, even by the gods, the asuras, the gandharvas and all the worlds. The worlds will regard this extremely marvellous battle as wonderful. Such a battle will never take place again. In the encounter, Bhishma is incapable of being vanquished by the intelligent Partha, even though he uses his bow, chariot, horses and arrows in the battle. In that fashion, in a battle, even the gods cannot conquer Pandava. Though he makes every endeavour, Bhishma cannot vanquish that archer in an encounter.' O lord of the earth! We heard these words of praise spoken about both Gangeya and Arjuna in that battle. O descendant of the Bharata lineage! While they fought, your warriors and those of the Pandaveyas, killed each other in the battle. They valiantly used polished and sharp swords, polished battleaxes, many kinds of arrows and diverse types of weapons and other arms. As long as that extremely terrible battle continued, the brave ones on either side killed one another. O king! There was a great encounter between Drona and Panchala.[108]"'

Chapter 909(49)

'Dhritarashtra said, "O Sanjaya! Tell me how the great archer Drona and Parshata Panchala fought and strove against each other in that battle. O Sanjaya! It is my view that destiny is superior to human endeavour, since Shantanu's son, Bhishma, could not vanquish Pandava in battle. When Bhishma is enraged in battle, he can destroy all mobile and immobile objects in the worlds. O Sanjaya! With his energy, why could he not escape from Pandava in that encounter?"

'Sanjaya replied, "O king! Be patient and hear about that extremely terrible battle. Pandava is incapable of being vanquished by the gods, together with Vasava. With sharp arrows, Drona wounded

[108]Dhrishtadyumna.

Dhrishtadyumna and used a broad-headed arrow to bring down his
charioteer from the safety of the chariot. O venerable one! Using
the best of arrows, the wrathful one wounded Dhrishtadyumna's
four horses. The brave Dhrishtadyumna smiled, and asking Drona
to wait, pierced him with nine sharp arrows. At this, Bharadvaja's
powerful son, immeasurable in his soul, enveloped the intolerant
Dhrishtadyumna with arrows. With a desire to kill Parshata, he then
grasped a terrible arrow. It was like Shakra's vajra to the touch and
resembled the staff of death. O descendant of the Bharata lineage!
On seeing that Bharadvaja's son was about to use it in battle, a
great lamentation arose from all the soldiers. We then witnessed
Dhrishtadyumna's extraordinary manliness. Like an immobile
mountain, the brave one remained stationed in battle. As the terrible
and flaming arrow rushed towards him, like his own death, he
sliced it down and unleashed a shower of arrows on Bharadvaja's
son. On witnessing that extremely difficult deed accomplished by
Dhrishtadyumna, all the Panchalas, together with the Pandavas,
were delighted and roared loudly. With a desire to kill Drona, the
valiant one then hurled a lance, decorated with gold and lapis lazuli,
with great force. On witnessing the gold-adorned lance suddenly
descending in the battle, Bharadvaja's son smiled and sliced it down
into three parts. O lord of men! Having seen that his lance had been
thus repulsed, the powerful Dhrishtadyumna unleashed a shower of
arrows in Drona's direction. But the greatly famous Drona repulsed
this shower of arrows and in the midst of this, sliced down the bow
of Drupada's son. When his bow had been sliced down in that battle,
the immensely famous and powerful one hurled a giant club towards
Drona. It was as firm as a mountain. Having been thus forcefully
hurled, the club headed towards Drona, for his destruction. We then
witnessed the extraordinary valour of Bharadvaja's son. He countered
the gold-adorned club with dexterity. Having repulsed the club,
he despatched broad-headed arrows towards Parshata. They were
extremely sharp and yellow. They were gold-tufted and had been
sharpened on stone. In that battle, they penetrated his armour and
drank his blood. Then the great-minded Dhrishtadyumna picked up
another bow. In that encounter, he used his valour to pierce Drona

with five arrows. Those two bulls among men were covered with blood. O king! They looked as beautiful as flowering kimshukas in the spring. O king! Intolerant with anger and displaying his valour at the head of his troops, Drona again sliced down the bow of Drupada's son. When the bow had been sliced down, the one with the immeasurable soul covered him with arrows with drooping tufts, like clouds raining on a mountain. He used a broad-headed arrow to bring down his charioteer from the safety of the chariot. With four sharp arrows, he brought down his four horses. He roared like a lion in that battle. With another broad-headed arrow, he sliced down the leather guard from his[109] hands. His bow was sliced down. He was without a chariot. His horses were killed. His charioteer was slain. Displaying great manliness, he tried to leap down, with a club in his hands. O descendant of the Bharata lineage! But before he could descend from his chariot, he[110] used his arrows to shatter the club into fragments and it was an extraordinary feat. The powerful one with the excellent arms[111] then grasped a large and divine sword and a huge and beautiful shield marked with the marks of one hundred moons. In a desire to kill Drona, he rushed towards him with force, like a lion looking for meat dashes towards a crazy elephant in the forest. O descendant of the Bharata lineage! We then witnessed the extraordinary manliness of Bharadvaja's son, his dexterity in the use of weapons and the strength of his arms. He repulsed Parshata with a shower of arrows. Though he was strong, he could not advance any further in that battle. We saw maharatha Dhrishtadyumna stationed there, using the shield in his hands to ward off the shower of arrows.

'"Then the mighty-armed and powerful Bhima suddenly arrived, wishing to aid the great-souled Parshata in that battle. O king! He pierced Drona with seven sharp arrows and swiftly took up Parshata on his own chariot. King Duryodhana despatched Kalinga to protect Bharadvaja's son, with a large number of soldiers. O lord of men!

[109]Dhrishtadyumna's.
[110]Drona.
[111]Dhrishtadyumna.

On the instructions of your son, that large army of Kalingas rushed towards Bhima. Drona, supreme among charioteers, abandoned Panchala and encountered and fought with the aged Virata and Drupada. In that battle, Dhrishtadyumna went to help Dharmaraja. A tumultuous battle commenced and it made the body hair stand up. This was between the Kalingas and the great-souled Bhima. It was terrible in form and awful, and was destructive of the universe."'

Chapter 910(50)

'Dhritarashtra asked, "The immensely strong and brave Bhimasena roams around with a club, like death with a staff in his hands. He is the performer of extraordinary deeds. Kalinga, the general of an army, was instructed. But with his soldiers, how did he encounter him[112] in battle?"

'Sanjaya replied, "O Indra among kings! Thus instructed by your son, the immensely strong one was protected by a large army and advanced towards Bhima's chariot. That large army of the Kalingas was full of chariots, elephants and horses and was armed with many mighty weapons. O descendant of the Bharata lineage! As the army of the Kalingas marched towards him, led by Ketuman and the son of Nishada, Bhimasena, accompanied by the Chedis, descended on it. Together with Ketuman, the angry Shrutayu[113] arranged his troops in battle formation and advanced before Bhima and Chedi in that battle. The king of Kalinga possessed many thousands of chariots. Other than Ketuman, the Nishadas had ten thousand elephants. O king! In that battle, they surrounded Bhimasena from all directions. With Bhimasena at the forefront, the Chedis, the Matsyas and the Karushas swiftly advanced against the Nishadas and the other kings. A fierce battle raged, terrible in form. In a desire to kill each other, the

---

[112]Bhima.

[113]Shrutayu was the king of Kalinga.

warriors on both sides dashed forward. The sudden battle that was
fought between Bhima and his enemies was terrible. O great king!
It was like that between Indra and the large army of the daityas. O
descendant of the Bharata lineage! As the armies fought on that field
of battle, a tumultuous noise arose, like the roar of the ocean. O lord
of the earth! The warriors killed each other. The entire ground was
like a cremation ground, strewn with flesh and blood. Driven by the
desire to kill, the warriors could not distinguish between their own
and those of the enemy. Those brave ones were invincible in battle
and even killed those from their own side. There was an extremely
fierce fight, between the few and the many.[114] O lord of the earth!
The Chedis fought with the Kalingas and the Nishadas. The extremely
strong Chedis exhibited their manliness, to the best of their capacity,
but then abandoned Bhimasena and retreated.

'"When the Chedis retreated, Pandava did not retreat. Resorting
to the strength of his own arms, he faced all the Kalingas. The
immensely strong Bhimasena remained stationary on his chariot.
He enveloped the Kalinga army with sharp arrows. The great archer
who was the king of Kalinga and his maharatha son, famous by the
name of Shakradeva, attacked Pandava with arrows. But the mighty-
armed Bhima brandished his beautiful bow. Resorting to the strength
of his arms, he fought with Kalinga. In that battle, Shakradeva shot
many arrows. In that battle, he killed Bhimasena's horses with those
arrows and showered down clouds of arrows, like a downpour at the
end of the summer. But the immensely strong Bhimasena remained
stationed on his chariot, despite his horses having been slain, and
hurled a club made completely of steel at Shakradeva.[115] O king!
The son of Kalinga was thus killed. With his standard and charioteer,
he fell down from the chariot onto the ground. On seeing that his
own son had been killed, the king of Kalinga surrounded Bhima

[114]The few were those on Bhima's side. The many were the Kalingas and
the Nishadas.

[115]The text uses the word *shaikyayasa*. This should be translated as steel.
However, it is also possible to break up the word into *shaikya* and *ayasa* and
thus translate it as sharp iron.

from every direction with many thousands of chariots. At this, the
mighty-armed Bhima discarded that giant club. He grasped a sword,
so as to accomplish a terrible deed. O bull among kings! That bull
among men also took up an unparalleled shield. It was marked with
stars and half-moons and was made out of gold. The enraged Kalinga
touched the string of his bow. He grasped a terrible arrow that was
like the venom of a serpent and despatched it at Bhimasena, desiring
to kill that lord of men. Despatched with force, that sharp arrow
descended. O king! However, Bhimasena sliced it into two with his
huge sword. He then roared in delight, frightening the soldiers. In
that encounter with Bhimasena, Kalinga became even angrier. He
swiftly hurled fourteen lances that had been sharpened on stone. O
king! But before they could reach him, the mighty-armed Pandava
used his supreme sword to swiftly cut them down in the sky.

'"The bull among men saw that Bhanuman[116] was advancing
towards him. Bhanuman enveloped Bhima with a shower of arrows
and roared powerfully, making the sound echo in the sky. But Bhima
was not prepared to tolerate that lion-like roar in that great battle.
He possessed a giant roar himself and roared loudly. At this shout,
the Kalinga soldiers were frightened. O bull among the Bharata
lineage! In that battle, they no longer regarded Bhima as human.
O great king! Bhima let out a loud roar. O venerable one! With the
sword in his hand, he used the supreme elephant's tusks[117] to climb
onto the back of that king of elephants. With that large sword, he
sliced Bhanuman down the middle. The scorcher of enemies killed
the duelling prince in this way. His sword was capable of bearing a
great load and he then made it descend on the neck of the elephant.
With its neck severed, that leader of elephants screamed and fell
down, like the summit of a mountain shattered by the battering
of the sea. O descendant of the Bharata lineage! That descendant
of the Bharata lineage then descended from the elephant that was
falling down.

[116]Shrutayu was the king of Kalinga and his sons were Bhanuman, Shakradeva
and Ketuman.
[117]Bhanuman's elephant.

"'Armoured, he stood on the ground, indomitable in soul and with a sword in his hand. He roamed around along many paths, bringing down frightened elephants. Everywhere, he looked like a whirling circle of fire. The lord slaughtered masses of horses, elephants, masses of chariots and large numbers of infantry, covering them with blood. Intoxicated with his valour, Bhima was seen in that battle, roaming around like a hawk amidst the enemy. With great force, he sliced off their bodies and their heads and also those who fought on elephants, using his sharp sword in that battle. He fought wrathfully on foot, increasing the terror of his enemies. He was like Yama at the time of destruction and confounded them. Only the foolish ones roared and advanced towards him, as he forcefully roamed around on that great field of battle, with his sword unsheathed. That powerful destroyer of enemies cut down chariots, the yokes of chariots and killed the horses yoked to chariots. Bhimasena was seen to display many different kinds of motions. He whirled around and leapt up. Pandava was seen to strike towards the sides and advance in front. The great-souled Pandava sliced down some with his supreme sword. Some shrieked as they were pierced in their inner organs and fell down, bereft of their lives. O descendant of the Bharata lineage! Many elephants had their tusks and trunks severed. Others had their temples shattered. Without any riders, they killed their own soldiers as they screamed and fell down. O king! Broken lances, the heads of the drivers of elephants, colourful seats on the elephants, the sides blazing in gold, spikes that adorned the collars,[118] standards, weapons, quivers and other machines, colourful bows, beautiful pots with fire in them, goads, different kinds of bells and hilts that were embellished with gold—all these were seen by us, already fallen, or falling down, together with the riders. The elephants were slain, with the front and rear of their bodies, and their trunks, shattered. That arena seemed to be strewn with mountains that had fallen down. Having killed many giant elephants, that bull among men began to destroy the horses. O descendant of the Bharata lineage! He brought down the foremost of horse-riders. O descendant of the Bharata lineage! The

[118]Of elephants.

battle between him and them was extremely terrible. In the great battle, we saw the hilts of swords, thongs, reins resplendent in gold, cushions, spikes, extremely expensive swords, armour, shields and colourful carpets strewn over the ground. There were also sparkling weapons with colourful inlays. He made the earth look as if it was strewn with lilies. The immensely strong Pandava leapt up and brought some charioteers down. He cut them and their standards down with his sword. The renowned one repeatedly dashed in all the directions. He astounded the people by traversing diverse paths. He killed some with his legs. He brought down others and pressed them down. He beheaded some with his sword and frightened others with his roars. The force of his thighs brought others down on the ground. Others fled on seeing him, dying out of terror.

'"Then the swift and large army of the Kalingas, which had surrounded Bhishma[119] in battle, attacked Bhimasena. O bull among the Bharata lineage! Shrutayu was at the head of the Kalinga army and on seeing him, Bhimasena attacked him. On seeing him advance, Kalinga, whose soul was immeasurable, pierced Bhimasena between the breasts with nine arrows. Struck by Kalinga's arrows, Bhimasena was like an elephant goaded with a hook and blazed in anger, like a fire into which kindling had been offered. Ashoka then brought a chariot decorated with gold and Bhimasena ascended this chariot with that supreme of charioteers.[120] Kounteya, the destroyer of enemies, swiftly climbed onto that chariot. He advanced towards Kalinga, exclaiming, 'Wait. Wait.' At this, the powerful Shrutayu was enraged and displaying the dexterity of his hands, despatched sharp arrows at Bhima. He was pierced by nine sharp arrows released from that supreme bow. O king! Having been thus wounded with force by Kalinga, the immensely famous Bhima was like a serpent that had been struck with a staff. Partha Bhima, the supreme among strong ones, was enraged and stretching his bow, killed the

[119]The Critical edition probably has a typo here. It should probably read Bhima rather than Bhishma.

[120]Bhima had earlier lost his chariot. Ashoka or Vishoka was the name of Bhima's charioteer.

king of Kalinga with seven iron arrows. With razor-like arrows, he despatched Satyadeva and Satya, the protectors of the chariot wheels of the immensely strong Kalinga, to Yama's abode. In that battle, Bhima, the one whose soul is immeasurable, then used iron arrows and sharp weapons to send Ketuman to Yama's abode.

'"The kshatriyas in the Kalinga army, with many thousands of soldiers, became wrathful and attacked the intolerant Bhimasena. O king! The Kalinga surrounded Bhimasena with lances, clubs, swords, spikes, scimitars[121] and battleaxes. They enveloped him with a terrible shower of arrows. However, though enveloped, the immensely strong Bhima swiftly grasped a club and sent seven hundred warriors to Yama's abode. The destroyer of enemies again sent two thousand Kalingas to the world of the dead and this was extraordinary. In that battle, the brave Bhima,[122] great in his vows, repeatedly killed the Kalinga soldiers. The great-souled Pandava robbed elephants of their riders. They were wounded with arrows and wandered around shrieking, like clouds struck by the wind, trampling their own soldiers. The powerful and mighty-armed Bhima blew on his conch shell and the hearts of all the Kalinga soldiers trembled. O scorcher of enemies! The Kalingas were overcome by confusion. O king! The soldiers and all the mounts trembled, as Bhima roamed around everywhere in that field of battle, like an Indra among elephants. He dashed around, following many different paths and repeatedly leaping up. Terrified of Bhimasena, confusion was engendered in the soldiers and they trembled, like a large lake that is agitated by a crocodile. Frightened by Bhima's extraordinary deeds, the brave ones fled in all directions and were then rallied again.

'"Parshata, the commander of the army of the sons of Pandu, told his soldiers to fight with all the Kalinga warriors. On hearing the words of the general, the cohorts, with Shikhandi at the forefront,

---

[121]The text states khadga and rishti. These are different types of swords. A rishti is not quite a scimitar, but we have used that term to distinguish between the two different types of swords.

[122]We have corrected this typo, since it doesn't make sense otherwise. The text says Bhishma.

came to help Bhima, with masses of chariots and warriors. Pandava
Dharmaraja followed all of them, on the back of a large number
of elephants with the complexion of clouds. Thus urging his own
soldiers, Parshata, surrounded by many virtuous men, went to guard
Bhimasena's flanks. To the king of Panchala,[123] there was no one in
the world as beloved as Bhima and Satyaki and he was engaged in
their welfare. The mighty-armed Parshata, the destroyer of enemy
warriors, saw that Bhimasena, the destroyer of enemies, was roaming
around amidst the Kalingas. O king! The scorcher of enemies uttered
many large shouts. In that battle, he blew on his conch shell and
roared like a lion. On seeing that gold-embellished chariot to which
horses with the colour of pigeons were yoked and the red standard,
Bhimasena was assured. On seeing Bhimasena, immeasurable in
his soul, attacked by the Kalingas, Dhrishtadyumna advanced to
his rescue. Beholding Satyaki from a distance, Dhrishtadyumna
and Vrikodara, the spirited and brave ones, began to fight with the
Kalingas in that battle. Swiftly advancing there, Shini's descendant,[124]
supreme among victorious ones and a bull among men, started to
protect Partha and Parshata's flanks. He grasped his bow and arrows
and created havoc there. In that encounter, he adopted a terrible form
and killed the enemy. Bhima caused a river of blood to flow there, with
mud created by the flesh and blood of the Kalingas. The immensely
strong Bhimasena traversed the impassable river that flowed between
the armies of the Kalingas and the Pandavas. O king! On seeing the
enraged Bhimasena there, the soldiers exclaimed, 'In Bhima's form,
this is death itself that is fighting with the Kalingas.' Hearing their
loud cries in battle, Bhishma, Shantanu's son, swiftly advanced
towards Bhima, surrounded by battle formations and soldiers.

   '"Satyaki, Bhimasena and Parshata Dhrishtadyumna advanced
towards Bhishma's gold-embellished chariot. In that encounter, they
surrounded Gangeya from all sides and without losing any time,
each of them pierced Bhishma with three terrible arrows. But your

---

[123]The king of Panchala is Drupada. However, the reference here is to
Dhrishtadyumna.
   [124]Satyaki.

father Devavrata, the great archer, pierced all of the striving ones
back in return, using straight-tufted arrows. Having countered those
maharathas with thousands of arrows, he used his arrows to kill
Bhima's horses, which were clad in golden armour. Although his
horses were slain, the powerful Bhimasena remained stationed on
his chariot. He powerfully hurled a spear towards Gangeya's chariot.
But in that battle, before that spear could reach him, your father
Devavrata sliced it into three and it fell down on the ground. O bull
among men! Bhimasena then grasped a large and heavy club made
out of steel[125] and leapt down from his chariot. Desiring to do that
which would bring pleasure to Bhima, Satyaki used his arrows to
swiftly bring down the aged Kuru's charioteer. When his charioteer
was killed, Bhishma, supreme among charioteers, was borne away
from the field of battle by horses that were as fleet as the wind. O
king! When the one who is great in his vows was thus carried away,
Bhimasena blazed, like a fire consuming dry grass. He remained
stationed in the midst of the Kalinga soldiers and killed them all.
O bull among the Bharata lineage! No one from your side dared to
oppose him. Dhrishtadyumna took up that supreme of charioteers
on his own chariot. In the sight of all the soldiers, he took away that
famous one. O bull among the Bharata lineage! Honoured by the
Panchalas and the Matsyas, he embraced Dhrishtadyumna and then
went to Satyaki. Satyaki, for whom his valour is truth, delightedly
told Bhimasena, while Dhrishtadyumna, tiger among men, looked
on, 'It is through good fortune that the king of Kalinga, the princes
Ketuman and Shakradeva of Kalinga and all the Kalingas have
been slain in battle. They possessed many elephants, horses and
chariots. The Kalingas possessed large battle formations. But through
the valour of your own arms, they have been vanquished by you
single-handedly.' Having said this, Shini's long-armed descendant,
the destroyer of enemies, swiftly ascended onto the chariot and
embraced Pandava. Then the maharatha again climbed onto his own

---

[125]The text uses the word shaikyayasa. This should be translated as steel.
However, it is also possible to break up the word into shaikya and ayasa and
thus translate it as sharp iron.

chariot and angrily began to kill those on your side, thus increasing Bhima's strength."'

Chapter 911(51)

'Sanjaya said, "O descendant of the Bharata lineage! When the forenoon of that day had passed, and when there was a great destruction of chariots, elephants, infantry and horse-riders, Panchala fought with three maharathas—Drona's son, Shalya and the great-souled Kripa. With ten sharp and swift arrows, Panchala's immensely strong heir[126] killed the horses of Drona's son, which were renowned in the world. Deprived of his mounts, Drona's son swiftly ascended Shalya's chariot and showered arrows on Panchala's heir. O descendant of the Bharata lineage! On seeing that Dhrishtadyumna was engaged in a duel with Drona's son, Subhadra's son quickly attacked, showering sharp arrows. O bull among men! He pierced Shalya with twenty-five arrows, Kripa with nine and Ashvatthama with eight. However, Drona's son also quickly pierced Arjuna's son with shafted arrows. Shalya pierced him with twelve and Kripa with three sharp arrows. On seeing that your grandson was thus engaged in battle, your grandson Lakshmana rushed at him in great anger and there was an encounter between the two.[127] O king! In that battle, Duryodhana's son angrily pierced Subhadra's son with nine arrows and it was an extraordinary sight. O bull among the Bharata lineage! O king! Abhimanyu was filled with ire and with dextrous hands, pierced his brother with five hundred arrows. At this, Lakshmana used shafted arrows to slice down his[128] bow at the handle. O great king! On seeing this, the people raised a loud shout. Then Subhadra's son, the destroyer of enemies, discarded

[126]Referring to Dhrishtadyumna.

[127]Both Abhimanyu and Lakshmana were Dhritarashtra's grandsons. Abhimanyu was the son of Arjuna and Subhadra. Lakshmana was the son of Duryodhana and Bhanumati.

[128]Abhimanyu's.

that shattered bow and picked up another bow that was more beautiful and stronger. Those two bulls among men happily fought against each other, countering each other's efforts and piercing each other with sharp and shafted arrows. On seeing that his maharatha son was thus assailed by your grandson, King Duryodhana, lord of men, rushed towards the spot. When your son advanced, all the kings used masses of chariots to surround Arjuna's son from every direction. O king! But he was a brave and invincible warrior, equal in valour to Krishna. Despite being surrounded by those heroes, he was not distressed.

'"On seeing that Subhadra's son was fighting there, Dhananjaya swiftly advanced there, intending to save his son. With chariots, elephants and horses and with Bhishma and Drona at the forefront, all the kings forcefully attacked Savyasachi. A thick dust suddenly arose from the ground, raised by the elephants, horses, chariots and infantry and it seemed to obstruct the path of the sun. When those thousands of elephants and hundreds of kings approached within striking distance of his[129] arrows, none of them could advance any further. All the beings lamented loudly and all the directions were covered in darkness. The army of the Kurus seemed to be terrible and dreadful. O foremost among the Bharata lineage! Because of the numerous arrows shot by Kiriti, the sky, the directions, the earth or the sun could not be seen. Elephants were deprived of the standards on their backs. Many charioteers were deprived of their horses. Having been deprived of their chariots, many charioteers were seen to be wandering around there. Other charioteers discarded their chariots and were seen to flee. They were seen there, weapons in their hands and with bracelets on their upper arms. O king! Because of their fear of Arjuna, horse-riders gave up their horses and elephant-riders their elephants. They fled in all the directions. The kings were seen to fall down from their chariots, elephants and horses. They were seen to fall down, oppressed by Arjuna. O lord of the earth! Assuming a terrible form there, Arjuna used his terrible arrows to cut down the upraised arms of men who held clubs, swords, lances, quivers, bows, arrows, goads and standards. O venerable one! O descendant of the

[129]Arjuna's.

Bharata lineage! Heavy maces and clubs, lances, catapults, swords, sharp battleaxes, javelins, shields and armour were shattered in that battle and fell down on the ground. O descendant of the Bharata lineage! Flags, shields, many kinds of whisks, umbrellas, golden rods and tassels were strewn around. O venerable one! There were whips, halters, thongs and reins. They were seen to be scattered on the field of battle. O descendant of the Bharata lineage! There was not a single man in your army who could advance against the brave Arjuna in battle. O lord of the earth! In that encounter, whoever advanced against Partha was pierced by sharp and shafted arrows and conveyed to the world of the dead. When all the warriors on your side were scattered, Arjuna and Vasudeva blew on their supreme conch shells.

'"On seeing that the army had been shattered in that battle, your father, Devavrata, smiled and told Bharadvaja's brave son, 'This brave and powerful son of Pandu is united with Krishna. He is dealing with our soldiers only as Dhananjaya can. No one is capable of vanquishing him in battle today. His form seems to be like that of the destroyer at the end of an era. It is impossible to rally our great army now. Behold. They are looking at each other and are running away. The sun can be seen aloft the supreme mountain Asta.[130] It is as if it has robbed the sight of the entire world. O bull among men! I think the time has come for retreat. The warriors are exhausted and frightened and will never fight.' Having spoken thus to the supreme preceptor Drona, maharatha Bhishma arranged that your army should be withdrawn. O descendant of the Bharata lineage! Your soldiers, and those of the others, were withdrawn. The sun set and evening set in."'

Chapter 912(52)

'Sanjaya said, "O descendant of the Bharata lineage! When night had passed and it was morning, Shantanu's son, Bhishma,

---

[130]The mountain over which the sun sets.

instructed that a battle formation should be created. Wishing to ensure victory for your sons, Shantanu's son, Bhishma, the grandfather of the Kurus, formed the great vyuha known as Garuda. Your father Devavrata stationed himself on Garuda's mouth and Bharadvaja's son and Satvata Kritavarma were the eyes. Ashvatthama and the famous Kripa were the head, supported by Trigartas, Matsyas, Kekayas and Vatadhanas. O venerable one! Bhurishrava, Shala, Shalya, Bhagadatta, Madrakas, Sindhus, Souviras and those from the land of the five rivers, together with Jayadratha, constituted the neck. King Duryodhana, together with his brothers and followers, constituted the back. O great king! Vinda and Anuvinda from Avanti, together with the Kambojas and the Shakas and the Shurasenas, constituted the tail. Magadhas and Kalingas, together with masses of Dasherakas, were armoured and stationed themselves on the right wing of the vyuha. Kananas, Vikunjas, Muktas, Pundravishas, together with Brihadbala, were stationed on the left wing.

'"On seeing this battle formation of your soldiers, Savyasachi, the scorcher of enemies, together with Dhrishtadyumna, arranged a counter vyuha for the encounter. This vyuha was in the form of a half-moon and this vyuha was extremely terrible. Bhimasena stationed himself on the right horn. He was surrounded by kings from many countries, wielding many different kinds of weapons. Maharatha Virata and Drupada were next to him. Next to him was Nila, accompanied by Nilayudha. Next to Nila was maharatha Dhrishtaketu. He was surrounded by the Chedis, the Kashis, the Karusha and the Pouravas. O descendant of the Bharata lineage! Dhrishtadyumna, Shikhandi, the Panchalas and the Prabhadrakas were stationed in the midst of the large army, ready for battle. Dharmaraja was also there, surrounded by an army of elephants. O king! Satyaki was also there, together with Droupadi's five sons. Abhimanyu was there and beyond him was Iravan. O king! Bhimasena's son[131] was there, together with the maharatha Kekayas. Next to him, on the left flank, was the foremost of men.[132] His protector was Janardana, the protector of the entire

[131]Ghatotkacha.
[132]Referring to Arjuna.

universe. It was thus that the Pandavas formed a giant vyuha as a counter vyuha, for the death of your sons and of those who have assembled on your side. The battle between those on your side and those of the enemy then commenced, seeking to kill each other in a melee of chariots and elephants. O lord of the earth! Masses of horses and masses of chariots were seen there. They were seen to descend on each other, seeking to kill each other. Masses of chariots dashed towards each other, or engaged each other individually. They created a tumultuous sound, mixed with the sound of drums. O descendant of the Bharata lineage! As they sought to kill each other in that tumultuous battle, the shouts of the brave men on your side, and on theirs, seemed to touch heaven."'

Chapter 913(53)

'Sanjaya said, "Your soldiers and those of the others were arranged in battle formation. O descendant of the Bharata lineage! After that, Dhananjaya slaughtered a large number of charioteers on your side. In that battle, he used his arrows to bring down large numbers of charioteers. They were thus killed by Partha, like death at the time of the destruction of a yuga. But in that encounter, the sons of Dhritarashtra endeavoured to repulse the Pandavas. They strove for blazing fame and preferred death to retreat. O king! Thus single-minded in their objective in that battle, they broke through the Pandava ranks in many places and were themselves broken. Both the Pandava and the Kourava were broken and fled, reassembling again. Nothing could be seen. A cloud of dust arose from the ground and shrouded the sun. No one was in a position to distinguish the directions or the sub-directions. The battle raged everywhere, through inferences drawn on the basis of signs, names and family names.[133]

---

[133]A trifle inaccurately, we have translated gotra as family name. Since nothing could be seen, the identities of the two sides had to be determined on the basis of such indications.

However, in that encounter, the vyuha of the Kouravas was protected by Bharadvaja's intelligent son, who was devoted to the truth, and it could not be broken. In that fashion, nor could the great vyuha of the Pandavas, protected by Savyasachi and guarded well by Bhima.

'"O king! Men, infantry, chariots and elephants emerged from the heads of both the armies and engaged in fighting with each other. In that great battle, those riding horses brought down those riding horses, using polished and sharp swords and lances in that encounter. In that terrible battle, charioteers used gold-decorated arrows to bring down charioteers. Those riding on elephants used iron arrows, arrows and spikes against those riding on elephants and used these to bring each other down. In that battle, large numbers of infantry engaged against infantry and happily cut each other down with catapults and battleaxes. In that battle, in both the armies, infantry brought down charioteers and charioteers brought down infantry, using sharp weapons. Those riding elephants brought down those riding horses. Those riding horses brought down those stationed on elephants and it was extraordinary. Here and there, the supreme among those riding on elephants brought down foot soldiers and warriors riding on elephants were seen to be brought down by them in return. Large numbers of infantry were slaughtered by those riding horses and large numbers of those riding horses were brought down by foot soldiers. They were seen to be brought down in hundreds and thousands. O foremost among the Bharata lineage! The ground was strewn with destroyed standards, bows, lances, javelins, clubs, maces, *kampanas*,[134] spears, colourful armour, *kanapas*,[135] goads, polished swords, gold-shafted arrows, cushions, carpets and extremely expensive coverlets and seemed to be strewn with garlands of flowers. In that great battle, the bodies of men, horses and fallen elephants made the ground impassable and mud was created by flesh and blood. The dust that had arisen from the ground settled down because of the blood from the battle. O lord of men! Because of this, the directions again became clearly visible.

[134]Unidentified weapon that makes the enemy tremble.
[135]A kind of lance.

O descendant of the Bharata lineage! Many headless torsos were seen to arise from the ground, as a portent that all the beings in the universe would be destroyed. In that extremely terrible and fearful battle, charioteers could be seen to flee in every direction.

'"Bhishma, Drona, Saindhava Jayadratha, Purumitra, Vikarna and Shakuni Soubala were invincible in battle and were like lions in their valour. They repeatedly broke the Pandava ranks in battle. O descendant of the Bharata lineage! In that way, Bhimasena, the rakshasa Ghatotkacha, Satyaki, Chekitana and Droupadi's sons oppressed your sons, together with all the kings, like the gods against the danavas. Those bulls among kshatriyas killed each other in that battle. Drenched in battle, they assumed terrible forms, like dazzling danavas. In both the armies, brave ones triumphed over their enemies and seemed to be like the best of planets in the firmament. With one thousand chariots, your son Duryodhana advanced to do battle with the Pandavas and the rakshasa Ghatotkacha. All the Pandavas, together with a large army, advanced to do battle with Drona and Bhishma, the brave scorchers of enemies. The enraged Kiriti advanced against the best of kings. Arjuna's son and Satyaki advanced against Soubala's army. An extremely terrible battle commenced between those on your side and those of the enemy, each trying to defeat the other, and it made the body hair stand up."'

Chapter 914(54)

'Sanjaya said, "The kings were angry and saw Phalguna in that battle. They surrounded him on all sides with many thousands of chariots. O descendant of the Bharata lineage! Having surrounded him with a large number of chariots, they enveloped him in all directions with many thousands of arrows. Enraged in battle, they hurled polished and sharp lances, clubs, maces, javelins, battleaxes, bludgeons and pestles towards Phalguna's chariot. That shower of weapons descended on him like a flight of locusts. But Partha countered all of them with gold-decorated arrows. O Indra among kings! On witnessing Bibhatsu's superhuman lightness of hand, the gods, the danavas, the gandharvas, the pishachas, the serpents and the rakshasas honoured Phalguna with words of praise. With a large army and together with Soubala, the brave ones from the land of Gandhara surrounded Satyaki and Abhimanyu in that battle. With many different kinds of weapons, the angry ones who were on Soubala's side wrathfully cut down Varshneya's supreme chariot into tiny fragments.[136] In that extremely fearful battle, Satyaki abandoned his chariot and the scorcher of enemies swiftly ascended onto Abhimanyu's chariot. Stationed on the same chariot, they swiftly countered Soubala's army and pierced it with many sharp and straight-tufted arrows. In that battle, Drona and Bhishma made endeavours to fight with Dharmaraja's army. They destroyed it with sharp arrows tufted with the feathers of herons. In the sight of all the soldiers, the king who was Dharma's son and the Pandavas who were Madri's sons began to oppress Drona's army. The great battle that was fought was tumultuous and made the body hair stand up. It was like the extremely terrible battle that was earlier fought between the gods and the asuras. Bhimasena and Ghatotkacha performed extremely great deeds. Then Duryodhana arrived and repulsed both of them. We witnessed the valour displayed by Hidimba's son[137] and it was extraordinary. O descendant of the Bharata lineage! When he fought, he surpassed his father in battle. Pandava Bhimasena was enraged. He smiled and pierced the intolerant Duryodhana in the chest with an arrow. At this, King Duryodhana lost his senses from this blow. He sank down on his chariot and fainted. O king! On seeing that he had lost his senses, the charioteer swiftly carried him away from the field of battle and his soldiers ran away. While the Kourava soldiers were running away in all directions, Bhima pursued them and killed them with sharp arrows.

'"In Drona's sight and in the sight of Gangeya, Parshata, foremost among charioteers, and the Pandava who was Dharma's son began

---

[136]Varshneya means someone of the Vrishni lineage. In this context, it is being used for Satyaki.

[137]Ghatotkacha.

to slaughter their soldiers with sharp and straight-tufted arrows that were capable of killing the enemy. In that battle, the soldiers of your sons started to run away. O lord of the earth! Maharatha Bhishma and Drona were incapable of restraining them, though Bhishma and Drona did try to restrain them. While both Drona and Bhishma looked on, the soldiers fled. Thousands of chariots fled in all directions. Subhadra's son and the bull among Shinis were stationed on a single chariot. In that battle, in every direction, they began to slaughter the soldiers of Soubala. Shini's descendant and the bull among the Kurus[138] were resplendent, like two suns in the firmament after the night of the new moon had passed. O lord of the earth! Arjuna angrily showered down arrows on the soldiers, like clouds pouring down rain. Thus slaughtered in that battle with Partha's arrows, the Kourava soldiers were overcome by sorrow and fright and trembled and ran away. On seeing that the soldiers were running away, maharatha Bhishma and Drona, became angry and having Duryodhana's welfare in mind, tried to restrain them. O lord of the earth! At this, King Duryodhana himself reassured the troops and restrained them from running away in every direction. O descendant of the Bharata lineage! Wherever your son could be seen, there the maharatha kshatriyas were restrained. O king! Wherever they were restrained, the ordinary soldiers saw them and were also restrained, ashamed and desiring to rival each other. O lord of the earth! That army was thus forcefully rallied and looked like a full ocean when the moon rises.

'"Having seen that the army had been rallied, King Suyodhana swiftly went to Bhishma, Shantanu's son, and spoke these words to him. 'O grandfather! O descendant of the Bharata lineage! Listen to the words I am speaking to you. O Kourava! When you are alive, and so is Drona, supreme among those who are skilled in weapons, together with his son and well-wishers, and so is the great archer Kripa, I do not think it is praiseworthy that my soldiers should flee in this way. I do not think that the Pandavas are a force capable of withstanding you in battle, or Drona, or Drona's son, or Kripa. O

[138]Satyaki and Abhimanyu respectively.

grandfather! The Pandavas are certainly being favoured by you. O brave one! That is the reason you are pardoning them this act of killing my soldiers. O king! You should have told me earlier, before this encounter commenced, that you would not fight in a battle with the Pandavas, or with Parshata, or with Satyaki. On hearing your words and those of the preceptor and of Kripa, together with Karna, I would then have reflected on what should be done. O bulls among men![139] If I do not deserve to be abandoned by both of you in this battle, then fight in accordance with your valour.' Having heard these words, Bhishma laughed repeatedly. His eyes were full of anger and he spoke these words to your son. 'O king! On many occasions, I have spoken words for your welfare and you should have accepted them. The Pandavas are incapable of being vanquished in battle even by the gods, together with Vasava. O supreme among kings! Though I am aged now, I will do what I am capable of doing and I will do it to the best of my capacity. Behold it with your relatives. While all the worlds look on, I will alone repulse the sons of Pandu now, together with their soldiers and relatives.' O lord of men! Having been thus addressed by Bhishma, your son was extremely delighted and instructed that conch shells and drums should be sounded. O king! Having heard this loud roar, the Pandavas blew on their conch shells and instructed that drums and tambourines should be sounded.'"

Chapter 915(55)

'Dhritarashtra asked, "When Bhishma was especially angered and distressed because of my son and took that terrible vow in that battle, what did Bhishma do when he encountered the Pandaveyas. O Sanjaya! Tell me what the Panchalas did to the grandfather."

'Sanjaya replied, "O descendant of the Bharata lineage! When the forenoon of that day had passed and when the great-souled

[139]Duryodhana is addressing both Bhishma and Drona now.

Pandavas were delighted at having accomplished victory, your father, Devavrata, learned in all kinds of dharma, advanced on the swiftest of steeds towards the army of the Pandavas. He was protected by a large army and by all your sons. O descendant of the Bharata lineage! A tumultuous battle ensued between us and the Pandavas, because you did not follow dharma. It made the body hair stand up. There was the twanging of bows there, as they struck against the palms. A tremendous sound arose and it was capable of splintering mountains. 'Wait', 'I am stationed here', 'Know this one', 'Retreat', 'Be steady', 'I am steady here', 'Strike'—these were the sounds that were heard everywhere. Golden body-armour, crowns and standards fell down and it was like the sound of boulders descending on stony ground. Hundreds and thousands of heads and ornamented arms fell down immobile on the ground. With the heads sliced off, some supreme among men still stood, with their bows raised and holding weapons. An extremely swift river of blood began to flow. Its mud was terrible with flesh and blood and the bodies of elephants were like stones in it. The bodies of excellent horses, men and elephants flowed in it then, as it flowed towards the world of the hereafter. It was delightful to vultures and jackals. O king! A battle like this has not been seen earlier, nor heard of. O descendant of the Bharata lineage! Such was the one between your sons and the Pandavas. Because of the warriors who had been brought down in battle, chariots could not find a path there. The bodies of fallen elephants were like blue summits of mountains. O venerable one! Strewn with colourful armour, standards and umbrellas, the field of battle was as beautiful as the autumn sky. Though they were oppressed and wounded by arrows, some armoured ones were seen to dash towards the enemy in battle, without any fear. Many who fell down in the battle cried, 'O father! O brother! O friend! O relative! O companion! O maternal uncle! Do not abandon me.' There were others who exclaimed, 'Come here. Why are you frightened? Where are you going? I am stationed in battle. Do not be afraid.'

"'Bhishma, Shantanu's son, was there, his bow always stretched in a circle. He released blazing arrows that were like the venom of virulent snakes. Rigid in his vows, he released arrows in all the

directions. O bull among the Bharata lineage! He picked out the
Pandava charioteers and killed them. With a dextrous hand, he
seemed to be dancing around in the chariot. O king! He could be seen
everywhere, like a circle of fire. Though the brave one was alone in
that battle, because of his dexterity, the Pandavas and the Srinjayas
saw him as many hundreds and thousands. Everyone there thought
that Bhishma had used maya on his own self. In one moment, he was
seen in the eastern direction. In the next moment, he was seen in the
western direction. They saw the lord in the north and immediately
saw him in the south. Thus the brave Gangeya was seen in that battle.
There was no one among the Pandaveyas who was capable of glancing
at him. They only saw many arrows shot from Bhishma's bow.
Having seen him perform such great feats in the battle there, with the
slaughter of the army, the brave ones uttered many lamentations. Your
father wandered around in superhuman form and driven by destiny,
thousands of kings fell down like insects, led to the fire of the angry
Bhishma. In that battle, not a single one of Bhishma's arrows failed to
be successful, because of the large numbers that were arrayed against
him, and descended on the bodies of men, elephants and horses. With
a single shafted arrow that was released well, he brought down an
armoured elephant, like the vajra shattering a mountain. With an
extremely sharp iron arrow, your father killed two or three elephant-
riders, armoured and standing together, at a single stroke. Whoever
approached Bhishma, tiger among men, in that battle, was seen to
be brought down onto the ground in an instant. Thus, Dharmaraja's
large army was slaughtered through Bhishma's valour and shattered
in a thousand ways. Tormented by the shower of arrows, the large
army trembled, while Vasudeva and the great-souled Partha looked
on. Though the brave ones made every endeavour, they could not
restrain the maharathas who were oppressed by Bhishma's arrows.
He slaughtered that large army with a valour that was like that of
the great Indra. O great king! It was routed such that no two persons
were seen together. Men, elephants and horses were pierced. Standards
and axle-shafts fell down. The soldiers of the sons of Pandu lost their
senses and lamented. Father killed the son and the son killed the
father. Driven by the force of destiny, a friend challenged a beloved

friend to a fight. O descendant of the Bharata lineage! Many soldiers
on the side of the sons of Pandu were seen to run away, with their
armour discarded and with their hair dishevelled. The soldiers of the
sons of Pandu, and even the leaders among them, were seen to be as
confounded as a herd of cattle. They lamented in woe.

'"On seeing that the soldiers were routed, Devaki's son[140] stopped
that supreme of chariots and spoke to Partha Bibhatsu. 'O Partha!
The hour that you desired, has now arrived. O tiger among men! If
you wish to be free from confusion, strike. O brave one! In earlier
times, in the assembly of kings, you had said that you would kill the
soldiers of the sons of Dhritarashtra, with Bhishma and Drona at the
forefront, with all the relatives and those who wished to fight against
you in battle. O Kounteya! O destroyer of enemies! Act accordingly
now and make your words come true. O Bibhatsu! Behold. Your
army is being driven back in every direction. Behold. All the kings
in Yudhishthira's army are running away, on having seen Bhishma in
battle, with his mouth gaping open. They are frightened and are being
destroyed, like small animals by a lion.' Having been thus addressed,
Dhananjaya replied to Vasudeva, 'Drive the horses through this ocean
of soldiers to where Bhishma is stationed.' O king! Madhava then
drove those silver-white steeds to the place where Bhishma's chariot,
which was like the sun and was difficult to look at, was stationed.
Having seen the mighty-armed Partha advance to fight in the battle
against Bhishma, Yudhishthira's great army rallied again.

'"Bhishma, foremost among the Kurus, roared repeatedly, like
a lion. He swiftly enveloped Dhananjaya's chariot with a shower
of arrows. In an instant, with the horses and with the charioteer,
the chariot disappeared. It was covered by that great shower of
arrows and could no longer be seen. But the spirited Vasudeva was
not agitated. Though the horses had been wounded by Bhishma's
arrows, he patiently continued to drive them. Partha picked up his
divine bow, with a twang that was like the clap of thunder. He sliced
down Bhishma's bow with three arrows. With his bow sliced down,
your father Kouravya again picked up a large bow and strung it in

[140]Krishna.

the twinkling of an eye. He drew the bow with his two hands and its twang was like the roar of the clouds. But the enraged Arjuna sliced down that bow too. At this, Shantanu's son applauded his dexterity. 'O Partha! O mighty-armed one! O descendant of Pandu! Wonderful. O Dhananjaya! Such a great deed is deserving of you. O son! I am pleased with you. Fight hard with me now.' Having thus praised Partha and having grasped another large bow, in that battle, the brave one released arrows towards Partha's chariot. Vasudeva displayed his supreme skill in handling horses. By driving around in swift circles, he avoided all those arrows. O venerable one! However, with great force, Bhishma used sharp arrows to pierce Vasudeva and Dhananjaya all over their bodies. Thus wounded by Bhishma's arrows, those two tigers among men were adorned like two roaring bulls, with the scratches of thorns on them. Yet again, extremely angry, Bhishma used straight-tufted arrows to cover the two Krishnas[141] on every side. Though enraged, Bhishma repeatedly smiled and used his sharp arrows to make Varshneya tremble and wonder.

'"Krishna witnessed Bhishma's valour in battle and saw the mildness with which the mighty-armed Partha countered him. In that encounter, Bhishma created an incessant shower of arrows. In the midst of the two armies, he was like the tormenting sun. He was killing the best of the best among the soldiers of Pandu's son. Bhishma was like the fire of destruction amidst Yudhishthira's army. The lord Keshava, the destroyer of enemy heroes, could no longer tolerate this. The one with the immeasurable soul thought that Yudhishthira's army would not be able to survive. In a battle, Bhishma was capable of destroying the gods and the danavas in a single day, not to speak of taking on the sons of Pandu, with their soldiers and their followers, in a fight. The large army of the great-souled Pandava began to flee. Having seen the Somakas shattered and fleeing in that battle, the Kouravas were delighted and advanced to the fight, gladdening the grandfather. He[142] thought, 'For the welfare of the Pandavas, I will armour myself and kill Bhishma today. I will relieve the burden

---

[141]Krishna is also one of Arjuna's names.
[142]Krishna.

of the great-souled Pandavas. Though Arjuna has been struck with sharp arrows in this battle, he does not know his duty in this encounter, on account of the respect he has for Bhishma.' While he was reflecting in this way, the wrathful grandfather again unleashed arrows towards Partha's chariot. Because of the many arrows that were flying around, all the directions were enveloped. The sky, the directions and the earth could not be seen. Nor could the sun, the possessor of the rays, be seen. The tumultuous wind seemed to be mixed with smoke. All the directions were agitated.

'"Drona, Vikarna, Jayadratha, Bhurishrava, Kritavarma, Kripa, Shrutayu, the lord and king of Ambashtha,[143] Vinda and Anuvinda, Sudakshina, those from the east, all the large numbers of Souviras, the Vasatayas, the Kshudrakas and the Malavas—on the instructions of the king who was Shantanu's son, all of these swiftly advanced to do battle with Kiriti. Shini's grandson saw that Kiriti was surrounded by a net with hundreds and thousands of horses, infantry and chariots and a large number of elephants. Shini's brave descendant, foremost among the wielders of arms, swiftly advanced to where the soldiers were, wielding a giant bow. The brave one from Shini's lineage suddenly arrived to aid Arjuna, like Vishnu helping the destroyer of Vritra. The elephants, horses, chariots and standards were shattered and all the warriors were frightened by Bhishma. Yudhishthira's soldiers were running away. On seeing this, Shini's brave descendant said, 'O kshatriyas! Where are you going? This is not the dharma of virtuous men, as it has been recounted in the ancient texts. O brave ones! Do not forsake your oaths. Follow the dharma of those who are brave.' Vasava's younger brother[144] was unable to tolerate the act of the foremost among the kings running away. In that battle, he saw that Bhishma was exerting all his powers, that Partha was mild and that the Kurus were advancing from every direction.

'"Unable to tolerate it, the great-souled and illustrious one, the protector of all the Dasharhas, spoke approvingly to Shini's

---

[143]There were two Shrutayus, one was the king of Kalinga and the other one was the king of Ambashtha. Ambashtha was located in the area of the Punjab.

[144]Krishna.

descendant. 'O brave descendant of the Shini lineage! Those who are running away, are indeed running away. O Satvata! Let those who are still here, also flee. Behold. In this battle, I will today bring down Bhishma from his chariot and also Drona and all their followers. O Satvata! There is no charioteer among the Kouravas who will escape when I am enraged in battle today. I will grasp the terrible chakra and rob the one who is great in his vows, of his life.[145] O descendant of Shini! I will kill Bhishma and his followers and Drona, the foremost among charioteers. I will act so as to bring pleasure to Dhananjaya, the king,[146] Bhima and the two Ashvins.[147] I will kill all the sons of Dhritarashtra and the foremost among kings who are on their side. In a cheerful frame of mind, I will today give the kingdom to King Ajatashatru.' Having said this, Vasudeva's son discarded the reins of the chariot and raised the chakra in his hand. It possessed an excellent handle and was like the sun in its radiance. It was like the vajra in its power. The great-souled one made the earth tremble with his footsteps. With great force, Krishna rushed towards Bhishma. The great Indra's younger brother was angry. He rushed towards Bhishma, as he was stationed in the midst of his troops. He was like a lion that wished to kill a king of the elephants. He was blind in his anger and agitated in his pride. The ends of his yellow garments trailed in the air and looked like a cloud charged with lightning in the sky. Sudarshana looked like a glorious lotus, with Shouri's beautiful arm as the stalk. It was like the original lotus, as resplendent as the morning sun, which emerged from Narayana's navel.[148] Krishna's anger was like the rising sun that caused the lotus to bloom and its beautiful petals were as sharp as a razor. On seeing that the great Indra's younger brother was angry and roaring and that he was wielding the chakra, all the

[145]The text uses the word *rathanga*. This can mean the wheel of a chariot, or it can mean a chakra. Krishna could have been referring to the sudarshana chakra, or to the more mundane wheel of the chariot. Either translation is correct.

[146]Yudhishthira.

[147]Nakula and Sahadeva.

[148]The original lotus is the lotus at the time of creation, which emerged from Vishnu's navel.

beings shrieked in lamentation. They thought that the destruction of the Kurus was nigh. Having grasped the chakra, Vasudeva looked like the fire of destruction that consumes the world of the living. The preceptor of the worlds arose like the fire of destruction that would destroy all beings. On seeing the god, foremost among men, advance with the chakra, Shantanu's son remained fearlessly stationed on his chariot, with the bow and arrows in his hand. He said, 'O lord of the gods! O one whose abode is the universe! O wielder of the Sharnga bow! O one with the chakra in your hand! Come. I am bowing down before you. O protector of the worlds! Bring me down from this supreme chariot. You are the wonderful refuge of everyone in a battle. O Krishna! If I am killed by you today, I will obtain supreme welfare in this world and in the next. O protector of the Andhakas and the Vrishnis! You have shown me great honour and my valour will be celebrated in the three worlds.' However, Partha swiftly descended from his chariot and ran after the foremost of the Yadus. With his thick and long arms, he seized Hari's large and thick arms. The original god, whose name is the great yogi, was consumed by great wrath. Though he was seized in this way, Vishnu dragged Jishnu after him with great force, like a great storm carries away a tree. But as he was swiftly advancing towards Bhishma, Partha forcibly grasped him by the feet. O king! Thus grasping him with force, Kiriti succeeded in stopping him at the tenth step. When Krishna had stopped, bedecked with a beautiful and golden garland, Arjuna happily bowed down before him and said, 'O Keshava! You are the refuge of the Pandavas. Control your anger. O Keshava! I swear in the names of my sons and brothers that I will not deviate from the acts that I have promised to carry out. O younger brother of Indra! Instructed by you, I will certainly destroy the Kurus.' Hearing the promise and the pledge, Janardana was happy and was pacified. He was always engaged in the welfare of the supreme among the Kouravas.[149] With the chakra, he again ascended on the chariot.

[149]Since Kuru was a common ancestor, the Pandavas can also be referred to as the Kouravas. This is presumably a reference to Arjuna, but can also be a reference to Yudhishthira.

'"The slayer of enemies again grasped the reins. Shouri grasped his conch shell Panchajanya and blew on it, making the directions resound with its roar. The foremost among the Kurus saw him, adorned with a necklace, armlets and earrings. His curved eyelashes were smeared with dust. With gleaming teeth, he grasped the conch shell and they set up a loud cry. Tambourines, drums, kettledrums and smaller drums began to sound, mixed with the sound of chariot wheels. Lion-like terrible roars were uttered among the Kuru soldiers. There was the roar of Partha's Gandiva, ascending into the sky and the directions like the clap of thunder. The bright and polished arrows released from Pandava's bow covered all the directions. Together with Bhishma and Bhurishrava and an army, the lord of the Kouravas[150] advanced against him. He held raised arrows in his hand and was like a fire[151] that would consume dry wood. Bhurishrava shot seven gold-tufted and broad arrows at Arjuna. Duryodhana hurled an extremely forceful lance, Shalya a club and Shantanu's son a spear. But he used seven arrows to counter the seven supreme arrows shot by Bhurishrava. With a razor-sharp arrow, he countered the lance that had been released from Duryodhana's hand. Shantanu's son had hurled a spear at him, as resplendent as lightning. But as it descended, the brave one used two arrows to cut this down and also the club that had been released from the arms of the king of Madra. He used the strength of his two arms to draw the beautiful bow Gandiva, whose energy was immeasurable. In accordance with the prescriptions, he invoked the extremely terrible and wonderful weapon of the great Indra and made it appear in the sky. The great-souled and great archer, Kiriti, used that weapon to counter all the soldiers. It showered down a mass of polished arrows, with the complexion of the fire. The many arrows that were released from Partha's bow cut down chariots, standards and bows and the arms that held them. They penetrated the bodies of the enemy

[150]Duryodhana.
[151]The word used in the text is *dhumaketu*. The natural meaning for this is comet or meteor. But the word also means fire and fire seems more appropriate, given that dry wood or grass is referred to.

kings, the gigantic elephants and the large number of horses. Having covered all the directions and the sub-directions with his extremely sharp arrows, Partha created terror in their minds with the twang of Gandiva. Thus did Kiriti oppress them and as that terrible encounter raged, the sounds of conch shells and kettledrums were surpassed by Gandiva's roar.

'"When they got to know the sound of Gandiva, the brave ones among men, with King Virata at the forefront, and the valiant King Drupada of Panchala, went to the spot, with uplifted hearts. But wherever the sound of Gandiva was heard, all your soldiers were immersed in despair there and not a single one would venture forth. In that extremely terrible slaughter of kings, many brave ones were slain, together with their chariots and charioteers. Elephants were tormented and brought down with iron arrows, with their giant banners and seats made out of pure gold. They lost their lives and were suddenly brought down, their bodies mangled by Kiriti. Partha used a firm hand to bring them down with the force of his sharp, polished and broad-headed arrows. The implements of war were shattered, the fortifications were destroyed. In that battle, Dhananjaya brought down large standards and the best of pennants and large numbers of infantry, chariots, horses and elephants. Struck by the arrows, they lost their lives. Their bodies became immobile and they fell down on the ground. O king! In that great battle, their armour and their bodies were mangled by the supreme weapon named after Indra. With a flood of sharp arrows, Kiriti made an extremely terrible river flow on the field of battle. The blood was the bodies of men wounded by weapons. The foam was human fat. Its expanse was broad and it flowed swiftly. The banks were formed by the dead bodies of elephants and horses. The mud was the entrails, marrow and flesh of men. Many hordes of rakshasas and demons populated it. The moss was formed by heads, with the hair attached. Thousands of bodies were borne in the flow and the waves were formed by many shattered fragments of armour. The bones of men, horses and elephants were the stones. A large number of crows, jackals, vultures and herons and many predatory beasts like hyenas were seen to line up along its banks, as that terrible and destructive river flowed towards the nether regions. That terrible river was as cruel as the great Vaitarani.[152] Created through the masses of Arjuna's arrows, that extremely fearful river conveyed fat, marrow and blood.

'"The Chedis, the Panchalas, the Karushas and the Matsyas, together with all the Parthas, began to roar. The soldiers and leaders of the army[153] were terrified, like a herd of deer at the sight of a lion. The wielder of the Gandiva and Janardana roared in great delight. The Kurus, together with Bhishma, Drona, Duryodhana and Bahlika, saw that Indra's terrible weapon had extended everywhere and was like the end of a yuga. Their limbs were sorely wounded from the weapon and they saw the sun was withdrawing its rays. They saw that twilight was near and that the sun was streaked with red. They decided to withdraw. Having performed deeds and won fame in the world, Dhananjaya had triumphed over the enemies. Having completed his tasks, together with his brothers, the lord of men retired to his camp for the night. When night set in, there was a terrible and great uproar among the Kurus. 'In the battle, Arjuna has killed ten thousand charioteers and seven hundred elephants. All those from the eastern regions, all the masses of Souviras, the Kshudrakas and the Malavas have been brought down. Dhananjaya has accomplished a great deed. No one else is capable of accomplishing this. O king!'[154] King Shrutayu, the lord of Ambashtha, Durmarshana, Chitrasena, Drona, Kripa, Saindhava, Bahlika, Bhurishrava, Shalya and Shala, together with Bhishma, have been vanquished by Kiriti, the maharatha of the world, through the valour of his own arms.' O descendant of the Bharata lineage! Having spoken these words, all those who were on your side went to their camps. There were thousands of torches to bring illumination and many beautiful lamps. All the warriors and leaders among the Kurus settled down for the night, terrified of Kiriti."'

[152]River that separates the world of the living from the world of the dead.
[153]Belonging to the enemy.
[154]This is being addressed to Duryodhana.

Chapter 916(56)

"Sanjaya said, "O descendant of the Bharata lineage! When night had passed, the great-souled Bhishma was full of anger. Placing himself at the head of the Bharata army and surrounded by a large number of troops, he advanced against the enemy. Drona, Duryodhana, Bahlika, Durmarshana, Chitrasena and the extremely strong Jayadratha, and many other powerful kings with their armies, surrounded him on all sides. O king! Surrounded by these great maharathas, all of whom possessed energy and valour, that supreme of kings was radiant at the forefront of those kings, like the wielder of the vajra when he is surrounded by the gods. Giant standards fluttered on the backs of mighty elephants stationed in front of the troops. They were beautiful and colourful—red, yellow, black and brown. That army had the king who was Shantanu's son, maharathas, elephants and horses. It was as dazzling as clouds tinged with lightning, or the sky when clouds gather at the onset of the monsoon. Protected by Shantanu's son, that great and large army of the Kurus suddenly rushed towards Arjuna to do battle, like a terrible and flowing river. It possessed diverse kinds of powerful forces, with innumerable elephants, horses, infantry and chariots along the sides. The vyuha was like a giant cloud. From a distance, the great-souled one with the king of apes on his standard saw it.[155] The brave bull among men, with the white horses, was stationed on his chariot with the tall standard. The great-souled one was at the head of a large army and advanced against all the forces of the enemy. He possessed excellent equipment and the shaft of the chariot was supreme. In that battle, he was aided by the bull among the Yadus. On seeing the ape on the standard, all the Kouravas, together with your sons, were dejected.

"'They saw that the king of vyuhas was protected by Kiriti, the maharatha of this world, with his weapons upraised. There were four thousand elephants at each of its four corners. This vyuha was like

---

[155]Arjuna had an ape on his standard.

the one that had been prepared the preceding day by Dharmaraja, the descendant of the Kourava lineage. The foremost among the Panchalas and the foremost among the Chedis advanced towards the spot. A great roar arose from every direction and thousands of drums were sounded. There was the blowing of conch shells, mixed with the sounds of drums. All the soldiers roared like lions. As the brave ones twanged their bows, there was the great sound of arrows. In an instant, the sky was filled with the loud sound of drums, kettledrums and cymbals and the great noise of conch shells being blown. Enveloped in that sound, the sky was also covered by fine dust that arose from the ground. On seeing that canopy spread all over, the brave warriors dashed forwards to battle each other. Rathas were brought down by rathas, together with their charioteers, horses, chariots and standards. Elephants were struck and brought down by elephants. Infantry was brought down by infantry. Those who advanced were brought down by others who advanced. The wounds from the arrows were wonderful to behold. Lances and swords fell down. Well-trained horses clashed against well-trained horses. The brave ones held excellent shields marked with the signs of golden stars and used them against excellent arrows. These were shattered by battleaxes, lances and swords and fell down on the ground. Some rathas and their charioteers were mangled by the tusks and mighty trunks of elephants and fell down. Bulls among elephant-riders clashed against bulls among rathas and killed by arrows, fell down on the ground. Having heard the wails of horse-riders struck by the force of elephants or the lamentations of horse-riders and infantry whose limbs were crushed by the tusks of elephants, many men were distressed and fell down.

'"Many elephants, horses and chariots were running away and there was a great terror among the horse-riders and infantry. Bhishma, surrounded by maharathas, saw the one who had the king of apes on his standard. Shantanu's son had a palm tree on his standard, embellished with the marks of five palm trees. He rushed against the valiant Kiriti, who possessed well-trained and swift horses and great weapons and arrows with the resplendence of the vajra. O king! Many other warriors, with Drona, Kripa, Shalya, Vivimshati,

Duryodhana and Somadatta's son at the forefront, advanced against Indra's son, who was like Shakra himself. Arjuna's brave son, Abhimanyu, was skilled in the knowledge of all weapons and was clad in golden and colourful armour. He rushed out from the mass of rathas and attacked. He confounded the great weapons of all those maharathas. Karshni[156] performed deeds that were incapable of being countered. He was like the illustrious fire on a sacrificial altar, when the one with the flames has been invoked with great mantras. In that battle, the spirited Bhishma swiftly created a river, with the blood of enemies as the foam. But he avoided Subhadra's son and attacked maharatha Partha. Kiriti grasped Gandiva, extraordinary to behold. Its roar was exceedingly loud. He cast out a net of arrows and repulsed the net of great weapons.[157] The supreme among all wielders of the bow, with the king of apes on his standard, then showered down a net of arrows and polished and broad-headed arrows on the great-souled Bhishma. All the worlds, the Kurus and the Srinjayas, witnessed the duel between Bhishma and Dhananjaya, the two spirited ones who were the foremost among virtuous men, accompanied by the terrible roars of the bows."'

Chapter 917(57)

'Sanjaya said, "O venerable one! Drona's son, Bhurishrava, Shalya, Chitrasena[158] and Samyamani's son[159] fought with Subhadra's son. While he was fighting with these five tigers among men alone, people saw that he was extremely energetic and was like a young lion against elephants. No one was equal to Krishna's son[160]

---

[156]Karshni means a descendant of Krishna. This is Abhimanyu. Hence, the Krishna in question is Arjuna.

[157]Released by Bhishma.

[158]In what follows, the warrior seems to be Shala and not Chitrasena.

[159]Samyamani is another name for Shala.

[160]The Krishna here is Arjuna and Krishna's son is Abhimanyu.

in sureness of aim, courage, valour, knowledge of weapons and dexterity. When Partha saw his son, the scorcher of enemies, thus displaying his valour in that battle, he uttered a roar like a lion. O lord of the earth! O Indra among kings! Having seen your grandson oppress your soldiers in this way, those on your side surrounded him from all directions. But Subhadra's son, the destroyer of enemies, was not dispirited. Using his energy and strength, he attacked the sons of Dhritarashtra. When he was fighting with the enemy in that battle and using his large bow, he was like the sun in radiance and was seen to use dextrous moves. He pierced Drona's son with one arrow and Shalya with five. He sliced down the standard of Samyamani's son with eight. Somadatta's son[161] hurled a gold-shafted and giant lance at him and it was like a serpent. But he cut it down with sharp arrows. Arjuna's heir repulsed the hundreds of extremely terrible arrows that Shalya shot and slew his four horses. Bhurishrava, Shalya, Drona's son, Samyamani's son and Shala were struck with terror at the strength of arms displayed by Krishna's son and could not withstand him.

"'O Indra among kings! The Trigartas, the Madras, the Kekayas, with a number of twenty-five thousand, were urged by your son. They were foremost among those who were skilled in the use of weapons and were incapable of being vanquished by enemies in battle. They surrounded Kiriti and his son, desiring to kill them. O king! The Panchala general, conqueror of enemies, saw from a distance that the father and son, bulls among charioteers, had been surrounded. With many thousands of elephants and chariots and surrounded by hundreds of thousands of horse-riders and infantry, the scorcher of enemies angrily stretched his bow and advanced against the army of Madras and Kekayas. Protected by the illustrious and firm wielder of the bow and with masses of chariots, elephants and horses, that army was resplendent as it advanced towards the fight. O descendant of the Kuru lineage! While he was advancing towards Arjuna, Panchala struck Sharadvat[162] in the shoulder with three arrows. He killed ten

---

[161]Bhurishrava.
[162]Kripa.

Madrakas with ten arrows. With a broad-headed arrow, he cheerfully killed Kritavarma's horses. With an iron arrow that was broad at the tip, the scorcher of enemies killed Damana, the heir of the great-souled Pourava. At this, Samyamani's son pierced Panchala, who was invincible in battle, with thirty arrows and his charioteer with another ten. Having been thus wounded, that great archer licked the corners of his mouth with his tongue and used a broad-headed and extremely sharp arrow to slice down the bow.[163] O king! He swiftly wounded him with another twenty-five and killed his horses and the two charioteers who protected his flanks.[164] O bull among the Bharata lineage! With his horses slain, Samyamani's son remained stationed on the chariot and looked at the great-souled son of Panchala.[165] Grasping an extremely terrible sword that was made out of iron, he advanced on foot towards the chariot of Drupada's son. He was like a large wave, or like a serpent descending from the sky. He whirled his sword and with the blazing sword, looked like the resplendent sun at the time of destruction. He was like a crazy elephant in his valour. The Pandavas and Parshata Dhrishtadyumna saw him. On seeing him advance towards him, with a sharp sword in his hand and holding a shield, Panchala's son was overcome with rage. He was beyond the range of arrows, but was swiftly advancing towards the chariot. The enraged general shattered his head with a club. O king! When he fell down dead, the extremely polished sword and shield were loosened from his hands and fell down on the ground. Thus did the great-souled son of the king of Panchala exhibit his terrible valour and having killed him with his supreme club, obtained supreme fame.

'"O venerable one! When the prince, the maharatha and great archer, was killed, loud cries of lamentation arose among your

---

[163]Of Samayamani's son.

[164]Parshnis. Parshni has different meanings. When four horses are attached to a chariot, it means one of the outside horses. It can also mean one of the two charioteers who drive the outside horses, as opposed to the main charioteer (sarathi), or someone who guards the axles.

[165]The word Panchala is being used both for Drupada and for his son, Dhrishtadyumna.

soldiers. Having seen that his son had been slain, Samyamani angrily and forcefully advanced against Panchala, invincible in battle. A great battle commenced between those two brave ones, both of whom were invincible in battle and all the kings among the Kurus and the Pandavas looked on. Samyamani, the destroyer of enemy heroes, struck Parshata with three arrows, like a mighty elephant with goads. Shalya, the adornment of any assembly, also angrily struck the brave Parshata on his chest and another encounter commenced."'

Chapter 918(58)

'Dhritarashtra said, "O Sanjaya! I think that destiny is superior to human endeavour, since the soldiers of my sons are being killed by the soldiers of Pandu. O son![166] You always tell me that those on my side are being slaughtered and you always tell me that the Pandavas are not being killed and are happy. O Sanjaya! You tell me that those on my side are devoid of manliness and have fallen down, or are falling down, or are being killed. They are fighting to the best of their capacity and are endeavouring for victory. But while those on my side are decaying, the Pandavas are obtaining victory. O son! I am always hearing about the great, terrible and intolerable misery that has been caused by Duryodhana's misdeeds. O Sanjaya! I do not see any means whereby the Pandavas may decay and those on my side are able to obtain victory in this battle."

'Sanjaya replied, 'O king! Be patient and listen to the slaughter of the bodies of men and the destruction of elephants, horses and chariots and all of this great evil originates with you. Shalya oppressed Dhrishtadyumna with nine arrows. He was enraged and oppressed the lord of Madra with iron arrows. We then witnessed Parshata's extraordinary valour, as he swiftly countered Shalya, the adornment of assemblies. As they engaged in battle, no gap could be seen and

---

[166]The word used is tata.

the battle between the two seemed to last only for an instant. O great
king! In that encounter, Shalya sliced down Dhrishtadyumna's bow
with a broad-headed, yellow and sharp arrow. O descendant of the
Bharata lineage! He enveloped him with a shower of arrows and it
was like clouds showering down rain on mountains at the time of the
monsoon. When Dhrishtadyumna was thus tormented, Abhimanyu
became angry. With great force, he dashed towards the chariot of
the king of Madra. Having reached the chariot of the lord of Madra,
Karshni, whose soul was immeasurable, pierced Artayani with three
arrows. O king! Those on your side wished to counter Arjuna's son
in battle. They surrounded the chariot of the king of Madra and
stationed themselves there. O descendant of the Bharata lineage!
O fortunate one! Duryodhana, Vikarna, Duhshasana, Vivimshati,
Durmarshana, Duhsaha, Chitrasena, Durmukha, Satyavrata and
Purumitra stationed themselves in battle, so as to protect the chariot of
the lord of Madra. O lord of the earth! At this, the angry Bhimasena,
Parshata Dhrishtadyumna, Droupadi's sons, Abhimanyu and the
Pandavas who were Madri's sons[167] discharged many different kinds
of weapons. In great delight, they sought to kill each other. O king!
It is because of your evil policy that they engaged in battle. When
that terrible encounter commenced between the ten rathas on either
side, all the other rathas, on your side and on those of the enemy,
became spectators. The maharathas discharged many different kinds
of weapons. They roared at each other and struck each other. They
were inflamed with anger and desired to kill each other. They were
intolerant of each other and discharged great weapons. Overcome
with anger in that great battle, Duryodhana pierced Dhrishtadyumna
with four sharp, swift and terrible arrows. Durmarshana pierced
him with twenty, Chitrasena with five, Durmukha with nine arrows,
Duhsaha with seven, Vivimshati with five and Duhshasana with three.
O Indra among kings! In return, Parshata, the tormentor of enemies,
displayed the dexterity of his hands and pierced each of them with
twenty-five. O descendant of the Bharata lineage! In that encounter,
Abhimanyu pierced Satyavrata and Purumitra with ten arrows

[167]There were ten charioteers on the Kourava side and ten on the Pandava side.

each. In that battle, the sons of Madri, the delight of their mother, enveloped their maternal uncle[168] with a wonderful torrent of arrows. O great king! The sons of his sister were supreme charioteers and were repulsing him. But Shalya enveloped them with many arrows. Despite being covered, the sons of Madri did not waver.

'"The immensely strong Bhimasena saw Duryodhana. Pandava grasped a club, thinking that he would bring an end to the strife. On seeing the mighty-armed Bhimasena with his upraised club, like the peak of Kailasa, your sons were terrified and fled. However, Duryodhana was angered. With ten thousand swift elephants, he engaged the army of Magadhas against him.[169] With that army of elephants, and placing the Magadhas in front of him, King Suyodhana advanced against Bhimasena. Vrikodara saw that army of elephants descending on him. Roaring like a lion, he leapt down from the chariot, with a club in his hand. He grasped the heavy and great club, with a heart like that of a mountain. He attacked that army of elephants, like death with a gaping mouth. Killing the elephants with the club, the powerful one wandered around in battle. The mighty-armed Bhimasena was like Vasava with the vajra. He let out a loud roar and this made the mind and the heart tremble. At Bhima's mighty roar, the elephants gathered together and lost all power of motion. The sons of Droupadi, Subhadra's maharatha son, Nakula, Sahadeva and Parshata Dhrishtadyumna were guarding Bhima's rear. They attacked the elephants with a shower of arrows, like clouds pouring down on mountains. With razor-sharp and broad-headed arrows and yellow *anjalika*s, the Pandavas severed the heads of those who were fighting on elephants.[170] The heads fell down and so did adorned arms and hands with goads held in them. It seemed like a shower of stones. Seated on the backs of elephants, those who were fighting on elephants lost their heads. They looked like broken trees

[168]Shalya was Madri's brother.

[169]Against Bhima.

[170]Four types of arrows are mentioned here—*kshura*s (with tips like razors), *kshurapra*s (arrows with sharp edges), bhallas (arrows with broad heads) and anjalikas (with heads shaped like crescents).

on the summits of mountains. We saw other large elephants slain and
brought down by Dhrishtadyumna, the great-souled Parshata. In that
battle, the king of Magadha advanced on an elephant that looked
like Airavata,[171] towards the chariot of Subhadra's son. On seeing
Magadha's mighty elephant advance towards him, Subhadra's son,
the destroyer of enemy heroes, killed it with an arrow. After depriving
him of his elephant, Karshni, the destroyer of enemy cities, used a
broad-headed and silver-shafted arrow to slice off the king's head.

   "'Pandava Bhimasena penetrated that army of elephants. He
roamed around the field of battle, crushing elephants, like Indra
against mountains. In that battle, we saw Bhimasena kill elephants
with a single stroke, like mountains shattered by the vajra. Elephants
had broken tusks, broken temples, broken bones, broken backs and
broken heads. They were slain like mountains. They trumpeted and
lay down on the ground. Other elephants refused to fight in the
battle. Some issued urine. In pain, others issued excrement. We saw
dead elephants strewn along whichever path Bhimasena took, like
mountains. Others vomited blood. Other giant elephants had their
frontal globes smashed. Some lost their senses and fell down on the
ground, like mountains on the face of the earth. Bhima wandered
around on the field of battle, like death with a staff in his hand. His
body was smeared with fat, blood, lard and marrow. Vrikodara
whirled his club, drenched with the blood of elephants. He seemed to
be as terrible as Pinaki, the wielder of Pinaka.[172] Crushed by the angry
Bhimasena, the remaining army of your elephants suddenly fled. The
charioteers and great archers, with Subdhadra's son at the forefront,
protected the brave one as he fought, like the wielder of the vajra is
by the immortals. He held the club that was drenched in blood and
was himself drenched in the blood of elephants. Bhimasena, terrible
in his soul, then seemed to be like death himself. O descendant of
the Bharata lineage! We saw him whirl his club in every direction.
In that battle, we saw him dancing around like Shankara. O great
king! We saw his terrible, heavy and devastating club, like Yama's

---

[171]Indra's elephant.
[172]Shiva's name is Pinaki and the name of his trident or bow is Pinaka.

staff and with a sound like that of Indra's vajra. It was covered in
hair and marrow and was smeared with blood. It was like Rudra's
Pinaka, when he angrily kills animals. Just as a herdsman uses a stick
to drive a herd of animals, your army of elephants was driven back
by Bhima's club. They were killed by that club and by arrows from
all directions. Your elephants were scattered and ran away, crushing
their own soldiers. Like a great storm that scatters the clouds, the
elephants were driven away in that tumult by Bhima. He stood, like
the wielder of the trident[173] in a cremation ground.'"

Chapter 919(59)

'Sanjaya said, "When that army of elephants was destroyed, your
son, Duryodhana, instructed all the soldiers to kill Bhimasena.
On your son's instructions, all the soldiers uttered terrible roars and
rushed against Bhimasena. That large army was incapable of being
assailed, even by the gods. It was as difficult to cross as the turbulent
ocean, on the night of the new or full moon. It was full of chariots,
horses and elephants. There was the sound of conch shells. There were
a large number of kings in it and it was incapable of being agitated. As
it advanced, Bhimasena stationed himself in the battle, against a large
ocean. He was like the shore, withstanding that ocean of soldiers.
O king! In that battle, we faithfully witnessed Bhimasena's wonderful,
extraordinary and superhuman deed. Without any hesitation,
Bhimasena countered all those kings, horses, chariots and elephants
with his club. That supreme of charioteers used his club to check
that large army. Bhima stood immobile in that melee, like Mount
Meru. At that extremely tumultuous and supremely dreadful time,
his brothers, his sons, Parshata Dhrishtadyumna, Droupadi's sons,
Abhimanyu and maharatha Shikhandi did not abandon Bhimasena,
because of the fear that was engendered from that great force.

[173]Shiva.

'"He[174] grasped a heavy and great club that was made of steel[175] and rushed against your soldiers, like Death with a staff in his hand. The lord smashed large numbers of chariots and large numbers of horses. Bhima wandered around in that battle, like the fire of destruction at the end of a yuga. He killed everyone in that encounter, like the lord of death at the end of a yuga. Pandava crushed large numbers of chariots with the force of his thighs. He was like a crazy elephant and all of them were like reeds before an elephant. He brought down charioteers from chariots and elephant-riders from elephants. He brought down horse-riders from the backs of horses and crushed infantry on the ground. With the dead bodies of men, elephants and horses, the field of battle looked like the abode of the dead. He was like Rudra with the Pinaka, destroying animals in his anger. With the terrible and destructive club, which made a sound like Indra's vajra, Bhimasena looked like Yama, with a staff in his hand. The great-souled Kounteya whirled his club and assumed an extremely terrible form, like death at the time of the destruction of a yuga. He repeatedly shattered that large army. He was seen to be like death himself and all of them became dispirited. O descendant of the Bharata lineage! Wherever Pandava cast his eye, with his club upraised, all the soldiers there seemed to vanish. He shattered the soldiers and was unvanquished by the army. He devoured the soldiers, like the destroyer with a gaping mouth. He grasped the great club and performed terrible deeds there.

'"On seeing Vrikodara thus, Bhishma swiftly advanced towards him. He was on a giant chariot with the radiance of the sun and it roared like the clouds. He enveloped everything with a shower of arrows, like clouds showering down rain. On seeing Bhishma advance, like the destroyer with a gaping mouth, the mighty-armed and intolerant Bhima rushed towards him. At that instant, Satyaki, the brave descendant of the Shini lineage, devoted to the truth,

---

[174]Bhima.

[175]The text uses the word shaikyayasa. This should be translated as steel. However, it is also possible to break up the word into shaikya and ayasa and thus translate it as sharp iron.

attacked the grandfather. He began to kill the enemy with his firm
bow and made the soldiers of your son tremble. He was borne on
silver steeds and unleashed arrows from his firm bow. O descendant
of the Bharata lineage! Among all those on your side, there was no
second one capable of withstanding him.[176] Alambusa, seated on
a supreme king of elephants, pierced him with sharp and terrible
arrows. But Shini's brave grandson pierced him with four arrows
and advanced on his chariot. On seeing the foremost of the Vrishni
lineage thus advancing, circling in the midst of the enemy, repeatedly
repulsing the bulls among the Kuru lineage and roaring, no one, not
even the best, was capable of withstanding him. He tormented like
the midday sun. O king! With the exception of Somadatta's son,
there was no one there who was not cheerless. O descendant of the
Bharata lineage! On seeing that all the charioteers on his side had
been routed, Bhurishrava, Somadatta's son, grasped a terrible and
powerful bow and advanced, desiring to fight with Satyaki."'

Chapter 920(60)

'Sanjaya said, "O king! Extremely enraged, like a gigantic
elephant, Bhurishrava pierced Satyaki with nine arrows.
While all the worlds looked on, Satyaki, immeasurable in his soul,
used straight-tufted arrows to repulse Kourava.[177] At this, King
Duryodhana, surrounded by his brothers, surrounded Somadatta's
son, who was striving in that battle. In the same fashion, the
immensely energetic Pandavas swiftly surrounded Satyaki in that
encounter and stationed themselves for battle. O descendant of the
Bharata lineage! Bhimasena was extremely angry. He raised his club
and confronted all your sons, with Duryodhana at the forefront.
Surrounded by several thousand chariots and inflamed with anger,

[176]The exception being Alambusa, or more likely, Bhurishrava.

[177]The word Kourava is being used because Bhurishrava was on the
Kourava side.

your son, Nandaka, pierced the immensely strong Bhimasena with
sharp arrows, tufted with the feathers of herons and sharpened on
stone. In that battle, Duryodhana was also angry and struck the
immensely strong Bhimasena in the chest with three sharp arrows. At
this, the mighty-armed and immensely strong Bhima climbed onto his
own chariot, supreme among chariots, and told Vishoka,[178] 'These
brave maharathas, the sons of Dhritarashtra, are extremely strong.
They are extremely angry and are trying to kill me in battle. While you
look on, there is no doubt that I will kill them today in this encounter.
O charioteer! Therefore, in this encounter, drive the horses carefully.'
Having said this, Partha pierced your son, Duryodhana, with nine
sharp arrows that were decorated with gold. He pierced Nandaka
in the chest with three arrows. Duryodhana pierced the immensely
strong Bhima with six. With another three extremely sharp arrows, he
pierced Vishoka. O king! In that encounter, as if he was smiling, the
king[179] sliced off Bhima's radiant bow from his hand with three sharp
arrows. On seeing that Vishoka was oppressed in that encounter by
the sharp arrows discharged by your archer son, Bhima was unable
to tolerate it. O great king! O descendant of the Bharata lineage! In
great rage, he grasped a divine bow, with the desire of killing your
son. In his anger, he grasped a kshurapra arrow, tufted with hair.
With this, Bhima sliced off the king's supreme bow. Discarding the
bow that was sliced down, he[180] was inflamed with wrath and swiftly
grasped another bow that was stronger. He took up an extremely
terrible arrow that was as radiant as destiny and death. In great
rage, he struck Bhimasena in the chest with this. Having been thus
deeply wounded in the chest, he was in pain and sunk down on the
floor of the chariot, having lost his senses. On seeing that Bhima was
thus wounded, all the Pandava maharathas and great archers, with
Abhimanyu at the forefront, could not tolerate this. Those extremely
energetic ones unleashed a tumultuous shower of terrible and sharp
weapons on your son's head. Meanwhile, the immensely strong

[178]Bhima's charioteer.
[179]Duryodhana.
[180]Duryodhana.

Bhimasena regained consciousness. He again pierced Duryodhana with five arrows. Pandava, the great archer, then pierced Shalya with twenty-five arrows that had golden tufts and thus pierced, he fled from the field of battle.

'"Fourteen of your sons then attacked Bhima—Senapati, Sushena, Jalasandha, Sulochana, Ugra, Bhimaratha, Bhima,[181] Bhimabahu, Alolupa, Durmukha, Dushpradharsha, Vivitsu, Vikata and Soma. Their eyes were red with rage and they shot many arrows towards Bhimasena, piercing him simultaneously. The immensely strong Bhimsena saw your sons and the brave one licked the corners of his mouth, like a wolf amidst smaller animals. With a kshurapra arrow, Pandava sliced off Senapati's head. He pierced Jalasandha and despatched him to Yama's abode. He killed Sushena and sent him to the land of the dead. With a bhalla arrow, he brought down Ugra's head, with the helmet and earrings and as handsome as the moon, to the ground. O venerable one! In that encounter, Bhima then used seven arrows to despatch Bhimabahu to the land of the dead, together with his horses, his standard and his charioteer. O king! Smilingly, Bhimasena swiftly despatched the brothers, Bhima and Bhimaratha, to Yama's abode. In the sight of all the soldiers, in that great encounter, Bhima used a kshurapra arrow to convey Sulochana to Yama's abode. On witnessing Bhimasena's terrible valour, your remaining sons were struck with fear on account of Bhima.[182]

'"Shantanu's son then spoke to all the maharathas. 'This Bhima, wielding a fierce bow, is angry in battle and is slaughtering the maharatha sons of Dhritarashtra, though they are wise, superior, brave and united and the kings are being scattered.' Having been thus addressed, all the soldiers on the side of the sons of Dhritarashtra angrily rushed at the immensely strong Bhimasena. O lord of the earth! Bhagadatta mounted an elephant with rent temples and swiftly descended on the spot where Bhima was stationed. Descending

---

[181]Not to be confused with Pandava Bhima.

[182]Only seven sons are directly mentioned as having been killed. However, all fourteen were killed by Bhima.

in that battle, he used arrows sharpened on stone, so that in the encounter, Bhimasena became invisible, like clouds covering the sun. Depending on the strength of their own arms, the maharathas, with Abhimanyu at the forefront, could not tolerate that Bhima should be thus enveloped. They released a shower of arrows from all directions. The elephant was pierced by arrows from all directions. The elephant of the king of Pragjyotisha was pierced by a shower of extremely energetic and excellent weapons of many types. It was oppressed and covered with blood. In that battle, it looked like a giant cloud that was tinged with the rays of the sun. The elephant was exuding musth. Goaded by Bhagadatta, it rushed against them, like Death urged by the Destroyer. It doubled its speed and made the earth tremble. On beholding its gigantic and extremely terrible form, all the maharathas thought that it was intolerable and became dispirited. O tiger among men! The maharatha king, who was a great archer, used an arrow with drooping tufts to strike him on the chest. Thus struck, his limbs stiffened and losing his senses, he grasped the pole of the standard.[183] On seeing that the others were terrified and that Bhimasena had lost his senses, the powerful and strong Bhagadatta began to roar.

"'O king! On seeing Bhima in this state, the rakshasa Ghatotkacha became angry. Assuming a terrible form, he created fearful maya, capable of creating terror among cowards. He disappeared in an instant and then again assumed a terrible form. He rode on Airavata, created through the use of his own maya. Other elephants that were the guardians of the directions followed it—Anjana, Vamana and Mahapadma.[184] Rakshasas were seated on these extremely radiant and giant elephants. O king! These three were gigantic in form and exuded a lot of musth. They were energetic, courageous and powerful and extremely strong and valiant. Ghatotkacha goaded his own

[183]Bhima was struck and lost his senses.

[184]There are eight elephants who guard the eight directions—Airavata, Pundarika, Vamana, Kumuda, Anjana, Pushpadanta, Sarvabhouma and Supratika. Airavata is also regarded as the king of elephants and is Indra's mount. Mahapadma is another name for either Pundarika or Kumuda.

elephant. The scorcher of enemies wished to kill Bhagadatta and his elephant. The other rakshasas, immensely strong, goaded the other elephants, each of which possessed four tusks. They descended on Bhagadatta's elephant and simultaneously pierced it with their tusks. Oppressed and pained by those elephants and wounded by the arrows, it uttered a giant roar, like the sound of thunder. On hearing the roar and the extremely terrible and fearful sound, Bhishma spoke to Drona and King Suyodhana. 'In fighting in this battle with Hidimba's evil-souled son, the great archer Bhagadatta confronts a mighty danger. This rakshasa resorts to great illusion and the king is also extremely wrathful. These extremely valorous ones will confront each other, like Death and the Destroyer facing each other. We can hear the great roars of the delighted Pandavas. We can hear the great lamentations of the frightened elephant.[185] O fortunate ones! Let us go and protect the king. If he is not swiftly protected in this encounter, he will lose his life. O extremely valiant ones! Therefore, let us proceed without delay. This great and terrible encounter has commenced and it is making the body hair stand up. This brave leader of an army[186] is devoted to us and has been born in a noble lineage. O ones without decay! It is appropriate that we should save him together.' On hearing these words of Bhishma, with Bharadvaja's son at the forefront, and accompanied by all the kings, they advanced to protect Bhagadatta.

'"With great speed, they advanced to the spot where he was stationed. On seeing that they were advancing, with Yudhishthira at the forefront, the Panchalas, together with the Pandavas, followed the enemy from behind. On seeing that large army, the powerful Indra among the rakshasas let out an extremely loud roar, which was like the sound of thunder. On hearing this roar and on seeing the fighting elephants, Shantanu's son, Bhishma, spoke to Bharadvaja's son. 'I do not wish to fight with Hidimba's evil-souled son. He is full of strength and valour now and has support. The wielder of the vajra himself is incapable of vanquishing him in battle now. He is certain

---

[185]Bhagadatta's elephant.
[186]Referring to Bhagadatta.

in his aims and can strike. Our mounts are exhausted and at the end of the day, are wounded and lacerated on account of the Panchalas and the Pandaveyas. Therefore, I do not think that we should fight any more with the victorious Pandavas. Let it be announced that we will withdraw for the day. Tomorrow, we will fight with the enemy again.' On hearing the grandfather's words, the Kouravas, who were oppressed by the fear of Ghatotkacha, were happy and resorted to the advent of night. The Kouravas retreated. O descendant of the Bharata lineage! The Pandavas were victorious and roared like lions, sounding conch shells and flutes. O bull among the Bharata lineage! Thus did the battle rage on that day, between the Kurus and the Pandavas, with Ghatotkacha at the front. O king! The Kouravas returned to their own camps. When night arrived, they were ashamed at having been defeated by the Pandaveyas. The bodies of the maharatha sons of Pandu were wounded by arrows. But they were delighted at the outcome of the battle and returned to their camps. O great king! They placed Bhimasena and Ghatotkacha in the front and in great delight, honoured them. They roared in many different kinds of ways and this mixed with the sounds of the trumpets. They roared like lions and this mingled with the sounds of conch shells. The great-souled ones roared and made the earth tremble. O venerable one! This agitated the hearts of your sons. When night fell, those scorchers of enemies retired to their camps. King Duryodhana was miserable at his brothers having been killed. He reflected on this for some time, overcome by sorrow and tears. He then made arrangements in all the camps, according to what is decreed. He was tormented by sorrow and pained, on account of his brothers.'"

Chapter 921(61)

'Dhritarashtra said, "O Sanjaya! I am struck by great fear and wonder on hearing of the deeds of the sons of Pandu. Even the gods will find it extremely difficult to accomplish these. O Sanjaya!

O suta! On hearing about the defeat of my sons in every way, I am overcome with grave thoughts about what will happen. Vidura's certain words are oppressing my heart. O Sanjaya! Because of destiny, it is seen that everything is occurring as he said it would. Bhishma is the foremost among brave ones and is supreme among those who possess the knowledge of weapons. That warrior is fighting with the army of the Pandavas. What do the great-souled and immensely strong sons of Pandu possess? O son![187] What supreme boons have they obtained? What knowledge have they accumulated? They do not suffer any decay, like masses of stars in the firmament. I cannot endure the repeated slaughter of my soldiers at the hands of the Pandavas. Because of destiny, this extremely terrible punishment is descending on me. The sons of Pandu cannot be killed and my sons are being slaughtered. O Sanjaya! I cannot detect any reason as to why this should be the case. Nor do I see any means of overcoming this misery. I am like a man who is trying to cross the mighty ocean with his arms. There is no doubt that all my sons will meet a terrible death. I do not see a brave one who can protect those on my side in battle. O Sanjaya! In this battle, the destruction of my sons is certain. O suta! Tell me the specific reason for this. I am now asking you about the true reason and you should tell me everything. What did Duryodhana do, on seeing that his troops were running away in battle? What about Bhishma, Drona, Kripa, Soubala, Jayadratha, the mighty archer who is Drona's son and the immensely strong Vikarna? What did those great-souled ones determine to do then? O immensely wise one! O Sanjaya! Did my sons retreat?"

'Sanjaya replied, "O king! Listen attentively to what you wish to hear. Nothing was accomplished because of mantras and nothing was caused by maya. O king! Nor did the Pandavas create a fresh calamity. They are fighting in a just cause and they are fighting according to their powers. O descendant of the Bharata lineage! They have performed all their deeds and tasks in accordance with dharma. The Parthas have always acted so as to obtain great fame. Resorting to dharma, those immensely strong ones have never retreated from

[187]The word used is tata.

a fight. They have obtained supreme prosperity. Where there is dharma, victory exists there. O king! That is the reason the Parthas cannot be killed in battle and that is the reason they are victorious. Your evil-souled son has always acted according to evil. He is cruel and has performed inferior deeds. That is the reason he is decaying in this battle. O lord of men! Your son has performed many violent deeds. He has deceived the sons of Pandu, acting like inferior men. They disregarded all the offences committed by your son. O Pandu's elder brother! The Pandavas have always ignored them. O lord of the earth! Your son has not shown them appropriate honour. This is the outcome of those evil deeds. These are the extremely terrible fruits of that, like that of *kimpaka*.[188] O great king! With your sons and well-wishers, you are tasting that. O king! Though you were restrained by your well-wishers, Vidura, Bhishma and the great-souled Drona, you did not realize this. I also tried to restrain you, but you did not accept those words. Those were beneficial words. They were like medicine. But you rejected them, like a dying man who does not accept medicines. You accepted the views of your sons and hoped to defeat the Pandavas. Listen to my words about the true reasons. You have asked me about them. O foremost among the Bharata lineage! I will tell you about the reasons behind the victory of the Pandavas. O scorcher of enemies! I will tell you exactly as I have heard it. Duryodhana himself asked the grandfather about this, when he saw that all his maharatha brothers were vanquished in the battle. When night fell, Kourava was overwhelmed with sorrow in his heart. In humility, he went to the immensely wise grandfather. O lord of men! Hear from me what your son said at that time.

"'Duryodhana said, 'You, Drona, Shalya, Kripa, Drona's son, Hardikya Kritavarma,[189] Sudakshina from Kamboja, Bhurishrava, Vikarna and the valiant Bhagadatta—all of these are renowned as maharathas and all of them have been born in noble lineages. It is my view that they are sufficient for all the three worlds. All the assembled Pandavas cannot stand before them in valour. A doubt

---

[188]Kimpaka is a pretty but bitter fruit, probably of the Trichosanthes variety.
[189]Kritavarma was the son of Hridika.

has therefore arisen in my mind and I am asking you about this. How are the Kounteyas obtaining victory at every step? Who is their support?'

'"Bhishma replied, 'O king! O Kourava! Listen to the words that I am going to speak to you. I often spoke to you. But you did not act in accordance with my words. O supreme among the Bharata lineage! I asked you to act so that there might be peace with the Pandavas. O lord! I thought that this would have been beneficial for both you and the world. O king! You would have happily enjoyed the earth with your brothers. You would have chastised all ill-wishers and delighted your relatives. O son![190] But on earlier occasions, you did not heed my words. Because you dishonoured the Pandus, you are now confronted with this calamity. They are the performers of unsullied deeds. O lord! O great king! I will tell you the reasons why they cannot be killed. Listen. There is no one in this world who can vanquish the Pandavas in battle. There has been no such person, nor will there be. They are protected by the wielder of the Sharnga bow.[191] O son! O one learned in dharma! Listen exactly to what was chanted and recounted in the ancient accounts, by sages whose souls were controlled. In ancient times, all the gods and rishis assembled and worshipped the grandfather[192] on Mount Gandhamadana. Seated in their midst, Prajapati[193] saw an excellent and blazing vimana stationed in the sky. Having got to know everything about it through his powers of meditation, Brahma joined his hands in salutation. With his soul filled with delight, he bowed before the supreme being, the supreme lord. On seeing that Brahma had stood up, all the rishis and gods also stood, hands joined in salutation, beholding that great marvel.

'"'Brahma, supreme among those who have knowledge of the brahman, worshipped him and said, "You are the end of the universe. You are the creator of the universe. You are supreme. You

[190]The word used is tata.
[191]Sharnga is the name of Krishna's bow, made out of horn.
[192]Brahma.
[193]Brahma.

are supreme dharma. You are the glory of the universe. You are the manifestation of the universe. You are the refuge of the universe. You are the action of the universe. You are the controller. You are the lord of the universe. You are Vasudeva. You are the soul of yoga. You are divinity and I seek refuge in you. Victory to the great god of the universe. Victory to the one who is engaged in the welfare of the worlds. Victory to the illustrious lord of all yoga. Victory to the one who is before and after yoga. The lotus was created from your navel. You possess large eyes. Victory to the one who is the lord of all the lords in the universe. You are the past, the present and the future. Victory to the one who creates tranquillity in the soul. You are the store of innumerable qualities. Victory to the one on whom everything depends. You are Narayana. You are impossible to comprehend. Victory to the one who is the wielder of the Sharnga bow. You are the one who possesses all the secret qualities. The universe is your form. You are free from disease. You are the lord of the universe. You are mighty-armed. Victory to the one who is engaged in the welfare of the worlds. O mighty serpent! O great boar! O one with the tawny mane! Victory to the lord. O one with the yellow garment! O one who is the lord of the directions. O one in whom the universe resides! O one without decay! You are the manifest. You are the unmanifest. You are in control of your senses. You possess vigorous senses. Your soul is beyond measure. You are the only one who knows about your own self. Victory to the deep one who satisfies all desires. You are infinite. You are known as the wise one. You are eternal. You are the one who causes all the worlds to be manifest. You accomplish all your tasks. You act according to wisdom. You know about dharma. You are the one who is the harbinger of victory. Your soul is mysterious. You are the soul of all beings. You are the origin of everything that comes into existence. You know about the nature of all beings. You are the lord of the worlds. Victory to the one who makes all beings appear. You are the self-creating one. You are the immensely fortunate one. You are the one who acts so as to bring about the destruction of everything. You are the one who inspires all thoughts in the mind. Victory to the brahman, beloved of all beings. You act for the sake of creation and destruction. O lord of desire!

O supreme lord! You are the origin of amrita. You are the origin of virtue. You are the fire at the end of a yuga. You are the one who grants victory. You are the lord of all Prajapatis. O god! The lotus was created from your navel. O immensely powerful one! You are the one who was created from his own self. You are the great being. You are the one with action in his soul. Victory to the one who is active. The goddess earth constitutes your feet. The directions are your arms. The firmament is your head. I am your form. The gods are your limbs. The sun and the moon are your eyes. O lord! Austerities performed because of truth, dharma and desire are your strength. The fire is your energy. The wind is your breath. Water is created from your sweat. The Ashvins are always your ears. The goddess Sarasvati is your tongue. The devoted sacraments of the Vedas are vested in. The universe finds refuge in you. You are the lord of yoga. It is impossible to know your measure, your dimensions, your energy, your valour, your strength or your yoga. The gods are devotedly faithful to you. They are immersed in your rules. O Vishnu! O supreme lord! O great lord! They always worship you. Through your favours, I have created rishis, gods, gandharvas, yakshas, rakshasas, serpents, pishachas, men, animals, birds and reptiles on earth. O one who created the lotus in your navel! O large-eyed one! O Krishna! O dispeller of all misery! You are the destination of all beings. You are the leader. You are the mouth of the universe. O lord of the gods! It is through your favours that the gods are always happy. O god! It is through your favours that the earth is always without fear. O large-eyed one! You have taken birth to extend the lineage of the Yadus, so that dharma may be established and the daityas destroyed. O lord! For upholding the universe, do what I have asked you to. O lord! O Vasudeva! Through your favours, I have exactly sung all that is extremely mysterious in your essence. Create the god Samkarshana[194] out of your own self. O Krishna! Create Pradyumna out of your own self.[195] Aniruddha is known

[194]Balarama.
[195]Pradyumna is the son of Krishna and Rukmini. Aniruddha is Pradyumna's son and Krishna's grandson.

as the undecaying Vishnu and create him out of Pradyumna. It is
Aniruddha who created me, Brahma, the upholder of the universe.[196]
I have been created by Vasudeva's essence and I have therefore been
created by you. O lord! Divide yourself into different parts and take
birth in the world of men. There, for the welfare of all the worlds,
act so that all the asuras can be killed. Establish dharma. Obtain
fame. Obtain the essence of yoga. O infinitely valorous one! The
brahmarshis of the world and the gods are devoted to you and chant
your names and about your supreme soul. They are all established
in you. All beings find refuge in you. You are the one who provides
them sanctuary. O well-armed one! You are the granter of boons.
You have no beginning. You have no middle. You have no end. You
possess the supreme yoga. You are a bridge for the worlds. That is
what the brahmanas sing." ' "

Chapter 922(62)

" " Bhishma said, 'Then the illustrious god, the lord of all
the lords of the world, replied to Brahma in a soft and
deep voice. "O son![197] Through yoga, I have come
to know everything that you desire. It will be as you wish." Saying
this, he instantly disappeared. At this, the gods, the rishis and the
gandharvas were filled with great wonder. All of them were filled with
great curiosity and spoke to the grandfather. "O lord! Who was the
one before whom your illustrious self bowed down? You worshipped
him using supreme praises. We desire to hear this." Thus addressed, the
illustrious grandfather replied to all the gods, the brahmarshis and the
gandharvas in soft and sweet words. "He is the supreme *Tat*.[198] He is

[196]Aniruddha as part of Vishnu and not as Pradyumna's son.
[197]The word used is tata.
[198]Tat means that. Aum Tat Sat is an expression used in the context of the
brahman. Aum stands for the brahman. Tat means that. Sat means the absolute

the one who exists now and he is the one who will exist in the future.
He is the supreme one. He is the lord who is the soul of all beings.
He is the brahman who is the supreme goal. O bulls among gods!
I had a conversation with that cheerful one. For the welfare of the
universe, I sought the favours of the lord of the universe. I requested
him to be born in the world of men and to be known as Vasudeva.
I asked him to be born on earth for the death of the asuras. The
immensely strong and terrible daityas, danavas and rakshasas, who
have been killed in the battle, have been born among men. It is for
their death that the illustrious and mighty one has been born in a
human womb and is roaming around on earth, accompanied by
Nara. The supreme rishis Nara and Narayana are ancient. They
are invincible in battle, even by the united immortals. Ignorant
ones will not know the rishis Nara and Narayana. Vasudeva is
the great god of all the worlds and should be worshipped by you.
I, Brahma, the lord of the universe, am his offspring. O supreme
among the gods! You should never disregard him as a mere man.
He is extremely valorous and holds the conch shell, the chakra and
the club. He is the supreme mystery. He is the supreme goal. He
is the supreme brahman. He is the supreme glory. He is without
decay. He is the one who is not manifest. He is the eternal one. He
is the supreme being whose praise is chanted as Purusha. But no
one knows him. He is supreme energy. He is supreme happiness.
He is the supreme truth praised by Vishvakarma. The illustrious
Vasudeva, whose valour is infinite, should not be disregarded as
a mere man by all the gods and Indra, or by all the worlds. The
evil-minded one, who disregards and speaks of Hrishikesha as a
mere man, is the worst of men. The great-souled yogi has adopted
a human form. He who disregards Vasudeva, is spoken of as one
who is immersed in darkness. That god is the soul of the mobile
and the immobile. He is the immensely radiant one who bears the

---

truth. Hence, Aum Tat Sat means the brahman is the absolute truth. One should
also mention the expression Tat Tvam Asi, an expression that features in the
Upanishads. Tvam means 'you' and Asi means 'are'. Therefore, Tat Tvam Asi
means that you are the brahman.

srivatsa mark.[199] The lotus sprouted from his navel. He who does
not know this is spoken of as one who is immersed in darkness. He
is diademed and wears the Koustubha jewel.[200] He is the one who
dispels the fear of his friends. He who disregards the great-souled one,
will be immersed in terrible darkness. O supreme among the gods!
Having known the truth about Vasudeva, the lord of the lords of the
worlds, all the worlds should show him obeisance." Having spoken
these words to the masses of gods in earlier times, the illustrious soul
of all the worlds returned to his own abode.

""'The gods, the gandharvas, the sages and the apsaras listened to
Brahma's chants, and happily returned to heaven. O son![201] In earlier
times, the learned rishis spoke about Vasudeva in their assembly and
I heard this. O one who knows about the sacred texts! I also heard
this from Rama, Jamadagni's son, the wise Markandeya, Vyasa and
Narada. Having heard the nature of the great-souled and illustrious
Vasudeva, the lord of the lords of the worlds and the undecaying
one, from whom was created Brahma, the father of the universe,
why should men not worship and show obeisance to Vasudeva? O
son! You have been restrained earlier by the sages, learned in the
Vedas, and been asked not to enter into a fight with the intelligent
Vasudeva and also with the Pandavas. But because of your delusion,
you did not understand. I think of you as a cruel rakshasa who is
immersed in darkness. That is the reason you hate Govinda and
Pandava Dhananjaya. O king! I am telling you that he is eternal
and undecaying. He is the eternal one who pervades all the worlds.
He is the controller. He is the creator. He is the eternal upholder.
He holds up all the three worlds. He is the lord and the preceptor
of the mobile and the immobile. He is the warrior. He is victory. He
is the victorious. He is the lord of all nature. O king! He is full of
truth. He is devoid of darkness and passion. Where there is Krishna,
dharma exists there. Where there is dharma, victory exists there.

---

[199]Vishnu bears the srivatsa mark (or curl) on his chest. This is the place
where Lakshmi resides.

[200]Vishnu's jewel that emerged from the churning of the ocean.

[201]The word used is tata.

His greatness is yoga and yoga is his own self. O king! It is because
the sons of Pandu hold this up that victory will be theirs. He always
provides beneficial counsel to the Pandavas. He always gives them
strength in battle and protects them from fear. He is the eternal god.
He is the auspicious one who is full of mystery. O descendant of the
Bharata lineage! You have asked me about the one who is famous
by the name of Vasudeva. Brahmanas, kshatriyas, vaishyas and
shudras, each with their respective marks, always perform their own
duties and serve the one who should be worshipped. At the end of
dvapara yuga and at the beginning of kali yuga, he is the one whom
Satvata Samkarshana eulogized in the appropriate way.[202] All the
worlds of gods and men, with the cities and right up to the frontiers
of the ocean, where men have lived for years and years, have been
repeatedly created by Vasudeva.'"'

Chapter 923(63)

"'"Duryodhana said, 'In all the worlds, Vasudeva is
spoken of as the great being. O grandfather! I wish
to know about his origin and his glory.'

"'"Bhishma replied, 'Vasudeva is the great being. He was created
with the gods. O bull among the Bharata lineage! No one superior
to Pundarikaksha can be seen. Markandeya spoke about Govinda's
extraordinary greatness. He is the great-souled Purushottama. He
is in all beings and is the soul of all beings. He created the three
elements of water, air and energy. He is the god who created the
earth. He is the lord of all the lords of the worlds. The great-souled
Purushottama was lying down on water. The god who is everywhere
was asleep in his yoga. He created fire from his mouth. He created
wind from his breath of life. Through his mind, the undecaying one

---

[202]However, at the time when this is being said, the present kali yuga has
not yet started.

created Sarasvati and the Vedas. He initially created the worlds, with
the gods and the masses of rishis. He decreed the decay and death
of all beings and also their birth and growth. He is dharma. He is
learned in dharma. He is the granter of boons. He is the one who
satisfies all desire. He is the actor. He is action. He is the ancient
god and is himself the lord. He created the past, the present and
the future, and everything. Janardana created the two sandhyas,[203]
the directions, the sky and the rituals. Govinda created the austere
rishis. The great-souled and undecaying lord created the universe.
He created Samkarshana, the first among all beings. He created the
god Shesha, whom the learned know of as Ananta. He holds up all
beings and the earth, with all its mountains.[204] Through their yoga
of meditation, brahmanas speak of him as the immensely energetic
one. The great asura named Madhu was born from the secretion
of his ears. He was extremely terrible in his deeds and terrible in
his intelligence. He was about to kill Brahma, but Purushottama
slew him. O son! Having killed him, the god Janardana came to be
worshipped by gods, danavas, men and rishis as Madhusudana.[205]
He is the boar. He is the lion. He is the lord with the three steps.[206]
He is the mother. He is the father. He is Hari for all beings. There is
no one superior to Pundarikaksha, nor will there ever be. O king!
He created the brahmanas from his mouth, the kshatriyas from his
arms, the vaishyas from his thighs and the shudras from his feet. He
is the refuge of all beings. He is the essence of the brahman. He is the
essence of yoga. One can attain the great god Keshava by devoutly
performing austerities on the nights of the new moon and the full
moon. Keshava is supreme energy. He is the grandfather of all the
worlds. O lord of men! The sages know him as Hrishikesha.[207] Know

---

[203]Dawn and dusk.

[204]The earth rests on the serpent Shesha.

[205]Madhusudana means the destroyer of Madhu.

[206]These are respective references to Vishnu's *varaha* (boar), *narasimha*
(man-lion) and *vamana* (dwarf) incarnations.

[207]Hrishikesha means the lord of the senses.

him to be the teacher, the father and the preceptor. When Krishna favours someone, he wins the undecaying worlds. If a man confronts fear and always seeks refuge with Keshava, or reads about this, such a man obtains sanctuary and happiness. Men who attain Krishna are never deluded. Janardana always saves those who are immersed in great fear. O descendant of the Bharata lineage! Yudhishthira knows about the truth of this. O king! With all his soul, he has sought refuge with the great-souled Keshava, the lord of the universe. He is the lord of yoga and he is the lord of the earth.'"'

Chapter 924(64)

Bhishma said, 'O great king! Hear this hymn from me. It was chanted by Brahma himself and, in ancient times, recounted to those on earth by the brahmarshis and the gods. "You are the god of the sadhyas. You are the illustrious god who is the lord of all the gods. You know about the creator of the worlds. Thus did Narada speak about you. Markandeya has described you as the past, the present and the future. You are the sacrifice among all sacrifices. You are austerity among all austerities. You are the god of all the gods. Thus did the illustrious Bhrigu describe you. You are the terrible and ancient form of Vishnu, the lord of all beings. You are Vasudeva among the Vasus. You are the one who established Shakra. You are the god of the gods and the god of all beings. Thus did Dvaipayana speak of you. In earlier times, at the time of the creation of all beings, you have been spoken of as Daksha Prajapati. You are the creator of all the worlds. Thus did Angiras speak of you. That which is not manifest is your body. That which is manifest is established in your mind. The gods have been created from your words. Thus did Devala speak of you. Your head extends up to heaven. Your two arms hold up the earth. The three worlds are in your stomach. You are the eternal Purusha. Men who are purified through austerities know of you in this way. To rishis who are satisfied with knowledge of the soul, you are truth. O Madhusudana! You are sole refuge of generous royal sages who do not retreat from the field of battle and who resort to the supreme forms of dharma." O son! This is the nature of Keshava and I have recounted it you, both briefly and in detail. With affection in your mind, turn towards Keshava.'"

'Sanjaya said, "O great king! Having heard this sacred account, your son formed a high opinion of Keshava and the maharatha Pandavas. O great king! Bhishma, Shantanu's son, again spoke to him. 'O son! You have heard about the glory of the great-souled Keshava and about the essence of Nara. You had asked me about them. You have heard about the reasons why Nara and Narayana have been born among men and why those two brave ones cannot be vanquished or slain in battle. O king! Nor can the Pandavas be worsted in battle. Krishna is firm in his devotion to the illustrious Pandavas. O Indra among kings! That is the reason I am telling you that you should strive for peace with the Pandavas. Enjoy the earth, with your powerful brothers around you. If you disregard the gods Nara and Narayana, you will be destroyed.' O lord of the earth! Having spoken in this way, your father became silent. Having taken his leave of the king, he left to sleep for the night. The great-souled king bowed to him and left for his own camp. O bull among the Bharata lineage! He spent the night on a white bed."'

Chapter 925(65)

'Sanjaya said, "O great king! When the night had passed and the sun had arisen, both the armies assembled to fight again. In great rage, wishing to kill each other, they advanced against each other. All of them glanced at each other and assembled for the encounter. O king! Because of your evil counsel, the Pandavas and the sons of Dhritarashtra arrayed themselves in vyuhas and counter-vyuhas.

They armed and arrayed themselves and attacked each other. O king! Bhishma protected himself in every direction in the form of a makara vyuha.[208] O king! The Pandavas also protected themselves in the form of a vyuha. Your father, Devavrata, advanced with a great army of chariots. He was surrounded by supreme charioteers and other chariots, infantry, elephants and horse-riders, all stationed in accordance with their appropriate ranks. The illustrious Pandavas saw that they were ready for battle. They arranged themselves for battle in the form of a *shyena*,[209] the invincible vyuha that is the king of all vyuhas. The immensely strong Bhimasena was radiant at the mouth. The invincible Shikhandi and Parshata Dhrishtadyumna were the eyes. The brave Satyaki, with truth as his valour, was the head. Wielding the Gandiva bow, Partha was stationed at the neck. With an entire akshouhini, the illustrious and great-souled Drupada, together with his sons, stationed himself for battle on the left wing. Kekaya, the leader of an akshouhini, was stationed on the right wing. Droupadi's sons and Subhadra's valiant son formed the back. The illustrious King Yudhishthira, handsome in his prowess, was himself at the rear, with his two intelligent brothers.[210]

"'The battle commenced with Bhima penetrating the makara's mouth. He advanced against Bhishma in that encounter and enveloped him with arrows. O descendant of the Bharata lineage! Using great weapons, Bhishma brought these down. In that great battle, he confounded the soldiers of the sons of Pandu, who were stationed in arrays. On seeing that the soldiers were confounded, Dhananjaya swiftly advanced. In the forefront of that battle, he pierced Bhishma with one thousand arrows. Having repulsed the weapons that had been released by Bhishma in that encounter, he delighted his own soldiers, who were stationed in battle. At this, King Duryodhana spoke to Bharadvaja's son. The supreme among strong ones had earlier witnessed the terrible slaughter of his

[208]A makara is a mythical aquatic animal and makara can loosely be translated as shark or crocodile.

[209]Hawk.

[210]Nakula and Sahadeva.

soldiers and the death of his brothers in the battle. Remembering
this, the maharatha said, 'O preceptor! O unblemished one! You
have always had my welfare in heart. We have sought refuge with
you and with Bhishma, the grandfather. With this, there is no doubt
that we can hope to vanquish even the gods in battle, not to speak
of the sons of Pandu, who are inferior in valour and power in this
encounter.' O venerable one! Having been thus addressed by your
son, while Satyaki looked on, Drona penetrated the Pandava ranks.
O descendant of the Bharata lineage! Satyaki countered Drona's
progress and a tumultuous battle commenced. It made the body hair
stand up. Bharadvaja's powerful son was enraged. In that encounter,
as if smiling, he pierced Shini's descendant on his shoulders with
ten sharp arrows. O king! At this, extremely enraged, Bhimasena
wished to protect Satyaki from Drona, supreme among the wielders
of weapons, and pierced him. O venerable one! In that battle, Drona,
Bhishma and Shalya angrily enveloped Bhimasena with arrows. O
venerable one! Abhimanyu became angry, and so did Droupadi's
sons. They used sharp arrows to wound all the warriors with
upraised weapons. In the great battle, the great archer, Shikhandi,
angrily advanced against the immensely strong Bhishma and Drona,
who were causing this torment. The brave and powerful one grasped
a bow that had the sound of a cloud. Shikhandi swiftly showered
arrows that shrouded the sun. However, on confronting him, the
grandfather of the Bharata lineage remembered that he had been a
woman earlier and withdrew from the battle. O great king! At this,
instructed by your son and with a desire to protect Bhishma, Drona
rushed to battle. Shikhandi confronted Drona, supreme among the
wielders of weapons, and fled from the field of battle, as if from the
fire that burns at the destruction of an era. O lord of the earth! With
a large army, your son advanced to protect Bhishma and desiring
a great victory. O king! But with Dhananjaya at the forefront, the
Pandavas advanced against Bhishma, firm in their resolution of
ensuring victory. A terrible and extremely wonderful battle ensued,
like that between the gods and the danavas. Each side desired victory
and eternal fame."'

Chapter 926(66)

'Sanjaya said, "Shantanu's son, Bhishma, then fought a tumultous
battle, wishing to save your sons from their fear of Bhimasena.
In the forenoon, there was an extremely terrible battle between the
kins on the Kuru and Pandava sides, with the destruction of the
foremost among warriors. While that extremely fearful battle was
raging on, there was a great and tumultuous sound that seemed to
touch the sky. Giant elephants roared. Horses neighed. There was
the sound of drums and conch shells and there was a mighty roar.
Those valiant and extremely strong ones fought with each other,
desiring victory. They roared at each other, like great bulls among
herds of cows. O bull among the Bharata lineage! In that battle, heads
were sliced down with sharp arrows and descended like a shower of
stones from the sky. They still wore earrings and helmets, blazing in
gold. O bull among the Bharata lineage! These heads were seen to
fall down. The bodies were wounded by arrows. The severed arms
still held on to bows. Adorned with ornaments, they were seen to be
strewn all over the ground. The bodies bore armour. The upper arms
were decorated with bracelets. The faces were like moons. The eyes
were red. O lord of the earth! There were all the bodies of elephants,
horses and men. In an instant, the earth was covered with a thick
dust. In that thick cloud of dust, the weapons were like lightning.
The sound made by the weapons was like the clap of thunder. O
descendant of the Bharata lineage! The ensuing tumultuous and fierce
encounter between the Kurus and the Pandavas made a river of blood
flow there. It was an extremely fearful, terrible and tumultuous fight
and it made the body hair stand up. Unassailable in that battle, the
kshatriyas showered down arrows. O supreme among the Bharata
lineage! Afflicted by the shower of arrows in that encounter, your
elephants, and those belonging to the enemy, screamed in agony. With
their riders slain, the horses ran around in the ten directions. O bull
among the Bharata lineage! Your warriors, and those of the enemy,
were oppressed and wounded by arrows. They leapt up and fell
down. O lord of the earth! Horses, elephants and chariots were seen

to whirl around in the battle there. Driven by destiny, the kshatriyas killed each other there with clubs, lances and arrows with drooping tufts. Other brave ones, skilled in battle, struck each other with bare arms that were like clubs made completely out of iron. O lord of the earth! The brave ones, on your side and that of the Pandavas, killed each other with clenched fists, thighs and palms. Charioteers were bereft of their chariots. Desiring to kill each other, they rushed at each other, with excellent swords in their hands. Surrounded by a large number of Kalingas and with Bhishma at the forefront, King Duryodhana charged against the Pandavas. At this, all the Pandavas surrounded Vrikodara. Inflamed with rage, they rushed against Bhishma on swift mounts."'

Chapter 927(67)

'Sanjaya said, "On seeing Bhishma engaged in a fight with his brothers and the other kings, Dhananjaya raised his weapons and rushed against Gangeya. At Panchajanya's[211] roar, Gandiva's twang and on seeing Partha's standard, all those on our side were overcome with terror. It was like a tree that did not waver, like a comet that had arisen.[212] It was colourful and possessed many hues. It was divine and bore the mark of the ape. O great king! We saw the wielder of the Gandiva's standard to be of this type. It was like lightning in the midst of clouds, resplendent in the sky. The maharatha warriors saw Gandiva, with a back encrusted with gold. We heard his loud roars, like the roars of Shakra himself, and the terrible sound with which he slapped his palms as he went about killing your soldiers. As he showered arrows in every direction and enveloped all the directions, it was like a torrential cloud that was charged with lightning. With terrible weapons, Dhananjaya advanced against Gangeya. We were

[211]The name of Krishna's conch shell.
[212]Referring to Arjuna's standard.

confounded by these weapons and could not distinguish between the eastern and the western direction. O bull among the Bharata lineage! Your warriors could not distinguish between the directions. They were overcome with exhaustion. They were bereft of their weapons. They were bereft of their senses. They clung to each other for comfort. With all your sons, they sought succour with Bhishma. In that battle, Bhishma, Shantanu's son, became the refuge of the oppressed ones. Overcome with terror, charioteers jumped down from their chariots and horse-riders from the backs of their horses. Even the infantry fell down on the ground. O descendant of the Bharata lineage! Having heard the roar of Gandiva, which was like the rumbling of thunder, all your soldiers were frightened and seemed to decay.

'"There were a large number of the best of Kamboja horses, fleet of foot. This was surrounded by a large army from the land of Govasana,[213] with many thousand gopas.[214] O lord of the earth! This was surrounded by Madras, Souviras, Gandharas, Trigartas, all the best among the Kalingas, the king of Kalinga,[215] nagas and a large number of men, with Duhshasana at the forefront. It was accompanied by King Jayadratha and all the kings. Instructed by your son, there were fourteen thousand supreme horse-riders and they surrounded Soubala. O bull among the Bharata lineage! In that battle, all these on your side assembled against Pandava, on separate chariots and mounts. The chariots, elephants, horses and infantry raised an extremely thick cloud of dust and it made the battle seem even more fearful. Bhishma was supported by a large army with spears, lances, iron arrows, elephants, horses, chariots and warriors and attacked Kiriti. The king of Avanti engaged the king of Kashi and Bhimasena engaged Saindhava. Ajatashatru fought with

---

[213]In the Mahabharata, Shaivya was the king of Govasana. In the Puranas, Govasana is given as the name of a king, and his daughter, Youdheyi, was married to Yudhishthira.

[214]A gopa is a herdsman or cowherd. Govasana can be translated as a region where cattle reside.

[215]There is an inconsistency, because the Kalingas have already been destroyed by Bhima and the king of Kalinga has been killed.

Shalya, bull among the Madras, together with his sons and advisers.
Vikarna fought with Sahadeva and Chitrasena with Shikhandi. O
lord of the earth! The king of Matsya engaged Duryodhana and
Shakuni. Drupada, Chekitana and maharatha Satyaki fought with
the great-souled Drona, together with his son. Kripa and Kritavarma
advanced against Dhrishtaketu. In this fashion, there was a melee
with horses, elephants and chariots. In every direction, the soldiers
fought with each other. Though there were no clouds, there was
terrible lightning. Dust enveloped the directions. O lord of the
earth! With terrible sounds, large meteors were seen to fall down.
A mighty storm began to blow and a shower of dust fell down. The
soldiers were shrouded in dust and the sun disappeared in the sky.
Covered by that dust, though they continued to fight with upraised
weapons, all the soldiers were confused and dispirited. As they were
released from the arms of brave ones, the net of arrows, capable of
piercing every kind of armour, raised a loud noise. O bull among
the Bharata lineage! Weapons were released from excellent arms
and blazed in the sky, like radiant stars. O bull among the Bharata
lineage! Shields were seen to be scattered around in all the directions.
They were colourful and made from the hides of bulls. They were
decorated with golden nets. Heads and bodies were seen to fall in
every direction, sliced off by swords with the complexion of the sun.
Maharathas fell down on the ground there. The wheels, axles and
shafts of their chariots were shattered. Their giant standards were
brought down. Their horses were slain. With the charioteers slain,
some horses were maimed with weapons and fell down, dragging
the chariots with them. O descendant of the Bharata lineage! Those
best of horses still had their harnesses on. But they were wounded
by arrows and their bodies were mangled. They could be seen there,
dragging the yokes after them. O king! Extremely powerful elephants
were seen to kill rathas who fought on chariots, with their charioteers
and horses, single-handedly. While large numbers of soldiers were
being killed, many elephants were seen to sniff in the air, inhaling the
scent of the musth exuded by other elephants. In the midst of that
large army, elephants were killed with lances and iron arrows and fell
down, deprived of their lives. In the midst of the army, the field was

strewn with the dead bodies of the best of elephants. The elephants crushed warriors as they fell down, with their elephant-riders and their standards. O great king! In that battle, the shafts of chariots were seen to be shattered by the trunks of elephants that resembled the king of elephants.[216] Tuskers shatterd large numbers of chariots. In that battle, they crushed and dragged down charioteers by the hair, as if they were the branches of trees. As chariots fought with chariots, the best of elephants dragged them down, running in all the directions with a loud noise. As they were thus dragged away by the elephants, they looked like masses of lotus stalks, dragged away from ponds by other elephants. Thus, the field of battle was strewn with a large number of horse-riders, infantry and maharathas, and their standards."'

Chapter 928(68)

'Sanjaya said, "O lord of the earth! With Virata of Matysa, Shikhandi swiftly attacked Bhishma, the mighty archer who was extremely difficult to vanquish. O bull on the earth! In that battle, Dhananjaya advanced against Drona, Kripa, Vikarna and many other brave kings who were great archers and extremely powerful, and also against the great archer Saindhava, together with his advisers and relatives and the kings from the west and the south. In that encounter, Bhimasena attacked your intolerant son Duryodhana, the great archer, together with Duhsaha. Sahadeva advanced against Shakuni and maharatha Uluka, the father and son who were great archers and were extremely difficult to vanquish in battle.[217] O great king! Maharatha Yudhishthira had been deceived by your sons. In that battle, he attacked the army of elephants.[218]

---

[216]The king of elephants is Airavata.

[217]Uluka was Shakuni's son.

[218]Of the Kouravas.

Pandava Nakula was a brave warrior who could make enemies
cry in battle. He attacked the excellent chariots of the Trigartas.
Satyaki, Chekitana and Subhadra's maharatha son were invincible in
battle and advanced against Shalva and the Kekayas. Dhrishtaketu
and rakshasa Ghatotkacha were extremely difficult to defeat. In
that encounter, they attacked the army of chariots that belonged
to your sons. General Dhrishtadyumna was immensely strong and
immeasurable in his soul. O king! In that battle, he attacked Drona,
whose deeds were extremely wonderful. Thus the great archers on
your side fought with the Pandavas. Having encountered each other
in battle, the brave ones proceeded to strike each other down. When
it was midday and the sun had reached the midpoint of the sky,
burning down with its fierce rays, the Kurus and the Pandavas began
to kill each other. Chariots roamed around on the field of battle.
They had standards decorated with gold and pennants. They were
covered with tiger skins and were beautiful. As they encountered
each other in that battle, wishing to kill each other and roaring like
lions, a tumultuous sound arose. In that battle, the brave Srinjayas
and Kurus performed extremely terrible deeds and struck each
other and it was an extraordinary sight. O king! O tormentor of
enemies! We could not see the sky, the directions, or the sun, or the
sub-directions. Arrows were released in every direction. There were
lances with polished tips, iron spears and yellow swords. These
possessed radiance like that of blue lotuses. There were colourful
armour and the brilliance of ornaments. The radiance from these
made the sky, the directions and the sub-directions blaze. O king!
The field of battle was resplendent. There were lions among rathas
and tigers among men and they confronted each other in battle. O
king! They blazed in that battle, like planets in the sky.

"'While all the soldiers looked on, Bhishma, foremost among
charioteers, angrily repulsed the immensely strong Bhimasena. In
that encounter, the arrows used by Bhishma were gold-tufted and
sharpened on stone. They were extremely forceful and washed in
oil and they wounded Bhima. O descendant of the Bharata lineage!
The immensely powerful Bhimasena was enraged. He hurled an
extremely powerful javelin that was like a venomous serpent. As

that gold-shafted and invincible lance suddenly descended in that encounter, Bhishma sliced it down with straight-tufted arrows. O descendant of the Bharata lineage! After this, using a broad-headed, yellow and sharp arrow, he sliced Bhimasena's bow into two. At this, Satyaki quickly attacked Bhishma in that battle. O lord of men! He shot many arrows at your father. Bhishma then affixed an extremely terrible and sharp arrow and brought down Varshneya's[219] charioteer from his chariot. O king! When the charioteer of the chariot was slain, the horses fled. They ran hither and thither, with the speed of the mind and the wind. At this, a tumultuous uproar arose from all the soldiers. There were lamentations of woe from those who were on the side of the great-souled Pandavas. 'Run', 'grab the horses', 'advance swiftly'—such loud noises followed Yuyudhana's chariot.[220] While this was going on, Bhishma, Shantanu's son, began to kill the Pandava soldiers, like the slayer of Vritra against the asuras. When the Panchalas and Somakas were being killed by Bhishma, the noble ones[221] resolved to fight and attacked Bhishma. With a desire to kill those in the army of your sons, the Parthas, with Dhrishtadyumna at the forefront, rushed against Shantanu's son in that encounter. O king! Your soldiers, with Bhishma and Drona at the forefront, advanced forcefully against the enemy and another battle commenced."'

Chapter 929(69)

'Sanjaya said, "With three arrows, Virata pierced maharatha Bhishma. With another three arrows, he pierced the maharatha's steeds. At this, Bhishma, Shantanu's son, the great archer, immensely strong and skilled in the use of his hands, used ten gold-tufted arrows

---

[219]Satyaki is being referred to as Varshneya.
[220]Yuyudhana is Satyaki's name.
[221]The word used is aryas.

to pierce him back in return. With a firm hand, Drona's son, the maharatha who was terrible in wielding the bow, used six arrows to pierce the wielder of Gandiva between his breasts. At this, Phalguna, the slayer of enemy heroes, sliced down his bow. The destroyer of enemies used extremely sharp arrows to wound him. He[222] became senseless with rage and grasped an even more powerful bow. In that encounter, he could not tolerate his bow being sliced down by Partha. O king! He pierced Phalguna with nine sharp arrows and pierced Vasudeva with seventy supreme arrows. At this, the eyes of Krishna and Phalguna became coppery red in wrath. They sighed long and deep and began to think repeatedly. The wielder of Gandiva, the destroyer of enemies, grasped his bow with his left hand. He angrily affixed sharp and straight-tufted arrows. They were terrible and were capable of robbing one of one's life. In that encounter, he swiftly pierced Drona's son, supreme among strong ones, with these. In that battle, they pierced through his armour and drank up his blood. But though pierced by the wielder of Gandiva, Drona's son was not distressed. Without being perturbed, he showered back arrows in return. O king! In that battle, he wished to protect the one who was great in his vows.[223] The bulls among men applauded this great deed of his, of being able to counter the two Krishnas[224] together. He remained fearlessly stationed in that battle, fighting all the soldiers. From Drona, he had learnt about releasing and withdrawing extremely difficult weapons. 'This is the son of my preceptor. This is Drona's beloved son. In particular, he is a brahmana and is worthy of my veneration.' Thinking this, the brave Bibhatsu, the tormentor of his enemies and foremost among charioteers, showed mercy towards Bharadvaja's son. In that battle, Kounteya, the tormentor of his enemies, gave up the fight with Drona's son. The brave one swiftly began to kill your soldiers.

"'Duryodhana pierced the mighty archer Bhimasena with ten gold-tufted arrows that had been sharpened on stone and were

[222]Ashvatthama.
[223]Bhishma.
[224] Arjuna and Krishna.

shafted with the feathers of vultures. Extremely enraged, Bhimasena grasped a colourful and firm bow, which was capable of slaying the enemy, and ten sharp arrows. He drew the bow back to his ear and aimed those sharp, forceful and extremely energetic arrows. With these, he powerfully pierced the king of the Kurus on his broad chest. A gem hung from his chest on golden threads. When he was pierced, this was as resplendent as the sun surrounded by planets. When oppressed by Bhimasena, your energetic son could not tolerate it, like a snake unable to bear the slap of a palm. O great king! He became extremely wrathful and desiring to protect his own soldiers, used gold-tufted arrows that were sharpened on stone to pierce Bhima. In that battle, they fought and wounded each other. Those two immensely strong sons of yours were like the gods.

'"Subhadra's son, the destroyer of enemy heroes, pierced Chitrasena, tiger among men, with ten arrows and Purumitra with seven. He was the equal of Shakra in battle and pierced Satyavrata with seventy. The brave one seemed to dance around on the field, causing great grief to us. Chitrasena pierced him back with ten arrows, Saytavrata with nine and Purumitra with seven. He was pierced and wounded and was covered with blood. However, Arjuna's son sliced down Chitrasena's great and colourful bow, which was capable of repulsing the enemy. He used an arrow to pierce his armour and oppress him. At this, all the brave and maharatha princes on your side united together and angrily began to pierce him with sharp arrows. But he was supreme in the knowledge of weapons and wounded all of them with sharp arrows. On witnessing this deed accomplished by him, your sons surrounded him. He was capable of consuming soldiers in a battle, like a fire consumes deadwood in the forest after the winter season is over. As he chastised your soldiers, Subhadra's son was radiant. O lord of the earth! On beholding the deeds of Satvati's son[225] in that battle, your grandson, Lakshmana, the bearer of auspicious marks, swiftly attacked him. Abhimanyu angrily pierced Lakshmana with six arrows and his charioteer with

---

[225] Subhadra belonged to the Yadava lineage and is being referred to as Satvati. Lakshmana was Duryodhana's son.

three. O king! But Lakshmana pierced Subhadra's son with sharp arrows. O great king! This seemed to be extraordinary. Subhadra's extremely powerful son used sharp arrows to slay Lakshmana's four arrows and his charioteer, and then attacked him. When the horses were killed, Lakshmana, the destroyer of enemy heroes, remained stationed on his chariot. He angrily hurled a javelin towards the chariot of Subhadra's son. It was terrible in form and unassailable and suddenly descended, like a snake. But Abhimanyu used sharp arrows to slice it down. At this, Goutama's son[226] took Lakshmana up on his own chariot and carried him away on the chariot, while all the soldiers looked on.

'"That extremely fearful battle raged on. Warriors violently struck each other, wishing to kill each other. The great archers on your side and the maharatha Pandavas fought each other in that battle, prepared to lay down their lives and killing each other. Their hair was dishevelled. They lost their armour. They were bereft of their chariots. Their bows were sliced down. The Srinjayas and the Kurus fought on, with their bare arms. The mighty-armed and immensely strong Bhishma, angrily began to kill the soldiers of the great-souled Pandavas with divine weapons. Horses, elephants, men, charioteers and horse-riders were slain and brought down there and the earth was covered with them."'

Chapter 930(70)

'Sanjaya said, "O king! The mighty-armed Satyaki, invincible in battle, drew a supreme bow, capable of withstanding a great burden, in that battle. He discharged many tufted arrows that were like virulent serpents. He displayed the deep, light and wonderful dexterity of his hands. He drew the bow, affixed arrows to it, discharged them and affixed others so swiftly that he seemed to be

[226]Kripa.

like a beautiful cloud that was showering down rain. He killed the enemies in that battle. O descendant of the Bharata lineage! King Duryodhana saw that he was blazing and despatched ten thousand chariots against him. But valiant Satyaki, for whom truth was valour, was a great and supreme archer. He used divine weapons to slay all of them. Having accomplished this terrible deed, he grasped his bow and confronted Bhurishrava, the extender of the deeds of the Kuru lineage, in that battle. On seeing that the soldiers had been brought down by Yuyudhana, he[227] angrily attacked him. He stretched an extremely large bow that had the complexion of Indra's weapon.[228] O great king! He displayed the dexterity of his hands and released thousands of arrows that were as virulent as serpents and were like the vajra. O king! These arrows were like the touch of death to Satyaki's followers and they fled, leaving the invincible Satyaki alone in that fight.

'"On seeing this, Yuyudhana's ten sons advanced against Bhurishrava, the great archer, in that battle. They were maharathas and immensely strong. They were clad in excellent armour and bore many different kinds of weapons and standards. All of them were extremely angry in that great battle and spoke to the one who had the mark of a sacrificial stake on his standard.[229] 'O immensely strong one! O relative of the Kouravas![230] Come and fight with us, either singly, or together. You will obtain great fame if you vanquish us in battle. Or we will vanquish you in battle and obtain great satisfaction.' Thus addressed, the immensely strong and brave one, who was foremost among men and prided himself on his valour, saw them stationed there and replied, 'O brave ones! You have spoken well. If that is your desire, fight with me now. I will endeavour to kill all of you in battle.' Having been thus addressed, the brave ones who were swift in action showered the great archer, the destroyer

[227]Bhurishrava.

[228]Indra's weapon is the rainbow.

[229]Bhurishrava had a sacrificial stake on his standard.

[230]Bhurishrava was the son of Somadatta and Somadatta was descended from Pratipa, who was also the ancestor of the Pandavas and the Kouravas.

of enemies, with arrows. O great king! That tumultuous encounter commenced when it was afternoon. In that field of battle, there was a single one on one side and many united ones on the other. They enveloped that single-handed and foremost warrior with arrows. O king! It was like clouds showering down on a giant mountain. When unleashed, that shower of arrows was like Yama's staff, or like the vajra. But before they could reach him, the maharatha swiftly sliced them down. We then beheld the extraordinary valour of Somadatta's son. He single-handedly fought with many, without any fear. O king! The ten maharathas created a shower of arrows. They surrounded the mighty-armed one, wishing to kill him. O descendant of the Bharata lineage! O king! In that battle, Somadatta's son used ten arrows to angrily slice down their bows. O king! When their bows had been sliced down, in that encounter, the maharatha instantly used sharp, straight-tufted and broad-headed arrows to slice off their heads. Thus slain, they fell down on the ground, like trees struck by lightning.

'"O king! On seeing that his brave and immensely strong sons had been killed in battle, Varshneya[231] roared and attacked Bhurishrava. In that battle, chariot dashed against chariot and the two immensely strong ones oppressed each other. In that encounter, they slew the horses of each other's chariot. Deprived of their chariots, the maharathas jumped down on the ground. They grasped great swords and supreme shields and attacked each other. As they were stationed for battle, those tigers among men were dazzling. Satyaki was wielding a supreme sword. O king! But Bhimasena swiftly approached him and took him up on his chariot. O king! And while all the archers looked on in that battle, your son picked up Bhurishrava on his chariot. O bull among the Bharata lineage! While that battle raged on, the angry Pandava began to fight with maharatha Bhishma. When the sun had assumed a reddish tinge, Dhananjaya swiftly killed twenty-five thousand maharathas. They had been instructed by Duryodhana to slay Partha. But they approached him and met their destruction, like insects before a flame. At this, the Matsyas and the Kekayas, skilled in the knowledge of fighting, surrounded maharatha Partha

[231]Satyaki.

and his son. At that moment, the sun disappeared and all the soldiers were overcome with confusion. O great king! It was evening and with his mounts exhausted, your father, Devavrata, instructed that the soldiers should withdraw. Having encountered each other, the Pandava and Kuru troops were filled with great fear and anxiously retired to their camps. O descendant of the Bharata lineage! Having retired to their own camps, the Pandavas and the Srinjayas, and the Kurus, rested, as was appropriate.'"

Chapter 931(71)

'Sanjaya said, "O king! The Kurus and the Pandavas spent the time in different ways and when night had passed, they emerged again to fight. O descendant of the Bharata lineage! A great sound arose from those on your side and theirs. The foremost among rathas prepared to do battle and elephants were readied. O descendant of the Bharata lineage! Infantry and horses were armoured. The tumultuous sound of conch shells and drums was everywhere. At this, King Yudhishthira spoke to Dhrishtadyumna. 'O mighty-armed one! Construct the vyuha known as makara, which is capable of tormenting the enemy.' O great king! Thus addressed by Partha, maharatha Dhrishtadyumna, foremost among rathas, accordingly instructed the rathas. Drupada and Pandava Dhananjaya were at the head. Maharatha Sahadeva and Nakula were the eyes. O great king! The immensely strong Bhimasena was the beak. Subhadra's son, Droupadi's sons, rakshasa Ghatotkacha, Satyaki and Dharmaraja were stationed at the neck of the vyuha. O great king! Virata, the leader of an army, was at the back, surrounded by Dhrishtadyumna and a large army. The five brothers from Kekaya were on the left flank. Dhrishtaketu, tiger among men, and the valiant Karakarsha were stationed on the right flank, so as to protect the vyuha. O great king! The illustrious maharatha Kuntibhoja and Shatanika were stationed at the feet, surrounded by a large army. The great and might archer Shikhandi, surrounded by the Somakas, and Iravat stationed themselves at the tail of the makara. O descendant of the Bharata lineage! Thus did the Pandavas array themselves in the form of a great vyuha. O great king! When the sun arose, they armoured themselves and stationed themselves for battle. They had elephants, horses, chariots and infantry. They raised their colourful standards and umbrellas. They armed themselves with sharp and polished weapons and swiftly advanced against the Kouravas.

'"O king! Your father, Devavrata, saw this vyuha and arranged his soldiers in the form of a giant counter-vyuha that had the shape of a curlew.[232] Bharadvaja's son, the great archer, was at its beak. O lord of men! Ashvatthama and Kripa were the eyes. Kritavarma, foremost among men and foremost among all archers, was at the head, together with the kings of Kamboja and Bahlika. O venerable one! O great king! Shurasena and your son, Duryodhana, were at the neck, surrounded by many kings. O foremost among men! The king of Pragjyotisha was at the chest, together with the Madras, Souviras and Kekayas, and surrounded by a large army. Together with his own army, Susharma, the king of Prasthala,[233] armoured and stationed himself along the left wing. O descendant of the Bharata lineage! The Tusharas, Yavanas, Shakas and Chuchupas stationed themselves along the right wing of that vyuha. O venerable one! Shrutayu, Shatayu and Somadatta's son were stationed at the rear of the vyuha, protecting each other.

'"The battle between the Pandavas and the Kouravas commenced. O great king! When the sun had arisen, there was a great encounter. Charioteers confronted charioteers and elephants confronted elephants. Those riding on horses advanced against those riding on horses. But those on chariots also attacked horse-riders. O king! In that great battle, chariot-riders not only attacked chariot-riders, but also elephants. Elephant-riders fought against chariot-riders and chariot-riders fought against horse-riders. Chariot-riders fought against infantry and horse-riders fought against infantry. O king!

[232]The *krouncha* bird.
[233]Susharma was the king of Trigarta and the capital of Trigarta was Prasthala.

They were full of wrath and attacked each other in that encounter. Protected by Bhima, Arjuna, the twins and the other maharathas, the army of the Pandavas was as beautiful as the night sky with stars. Your army was also resplendent with Bhishma, Kripa, Drona, Shalya, Duryodhana and the others, like the firmament circled by planets.

'"On seeing Drona, the valiant Kounteya Bhimasena, borne by swift horses, advanced against the men who were in the army of Bharadvaja's son. Drona was enraged in the battle. O king! In that encounter, the valiant one pierced Bhima in his inner organs with nine iron arrows. However, though Bhima was forcefully struck in that conflict, he despatched the charioteer of Bharadvaja's son to Yama's abode. Bharadvaja's powerful son began to control the mounts himself. He consumed the Pandava soldiers, like a fire amidst a mass of cotton. O supreme among men! Thus slaughtered by Drona and Bhishma, the Srinjayas and the Kekayas were defeated and began to run away. Your soldiers were also mangled by Bhima and Arjuna. They lost their senses there, like a proud and beautiful woman.[234] Both the vyuhas were penetrated and there was a destruction of the best of brave ones. O descendant of the Bharata lineage! There was terrible distress in your army and in theirs. O descendant of the Bharata lineage! We witnessed the extraordinary sight of all your soldiers and those of the enemy fighting with a single objective in mind. O lord of the earth! The maharatha Pandavas and Kouravas fought with each other. They repulsed each other's weapons."'

Chapter 932(72)

'Dhritarashtra said, "Our army is supreme and possesses many qualities. It has many different components. O Sanjaya! It has been arranged in a vyuha according to the sacred texts and

---

[234] The imagery seems to be that of a beautiful woman whose pride has been hurt.

should be unassailable. We have sustained it and it has always been extremely devoted to us. The soldiers are disciplined and free from vice and they have exhibited their valour earlier. They are not too old. Nor are they too young. They are not lean. Nor are they fat. They are active and tall. Their bodies are well-developed and they are free from disease. They are armoured and trained in the use of weapons. They possess many kinds of weapons. They are skilled in fighting with swords, bare arms and in fighting with clubs. Lances, swords, clubs, iron maces, catapults, javelins and all kinds of maces, kampanas, bows, kanapas, different kinds of slings, fighting with the bare fists—they are skilled in all these. They are devoted to training. They have persevered in exercises. They have devotedly learned everything about the handling of weapons. They have trained in mounting and descending, riding, moving forward, stepping back, striking effectively, advancing and retreating and are skilled. In many ways, they have been tested with elephants, horses, chariots and vehicles. Having been appropriately tested, they have been given the right kind of pay. This has not been influenced by lineage, favours, relationships, the strength of friendship, or connections of birth or marriage. They are prosperous people and noble. Their relatives have been treated well by us and are satisfied. We have shown them many favours. They are famous and honoured. O son![235] They are protected by many victorious ones who are the foremost among men, famous in the worlds because of their prominent deeds. They are like the guardians of the worlds. They are protected by many kshatriyas, who are honoured by all the people on earth. They have to come because of their own wishes, with their armies and their followers. This is like a large ocean, with rivers flowing into it from all directions. There are many elephants and chariots. Though these do not actually have wings, they seem to possess wings. Our many warriors constitute the terrible waters. The mounts are the waves. It is full of slings, swords, clubs, lances, bows and javelins. There are standards and ornaments that are embellished with jewelled cloth. The advancing mounts are like the agitating force of the wind. It is

---

[235]The word used is tata.

like a great and roaring ocean, without any limits. It is protected
by Drona and Bhishma and also protected by Kritavarma, Kripa
and Duhshasana and others who are led by Jayadratha. It is also
protected by Bhagadatta and Vikarna, Drona's son, Soubala and
Bahlika and many other great-souled ones who are the foremost
warriors of the world. That this should be slaughtered in battle can
only be because of earlier destiny. O Sanjaya! Such a preparation[236]
on earth has never been seen before, by men, or by the immensely
fortunate and ancient rishis. This large army is prosperous with
every kind of weapon. If it should be killed in battle, how can that
be anything other than destiny? O Sanjaya! To me, everything seems
to be contrary. Such a terrible army cannot fight with the Pandavas
in battle. Perhaps the gods have assembled here in the cause of the
Pandavas. O Sanjaya! Perhaps they are fighting against my soldiers
and that is the reason they are being killed. O Sanjaya! Vidura had
earlier spoken about what was beneficial medicine for me. But my
evil-minded son, Duryodhana, did not accept it. It is my view that
the great-souled and omniscient one had known all this earlier. O
son! He knew what was going to happen. It was preordained destiny.
O Sanjaya! Perhaps all this is exactly as the creator had ordained it
earlier. That is the reason it cannot be countered."'

Chapter 933(73)

'Sanjaya replied, "O king! O bull among the Bharata lineage! It is
because of your own sins that you have confronted this calamity.
O king! Duryodhana failed to foresee what you saw as the outcome
of adharma in action. O lord of the earth! It was because of your
sins that the gambling match had taken place earlier. It is because of
your sins that the battle with the Pandavas has commenced. Having
committed the evil yourself, you must now enjoy the fruits. O king!

[236]For war.

One must bear the consequences of the deeds one commits, in this world or in the next, and you have obtained what is appropriate. O king! Therefore, though you confront this great calamity, be patient. O venerable one! Listen, while I describe the account of the battle.

'"With sharp arrows, Bhimasena penetrated your great army. The brave one then confronted all of Duryodhana's younger brothers—Duhshasana, Durvishaha, Duhsaha, Durmada, Jaya, Jayatsena, Vikarna, Chitrasena, Sudarshana, Charuchitra, Suvarmana, Dushkarna, Karna[237]—and a large number of other maharathas. When he approached and saw these sons of Dhritarashtra, the immensely strong Bhima was excited with rage. In that battle, the great army was protected by Bhishma. But he penetrated into it. On seeing him there, those lords of men spoke to each other. 'Vrikodara Bhima is here. Let us rob him of his life.' Partha was thus surrounded by the brothers, who had made up their minds. He was like the sun, surrounded by large and evil planets at the time of the destruction of all beings. Though Pandava was in the midst of the vyuha, he was not frightened. It was like the great Indra, when he confronted the danavas in the battle between the gods and the asuras. O lord! Hundreds and thousands of rathas covered the single-handed one from all directions, with terrible arrows and he reciprocated. In that battle, the brave one paid no attention to the sons of Dhritarashtra and killed the foremost of brave warriors, on elephants, horses and chariots. O king! The great-minded Bhimasena knew the intentions of his relatives and had made up his mind to kill all of them. Pandava descended from his chariot and grasped a club. With this, he began to kill the soldiers of the sons of Dhritarasthra, which was like a great ocean.

'"When Bhimasena had penetrated, Parshata Dhrishtadyumna swiftly abandoned Drona[238] and went to where Soubala was. That bull among men shattered your large army. In that battle, he came upon Bhimasena's empty chariot. In that encounter, he saw

[237]Not to be confused with the famous Karna, who was not fighting at this stage.

[238]He had been fighting with Drona.

Bhimasena's charioteer, Vishoka. O great king! Dhrishtadyumna was
distressed and lost his senses. Exremely miserable, he asked in a voice
that was choked with tears, the words emerging through his sighs.
'Where is Bhima? I love him more than my own life.' Vishoka joined
his hands in salutation and told Dhrishtadyumna, 'The powerful
and strong Pandaveya instructed me to wait here and plunged into
the army of the sons of Dhritarashtra, as large as an ocean. That
tiger among men cheerfully spoke these words to me. "O charioteer!
Control the horses and wait here for an instant, while I swiftly slay
those who have raised their weapons against me." When they saw
the immensely strong one advance with the club in his hand, all the
others on our side also advanced to fight. A tumultuous and fearful
battle commenced. O king! Your friend penetrated that great vyuha
and entered. 'Parshata Dhrishtadyumna heard Vishoka's words. In
that field of battle, the immensely strong one replied to the charioteer.
'O suta! If I abandon my affection for the Pandavas and abandon
Bhimasena in the battle, there is no reason for me to remain alive.
What will the kshatriyas say, if I return without Bhima? After all, I
was present when Bhima showed such single-mindedness in battle.
With Agni at the forefront, the gods inflict harm on those who forsake
their aides and return home unharmed. The immensely strong Bhima
is my friend and my relative. That destroyer of enemies is devoted to
me and I am devoted to him. I will therefore go where Vrikodara has
gone. Behold me slay the enemies, like Vasava against the danavas.'
Having said this, the brave one penetrated the midst of the Bharata
soldiers,[239] following the path traversed by Bhimasena, marked
out by elephants ravaged with the club. He saw Bhima consuming
the ranks of the enemy. He shattered those kings in battle, like a
powerful wind devastating trees. In that battle, charioteers, horse-
riders, infantry and elephant-riders were killed and roared loudly in
lamentation. O venerable one! There were cries of woe among your
soldiers, as Bhimasena, wonderful in different means of fighting, slew
them. All those who were skilled in the use of weapons surrounded
Vrikodara from all sides. Without any fear, they showered weapons

---

[239]That is, the Kourava army.

at him from all directions. Parshata saw that Pandava Bhimasena, foremost among the wielders of weapons, was attacked on all sides by those brave ones of the world, accompanied by their terrible assembly of soldiers. His limbs were mangled from the arrows. He was treading on the ground with a club in his hand, vomiting the poison of his wrath. He was like death at the time of destruction. Parshata went and comforted Bhimasena. The great-souled one removed the arrows from his body and lifted him up onto his own chariot. He embraced and comforted Bhimsena, in the midst of the enemy.

'"While that great battle was going on, your son approached his brothers and told them, 'This son of Drupada is evil in his soul. He has arrived to help Bhimasena. All of you go and kill him. Let the enemy not seek out our soldiers.' The sons of Dhritarashtra were incited by their elder brother. They heard his words and attacked in intolerance. They raised their weapons with a desire to kill, like terrible comets at the time of the destruction of a yuga. The brave ones grasped colourful bows. They made the earth tremble with the twang of their bows and the roar of their chariot wheels. They showered arrows on Drupada's son, like clouds pouring down water on the tops of mountains. But that colourful warrior[240] was not perturbed in the battle and sliced them all down with his own sharp arrows. Your brave sons were stationed around him in that battle, striving their utmost. But Drupada's young and fierce son was determined to kill them. O king! Extremely angry, the maharatha released the weapon known as *pramohana*[241] at your sons, like the great Indra in a battle against the daityas. In that battle, those brave ones among men lost their senses. Afflicted by the pramohana weapon, they lost their minds and their spirits. When they saw that your sons were unconscious and had lost their senses, as if their time had come, all the Kurus fled in all the directions, together with the horses, the elephants and the chariots.

'"At that time, Drona, foremost among the wielders of weapons, confronted Drupada and pierced him with three terrible arrows. O

[240]Dhrishtadyumna.

[241]A divine weapon that causes loss of consciousness.

king! Having been thus pierced by Drona in the field of battle, King Drupada remembered his earlier enmity.[242] O king! He fled. Having thus defeated Drupada, the powerful Drona blew on his conch shell. On hearing the sound of this conch shell, all the Somakas were frightened. The energetic Drona, supreme among the wielders of weapons, heard that your sons had become unconscious in battle because of the pramohana weapon. O king! In his anxiety, Drona swiftly went to that part of the battlefield. Bharadvaja's powerful son, the great archer, saw Dhrishtadyumna and Bhima wandering around in that great field of battle. The maharatha saw that your sons were overcome by unconsciousness. He unleashed the weapon known as *prajna*, to counter the *mohana* weapon.[243] Your maharatha sons again regained their breath of life. They returned to the battle against Bhima and Parshata.

'"Yudhishthira summoned and addressed his own soldiers. 'Let twelve brave rathas armour themselves. And with Subhadra's son at the forefront, to the best of their ability, follow the footsteps of Bhima and Parshata in the battle. Let us find out what has happened to them. My mind is not at peace.' Having been thus addressed, those brave and valiant warriors, all of whom prided themselves on their manliness, agreed and accepted what they had been asked to do. They departed together, when the sun had reached the midpoint in the sky. The Kekayas, Droupadi's sons and the valiant Dhrishtaketu had Abhimanyu at the forefront and were surrounded by a large army.[244] In that battle, those destroyers of enemies arranged themselves in the vyuha known as *suchimukha*.[245] In that battle, they broke through the ranks of chariots that belonged to the sons of Dhritarashtra. Those great archers advanced, with Abhimanyu at the forefront.

[242]The enmity between Drona and Drupada doesn't quite explain why Drupada should flee. Drupada probably remembered that Dhrishtadyumna had been born so that Drona might be killed.

[243]Prajna means wisdom or intelligence. Mohana and pramohana have the same meaning.

[244]The five Kekaya princes, five of Droupadi's sons, Dhrishtaketu and Abhimanyu—these were the twelve.

[245] The mouth of a needle.

O lord of men! Your soldiers were terrified of Bhimasena and had
lost their senses because of Dhrishtadyumna. They were incapable
of resisting and were like a woman in the streets, who faces a
person who is drunk. Those great archers advanced with standards
that were decorated with gold. They advanced swiftly to protect
Dhrishtadyumna and Vrikodara. On seeing the great archers, with
Abhimanyu at the forefront, those two were delighted and began to
slaughter your soldiers.

'"Brave Parshata of Panchala suddenly saw his preceptor
advancing towards him.[246] He gave up the desire to kill your sons.
He made Kekaya take Vrikodara up on his chariot and advanced
in great rage against Drona, skilled in the use of weapons. At this,
Bharadvaja's powerful son, the destroyer of enemies, became angry
and used a broad-headed arrow to slice down his bow. For the sake
of Duryodhana's welfare and remembering the food he had obtained
from his master,[247] he released hundreds of arrows towards Parshata.
But Parshata, the destroyer of enemy heroes, took up another bow
and pierced Drona with seventy gold-tufted arrows that had been
sharpened on stone. Drona, the destroyer of enemies, sliced down
his bow yet again. The valiant one then swiftly used four supreme
arrows to despatch his four horses to Vaivasvata's[248] eternal and
terrible abode. He despatched another broad-headed arrow and killed
his charioteer. With his horses killed, the mighty-armed maharatha
descended from his chariot and climbed onto Abhimanyu's great
chariot. While Bhimasena looked on and while Parshata looked on,
the infinitely energetic Drona shattered the forces and made their army
of chariots, horses and elephants tremble. The assembled maharathas
were powerless to counter this. Having been killed by Drona's sharp
arrows, those soldiers swayed, like a turbulent ocean. When they saw
those soldiers in that state, your troops were delighted. They saw the
enraged preceptor consume the ranks of the enemy. O descendant of
the Bharata lineage! All the warriors roared in applause."'

[246]Dhrishtadyumna had studied under Drona.
[247]Duryodhana.
[248]Yama's.

Chapter 934(74)

'Sanjaya said, "Having regained his senses, King Duryodhana once again repulsed the undecaying Bhima with showers of arrows. Yet again, your maharatha sons united together. With raised weapons, they fought with Bhima in that battle. In that battle, Bhimasena again climbed onto his own chariot. The mighty-armed one went to the spot where your sons were. He grasped an extremely forceful, firm and colourful bow that was capable of slaying the enemy. In the battle, he pierced your sons with arrows. At this, King Duryodhana pierced the immensely strong Bhimasena in his vital parts with an extremely sharp iron arrow. Thus pierced by your archer son, the great archer's eyes became red with rage. He forcefully drew his bow and wounded Duryodhana in the arms and the chest with three arrows. But despite being wounded, the king remained there, like an immobile king of mountains. All of Duryodhana's brave younger brothers were ready to give up their lives. In the battle, they saw the two angry ones striking one another and remembered their earlier resolution of afflicting the one whose deeds were terrible. O great king! As they descended on him, the immensely strong Bhimasena rushed against them, like an elephant against other elephants. O great king! In great rage, the energetic one struck your immensely famous son, Chitrasena, with an iron arrow. O descendant of the Bharata lineage! He also struck your other sons in that conflict, with many different kinds of arrows, gold-tufted and extremely fast.

'"Those twelve maharathas, Abhimanyu and the others, had been sent by Dharmaraja to follow in Bhimasena's footsteps. O great king! They advanced against your immensely strong sons. Those brave ones were stationed on chariots that were like the sun and the fire in their energy. All of them were great archers and blazed in their prosperity. On seeing them resplendent in that great battle, with shining and golden armour, your immensely strong sons gave up the fight with Bhima. But Kounteya was unable to tolerate the sight of their leaving alive. In that battle, Abhimanyu, accompanied by Bhimasena, attacked. On seeing them, and on seeing Parshata, your maharatha soldiers, Duryodhana and the others, grasped their bows. Borne by fast horses, they went to the spot where those rathas were stationed. O king! O descendant of the Bharata lineage! In the afternoon, there was a terrible battle between the powerful ones on your side and on the side of the enemy. Abhimanyu killed Vikarna's extremely swift horses. He then pierced him with twenty-five *kshudraka*[249] arrows. O king! With his horses slain, maharatha Vikarna abandoned his chariot and climbed onto Chitrasena's radiant chariot. O descendant of the Bharata lineage! Stationed on a single chariot, those two brothers, the extenders of the Kuru lineage, enveloped Arjuna's son with a net of arrows. Durjaya and Vikarna pierced Krishna's son[250] with five iron arrows. However, Krishna's son did not waver and was immobile, like Mount Meru. O venerable one! In that encounter, Duhshasana fought with the five from Kekaya. O Indra among kings! It was an extraordinary fight. Enraged in battle, Droupadi's sons repulsed Duryodhana. O lord of the earth! Each of them pierced your son with three arrows. But your son was invincible in that battle with Droupadi's sons. O king! He wounded each of them separately with sharp arrows. Pierced in return, he was covered in blood and was radiant. He was like a mountain, with streams mixed with minerals flowing down it.

"'O king! In that battle, the powerful Bhishma killed the Pandava soldiers, like a herdsman driving large numbers of animals. O lord of the earth! The roar of Gandiva was heard then, as Partha began to slaughter the soldiers along the right flank. O descendant of the Bharata lineage! In that battle, headless torsos stood up in every direction, amongst the soldiers of both the Kurus and the Pandavas. It was like an ocean of blood, with the chariots as the eddies. The elephants were the islands and the horses were the waves. The chariots were boats that tigers among men used to cross that ocean of soldiers. The best of men were without arms, without armour and without bodies. They were seen to fall down, in hundreds and thousands. Crazy elephants were slain, their bodies splattered with

---

[249]Small arrow.
[250]Arjuna is being referred to as Krishna here.

blood. O foremost among the Bharata lineage! The earth seemed to be strewn with mountains. O descendant of the Bharata lineage! We witnessed an extraordinary sight, both among those on your side and theirs. There was no man there who did not wish to do battle. Thus did the brave ones fight, striving for great fame. Those on your side fought with the Pandavas, desiring victory in battle.'"

Chapter 935(75)

'Sanjaya said, "The sun assumed a reddish tinge. Desiring victory and wishing to kill him, King Duryodhana attacked Bhima. On seeing that brave one amongst men, firm in his enmity, advance towards him, Bhimasena was extremely enraged and spoke these words. 'I have desired this moment for many years and the time has now arrived. If you do not flee from the battle, I will kill you today. I will dispel the misery of Kunti today and the difficulties we faced during our exile in the forest. I will kill you and dispel Droupadi's woes. At the time of gambling with the dice, you insulted the Pandavas. O Gandhari's son! Witness the calamity that has befallen you because of your evil act. In earlier times, you relied on the views of Karna and Soubala. You did not think of the Pandavas and did as you wished. When Dasharha came as a supplicant,[251] you disregarded him because of your delusion. In delight, you gave Uluka a message to deliver to us. I will kill you today, with your relatives and your kin. I will avenge all the evil deeds you have committed earlier.' Having said this, he repeatedly stretched his terrible bow. He took up terrible arrows that were as radiant as the great vajra. In great anger, he swiftly shot twenty-six arrows at Suyodhana. They were flaming, with crests like fire, and they had tongues like the vajra. After that, he struck his bow with two and his charioteer with another two. With

---

[251]A reference to Krishna's mission of peace.

four arrows, he despatched his[252] swift horses to Yama's abode. The scorcher of enemies then used two arrows that were released with great force. With these, he sliced down the king's umbrella from his supreme chariot. With three more, he sliced down the flaming and supreme standard. Having sliced it down, while your son looked on, he emitted a loud roar. That handsome standard, decorated with many gems, fell down from the chariot. It suddenly fell down on the ground, like lightning from the clouds. It was resplendent like the sun and was beautiful with jewels. It was marked with the sign of an elephant. All the kings saw that the standard of the lord of the Kurus had been brought down. In that battle, as if he was smiling, Bhima then used ten arrows to slay his mighty elephant.

"'At this, Jayadratha, the king of Sindhu, foremost among rathas, stationed himself on Duryodhana's flank, supported by many good warriors. O king! Kripa, foremost among rathas, picked up the infinitely energetic Kouravya, the intolerant Duryodhana, on his own chariot. He had been deeply pierced and wounded in that battle with Bhimasena. O king! Duryodhana sat down on the floor of the chariot. Desiring to kill Bhima, Jayadratha surrounded him from all sides. There were many thousand chariots on all of Bhima's directions. O king! Then Dhrishtaketu, the valiant Abhimanyu, the Kekayas and Droupadi's sons fought with your sons.

"'O king! The delicate and famous Abhimanyu's chariot was surrounded from all directions by eight great archers—Chitrasena, Suchitra, Chitrashva, Chitradarshana, Charuchitra, Sucharu, Nanda and Upanandaka. But the great-souled Abhimanyu swiftly wounded each of them with five straight-tufted arrows. These were like the vajra, or like death itself, and were released from his colourful bow. All of them were unable to tolerate this. They showered down sharp arrows on the supreme chariot of Subhadra's son, like clouds showering down on Mount Meru. Though he was skilled in weapons and invincible in battle, he was oppressed in that encounter. O great king! But Abhimanyu made all of them tremble, like the wielder of the vajra against the great asuras, in the battle between the gods

[252]Duryodhana's.

and the asuras. O descendant of the Bharata lineage! The foremost among charioteers despatched fourteen broad-headed and terrible arrows towards Vikarna. They were like venomous serpents. With these, he cut down his standard, his chariot and his horses and seemed to be dancing around in the battle. Subhadra's immensely strong son then again used yellow arrows that did not waver from their course. They were pointed and had been sharpened on stone and were shafted with the feathers of herons and peacocks. They descended on Vikarna and pierced his body. Having done this, they penetrated the ground, like flaming serpents. Those gold-tufted and gold-tipped arrows could be seen stuck to the ground. They were drenched with Vikarna's blood and seemed to be vomiting blood. On seeing that Vikarna had been thus wounded in the battle, all his other brothers attacked those charioteers, with Subhadra's son at the forefront. They swiftly advanced on their own chariots and attacked those other chariots, which were as radiant as the sun. Invincible in battle, they began to pierce each other in that encounter.

'"Durmukha pierced Shrutakarma[253] with seven swift arrows, sliced down his standard with one and pierced his charioteer with seven. Shurtakarma's horses were caparisoned with nets of gold and were as fleet as the wind. He advanced closer and killed them with six arrows and then brought down his charioteer. But despite his horses having been slain, maharatha Shrutakarma remained stationed on the chariot. In great anger, he hurled a flaming javelin that was like a giant meteor. The illustrious Durmukha's large armour was penetrated. Having shattered the armour, it penetrated the ground, blazing in its great energy. The immensely strong Sutasoma saw that he[254] was without a chariot. While all the soldiers looked on, he took him up on his own chariot. O king! The brave Shrutakirti[255] then attacked your son Jayatsena in that battle, wishing to kill the illustrious

[253]The names of Droupadi's sons were Prativindhya (through Yudhishthira), Sutasoma (through Bhima), Shrutakarma (through Arjuna), Shatanika (through Nakula) and Shrutasena (through Sahadeva).

[254]Shrutakarma.

[255]Shrutakirti is another name for Shrutakarma.

one. O king! O descendant of the Bharata lineage! When the great-souled Shrutakirti stretched his bow in battle, smilingly, your son, Jayatsena, sliced it down with an extremely sharp kshurapra arrow. Shatanika saw that his brother's bow had been sliced down. The energetic one swiftly arrived there, roaring repeatedly like a lion. In that battle, Shatanika firmly drew his bow and pierced Jayatsena with ten arrows. Using another extremely sharp arrow that was capable of penetrating all kinds of armour, Shatanika powerfully struck Jayatsena in the chest. Dushkarna was near his brother then. Senseless with rage, he sliced down the bow of Nakula's son in that battle. However, the immensely strong Shatanika took up another supreme bow that was capable of bearing a great load and affixed sharp arrows. In the presence of his brother,[256] he asked Dushkarna to wait and released sharp arrows that were like flaming serpents. O venerable one! He sliced down his bow with one arrow and killed his charioteer with two. In that battle, he then pierced him with seven more. With twelve sharp arrows, the unblemished one killed all his horses, which were speckled and were as swift as the mind. In that battle, he used another broad-headed and well-released arrow to angrily pierce Dushkarna deeply in the chest. O king! On seeing that Dushkarna had been smitten,[257] five maharathas surrounded Shatanika from all sides, wishing to kill him. They enveloped the illustrious Shatanika with a torrent of arrows.

'"Extremely wrathful, the five brothers from Kekaya advanced to the attack. O great king! On seeing them advance, like elephants against giant elephants, your maharatha sons—Durmukha, Durjaya, the youthful Durmarshana, Shatrunjaya and Shatrusaha, all of them wrathful and illustrious, countered the brothers from Kekaya. Their chariots were like cities, with many colours and decorated with flags, and horses as fleet as thought had been yoked to them. The

[256]Referring to Jayatsena.

[257]The text is such that it can also be translated as 'slain', but smitten is indicated. There are two reasons why slain can't be right. First, Dushkarna wasn't killed and surfaces again in Drona Parva. Second, Duryodhana and all his brothers were killed by Bhima.

brave ones held supreme bows and were adorned with colourful
armour and standards. They descended on the enemy soldiers, like
lions moving from one forest to another forest. A tumultuous battle
ensued, with chariots and elephants. It was extremely terrible, where
they sought to kill each other. O king! Because of enmity towards
each other, they increased the numbers in Yama's kingdom. But since
the sun was about to set, that extremely terrible battle lasted only
for a short while. Thousands of charioteers and horse-riders were
strewn around. Bhishma, Shantanu's son, was excited with rage. He
used straight-tufted arrows to slaughter the soldiers of the great-
souled ones. He used his arrows to despatch the Panchala soldiers
to Yama's undecaying realm. O king! Having thus shattered the
Pandava army, the great archer withdrew his soldiers and returned
to his own camp. Having seen Dhrishtadyumna and Vrikodara,
Dharmaraja inhaled the fragrances of their heads and happily retired
to his own camp."'

Chapter 936(76)

'Sanjaya said, "O great king! Those brave ones were driven by
enmity towards each other. They retired to their respective
camps, drenched in blood. Having rested for some time, they
honoured each other in accordance with the proper forms. They
were then seen armoured again, desiring to do battle. O king! Your
son was overwhelmed with anxiety and blood was trickling from his
limbs. He told the grandfather, 'Our soldiers are terrible and fierce.
They are arrayed and bear many standards. But the brave Pandava
rathas have swiftly shattered, slain and oppressed us. Having
confounded all our warriors, they have obtained fame. The makara
vyuha was like the vajra. But Bhima penetrated it and wounded me
with arrows that were like the staff of death. O king! On seeing
him enraged, I was overcome with fear and lost my senses. I cannot
find peace even now. You are truthful in your vows. Through your

favours, I wish to obtain victory and slay the Pandavas.' When he was thus addressed, Ganga's great-souled son, foremost among the wielders of weapons, knew that Duryodhana was overcome by grief. Though his mind was distracted, the intelligent one replied, 'O prince! I will make supreme efforts to penetrate their army, as much as I can. I wish to grant you victory and joy. But I will not hide anything for your sake. These maharathas are terrible and many. There are illustrious and supreme among brave ones. They are skilled in the use of weapons. They have become the aides of the Pandavas in battle. They have overcome fatigue and they are vomiting the venom of their wrath. Those brave ones are firm in their enmity towards you. They are incapable of being vanquished easily. O king! O brave one! But for your sake, I will strive against them to the best of my ability, giving up my life. O high-minded one! In this battle, for your sake, I will no longer attempt to remain alive today. For your sake, I will take on the gods, the daityas and all the worlds, not to speak of the enemies here. O king! To bring you pleasure, I will fight with the Pandavas and do everything that you desire.' On hearing these words, Duryodhana was supremely content and delighted.

'"He cheerfully instructed all the soldiers and all the kings to advance. On hearing his instructions, the chariots, horses, infantry and elephants began to advance. O king! They were happy and were armed with a large number and many kinds of weapons. O king! With elephants, horses and infantry, your army was extremely resplendent. There were masses of tuskers, stationed in arrays and commanded well. The warriors, gods among men and skilled in the use of weapons, stationed themselves amidst the masses of soldiers. The arrays of chariots, infantry, elephants and horses advanced, proceeding along the proper formations. They raised a dust that was tinged like the morning sun and shrouded the sun's rays. There were bright standards on chariots and elephants. In every direction, they fluttered in the air. O king! In that battle, their different colours looked like clouds tinged with lightning in the sky. The kings twanged their bows and a tumultuous and terrible sound arose. This was like the roar of the ocean, when it was churned by the gods and the great

asuras in the first yuga.[258] With that great roar and with many forms
and colours, the army of yoru sons was greatly agitated. The soldiers
were ready to kill the soldiers of the enemy and looked like masses
of clouds at the end of a yuga.'"

Chapter 937(77)

'Sanjaya said, "O foremost amongst the Bharata lineage! Gangeya
saw that your son was still immersed in thought. He then again
spoke these pleasing words to him. 'O king! I, Drona, Shalya, Satvata
Kritavarma, Ashvatthama, Vikarna, Somadatta's son, Saindhava,
Vinda and Anuvinda from Avanti, Bahlika and the Bahlika forces,
the powerful king of Trigarta, the invincible king of Magadha,
Brihadbala from Kosala, Chitrasena, Vivimshati, many thousand
rathas with radiant and giant standards, horses from many countries
and horse-riders astride them, crazy kings of elephants with musth
issuing from their shattered temples and mouths, brave infantry
armed with many different kinds of weapons, warriors with raised
weapons who have assembled in your cause from many countries—
these and many others have assembled in your cause, ready to give
up their lives. It is my view that they are capable of defeating even the
gods in battle. O king! But I must always tell you words that are for
your own welfare. The Pandavas are incapable of being vanquished,
even by the gods, with Vasava. They have Vasudeva as their aide and
are like the great Indra in their valour. O Indra among kings! In every
way, I will act according to your words. I will defeat the Pandavas
in battle, or they will defeat me.' Having thus spoken, he gave him
the sacred *vishalyakarani*.[259] This herb possessed great efficacy and
he[260] used it to heal his wounds.

[258]The first yuga means satya or krita yuga.
[259]A herb with wonderful healing properties. Literally, something that
removes pain.
[260]Duryodhana.

'"When it was morning and the sky was clear, the valiant Bhishma, skilled about vyuhas, himself arranged his soldiers in an array that was in the form of the *mandala* vyuha.[261] O foremost among men! It abounded in many different kinds of weapons. It was full of the foremost warriors, tuskers and infantry. There were many thousands of chariots in every direction. There were large numbers of horse-riders, wielding swords and lances. There were seven chariots near every elephant and there were seven horses near every chariot. There were ten archers near every horse-rider and there were seven with shields near every archer. O great king! Such was the vyuha in which your maharatha soldiers were arrayed. Protected by Bhishma, they were stationed, ready for the great battle. Ten thousand horses, as many elephants, ten thousand chariots and your armoured sons, the brave Chitrasena and the others, protected the grandfather. He was seen to be protected by those brave ones and those immensely strong kings were themselves armoured. In that battle, Duryodhana was armoured and was stationed on his chariot. He blazed in prosperity, like Shakra in heaven. O descendant of the Bharata lineage! A great roar arose from the army of your sons. There was the tumultuous sound of chariot wheels and the noise made by musical instruments. Arrayed by Bhishma, the battle formation of the sons of Dhritarashtra advanced towards the west. It was in the form of a giant vyuha known as mandala, impenetrable and the destroyer of the enemy. O king! It was beautiful in every direction and was incapable of being assailed by the enemy.

'"On seeing the extremely terrible vyuha known as mandala, King Yudhishthira himself created the vyuha known as vajra. The different divisions were stationed in the form of this array. The charioteers and horse-riders roared like lions. Desiring to do battle, the warriors wished to break each other's vyuhas. Here and there, with their soldiers, the brave ones began to strike. Bharadvaja's son advanced against Matsya and Drona's son against Shikhandi. King Duryodhana attacked Parshata himself. O king! Nakula and Sahadeva advanced against the lord of Madra. Vinda and Anuvinda from Avanti attacked

---

[261]Mandala means circular.

Iravat.[262] In that encounter, all the kings fought against Dhananjaya. Bhimasena strove in that battle and countered Hardikya.[263] O king! In that battle, Arjuna's illustrious son[264] fought with your sons Chitrasena, Vikarna and Durmarshana. Hidimba's son, supreme among rakshasas, advanced forcefully against the great archer from Pragjyotisha and it was like a crazy elephant encountering another crazy elephant.[265] O king! The rakshasa Alambusa was enraged in that war. He attacked Satyaki, invincible in battle, together with his soldiers. Bhurishrava made every effort in that battle and fought against Dhrishtaketu. Yudhishthira, Dharma's son, confronted King Shrutayu.[266] In that battle, Chekitana fought against Kripa. The remaining ones fought against maharatha Bhima.

"'Thousands of kings surrounded Dhananjaya, with spears, lances, iron arrows, maces and clubs in their hands. Arjuna became extremely angry and told Varshneya, 'O Madhava! Look at the soldiers of the sons of Dhritarashtra, arrayed for battle. They have been arranged in this formation by the great-souled Gangeya, knowledgeable about vyuhas. O Madhava! Look at these armoured and brave ones, wishing to do battle. O Keshava! Behold the king of Trigarta, together with his brothers. O Janardana! While you look on, I will kill all of them today. O foremost among the Yadu lineage! They are wishing to fight against me in this field of battle.' Having spoken thus, Kounteya touched the string of his bow and showered arrows towards the masses of kings. Those supreme archers also showered back arrows in return and it was like clouds pouring down onto a lake during the monsoon season. O lord of the earth! In that great battle, the two Krishnas were seen to be completely covered through those showers of arrows and a great lamentation arose amidst the soldiers. The gods, the devarshis, the gandharvas and the giant serpents were struck with great wonder, when they saw the two Krishnas in

---

[262]Iravat or Iravan was the son of Arjuna and the naga princess Ulupi.
[263]Kritavarma.
[264]Abhimanyu.
[265]Ghatotkacha and Bhagadatta respectively.
[266]Equivalently, Shrutayush.

that state. O king! At this, Arjuna was enraged and unleashed the
aindra[267] weapon. We witnessed Vijaya's extraordinary valour. The
showers of weapons released by his enemies were repulsed by his
innumerable arrows. O lord of the earth! Among those thousands
of kings, horses and elephants, there was not a single one who was
not wounded. O venerable one! Partha pierced others with two or
three arrows each. Having been thus killed by Partha, they sought
refuge with Bhishma, Shantanu's son. At that time, they seemed to be
immersed in fathomless waters and Bhishma became their protector.
Your soldiers confronted a calamity there and were scattered. O great
king! They were agitated, like the great ocean in a storm.'"

Chapter 938(78)

'Sanjaya said, "Susharma[268] retreated from the battle. The brave
ones were routed by the great-souled Pandava. However, the
battle continued. Your army, which was like the ocean, had been
agitated. Gangeya swiftly advanced towards Vijaya. O king! On
witnessing Partha's valour in battle, Duryodhana hastened towards
all those kings and spoke to them. The brave and immensely strong
Susharma was at the forefront and was stationed in the midst of all
the soldiers. These words delighted them. 'This Bhishma, Shantanu's
son, wishes to fight with Dhananjaya with all his heart. He is the
best of the Kurus and is willing to give up his own life. With all the
soldiers of the Bharata army, he will advance against the army of the
enemy. All of you unite in the battle and protect the grandfather.'
O great king! Having been thus urged, all the divisions of all those
kings of men followed the grandfather. Bhishma, Shantanu's son,
swiftly went to where Arjuna was and the immensely strong one of
the Bharata lineage had also been advancing towards him. He was

[267]Divine missile named after Indra.
[268]The king of Trigarta.

resplendent on a great chariot that roared like the clouds. Large white horses were yoked to it and the terrible ape was on the standard. On seeing Dhananjaya Kiriti advance in battle, all the soldiers in your army were frightened and let out a tumultuous roar. Krishna held the reins in that battle and looked as dazzling as the sun in midday. They were unable of glancing at him. Like that, the Pandavas were incapable of glancing at Bhishma, Shantanu's son. His horses were white and he held a white bow. He looked like the white planet when it has risen.[269] He was surrounded on every side by the extremely great-souled Trigarta and his brothers, your sons and many other maharathas.

'"Bharadvaja's son pierced Matsya with an arrow in that encounter. He brought his standard down with one arrow and sliced down his bow with another. Discarding his broken bow, Virata, the leader of an army, quickly took up another bow that was powerful and could bear a great burden. He used venomous arrows that were like flaming serpents. He pierced Drona with three of these and his horses with four. He pierced his standard with one and his charioteer with five. With a single arrow, he pierced his bow. Drona, bull among brahmanas, became angry. O foremost among the Bharata lineage! Using eight straight-tufted arrows, he killed his horses and his charioteer with a single one. With his horses slain and his charioteer also slain, the best of charioteers jumped down from his chariot and swiftly ascended Shankha's chariot.[270] The father and the son were on the same chariot and powerfully countered Bharadvaja's son with a great shower of arrows. O lord of men! Bharadvaja's son became enraged in that battle. He despatched an arrow that was like a venomous serpent towards Shankha. In that encounter, it pierced his heart and drank up his blood. Then the arrow fell down on the ground, smeared in blood. Killed by the arrow released by Bharadvaja's son, he fell down from the chariot. While his father looked on, the bow and arrows dropped from his grasp. On seeing that his son had been killed, Virata gave up the fight and fled in fear.

[269]White planet probably means Venus, but it can also signify the moon.
[270]Shankha was Virata's son.

Drona was like death with a gaping mouth. Bharadvaja's son swiftly attacked the great army of the Pandavas. In that battle, he scattered hundreds and thousands of them.

'"O great king! Shikhandi confronted Drona's son in battle and struck him between the brows with three swift and iron arrows. With those three adhering to his forehead, that tiger among men looked like Mount Meru with three golden peaks. O king! Ashvatthama became angry. In that encounter, in an instant, he showered down many arrows at Shikhandi's charioteer, standard, horses and weapon and brought them down. With his horses slain, the supreme of rathas descended from his chariot. He grasped a sharp sword and a polished shield. O great king! Shikhandi, the scorcher of enemies, strode around in the field of battle with a sword, like an angry hawk. Drona's son did not find an opportunity to strike him and it was extraordinary. O bull among the Bharata lineage! Supremely enraged, Drona's son unleashed many thousand arrows in that battle. But when that extremely terrible shower of arrows descended in that encounter, the supreme among strong ones struck them down with his sharp sword. The shield was polished and was decorated with a hundred moons on it. In that encounter, Drona's son shattered his shield and his sword. O king! He pierced him with many sharp arrows. Though pierced and wounded, Shikhandi whirled the fragment of the sword that had been shattered by the arrows and swiftly hurled it, like a blazing serpent. It suddenly descended, as radiant as the fire of destruction. But in that encounter, Drona's son displayed the dexterity of his hands. He sliced it down and pierced Shikhandi with many iron arrows. O king! Shikhandi was severely wounded by those sharp arrows. He quickly ascended the chariot of the great-souled Madhava.[271]

'"The angry Satyaki, strongest among strong ones, attacked the cruel rakshasa Alambusa in that battle and pierced him with many terrible arrows. O descendant of the Bharata lineage! But in that encounter, the Indra among rakshasas sliced his bow down with an arrow that was in the shape of a half-moon and pierced him with

[271]Meaning Satyaki.

many arrows. He used the maya of rakshasas and showered down arrows on him. We then witnessed the extraordinary valour of Shini's descendant. Despite being pierced by sharp arrows in that encounter, he disregarded them. O descendant of the Bharata lineage! Varshneya then invoked the aindra weapon, which the illustrious Madhava had obtained from Vijaya.[272] Using that weapon, he reduced the maya of rakshasas to ashes. From every direction, he showered Alambusa with terrible arrows, like the slayer of Bala[273] showering rain on mountains. He was thus oppressed by the great-souled Madhava. Out of fear, the rakshasa gave up the fight with Satyaki and fled. While your warriors looked on, Shini's descendant triumphed over the Indra among rakshasas, whom even Maghavan found difficult to defeat, and roared. Satyaki, with truth as his valour, killed your soldiers with many sharp arrows and they ran away in fear.

"'O great king! At that time, Dhrishtadyumna, Drupada's powerful son, encountered your son, lord among men, and in that encounter, enveloped him with straight-tufted arrows. O descendant of the Bharata lineage! He was shrouded by Dhrishtadyumna's arrows. But your son, lord of men and Indra among kings, was not perturbed. In that encounter, he pierced Dhrishtadyumna back with ninety arrows and it was extremely wonderful. O venerable one! The commander[274] became angry and sliced his bow down. The maharatha swiftly killed his four horses and quickly pierced him with seven extremely sharp arrows. When his horses were killed, the mighty-armed one, strong among rathas, leapt down from his chariot. He advanced on foot towards Parshata, with a sword in his hand. The immensely strong Shakuni, who was devoted to the king, arrived. He took the king of all the worlds up on his own chariot. Having defeated the king, Parshata, the destroyer of enemy heroes, began to slaughter your troops, like the wielder of the vajra against the asuras.

"'In that battle, Kritavarma attacked maharatha Bhima and covered him with arrows. He was enveloped, like the sun with large

---

[272]Satyaki studied the art of war from Arjuna.

[273]Indra.

[274]Dhrishtadyumna was the overall commander of the Pandava army.

clouds. But Bhimasena, scorcher of enemies, laughed in that battle. Extremely angry, he unleashed arrows on Kritavarma. O great king! But the atiratha from the Satvata lineage, skilled in the use of weapons, did not waver. He enveloped Bhima with sharp arrows. The immensely strong Bhimasena killed his four horses. He brought down his charioteer and his beautiful standard. The destroyer of enemy heroes covered him with many arrows. He was wounded in every limb and looked like a porcupine. O great king! With his horses slain, he quickly abandoned his chariot and went to the chariot of your brother-in-law Vrishaka, while your son looked on.[275] Bhimasena angrily rushed to attack your soldiers. He began to slaughter them in great rage, like Death with a staff in his hand.”’

Chapter 939(79)

‘Dhritarashtra said, “O Sanjaya! As you have described them, I have heard about the many wonderful duels that took place between those on the side of the sons of Pandu and those on my side. O Sanjaya! But you have never spoken about those on my side being happy. You have always described the sons of Pandu as happy and as those who are never routed. O suta! You have spoken about those on my side being distressed and deprived of energy in the battle. There is no doubt that this is because of destiny.”

‘Sanjaya replied, “O bull among men! Those on your side are striving to do battle, to the best of their capacity and the best of their enterprise. They are displaying supreme manliness, to the best of their capability. The water of Ganga, the river of the gods, is sweet. But when it merges into the great ocean, it attains the quality of salinity. O king! The manliness of the great-souled ones on your side is like that. When they confront the brave sons of Pandu in battle,

[275]Vrishaka and Achala were the sons of the king of Gandhara (Subala) and were thus brothers to Shakuni and brothers-in-law to Dhritarashtra.

they obtain no success. They are trying to the best of their strength and are performing extremely difficult tasks. O foremost among the Kurus! You should not censure them because they have merged with the Kouravas. O lord of the earth! This great and terrible destruction of the earth, and the extension of Yama's kingdom, has come about because of your crimes and those of your sons. O king! Since it is because of your own sins, you should not grieve over this. The lords of the earth desire the worlds that can be obtained by performing good deeds in battle. Striving for heaven, they are fighting and penetrating the army formations. O great king! On the forenoon of that day, there was a great destruction of people, like that in the battle between the gods and the asuras. Listen with single-minded attention.

"'The two great-souled and great archers from Avanti, immensely strong, saw Iravat in that battle and encountered him with ferocity. The battle that took place between them was tumultuous and made the body hair stand up. Iravat was extremely enraged. He quickly pierced those brothers, who were like gods, with sharp and straight-tufted arrows. In that encounter, those wonderful warriors pierced him back. O king! They fought on and there was nothing to differentiate the two parties. They sought to kill the enemy and neutralized each other's endeavours. O king! Iravat used four arrows to despatch his four horses to Yama's abode.[276] O venerable one! With two extremely sharp and broad-headed arrows, he sliced off his bow and standard. O king! In that encounter, this was extraordinary. At this, Anuvinda discarded his chariot and climbed onto Vinda's chariot. He grasped a supreme and new bow that was capable of bearing a great burden. In that battle, those two brave ones from Avanti, supreme among rathas, were stationed on the same chariot. They swiftly showered arrows on the great-souled Iravat. They released extremely swift arrows, decorated with gold. They covered the sky and reached the path of the sun. Iravat became extremely angry in that battle and showered down arrows on those maharatha brothers. He brought down their charioteer. Having lost his life, the charioteer fell down on the ground. The horses were no longer controlled and dragged

---

[276]Succeeding sentences show that this means Anuvinda's horses.

the chariot off in various directions. O great king! The son of the
naga king's daughter triumphed in this way. He quickly displayed
his manliness and began to slaughter your soldiers. Thus killed in
battle, the great army of the sons of Dhritarashtra reeled around in
many directions, like a man who has drunk poison.

'"Hidimba's son, Indra among the rakshasas, advanced against
Bhagadatta. The immensely strong one was on a chariot that had
the complexion of the sun and possessed a standard. The king of
Pragjyotisha was seated on a king of elephants, like the wielder of
the vajra in ancient times, in the *tarakamaya* battle.[277] The gods,
together with the gandharvas, and the rishis assembled and were
unable to differentiate between Hidimba's son and Bhagadatta. Just
as Shakra, the lord of the gods, had driven the danavas away with
weapons, in that encounter, the king[278] drove the Pandavas away in
all directions. O descendant of the Bharata lineage! The Pandavas
were driven away in all the directions and within their own ranks,
could not find a single one who could protect them. O descendant
of the Bharata lineage! But we saw Bhimasena's son stationed on his
chariot there, though the other maharathas had fled with dispirited
hearts. O descendant of the Bharata lineage! When the soldiers of
the Pandus returned again, in that encounter, your soldiers let out
a terrible roar. O king! In that great battle, Ghatotkacha enveloped
Bhagadatta with arrows, like clouds raining down on Mount Meru.
The king repulsed the arrows released from the rakshasa's bow
and in that battle, quickly pierced Bhimasena's son in all his inner
organs. He oppressed him with many straight-tufted arrows. But the
Indra among rakshasas was not distressed and was like an immobile
mountain. At this, Pragjyotisha became angry. In that encounter, he
hurled fourteen javelins. However, the rakshasa sliced them down.
Having sliced the javelins down with his sharp arrows, the mighty-
armed one pierced Bhagadatta with seventy gold-tufted arrows.

---

[277]Famous battle that took place between the gods and the demons. This is
sometimes described to have been over Tara (Brihaspati's wife) and sometimes
described to have been over Taraka (a demon).

[278]Bhagadatta.

O king! O descendant of the Bharata lineage! But Pragjyotisha only laughed. In that battle, he used arrows to bring down his four horses. Though the horses were slain, the powerful Indra among rakshasas remained stationed on his chariot. He powerfully hurled a javelin towards Pragjyotisha's elephant. This possessed a golden shaft and was extremely swift. As it suddenly descended, the king cut it down into three and shattered, it fell down on the ground. On seeing that the javelin had been destroyed, Hidimba's son fled and left the field of battle, like in ancient times, Namuchi, supreme among daityas, had fled from Indra.[279] The brave and valiant one,[280] famous for his manliness, won that battle. O king! He was invincible in battle, like Yama and Varuna. O king! In that battle, he began to crush the Pandava soldiers with his elephant, like a wild elephant destroying the stalks of lotuses.

'"In that battle, the lord of Madra fought with the twins, the sons of his sister. He enveloped the sons of Pandu with a cloud of arrows. Finding himself engaged in battle with his maternal uncle, Sahadeva repulsed him with a shower of arrows, like clouds shrouding the sun. Covered by that shower of arrows, he seemed to be happy.[281] On account of their mother, the twins were also extremely delighted. O king! In that battle, smilingly, the maharatha[282] used four supreme arrows to despatch Nakula's four horses to Yama's abode. With the horses slain, the maharatha[283] quickly descended from his chariot and ascended onto his illustrious brother's vehicle. In that battle, the brave ones stretched their bows while stationed on the same chariot. In a short while, they angrily covered the chariot of the king of Madra with arrows. He was shrouded with many straight-tufted arrows released by his sister's sons. But the tiger among men did not waver and was like a mountain. As if laughing, he destroyed that shower of arrows. Sahadeva became angry. O descendant of the

---

[279]Namuchi was a demon killed by Indra.
[280]Bhagadatta.
[281]He was proud, because they were his sister's sons.
[282]Shalya.
[283]Nakula.

Bharata lineage! The valiant one picked up an arrow and released it in the direction of the king of Madra. That arrow released by him was as forceful as Garuda. It pierced the king of Madra and fell down on the ground. Having been severely wounded and pained, the maharatha sat down on the floor of his chariot. O great king! He lost his consciousness. On seeing that he had fallen down and had lost his senses in that encounter and had been oppressed by the twins, his charioteer drove his chariot away. On seeing that the chariot of the lord of Madra had retreated, the sons of Dhritarashtra lost heart. All of them were distressed and thought that he was no longer alive. Having vanquished their maternal uncle in battle, Madri's maharatha sons were delighted. They blew their conch shells and roared like lions. O lord of the earth! O king! Filled with joy, they attacked your soldiers, like the immortal Indra and Upendra[284] attacking the army of the daityas."'

Chapter 940(80)

'Sanjaya said, "When the sun reached the midpoint, King Yudhishthira saw Shrutayu and urged his horses towards him. The king attacked Shrutayu, the scorcher of enemies and pierced him with nine sharp and straight-tufted arrows. But, in that encounter, the king, the great archer, countered the arrows shot by Dharma's son and struck Kounteya with seven arrows. In that battle, these penetrated his armour and drank up his blood, as if all the vital forces in the great-souled one's body had been sucked out. Pandava was severely wounded by the great-souled king. However, in that encounter, he pierced the king in the heart with an arrow that was like a boar's ear. With another broad-headed arrow, Partha, foremost among rathas, quickly brought down the great-souled one's standard from his chariot and made it fall down on the ground. O king! On seeing

[284]Indra's younger brother, Vishnu.

that his standard had been brought down, King Shrutayu pierced Pandava with seven sharp arrows. At this, Yudhishthira, Dharma's son, blazed up in anger, like the fire that burns at the end of a yuga and consumes all beings. O great king! On seeing Pandava enraged, the gods, the gandharvas and the rakshasas were pained and anxious. All the beings thought that, thus enraged, the king would destroy the three worlds then. O king! When Pandava was thus angered, the rishis and the gods uttered great words of benediction so that there might be peace in the worlds. He was overcome with rage and licked the corners of his mouth. His appearance was as terrible as that of the sun at the time of the destruction of a yuga. O lord of the earth! O descendant of the Bharata lineage! All the soldiers in your army became distressed and thought that they would no longer remain alive. But the immensely famous one controlled his anger through patience. He sliced down Shrutayu's great bow from his hand. After the bow had been sliced down, while all the soldiers looked on in that battle, the king used an iron arrow to pierce him between the breasts. O king! Nimble on his feet, the great-souled and extremely strong one, then used sharp arrows to kill his mounts and his charioteer. On witnessing the king's manliness and with his horses slain, Shrutayu gave up his chariot and swiftly fled from the field of battle. Dharma's son defeated the great archer in that encounter. O king! Because of this, all of Duryodhana's soldiers became reluctant to do battle. O great king! Having accomplished this, Yudhishthira, Dharma's son, began to slaughter your soldiers, like Death with a gaping mouth.

'"While all the soldiers looked on, Varshneya Chekitana enveloped Goutama, supreme among charioteers, with arrows. In that encounter, Kripa, Sharadvat's son, countered all those arrows. O king! Fighting with care in that battle, he pierced Chekitana with arrows. O venerable one! He used another broad-headed arrow to slice down his bow. Displaying his lightness of hand in that encounter, he brought down his charioteer. O king! He killed his horses and the two charioteers who protected his flanks.[285] Satvata[286]

[285]Parshnis.
[286]Chekitana.

swiftly leapt down from his chariot and grabbed a club. With that club, capable of killing heroes, that supreme among wielders of clubs killed Goutama's horses and brought down his charioteer. Goutama stood on the ground and shot sixteen arrows at him. Those arrows pierced Satvata and entered the ground. Chekitana became angry. Wishing to kill Goutama, like Purandara against Vritra, he again hurled his club. That polished and great club was as hard as stone. On seeing it descend, Goutama repulsed it with thousands of arrows. O descendant of the Bharata lineage! Chekitana drew his sword out from its sheath. With supreme lightness, he attacked Goutama. Goutama discarded his bow and took up an extremely sharp sword. O king! He advanced with great speed towards Chekitana. Both of them were extremely strong and both wielded supreme swords. They began to strike each other with those extremely sharp swords. Those bulls among men were struck with the force of each other's swords and fell down on the ground, the abode of all beings. Their limbs became unconscious and they were exhausted because of their exertions. Because of his affectionate feelings, Karakarsha, invincible in battle, swiftly rushed to the spot. He saw that Chekitana was in that state and while all the soldiers looked on, took him up on his own chariot. O lord of the earth! The brave Shakuni, your brother-in-law, swiftly took Goutama, supreme among rathas, up on his chariot.

'"O king! In anger, the immensely strong Dhrishtaketu pierced Somadatta's son[287] in the chest with ninety arrows. O great king! With those arrows on his chest, Somadatta's son looked resplendent, like the sun with its rays at midday. However, in that battle, Bhurishrava killed maharatha Dhrishtaketu's horses and charioteers with supreme arrows and he was deprived of his chariot. On seeing that he had been deprived of his chariot and that his horses and his charioteer had been slain in that encounter, he enveloped him with a great shower of arrows. O venerable one! The great-minded Dhrishtaketu then abandoned his chariot and ascended Shatanika's vehicle.

'"O king! The rathas Chitrasena, Vikarna and Durmarshana were clad in golden armour and attacked Subhadra's son. O king!

[287]Bhurishrava.

A terrible encounter commenced between Abhimanyu and those armed ones, like that in the body between *vata*, *pitta* and *kapha*.[288] O king! In that great battle, he deprived your sons of their chariots. But remembering Bhima's pledge, the tiger among men did not kill them.[289] Bhishma was unassailable, even to the gods. In that battle, surrounded by many kings and hundreds of elephants, horses and chariots, he swiftly advanced to rescue your sons. On seeing this and on seeing that maharatha Abhimanyu, who was only a child, was alone, Kounteya, the one borne on white steeds, told Vasudeva, 'O Hrishikesha! Drive the horses to the spot where those numerous chariots are. There are many brave ones there, skilled in the use of weapons and invincible in battle. O Madhava! Drive the horses so that they cannot slay our soldiers.' Thus urged by the infinitely energetic Kounteya, in that encounter, Varshneya drove the chariot yoked to the white horses there. O venerable one! When Arjuna angrily advanced into battle, a great uproar was created by your troops. Kounteya advanced to the kings who were protecting Bhishma. O king! He spoke these words to Susharma. 'I know that you are the foremost among warriors and that you bear extreme enmity towards us from earlier times. You will now behold the extremely terrible fruits of that. I will today show you your deceased ancestors.' Having heard these harsh words spoken by Bibhatsu, the slayer of enemies, Susharma, the leader of a large number of charioteers, did not speak anything in reply, pleasant or unpleasant. But he advanced against the brave Arjuna, surrounded by a large number of kings. O unblemished one! In that battle, Arjuna was surrounded by your sons from every direction, to the front, the rear and the sides. They enveloped him with arrows, like clouds covering the sun. O descendant of the Bharata lineage! An extremely terrible battle commenced between those on your side and the Pandavas and in that encounter, blood flowed like water.'''

[288]These can be loosely translated as wind, bile and phlegm. In Ayurveda, these are the three *dosha*s or humours in the body and they are always striving against each other.

[289]Bhima had taken an oath that he would kill Duryodhana and his brothers.

Chapter 941(81)

'Sanjaya said, "The powerful Dhananjaya was breathing like a snake that had been trodden on with the foot. He raised his arrows. In that battle, he continuously used arrows to slice down the bows of those maharathas. In that battle, he instantly sliced down the bows of those valiant kings. The great-souled one simultaneously pierced them with arrows, wishing to slay those illustrious ones. O king! Some of those kings fell down on the ground, drenched in blood. They were oppressed by Shakra's son. Their bodies were mangled and their heads fell down. Some died because their armour and their bodies were penetrated. They were overcome by Partha's strength and resorted to the ground. They assumed wonderful forms and were simultaneously destroyed. On seeing that those warriors and princes had perished, the king of Trigarta quickly advanced towards Partha. Thirty-two charioteers, who were protecting from the rear, were also with him. They surrounded Partha and drew their bows with a loud noise. They showered him with a great rain of arrows, like clouds pouring down rain on a mountain. In that encounter, Dhananjaya was oppressed by that shower of arrows and anger was engendered in him. He used sixty arrows that had been washed in oil and killed the ones who had been protecting from the rear. Having vanquished the sixty rathas, the illustrious Dhananjaya was delighted.[290] Having killed the forces of those kings, Jishnu advanced to slay Bhishma. The king of Trigarta saw that the ranks of his maharatha relatives had been killed. He swiftly advanced to kill Partha in battle, with the lords of the earth following him. On seeing that they were advancing against Dhananjaya, foremost among the wielders of weapons, with Shikhandi at the forefront, they[291] advanced to protect Arjuna's chariot. They raised sharp weapons in their hands. Partha also saw that those brave ones were advancing against him, together with the king of Trigarta. In that battle, he pierced them with sharp arrows shot from the bow Gandiva. The skilled warrior wished to fight with

---

[290]There is an inconsistency between the number of thirty-two and sixty.
[291]The Pandava warriors.

Bhishma and saw Duryodhana and Saindhava and the other kings. For a brief moment, the brave Jishnu used his strength to counter them. But then the infinitely valorous and greatly energetic one avoided those kings, Jayadratha and the other kings. With a bow and arrow in his hand, the spirited one, terrible in his strength, went to where Gangeya was.

'"The great-souled Yudhishthira, terrible in his strength, also advanced swiftly, his anger having been excited. In that encounter, he avoided the lord of Madra, whose deeds were infinite and who had been assigned as his share.[292] To do battle, with the sons of Madri and Bhimasena, he went to the spot where Bhishma, Shantanu's son, was stationed. Ganga's son was wonderful in battle. He was set upon by all the maharathas together. But Shantanu's great-souled son was not distracted. King Jayadratha was terrible in his valour and spirited. He was a warrior who was unwavering in his aim. He advanced against those maharathas and sliced down their bows with his supreme bow. The great-souled Duryodhana was overcome with the poison of anger. His wrath having been ignited, he used arrows that were like fire to fight with Yudhishthira, Bhimasena, the twins and Partha. They were also pierced with arrows shot by Kripa, Shalya, Shala and the lord Chitrasena and their[293] anger increased, like the gods when they confronted the assembled daityas. Shikhandi's weapon had been sliced down by the king who was Shantanu's son. On seeing that he was running away in that battle, the great-souled Ajatashatru became wrathful and spoke these words of anger to Shikhandi. 'You spoke these words to me, in the presence of your father. "Using arrows that are clear and have the complexion of the sun, I will kill Bhishma, who is great in his vows. I say this truthfully." This was the pledge you took and you are not making it come true. You are not killing Devavrata in battle. O brave one among men! You have become false in your oath. Protect your dharma and the fame of your lineage. Behold. Bhishma is fighting with terrible force. He is tormenting the masses of my soldiers. The net of his arrows is fierce in its energy. Like Death

---

[292]It had been agreed that Yudhishthira would kill Shalya.
[293]That of the Pandavas.

himself, he is killing everything in an instant. Your bow has been sliced
down by the king who is Shantanu's son. You have been vanquished
and are running away from the field of battle. You are abandoning
your relatives and your brothers. Where are you going! This is not
becoming of you. Bhishma is infinite in his valour. On seeing him, our
soldiers are routed and are fleeing. O Drupada's son! You are certainly
frightened. The complexion of your face is distressed. O brave one
among men! Honouring his commands, Dhananjaya is engaged in
this great battle. O brave one! You are famous on earth! Why are
you now frightened of Bhishma?' Dharmaraja's words were harsh.
But he heard them and perceived them to be full of sound reason.
O king! Having honoured these instructions, the great-souled one
swiftly set about the task of killing Bhishma.

'"Shikhandi advanced towards Bhishma with great force. Shalya
countered him with weapons that were terrible and extremely
difficult to resist. O king! However, Drupada's son was like Indra
in his power. He saw those weapons, which were as powerful as
the fire at the destruction of a yuga, and was not confounded at all.
The great archer countered those weapons with his own arrows. To
counter them, Shikhandi took up another terrible weapon known as
Varuna. The gods stationed in the firmament and the sky saw those
weapons[294] repulsed by this weapon. O king! In that battle, the
great-souled and brave Bhishma sliced down the bow and colourful
standard of Pandu's son, King Yudhishthira Ajamidha. On seeing
that Yudhishthira was overcome with fear and had cast aside his bow
and arrows in that battle, Bhimasena grabbed a club and advanced
on foot against Jayadratha. On seeing Bhimasena advance with great
speed with the club, Jayadratha pierced him from every direction with
five hundred sharp and terrible arrows that were like Yama's staff.
But the swift Vrikodara, his heart full of rage, paid no attention to
these arrows. In that battle, he slew the mounts which bore the king
of Sindhu in that encounter, ones that had been born in Aratta.[295]

---

[294]Shalya's weapons.

[295]Aratta is a distant kingdom. It is difficult to pinpoint its precise location,
though it figures prominently in Sumerian literature.

Your son[296] was unrivalled in his prowess and was like the king of the gods. On seeing Bhimasena, he swiftly advanced on his chariot to kill him, with his weapons raised. Bhima suddenly roared. Uttering threats, he rushed towards him with a club. In every direction, the Kurus saw this upraised club, like Yama's staff. All of them wished to avoid the descent of the terrible club and abandoned your son. O descendant of the Bharata lineage! There was a tumultuous and extremely terrible melee and they were all confounded. But despite seeing the great club descend, Chitrasena did not lose his senses. He discarded his chariot and resorted to fighting on foot, grasping a polished sword and shield. He leapt down, like a lion from the peak of a mountain, and resorted to the face of the earth. In that battle, the club descended on the colourful chariot and killed the horses and the charioteer. It then fell down on the ground, like a flaming and giant meteor that has been dislodged from the sky and has fallen down. O descendant of the Bharata lineage! On witnessing the extraordinary, extremely great and unrivalled feat accomplished by your son,[297] all the soldiers were delighted and honoured him. They uttered a roar in every direction."'

Chapter 942(82)

'Sanjaya said, "On seeing that the spirited Chitrasena was without a chariot, your son, Vikarna, picked him up on his own chariot. An extremely tumultuous and fierce battle raged there. Bhishma, Shantanu's son, swiftly attacked Yudhishthira. With their chariots, elephants and horses, the Srinjayas trembled. They thought that Yudhishthira was already inside the mouth of death. However, the lord Kouravya Yudhishthira, together with the twins, attacked the great archer and tiger among men, Bhishma, Shantanu's son. In that

[296]Later sentences identify this son as Chitrasena.
[297]Of avoiding the club.

battle, Pandava shot thousands of arrows. They enveloped Bhishma,
like clouds covering the sky. O descendant of the Bharata lineage!
Gangeya received a net of innumerable arrows, in hundreds and
thousands. O venerable one! Bhishma also released a net of arrows.
It looked like a swarm travelling through the sky. In that battle, in
an instant, Bhishma, Shantanu's son, made Kounteya invisible in
the encounter through the net of arrows he shot in groups. King
Yudhishthira was enraged and despatched an iron arrow at the
great-souled Kouravya. It was like a virulent serpent. O king! But
before it could reach him in that encounter, maharatha Bhishma
used a kshurapra arrow to slice down the weapon released from
the bow. Having destroyed the iron arrow in battle, which was like
death, Bhishma killed the horses, decorated with gold, of the Indra
among Kouravas. With the horses slain, Yudhishthira, Dharma's
son, abandoned the chariot and swiftly ascended the chariot of the
great-souled Nakula. Bhishma, the destroyer of enemy cities, was
extremely enraged in that battle. He attacked the twins and covered
them with arrows. O great king! On seeing that they were oppressed
by Bhishma's arrows, he[298] desired Bhishma's death and anxiously
thought about the means.

"'Yudhishthira addressed all the kings and well-wishers who
were following him. 'All of you unite and kill Bhishma, Shantanu's
son.' All the kings heard the words that Partha had addressed and
they surrounded the grandfather with a large number of chariots.
Your father, Devavrata, was surrounded in every direction. O king!
He seemed to be playing with his bow and brought down those
maharathas. While all the Parthas looked on, Kourava strode around
on that field of battle, like a lion cub in the forest amidst a herd of
deer. He roared in the battle and frightened the brave ones with his
arrows. O great king! They were frightened on seeing him, like a
herd of deer at a lion. The kshatriyas saw the movements of that
lion among the Bharata lineage in that battle. He was like a fire
consuming dry wood, aided by the wind. In that encounter, Bhishma
brought down the heads of the rathas, like a skilled man bringing

---

[298]Yudhishthira.

down ripe fruit from a palm tree. O great king! As those heads fell
down on the ground, there was a tremendous sound, like that of
stones falling down. There was a tumultuous and extremely terrible
battle. There was great and extreme confusion among all those
soldiers. The vyuhas of the kshatriyas were thus shattered. In that
battle, they challenged one another to a fight. Shikhandi forcefully
approached the grandfather of the Bharatas, asking him to wait. But
Bhishma avoided Shikhandi in that battle, remembering Shikhandi's
feminine nature.[299] Instead, he angrily attacked the Srinjayas. On
seeing maharatha Bhishma, the Srinjayas were delighted. They roared
like lions and uttered many other shouts. These mingled with the
sound of conch shells. O lord! This was a time when the sun was
stationed on the other side of the directions.[300] A battle with chariots
and elephants commenced.

"'Panchala Dhrishtadyumna and maharatha Satyaki oppressed
the soldiers terribly, using a shower of spears and javelins. O king!
In that battle, they used many arrows to strike down those on your
side. O bull among men! Though those on your side were killed in
that battle, the noble ones were resolved to fight in that battle and
did not retreat from the encounter. In that battle, those maharatha
men strove to the best of their endeavours. But a great lamentation
arose among the great-souled ones on your side. On hearing this
terrible lamentation amidst the maharathas on your side, Vinda and
Anuvinda from Avanti attacked Parshata. Those swift maharathas
slew his horses. They enveloped Parshata with a shower of arrows.
At this, the extremely strong Panchala quickly jumped down from his
chariot. He swiftly ascended the chariot of the extremely great-souled
Satyaki. King Yudhishthira was surrounded by a large army. With
this, in that battle, he angrily attacked the scorchers of enemies from
Avanti. O venerable one! Your sons made every effort to surround
Vinda and Anuvinda from Avanti. O bull among the kshatriya
lineage! Arjuna angrily fought against the kshatriyas. He fought in
that battle, like the wielder of the vajra against the asuras. Drona

[299]Earlier, Shikhandi had been the lady Amba.
[300]It was afternoon and the sun was in the western sky.

was also angry in that battle, wishing to do that which would bring
your son pleasure. He began to consume all the Panchalas, like a
fire amidst a mass of cotton. O lord of the earth! With Duryodhana
at the forefront, your sons surrounded Bhishma in that battle and
fought against the Pandavas.

'"O descendant of the Bharata lineage! When the sun assumed a
reddish tinge, King Duryodhana spoke to all those who were on your
side. 'Do not delay.' They fought on and accomplished extremely
difficult tasks. But the sun ascended the Asta mountain[301] and could
no longer be seen. An extremely terrible river began to flow and its
current and waves were made out of blood. It was infested with masses
of jackals and it was the moment of twilight. Jackals let out fearful
howls and it was inauspicious. The terrible field of battle was infested
with the spirits of the dead. Rakshasas, pishachas and others who
fed on flesh were seen in every direction, in hundreds and thousands.
Arjuna vanquished the kings who followed Susharma, together with
their followers. In the midst of his divisions, he then proceeded
towards his own camp. O Indra among kings! Since it was night,
surrounded by the soldiers and with his brothers, King Kourvaya
Yudhishthira also went to his own camp. Having vanquished the
rathas headed by Duryodhana in battle, Bhimasena also went to his
own camp. In the great battle, Duryodhana was surrounded by the
kings. With Bhishma, Shantanu's son, he swiftly went to his camp.
Surrounded by all their armies, Drona, Drona's son, Kripa, Shalya and
Satvata Kritavarma also went to their camps. O king! Surrounded in
the battle by all the warriors, Satyaki and Parshata Dhrishtadyumna
also went to their camps. O great king! When it was night, thus did
the scorchers of enemies, on your side and on that of the Pandavas,
retreat. The Pandavas and the Kurus went to their own camps. O great
king! They entered and honoured each other. The brave ones made
arrangements for protecting themselves and set up outposts, according
to the prescribed methods. They removed the stakes[302] and bathed
in different kinds of water. Benedictions were pronounced and all of

[301]Mountain behind which the sun sets.
[302]From the wounds.

them were praised by bards. Those illustrious ones sported, to the sound of singing and the playing of musical instruments. For a short while, everything seemed to be like heaven. The maharathas did not speak at all about what transpired in the battle. O king! Having been exhausted, all the people in the armies slept. O king! With the large numbers of elephants and horses, it was seen to be beautiful.'"

Chapter 943(83)

'Sanjaya said, "Those lords of men spent the night happily, engrossed in sleep. Then the Kurus and the Pandavas again emerged to fight. A great sound arose from both the armies, as they emerged to do battle. It was like the great ocean. King Duryodhana, Chitrasena, Vivimshati, Bhishma, supreme among rathas, and the brahmana who was Bharadvaja's son united themselves and arrayed the great army of the Kouravas. O king! They armoured themselves and formed a vyuha to counter the Pandavas. O lord of the earth! Your father, Bhishma, constructed a great vyuha. It was as terrible as the ocean, with the mounts as its waves. Bhishma, Shantanu's son, advanced at the forefront of all the soldiers. He was supported by the Malavas, those from the south and those from Avanti. Bharadvaja's powerful son was next to him. The Pulindas, the Paradas and the lesser Malavas were with him. O lord of the earth! The powerful Bhagadatta was next to Drona, together with the Magadhas, the Kalingas and the Pishachas. Brihadbala, the king of Kosala, was behind Pragjyotisha, together with the Mekalas, the Tripuras and the Chichchilas. Next to Brihadbala was the brave Trigarta, the lord of Prasthala. He was accompanied by a large number of Kambojas and thousands of Yavanas. O descendant of the Bharata lineage! Drona's brave son was next to Trigarta and advanced to do battle. He roared like a lion and made the earth resound. Surrounded by his brothers, Duryodhana was next to Drona's son and Kripa Sharadvat was behind him. It was thus that the great vyuha advanced, like an ocean. O lord! There were resplendent flags and dazzling umbrellas. There were colourful bracelets and extremely expensive bows.

'"On seeing the great vyuha of your soldiers, maharatha Yudhishthira quickly addressed Parshata, the supreme commander. 'O great archer! Behold the vyuha that has been constructed. It is like an ocean. O Parshata! Without any delay, create a counter vyuha.' Having been thus addressed, the brave Parshata constructed an extremely terrible vyuha. O great king! It was called Shringataka[303] and it was destructive of the vyuhas of enemies. Bhimasena and maharatha Satyaki were at the two horns, with many thousands of chariots, horses and infantry. The foremost of men, the one with the white horses and the ape on his standard, was next to them. King Yudhishthira was in the centre, with the Pandavas who were Madri's sons. Other kings who were great archers, skilled in the use of weapons, filled up the vyuha with their soldiers. Abhimanyu was at the rear, with maharatha Virata, Droupadi's delighted sons and the rakshasa Ghatotkacha. O descendant of the Bharata lineage! Thus did the Pandavas array themselves in the form of a gigantic vyuha. The brave ones stationed themselves in that battle, wishing to fight and desiring victory. The tumultuous sound of drums mingled with the sound made by conch shells. Armpits were slapped and a terrible noise arose in all the directions.

'"In that battle, the brave ones then confronted each other. O king! They glanced at each other in rage, without blinking their eyes. O Indra among men! They challenged each other, summoning each other by name first. A battle commenced. The battle that started was terrible in form and fearful. Those on your side, and those of the enemy, sought to kill each other. O descendant of the Bharata lineage! Sharp iron arrows descended in that battle. They were like fearful snakes with gaping mouths. There were polished and extremely energetic lances that had been washed in oil. O king! They were as radiant as lightning[304] in the clouds. There were polished and thick

---

[303]Meaning that it had cusps or horns.

[304]The word used is *shatahrada*. Literally, this means something with a hundred rays of light.

clubs, covered in cloth and decorated with gold. They were seen to descend, like beautiful summits of mountains. There were radiant swords, as clear as the sky. O descendant of the Bharata lineage! There were shields made out of the hides of bulls, with a hundred moons marked on them. O king! They were resplendent in that battle, as they descended in every direction. O lord of men! The two armies encountered each other in that battle. They dazzled like the armies of the gods and the daityas, when arrayed against each other. In that battle, they clashed against each other in every direction. In that supreme battle, chariots quickly clashed against chariots. As those bulls among men fought, the yokes of one got entangled with the yokes of another. O foremost among the Bharata lineage! Tuskers fought with tuskers and because of the friction, flames were seen in every direction, mingled with smoke. In all directions, struck by lances, some warriors on elephants were seen to fall down, like the summits of mountains. Infantry was seen to kill each other. The brave ones fought in many colourful ways and used lances and bare nails. Thus did the soldiers of the Kurus and the Pandavas attack each other. Many terrible weapons were used in that battle, to despatch others to the eternal worlds.[305] The chariot of Bhishma, Shantanu's son, roared in that battle. He advanced against the Pandus and confounded them with the twang of his bow. The chariots of the Pandavas also emitted a terrible roar. With Dhrishtadyumna at the forefront, they advanced together. O descendant of the Bharata lineage! Thus did the battle between you and them commence. Men, horses, chariots and elephants got entangled with each other.'"

Chapter 944(84)

'Sanjaya said, "In that battle, the powerful Bhishma was enraged. Like the sun, he tormented in every direction and the Pandavas

[305]The land of the dead.

were incapable of glancing towards him. On the instructions of Dharma's son, all the soldiers rushed towards Gangeya, who was causing oppression with his sharp arrows. But the great archer Bhishma prided himself in battle. With his arrows, he brought down the Somakas, together with the Srinjayas and the Panchalas. Though they were slaughtered by Bhishma, the Panchalas and the Somakas gave up their fear of death and quickly attacked Bhishma. O king! In that battle, the brave Bhishma, Shantanu's son, powerfully sliced off the arms and the heads of those rathas. Your father, Devavrata, deprived the rathas of their chariots. The heads of horse-riders fell down from the horses. O great king! Confounded by Bhishma's weapons, we saw elephants lying around like mountains, deprived of their riders. O lord of the earth! Among the Pandavas, there was no one other than the immensely strong Bhimasena, foremost among rathas, who could resist him. In that encounter, he was the one who engaged Bhishma. There was a terrible battle between Bhishma and Bhima and an extremely terrible and fearful roar arose from all the soldiers.[306] The delighted Pandavas also roared like lions. Surrounded by his brothers, King Duryodhana protected Bhishma in that battle, which resulted in a destruction of men. Bhishma was supreme among rathas. But Bhima slew his charioteer. The horses were no longer controlled and dragged the chariot away in all directions.

'"With a swift arrow, the destroyer of enemies sliced off Sunabha's head. He was slain by that extremely sharp kshurapra and fell down on the ground. O great king! When your maharatha son was killed in that battle, seven of his brothers could not tolerate this. Adityaketu, Bahvashi, Kundadhara, Mahodara, Aparajita, Panditaka and the invincible Vishalaksha attacked Pandava in that encounter. They were clad in colourful armour and sported diverse standards. Those scorchers of enemies attacked in that battle, wishing to fight. In that encounter, Mahodara pierced Bhimasena with nine arrows, like the killer of Vritra against Namuchi. Each was like the vajra. Adityaketu pierced him with seventy, Bahvashi with five, Kundadhara with ninety and Vishalaksha with seven. O great king! Maharatha Aparajita, the

---

[306]Meaning the soldiers on the Kourava side.

vanquisher of enemies, pierced the immensely strong Bhimasena with many arrows. In that encounter, Panditaka also pierced him with three arrows. But in that battle, Bhima did not tolerate the attacks of his enemies. The destroyer of enemies grasped the bow in his left hand. Your son, Aparajita, possessed an excellent nose. In that battle, he used an arrow with a drooping tuft to slice off his head. In that encounter, he was defeated by Bhima and his head fell down on the ground. While all the people looked on, he used another broad-headed arrow to despatch maharatha Kundadhara to the land of the dead. O descendant of the Bharata lineage! In that battle, the one with the immeasurable soul then grasped another arrow and despatched it towards Panditaka.[307] The arrow killed Panditaka and penetrated the ground. It was like a serpent that kills a man whose time has come. Remembering his earlier hardships, the one whose soul is not depressed then used three arrows to slice off Vishalaksha's head and make it fall down on the ground. The great archer then struck Mahodara between the breasts with an iron arrow. O king! Pierced in the battle, he was slain and fell down on the ground. In the encounter, he sliced off Adityaketu's standard with an arrow. He used an extremely sharp and broad-headed arrow to slice off the enemy's head. The angry Bhima then used an arrow with a drooping tuft to despatch Bahvashi towards Yama's abode. O lord of the earth! Your other sons fled. They remembered the words that he had spoken in the assembly hall.[308]

'"Because of his brothers, King Duryodhana was distressed. He spoke to all the warriors, 'There is Bhima. Let him be killed in battle.' O lord of the earth! Having been thus addressed, your sons, the great archers, saw that their brothers had been killed and remembered the beneficial words that the immensely wise Kshatta[309] had spoken. The words of the one who could foresee were now coming true. O lord of men! You were overcome by avarice and confusion, because of affection towards your sons. In earlier times, you did not understand

---

[307]The text says Pandita. But Pandita is the same as Panditaka.
[308]The promise that he would kill Duryodhana and his brothers.
[309]Vidura.

the purport of those great and beneficial words. Given the way the powerful Pandava is killing your sons, it seems that the mighty-armed one has been born for the sake of killing the Kouravas. O venerable one! King Duryodhana was overcome by great grief and distress. He went to Bhishma and began to lament. 'My brave brothers have been killed by Bhimasena in battle. All the soldiers are fighting to the best of their capacity. But they are being killed. You seem to be neutral and are constantly disregarding us. I have chosen to traverse an evil path. Behold my destiny.' On hearing Duryodhana's cruel words, your father, Devavrata's, eyes filled with tears and he spoke these words. 'O son![310] I uttered these words earlier, and so did Drona, Vidura and the illustrious Gandhari. But you did not understand. O destroyer of enemies! It was decided by me earlier that I will not escape from this battle with my life. Neither will the preceptor. I tell you truthfully that whichever son of Dhritarashtra Bhima sets his eyes on in this battle will be killed by him in the encounter. O king! Therefore, be patient. Be firm in your resolution to fight. Fight with the Parthas in this battle, setting your sights on heaven as the objective. No one is capable of vanquishing the Pandavas, the gods with Indra, or the asuras. O descendant of the Bharata lineage! Therefore, fix your mind on the battle. Be patient and fight.'"

Chapter 945(85)

'Dhritarashtra said, "O Sanjaya! On seeing that many of my sons are being killed by a single person, what did Bhishma, Drona and Kripa do in that battle? O Sanjaya! From one day to another, my sons are going to their perdition. O suta! I think that they have been completely overtaken by terrible destiny, since all my sons are being defeated and are never victorious. O son![311] My sons are in

[310]The word used is tata.
[311]The word used is tata.

the midst of Bhishma, Drona, the great-souled Kripa, Somadatta's
valiant son, Bhagadatta, Ashvatthama and many other brave and
extremely great-souled warriors. Yet they are being killed in the
battle. Other than destiny, what can this be? The evil Duryodhana
did not comprehend the words that I had spoken earlier. O son! He
was restrained by me, and by Bhishma and Vidura. So did Gandhari,
always desiring his welfare. But because of his delusion, the wicked
one did not understand earlier and is now reaping the fruits. In this
battle, the angry Bhimasena is killing and conveying my insensate
sons to Yama's abode."

'Sanjaya replied, "Kshatta's supreme words were for your own
welfare. They have now come true. O lord! You did not comprehend
them then. Vidura had asked you to restrain your sons from the
gambling match with the Pandavas and not oppress them. He is
a well-wisher with your welfare in mind and spoke truthfully. But
you did not heed his words, like a dying man who refuses good
medicine. The words spoken by the virtuous have now come to be
true. Vidura, Drona, Bhishma and other well-wishers spoke beneficial
words that were not accepted and the Kouravas are headed towards
destruction. O lord of the earth! All of this is the consequence of what
transpired earlier. Now listen to the account of the battle, exactly
as it unfolded. It was midday and an extremely great and terrible
encounter commenced. O king! There was destruction of men. Listen,
as I describe it. On the instructions of Dharma's son, all the soldiers
were enraged and attacked Bhishma, wishing to kill him. O great
king! Dhrishtadyumna, Shikhandi, maharatha Satyaki, together with
their armies, advanced against Bhishma. In that encounter, Arjuna,
Droupadi's sons and Chekitana united and advanced against the kings
who were following Duryodhana's command. The brave Abhimanyu,
Hidimba's maharatha son and Bhimasena were enraged and attacked
the Kouravas. The Pandavas divided themselves into three parts and
fought against the Kouravas. O king! The Kouravas also began to
kill the enemies in battle.

'"Drona, best among rathas, angrily advanced against and fought
with the Somakas and the Srinjayas, despatching them to Yama's
eternal abode. O king! When they were slaughtered in battle by the

archer who was Bharadvaja's son, a great lamentation arose among the great-souled Somakas. Drona killed many kshatriyas in that battle. They were seen to be unconscious, like men afflicted with disease. There were groans, moans and shrieks in that field of battle. There were continuous sounds, like those uttered by men overcome with hunger. The immensely strong and angry Bhimasena was like terrible death amidst the Kouraveyas and caused carnage. In that great battle, soldiers killed each other. A terrible river began to flow, with waves of blood. O great king! That battle between the Kurus and the Pandavas was great and assumed a terrible form. It extended Yama's kingdom. In particular, Bhima was incited with rage in that battle. He descended on the army of elephants and despatched them to the land of the dead. O descendant of the Bharata lineage! Elephants were struck by Bhima's iron arrows. Some of them fell down. Others were paralysed. Others shrieked. Still others ran away in different directions. O venerable one! Great elephants had their trunks sliced off, their feet sliced off. Terrified, they shrieked like cranes. They fell down on the ground. Nakula and Sahadeva attacked the army of horses. The horses possessed golden harnesses. Their caparisons were made out of gold. They were seen to be slain in hundreds and thousands. O king! The earth was strewn with horses that had fallen down. Some lost their tongues. Others could not breathe. Still others shrieked in agony and lost their lives. O best of men! The earth was beautiful with horses of many different forms. O descendant of the Bharata lineage! O lord of the earth! The earth looked resplendent, yet terrible, because in that encounter, Arjuna also killed many horses. O king! There were broken chariots, shattered standards, extremely dazzling umbrellas, golden necklaces, bracelets, heads with earrings, loosened headdresses, pennants and the beautiful floors, yokes and reins of chariots everywhere. The earth was as beautiful as spring with its flowers. O descendant of the Bharata lineage! The Pandus were also confronted with this kind of destruction when the angry Bhishma, Shantanu's son, Drona, supreme among rathas, Ashvatthama, Kripa and Kritavarma were enraged. And when those on the other side became angry, those on your side met with decay."'

Chapter 946(86)

'Sanjaya said, "O king! When that terrible destruction of brave ones was going on, the illustrious Shakuni Soubala attacked the Pandavas. O king! Hardikya Satvata,[312] the destroyer of enemy heroes, attacked the army of the Pandavas in that encounter. Pandava's brave powerful son, the scorcher of enemies, attacked your soldiers in a cheerful frame of mind. He possessed the foremost of speedy horses, the best of those from Kamboja and from the land of the rivers, those from Aratta, Mahi, Sindhu, white ones from Vanayu and others from mountainous regions. There were other swift ones of the Tittira breed, as fleet as the wind. They were armoured and ornamented in gold. They were trained well. This brave son of Arjuna was named Iravat. He was born from the intelligent Partha and was the son of the daughter of the king of the nagas. When her husband was slain by Suparna,[313] she was distressed and depressed in her mind. She was also childless and was bestowed by the great-souled Airavata.[314] She was overcome by the pangs of desire and Partha accepted her as his wife. Thus it was that Arjuna's son was born in another one's field.[315] Protected by his mother, he grew up in the world of the nagas. Because of his hatred for Partha, his evil-souled uncle abandoned him.[316] He was handsome and brave and possessed all the qualities. Truth was his valour. He quickly went to Indra's world when he heard that Arjuna had gone there. The one for whom truth was his valour, went to his great-souled father. He anxiously bowed before him. Joining his hands in salutation, he

---

[312]Kritavarma.

[313]Garuda.

[314]Bestowed on Arjuna. Her father Kouravya was the king of the nagas and was descended from Airavata. Thus, Kouravya can also be referred to as Airavata. The story has been recounted in Section 16 (Volume 2).

[315]Meaning another person's wife.

[316]This is left dangling It is probably a reference to the naga Takshaka, who bore an animosity towards Arjuna because of the destruction of nagas in Khandava.

humbly said, 'O fortunate one! O lord! I am Iravat. I am your son.'
He told Pandava everything and reminded him of the circumstances
about how he had met with his mother. He embraced his son, who
was exactly like him in all the qualities. In the abode of the king of
the gods, Partha was delighted. O king! O descendant of the Bharata
lineage! The mighty-armed Arjuna then commanded him in the world
of the gods and affectionately told him about his duty. 'Come to us
when it is the time for war.' O lord! He agreed and went away. In
accordance with those words, he presented himself, since the time for
battle has come. O king! He was surrounded by many swift horses,
with all the complexions that one desires. Those horses bore golden
harnesses and were of many hues. They were as swift as thought.
O king! They suddenly arrived and were like swans in the great
ocean. They attacked the large numbers of your horses, which were
also exceedingly fast. They struck each other on the chests and on
the noses. O king! Those extremely swift horses suddenly fell down
on the ground. Those masses of horses clashed against each other
and were shattered and fell down. An extremely terrible sound was
heard, like that when Suparna descends. O great king! Thus it was
that they clashed against each other in the battle. The horse-riders
fiercely began to kill each other. A tumultuous and fearful encounter
raged. On both sides, large numbers of horses dashed around in all
directions. The brave ones were mutilated with arrows. The horses
were slain. They were overcome with exhaustion. They began to
diminish in number, destroying each other with their swords.

"'O descendant of the Bharata lineage! When the armies of
horses were whittled away and only a few were left, Soubala's brave
younger brothers rode out in the forefront of that battle. They were
astride supreme horses that were like the touch of the wind in their
speed. They were as fleet as the wind. They were well-trained and
not too old or young. Those six were powerful—Gaja, Gavaksha,
Vrishaka, Charmavat, Arjava and Shuka.[317] They advanced with a
great army and were supported by Shakuni and their own extremely
strong warriors. They were armoured and skilled in battle. They were

---

[317]The names of Shakuni's six brothers. Their father was Subala.

terrible in form and extremely strong. O mighty-armed one! With that
extremely large army, desiring heaven and victory, they penetrated
that supremely invincible army.[318] Unassailable in battle, those from
Gandhara cheerfully entered there. On seeing that they had cheerfully
penetrated, the valiant Iravat spoke to his own warriors, who were
adorned with colourful ornaments and weapons in that battle. 'Act
according to the decreed policy, so that all the warriors of the sons
of Dhritarashtra can be killed in this battle, together with their
followers and their mounts.' Agreeing, all of Iravat's warriors began
to slay the ranks of the enemy, though the enemy was invincible in
battle. On witnessing that their ranks were being brought down in
that battle, all of Subala's sons could not tolerate this state of affairs
in the encounter. All of them attacked and surrounded Iravat. They
incited each other to attack him with sharp lances. The brave ones
dashed around and created a great melee. The great-souled Iravat
was pierced by those sharp lances. Blood began to flow from his
body and he looked like an elephant wounded by a goad. He was
severely wounded on his chest, his back and his sides. O king! He was
alone and faced many. But he was not distressed and did not lose his
fortitude. Iravat was enraged in that battle. The destroyer of enemy
cities confounded all of them by piercing them with sharp arrows.
The scorcher of enemies uprooted all the lances from his own body
and used them to strike Subala's sons in that battle. He unsheathed
a sharp sword and grasped a shield. He swiftly advanced on foot,
wishing to kill Subala's sons in that encounter. Having regained their
senses, all of Subala's sons became angry and advanced against Iravat.
But displaying the dexterity of his hands with the sword and proud
of his strength, Iravat attacked all those sons of Subala. He roamed
around with such great speed, that Subala's sons, though they were
on fleet horses, could not find an opportunity to strike him. However,
in that battle, seeing him stationed on the ground again, all of them
surrounded him at close quarters, wishing to capture him. The
destroyer of enemies saw that they were near him. He used his sword
to slice off their right hands and their left and mutilated other parts

[318]Referring to Iravat's army.

of their bodies. All their arms were adorned with various ornaments. They were seen to fall down. They too, without their limbs, fell down on the ground, devoid of their lives. O great king! In that extremely terrible battle where brave warriors were slaughtered, only Vrishaka escaped, though he was severely wounded.[319]

'"On seeing that all of them had fallen down, Duryodhana was frightened. He spoke to the extremely terrible rakshasa who was terrible in form. The scorcher of enemies was a great archer and was skilled in maya. He was the son of Rishyashringa.[320] He had earlier become an enemy of Bhimasena on account of the slaying of Baka.[321] 'O brave one! Witness the strength of Phalguna's son. He is skilled in maya and has caused the unpleasant and terrible destruction of my forces. O son![322] You are capable of going anywhere at will. You are skilled in the use of weapons of maya. You are the sworn enemy of Partha. Therefore, kill him in battle.' The rakshasa, terrible in form, agreed to these words. He roared like a lion and advanced to where Arjuna's young son was. He was surrounded by his own soldiers, who were brave and armed. They were accomplished in fighting, were astride mounts and were armed with polished lances. He wished to kill the immensely powerful Iravat in battle. The valiant and swift Iravat was enraged. The slayer of enemies countered the rakshasa who was seeking his death. On seeing that he was descending on him, the extremely powerful rakshasa swiftly resorted to his powers of maya. He created a large number of illusory horses. They were ridden by terrible rakshasas, who wielded spears and javelins. Two thousand of these armed ones angrily advanced. The two sides clashed and quickly sent each other to the land of the dead. When the soldiers on both sides had been killed, the two of them, invincible in battle, attacked each other in that encounter, like Vritra against Vasava. On seeing the rakshasa, invincible in battle, advance against him, the extremely strong Iravat was enraged and attacked him. When

---

[319]Vrishaka was the only one of Subala's sons who survived.

[320]Rishyashringa was a famous sage.

[321]Bhima had killed a rakshasa named Baka.

[322]The word used is tata.

the evil-minded one approached close, he used his sword to slice off his blazing sword and shattered his shield into five parts. On seeing that the bow had been severed, he quickly resorted to the sky and angrily confounded Iravat with his maya. But Iravat also rose up into the sky and confounded the rakshasa with his own maya. He was invincible too and could assume any form at will. He knew about the body's inner organs and pierced his body with his arrows. O great king! The foremost among rakshasas was repeatedly wounded through these arrows, but he became hale again and regained his youth. Maya is natural to them, and according to their wishes, so are energy, age and beauty. Thus, though the rakshasa's limbs were repeatedly mangled, they healed. Iravat used his sharp battle axe to repeatedly slice angrily at the immensely strong rakshasa. That brave and powerful rakshasa was repeatedly sliced like a tree and roared terribly, making a tumultuous sound. Wounded by the battleaxe, the rakshasa began to profusely shed blood. The powerful one became enraged and continued to battle forcefully. On seeing that the enemy was so energetic in the battle, Rishyashringa's son assumed an extremely terrible and gigantic form. While everyone looked on, he tried to grasp him in the forefront of that battle. But seeing this maya employed by the great-souled rakshasa, Iravat angrily created his own maya. He was overcome by anger and he was one who never retreated from battle. O king! His mother's relatives approached him and he was surrounded by many nagas in that battle, assuming a great form like Bhogavat.[323] The rakshasa was enveloped by many kinds of nagas. Enveloped by those nagas, that bull among rakshasas thought and assumed the form of Suparna,[324] so that he could devour the nagas. On seeing that his mother's relatives were devoured through maya, Iravat was confused. And the rakshasa killed him with his sword. Iravat's head was adorned with earrings and a diadem and was as radiant as a lotus or the moon. The rakshasa made it fall down on the ground.

[323]Bhogavati is the capital of the nagas and Bhogavat can mean any of the serpents residing there. But it is probably a reference to Ananta.

[324]Garuda.

'"On seeing that Arjuna's brave son had been slain by the rakshasa, the sons of Dhritarashtra, together with the kings, became free from sorrow. The great and terrible battle commenced again. The armies attacked each other and the carnage was great and terrible. Horses, elephants and infantry became mixed with each other and were killed by tuskers. Chariot-riders and elephants were also killed by foot soldiers. O king! Rathas, on your side and on theirs, killed masses of infantry and chariot-riders and many horses in that encounter. Arjuna did not know that his son had been killed and in that battle, slew many kings who were protecting Bhishma. O king! The immensely strong ones, on your side and on that of the Srinjayas, fought each other in that battle, offering their lives as oblations. Their hair was dishevelled. They were without armour. They were without chariots and their bows had been severed. But they confronted each other and fought with their bare arms. The immensely strong Bhishma killed many maharathas with arrows that penetrated the innards and made the soldiers of the Pandavas tremble. He killed many men in Yudhishthira's army, and many elephants, horse-riders, chariot-riders and horses. O descendant of the Bharata lineage! On witnessing Bhishma's valour in that battle, we thought that it was as extraordinary as Shakra's valour. O descendant of the Bharata lineage! Bhimasena and Parshata were also like that. The battle fought by the Satvata archer[325] was also terrible. On witnessing Drona's valour, the Pandavas were overcome by fear. They thought that he was alone capable of killing all the soldiers in battle, not to speak of a situation where he was surrounded by warriors whose bravery was famous on earth. O great king! Oppressed by Drona in that battle, they spoke in this fashion. O bull among the Bharata lineage! While that terrible encounter continued between the two armies, the brave ones did not pardon each other. Those immensely strong ones were engrossed in that battle, as if they were overcome by rakshasas and demons. The archers on your side, and those of the Pandaveyas, were enraged. We did not see anyone seeking to

[325]Satyaki.

protect his life. O lord of men! It was a battle like that of warriors
from among the daityas themselves.'"

Chapter 947(87)

'Dhritarashtra asked, "O Sanjaya! On seeing that Iravat had
been killed in the battle, what did the maharatha Parthas
do?"

'Sanjaya said, "On seeing that Iravat had been killed in the
battle, Bhimasena's son, the rakshasa Ghatotkacha, let out a loud
roar. O king! At the sound of this roar, the earth, up to the frontiers
of the ocean, with its mountains and forests, seemed to tremble
violently. So did the sky, the directions and all the sub-directions.
O descendant of the Bharata lineage! On hearing this extremely
loud roar, the thighs and other limbs of all your soldiers began
to tremble. They quaked and began to sweat. O Indra among
kings! All those on your side became dispirited. They seemed to
be in the coils of a snake and were like elephants frightened of a
lion. The rakshasa let out that extremely loud roar. He raised a
flaming spear and assumed a terrible form. He was surrounded
by terrible bulls among rakshasas, wielding many weapons. They
advanced in great anger, like Yama at the destruction of an yuga.
On witnessing him advance, in anger and with a terrible form and
beholding that his own soldiers were frightened and were running
away, King Duryodhana attacked Ghatotkacha. He grasped a
large bow and repeatedly roared like a lion. The lord of Vanga
himself followed him at the back, with ten thousand elephants
that were like mountains and were exuding musth. O great king!
On seeing that your son was advancing, surrounded by an army of
elephants, the traveller of the night[326] became angry. O Indra among
kings! A tumultuous battle commenced between the rakshasa and

---

[326]Ghatotkacha.

Duryodhana's soldiers and it made the body hair stand up. That army of elephants was like a mass of clouds, charged with lightning. On beholding it advance, the angry rakshasas grasped weapons in their hands. They roared in many different ways, like thundering clouds full of lightning. They began to strike down the elephant-riders with arrows, javelins, swords, iron arrows, catapults, spears and battleaxes. They killed the mighty elephants with the peaks of mountains and trees. Their temples were shattered. Blood began to flow from the mangled bodies of the elephants. O great king! We saw that they were killed by those travellers of the night. The warriors on elephants were scattered. O great king! On seeing this, Duryodhana attacked the rakshasas. He was overcome by intolerance and gave up all desire to protect his own life. The immensely strong one released arrows towards the rakshasas. The great archer slew the foremost among the rakshasas. O best of the Bharata lineage! Your son, Duryodhana, was angry. The maharatha used four arrows to kill four of them—Vegavat, Maharoudra, Vidyutjihva and Pramathi. O best of the Bharata lineage! The one whose soul is immeasurable showered down arrows that were irresistible, towards that army of travellers in the night. O venerable one! On seeing that great deed of your son, Bhimasena's extremely strong son blazed forth in anger. He twanged his great bow, with a sound like that of Indra's vajra. The scorcher of enemies forcefully attacked Duryodhana. O great king! On seeing him advance, like Death urged on by the Destroyer, your son, Duryodhana, was not distressed. The cruel one[327] angrily spoke to him, his eyes red with rage. 'It is because of your great cruelty that they were exiled for a long time. O king! You defeated the Pandavas in a deceitful game of dice. O one with evil intelligence! It was because of this that Droupadi Krishna was brought to the assembly hall, though she was in her menses and was clad in a single garment. You caused her hardship in many ways. While they dwelt in the hermitage, it was to bring you pleasure that the evil-souled Saindhava tormented her, disrespecting my fathers. O worst of your lineage! Because of

[327]Ghatotkacha.

this and many other insults, I will bring about your end today, if you do not flee from the field of battle.' Having said this, Hidimba's son drew his gigantic bow. He bit his lip[328] and licked the corners of his mouth. He covered Duryodhana with a great shower of arrows, like the slayer of Bala[329] bringing down a shower of rain on a mountain during the monsoon.'"

Chapter 948(88)

'Sanjaya said, "That shower of arrows was difficult to withstand, even by the danavas. But that Indra among kings withstood it in battle, like a giant elephant bearing rain. Overcome with rage, he sighed like a serpent. O bull among the Bharata lineage! Your son confronted a supreme danger. He released twenty-five extremely sharp iron arrows. O king! They suddenly descended on that bull among rakshasas, like angry and violent serpents on Mount Gandhamadana. He was pierced by them and blood began to flow. He was like an elephant with a shattered temple. The maneater then made up his mind to destroy the king. He grasped a giant javelin that was capable of shattering a mountain. It blazed like a giant meteor and was like Maghavan's vajra. The mighty-armed one raised it, wishing to kill your son. The lord of Vanga was astride an elephant that was like a mountain.[330] On seeing it raised, he swiftly advanced towards the rakshasa. That supreme of elephants was powerful and was extremely fast. He reached the path where Duryodhana's chariot was stationed and protected your son's chariot with the elephant. O great king! On seeing that the path had been restricted by the intelligent king of Vanga, Ghatotkacha's eyes became red with rage. He raised a giant javelin and hurled it towards the elephant. O king!

[328]The lower lip.
[329]Indra killed a demon named Bala.
[330]Although described as the lord of Vanga, this is Bhagadatta.

When it was hurled from his arms, the elephant was struck. It was covered with blood and hurt grievously, fell down and died. When the elephant fell down, the powerful lord of Vanga quickly jumped down and resorted to the ground.

'"Duryodhana saw that the supreme of elephants had fallen down and that his soldiers were scattered. He was gravely distressed. He held the dharma of kshatriyas to be of paramount importance and was also proud of his own self. Though he had been defeated, the king remained as immobile as a mountain. He affixed a sharp arrow that was like the fire at the time of destruction and in great rage, unleashed it at the terrible traveller of the night. The arrow was as radiant as Indra's vajra. On seeing it descend, the gigantic Ghatotkacha avoided it through his dexterity of movement. He roared terribly again, his eyes red with anger. This frightened all beings, like clouds at the end of a yuga. On hearing the fearful roar of the terrible rakshasa, Bhishma, Shantanu's son, went to the preceptor and said, 'I have heard the terrible roar emitted by the rakshasa. I have no doubt that Hidimba's son is fighting with King Duryodhana. No being is capable of vanquishing him in battle. O fortunate one! Therefore, go there and protect the king. The immensely fortunate one has been attacked by the evil-souled rakshasa. O scorchers of enemies![331] This is the supreme duty for all of us now.' On hearing the words of the grandfather, the maharathas used the utmost speed to quickly go to the spot where Kourava was—Drona, Somadatta, Bahlika, Jayadratha, Kripa, Bhurishrava, Shalya, Chitrasena, Vivimshati, Ashvatthama, Vikarna, the one from Avanti[332] and Brihadbala. Many thousand rathas followed them. They advanced to rescue Duryodhana, your son, who was oppressed. That invincible army was protected by the best in the worlds. The supreme of rakshasas saw that it was advancing to kill him. However, like Mount Mainaka, the mighty-armed one did not tremble at all. Surrounded by his relatives, he grasped a giant

---

[331]Bhishma is addressing others too.

[332]It is not clear which of the two from Avanti is meant.

bow. With spears, clubs, bare hands and many kinds of weapons, a tumultuous battle commenced and it made the body hair stand up. The rakshasas were on one side and the foremost of Duryodhana's soldiers on the other. O great king! The tremendous sound of bows being twanged could be heard everywhere, as if bamboos were being burned. Weapons descended on bodies protected by armour. O king! That sound was like that of mountains being shattered. O lord of the earth! Javelins were hurled from the arms of brave ones and as they travelled through the sky, they looked like snakes. The Indra among rakshasas became extremely angry. The mighty-armed one drew his extremely large bow and let out a terrible roar. In anger, he used an arrow in the shape of a half-moon to slice down the preceptor's bow. He roared and used a broad-headed arrow to bring down Somadatta's standard. He used three arrows to pierce Bahlika between the breasts. He pierced Kripa with one arrow and Chitrasena with three. He drew his bow to the full extent and used a well-aimed arrow to strike Vikarna in the joint of his shoulders. Covered in blood, he sank down on the floor of his chariot. O bull among the Bharata lineage! The one whose soul was immeasurable was wrathful. He despatched fifteen iron arrows in the form of half-moons towards Bhurishrava. These swiftly penetrated his armour and penetrated the ground. He next struck Vivimshati and Drona's charioteers. They fell down on the floors of their chariots, giving up the reins of their horses. The standard of the king of Sindhu bore the mark of a boar and was decorated with gold. O great king! He uprooted that with an arrow in the shape of a half-moon and used another to sever his bow. The great-souled one's eyes were red with rage. He used four iron arrows to slay the four horses of Avanti. O great king! He stretched his bow back to the fullest extent and used a yellow and sharp arrow to pierce Prince Brihadbala. Gravely pierced and wounded, he sank down on the floor of the chariot. The lord of the rakshasas was full of great rage and was stationed on his chariot. He shot many arrows that were sharp at the tip and were like venomous serpents. O great king! Though Shalya was skilled in battle, they pierced him.'"

Chapter 949(89)

'Sanjaya said, "In that battle, the rakshasa made all those on your side retreat from battle. O best of the Bharata lineage! He then rushed at Duryodhana, wishing to kill him. On seeing him forcefully descend on the king, many on your side, unassailable in battle, attacked him, wishing to kill him. Those immensely strong ones twanged bows that were as long as palm trees. They roared like a group of lions and together, attacked the one who was alone. They surrounded him from every direction and showered down arrows. It was like the slayer of Bala showering rain on mountains during the autumn. He was severely pierced and wounded, like an elephant with a goad. He quickly rose up into the sky, like Vinata's son.[333] Stationed there, he uttered mighty roars, like clouds during the autumn. His terrible roars echoed in the sky, the directions and the sub-directions. O best of the Bharata lineage! On hearing the sounds emitted by the rakshasa, King Yudhishthira spoke these words to Bhimasena. 'The rakshasa is certainly fighting with the maharatha sons of Dhritarashtra. That is the reason we are hearing the sounds of these terrible roars. O son![334] I see that the burden he has taken on is too much. The angry grandfather is ready to kill the Panchalas. For the sake of protecting them, Phalguna is fighting with the enemy. O mighty-armed one! Two tasks now present themselves.[335] Having heard this, go and protect Hidimba's son. He confronts a great danger.' Obeying the words of his brother, Vrikodara swiftly advanced. He roared like a lion, frightening all the kings. O king! He proceeded with great force, like the ocean at the time of the new moon or the full moon. He was followed by Satyadhriti and Souchitti, invincible in battle, Shrenimat, Vasudana and the lord who was the son of the king of Kashi. There were many other maharathas, with Abhimanyu at the forefront, Droupadi's sons, the valiant Kshatradeva, Kshatradharma and Nila, the lord of

---

[333]Garuda.

[334]The word used is tata.

[335]Fighting with the enemy and protecting Ghatotkacha.

the marshy regions, together with his own soldiers. They surrounded Hidimba's son with a large number of chariots. There were six thousand elephants that were always crazy, with riders prepared to strike. They advanced to protect Ghatotkacha, Indra among the rakshasas. They roared like lions. There was a great sound from the wheels of the chariots. There was a roar from the sound of the hooves. The earth began to tremble. On hearing the sounds of those advancing ones, the faces of your soldiers paled. They were anxious because of their fear of Bhimasena. O great king! They abandoned Ghatotkacha and fled from the field of battle.

"'A battle then commenced between the great-souled ones on your side and those of the enemy. Neither side wished to retreat from the encounter. The maharathas used many different kinds of weapons. They attacked each other and struck each other. That extremely terrible battle struck terror in the minds of those who were cowards. Horse-riders encountered elephant-riders, infantry clashed with chariot-riders. O king! In that encounter, they challenged each other and attacked each other. Because of that clash, a terrible and great dust arose, from chariots, horses, elephants, infantry, footsteps and wheels. That dust was thick, like red smoke, and covered the arena of the battle. O king! It was impossible to distinguish those on one's own side from those of the enemy. The father did not recognize the son. The son did not recognize the father. No mercy was shown in the encounter and it made the body hair stand up. O best of the Bharata lineage! There was the sound of weapons and the roar of men. There was an extremely large din, like that of bamboos being burnt. A river of blood began to flow there and the waves were elephants, horses and men. The hair[336] constituted the weeds and moss. The heads and bodies of men fell down in that battle and a great sound was heard, like that of stones falling down. The earth was strewn with the torsos of men, the mangled bodies of elephants and the mutilated bodies of horses. The maharathas released many different kinds of weapons. They attacked each other and struck each other. Urged by horse-riders, horses clashed against horses. In

[336]Of the fighters.

that battle, they dashed against each other and fell down, devoid of life. Men attacked men, their eyes extremely red with rage. They struck each other with their chests and thus killed each other. Urged by the trainers, elephants attacked the elephants of the enemy. And in that encounter, they slew the others with the points of their tusks. They were adorned with pennants and were covered in blood. In that clash, they looked like clouds tinged with lightning. Some had their trunks sliced into two. Others had their bodies lacerated. They fell down in that tumult, like mountains with their wings sliced off.[337] Some supreme elephants had their sides ripped open by other elephants. They shed large quantities of blood, like mountains exuding minerals. Some were slain through iron arrows, others were pierced by javelins. Without their riders, they were seen to be like mountains without summits. Some of them were blind with anger and madness. No longer controlled, they crushed hundreds of chariots, horses and infantry in that encounter. Horse-riders pierced horses with spears and javelins. They rushed against each other, confused about the directions. Rathas born in noble lineages fought with other rathas, ready to give up their bodies. They resorted to the best of their strength and acted without any fear. O king! Those skilled in battle sought fame, or heaven, and fought each other, as if in a svayamvara. Thus the battle raged there, and it made the body hair stand up. The great army of the sons of Dhritarashtra were generally made to retreat.'"

Chapter 950(90)

'Sanjaya said, "On seeing that his own soldiers had been killed, King Duryodhana angrily attacked Bhimasena, the destroyer of enemies. He grasped a giant bow, which had a sound like that of

---

[337]Mountains are believed to possess wings, until Indra lopped them off. Mount Mainaka was the only one which escaped.

Indra's vajra. He covered Pandava with a great shower of arrows.
He was full of rage. He affixed an extremely sharp arrow that was
in the shape of a half-moon and was tufted with hair. He sliced
down Bhimasena's bow with this. Thereafter, the maharatha saw an
opportunity. He affixed an extremely sharp arrow that was capable
of shattering a mountain. With this, the mighty-armed one struck
Bhimasena in the chest. He was severely pierced and wounded
and licked the corners of his mouth. The energetic one sought the
support of his standard, which was decorated with gold. On seeing
Bhimasena in that dispirited state, Ghatotkacha blazed up in anger,
like a fire that can consume everything. With Abhimanyu at the
forefront, all the maharatha Pandavas dashed angrily towards the
king, roaring loudly. On seeing them advance, in fury and rage,
Bharadvaja's son spoke these words to the maharathas on your
side. 'O fortunate ones! Go swiftly and protect the king. I think he
confronts a great danger and is submerged in an ocean of distress.
These maharatha Pandavas are great archers and are angry. With
Bhimasena at the forefront, they are attacking Duryodhana. With
victory in mind, they are using many different kinds of weapons.
They are uttering terrible roars and are terrifying the kings.'[338] On
hearing the words of the preceptor, with Somadatta at the forefront,
many on your side attacked the army of the Pandavas—Kripa,
Bhurishrava, Shalya, Drona's son, Vivimshati, Chitrasena, Vikarna,
Saindhava, Brihadbala and the two great archers from Avanti. They
surrounded Kourava. They advanced only twenty steps and began
to strike each other. The Pandavas and the sons of Dhritrashtra
sought to kill each other.

"'Having spoken those words, Bharadvaja's mighty-armed son
stretched his own gigantic bow and pierced Bhima with twenty-six
arrows. Yet again, the mighty-armed one quickly enveloped him with
arrows. It was like the slayer of Bala showering rain on a mountain
during autumn. However, Bhimasena was extremely strong. The
great archer swiftly pierced him back on the left side with ten arrows.
O descendant of the Bharata lineage! He was severely pierced and

[338]Obviously, on the Kourava side.

wounded. He was also elderly in years. He became unconscious and
suddenly sat down on the floor of his chariot. On seeing that the
preceptor was wounded, King Duryodhana himself, and Drona's
son, became angry and attacked Bhimasena. Each of them was like
Yama at the end of a yuga. On seeing them advance, the mighty-
armed Bhimasena quickly grasped a club. He instantly descended
from his chariot and stood, as immobile as a mountain. That heavy
club looked like Yama's staff, raised in battle. On seeing him with
the upraised club, like the summit of Kailasa, Kourava and Drona's
son rushed at him, together. Vrikodara also swiftly rushed at those
supreme among strong ones, as they forcefully advanced against him.
On seeing him advance in rage, terrible in his visage, many Kourava
maharathas quickly attacked him. With Bharadvaja's son[339] at the
forefront, all of them wished to kill Bhimasena. They hurled many
different kinds of weapons towards Bhima's chest. Together, all of
them oppressed Pandava from every direction. On beholding that
the maharatha was oppressed and faced a great danger, Abhimanyu
and the other Pandava maharathas advanced to rescue him, ready to
give up their lives. The brave lord of the marshy regions was Bhima's
beloved friend. Nila possessed a complexion that was blue like the
clouds and in anger, he attacked Drona's son. The great archer had
always sought to challenge Drona's son. He drew his large bow and
pierced Drona's son with arrows. O great king! It was like Shakra
piercing the invincible danava Viprachitti, who was the terror of the
gods, in earlier times. Through his anger and energy, he had terrified
the three worlds. In that way, Nila pierced him with arrows that
were well-tipped.[340] Drona's son was wounded and covered with
blood and overcome with rage. He drew his colourful bow, with a
roar like that of Indra's vajra. The supreme among intelligent ones
made up his mind to destroy Nila. He affixed polished and broad-
headed arrows that had been crafted by a blacksmith and slew

[339]This actually means Ashvatthama, the word son being used in a loose sense.
[340]Viprachitti was a famous demon and was the son of Kashyapa and Danu.
Kashyapa and Danu had 100 sons and Viprachitti is described as the most
powerful of the lot.

his[341] four horses and brought down his standard. With a seventh broad-headed arrow, he pierced Nila in the breast.[342] He was severely pierced and wounded and sat down on his chariot.

'"King Nila possessed the complexion of the clouds. On seeing that he was unconscious, Ghatotkacha became angry. Surrounded by his brothers, he impetuously rushed towards Drona's son, who was the ornament of any battle. In that fashion, many other rakshasas, invincible in battle, also advanced. On seeing that rakshasa, terrible in form, advance towards him, Bharadvaja's spirited son became angry and killed many rakshasas, who were terrible in form, especially those enraged rakshasas who were leading from the front. On seeing that they were repulsed as a consequence of the arrows released from the bow of Drona's son, Ghatotkacha, Bhimasena's son who was gigantic in size, became angry. He resorted to great maya that was fearful in form and extremely terrible. In that encounter, the lord of the rakshasas, skilled in the use of maya, confounded Drona's son. Because of that maya, all those on your side retreated. They saw each other lying down immobile on the face of the ground, writhing in convulsions, miserable and covered in blood. Drona, Duryodhana, Shalya, Ashvatthama and the other great archers who were generally regarded as the foremost among the Kouravas were also in that state. All the chariots seemed to be shattered, the elephants brought down. Horses and horse-riders were cut down in thousands.[343] On seeing this, all the soldiers on our side fled towards their camps. O king! I[344] and Devavrata shouted, 'Fight. Do not run away. This is the maya of rakshasas in battle. It has been applied by Ghatotkacha.' But they were confounded and did not stay. Though both of us shouted in this way, they were frightened and did not pay attention to our words.

[341]Nila's.

[342]Some non-critical versions mention the charioteer too. In that event, we have a tally for the seven arrows—four for the horses, one for the charioteer, one for the standard and one for Nila.

[343]All of this was the outcome of an illusion and wasn't real. But the Kourava soldiers didn't see it that way.

[344]Sanjaya saying this is unusual. However, the text allows for no other translation.

On seeing that they were running away, the Pandavas thought that they were victorious. Together with Ghatotkacha, they roared like lions. The roars and the sounds of conch shells and drums resounded in every direction. Thus all your soldiers were routed by Hidimba's evil-souled son and fled in different directions. It was time for the sun to set.'"

Chapter 951(91)

'Sanjaya said, "After that mighty battle, King Duryodhana went to Gangeya. He honoured him and in humility, told him everything exactly as it had happened, about Ghatotkacha's victory and about his own defeat.[345] O king! While narrating, the invincible one sighed repeatedly. He then spoke these words to Bhishma, the grandfather of the Kurus. 'O lord! We sought refuge with you, just as the enemy resorted to Vasudeva, and we embarked on this terrible conflict with the Pandavas. I possess eleven illustrious akshouhinis. O scorcher of enemies! They are with me and follow your command. O tiger among the Bharata lineage! But I have been defeated by the Pandava warriors, led by Bhimasena. They have resorted to Ghatotkacha. My body is burning, like a dry tree being consumed by a fire. O immensely fortunate one! O scorcher of enemies! I desire your favours. O grandfather! I wish to kill that outcast among rakshasas myself.' O supreme among the Bharata lineage! On hearing these words of the king, Bhishma, Shantanu's son, spoke these words to Duryodhana. 'O king! O Kourava! Listen to the words that I am speaking to you. O great king! O scorcher of enemies! This is about how you should conduct yourself. O son![346] O destroyer of enemies! One's own self must always be protected in battle, in every situation. O unblemished one! It is your duty to fight with Dharmaraja, Arjuna, the twins and

[345]However, there was no reason for Bhishma not to have known that. This is really a prelude to what follows.
[346]The word used is tata.

Bhimasena. Upholding the dharma of a king, a king must strike at
a king. I, Drona, Kripa, Drona's son, Satvata Kritavarma, Shalya,
Somadatta's son, maharatha Vikarna and your brave brothers, with
Duhshasana at the forefront, will fight against the immensely strong
rakshasa for your sake. However, if your hatred for that terrible
Indra among the rakshasas is great, let King Bhagadatta advance in
battle and fight against the evil-minded one. He is Purandara's equal
in battle.' Having said this, in the presence of the king, the one who
was eloquent with words, spoke these words to King Bhagadatta. 'O
great king! Swiftly advance against Hidimba's son, who is invincible
in battle. While all these archers look on, take care and counter the
rakshasa, evil in deeds, in the battle, just as Indra resisted Taraka in
ancient times.[347] O scorcher of enemies! Your weapons are celestial
and so is your valour. In earlier times, you have had many encounters
with asuras. O tiger among kings! In this great battle, you will be
able to resist him. O king! Surrounded by your own soldiers, you
will be able to vanquish the bull among the rakshasas.' On hearing
Bhishma's words, the leader of an army roared like a lion and swiftly
advanced towards the enemy.

"'O venerable one! On seeing him advance, roaring like a cloud,
the Pandava maharathas became enraged and dashed towards him—
Bhimasena, Abhimanyu, the rakshasa Ghatotkacha, Droupadi's sons,
Satyadhriti, Kshatradeva, the lord of Chedi, Vasudana and the lord
of Dasharna. Bhagadatta advanced against them on Supratika.[348]
A terrible and fearful encounter started between the Pandus and
Bhagadatta and it extended Yama's kingdom. The rathas released
extremely energetic arrows, fierce in their speed. O great king! These
descended on the elephants and the chariots. They shattered the great
elephants that were urged by the elephant-riders. They clashed and fell
against each other, without any fear. They were blind with madness
and overcome with rage and in that great battle, attacked each other
with the tips of tusks that looked like clubs. They gored each other
with these. The horses possessed bushy tails and their riders had

---

[347]However, Indra was actually vanquished by Taraka.
[348]Supratika was the name of Bhagadatta's elephant.

lances in their hands. Goaded by the riders, they swiftly attacked each other. Foot soldiers attacked foot soldiers with spears and javelins. Hundreds and thousands fell down on the ground. O king! In that encounter, brave rathas used barbed and hollow arrows and slew each other, roaring like lions. The battle raged and it made the body hair stand up. The great archer, Bhagadatta, attacked Bhimasena on an elephant with shattered temples, with musth strewing down in seven streams. It was like a mountain with rainwater flowing down from it in every direction. O unblemished one! He was stationed on Supratika's head and showered down thousands of arrows, like Maghavan showering rain from Airavata. The king tormented Bhima with that shower of arrows, like the slayer of Bala showering down rain on a mountain during the monsoon. Bhimasena became angry. Enraged, the great archer showered down arrows and slew more than one hundred soldiers who were protecting his[349] feet. On seeing that they had been slain, the powerful Bhagadatta became angry. He urged that Indra among elephants towards Bhimasena's chariot. Thus urged, the elephant advanced forcefully towards Bhimasena, the scorcher of enemies, like an arrow released from the string of a bow. On witnessing it advance, the Pandava maharathas, with Bhimasena at the forefront, impetuously advanced towards it. O venerable one! They were those from Kekaya, Abhimanyu, all of Droupadi's sons, the lord of Dasharna, the brave Kshatradeva, the lord of Chedi and Chitraketu. All of them were angry. These immensely strong ones exhibited their supreme and divine weapons. They angrily surrounded the elephant from every direction. Pierced by many arrows, that giant elephant was covered with blood from its wounds and looked like a colourful king of mountains with minerals flowing from it.

'"The lord of Dasharna was on an elephant that looked like a mountain. Stationed on that, he attacked Bhagadatta's elephant. But in that encounter, Supratika, the king of elephants withstood the advancing elephant, like the shoreline counters the ocean. On seeing that the great-souled Dasharna's king of elephants was repulsed, even the Pandava soldiers applauded. O supreme among

---

[349]Bhagadatta's.

kings! Pragjyotisha then angrily hurled fourteen javelins towards the elephant. These swiftly penetrated the excellent armour, embellished with gold, and shattered it, like serpents entering a termite hill. O supreme among the Bharata lineage! Severely pierced and wounded, the elephant quickly and forcefully retreated, its craziness pacified. It fled with great speed, uttering loud shrieks and crushing its own ranks, like a violent storm amidst trees. When that elephant was vanquished, the Pandava maharathas roared like lions and advanced to do battle. With Bhima leading, they attacked Bhagadatta. They released many kinds of arrows and used different kinds of weapons. O king! They were angry and intolerant. On seeing them advance and on hearing their terrible roars, Bhagadatta, the great archer, angrily and fearlessly urged his own elephant. That supreme of elephants was urged by the goad and the toe. It assumed the form of the fire of destruction.[350] It crushed a large number of chariots, elephants and horses, together with their riders. It angrily crushed hundreds and thousands of foot soldiers. O king! It began to rampage around everywhere in that battle. O great king! Agitated, that large army of the Pandus seemed to diminish, like leather that is exposed to the fire.

'"On seeing that his own ranks were scattered by the intelligent Bhagadatta, Ghatotkacha became angry and attacked Bhagadatta. O king! His visage was gruesome, harsh and flaming. His eyes burnt. Burning with rage, he assumed a terrible form. He grasped a giant spear that was capable of shattering a mountain. The immensely strong one hurled it forcefully, wishing to kill the elephant. It was surrounded by sparks of flaming fire in every direction. On seeing it forcefully descend towards him in that battle, flaming away, the king sliced it down with a beautiful arrow that was in the shape of a half-moon. He severed that extremely large spear with a powerful arrow. Divided into two and dislodged, the spear, decorated with gold, fell down on the ground. It was like the great vajra, released by Shakra and coursing through the sky. On seeing that the spear

---

[350]This fire is called *samvartaka* and appears at the time of the dissolution of the universe.

had been severed into two and brought down, the king grasped a mighty javelin with a golden handle. It was like the flame of a fire. Asking the rakshasa to wait, he hurled it at him. On seeing it descend towards him from the sky, like lightning, the rakshasa roared. He leapt up and grasped it quickly. O descendant of the Bharata lineage! While all the lords of the earth looked on, he placed it on his thighs and broke it. It was extraordinary. Having witnessed this deed accomplished by the powerful rakshasa, the gods in heaven, together with the gandharvas and the sages, were astounded. With Bhimasena at the forefront, the great archers among the Pandavas made the earth resound with their roars of applause.

'"However, the powerful Bhagadatta, the great archer, could not bear to hear the roars of delight uttered by those great-souled ones. He stretched his great bow, which had a sound like that of Indra's vajra. He quickly attacked the maharatha Pandavas. He shot many polished and sharp iron arrows that were as radiant as the fire. He pierced Bhima with one arrow and the rakshasa with nine, Abhimanyu with three and the Kekayas with five. In that battle, he stretched his bow back to its full extent and used a gold-tufted arrow to pierce Kshatradeva's right arm, so that his supreme bow, with the arrow affixed to it, fell down on the ground. He struck Droupadi's five sons with five. He angrily killed Bhimasena's horses and used three arrows to bring down his standard, bearing the mark of a lion. With three other arrows, he pierced his charioteer. O best of the Bharata lineage! Severely pierced and wounded by Bhagadatta in that battle, Vishoka sank down on the floor of the chariot. O great king! Bereft of his chariot, Bhima, supreme among rathas, quickly leapt down from his large chariot and grasped a club. O descendant of the Bharata lineage! On seeing him with the upraised club, like a mountain with a summit, all those on your side were overcome with terrible fear. At this time, Pandava, with Krishna as his charioteer, arrived, slaughtering the enemy in thousands. Those tigers among men, scorchers of enemies, father and son, Bhimasena and Ghatotkacha, were fighting with Pragjyotisha there. O king! O best of the Bharata lineage! On seeing that the maharathas were fighting there, Pandava quickly began to shower down arrows. Maharatha King Duryodhana

swiftly urged his soldiers, full of chariots, elephants and horses.
As that great army of the Kouravas forcefully advanced, Pandava,
borne on white steeds, powerfully countered them. O descendant
of the Bharata lineage! Mounted on his elephant in that encounter,
Bhagadatta scattered the Pandava army and advanced towards
Yudhishthira. O venerable one! A tumultuous battle commenced
between Bhagadatta and the Panchalas, Srinjayas and Kekayas,
with the warriors raising their weapons. In the course of that battle,
Bhimasena told Keshava and Arjuna the detailed account of how
Iravat had been killed, exactly as it had occurred.'"

Chapter 952(92)

'Sanjaya said, "On hearing that his son Iravat had been killed,
Dhananjaya was overcome by great grief. He sighed like a
serpent. O king! In that battle, he spoke these words to Vasudeva.
'There is no doubt that the immensely wise Vidura had foreseen
all this earlier. The one with great intelligence had known about
the terrible destruction of the Kurus and the Pandavas. It was for
this reason that he tried to restrain Dhritarashtra, the lord of men.
O Madhusudana! Many brave ones who cannot be slain have been
killed by the Kouravas in this battle. We have also killed those on
their side. O best of men! Evil acts are being perpetrated for the sake
of artha. Shame on artha. For its sake, this slaughter of kin is being
perpetrated. For one who possesses no wealth, death is preferable
to this acquisition of wealth through the slaughter of relatives.
O Krishna! What will we gain by killing these assembled relatives?
Because of Duryodhana's crimes, and those of Shakuni Soubala,
and because of Karna's evil counsel, all the kshatriyas are headed
towards destruction. O Madhusudana! O mighty-armed one! I
now understand the king's wise act, when he sought only half the
kingdom from Suyodhana, or only five villages. But the evil-minded
one did not grant it. On seeing so many brave kshatriyas lying down

on the ground, I censure myself severely. Shame on the livelihood of kshatriyas. In this battle, the kshatriyas will know me as incapable. O Madhusudana! I no longer derive pleasure from this battle with relatives. However, swiftly drive the horses towards the army of the sons of Dhritarashtra. With my two arms, I will cross the ocean that this battle is, one that is difficult to cross. O Madhava! This is not the time to act like a eunuch.' Thus addressed by Partha, Keshava, the destroyer of enemy heroes, urged those white horses, which were as fleet as the wind. O descendant of the Bharata lineage! A great roar arose amidst your soldiers. It was like the ocean at the time of the new moon or the full moon, agitated by the force of the wind.

'"O great king! It was afternoon and a battle commenced between Bhishma and the Pandavas, with a roar like that of the clouds. O king! In that encounter, your sons surrounded Drona, like the Vasus around Vasava, and attacked Bhimasena. Bhishma, Shantanu's son, Kripa, supreme among rathas, Bhagadatta and Susharma attacked Dhananjaya. Hardikya and Bahlika attacked Satyaki. King Ambashtha countered Abhimanyu. O great king! Others who were left encountered other maharathas. A terrible battle that was fearful in form commenced. O lord of men! On seeing Bhimasena, your son blazed in that battle, like oblations being poured onto a sacrificial fire. At that time, your sons covered Kounteya with arrows. O great king! It was like monsoon clouds pouring down on mountains. O lord of men! He was thus enveloped by your sons in many ways and licked the corners of his mouth. The brave one was as proud as a tiger. O king! Bhima brought down Vyudoraska with an extremely sharp and broad-headed arrow and he was deprived of his life. With another sharp, yellow and broad-headed arrow, be brought down Kundalina, like a lion bringing down a small animal.[351] O venerable one! Having approached your sons, he swiftly took up seven extremely sharp and yellow arrows. Firm in wielding the bow, Bhimasena despatched these arrows and brought down your sons, extremely great maharathas, from their chariots. These were Anadhrishti, Kundabheda, Vairata, Dirghalochana, Dirghabahu,

---

[351]Both Vyudoraska and Kundalina are Duryodhana's brothers.

Subahu and Kanakadhvaja. O bull among the Bharata lineage! As they fell down, these brave ones were radiant, like blossoming and dappled trees that fall down during the spring. O lord of the earth! Your remaining sons fled. They thought that the immensely strong Bhimasena was like Death himself. On seeing that the brave one had consumed your sons in the battle, Drona showered arrows on him from every direction, like rain pouring on a mountain. We beheld the manliness of Kunti's son and it was extraordinary. Though he was restrained by Drona, yet he killed your sons. Like a bull bears a downpour of rain from above, Bhima tolerated the shower of arrows released by Drona. O great king! Vrikodara performed a wonderful deed. While repulsing Drona, he killed your sons in that battle. Arjuna's elder brother played with your brave sons, like an immensely strong tiger roaming around amidst deer, or like a wolf stationing itself amidst animals and driving those animals away. Thus did Vrikodara drive your sons away in that battle.

'"Gangeya, Bhagadatta and maharatha Goutama countered the violent Pandava Arjuna. In that encounter, the atiratha repulsed all their weapons with his own weapons. He despatched many brave soldiers on your side to the land of the dead. Abhimanyu used his arrows to deprive King Ambashtha, famous in the world and foremost among rathas, of his chariot. Deprived of his chariot, he was about to be slain by Subhadra's illustrious son. O lord of men! In shame, he quickly leapt down from his chariot. In the battle, he hurled his sword at Subhadra's great-souled son and ascended onto the chariot of the great-souled Hardikya. Subhadra's son was the destroyer of enemy heroes and was skilled in all the techniques of war. On seeing the sword descend towards him, he avoided it through his dextrous movements. O lord of the earth! At this, loud sounds of applause were heard among all the soldiers. With Dhrishtadyumna at the forefront, others fought with your soldiers. And those on your side fought with the soldiers of the Pandus. O descendant of the Bharata lineage! There was a great battle between those on your side and theirs. They killed each other fiercely and performed extremely difficult deeds. O venerable one! In that battle, the brave ones seized each other by the hair. They fought with their nails and teeth and with their fists and thighs. They used their arms and palms and extremely sharp swords. They sought out each other's weakness and despatched each other to Yama's abode. The father killed the son and the son the father in that battle. Those men fought there, desperate and firm in their resolution.

'"O descendant of the Bharata lineage! In that battle, beautiful bows with golden handles and extremely expensive ornaments were loosened from the hands of those who had been slain. There were sharp arrows, with tufts made of pure gold and silver and washed in oil. They were as resplendent as snakes that have cast off their skin. There were swords decorated with gold, with handles made out of ivory. There were shields and bow-sheaths for the archers, with golden backs. There were spears, javelins, swords and spikes. All of these were decorated with gold and embellished with gold. They were as bright as gold. O venerable one! Heavy clubs were destroyed and fell down. There were maces, battleaxes and catapults. Colourful spears, decorated with gold, fell down. There were many types and forms of carpets and whisks and fans. There were many types of weapons, dislodged from men who had fallen down. Though they had lost their lives, the maharathas seemed to be alive. Their bodies were shattered through clubs. Their heads were smashed through maces. The men lay on the ground, crushed by elephants, horses and chariots. O king! The earth was strewn everywhere with the bodies of slain horses, men and elephants, which looked like mountains, and seemed to be beautiful. Spears, swords, arrows, javelins, scimitars, spikes, lances, darts, battleaxes, clubs, catapults and *shataghnis*[352] fell down on the field of battle there. The earth was strewn with bodies that had been shattered by weapons. Some were silent. Others made slight sounds. They were covered with blood. The earth was strewn with the bodies of those who had been killed by the enemy and looked beautiful. The arms of the spirited ones had leather guards and bracelets and were smeared with sandalwood paste. Their shattered thighs were like the trunks of elephants. The crowns of the heads were adorned with jewels. The heads bore earrings. O descendant of the Bharata lineage! The earth

[352]Unidentified weapon that could kill one hundred people at one go.

was resplendent with the bull-eyed ones who had fallen down. The
earth was covered with armour and golden ornaments drenched in
blood. It looked as beautiful as a fire with calm flames. Ornaments
were strewn around and bows had fallen down. Bows and gold-tufted
arrows were scattered in every direction. There were many shattered
chariots, garlanded with nets of bells. Dead horses were lying around,
with protruding tongues and drenched in blood. There were the floors
of chariots, standards, quivers and pennants. Large and white conch
shells belonging to the brave ones were scattered around. Elephants
were supine on the ground, their trunks severed and the earth looked
as beautiful as a lady adorned with many different kinds of ornaments.
There were tuskers in great pain, pierced with lances. They repeatedly
let out moans through their trunks. That field of battle was beautiful,
as if with mobile mountains. There were carpets of many different
hues and cushions for the elephants. Dazzling goads, with handles
made of lapis lazuli, fell down. Bells for the kings among elephants
were scattered around everywhere. There were colourful seats and
hides of *ranku* deer. There were colourful necklaces and golden
harnesses for the elephants. There were many shattered implements
and lances and kampanas. There were shattered golden breastplates
for the horses, soiled with dirt. The severed arms of the horse-riders
fell down, with the bracelets still there. There were polished and sharp
javelins and polished swords. Torn headdresses were scattered around
there. There were colourful arrows in the shape of the half-moon,
decorated with gold. There were cushions for the horses and the hides
of ranku deer. There were colourful and extremely expensive gems
for the crests of those Indras among men. Umbrellas were scattered
around, and whisks and fans. The faces were as beautiful as the lotus
or the moon and were still adorned with earrings. The brave ones were
ornamented and their beards were well-trimmed. O great king! They
were beautiful and radiant, with golden earrings. The earth looked
like the sky, with its array of planets and stars. O descendant of the
Bharata lineage! Thus did those two large armies, yours and that of
the enemy, clash against each other in that battle. O descendant of the
Bharata lineage! They were exhausted, scattered and routed. Night
set in and nothing could be seen in the field of battle. The soldiers of

the Kurus and the Pandavas retreated. The terrible and fearful night set in and the Kurus and the Pandavas withdrew from that extremely terrible encounter. With the time having come, they retreated to their own camps."'

Chapter 953(93)

'Sanjaya said, "O great king! Then King Duryodhana, Shakuni Soubala, your son Duhshasana and the invincible son of the suta assembled and consulted each other. How could the sons of Pandu, together with their followers, be vanquished in battle? King Duryodhana spoke to all his advisers, addressing particularly the son of the suta and the immensely strong Soubala. 'I do not know the reason why Drona, Bhishma, Kripa, Shalya and Somadatta's son are unable to resist the Parthas in this battle. They are not being killed, but are demolishing my army. O Karna! In this battle, my army is becoming weaker and my weapons are being exhausted. I have been deceived by the Pandavas. They cannot be slain, even by the gods. I am full of doubt as to what I should do in this battle.' O great king! The son of the suta then spoke to the king. 'O best of the Bharata lineage! Do not grieve. I will do what is agreeable to you. Let Bhishma, Shantanu's son, withdraw from this great battle. O descendant of the Bharata lineage! When Gangeya has withdrawn from the battle and has cast aside his weapons, I will kill the Parthas, together with all the Somakas, while Bhishma witnesses the battle. O king! This is the pledge I truthfully take. O king! Bhishma has always acted kindly towards the Pandavas. Bhishma is incapable of vanquishing those maharathas in battle. Bhishma is proud of his prowess in battle and always loves an encounter. O father![353] How

---

[353]The word used is tata, used not just for father, but anyone who is senior. In this context, 'father' is singularly inappropriate. But we have stuck to it for the sake of consistency.

can he defeat the Pandavas when he encounters them in battle?[354]
Therefore, you should quickly go to Bhishma's camp. O descendant
of the Bharata lineage! You should request Bhishma to cast aside his
weapons in battle. When Bhishma casts aside his weapons, you will
see the Pandavas killed. O king! I will alone accomplish this in the
battle, together with their well-wishers and their relatives.' Having
been thus addressed by Karna, your son, Duryodhana, spoke these
words to his brother, Duhshasana. 'O Duhshasana! Let all those,
who will come with me, be appropriately dressed. Quickly make
all the arrangements.' O king! Having thus spoken, the lord of
men then addressed Karna. 'O supreme among men! O scorcher of
enemies! Having requested Bhishma to withdraw from the battle, I
will swiftly return and come before you. O tiger among men! You
will then act in this battle.' O lord of the earth! Without any delay,
your son departed.

"'He left with his brothers, like Shatakratu with all the gods.
His brother, Duhshasana, quickly made his brother, who was a tiger
among kings and with the valour of a tiger, ascend a horse. The king
was adorned with armlets and bracelets and wore a crown on his
head. O great king! Dhritarashtra's son was as resplendent as the
great Indra. He was smeared with fragrant sandalwood paste. He
looked like a *bhandi* flower[355] and had a golden complexion. He
was clad in garments that had no dirt on them. The king proceeded
with the sporting gait of a lion. He was as beautiful as an autumn
sun with unblemished rays. That tiger among men departed for
Bhishma's camp. He was followed by great archers, who were
famous in all the worlds as archers. His brothers, great archers,
also followed him, like the thirty gods with Vasava. O descendant
of the Bharata lineage! There were others astride horses, and still
others astride elephants. Others on chariots, the foremost of men,
surrounded him in every direction. His well-wishers had taken up
arms for the sake of protecting the lord of the earth. They were

---

[354]The implicit sense seems to be that if Bhishma defeats the Pandavas, the
encounter will be over. Hence, Bhishma is unnecessarily prolonging it.
[355]*Rubia manjith*, the Indian madder.

with him, like the immortals with Shakra in heaven. The maharatha among the Kouravas was worshipped by the Kurus. O king! He went towards the illustrious Gangeya's abode. The king was followed and surrounded by his brothers in every direction. Occasionally, he raised his right arm. It was as muscular as the trunk of an elephant and was capable of destroying all enemies. He raised that arm and accepted the worship of the kings, who were in every direction, hands joined in salutation. He heard sweet words from the residents of many countries. The immensely illustrious one was praised by bards and minstrels. The lord of all the lords of the worlds honoured all of them in return. Great-souled ones surrounded him in every direction with golden lamps, with fragrant oil as fuel. The king was surrounded by these auspicious and golden lamps. He was as beautiful as the moon, surrounded by the resplendent large planets. There were attendants with golden headdresses, and with drums and sticks in their hands. They gently asked the people in every direction to make way. Having reached Bhishma's beautiful abode, the lord of men got down from his horse and approached Bhishma. He paid his respects to Bhishma and sat down on an excellent and golden seat. It was beautiful everywhere and was covered with a wonderful carpet.

'"He joined his hands in salutation and spoke to Bhishma, his voice choking and his eyes full of tears. 'O destroyer of enemies! We sought your protection and resorted to this war. In the battle, we thought we possessed the enterprise to defeat the gods and the asuras combined, together with Indra, not to speak of the brave sons of Pandu, with their well-wishers and their relatives. O lord! O Gangeya! Therefore, you should show your compassion towards me. Slay the brave sons of Pandu, like the great Indra against the danavas. O mighty-armed one! O descendant of the Bharata lineage! You earlier said that you would kill the Somakas and the Panchalas, together with the Pandavas. Act accordingly and make your words come true. Kill the assembled Parthas and the great archers, the Somakas. O descendant of the Bharata lineage! Make those words come true. O lord! O king! If you protect the Pandavas because of compassion, because of your hatred of me, or because of my misfortune, then I seek your permission to allow Karna, the ornament of any battle, to fight. He will defeat the Parthas, with their well-wishers and their relatives, in battle.' Having said this, the king, your son Duryodhana, did not say anything more to Bhishma, whose valour was terrible."'

Chapter 954(94)

'Sanjaya said, "These words spoken by your son were like stakes and Bhishma was pierced by them. He was overcome by great grief, but did not say anything unpleasant in reply. Overcome by grief and anger, he thought for a very long time. Wounded by these stakes, he sighed like a serpent. O descendant of the Bharata lineage! The supreme among those who know the worlds then raised his eyes. He seemed to burn the worlds, with the gods, the asuras and the gandharvas, with his anger. However, he spoke these conciliatory words to your son. 'O Duryodhana! Why are you piercing me with words that are like stakes? To the best of my strength, I have always sought to do that which brings you pleasure. Desiring your welfare, I am ready to give up my life in this battle. When the brave Pandava gratified Agni in Khandava, he defeated even Shakra in battle. That is proof.[356] O mighty-armed one! When the gandharvas captured you, Pandu's energetic son freed you. That is proof. O lord! At that time, all your brave brothers ran away. And so did Radheya, the son of a suta. That is proof. In Virata's city, he singly attacked all of us together. That is proof. He was angry and defeated both me and Drona in battle. He robbed the garments of Karna, Drona's son and the great maharatha Kripa. That is proof. Partha vanquished the Nivatakavachas in battle, whom even Vasava found to be invincible in an encounter. That is proof. Who is capable of vanquishing Pandava, who prides himself in an encounter, in battle? O Suyodhana! Because of your delusion, you do not know what should be said and what

[356]That the Pandavas are invincible.

should not be said. A man who is about to die thinks that all trees are made of gold. O Gandhari's son! In that fashion, you are looking at everything in a contrary way. You have yourself created this great enmity with the Pandavas and the Srinjayas. Fight with them in the battle now and show us your manliness. O tiger among men! I will myself kill all the assembled Somakas and the Panchalas, avoiding Shikhandi. Slain by them in battle, I will go to Yama's abode. Or, I will kill them in battle and give you pleasure. Shikhandi was earlier born as a girl in the king's abode. By virtue of a boon, she was born as a man.[357] This is that lady Shikhandi. O descendant of the Bharata lineage! I will not kill him, even if it means giving up my own life. Shikhandi is the one whom the creator made a lady earlier. O Gandhari's son! Sleep happily. I will fight a great battle tomorrow, one that will be spoken about as long as the earth exists.' O lord of men! Having been thus addressed, your son departed. He paid respects to his elder by lowering his head and left for his own residence. Having returned, the king asked his attendants to leave. The destroyer of enemies quickly entered and having entered, the king passed the night."'

Chapter 955(95)

'Sanjaya said, "When night passed and it was morning, the king arose. The king instructed all the warriors, 'Prepare for battle. In the encounter today, the angry Bhishma will kill all the Somakas.' O king! On hearing Duryodhana's many lamentations in the night, he[358] regarded them as instructions unto himself. He was supremely depressed and censured what the other had said. Shantanu's son thought for a long time and desired to encounter Arjuna in battle. O great king! Duryodhana understood from the signs what Gangeya

[357]The story of Amba becoming Shikhandi has been recounted in Section 60.
[358]Bhishma.

had been thinking about and instructed Duhshasana. 'O Duhshasana! Let chariots quickly be yoked, so that Bhishma can be protected. Let thirty-two entire divisions be instructed accordingly. What we have thought about for many years has now come to pass. With their soldiers, the Pandavas will be slain and the kingdom will be obtained. I think that Bhishma's protection is our task now. Protected by us, he will cheerfully slaughter the Parthas in this battle. The one with the pure soul said, "I will not kill Shikhandi. He was a lady earlier. Therefore, I should avoid him in battle. O mighty-armed one! The world knows that, in an attempt to bring pleasure to my father, I gave up women and a prosperous kingdom earlier.[359] O foremost among men! Therefore, I will not kill in battle anyone who has been born a woman, or has been a woman earlier. I am telling you this truthfully. O king! Shikhandi was a woman earlier and you have heard me tell you this when preparations were being made for the war. She was born as Shikhandini. O descendant of the Bharata lineage! Having been a woman, she was born as a man and wishes to fight. But I can never release arrows at her. O son![360] But if there are any other kshatriyas who desire the victory of the Pandavas in battle, I will kill them all—as soon as they come within reach of my arrows." These were the words spoken to me by Gangeya, foremost among the Bharata lineage and skilled in knowledge of the sacred texts. Therefore, with all my heart, I think that Bhishma's protection is most important. In the great forest, a wolf can kill a lion that is unprotected. Let Shikhandi not be like a wolf that kills a tiger. Let our maternal uncle, Shakuni, Shalya, Kripa, Drona and Vivimshati make endeavours to protect Gangeya. If he is protected, victory is certain.' On hearing Duryodhana's words, all the kings surrounded Gangeya from every direction, with a large number of chariots. Your sons surrounded Gangeya and got ready to fight. The earth and the firmament trembled and the Pandavas were agitated. The maharathas[361] possessed chariots and well-trained elephants.

---

[359]Referring to Bhishma's vow of celibacy, so that Shantanu could marry Satyavati.

[360]The word used is tata.

[361]On the Kourava side.

Armoured, they stationed themselves and surrounded Bhishma in that battle. Just as the thirty gods protect the wielder of the vajra in a battle between the gods and the asuras, in that way, all of them were stationed to protect the maharatha.

'"King Duryodhana again spoke to his brothers. 'Yudhamanyu is protecting Arjuna's left wheel and Uttamouja the right, while Arjuna is protecting Shikhandi. O Duhshasana! Act so that he cannot kill Bhishma, while protected by Partha and while he[362] is abandoned by us.' On hearing his brother's words, your son, Duhshasana, left with the army, with Bhishma at the forefront. On seeing Bhishma surrounded by that large number of chariots, Arjuna, best of rathas, spoke to Dhrishtadyumna. 'O unblemished one! Let Shikhandi, tiger among men, be placed in front of Bhishma. O one without decay! Establish the Panchala there and I will myself be his protector.' Bhishma, Shantanu's son, then advanced with his soldiers. In that encounter, he stationed his soldiers in the form of a large vyuha known as *saravatobhadra*.[363] O descendant of the Bharata lineage! Kripa, Kritavarma, maharatha Shaibya, Shakuni, Saindhava, Sudakshina from Kamboja and all your sons were stationed in front of all the soldiers and in front of the vyuha, together with Bhishma. O venerable one! Drona, Bhurishrava, Shalya and Bhagadatta armoured and stationed themselves on the right flank of the vyuha. Ashvatthama, Somadatta and the two maharathas from Avanti protected the left flank, together with a large army. O great king! O king! O descendant of the Bharata lineage! To counter the Pandavas, Duryodhana stationed himself in the midst of the vyuha, surrounded by the Trigartas. Alambusa, best among rathas, and maharatha Shrutayu armoured and stationed themselves at the rear of the vyuha and behind all the soldiers. O descendant of the Bharata lineage! Thus did those on your side construct a vyuha. When they were armoured, they looked like blazing fires. At this, King Yudhishthira, Pandava Bhimasena and Madri's sons, Nakula and

---

[362]Bhishma.

[363]Literally, something that is fortunate in every direction. Probably in the form of a square.

Sahadeva, armoured and stationed themselves in the vyuha, ahead of all the soldiers. Dhrishtadyumna, Virata and maharatha Satyaki, the destroyers of enemy ranks, stationed themselves, with a large army. O great king! Shikhandi, Vijaya,[364] the rakshasa Ghatotkacha, the mighty-armed Chekitana and the valiant Kuntibhoja were ready for battle, surrounded by a large army. The great archer, Abhimanyu, maharatha Drupada and the five brothers from Kekaya were armoured and stationed ready for battle. O venerable one! Thus did the brave Pandavas, invincible in battle, create a great vyuha as a counter-vyuha in that encounter and were ready to fight.

'"In that encounter, the kings on your side suddenly rushed, with great enterprise, to do battle. O king! Placing Bhishma in the front, they advanced against the Parthas in that battle. O king! In a similar way, the Pandavas placed Bhimasena at the forefront, wishing to fight against Bhishma and desiring victory in that encounter. There were war cries and sounds of joy. There were the sounds of saws and cow horns. The Pandavas played on battledrums, drums, cymbals and smaller drums and there was a terrible roar, as they advanced. There were the sounds of battledrums, drums, other drums and conch shells on our side. There were delighted roars, like those of lions, and other shouts, as we roared back in return and quickly advanced against them. We advanced forcefully and angrily and a tumultuous sound arose. They rushed against each other and struck each other. Because of that great sound, the earth began to tremble. Birds uttered terrible shrieks and began to fly around. The sun had risen with all its rays, but now seemed to be dimmed. There was a turbulent wind, signifying great disaster. Fearful jackals began to roam around, howling terribly. O great king! All of this seemed to tell us that a great calamity was at hand. O king! The directions blazed and ash began to shower down. There was a shower of bones mixed with blood. The mounts began to weep and tears began to fall from their eyes. O lord of the earth! Because of their anxiety, they discharged urine and excrement. Man-eating rakshasas began to roar in terrible tones. We saw that jackals, cranes and crows began

[364]Arjuna.

to swoop down. Dogs uttered many terrible howls. Flaming meteors struck against the sun and suddenly fell down on the ground. All this signified a great fear. In that great encounter, the two large armies of the Pandavas and the sons of Dhritarashtra clashed. There was the din of conch shells and drums and this caused a tremor, like that of a forest agitated by a storm. In that inauspicious moment, kings, elephants and horses clashed against each other and the tremendous noise was like that of oceans agitated by a tempest."'

Chapter 956(96)

'Sanjaya said, "The energetic Abhimanyu, foremost among rathas, was borne on steeds that were of a tawny colour and advanced against Duryodhana's large army. He brought down a shower of arrows, like clouds pouring down rain. The bulls among the Kurus who were on your side could not resist Subhadra's angry son in battle. That destroyer of enemies possessed a great number of weapons and he immersed himself in that inexhaustible ocean of soldiers. O king! In that encounter, he released many arrows that destroyed enemies. They conveyed the brave kshatriyas to the abode of the king of the dead. In that battle, Subhadra's angry son unleashed arrows that were like Yama's staff. They were flaming and terrible, like poisonous serpents. Phalguna's son quickly brought down charioteers from their chariots, horse-riders from the backs of horses and elephant-riders together with the elephants. In that great battle, the lords of the earth cheerfully honoured his extraordinary deeds and praised Phalguna's son. Subhadra's son drove away many colourful armies, like masses of cotton blown away by the wind in every direction. O descendant of the Bharata lineage! Driven away by him, your soldiers could not find a protector and were like elephants stuck in the mud. O king! Having driven all your soldiers away, Abhimanyu, supreme among men, stood like a flaming fire, without any smoke. All those on your side could not counter that destroyer of enemies and were like

insects, driven by destiny, before a flaming fire. Having struck all the
enemies of the Pandavas, the maharatha and great archer was like
the wielder of the vajra with his vajra. His bow had a golden back.
O king! As it was moved around in every direction, it was seen to be
as radiant as lightning.[365] The arrows released from his bow in that
battle were sharp and yellow. They were like flocks of bees, visiting
blossoming trees in the forest. That is the way Subhadra's great-souled
son roamed around. His chariot roared like the clouds and people
could not find an opportunity to strike him. He confounded Kripa,
Drona, Drona's son, Brihadbala and Saindhava, the great archer.
He moved around with skill and dexterity. O venerable one! As he
tormented your army, I saw that his bow was drawn in the shape of
a circle and was like the circular halo that is around the sun. Brave
kshatriyas saw this and were tormented by his arrows. Because of
his deeds, they thought the world now had two Phalgunas. O great
king! Oppressed by him, that great army of the Bharatas ran here
and there, like a woman intoxicated with liquour. He drove away
your soldiers and made the maharathas tremble and delighted his
well-wishers, like Vasava after vanquishing Maya.[366] Driven away
by him in that battle, your soldiers uttered lamentations of woe and
these sounded like the roar of the clouds.

'"O venerable one! On hearing that awful wail amidst your
soldiers, like that of the ocean agitated by the force of the wind at
the time of the new moon or the full moon, King Duryodhana spoke
to Rishyashringa's son. 'This great archer who is Krishna's son[367]
is like a second Phalguna. He is driving away the soldiers in rage,
like Vritra against the army of the gods. I do not see any other great
medicine against him in this battle, except your own self. O best of
the rakshasas! You are skilled in all forms of knowledge. O brave
one! Go swiftly and slay Subhadra's son in battle. We will kill Partha,
with Bhishma and Drona leading us.' Thus addressed and following
the instructions of your son, the powerful and strong Indra among

---

[365]Shatahrada.
[366]Maya was a famous danava. He was also the architect of the demons.
[367]Arjuna is also named Krishna.

the rakshasas quickly advanced to do battle. He emitted a loud roar, like the slayer of Bala at the time of the monsoon. O king! At this great sound, the mighty army of the Pandavas trembled in every direction, like a full ocean. O king! Frightened by that roar, many men gave up their beloved lives and fell down on the ground. Krishna's son was delighted and grasped his bow and arrows. He seemed to be dancing around on his chariot and attacked the rakshasa. The rakshasa was enraged and approached Arjuna's son in that battle. Stationing himself at a short distance, he started to drive away the soldiers. In that battle, he killed the great army of the Pandavas. The rakshasa attacked them in the encounter, like Bali against the army of the gods. O venerable one! There was great oppression and slaughter among those soldiers. The rakshasa, terrible in form, killed them in that battle. He released thousands of arrows on the great army of the Pandavas. The rakshasa displayed his valour and drove them back in that battle. Thus slaughtered by the rakshasa, terrible in form, the army of the Pandavas was frightened and fled from the field of battle. He crushed those soldiers, like an elephant amidst lotuses.

"'In that encounter, the immensely strong one then attacked the sons of Droupadi. The great archers who were Droupadi's sons were armoured and became wrathful. All of them advanced against the rakshasa, like five planets against the sun. Prativindhya swiftly pierced the immensely strong rakshasa with sharp, vigorous and iron arrows. They penetrated his armour and the supreme among rakshasas looked resplendent. He was like a giant mass of rain clouds, penetrated by the rays of the sun. O king! He was struck by arrows that were embellished with gold and Rishyashringa's son looked like a mountain with a flaming summit. In that great battle, the five brothers pierced the Indra among rakshasas with sharp arrows that were embellished with gold. O king! Pierced by terrible arrows that were like angry snakes, Alambusha became as angry as a king of elephants. O great king! O venerable one! He was pierced within a short instant. Having been wounded, the maharatha remained unconscious for a long time. When he regained consciousness, in his rage, he increased his dimensions to double of what they were. He sliced down their arrows, standards and bows. As if smiling, he pierced each of them with three arrows. Maharatha Alambusa seemed to be dancing around on his chariot. The rakshasa was angry and in his rage, the immensely strong one killed the horses and the charioteers of the great-souled ones. In great delight, he again pierced them with extremely sharp arrows. He used many different kinds of arrows, in hundreds and thousands. Those great archers were bereft of their chariots by the rakshasa and the traveller of the night swiftly rushed against them, wishing to kill them. On seeing them thus oppressed in battle by the evil-souled rakshasa, Arjuna's son attacked the rakshasa in that battle. The battle that commenced was like that between Vritra and Vasava. All those on your side and the maharatha Pandavas witnessed it. They encountered each other in that great battle and blazed with rage. O great king! They were immensely strong and their eyes were red with rage. The warriors glanced towards each other, like the fire at the destruction of a yuga. There was a terrible encounter that was fierce and awful. It was like that between Shakra and Shambara,[368] during the battle between the gods and the asuras.'"

Chapter 957(97)

'Dhritarashtra asked, "O Sanjaya! Arjuna's brave son killed many maharathas in battle. How did Alambusa counter him in the encounter? How did Subhadra's son, the destroyer of enemy heroes, fight with Rishyashringa's son? Tell me all this in detail, exactly as it occurred in the course of the battle. O Sanjaya! What did Dhananjaya do against my soldiers, and Bhima, foremost among strong ones, rakshasa Ghatotkacha, Nakula, Sahadeva and maharatha Satyaki? O Sanjaya! Tell me all this, because you are skilled."

[368]There are various demons named Shambara. This is the one whom Indra defeated to obtain soma.

'Sanjaya replied, "O venerable one! I will later tell you about
the battle that took place between the Indra among the rakshasas
and Subhadra's son. It made the body hair stand up. I will also
recount to you the valour of Arjuna and Pandava Bhimasena in the
battle and that of Nakula and Sahadeva in the encounter. I will also
tell you about the extraordinary and wonderful deeds of those on
your side, performed without fear and with Bhishma and Drona
at the forefront. In that encounter against maharatha Abhimanyu,
Alambusa roared extremely loudly. He advanced, roaring again and
again, and asking him[369] to wait. O king! In that battle, Subhadra's
son also roared repeatedly like a lion. He attacked the great archer
who was Rishyashringa's son and was also a sworn enemy of his
fathers. The man and the rakshasa, foremost among rathas, swiftly
confronted each other in battle on their respective chariots, like a
god and a danava. The foremost among rakshasas was skilled in
maya and Phalguna's son was skilled in the use of divine weapons.
O great king! Krishna's son used three sharp arrows to pierce
Rishyashringa's son in that battle and then again pierced him with
five arrows. Alambusa became angry and pierced Krishna's son
in the chest with nine swift arrows, like forcefully striking a giant
elephant with a goad. O descendant of the Bharata lineage! In that
battle, the traveller of the night, swift in action, used a thousand
arrows to oppress Arjuna's son. Abhimanyu became angry. He shot
nine sharp arrows with drooping tufts at the rakshasa's giant chest.
They quickly pierced his body and penetrated his inner organs. O
king! The limbs of that supreme among rakshasas were mangled
and he was as beautiful as a mountain with blossoming kimshukas.
Bearing those gold-encrusted arrows, the best of the rakshasas,
immensely strong, was as dazzling as a flaming mountain. O great
king! At this, Rishyashringa's immensely strong son became wrathful.
He enveloped Krishna's son, who was like the great Indra, with
arrows. He released sharp arrows that were like Yama's staff. These
pierced Abhimanyu and fell down on the ground. Arjuna's son shot
arrows that were decorated with gold. They pierced Alambusa and

[369]Abhimanyu.

penetrated the ground. In that battle, Subhadra's son used straight-tufted arrows to make the rakshasa retreat, like Shakra in a battle against Maya. Having been repulsed, the rakshasa, the scorcher of enemies, wished to kill his enemies in the battle and resorted to his great powers of dark maya. He caused everything on the ground to be enveloped in darkness. Abhimanyu could not be seen. And those on one's own side, or that of the enemy, could not be distinguished in that battle. On seeing that terrible and great gloom, Abhimanyu, the descendant of the Kuru lineage, invoked the supreme weapon known as *bhaskara*.[370] O lord of the earth! At this, everything in the universe again became visible. Thus, the maya of the evil-souled rakshasa was destroyed. In that encounter, the greatly valorous Indra among rakshasas became angry. He shrouded the supreme of men with straight-tufted arrows. The rakshasa used many other kinds of maya. But Phalguna's son, skilled in the use of all weapons and with an immeasurable soul, countered all of them. The rakshasa's maya was destroyed and he was wounded with arrows. He discarded his chariot and fled in great fear.

'"After having defeated the rakshasa, who used deceitful means to fight, Arjuna's son began to crush your soldiers in the battle. He was like a wild king of elephants, crazy with musth, agitating a pond that was full of lotuses. Bhishma, Shantanu's son, saw that the soldiers were being routed. He surrounded Subhadra's son with a large number of chariots. Many brave maharathas among the sons of Dhritarashtra created a circle around him. A single one fought against many and they struck him with firm arrows. That brave ratha was like his father in valour. He was Vasudeva's equal in valour and strength. He was supreme among all wielders of weapons and in that battle, performed many deeds that were like the two of them, his father and his maternal uncle.[371] O king! Dhananjaya began to destroy your soldiers. Wishing to rescue his son, the intolerant one arrived at the spot where he[372] was fighting with Bhishma. O king! In

---

[370]*Bhaskara* means the sun, or something that brings light.

[371]Arjuna and Krishna respectively.

[372]Abhimanyu.

that battle, your father, Devavrata, attacked Partha in the encounter,
like Svarbhanu[373] against the sun. O lord of the earth! With chariots,
elephants and horses, your sons surrounded Bhishma in that battle,
wishing to protect him in every direction. O king! In that fashion,
the Pandavas surrounded Dhananjaya. O bull among the Bharata
lineage! The armoured ones engaged in a great battle.

'"O king! Sharadvata stationed himself in front of Bhishma. He
pierced Arjuna with twenty-five arrows. To accomplish a pleasant task
for Pandava, Satyaki attacked him, like a tiger against an elephant,
and pierced him with sharp arrows. Goutama was enraged. In return,
he swiftly pierced Madhava[374] in the chest with nine arrows that
were tufted with the feathers of herons. Shini's descendant became
extremely angry at having been pierced. The maharatha unleashed
a terrible arrow at Goutama, one capable of taking his life away.
On seeing it descend with great force, as radiant as Shakra's vajra,
Drona's son, driven by supreme rage, angrily sliced it down into two.
Avoiding Goutama, supreme among rathas, in that battle, Shini's
descendant then attacked Drona's son in that encounter, like Rahu
in the sky against the moon. O descendant of the Bharata lineage!
However, Drona's son sliced his bow into two and once his bow had
been severed, oppressed him with arrows. The destroyer of enemies
picked up another bow that was capable of bearing a great burden.
O great king! He struck Drona's son in the arms and the chest with
six arrows. Having been thus pierced and wounded, he lost his senses
for some time. He sat down on the floor of his chariot, using the
pole of his standard for support. Having regained his senses, Drona's
powerful son angrily pierced Varshneya[375] in that encounter with iron
arrows. These pierced Shini's descendant and penetrated the ground,
like a powerful and young snake entering a hole during the spring. In
that encounter, Drona's son roared like a lion. He used another broad-
headed arrow to sever Madhava's supreme standard. O descendant
of the Bharata lineage! O great king! He again unleashed a shower

[373]Rahu.
[374]Satyaki.
[375]Descended from the Vrishni lineage. In this context, Satyaki.

of arrows to envelope him, like clouds covering the sun at the end of summer. O great king! Satyaki destroyed that net of arrows and quickly covered Drona's son with many nets of arrows. He was like the sun that had emerged from a net of clouds. Shini's descendant, the destroyer of enemy heroes, scorched Drona's son. The immensely strong Satyaki roared and again enveloped him with thousands of arrows. On seeing that his son was eclipsed, like the moon afflicted by Rahu, Bharadvaja's powerful son attacked Shini's descendant. O king! In that great battle, he pierced him with extremely sharp arrows, desiring to rescue his son, who was being tormented by Varshneya. In that battle, having defeated the maharatha son of his preceptor, Satyaki then pierced Drona with twenty arrows that were completely made out of iron. Kounteya, borne on white steeds, was immeasurable in his soul. In that encounter, the maharatha angrily attacked Drona. O great king! In that great battle, Drona clashed against Partha and it was like Budha and Shukra[376] meeting each other in the firmament.''

Chapter 958(98)

'Dhritarashtra asked, "O Sanjaya! How did those brave and great archers, Drona and Pandava Dhananjaya, encounter each other in that battle? Tell me. Pandava was always the beloved of Bharadvaja's intelligent son. O Sanjaya! In any encounter, the preceptor was always the beloved of Partha. Those two rathas are proud in battle and are as fierce as lions. How did Dhananjaya and Bharadvaja's son clash against each other in the encounter?"

'Sanjaya replied, "In a battle, Drona does not know Partha as someone who is dear to himself. Placing the dharma of kshatriyas at the forefront, Partha does not acknowledge a preceptor in an encounter. O king! Kshatriyas do not avoid each other in an

---

[376]Mercury and Venus respectively.

encounter. Without any fear, they fight with their fathers and their brothers. O descendant of the Bharata lineage! In that battle, Partha pierced Drona with three arrows. But he[377] paid no heed to the arrows that had been released from Partha's bow in that battle. In that battle, Partha again covered him with a shower of arrows and he[378] blazed in anger, like a conflagration in a deserted forest. In that battle, Drona released straight-tufted arrows towards Arjuna. O descendant of the Bharata lineage! O Indra among kings! But those were speedily countered. O king! King Duryodhana instructed Susharma to protect Drona's flank in that battle. The angry king of Trigarta drew his bow and in that battle, enveloped Partha with arrows with iron heads. O king! The arrows released by both of them[379] were resplendent in the sky. O great king! They looked like swans in the autumn sky. O lord! Those dazzling arrows reached Kounteya and penetrated, like birds entering a tree that is lowered from the burden of succulent fruit. Arjuna, supreme among rathas, roared in that battle. In that encounter, he pierced the king of Trigarta and his sons with arrows. Partha pierced them, like the fire at the destruction of a yuga. But having made up their minds to die, they did not retreat from the encounter with Partha. They showered arrows towards Pandava's chariot. O Indra among kings! Pandava countered that shower of arrows with his own shower of arrows. He was like a mountain receiving a downpour of rain. We witnessed the extraordinary dexterity of Bibhatsu's hands. The brave one countered many showers of arrows that were difficult to withstand, like the wind scattering masses of clouds. The gods and the danavas were delighted with Partha's deeds. O descendant of the Bharata lineage! Partha angrily advanced against Trigarta in battle. O great king! He released the vayavya weapon against the head of their army. A turbulent wind arose in the sky. It brought down masses of trees and killed the soldiers. Drona beheld that extremely terrible vayavya weapon. O great king! He released the extremely terrible

---

[377]Drona.

[378]Drona.

[379]Drona and Susharma.

weapon known as *shaila*.[380] When Drona released this weapon in
the great battle, the wind was pacified and the directions became
placid. But Pandu's brave son made the Trigartas, roaming around
on their chariots, dispirited in that battle. They lost their valour
and retreated.

"'King Duryodhana, Kripa, supreme among rathas, Ashvatthama,
Shalya, Sudakshina from Kamboja, Vinda and Anuvinda from Avanti
and Bahlika and the army of the Bahlikas surrounded Partha from
every direction with a great number of chariots. In a similar way,
Bhagadatta and the immensely strong Shrutayu surrounded Bhima
from every direction with a large army of elephants. O lord of the
earth! Bhurishrava, Shala and Soubala quickly countered Madri's
sons with many colourful arrows. With all the sons of Dhritarashtra
and their soldiers, Bhishma attacked Yudhishthira and surrounded
him from every direction. On seeing that army of elephants descend,
the brave Partha Vrikodara licked the corners of his mouth, like a king
of deer in a forest. The best of rathas grasped a club in the great battle.
He swiftly got down from his chariot and terrified your soldiers.
On seeing him, with the club in his hand, the elephant-riders made
endeavours to surround Bhimasena from every side in that battle. But
Pandava penetrated the midst of the elephants and began to roam
around. He was like the sun in the middle of a large mass of clouds.
The bull of the Pandava lineage slew that army of elephants with his
club. He was like the wind, scattering a large mass of clouds. Those
tuskers were slaughtered by the powerful Bhimasena. They shrieked
in that battle, roaring like clouds. There were many wounds on his
body, resulting from the tusks of the elephants. Partha dazzled in
the forefront of that battle, like a flowering ashoka tree. He seized
some elephants by their tusks and uprooted their tusks. He used
those tusks to strike the elephants on their temples. He brought
them down in that battle, like Yama with the staff in his hand. The
club was covered with blood and his body was spattered with fat
and marrow. With blood on his armlets, he seemed to be like Rudra.
O king! Thus slaughtered, the remaining mighty elephants fled in

[380]As an adjective, shaila means something that is made out of stone.

all the directions, crushing their own soldiers in the process. O bull among the Bharata lineage! The gigantic elephants were driven away in all the directions. All of Duryodhana's soldiers retreated from the field of battle.'"

Chapter 959(99)

'Sanjaya said, "O great king! It was midday and the encounter raged. There was a terrible battle, destructive of people, between Bhishma and the Somakas. Gangeya, best among rathas, pierced the Pandava soldiers with hundreds and thousands of sharp arrows. Your father, Devavrata, crushed those soldiers, like a herd of cattle, crushing reaped paddy. Dhrishtadyumna, Shikhandi, Virata and Drupada attacked Bhishma in that battle and struck the maharatha with arrows. He pierced Dhrishtadyumna and Virata with three arrows each. O descendant of the Bharata lineage! He then dispatched an iron arrow towards Virata. O king! Pierced by Bhishma, the destroyer of enemies, in that battle, those great archers became as angry as serpents that have been trod upon. Shikhandi pierced the grandfather of the Bharatas. But the undecaying one thought him to be a woman and did not strike him back. In that battle, Dhrishtadyumna was overcome with rage, like a flaming fire. He used three arrows to pierce the grandfather in the arms and the chest. Drupada pierced Bhishma with twenty-five arrows, Virata with ten arrows and Shikhandi with twenty-five. O great king! The great-souled Bhishma was pierced in that battle and was as beautiful as a blossoming red ashoka tree in the spring. Gangeya pierced them back with three arrows that travelled straight.[381] O venerable one! He severed Virata's bow with a broad-headed arrow. In the forefront of that battle, he took up another bow and pierced Bhishma with five

---

[381]Three arrows for Dhrishtadyumna, Drupada and Virata. He did not touch Shikhandi.

sharp arrows and his charioteer with three. O great king! Bhima, Droupadi's five sons, the five brothers from Kekaya and Satvata Satyaki, desiring Yudhishthira's welfare, attacked Gangeya. They wished to protect Panchala Dhrishtadyumna in that battle. O lord of men! All those on your side raised their weapons to protect Bhishma and attacked the Pandu soldiers with their own soldiers.

'"There was an extremely terrible battle between those on your side and those on their side. It involved men, horses, chariots and elephants and extended Yama's kingdom. Charioteers clashed with charioteers and sent them to Yama's abode. Others attacked, men, elephant-riders and horse-riders. They used straight-tufted arrows to dispatch each other to the hereafter. O lord of the earth! Many terrible weapons were used there. Chariots lost their horses, rathas and charioteers and in that battle, were dragged away in different directions. O king! In that battle, they crushed many men and horses. They seemed to be like the wind, or like the cities of the gandharvas. Energetic and armoured rathas were bereft of their chariots. They were adorned with earrings and headdresses and all of them were ornamented with golden armlets. They were the equals of the sons of the gods in beauty and bravery and Shakra's equal in fighting. They surpassed Vaishravana[382] in prosperity and Brihaspati in wisdom. O lord of the world! The brave ones who were there were the lords of all the worlds. They were seen to be driven away, like ordinary men. O best of men! The tuskers were bereft of the best of riders. They ran around and fell down, shrieking loudly and crushing their own ranks. O venerable one! Their armour, whisks, umbrellas and standards were strewn around, as were the housings, bells and lances. Devastated, they were seen to run away in the ten directions. They were like mountains or clouds and roared like rain clouds. O lord of the earth! Some elephant-riders were deprived of their elephants, both on your side and on theirs. They were seen to run away in that encounter. There were horses that had come from many countries and were decorated with gold. They were as fast as the wind and were there in hundreds and thousands. With the horses slain, horse-riders

[382]Kubera.

grasped swords in every direction. They were seen to run away, or chase others away, in that encounter. In that great battle, elephants clashed with elephants that were running away and swiftly crushed infantry and steeds. O king! In that battle, elephants crushed chariots and chariots clashed against infantry and horses. O king! In that battle, horses crushed men in the course of the encounter. O king! In this fashion, they crushed each other in diverse ways. That terrible battle raged and it gave rise to great fear. A fearful river began to flow, with blood as its waves. It was choked with masses of bones and the hair[383] was like moss and weeds. Chariots were the lakes and arrows were the currents, with horses as the unassailable fish. It was covered with heads as pebbles. It was infested with elephants as crocodiles. Armour and headdresses constituted the foam. Bows were islands and swords were turtles. Flags and pennants were trees along the banks. Men were the banks that the river destroyed. It was infested with large numbers of predatory creatures and it extended Yama's kingdom. O king! In that great battle, many brave kshatriyas gave up their fear. They sought to cross the river on boats made out of horses, elephants and chariots. In that battle, this river conveyed all the cowards who had become overcome by lassitude, just as Vaitarani conveys all those who are dead to the capital of the king of the dead. The kshatriyas present witnessed the great carnage. They exclaimed, 'It is because of Duryodhana's crimes that the Kouravas are headed towards destruction. The sons of Pandu possess many qualities. Why did Dhritrashtra's son, the lord of men, hate them? He is evil in his soul. He has been overcome by avarice.' O descendant of the Bharata lineage! Many words of this kind were heard there. They were full of praise for the Pandavas and were extremely terrible about your sons. O descendant of the Bharata lineage! On hearing these words spoken by all the warriors, your son, Duryodhana, who had caused offence to all the worlds, spoke these words to Bhishma, Drona, Kripa and Shalya. 'Fight with pride. What is the reason for delay?' O king! The extremely terrible battle between the Kurus and the Pandavas raged again, a consequence of the gambling

---

[383]Of slain combatants.

with the dice. O Vichitravirya's son! You paid no attention when
the great-souled ones tried to restrain you then. Behold the fruits of
that. O king! O lord of the earth! The sons of Pandu, their soldiers,
their followers and the Kouravas do not desire to protect their lives
in this battle. That is the reason there is this terrible destruction of
people. O tiger among men! O king! It has been caused by destiny
and your evil policy."'

Chapter 960(100)

'Sanjaya said, "O tiger among men! There were kings who were
following Susharma's lead and Arjuna used sharp arrows to
dispatch them to the abode of the king of the dead. In that battle,
Susharma pierced Partha with arrows. He again pierced Vasudeva
with seventy and Partha with nine. The maharatha who was Shakra's
son repulsed them with his own shower of arrows. In that battle, he
dispatched Susharma's warriors to Yama's abode. They were slain
by Partha, like the fire at the destruction of a yuga. O king! Those
maharathas were overcome with fear and fled from the field of
battle. O venerable one! Some abandoned their horses. Others gave
up their chariots. And still others discarded their elephants and fled
in the ten directions. Others fled from the field of battle, with their
horses, elephants and chariots. O lord of the earth! They ran away
with great speed. In that great battle, foot soldiers threw away their
weapons. O descendant of the Bharata lineage! As they ran away,
they ignored everything else. They were repeatedly restrained by
Susharma of the Trigartas and by other chiefs among the kings. But
they did not stay in that battle.

'"On seeing that his army was being routed, your son,
Duryodhana, placed Bhishma at the forefront of the battle, ahead
of all the soldiers. Using the best of his great endeavour, he attacked
Dhananjaya, for the sake of protecting the life of the lord of
Trigarta. He alone remained stationed in the battle, together with

all his brothers, and showered many different kinds of arrows. The remaining men ran away. O king! The Pandavas were armoured. For Phalguna's sake, they used their best endeavours to go to the spot where Bhishma was. They knew that the wielder of Gandiva was invincible. But cries of lamentation had arisen in all directions from the spot where Bhishma was. In that encounter, the brave one with the palm tree on his standard used straight-tufted arrows to shroud the army of the Pandavas. All the Kurus and the Pandavas seemed to be one single mass. O great king! They fought and the sun reached midday. Satyaki pierced Kritavarma with five iron arrows. The brave one remained stationed in the battle, releasing thousands of arrows. King Drupada pierced Drona with sharp arrows. He again pierced him with seventy arrows and his charioteer with seven. Bhimasena pierced his great-grandfather, King Bahlika, and emitted a loud roar, like a tiger in a forest.[384] Arjuna's son pierced Chitrasena with many fast arrows. Chitrasena was severely pierced in the chest with three arrows. These two great ones among men encountered each other in the battle and were radiant. O king! They were like the extremely terrible Budha and Shanaishchara in the sky.[385] Subhadra's son, the destroyer of enemy heroes, roared powerfully, after having slain his horses with four arrows and his charioteer with nine. O lord of the earth! With his horses slain, the maharatha swiftly descended from his chariot and climbed onto Durmukha's chariot. Drona pierced Drupada with straight-tufted arrows and the valorous one also swiftly pierced his charioteer. At the head of his soldiers, King Drupada was thus oppressed. Remembering his earlier hostility, he retreated on swift horses. In an instant, Bhimasena deprived King Bahlika of his horses, charioteer and chariot, while all the soldiers looked on. O

[384]Bahlika is the name of a kingdom, rather than of a specific king. Pratipa had three sons, Devapi, Bahlika and Shantanu. Shantanu became a king because his elder brothers, Devapi and Bahlika could not, or did not. This passage suggests that the Bahlika who took part in the war was Shantanu's elder brother and was thus Bhima's great-grandfather. Given the age, this seems unlikely. Somadatta, Bhurishrava and Shala were descended from this Bahlika and they are more likely candidates as the Bahlika who took part in the war.

[385]Mercury and Saturn respectively.

great king! Bahlika, supreme among men, was overcome by panic and confronted a great danger. He swiftly climbed onto maharatha Lakshmana's chariot. Satyaki repulsed maharatha Kritavarma. O king! He attacked the grandfather with many arrows. He pierced Bharata[386] with sixty sharp arrows that were tufted with hair and seemed to be dancing around on his chariot, brandishing his large bow. The grandfather hurled a giant and iron javelin towards him. It was decorated with gold and was extremely swift. It was as beautiful as a maiden of the serpents. On seeing it suddenly descend, extremely energetic and like death, the immensely famous Varshneya destroyed it with his dexterity. That extremely terrible javelin could not touch Varshneya. It fell down on the face of the ground, like a giant meteor that has lost its brilliance. O king! At this, Varshneya forcefully grasped and hurled a javelin towards the grandfather's chariot. It was terrible to behold. In that great battle, it was hurled through the force of Varshneya's arms. It advanced with great force, like a fatal night advancing towards a man. O descendant of the Bharata lineage! On seeing it suddenly descend, Gangeya used two extremely sharp kshurapra arrows to slice it into two, so that it fell down on the ground. Having severed the javelin, he angrily struck Satyaki on the chest with nine arrows and the destroyer of enemies smiled as he did this. O Pandu's elder brother! The Pandavas surrounded Bhishma in that battle, with their chariots, elephants and horses, so that Madhava[387] might be rescued. A tumultuous battle commenced and it made the body hair stand up. In that encounter, both the Pandavas and the Kurus desired victory.'"

Chapter 961(101)

'Sanjaya said, "O great king! Duryodhana saw that Bhishma was angry in the battle. O great king! He also saw that he was

[386]Bhishma.
[387]Satyaki.

surrounded by the Pandavas, like clouds in the sky surrounding the sun after summer is over. He addressed Duhshasana. 'This brave and great archer, Bhishma, is the destroyer of enemies. O bull among the Bharata lineage! He has been covered on all sides by the brave Pandavas. O brave one! It is your duty to protect the extremely great-souled one. In this battle, protect Bhishma, our grandfather, so that he can kill the Panchalas and the Pandavas in this encounter. I think that it is our duty to protect Bhishma. Bhishma, the great archer, is our protector and is also our grandfather. With all your soldiers, surround the grandfather. If you protect him, you will perform a difficult task in this battle.' In the encounter, having been thus addressed, your son, Duhshasana, stationed himself around Bhishma, surrounding him with a large army. Subala's son had many hundreds and thousands of horses. The riders had polished spears and wielded swords and spikes. They were proud and extremely swift. This was a force with standards. These supreme among men were trained and skilled in battle. They surrounded Nakula, Sahadeva and Pandava Dharmaraja from every direction and repulsed those best of men. King Duryodhana sent ten thousand brave horse-riders to restrain the Pandavas. They penetrated with great force, like Garudas advancing to do battle. O king! The earth was struck with the hooves and trembled because of the sound. A great noise from the hooves of the horses could be heard then. It was like a large forest of bamboos being burnt on a mountain. As they advanced there, a great cloud of dust arose. It rose up into the path of the sun and shrouded the sun. The army of the Pandavas was agitated because of the force of these horses, as if a flock of swans had descended onto a large lake with great force. Nothing could be heard because of the sounds of neighing.

"'O great king! In that battle, King Yudhishthira and the Pandavas who were Madri's sons spiritedly checked the force of those horse-riders, like the shoreline checks the forceful waves of the great ocean on the night of the full moon, when the waters are full because of the rains. O king! The rathas used straight-tufted arrows to sever the heads of the horse-riders from their bodies. O great king! They were slain and brought down by those who wielded firm bows. It was like elephants killed by mighty elephants and hurled into

mountainous caverns. They[388] roamed around in the ten directions
and used extremely sharp javelins and straight-tufted arrows to slice
off the heads. O bull among the Bharata lineage! The horse-riders
were struck by swords. Their heads fell down, like fruit from large
trees. O king! Horses and their riders were seen to be slain there.
They fell down and were falling down, in hundreds and thousands.
Having been thus slaughtered, the horses were overcome by fear
and fled. It was like deer trying to protect their lives at the arrival of
a lion. O great king! In that great battle, the Pandavas vanquished
the enemy. Having driven the enemy away in the battle, they blew
on their conch shells and sounded their drums.

'"In the midst of the soldiers, Duryodhana was seen to be
distressed. O best of the Bharata lineage! He spoke these words to the
king of Madra. 'This eldest son of Pandu has vanquished my maternal
uncle. O mighty-armed one! While you have looked on, the powerful
one has driven my soldiers away. O mighty-armed one! Repulse him,
the way the shoreline beats back the abode of makaras. On account
of your strength and valour, you are known to be irresistible.' Having
heard the words of your son, the powerful Shalya advanced with a
large number of chariots to the spot where King Yudhishthira was
stationed. Shalya suddenly descended with an extremely large force,
with the thrust of the great ocean. Pandava countered him in that
battle. In that encounter, maharatha Dharmaraja used ten arrows
to swiftly strike the king of Madra between the breasts. Nakula and
Sahadeva struck him with three arrows that were aimed straight. The
king of Madra pierced each of them with three arrows. He again
pierced Yudhishthira with sixty sharp arrows. Overcome with anger,
he struck the two sons of Madri with two arrows. The mighty-armed
Bhima then beheld the king in that battle. He approached the king
of Madra, as if advancing into the jaws of death. The vanquisher of
enemies advanced to the spot where Yudhishthira was stationed in
the battle. An extremely terrible and fearful battle raged. The sun
was blazing in the other direction then."'[389]

---

[388]The Pandava warriors.
[389]Noon had passed and the sun was in the western horizon.

Chapter 962(102)

'Sanjaya said, "Your father was enraged. In that battle, he used supreme and sharp arrows to pierce the Parthas and their soldiers in every direction. He pierced Bhima with twelve arrows and Satyaki with nine, Nakula with three arrows and Sahadeva with seven. He struck Yudhishthira with twelve arrows in his chest and arms. The immensely strong one then pierced Dhrishtadyumna and roared. Nakula pierced him with twelve arrows and Madhava[390] with three. Dhrishtadyumna pierced the grandfather back with seventy arrows, Bhimasena with five and Yudhishthira with twelve. Having pierced Satyaki, Drona pierced Bhimasena. He pierced each of them with five sharp arrows that resembled Yama's staff. But each of them pierced the bull among brahmanas back with three arrows that were straight in their aim and were like giant snakes. The Souviras, the Kitavas, those from the east, those from the west, those from the north, the Malavas, the Abhishahas, the Shurasenas, the Shibis and the Vasatayas did not avoid Bhishma in that battle, though they were slaughtered by his sharp arrows. Other great-souled ones on the side of the Pandaveyas were slaughtered. The Pandavas were attacked by those who wielded many weapons in their hands. O king! But the Pandavas still surrounded the grandfather. The invincible one was surrounded on all sides by a large number of chariots. Consuming the enemy, he blazed up like a fire engendered in a deserted forest. His chariot was the source of the fire. The bow, swords, javelins and clubs were the kindling. His arrows were the sparks. Bhishma was himself the fire that consumed the bulls among the kshatriyas. His arrows had golden tufts and the feathers of vultures. They were extremely energetic. He enveloped the enemy force with barbed, hollow and iron arrows. He used sharp arrows to bring down elephants and chariots. That large number of chariots looked like a forest of palm trees with the heads lopped off. O king! In that battle, the mighty-armed one, supreme among all wielders of

[390]Satyaki.

weapons, deprived chariots, elephants and horses of their riders. The
twang of his bow-string and the slapping of his palms were like the
clap of thunder. O descendant of the Bharata lineage! All the beings
were agitated and trembled. O bull among the Bharata lineage!
Your father's arrows were incapable of being countered. Released
from Bhishma's bow, those arrows did not only strike the armour
on the bodies. O king! Brave ones were slain on their chariots. O
great king! With the swift horses still yoked, we saw them[391] being
dragged around all over the field of battle. There were fourteen
thousand maharathas from the Chedis, the Kashis and the Karushas.
They were famous, born in noble lineages and were ready to give
up their lives. Their standards were decorated with gold and all of
them refused to retreat from the field of battle. They clashed against
Bhishma in that battle, as if against Death with a gaping mouth. All
of them were submerged in the world of the hereafter, together with
their horses, chariots and elephants. O king! We saw hundreds and
thousands of chariots. Some had their floors and axles chattered.
Others had completely broken wheels. The bumpers of the chariots
were fragmented and the charioteers were brought down. O lord of
the earth! O venerable one! Arrows, excellent armour, spikes, clubs,
maces, swords, arrows with iron heads, the floors of chariots, quivers
and wheels were broken and were strewn around. There were arms
that still held bows and swords. There were heads with earrings.
There were palm-guards and finger-guards and standards that had
been brought down. There were bows shattered into many fragments.
All these were scattered on the ground. O king! There were elephants
with the riders slain and horses devoid of riders. They lay there, in
hundreds and thousands. The brave ones[392] made every effort to
restrain the maharathas who were running away. But they did not
succeed, because of the oppression created by Bhishma's arrows. With
valour like that of the great Indra, he slaughtered that large army.
O great king! It was destroyed in such a way that no two people
ran away together. Chariots, elephants and horses were pierced and

[391]The chariots.
[392]The Pandavas.

standards and seats brought down. There was lamentation in the army of the sons of Pandu and they lost their senses. Father killed the son and the son killed the father. Driven by the force of destiny, a friend attacked a beloved friend. Many soldiers in the army of the sons of Pandu tore apart their armour. O descendant of the Bharata lineage! With disheveled hair, they were seen to run away. They were like a herd of cattle, crazy with fear and running around. Chariot-riders, elephants and soldiers in the army of the sons of Pandu were seen to be shrieking in piteous tones.

'"On seeing that the army was routed, the descendant of the Yadava lineage controlled the supreme chariot and spoke to Partha Bibhatsu. 'O Partha! The moment that you have wished for, has now arrived. O tiger among men! Strike and free yourself from this confusion. O brave one! O Partha! Earlier, in the assembly of kings, in Virata's city and in Sanjaya's presence, you said, "I will slay all the soldiers in the army of the sons of Dhritarashtra, with Bhishma and Drona at the forefront. I will kill them and their followers and all those who fight against me in the battle." O Kounteya! O destroyer of enemies! Do this and make your words come true. O bull among the Bharata lineage! Remember the dharma of kshatriyas and fight.' Thus addressed by Vasudeva, Bibhatsu lowered his face and cast a sideways glance. As if unwillingly, he spoke these words. 'Having killed those who should not be killed, I will obtain the kingdom, with hell as the ultimate objective. Or is it better to suffer the misery of dwelling in the forest? Which will be better for me? Drive the horses towards Bhishma. I will do what you have asked me to. I will bring down the aged and invincible grandfather of the Kurus.' At this, Madhava urged the horses that had the complexion of silver. O king! He took them to the spot where Bhishma was, difficult to look at, like the sun with its rays. On seeing the mighty-armed Partha ready to fight with Bhishma in that battle, Yudhisthira's large army returned again. Bhishma, best of the Kuru lineage, roared repeatedly like a lion. He swiftly showered down arrows on Dhananjaya's chariot. In an instant, because of that great shower of arrows, nothing could be seen of the chariot or the charioteer. However, Vasudeva was without fear. Satvata resorted to patience and goaded the horses, which had been wounded by Bhishma's arrows. Partha grasped his divine bow that roared like the clouds. He used sharp arrows to sever Bhishma's bow and made it fall down. With the bow severed, Kouravya again grasped a giant bow. In only an instant, your father strung the bow, which made a sound like that of the clouds. But in his anger, Arjuna sliced down this second bow too. At this, Shantanu's son praised his dexterity. 'O Partha! Well done. O mighty-armed one! O Kunti's son! Well done.' Having thus addressed him, he grasped another beautiful bow. In that battle, Bhishma released many arrows towards Partha's chariot. Vasudeva displayed supreme skill in handling the horses. He executed circular motions and avoided all those arrows. Wounded by arrows, Bhishma and Partha, tigers among men, looked beautiful. They were like two angry bulls, marked with the signs of horns.

'"Vasudeva saw that Partha was fighting mildly. Bhishma was continuously showering down arrows in the battle. Stationed between the two armies, he was as scorching as the sun. He was killing the best of the best in the army of Pandu's son. Against Yudhishthira's forces, Bhishma was like the destruction at the end of a yuga. The mighty-armed Madhava, the destroyer of enemy heroes, could not tolerate this. O venerable one! He abandoned Partha's horses, which had the complexion of silver. Full of anger, the great yogi descended from the great chariot. The powerful one advanced towards Bhishma, with his arms as weapons. The spirited one had a whip in his hand and roared repeatedly like a lion. The lord of the universe seemed to make the earth shatter with his footsteps. Krishna's eyes were coppery red with anger. The infinitely radiant one wished to kill him. In the great battle, those on your side lost their senses. They saw Madhava advance against Bhishma in that battle, as if he would swallow him up. 'Bhishma has been slain. Bhishma has been slain.' Such lamentations were uttered by the soldiers. All the men were frightened at the sight of Vasudeva advancing. Janardana was dressed in yellow garments. He was dark blue, like a jewel. As he advanced against Bhishma, he was as beautiful as a cloud with a garland of lightning. It was like a lion advancing on an elephant, or the leader of a herd advancing against another bull. The spirited bull among the Yadava lineage roared and advanced. On seeing Pundarikaksha descend on

him in the battle, Bhishma was not frightened. He stretched his great
bow in the encounter and addressed Govinda without any fear in
his heart. 'O Pundarikaksha! Come. O god of the gods! I bow down
before you. O best of the Satvata lineage! Bring me down in this
great battle. O god! O unblemished one! Slain by you in this battle,
I will obtain supreme welfare in this world and in the next world.
O Govinda! In the three worlds, I have obtained great honour in
the battle today.' The mighty-armed Partha ran after Keshava and
embraced him in his two arms. But despite being grasped by Partha,
the lotus-eyed Purushottama Krishna still proceeded with great force,
dragging him along. Partha, the destroyer of enemy heroes, now
grasped Hrishikesha's legs with force and managed to stop him at
the tenth step. His[393] eyes were full of rage and he was sighing like
a serpent. Arjuna, the destroyer of enemy heroes, spoke these words
of distress to him. 'O mighty-armed one! Refrain. You should not do
this. O Keshava! You earlier said that you would not fight in this war.
O Madhava! The world will say that you have uttered a falsehood.
Let the entire burden be on me. I will kill the one who is rigid in his
vows. O Madhava! If it is otherwise in this battle, let there be a curse
on my truth and my good deeds. O destroyer of enemies! I will do
everything so that the end of the foes is ensured. Behold. As I wish,
I will bring down the invincible one who is great in his vows today,
like the full moon at the end of an era.' Madhava heard these words
of the great-souled Phalguna. He did not say anything. But in great
rage, he again ascended onto the chariot.

'"Those two tigers among men were stationed on the chariot.
Bhishma, Shantanu's son, again showered down arrows, like
clouds raining down on a mountain. Your father, Devavrata, took
the lives of the warriors, like the rays of the sun absorb energy
from everything after winter has passed. Just as the Pandavas had
shattered the ranks of the Kurus in battle, your father shattered
the ranks of the Pandava soldiers in battle. The soldiers were slain
and routed. They lost their enterprise and were bereft of their
senses. In that battle, they were incapable of looking at Bhishma.

[393]Krishna's.

Scorching them with his own energy, he was like the midday sun.
They were slain by Bhishma, as if he was Death at the time of the
destruction of a yuga. O great king! The Pandavas were afflicted
with fear and glanced at him. They could not find a protector, like
cattle that had sunk into mire. In the battle, they were like weak
ants afflicted by a strong person. O descendant of the Bharata
lineage! The maharatha was unassailable. He scorched the kings
with his arrows. They were incapable of looking at Bhishma. His
arrows scorched like the rays of the sun. While the soldiers of the
Pandus were routed, the one with the thousand rays[394] began to
set. The soldiers were overcome by fatigue. Their hearts were set
on withdrawing."'

Chapter 963(103)

'Sanjaya said, "While they were still fighting, the sun set. Terrible
twilight set in and the field of battle could no longer be seen.
O descendant of the Bharata lineage! King Yudhishthira saw that
twilight had set in and that his own soldiers were being slaughtered
by Bhishma, the destroyer of enemies. They had discarded their
weapons and, surrounded by the enemy, had begun to run away. In
the battle, maharatha Bhishma was incited by supreme anger. He saw
that the Somakas had been vanquished and that the maharathas were
dispirited. He thought for a short while and gave the instructions for
withdrawal. King Yudhishthira instructed that the soldiers should be
withdrawn. In a similar way, your soldiers were also withdrawn at
the same time. O best of the Kurus! Having withdrawn the soldiers,
the maharathas entered their camps, having been wounded in the
battle. The Pandavas reflected on what should be done vis-à-vis
Bhishma in the battle. Oppressed by Bhishma, they could not find
any peace. In the battle, Bhishma had vanquished the Pandavas,

[394]The sun.

together with the Srinjayas. O descendant of the Bharata lineage! He was worshipped by your sons and praised by them. With the delighted Kurus surrounding him in every direction, he entered his camp. It was night and all the beings lost their senses. Towards the beginning of that terrible night, the Pandavas, the Vrishnis and the invincible Srinjayas sat down to have a consultation. All those immensely powerful ones thought that the time had come to consult about what would be beneficial for them. Those wise ones anxiously consulted to determine what would be best.

'"O king! King Yudhishthira consulted for a long time. He glanced towards Vasudeva and spoke these words. 'O Krishna! Behold the great-souled Bhishma, terrible in his valour. He crushes my soldiers like an elephant amidst a clump of lotuses. We do not even have the enterprise to glance at the great-souled one. He is like an expanding fire that is consuming my soldiers. He is like the terrible and great serpent Takshaka, whose venom is virulent. O Krishna! In the battle, the powerful Bhishma uses sharp weapons. He grasps his bow in the encounter and releases sharp arrows. It is possible to vanquish an angry Yama, the king of the gods with the vajra in his hand, Varuna with his noose and the lord of riches with his club. But if he is enraged, it is impossible to defeat Bhishma in a great battle. O Krishna! It is because of this reason that I am immersed in an ocean of grief. Having confronted Bhishma in the battle, I am suffering from weakness of intelligence. O invincible one! I will go to the forest. It is beneficial that I should go there. O Krishna! I have no desire to fight. Bhishma always kills us. He is like a flaming fire, towards which insects are attracted. I will obtain the same result of death by daring to fight with Bhishma. O Varshneya! Despite being valorous, for the sake of the kingdom, I am being conveyed towards destruction. My brave brothers are sorely afflicted through arrows. It is because of me, and because of affection towards their brother, that they were dislodged from the kingdom. O Madhusudana! Krishna[395] was oppressed because of what I had done. I think that being alive has great value. But it is now extremely difficult to remain alive. If

---

[395]Krishnaa, Droupadi.

I remain alive today, I will spend the remaining part[396] in pursuing supreme dharma. O Keshava! If you show your favours towards me and towards my brothers, tell me what I should do. O Keshava! But this should be without contravening my own dharma.' Krishna heard these words and their detailed description.

"'Overcome by compassion, he comforted Yudhishthira and replied, 'O Dharma's son! You should not grieve. You are devoted to the truth. Your brave brothers are invincible and are the destroyers of enemies. Arjuna and Bhimasena are as energetic as Vayu and Agni. Madri's two sons are as valorous as the lord of the thirty gods. O Pandava! For the sake of the good relationship that exists between us, employ me to fight with Bhishma. O king! Instructed by you, there is nothing I will not do in this great battle. While the sons of Dhritarashtra look on, if Phalguna does not desire it, I will challenge Bhishma, the bull among men, in this battle and kill him. O Pandava! If you see that Bhishma's death will ensure that you win the kingdom, alone on a chariot, I will slay the aged grandfather of the Kurus today. O king! Witness my valour in this battle, like that of the great Indra. I will use great weapons and bring him down from his chariot. There is no doubt that someone who is an enemy to the sons of Pandu is my foe too. My welfare is your welfare. All that is mine is yours. Your brother is my friend, relative[397] and disciple. O lord of the earth! For Arjuna's sake, I can slice off and give my own flesh. This tiger among men will also lay down his life for my sake. O father![398] This is our understanding, that we will protect each other. O Indra among kings! Employ me, so that I can be your protector. In Upaplavya, Partha earlier took an oath before many people. "I will slay Gangeya." I should protect the oath that the intelligent Partha took. If Partha gives me permission, there is no doubt that I should perform this task. Or let Phalguna bear this limited burden in battle. Let him kill Bhishma, the destroyer of enemy cities, in battle. If Partha stirs himself, there is nothing that he cannot accomplish in battle, even if the thirty gods

---

[396]Of the life.
[397]Referring to the matrimonial alliance through Subhadra.
[398]The word used is tata.

have raised their arms against him, together with the daityas and the danavas. O lord of men! They can be killed by Arjuna in battle, not to speak of Bhishma. Bhishma, Shantanu's immensely valorous son, has now become perverse and has lost his intelligence. He will not live for long. He no longer understands what his duty is.'

'"Yudhishthira replied, 'O mighty-armed one! O Madhava! It is exactly as you have spoken. All of them together are not capable of withstanding your force. O tiger among men! With an immensely strong one like you as my protector, I am always certain of obtaining everything that I desire. O supreme among victorious ones! With Govinda as a protector, I can vanquish the gods, together with Indra, in battle, not to speak of Bhishma in this great battle. But I cannot make your words come false for the sake of glorifying my own objective. O Madhava! As you had promised, help us, but without taking part in the fight. O Madhava! Bhishma had come to an agreement with me. "For your sake, I will proffer advice. But I will never fight for you. O lord! I tell you truthfully that I will fight for Duryodhana's cause." O Madhava! He may provide counsel, as to how we can obtain the kingdom. Let all of us go to Devavrata, to ask him about the means whereby he may be killed. O Madhusudana! Together with you, let all of us go and ask him. O supreme among men! Together with you, let all of us quickly go to Bhishma. O Varshneya! If this seems desirable to you, let us go and seek Kourava's counsel. O Janardana! He will offer us beneficial and truthful advice. O Krishna! In this battle, let us do what he asks us to do. The one who is rigid in his vows will give us counsel and victory. We lost our father when we were children and he reared us. O Madhava! This is the aged grandfather whom I wish to kill. He is the father of our beloved father. Shame on the livelihood of kshatriyas.'"

'Sanjaya said, "O great king! On hearing these words, Varshneya spoke to the descendant of the Kuru lineage. 'O mighty-armed one! I have always liked whatever you have said. Devavrata Bhishma is accomplished. He can burn down with his glance. Let us go to the one who is the son of the one who goes to the ocean[399] to ask about

---

[399]Ganga goes to the ocean.

the means of his death. He will certainly speak the truth, especially
if he is asked by you. Let us go there, to ask the grandfather of the
Kurus.' 'O Madhava! Let us bow down our heads and go and ask him
for counsel. He will offer us counsel about how we can fight with the
enemy.'[400] O Pandu's elder brother! Having thus consulted, all the
brave Pandavas, together with the valiant Vasudeva, departed. They
discarded their weapons and armour and proceeded to Bhishma's
residence. They entered and bowed their heads in obeisance before
Bhishma. O great king! O bull among the Bharata lineage! The
Pandavas worshipped him. They lowered their heads and sought
Bhishma's protection. The mighty-armed Bhishma, the grandfather
of the Kurus, told them, 'O Varshneya! Welcome. O Dhananjaya!
Welcome. O Dharma's son! O Bhima! O twins! Welcome. What is
the task that I can accomplish for you now? What will extend your
pleasure? Even if it should prove to be extremely difficult, I will do it
with all my heart.' With affection, Gangeya repeatedly spoke in this
way. Yudhishthira, Dharma's son, was miserable in his soul and spoke
these words. 'O one who is learned in dharma! How will we obtain
victory and the kingdom? How can this destruction of subjects be
stopped? O lord! Tell us this. You yourself tell us the means whereby
we can bring about your own death. O king! How will we be able
to withstand you in battle? O grandfather of the Kurus! You do not
exhibit the slightest bit of weakness. In the battle, your bow is always
seen, whirling around in a circle. No one can distinguish when you
affix an arrow, aim or stretch your bow. O mighty-armed one! We
see you stationed on your chariot, like the sun. O slayer of enemy
heroes! You slaughter men, horses, chariots and elephants. O bull
among the Bharata lineage! Which man is capable of killing you?
O supreme among men! You bring down a great shower of arrows.
Because of you, my large army is decaying from one day to another.
How can we defeat you in battle? How can the kingdom be ours?
How can there be peace among my soldiers? O grandfather! Tell
us this.' O Pandu's elder brother! Shantanu's son then spoke these
words to Pandava. 'O Kounteya! As long as I am alive in battle, your

---

[400]Though not explicitly stated, this is Yudhishthira speaking now.

prosperity will never be seen. I tell you this truthfully. After you have vanquished me in battle, your victory over the Kouravas is certain. If you wish to obtain victory in this battle, strike me down quickly. O Partha! You have my permission to happily strike at me. I think it is good for you that you know my nature.[401] After I have been killed, everyone else will be killed. Therefore, do as I am asking you to.'

'"Yudhishthira said, 'Tell us the means whereby we may defeat you in battle. When you are enraged in battle, you are like Yama with a staff in his hand. It is possible to defeat the wielder of the vajra, or Varuna, or Yama. But you are incapable of being defeated in battle, even by the gods and the asuras, together with Indra.'

'"Bhishma replied, 'O mighty-armed one! O Pandava! What you have said is true. I am incapable of being defeated in battle, even by the gods and the asuras, together with Indra. But this is when I grasp my weapons in battle and grasp my supreme bow. O king! But when I cast aside my weapons, the maharathas can kill me in battle. I do not wish to fight with someone who has cast his weapons aside, someone who has fallen down, someone whose armour and standard have been dislodged, someone who is running away, someone who is frightened, someone who solicits sanctuary, someone who is a woman, someone who bears the name of a woman, someone who is disabled, someone who only has one son, someone who does not have a son and someone who is difficult to look at. O Partha! Hear about the vow that I took a long time ago. I will never fight if I see an inauspicious sign on the standard. O king! This son of Drupada is a maharatha in your army. Shikhandi is a brave and victorious one who always desires to fight. But he was a woman earlier. He became a man later. All of you know everything about how this came about. In the battle, let the brave Arjuna place Shikhandi ahead of him. Let the armoured one attack me with sharp arrows. I will see an inauspicious sign on the standard then, especially that of someone who was earlier a woman. Even if I have grasped my bow, I will never strike him then. O bull among the Bharata lineage! Let Pandava Dhananjaya then

---

[401]It is not immediately obvious what this means. It probably means that everyone knows that Bhishma will not fight with Shikhandi.

strike me from every side with his arrows. Truly, with the exception of the immensely fortunate Krishna and Pandava Dhananjaya, I do not see anyone in the worlds who is capable of killing me. Therefore, placing him[402] at the front, let Bibhatsu strive his utmost to bring me down. Victory will be obtained. O Kounteya! Act in accordance with the words I have spoken. You will then be able to defeat the assembled sons of Dhritarashtra in the battle.'"

'Sanjaya said, "Having taken his permission and having shown their respects to the great-souled Bhishma, the grandfather of the Kurus, the Parthas then returned to their own camp. Gangeya prepared himself for his departure to the next world. Arjuna was tormented by grief and he was overcome with shame. He said, 'O Madhava! How can I fight with my senior, the aged one of the lineage? He is accomplished in wisdom and intelligence. How can I fight with the grandfather in a battle? O Vasudeva! As a child, I used to play with the great-minded one. O Gada's elder brother! I used to sully the great-souled one's garments with the dust on my body, when I used to climb onto his lap as a child. He is the father of my father, the great-souled Pandu. "O descendant of the Bharata lineage! I am not your father, but your father's father." These are the words he used to tell me in my childhood. How can he be killed by me now? I wish that my soldiers are killed. I cannot fight with that great-souled one. O Krishna! Which do you think is superior, victory or death?' Krishna replied, 'O Jishnu! Earlier, you have promised to kill Bhishma in the battle. O Partha! Established in the dharma of kshatriyas, how can you not kill him now? O Partha! Bring him down from his chariot, like a tree that has been struck by lightning. Without killing Gangeya in battle, victory cannot be obtained. This has been determined by destiny earlier. The killing has been ordained by destiny. Bhishma's killer is an earlier Indra.[403] It cannot but be otherwise. O

[402]Shikhandi.

[403]Indra is a title and there have been earlier Indras. The present one is Purandara. But having said this, it is difficult to make sense of the text. No earlier Indra is associated with any of the Bhishma stories. It is possible that this is an oblique reference to Arjuna being Indra's son. In all probability, this is a typo, since non-critical versions don't have this expression.

invincible one! Bhishma is like Death with a gaping mouth. No one other than you is capable of fighting with him, not even the wielder of the vajra himself. O mighty-armed one! Kill Bhishma. Listen to these words of mine. This is what the immensely intelligent Brihaspati told Shakra in earlier times. "O Shakra! One must kill someone who possesses all the qualities, if he comes as an assassin, or if he arrives to kill." O Dhananjaya! This is the eternal dharma in which kshatriyas have been established. They must fight, protect and perform sacrifices, without any malice.' Arjuna replied, 'O Krishna! It is certain that Shikhandi will be the cause of Bhishma's death. As soon as he sees Panchala, Bhishma will withdraw. Therefore, we will place Shikhandi ahead of all of us. It is my view that this is the means for bringing about Gangeya's downfall. I will restrain the other great archers with my arrows. Shikhandi will fight with Bhishma, the best of warriors. I have heard from the chief of the Kurus that he will not kill Shikhandi. He was born as a maiden earlier and became a man later.' Having decided this, the Pandavas, together with Madhava, retired to their own beds. The bulls among men were happy."'

Chapter 964(104)

'Dhritarashtra asked, "O Sanjaya! How did Shikhandi fight with Gangeya in that battle? How did Bhishma advance against the Pandavas? Tell me this."

'Sanjaya replied, "The morning was clear and it was time for the sun to rise. Many drums, kettledrums and tambourines were sounded. Conch shells with the complexion of curds were blown in every direction. The Pandava warriors placed Shikhandi at the forefront and marched out. O great king! They constructed a vyuha that was capable of destroying all enemies. O lord of the earth! Shikhandi was stationed at the forefront of all the soldiers. Bhimasena and Dhananjaya protected his wheels. Droupadi's sons and Subhadra's valiant son were behind him. Satyaki and maharatha Chekitana protected them. Dhrishtadyumna was behind them, protected by the Panchalas. O bull among the Bharata lineage! The lord, King Yudhishthira, marched out, together with the twins, roaring like lions. Virata was behind him, surrounded by his soldiers. O great king! Drupada advanced behind him. O descendant of the Bharata lineage! The five brothers from Kekaya and the valiant Dhrishtaketu protected the Pandu soldiers from the rear. The Pandavas arranged the large army of soldiers in the form of this vyuha. They advanced in the battle, ready to give up their lives. O king! In that fashion, the Kurus placed the immensely strong Bhishma at the forefront of all their soldiers and advanced against the Pandavas. He was protected by your invincible and extremely strong sons. The great archer, Drona, was behind them, together with his maharatha son. Bhagadatta was behind him, surrounded by a large army of elephants. Kripa and Kritavarma followed Bhagadatta. Sudakshina, the powerful king of Kamboja, was behind them, as were Jayatsena from Magadha, Soubala and Brihadbala. There were many other great archers and kings, with Susharma at the forefront. O descendant of the Bharata lineage! They protected your army's rear. From one day to another, Bhishma, Shantanu's son, created a different kind of vyuha for the battle—sometimes it was asura, sometimes it was pishacha, sometimes it was rakshasa.

'"O descendant of the Bharata lineage! The battle between those on your side and those of the enemy commenced. O king! They struck each other and extended Yama's kingdom. The Parthas, with Arjuna at their head, placed Shikhandi at the forefront. They advanced against Bhishma in the battle and released many kinds of arrows. O descendant of the Bharata lineage! Those on your side were oppressed by Bhima's arrows. They were covered in blood and left for the next world. Nakula, Sahadeva and maharatha Satyaki advanced against your soldiers and afflicted them with energy. O bull among the Bharata lineage! Those on your side were being slain in that battle. They were incapable of resisting the great army of the Pandavas. Your soldiers were slaughtered in every direction. O king! They were oppressed by those maharathas and were seen to run away in different directions. O bull among the Bharata lineage! Those on

your side could not find a protector. They were slaughtered by the
sharp arrows of the Pandavas, together with the Srinjayas."

'Dhritarashtra said, "On seeing that the army was thus oppressed
by the Parthas, what did the valiant Bhishma do, when he became
enraged in that battle? O Sanjaya! How did the scorcher of enemies
advance against the Pandavas in battle? O Sanjaya! How did he kill
the brave Somakas? Tell me this."

'Sanjaya replied, "O great king! When the soldiers of your sons
were oppressed by the Pandavas and the Srinjayas, I will tell you what
the grandfather did. O Pandu's elder brother! The brave Pandavas
were delighted. They advanced and began to slaughter your son's
army. O Indra among men! There was a destruction of men, elephants
and horses. Bhishma could not tolerate that the enemy was slaying
the soldiers in the battle. The great archer attacked the Pandavas, the
Panchalas and the Srinjayas. He was invincible and was prepared to
give up his own life. O king! He attacked the five supreme maharathas
among the Pandavas.[404] These were the ones who were exerting
themselves in the battle and he checked them with his arrows. He
used iron arrows, *vatsadantas*[405] and sharp anjalikas. He was angry
and killed many elephants and horses in that battle. O king! That
bull among men brought down charioteers from their chariots,
horse-riders from the backs of horses, assembled foot soldiers and
elephant-riders from the backs of elephants. He terrified the enemy.
In that battle, the maharatha Pandavas quickly attacked Bhishma
together, like the wielder of the vajra assailed by asuras. He released
sharp arrows that were like Shakra's vajra to the touch. He was seen
in every direction, having assumed a terrible form. As he fought in
that battle, his bow was always seen whirling around in a circular
motion, like Shakra's giant bow. O lord of the earth! On witnessing
his deeds in that battle, your sons were filled with supreme wonder
and honoured the grandfather. The Parthas were dispirited at the way
your brave father was fighting in the battle. They glanced towards

[404]It is not clear which of the five are meant, unless it means the five Pandava
brothers.
[405]A vatsadanta is an arrow that has a head like the tooth of a calf.

him, like the immortals towards Viprachitti. They could not resist the one who was like death with a gaping mouth.

'"On the tenth day of the battle, he began to consume Shikhandi's array of chariots with his sharp arrows, like the one with the black trails[406] burns a forest. Shikhandi pierced him between the breasts with three arrows. Bhishma was like an angry and virulent serpent, like the Destroyer who had been created by Death. Having been thus severely pierced, he glanced towards Shikhandi. He was enraged, but was unwilling.[407] He smiled and said, 'Whether you desire it or not, I will never fight with you. You are still the Shikhandini[408] that the creator made.' On hearing these words, Shikhandi became senseless with anger. In the battle, he licked the corners of his mouth and spoke to Bhishma. 'O mighty-armed one! I know you to be the destroyer of the kshatriyas. I have heard about your battle with Jamadagni's son. I have also heard many things about your divine powers. Knowing of your prowess, I wish to fight with you today. O supreme among men! I wish to do what is pleasant for the Pandavas and for my own self. O supreme among men! I wish to fight against you in the battle today. It is certain that I will kill you. I am swearing this truthfully, in front of you. Having heard these words of mine, do what you must do. Whether you wish to strike me or whether you do not, you will not escape with your life. O Bhishma! O victorious one! Take a final look at this world.' O king! Having said this, he pierced Bhishma with five straight-tufted arrows, having already wounded him with the arrows of his words. On hearing his words, Savyasachi, the scorcher of enemies, thought that the time had come and incited Shikhandi. 'I will now fight behind you and destroy the enemy with my arrows. Ignited with rage, attack Bhishma, whose valour is terrible. The immensely strong one will not be able to cause you any pain in the battle. O brave one! O mighty-armed one! Therefore, attack Bhishma. O venerable one! If you return without killing Bhishma in battle, the worlds will look at you, and at me, with disrespect. O brave one!

[406]A fire.
[407]Unwilling to fight.
[408]That is, the lady.

Exert yourself in this great battle so that we are not ridiculed. Make endeavours in the battle and repulse the grandfather. Drona, Drona's son, Kripa, Suyodhana, Chitrasena, Vikarna, Saindhava Jayadratha, Vinda and Anuvinda from Avanti, Sudakshina from Kamboja, the brave Bhagadatta, the maharatha from Magadha, Somadatta's son, the rakshasa who is Rishyashringa's son and is brave in battle, the king of Trigarta and all the other maharathas—I will restrain them in battle, like the shoreline holds back the dwelling place of makaras. I will hold back in battle all the Kurus, together with their soldiers. You strive against the grandfather.'"

Chapter 965(105)

'Dhritarashtra asked, "How did Panchala Shikhandi attack the grandfather Gangeya, when he was enraged in battle? He has dharma in his soul and is rigid in his vows. When Shikhandi raised his weapons, who protected the army of the Pandavas? Those maharathas desired victory and acted swiftly when it was the time to act fast. How did the immensely valorous Bhishma, Shantanu's son, fight on the tenth day with the Pandavas and the Srinjayas? I cannot tolerate the thought of Bhishma being overthrown by Shikhandi in battle. Was his[409] chariot shattered? Did his bow break into fragments?"

'Sanjaya said, "O bull among the Bharata lineage! When he fought in that battle, Bhishma's bow was not shattered. Nor was his chariot broken. He used straight-tufted arrows to kill the enemies in that encounter. O king! Many hundred and thousand maharathas on your side and large numbers of chariots, elephants and horses, with excellent harnesses, advanced to do battle, placing the grandfather at the forefront. O Kouravya! The victorious one stuck to his vow. Bhishma continuously slaughtered the soldiers of

[409]Bhishma's.

the Parthas. The great archer fought and killed the enemy with his arrows. All the Panchalas, together with the Pandavas, could not resist him. When the tenth day arrived, he scorched the army of the enemy. He released sharp arrows in hundreds and thousands. O Pandu's elder brother! The Pandavas were incapable of defeating Bhishma, the great archer, in battle. He was like Yama with a noose in his hand. O great king! Savyasachi, the scorcher of enemies and the one who was never defeated, arrived at the spot, causing terror among all the rathas. He roared like a lion. He repeatedly drew his bow and released a shower of arrows. Partha roamed around on the field of battle, like Death. O bull among the Bharata lineage! Those on your side were frightened at the sound. O king! They fled in great fear, like deer because of a lion. On witnessing that Partha was victorious and that your soldiers were oppressed by him, Duryodhana was greatly tormented and spoke to Bhishma. 'O father![410] This son of Pandu is borne by white horses and has Krishna as a charioteer. He is scorching all those on my side, like the one with the black trails in a forest. O Gangeya! Behold. The soldiers are running away in every direction. O foremost among warriors! They are being slaughtered and driven away by Pandava in this battle. They are like a herd of cattle being driven by a herdsman in the forest. O scorcher of enemies! My soldiers are being driven away. They are being shattered by Dhananjaya's arrows. They are running away, here and there. It is like a herdsman driving away a herd of cattle in the forest. O scorcher of enemies! My soldiers are being driven away in that fashion. They are being shattered through Dhananjaya's arrows and are fleeing in different directions. The invincible Bhima is driving away my soldiers. Satyaki, Chekitana, the Pandavas who are Madri's sons and the valiant Abhimanyu are scorching my army. The brave Dhrishtadyumna and rakshasa Ghatotkacha, immensely strong, are impetuously driving away my soldiers. In every way, my soldiers are being slaughtered by those immensely strong ones. O descendant of the Bharata lineage! In making them remain in this battle, I do not see any succour other

[410]The word used is tata.

than you, tiger among men and like the gods in your valour. You are my refuge in this oppression. You should swiftly counter them.' O great king! Thus addressed, your father, Devavrata, thought for some time and made up his mind.

'"Shantanu's son consoled your son. 'O Duryodhana! O lord of the earth! Be patient and listen to what I have to say to you. O immensely strong one! In earlier times, I had taken a pledge that I would kill ten thousand great-souled kshatriyas every day and would then return from the battle. O bull among the Bharata lineage! For the sake of your welfare, I have carried out the pledge I made to you. I will perform an even greater task in this great battle today. I will sleep after being slain, or I will kill the Pandavas today. O tiger among men! I will today free myself from the great debt I owe you. O king! You offered me food as my master. I will be slain at the forefront of the army.' Having spoken these words, the best of the Bharata lineage scattered arrows among the kshatriyas. The invincible one attacked the Pandava army. O bull among the Bharata lineage! Gangeya stationed himself in the midst of the army, like an angry and virulent serpent, and the Pandavas surrounded him. On the tenth day, he exhibited his strength. O king! The descendant of the Kuru lineage killed hundreds and thousands. He sucked out the energy from the best of the Panchalas and the immensely strong princes, like the sun sucking up water with its rays. O great king! The spirited one killed ten thousand elephants and then killed ten thousand horses, with their riders. The best of men killed two hundred thousand foot soldiers. Bhishma was dazzling in that battle, like a flame without smoke. No one among the Pandaveyas was capable of looking at him. He was like the scorching sun, when it is on its northern path. But though they were oppressed, the Pandaveyas, great archers, together with the maharatha Srinjayas, attacked and sought to kill Bhishma. There were many who fought with Bhishma, Shantanu's son, then. The mighty-armed one looked like a mountain that was occupied by clouds. Your sons surrounded Gangeya from every direction, together with a large army, and the battle raged on."'

Chapter 966(106)

'Sanjaya said, "O king! Arjuna then witnessed Bhishma's valour in battle. He told Shikhandi, 'Advance towards the grandfather. You should not exhibit the slightest fear of Bhishma today. I will bring down the supreme of rathas with sharp arrows.' O bull among the Bharata lineage! Having been thus addressed by Partha and having heard what Partha had said, Shikhandi attacked Gangeya. O king! Having heard what Partha had said, Dhrishtadyumna, and the maharatha who was Subhadra's son, cheerfully attacked Bhishma. The aged Virata and Drupada and the armoured Kuntibhoja attacked Bhishma, while your son looked on. O lord of the earth! Nakula, Sahadeva, the valorous Dharmaraja and all the other soldiers attacked Gangeya, having heard what Partha had said. The maharathas on your side united and counter-attacked, according to their capacity and according to their endeavour. Listen. I will describe it. O great king! Chitrasena attacked Chekitana, who was advancing in the battle against Bhishma, like a young tiger attacks a bull. O great king! In the encounter, Dhrishtadyumna had swiftly approached Bhishma and Kritavarma repulsed him. Bhimasena was enraged and wished to kill Bhishma. O great king! Somadatta's son quickly countered him. The brave Nakula released many arrows. Wishing to ensure that Bhishma remained alive, Vikarna repulsed these. Sahadeva was advancing towards Bhishma's chariot. In the battle, Sharadvata Kripa angrily countered him. On seeing that Bhimasena's immensely strong son, the rakshasa who performed cruel deeds, wished to kill Bhishma, Durmukha powerfully attacked him. In the encounter, Rishyashringa's son angrily repulsed Satyaki. O great king! Abhimanyu was advancing towards Bhishma's chariot. O great king! Sudakshina of Kamboja repulsed him. The aged Virata and Drupada, the destroyers of enemies, had united. O descendant of the Bharata lineage! Ashvatthama was enraged and repulsed them. The eldest of Pandu's sons wished to kill Bhishma. Bharadvaja's son made efforts in the battle to counter Dharma's son. Arjuna was hastening in the battle, with Shikhandi at the forefront. O great king! He was

approaching Bhishma, scorching the ten directions. Duhshasana, the
great archer, countered him in the battle. There were other Pandava
maharathas who were advancing towards Bhishma in the battle.
Other warriors on your side countered their advance.

"'Dhrishtadyumna forcefully advanced against the immensely
strong Bhishma alone. He repeatedly addressed the soldiers. 'This
Arjuna, the descendant of the Kuru lineage, is advancing against
Bhishma in battle. Advance. Do not be frightened. Bhishma will
not be able to touch you. When Arjuna fights in a battle, even
Vasava loses interest, not to speak of Bhishma. The brave one has
lost his spirits in the battle. He has but a short time to live.' On
hearing the words of their commander, the Pandava maharathas
cheerfully advanced towards Gangeya's chariot. The bulls among
men on your side cheerfully resisted them, as they advanced in that
battle, like a powerful storm. O great king! Maharatha Duhshasana
abandoned his fear. He wished to ensure that Bhishma remained alive
and attacked Dhananjaya. In that encounter, the brave Pandavas
advanced towards Gangeya's chariot and towards your maharatha
sons. O lord of the earth! We witnessed a wonderful and colourful
incident. Having reached Duhshasana's chariot, Partha was checked.
He was restrained, like the shoreline checks the turbulent and great
ocean. The angry Pandava was repulsed by your son. O descendant
of the Bharata lineage! Both of them were the best of rathas and
were invincible. O descendant of the Bharata lineage! Both of them
were radiant and were as handsome as the moon or the sun. Both of
them were overcome with anger and wished to kill each other. They
clashed in that great battle, like Maya and Shakra in earlier times.
O great king! Duhshasana wounded Pandava with three arrows and
Vasudeva with twenty. On seeing that Varshneya was wounded,
Arjuna was overcome with rage. He pierced Duhshasana with one
hundred iron arrows. In the encounter, they penetrated his armour
and drank his blood. O best of the Bharata lineage! Duhshasana was
angered at this. He pierced Partha in the forehead with five straight-
tufted arrows. O great king! With those arrows on his forehead, the
supreme of Pandavas was radiant, like Meru's lofty peaks. Pierced by
your archer son in the battle, Partha, the great archer, looked like a

blossoming kimshuka tree. Thus wounded, Pandava became angry. Extremely angry, he attacked Duhshasana, like Rahu attacking the moon on the night of the new moon or full moon. O lord of the earth! Your son was afflicted by the powerful one. In the battle, he pierced Partha with arrows that were sharpened on stone and tufted with the feathers of herons. The spirited and valorous Partha sliced down his bow. After this, he struck your son with nine arrows. Stationing himself in front of Bhishma, he[411] grasped another bow and shot twenty-five arrows at Arjuna's chest and arms. O great king! At this, Pandava, the destroyer of enemies, became angry. He released many arrows that were like Yama's staff. But though they were released by Partha, your son sliced them down before they could reach him. It was wonderful. Your son pierced Partha with sharp arrows. Partha became wrathful in that battle and fixed arrows to his bow. They were gold-tufted and sharpened on stone and he released them in the encounter. O great king! These penentrated the great-souled one's body, like swans entering a pond. O great king! O descendant of the Bharata lineage! Your son was afflicted by the great-souled Pandava. He avoided Partha in the battle and swiftly found refuge in Bhishma's chariot. He seemed to be submerged in fathomless waters and Bhishma was like an island. O lord of the earth! Your son was brave and valiant. When he regained consciousness, he again restrained Partha with extremely sharp arrows, like Vritra against Purandara. Though he was pierced by the immensely valorous one, Arjuna was not distressed."'

Chapter 967(107)

'Sanjaya said, "The armoured Satyaki raised his weapons against Bhishma in the battle. The great archer who was Rishyashringa's son repulsed him in the encounter. O king! O descendant of the

---

[411]Duhshasana.

Bharata lineage! Madhava[412] was enraged in the battle and, as if he was smiling, pierced the rakshasa with nine arrows. O king! O Indra among kings! The enraged rakshasa wounded Madhava, the bull among the Shini lineage, with sharp arrows. Madhava, Shini's descendant and the destroyer of enemy heroes, became wrathful in the battle and released a shower of arrows towards the rakshasa. The rakshasa roared like a lion and pierced Satyaki, the mighty-armed one for whom truth was his valour, with sharp arrows. In the battle, Madhava was severely wounded by the rakshasa. But the spirited one resorted to his patience. He laughed and roared. In the encounter, the angry Bhagadatta wounded Madhava with sharp arrows, like a mighty elephant being goaded. Shini's descendant, supreme among rathas, gave up the encounter with the rakshasa. He released straight-tufted arrows towards Pragjyotisha. The king of Pragjyotisha, skilled in the use of his hands, grasped a sharp and broad-headed arrow and sliced down Madhava's giant bow. The destroyer of enemy heroes grasped another one that was even more powerful. In the encounter, he angrily pierced Bhagadatta with sharp arrows. The great archer was pierced and repeatedly licked the corners of his mouth. He grasped a firm and iron javelin that was decorated with gold and lapis lazuli. It was as terrible as Yama's staff and he hurled this towards Satyaki. It was hurled through the force of his arms. O king! On seeing it suddenly descend in the battle, Satyaki severed it into three fragments with his arrows. It fell down on the ground, like a giant meteor that has lost its brilliance. O lord of the earth! On seeing that the javelin had been destroyed, your son[413] surrounded Madhava with a large number of chariots. On seeing that maharatha Varshneya had been surrounded, Duryodhana was extremely happy and spoke to all his brothers. 'O Kouravas! Act so that the warrior Satyaki may not escape with his life. Go there with a large number of chariots. If he is killed, I think that the great army of the Pandavas will also be slain.' The maharathas accepted his words and agreed to do this. With Bhishma at the forefront, they began to fight with Shini's descendant.

---

[412]Satyaki.
[413]Duryodhana.

'"Abhimanyu was advancing against Bhishma in the battle. The powerful king of Kamboja restrained him in the encounter. Arjuna's son pierced the king with straight-tufted arrows. O king! He again pierced the king with sixty-four arrows. Wishing to see that Bhishma remained alive, in that encounter, Sudakshina pierced Krishna's son with nine arrows and his charioteer with nine. When those two valorous ones clashed, the encounter was wonderful and great. Shikhandi, the scorcher of enemies, attacked Gangeya. Virata and Drupada, the aged maharathas, rushed forward to battle Bhishma, resisting that large army. Ashvatthama, supreme among rathas, became angry and repulsed them. O descendant of the Bharata lineage! A battle commenced between them. O king! O scorcher of enemies! Virata used ten broad-headed arrows to strike Drona's son, the great archer who was the ornament of any battle. Drupada also used three sharp arrows to pierce him. The preceptor's son stationed himself in front of Bhishma. As the aged Virata and Drupada advanced towards Bhishma, Ashvatthama pierced them with ten arrows. We witnessed the extraordinary and great conduct of those aged ones. In the battle, they repulsed the terrible arrows shot by Drona's son. Sharadvata Kripa rushed against the advancing Sahadeva, like an angry elephant attacks another elephant in the forest. O king! In that battle, maharatha Kripa quickly struck Madri's son with seventy arrows decorated in gold. But Madri's son used his arrows to slice down his bow into two. Once the bow had been severed, he pierced him with nine arrows. Wishing to ensure that Bhishma remained alive, he[414] grasped another bow that was capable of bearing a great burden. In anger, but cheerfully, he struck Madri's son in that battle with ten sharp arrows. O king! Desiring to kill Bhishma, Pandava was angry and struck back the intolerant one. The battle that raged was terrible and fearful. Wishing to ensure that Bhishma remained alive, Vikarna, the scorcher of enemies, angrily pierced Nakula in that battle with sixty arrows. Nakula was severely wounded by your archer son. But he pierced Vikarna back with seventy-seven arrows that had been sharpened on stone. For the sake of Bhishma, those

[414]Kripa.

scorchers of enemies and tigers among men bravely fought against each other, like two bulls fighting in a pen.

'"Ghatotkacha was engaged in fighting, slaying your soldiers. For Bhishma's sake, your valiant son, Durmukha, confronted him in battle. O king! But Hidimba's son was enraged. He struck Durmukha, the scorcher of enemies, in the chest with ninety sharp arrows. The brave Durmukha used sixty arrows that were crafted well at the tip to pierce Bhimasena's son and in the forefront of the battle, roared in great delight. Wishing to kill Bhishma, Dhrishtadyumna advanced in the battle. But wishing to ensure that Bhishma remained alive, Hardikya countered him. Varshneya struck the brave Parshata with five iron arrows and again quickly struck him between the breasts with fifty arrows.[415] O king! Parshata struck Hardikya with nine sharp arrows that were decorated with the feathers of herons. For Bhishma's sake, they severely confronted each other in that great battle. They encountered each other like Vritra and the great Indra. The immensely strong Bhimasena advanced against Bhishma. In the battle, Somadatta's son used an extremely sharp and gold-tufted iron arrow to strike Bhima between the breasts. O supreme among kings! With that stuck to his chest, the powerful Bhimasena looked like Krouncha in earlier times, struck by Skanda's javelin.[416] They angrily attacked each other in that battle and repeatedly released arrows that were like the sun and had been polished by artisans. Wishing to kill Bhishma, Bhima fought with the maharatha who was Somadatta's son. Wishing to ensure Bhishma's victory, Somadatta's son fought with Pandava. They performed tasks and out-performed each other in that battle. O great king! Surrounded by a large army, Yudhishthira advanced towards Bhishma and was countered by Bharadvaja's son. The roar of Drona's chariot was like the sound of the clouds. O king! O venerable one! On hearing it, the Prabhadrakas trembled. O king! In the battle, the great army of Pandu's son was checked by Drona and could not move a single step. O lord

---

[415]In this context, Varshneya means Hardikya Kritavarma, descended from the Vrishni lineage, while Parshata means Dhrishtadyumna.

[416]In fighting against the demon Taraka, Skanda (Kartikeya) hurled a javelin at Mount Krouncha, within which, Taraka was hiding.

of men! Chekitana was enraged in the battle and advanced towards Bhishma. But your son, Chitrasena, repulsed the one who was angry in form. O descendant of the Bharata lineage! For Bhishma's sake, the brave maharatha Chitrasena fought against Chekitana to his utmost capacity. Chekitana also fought against Chitrasena and the battle between the valiant ones was extraordinary. Arjuna was restrained in many different kinds of ways. But he repulsed your son[417] and crushed his soldiers. O descendant of the Bharata lineage! Duhshasana resisted Partha to his utmost capacity, having determined that Bhishma could not be killed. The soldiers of your son were slaughtered in the battle. O descendant of the Bharata lineage! They were agitated there by the best of the rathas.'"[418]

Chapter 968(108)

'Sanjaya said, "The brave and great archer was like a crazy elephant in his valour. He grasped a giant bow that was capable of restraining a crazy elephant. He brandished that best of bows and drove away the maharathas. The maharatha slaughtered the army of the Pandaveyas. The valiant one was skilled in reading portents and glanced in every direction. Having tormented the soldiers, Drona addressed his son. 'O son! This is the day when maharatha Partha will try his utmost to slay Bhishma in battle. My arrows are rising up and my bow is outstretched. But when I try to fix my weapons, they are falling off. My mind is without cheer. The peaceful directions have turned terrible and birds and animals are wandering around. Inferior vultures are swooping down towards the army of the Bharatas. The sun has lost its splendour and all the directions have turned red. The earth seems to be suffering and the mounts seem to have been destroyed. Herons, vultures and cranes are repeatedly

[417]This seems to be a reference to Duhshasana.
[418]On the Pandava side.

shrieking. Jackals are howling in inauspicious tones and this signifies a great calamity. Giant meteors are falling down from the centre of the sun's disc. The headless torso of parigha is stationed, covering the sun.[419] The discs of the sun and the moon have become terrible. They signify a terrible danger, pertaining to the mangling of the bodies of kings. In the temples of the Indra among the Kouravas, the gods are trembling, laughing, dancing and weeping. The planets are circling inauspiciously, keeping the moon to the left. O illustrious one! The moon is rising with its crescent inverted. The bodies of the kings seem to be destroyed. Though they are armoured, the soldiers of the sons of Dhritarashtra are no longer radiant. A great sound has arisen amidst both the armies, because of Panchajanya's roar and Gandiva's sound. It is certain that Bibhatsu will use supreme weapons in this battle. He will avoid all the others in the encounter and advance towards the grandfather. The pores in my body are contracting. My mind is weakening. O mighty-armed one! I am thinking about the encounter between Bhishma and Arjuna. Partha is conversant with deceit. He will place the evil-minded Panchala at the forefront of the battle and advance to fight with Bhishma. Bhishma had earlier said that he would not kill Shikhandi. The creator made him a woman and he later became a man through destiny. Yajnasena's maharatha son[420] bears an inauspicious mark on his standard. The son of the one who goes to the ocean[421] will not strike someone who bears an inauspicious mark on his standard. Having thought of all these things, my mind is severely distressed. In the battle today, Partha will attack the aged one of the Kuru lineage. Yudhishthira's anger, the encounter between Bhishma and Arjuna and the rage of my weapons in battle certainly portend ill for all subjects. Pandava is spirited, powerful and brave. He is skilled in the use of weapons and is firm in his valour. He can shoot from a great distance and can strike powerfully. He is skilled in understanding the signs. He

[419]In astrology, parigha is an inauspicious yoga or conjunction of the stars, signifying obstructions.

[420]Shikhandi. Yajnasena is Drupada's name.

[421]Ganga.

is invincible in battle, even by the gods, with Vasava. He is strong
and intelligent. He has conquered exhaustion. He is supreme among
warriors. Pandava possesses terrible weapons and is always victorious
in battle. Avoid his path and go to the spot where the one who is
rigid in his vows is stationed. O mighty-armed one! Behold the visage
of what is about to transpire. The armours of the brave ones are
decorated with gold. They are expensive and beautiful. They will
be shattered with straight-tufted arrows. The tops of the standards,
the javelins and the bows will be fragmented. There are polished
and sharp spears and lances blazing in gold. There are pennants on
elephants and all these will be destroyed by the angry Kiriti. O son!
This is not the time when dependents should seek to protect their
lives. Go, placing heaven at the forefront, and fame and victory. The
whirlpool of horses, elephants and chariots is extremely terrible and
is difficult to cross. The one with the ape on his banner is crossing
the river of battle on his chariot. Regard for brahmanas, self-control,
generosity, austerities and greatness in conduct—these can be seen in
the king.[422] Dhananjaya is his brother. Bhimasena is powerful and
so are the Pandavas who are Madri's sons. Varshneya Vasudeva is
stationed as their protector. The evil-minded sons of Dhritarashtra
are overcome by anger. While he[423] has scorched his body through
austerities, the Bharatas have been scorched through anger. Partha
can be seen, with Vasudeva as his refuge. He is shattering all the
soldiers of the sons of Dhritarashtra, in every direction. Kiriti can
be seen to be agitating the soldiers, like a giant whale agitating large
fish at the mouth of a river. Sounds of lamentation and woe can be
heard at the head of the army. Go and confront the son of Panchala.
I will go and confront Yudhishthira. The centre of the infinitely
energetic king's vyuha is difficult to penetrate. It is like the interior
of the ocean and atirathas are stationed in every direction. Satyaki,
Abhimanyu, Dhrishtadyumna, Vrikodara and the twins, lords among
men, are protecting the king. He is like Upendra[424] and is dark. He

[422]Yudhishthira.
[423]Yudhishthira.
[424]Indra's younger brother, Vishnu. This is a description of Abhimanyu.

is as tall as a giant shala tree. He is advancing amidst the soldiers, like a second Phalguna. Take up your supreme weapons and grasp your giant bow. Advance against King Parshata[425] and fight with Vrikodara. Who does not wish that his beloved son may live for an eternal period? However, placing the dharma of kshatriyas at the forefront, I am employing you in this task. In this battle, Bhishma is scorching the great army. O son! In battle, he is the equal of Yama and Varuna.'"'

Chapter 969(109)

'Sanjaya said, "Bhagadatta, Kripa, Shalya, Satvata Kritavarma, Vinda and Anuvinda from Avanti, Saindhava Jayadratha, Chitrasena, Vikarna and the youthful Durmarshana—these ten warriors from your side fought against Bhimasena. They were accompanied by a large army that had come from many countries. O king! In the battle over Bhishma, they sought great fame. Shalya struck Bhimasena with nine arrows, Kritavarma with three arrows and Kripa with nine arrows. O venerable one! Chitrasena, Vikarna and Bhagadatta struck Bhimasena with ten broad-headed arrows each. Saindhava struck him with three arrows in the joints of his shoulders. Vinda and Anuvinda from Avanti struck him with five arrows each. Durmarshana struck Pandava with twenty sharp arrows. O great king! The illustrious one struck all the maharathas from the side of the sons of Dhritarashtra, brave ones in all the worlds, separately. The immensely strong Bhimasena pierced them with many arrows. He pierced Shalya with fifty and Kritavarma with eight. O descendant of the Bharata lineage! He severed Kripa's bow, with an arrow fixed to it, from the middle. After severing the bow, he pierced him with five arrows. He pierced Vinda and Anuvinda

---

[425]This is probably a reference to Dhrishtadyumna. Shikhandi is also possible, but unlikely.

with three arrows each, Durmarshana with twenty and Chitrasena with five. Bhima pierced Vikarna with ten arrows and Jayadratha with five. He again struck Saindhava with three arrows and roared in delight. Goutama, supreme among rathas, grasped another bow and angrily pierced Bhima with ten sharp arrows. He was pierced by those many arrows, like a giant elephant that has been goaded. The mighty-armed and powerful Bhimasena became angry. In that battle, he wounded Goutama with many arrows. As dazzling as Yama at the end of an era, he pierced Saindhava's horses and his charioteer with three arrows and sent them to the land of the dead. With his horses slain, the maharatha quickly jumped down from his chariot. In that battle, he released many sharp arrows towards Bhimasena. O descendant of the Bharata lineage! O best of the Bharata lineage! But Bhima used a broad-headed arrow to sever the bow of the great-souled Saindhava into two, from the middle. O king! With his bow severed, bereft of a chariot and with his horses and charioteer slain, he quickly climbed onto Chitrasena's chariot. In the battle there, Pandava performed an extraordinary deed. The maharatha pierced all those maharathas with his arrows and repulsed them. While all the worlds looked on, he deprived Saindhava of his chariot.

'"Shalya could not tolerate Bhimasena's valour. He affixed sharp arrows that had been polished by an artisan. Asking Bhima to wait, he pierced him with seventy arrows. O venerable one! In that battle, for Shalya's sake, Kripa, Kritavarma, Bhagadatta, Vinda and Anuvinda from Avanti, Chitrasena, Durmarshana, Vikarna and the valiant king of Sindhu, scorchers of enemies, quickly pierced Bhima. He pierced each of them back with five arrows. He pierced Shalya with seventy arrows and yet again with ten. Shalya pierced him with nine arrows and yet again with five. He then used a broad-headed arrow to severely strike his charioteer in his inner organs. On seeing that Vishoka[426] had been wounded, the powerful Bhimsena struck the king of Madra in the arms and the chest with three arrows. He pierced each of the other great archers with three arrows each. Having wounded them in that battle, he roared like a

---

[426]Bhima's charioteer.

lion. Pandava was unassailable in battle. But the great archers made great efforts. Without any hesitation, each of them severely wounded him in the inner organs with three arrows each. But despite being pierced, Bhimasena, the great archer, was not distressed. He was like a mountain on which showers of rain were pouring down from the clouds. The immensely illustrious one severely pierced Shalya with nine arrows. O king! He firmly pierced Pragjyotisha with one hundred arrows. Using an extremely sharp kshurapra and displaying the dexterity of his hands, he severed the great-souled Satvata's bow, with an arrow fixed to it. O scorcher of enemies! Kritavarma grasped another bow and struck Vrikodara in the midst of his forehead with an iron arrow. In that encounter, Bhima pierced Shalya with nine iron arrows, Bhagadatta with three and Kritavarma with eight. He pierced Goutama and the other rathas with two arrows each. O king! In that encounter, they pierced him back with sharp arrows. He was thus afflicted in every direction by those maharathas. But he disregarded them like straw and roamed around, without any pain. Those best of rathas were not distracted and released hundreds and thousands of sharp arrows towards Bhima.

'"The brave maharatha Bhagadatta hurled an immensely forceful javelin in the battle. It was extremely expensive and possessed a golden handle. The strong-armed King Saindhava hurled a spear and a lance. O king! In that encounter, Kripa used a shataghni and Shalya an arrow. The other great archers released five energetic arrows each, in Bhimasena's direction. But the son of the wind god used a kshurapra to slice down the spear. He severed the lance with three arrows, as if it were the stalk of a sesamum plant. He shattered the shataghni with nine arrows that were tufted with the feathers of herons. The immensely strong one sliced down the arrow shot by the king of Madra and severed the javelin that had been suddenly and forcefully hurled by Bhagadatta in the battle. As for the other terrible arrows, he used straight-tufted arrows to strike them down. Bhimasena was proud in battle and struck each of them with three arrows. Each of those great archers was wounded with three arrows. In the great battle, Dhananjaya arrived there. He arrived on his own chariot and beheld maharatha Bhima, striking the enemy warriors in the battle with his arrows. O bull among men! On seeing the two great-souled Pandavas united, all those on your side gave up all hope of victory. In the battle, Arjuna advanced to fight with maharatha Bhishma. Wishing to kill Bhishma, he placed Shikhandi at the forefront. O descendant of the Bharata lineage! O king! Those ten warriors on your side had been fighting in the battle with Bhima. On seeing them stationed there and wishing to do that which would bring pleasure to Bhima, Bibhatsu attacked them. King Duryodhana incited Susharma for the death of both Arjuna and Bhimasena. 'O Susharma! Go swiftly, surrounded by your large army. Vanquish the sons of Pandu, Dhananjaya and Vrikodara.' On hearing this instruction, Trigarta, the lord of Prasthala, attacked the archers Bhima and Arjuna in the battle. He surrounded them with many thousands of chariots in every direction. A battle commenced between Arjuna and the enemy."'

Chapter 970(110)

'Sanjaya said, "In the battle, maharatha Arjuna exerted himself against Shalya. In the encounter, he shrouded him with straight-tufted arrows. He pierced Susharma and Kripa with three arrows each. O Indra among kings! In the battle, he wounded Pragjyotisha, Saindhava Jayadratha, Chitrasena, Vikarna, Kritavarma, Durmarshana and the two maharathas from Avanti with three arrows each. These were swift and were tufted with the feathers of herons and peacocks. In the battle, the atiratha oppressed your army with arrows. O descendant of the Bharata lineage! In the encounter, Jayadratha pierced Partha with arrows and while stationed on Chitrasena's chariot, swiftly pierced Bhima. In the battle, Shalya and Kripa pierced the mighty-armed Jishnu, supreme among rathas, with many arrows that struck at the inner organs. O lord of the earth! O venerable one! In the encounter, your sons, Chitrasena and the others, struck each of them, Arjuna and Bhimasena, with five sharp arrows. But those foremost of rathas, the Kounteyas, bulls among the Bharata

lineage, continued to oppress the large army of the Trigartas in the
encounter. In the battle, Susharma pierced Partha with many sharp
arrows. The powerful one roared and the sound echoed in the sky.
Other brave rathas pierced Bhimasena and Dhananjaya with sharp
and swift arrows that were tufted with gold. In the midst of those
rathas, the Kounteyas, supreme among rathas, looked beautiful as
they seemed to be sporting and roamed around in their chariots. They
were like powerful lions amidst a herd of cattle. They shattered the
bows and arrows of many brave ones in the battle. They brought
down the heads of hundreds of brave kings. They shattered many
chariots and killed hundreds of horses. In the great battle, they
brought down elephant-riders from their elephants. O king! Many
charioteers and riders were seen to be devoid of their lives. O king!
They were immobile in every direction. Elephants were slain. Foot
soldiers and horses lost their lives. The earth was strewn with many
shattered chariots. Many umbrellas and standards were broken and
were brought down. O descendant of the Bharata lineage! There were
discarded goads and cushions, diadems, armlets, necklaces, hides of
ranku deer and discarded headdresses, whisks and fans. There were
severed arms with sandalwood paste smeared on them. The earth
was strewn with the thighs of Indras among men.

'"We witnessed Partha's extraordinary valour in the battle.
He used his arrows to restrain and strike all the warriors in your
army. On seeing that Bhima and Arjuna were united, your son was
frightened and quickly rushed towards Gangeya's chariot, in great
fear. Kripa, Kritavarma, Saindhava Jayadratha and Vinda and
Anuvinda from Avanti were the ones who did not give up the battle
then. In the encounter, Bhima, the great archer, and maharatha
Phalguna crushed the army of the Kouravas in terrible fashion. In
the encounter, tens of thousands and millions of arrows were quickly
showered down on Dhananjaya's chariot. The maharatha repulsed
that net of arrows. In the encounter, Partha began to send them to the
land of the dead. Maharatha Shalya became enraged in that battle.
As if playing, he struck Jishnu in the chest with a straight-tufted and
broad-headed arrow. Partha used five arrows to sever the bow from
his hand. He then used other sharp arrows to severely wound him

in his inner organs. In the battle, the lord of Madra grasped another
bow that was capable of bearing a heavy burden. O great king! He
angrily wounded Jishnu with three arrows and Vasudeva with five.
He struck Bhimasena in the chest and the arms with nine. O great
king! Drona and the maharatha from Magadha were instructed
by Duryodhana and came to the spot where Partha and Pandava
Bhimasena were. O great king! The maharathas were slaying the
great army of the Kouravas. O bull among the Bharata lineage! In
the encounter, the young Jayatsena pierced Bhima, who possessed
terrible weapons, with eight sharp arrows. Bhima pierced him back
with ten arrows and again with seven. With a broad-headed arrow,
he brought down his charioteer from the seat of the chariot. The
horses were no longer controlled and fled in different directions,
dragging away the king of Magadha, while all the soldiers looked
on. Detecting a weakness, Drona pierced Bhimsena with sixty-five
extremely sharp iron arrows that had been sharpened on stone. O
descendant of the Bharata lineage! Bhima prided himself in battle.
In the encounter, he pierced his preceptor, who was like his father,
with nine broad-headed arrows and followed it up with another sixty.
Arjuna pierced Susharma with many iron arrows and scattered his
soldiers, like the wind dispersing a mass of clouds.

"'Bhishma, the king,[427] Soubala and Brihadbala angrily attacked
Bhimasena and Dhananjaya. The brave Pandavas and Parshata
Dhrishtadyumna attacked Bhishma, who was advancing in the
battle, like death with a gaping mouth. Shikhandi approached the
grandfather of the Bharatas. He was cheerful and had abandoned
fear. He attacked the one who was rigid in his vows. The Parthas,
headed by Yudhishthira, placed Shikhandi at the forefront. Together
with the Srinjayas, they fought against Bhishma in that battle. All
those on your side placed the one who was rigid in his vows at
the forefront. They fought against the Parthas in that battle, with
Shikhandi at the forefront. For the sake of victory over Bhishma, the
battle that commenced there among the Kouravas[428] was terrible. O

[427]Duryodhana.
[428]The Pandavas are being included as part of the Kouravas.

lord of the earth! The sons of Pandu wished to triump over Bhishma
and those on your side wished Bhishma's victory in the battle. It was
like gambling with the dice and victory or defeat became the stake.
O great king! Dhrishtadyumna incited all the soldiers. 'O supreme
among men! Attack Gangeya. Do not be scared.' On hearing the
words of the commander, the army of the Pandavas quickly advanced
against Bhishma. In that great battle, they were ready to give up their
lives. O great king! Bhishma, best of rathas, resisted that army as it
descended on him, like the shoreline against the great ocean.'''

Chapter 971(111)

'Dhritarashtra asked, "O Sanjaya! How did the immensely
valorous Bhishma, Shantanu's son, fight on the tenth day
of the battle against the Pandavas and the Srinjayas? How did the
Kurus repulse the Pandavas in the battle? Tell me about the great
battle fought by Bhishma, the ornament of all battles."

'Sanjaya replied, "O descendant of the Bharata lineage! I will
describe to you the battle between the Kurus and the Pandavas and
the detailed account of that encounter. Listen. Using his supreme
weapons, from one day to another, Kiriti killed the angry charioteers
on your side and sent them to the next world. The victorious
Kouravya, Bhishma, also stuck to his pledge and always created a
great destruction among the army of the Parthas. On seeing Bhishma
fight amidst the maharatha Kurus and Arjuna with the Panchalas,
people were uncertain.[429] On the tenth day, Bhishma and Arjuna
encountered each other. There was an extremely dreadful carnage.
O king! Bhishma, Shantanu's son and the scorcher of enemies,
skilled in supreme weapons, slaughtered many tens of thousands
of warriors. O king! There were many whose families, names and
lineages were not known. All of them refused to retreat and the brave

[429]As to which side would be victorious.

ones were slain by Bhishma's weapons. Having scorched the army of the Pandavas for ten days, the scorcher of enemies, with dharma in his soul, gave up all desire to remain alive. He desired a quick death and stationed himself at the forefront of the battle. 'I will no longer kill the best of men in the forefront of the battle.' O great king! Having thought in this way, Devavrata, your mighty-armed father, addressed these words to the Pandava who was near him. 'O Yudhishthira! O immensely wise one! O one who is knowledgable in all the sacred texts! O son![430] Listen to my words. They are about attaining dharma and heaven. O son! O descendant of the Bharata lineage! I am extremely disgusted with this body of mine. I have spent a lot of time in slaying a large number of beings in battle. Therefore, place Partha at the forefront, with the Panchalas and the Srinjayas. If you wish to do that which brings me pleasure, make endeavours to kill me.' Knowing that this was his command, Pandava, who knew about the truth, made efforts to fight against Bhishma in the battle, together with the Srinjayas. O king! On hearing Bhishma's words, Dhrishtadyumna and Pandava Yudhishthira instructed their army. 'Advance and fight. Vanquish Bhishma in the battle. You will be protected by Jishnu, who is unwavering in his aim and who is triumphant over enemies. This great archer, Parshata, is the commander. It is certain that Bhimasena will protect you in the battle. There is no need to fear Bhishma. The Srinjayas have no task other than to fight. With Shikhandi at the forefront, there is no doubt that we will obtain victory over Bhishma.' On the tenth day, the Pandavas took a vow to triumph or to go to Brahma's world. They advanced, senseless with rage. They placed Shikhandi and Pandava Dhananjaya at the forefront. They resorted to supreme efforts to bring about Bhishma's downfall.

'"The kings of many countries were instructed by your son. They were with Drona and his son and with an immensely strong army. The powerful Duhshasana was there, with all his brothers. Bhishma was in the midst of the battle and they sought to protect him. The brave ones on your side placed the one who was rigid in his vows at

---

[430]The word used is tata.

the forefront. In the battle, they fought with the Parthas, who had placed Shikhandi at the forefront. With Shikhandi at the forefront, the Chedis, the Panchalas and the one with the monkey on his banner advanced towards Bhishma, Shantanu's son. Drona's son fought with Shini's grandson and Dhrishtaketu with Pourava. Yudhamanyu fought with Duryodhana and his advisers, Virata and his soldiers with Jayadratha, the scorcher of enemies and Vriddhakshatra's heir,[431] and his soldiers. The great archer, the king of Madra, fought with Yudhishthira and his soldiers. With due protection, Bhimasena advanced against the army of elephants. Drona was invincible and impossible to resist. He was supreme among those who wielded all weapons. Panchala[432] and the Somakas advanced against him. Prince Brihadbala had a lion on his standard. He advanced against Subhadra's son, the scorcher of enemies who had a karnikara flower on his standard. Together with the kings, your sons attacked Shikhandi and Pandava Dhananjaya in the battle, wishing to kill them.

'"Both the armies were valorous and the advance against each other was extremely terrible. As the soldiers advanced, the earth trembled. O descendant of the Bharata lineage! The two armies clashed against each other. Both those on your side and those of the enemy were delighted to see Shantanu's son in the battle. O descendant of the Bharata lineage! As they angrily advanced against each other, a terrible sound arose in every direction. There was the sound of conch shells and drums. Elephants trumpeted. The soldiers roared terribly, like lions. All the Indras among men had complexions like that of the sun and the moon. The armlets and diadems the brave ones wore lost their brilliance because of the cloud of dust that was raised. The weapons seemed to be flashes of lightning. The terrible twang of bows could be heard. There was the sound of arrows and conch shells and the great roar of drums. In both the armies, the clatter of the chariots could be heard. There were large numbers of spears, lances, swords and masses of arrows hurled by

[431]Jayadratha was Vriddhakshatra's son.
[432]Dhrishtadyumna.

both the armies, and because of this, the sky lost its lustre. In that great battle, charioteers and riders struck each other. Elephants fought with elephants, infantry with infantry. A great battle raged between the Kurus and the Pandavas for the sake of Bhishma. O tiger among men! It was like hawks fighting over a piece of meat. O descendant of the Bharata lineage! There was a terrible encounter between the warriors. They sought to kill each other and defeat each other in that battle.'"

Chapter 972(112)

'Sanjaya said, "O great king! Abhimanyu fought against your valiant son, who was supported by a large army for Bhishma's sake. In the battle, Duryodhana struck Krishna's son with nine arrows with drooping tufts. He was enraged in the battle and again struck him with three arrows. In that encounter, Krishna's son angrily hurled a javelin towards Duryodhana's chariot. It was terrible and seemed to have been created by Death itself. O lord of the earth! On seeing it suddenly descend, dreadful in form, your maharatha son severed it into two with a kshurapra. On seeing the javelin fall down, Krishna's son became extremely enraged. He struck Duryodhana in the arms and the chest with three arrows. O best of the Bharata lineage! He again struck the king, the intolerant Duryodhana, between the breasts with ten terrible arrows. O descendant of the Bharata lineage! The battle between the two was dreadful and wonderful. It created pleasure among those who witnessed it and was applauded by all the kings. For the sake of Bhishma's death and Partha's victory, those brave ones, Subhadra's son and the bull among the Kurus, fought in that battle.

'"Drona's son, bull among the brahmanas, was enraged in the battle. The scorcher of enemies struck Satyaki in the chest with an iron arrow. O descendant of the Bharata lineage! Shini's descendant, immeasurable in his soul, struck the preceptor's son in all of his

inner organs with nine arrows shafted with the feathers of herons.
In the encounter, Ashvatthama struck Satyaki with nine arrows and
again wounded him in the arms and the chest with thirty. Having
been thus pierced by Drona's son, the immensely illustrious and
great archer from the Satvata lineage pierced Drona's son back with
three arrows.

'"In the battle, maharatha Pourava covered Dhrishtaketu
with arrows and severely wounded the great archer. However, the
extremely strong maharatha, Dhrishtaketu, pierced Pourava in the
encounter with thirty sharp arrows. Maharatha Pourava severed
Dhrishtaketu's bow and having pierced him with sharp arrows,
emitted a powerful roar. O great king! He grasped another bow
and pierced Pourava with seventy-three sharp arrows that had been
whetted on stone. Those two noble maharathas who were great
archers rained down a great shower of arrows towards each other.
O descendant of the Bharata lineage! They severed each other's bows
and slew each other's horses. Bereft of their chariots, the maharathas
began to fight with each other with swords. Each had a beautiful
shield made out of the hide of a bull, decorated with the signs of one
hundred moons and marked with the signs of one hundred stars.
O king! They grasped extremely brilliant and polished swords and
rushed towards each other. They were like lions in the great forest,
wishing to have intercourse with the same female. They circled in
wonderful motions, advanced and retreated. They exhibited their
movements, wishing to strike each other. Incited with rage, Pourava
asked Dhrishtaketu to wait and struck him on his frontal bone
with the large sword. In the encounter, the king of Chedi[433] struck
Pourava, bull among men, on the shoulder joint with the sharp tip of
his giant sword. O great king! Those destroyers of enemies advanced
against each other in the great battle. They struck each other with
great force and both of them fell down. O king! Your son, Jayatsena,
took Pourava up on his own chariot and carried him away from
the field of battle. O king! In the encounter, the powerful Sahadeva,

---

[433]Dhrishtaketu.

Madri's son and the scorcher of enemies, carried Dhrishtaketu away from the battle.

'"Chitrasena pierced Susharma with nine swift arrows.[434] He again pierced him with sixty and yet again with nine arrows. O lord of the earth! In that battle, Susharma became enraged with your son and pierced him with one hundred sharp arrows. O king! Chitrasena became angry in the battle and pierced him with thirty arrows with drooping tufts and was pierced back in return.

'"O king! In the battle over Bhishma, which increased fame and honour, Subhadra's son fought with Prince Brihadbala. The king of Kosala pierced Arjuna's son with five iron arrows and again pierced him with twenty straight-tufted arrows. Subhadra's son pierced Brihadbala with nine iron arrows. But despite piercing him again and again, he could not make him waver in the battle. Phalguna's son then severed the bow of the king of Kosala and wounded him with thirty arrows that were tufted with the feathers of herons. But Prince Brihadbala grasped another bow and in that battle, angrily pierced Phalguna's son with many arrows. O scorcher of enemies! They fought this battle for Bhishma's sake. O great king! In that battle, those wonderful fighters were excited with anger and were like Maya and Vasava in the battle between the gods and the asuras.

'"Bhimasena fought against that army of elephants. He was as resplendent as Shakra, with the vajra in his hand, after shattering mountains. Bhima killed elephants that were like mountains. They fell down in large numbers, making the earth resound with their roars. Those shattered elephants were like large mountains made out of collyrium. They were strewn over the ground, like shattered mountains.

'"In the battle, the great archer, Yudhishthira, fought with the king of Madra. He was protected by a large army and oppressed him. In

---

[434]The only Susharma we know of is the king of the Trigartas. He fought on the Kourava side and Chitrasena is Duryodhana's brother. Clearly, this must be some other Susharma, fighting on the Pandava side. However, no such other Susharma has ever been mentioned. Therefore, these shlokas have probably just been thrown in. In any event, they are irrelevant.

that encounter for the sake of Bhishma, the valiant king of Madra
was enraged and afflicted the maharatha who was Dharma's son.

'"The king of Sindhu pierced Virata with nine straight-tufted
and sharp arrows and again wounded him with another thirty. O
great king! In the forefront of that battle, Virata struck Saindhava
between the breasts with thirty sharp arrows. Matsya and Saindhava
possessed colourful bows and swords. Their armour, weapons and
standards were handsome. They looked handsome and resplendent
in that battle.

'"Drona advanced against the son of Panchala[435] in the great
battle and used straight-tufted arrows in the great clash. O great king!
Drona severed Parshata's giant bow and wounded Parshata with fifty
arrows. But Parshata, the destroyer of enemy heroes, grasped another
bow and in that encounter, fiercely unleashed arrows at Drona. The
maharatha repulsed those arrows with his own shower of arrows.
Drona released five arrows towards Drupada's son. O great king!
Parshata, the destroyer of enemy heroes, became enraged at this. In
the battle, he hurled a club towards Drona and it was like Yama's
staff, decorated with golden garments. On seeing it suddenly descend
towards him in that battle, Drona countered it with fifty arrows.
O king! Because of the unassailable arrows released by Drona, it
shattered into many fragments. Shattered and fragmented, it fell
down on the ground. On seeing the club destroyed, Parshata, the
destroyer of enemies, hurled a javelin towards Drona. It was beautiful
and was completely made out of iron. O descendant of the Bharata
lineage! In that battle, Drona sliced it down with nine arrows. In
that encounter, he afflicted Parshata, the great archer. In this fashion,
there was a great battle between Drona and Parshata. O great king!
It was fearful and dreadful and was fought over Bhishma.

'"Arjuna approached Gangeya and oppressed him with sharp
arrows. He angrily advanced against him, like a crazy elephant
attacking another in the forest. The powerful and immensely strong
Bhagadatta counter-attacked Partha on a crazy elephant that had
musth flowing down three streams. On seeing it suddenly descend

---

[435]Dhrishtadyumna.

towards him, like the great Indra's elephant, Bibhatsu took the greatest care in repulsing it. In that encounter, the powerful King Bhagadatta was astride an elephant and countered Arjuna with a shower of arrows. In the great encounter, Arjuna used extremely sharp and polished arrows that had the complexion of silver to pierce the elephant in battle. O great king! Kounteya kept addressing Shikhandi. 'Proceed. Proceed. Go towards Bhishma. Kill him.' O Pandu's elder brother! O king! Pragjyotisha abandoned Pandava and quickly went towards Drupada's chariot. O great king! Placing Shikhandi at the forefront, Arjuna advanced against Bhishma and in that battle, an encounter commenced, when the brave ones on your side fiercely attacked Pandava. All of them advanced, roaring in rage, and it was extraordinary. O lord of men! There were many divisions in the army of your sons. Arjuna scattered them, like the wind disperses a mass of clouds in the sky. Shikhandi approached the grandfather of the Bharatas. Quickly and eagerly, he pierced him with many arrows.

'"In the battle, Bhishma killed the Somakas who were following Partha. He repulsed the soldiers of the maharatha Pandava. The chariot was the storehouse for the fire. The bow constituted the flames. The javelins and clubs were the kindling. He released a great shower of flaming arrows and consumed the kshatriyas in the battle. He was like a large fire that consumes deadwood when it moves around, driven by the wind. Bhishma blazed like that, showering his divine weapons. There were gold-shafted, straight-tufted and sharp arrows. The immensely illustrious Bhishma roared in the directions and the sub-directions. O king! He brought down chariots and elephants, with their riders. The chariots roamed around, like palm trees that had been shorn of their tops. O king! In that battle, chariots, elephants and horses were bereft of men. Bhishma, supreme among those who wield all weapons, roamed around. The clap of his palms and the twang of his bow were like the clapping of thunder. O king! In every direction, the soldiers were disturbed and trembled. O lord of men! The arrows of your father were invincible. The unassailable arrows released by Bhishma never failed to penetrate the bodies. O king! The chariots had no men. But they were still yoked to swift horses. O lord of the earth! With the speed of the wind, we saw them being dragged around in different directions. There were fourteen thousand famous maharathas from the Chedis, the Kashis and the Karushas. They were born in noble lineages and were ready to give up their lives. These brave ones did not retreat from battle. Their standards were decorated in gold. With their horses, chariots and elephants, they advanced in battle against Bhishma and confronting the one who was like death with a gaping mouth, they left for the other world. O great king! There was not a single maharatha among the Somakas, who having approached Bhishma in that battle, returned alive from the engagement. In that battle, he sent all those warriors to the capital of the king of the dead. On seeing them conveyed there, all the people witnessed Bhishma's valour.

'"The only exceptions were Pandu's brave son, borne on white horses and with Krishna as his charioteer, and Panchala Shikhandi, who was infinitely energetic in battle. O bull among the Bharata lineage! Shikhandi approached Bhishma in that battle and in that great encounter, struck him with one hundred arrows. Gangeya glanced at Shikhandi with anger blazing in his eyes. O descendant of the Bharata lineage! He seemed to burn him down with the look in his eyes. O king! But while all the world looked on, he remembered that he was a woman. Bhishma did not strike him in battle, though he[436] did not understand the reason. O great king! Arjuna addressed Shikhandi. 'Advance quickly and kill the grandfather. O brave one! What do you wish to say? Kill maharatha Bhishma. I do not see anyone else in Yudhishthira's army who can kill him. Nor is there anyone who can fight with grandfather Bhishma in this battle. You are the exception. O tiger among men! I am telling this truthfully.' O bull among the Bharata lineage! Having been thus addressed by Partha, Shikhandi quickly pierced the grandfather with many kinds of arrows. Your father, Devavrata, paid no heed to these arrows. Enraged in the battle, he

---

[436]Shikhandi. However, there was no reason for Shikhandi not to understand, since Bhishma had already mentioned the reason.

countered Arjuna with arrows. O venerable one! In that encounter, he released sharp arrows and dispatched all the soldiers of the maharatha Pandava to the other world. O king! Supported by their large army, the Pandavas surrounded Bhishma and enveloped him, like clouds around the sun. O bull among the Bharata lineage! The descendant of the Bharata lineage was covered in every direction. In that battle, he consumed the enemy, like a flaming fire burns down a forest.

'"We then beheld the extraordinary manliness of your son. So as to protect the one who was rigid in his vows, he fought with Partha. All the worlds were gratified at the deeds of your great-souled archer son, Duhshasana, in that battle. In that battle, he alone fought with Partha and his followers and fought so fiercely that the Pandavas were unable to resist him. O great king! In that encounter, Duhshasana deprived rathas of their chariots and tuskers of their riders. He shattered them with sharp arrows and brought them down on the ground. With other arrows, he drove the tuskers away in different directions. He was like a fire that has obtained kindling and blazes with fierce flames. In that way, your son blazed and consumed the Pandavas. No Pandava maharatha could defeat the noble one of the Bharata lineage. Nor did anyone venture against him. The only exception was the great Indra's son, borne on white steeds and with Krishna as his charioteer. O king! Vijaya Arjuna defeated him in that encounter. While all the soldiers looked on, he then advanced against Bhishma. Though he had been vanquished, your son resorted to the strength of Bhishma's arms. O king! Intoxicated in that battle, he repeatedly comforted his side and continued to fight resplendently against Arjuna. O king! In that battle, Shikhandi pierced the grandfather with arrows that were like the vajra to the touch and were like the poison of serpents. O lord of men! But these did not cause your father any pain. Gangeya received all these arrows with a smile, like a man suffering from heat craves the pouring down of rain. In that fashion, Gangeya received the shower of arrows from Shikhandi. O great king! As Bhishma consumed the soldiers of the great-souled Pandavas, the kshatriyas saw his terrible visage in that battle.

'"O venerable one! Your son[437] spoke to all the soldiers. 'Attack Phalguna in the battle and surround him with chariots from all sides. Bhishma is knowledgable about dharma and will protect all of us in this battle. Give up your great fear and counter-attack the Pandavas. There is the blazing palm tree.[438] Bhishma is stationed there and is protecting us, and the honour and the armour of all the sons of Dhritarashtra in this battle. Even if the thirty gods endeavour, they cannot assail Bhishma, not to speak of the great-souled Partha and his soldiers. They are mortal beings. O warriors! Therefore, do not run away. We have obtained Phalguna in this battle. I will endeavour to fight against Phalguna in the battle today, together with all of you. O lords of the earth! Make efforts.' O king! On hearing the words of your archer son, the powerful maharathas united against Arjuna—Videhas, Kalingas and large numbers of Dasherakas. With the Nishadas and the Souviras, the Bahlikas, the Daradas, those from the east, those from the west, the Malavas, the Abhishahas, the Shurasenas, the Shibis, the Vasatayas, the Shalvas, the Shrayas, the Trigartas, the Ambashthas and the Kekayas advanced in the great battle. They attacked Partha in the encounter, like insects drawn to a fire. O great king! The maharathas were with all their armies. Dhananjaya invoked and affixed divine weapons. Bibhatsu, the immensely strong one, quickly released those extremely forceful weapons and consumed them with his arrows, like a fire before insects. The one with the firm bow created thousands of arrows. Gandiva was seen to be blazing in the sky. O great king! Oppressed by those arrows, the chariots and the standards were shattered. The kings could not approach the one with the monkey on his banner. Rathas were brought down with their standards, horses with their riders, elephants with elephant-riders. They were afflicted by Kiriti's arrows, created through Arjuna's arms. The earth was strewn in all directions with the many forces of the kings, which were running away. The mighty-armed Partha drove away those armies.

[437]Duryodhana.
[438]On Bhishma's standard.

'"In that encounter, he then dispatched arrows towards Duhshasana. They possessed iron heads and they pierced your son, Duhshasana. All of them then entered the ground, like snakes penetrating a termite hill. He killed his horses and brought down his charioteer. The lord used twenty arrows to deprive Vivimshati of his chariot. He severely wounded him with five arrows with drooping tufts. He pierced Kripa, Shalya and Vikarna with many iron arrows. Kounteya, borne on white steeds, deprived them of their chariots. O venerable one! Having been deprived of their chariots and having been vanquished in battle by Savyasachi, these five—Kripa, Shalya, Duhshasana, Vikarna and Vivimshati—fled. O king! Having defeated those maharathas in the forenoon, Partha blazed in the battle, like a fire without any smoke. He showered down arrows, like the rays of the sun. O great king! He brought down many other kings. O descendant of the Bharata lineage! Because of that shower of arrows, the maharathas retreated from the field of battle and a great river of blood began to flow between the armies of the Kurus and the Pandavas. Elephants, horses and large numbers of rathas were slain by the rathas. Rathas killed elephants and elephants killed horses and infantry. Bodies were sliced in the middle and heads lopped off. Elephants, horses, chariots and warriors fell down in all directions. The shattered bodies were still radiant with expensive earrings and armlets. Princes and maharathas fell down, or were falling down. Some were mangled by the wheels of chariots, others were trod on by elephants and horses. Foot soldiers, horses, horses with horse-riders, elephants, horses and masses of chariots were seen to fall down in every direction. The earth was littered with broken chariots and shattered wheels, yokes and standards. The masses of elephants, horses and chariots were covered with blood. It looked as beautiful as an autumn sky covered with red clouds. Dogs, crows, vultures, wolves, jackals and other dreadful animals and birds howled at the sight of the feast of flesh. Many kinds of winds were seen to blow in all the directions. Rakshasas and demons were seen to be roaring. Golden ropes and expensive flags were seen to be covered in smoke, suddenly stirred by the wind. There were thousands of white umbrellas and pennants of the maharathas. They were seen to be scattered around in hundreds and thousands. Elephants were afflicted by arrows and fled in all directions, with their standards. O Indra among men! Kshatriyas, holding clubs, javelins and bows, were seen to have fallen down on the ground.

'"O great king! Bhishma used a divine weapon and in the sight of all the archers, advanced against Kounteya. In the battle, the armoured Shikhandi also endeavoured to attack. At this, Bhishma withdrew that weapon, which was like the fire. At this time, Kounteya, borne on white horses, confounded the grandfather and killed your soldiers."'

Chapter 973(113)

'Sanjaya said, "O descendant of the Bharata lineage! There were many in the ranks of both the sides and they were arrayed in vyuhas. All of them advanced, aspiring to attain Brahma's world. In the encounter that followed, similar types of soldiers did not fight. Rathas did not fight with rathas, nor foot soldiers with foot soldiers. Horses did not fight with horses, nor elephants with warriors on elephants. In that great and dreadful clash between the armies, there were perversions. There were men, elephants and chariots scattered all over the place. In that great and terrible destruction, there was no discrimination.

'"O descendant of the Bharata lineage! Shalya, Kripa, Chitrasena, Duhshasana and Vikarna quickly resorted to their chariots. Those brave ones made the standards of the Pandavas tremble in the battle. In the encounter, the soldiers of the Pandus were slaughtered by those great-souled ones. They could not find a protector and were like a boat submerged in the water. Just as the winter strikes the inner organs of cattle, like that, Bhishma wounded the inner organs of the sons of Pandu. The great-souled Partha did likewise towards your soldiers. Many elephants that were like mountains or clouds were brought down. Partha was also seen to bring down leaders among men. He struck them with thousands of iron arrows. The great elephants were seen to fall down there, shrieking piteously. Great-souled ones were killed, their bodies still adorned with ornaments. There were beautiful and scattered heads, still wearing earrings. O king! That extremely terrible encounter was destructive of the supreme among brave ones. Bhishma fought with the valiant Pandava Dhananjaya. O king! On witnessing the valour with which the grandfather fought, the Kouravas placed Brahma's world at the forefront and did not retreat. They wished to be killed in battle, so that they might attain heaven. The Pandavas did not retreat from that destruction of the supreme among brave ones either. O great king! O lord of men! The Pandavas remembered the many and varied hardships that they had to suffer earlier on account of you and your son. The brave ones abandoned fear in that battle and placed Brahma's world at the forefront. They cheerfully fought with your sons and those on your side.

"'In the battle, the maharatha commander[439] addressed the soldiers. 'O Somakas! Together with the Srinjayas, attack Gangeya.' On hearing the words of the commander, the Somakas, together with the Srinjayas, attacked Gangeya and showered down weapons on him from every direction. O king! Thus assailed, your father, Shantanu's son, became intolerant and started to fight with the Srinjayas. O father![440] His achievements were glorious. In earlier times, the intelligent Rama[441] had imparted an instruction of weapons to him, one that could destroy the armies of enemies. He resorted to that instruction, capable of destroying the forces of the enemy. The aged grandfather of the Kurus, Bhishma, slew ten thousand of enemy heroes from the ranks of the Parthas every day. O descendant of the Bharata lineage! But with the tenth day having been reached, Bhishma alone slew seven maharathas from the Matsyas and the Panchalas in the encounter and killed innumerable elephants and horses. In the great battle, the great-grandfather killed five thousand rathas and

---

[439]Dhrishtadyumna.
[440]The word used is tata.
[441]Parashurama.

fourteen thousand men. He again killed one thousand elephants and ten thousand horses. O lord of the earth! Your father killed them through the strength of his instruction. He agitated the ranks of all the kings and brought down Virata's beloved brother, Shatanika. O great king! Having killed Shatanika in the battle the powerful Bhishma brought down another one thousand kings with broad-headed arrows. In the army of the Parthas, there were kings who had followed Dhananjaya. Whichever one among these approached Bhishma was sent to Yama's abode. In this way, Bhishma remained at the head of the army and surpassed the soldiers of the Parthas. He covered them and all the ten directions, with his net of arrows. He performed extremely great deeds on the tenth day. With the bow and arrows, he was stationed between the two armies. O king! None of the kings were capable of glancing at him. He was like the scorching midday sun in the sky, during the summer. O descendant of the Bharata lineage! Just as Shakra scorched the army of the daityas in battle, Bhishma scorched that of the Pandaveyas.

'"On witnessing his valour, Madhusudana, the son of Devaki, affectionately spoke these words to Dhananjaya. 'This Bhishma, Shantanu's son, is stationed between the two armies. Kill him with your power and become victorious. He is shattering our soldiers there. Go and use your strength to repulse him there. O lord! No one other than you is capable of withstanding Bhishma's arrows.' O king! The one with the monkey on his banner was incited at that moment. He used his arrows to make Bhishma, his standard, his chariot and his horses disappear. But the bull, the foremost among the Kurus countered Pandava's arrows with his own torrent of arrows and dispersed the many showers of arrows that had been targeted towards him. O great king! The valiant Dhrishtaketu, the king of Panchala, Pandava Bhimasena, Parshata Dhrishtadyumna, the twins, Chekitana, the five from Kekaya, Satyaki, Subhadra's son, Ghatotkacha, Droupadi's sons, Shikhandi, the brave Kuntibhoja, Susharma,[442] Virata and many other immensely strong ones among the Pandaveyas were oppressed by Bhishma's arrows and were

---

[442]The Susharma on the Pandava side mentioned earlier.

immersed in an ocean of grief. Phalguna rescued them. With great force, Shikhandi grasped a supreme weapon. Protected by Kiriti, he dashed towards Bhishma. Knowing what must be done in the battle, the victorious Bibhatsu killed all the followers[443] and himself rushed against Bhishma. Satyaki, Chekitana, Parshata Dhrishtadyumna, Virata, Drupada and the Pandavas who were Madri's sons also attacked Bhishma, protected by the one whose bow was firm. In that battle, Abhimanyu and Droupadi's five sons also attacked Bhishma in the encounter, holding up great weapons. All of them were firm in wielding the bow and never ran away from the field of battle. They pierced Bhishma with well-aimed arrows all over his body. However, the one whose soul was never distressed disregarded all those arrows released by the best of kings. He penetrated the Pandava army. As if smiling, the grandfather repulsed all those arrows. Bhishma smiled repeatedly at Panchala Shikhandi and remembering that he had been a woman, did not target a single arrow at him. But he killed seven maharathas from Drupada's army of rathas. Cries of lamentation then arose among the Matsyas, the Panchalas and the Chedis, all of whom had attacked the solitary one. With supreme horses, a cluster of chariots, elephants and foot soldiers, they enveloped the solitary one, like clouds around the sun. Bhishma, the son of Bhagirathi, scorched many enemies in that battle. There was a battle between Bhishma and Kiriti, who placed Shikhandi at the forefront, there, like that between the gods and the asuras."'

Chapter 974(114)

'Sanjaya said, "All the Pandavas placed Shikhandi at the head. O descendant of the Bharata lineage! In that encounter, they surrounded Bhishma from all sides and wounded him, using extremely terrible shataghnis, javelins, battleaxes, clubs, maces,

---

[443]Bhishma's followers.

spears, many types of catapults, gold-tufted arrows, spikes, lances, kampanas, iron arrows, vatsadantas and slings. Together with all the Srinjayas, they assailed Bhishma. His armour was shattered and he was oppressed everywhere, in many ways. But despite having been pierced in his inner organs, Gangeya was not distressed. The radiant bow and arrows and weapons seemed to be like the flames of a fire, fanned by the wind. The roar of the wheels of his chariot was the heat. His great weapons constituted the fire itself. His colourful bow was extremely resplendent and the one with the great bow was the destroyer of brave ones. Bhishma was like the fire at the end of a yuga, traversing through the enemy. He passed and brought down masses of chariots in that battle. He was again seen, roaming around in the midst of those kings among men. He ignored the king of Panchala and Dhrishtaketu and forcibly penetrated into the midst of the Pandava army. He pierced Satyaki, Bhima, Pandava Dhananjaya, Drupada, Virata and Parshata Dhrishtadyumna with extremely forceful arrows that could penetrate the armour of enemies. These six were struck with arrows that made a terrible roar and were as radiant as the sun. However, the maharathas repulsed those sharp arrows. Each of them struck Bhishma with great energy, using ten arrows each. In that battle, Shikhandi released arrows towards the one who was great in his vows. These were gold-tufted and sharpened on stone and swiftly penetrated Bhishma. Placing Shikhandi at the forefront, Kiriti impetuously attacked Bhishma and severed his bow. When Bhishma's bow was sliced down, the maharathas—Drona, Kritavarma, Saindhava Jayadratha, Bhurishrava, Shala, Shalya and Bhagadatta could not tolerate this. Extremely enraged, these seven attacked Kiriti. The maharathas displayed supreme and divine weapons. They attacked in great anger and enveloped Pandava. As they advanced towards Phalguna, sounds could be heard. It was like the sound being raised by the oceans at the time of the destruction of a yuga. 'Bring forward.[444] Grasp. Fight. Slice off.' Such were the tumultuous sounds as they advanced towards Phalguna's chariot.

[444]The army.

O bull among the Bharata lineage! On hearing that dreadful sound, the Pandava maharathas attacked, so as to protect Phalguna. Satyaki, Bhimasena, Parshata Dhrishtadyumna, Virata, Drupada, rakshasa Ghatotkacha and Abhimanyu—these seven were enraged and became senseless with anger. They wielded colourful bows and swiftly advanced. The battle that commenced was dreadful and made the body hair stand up. O best of the Bharata lineage! It was like the battle between the gods and the danavas.

"'Kiriti, best among rathas, was protected by Krishna and in that battle, after Bhishma's bow had been severed, pierced him with ten arrows. He struck down his charioteer with ten and his standard with one. Gangeya grasped a bow that was more powerful. However, Phalguna sliced that down with a sharp and broad-headed arrow. Pandava was enraged and one after another, Savyasachi, the scorcher of enemies, severed every bow that Bhishma took up. When the bows were severed, he[445] became wrathful and licked the corners of his mouth. In great wrath, he grasped a javelin that was capable of shattering mountains. In anger, he hurled this towards Phalguna's chariot. On seeing it descend, like the flaming vajra, the descendant of the Pandava lineage brought the javelin down with five sharp and broad-headed arrows. O best of the Bharata lineage! When that javelin, hurled angrily by Bhishma's powerful arms, was severed with five arrows by the enraged Kiriti, it was shattered and fell down on the ground, like lightning[446] dislodged from a mass of clouds. On seeing that the javelin had fallen down, Bhishma was overcome with anger. In the battle, the brave and intelligent one, the destroyer of the cities of enemies, began to think. 'I am capable of slaying all the Pandavas with a single bow, had the immensely strong Vishvaksena[447] not been their protector now. There are two reasons for me not to fight with the Pandavas—the Pandus cannot be killed[448] and Shikhandi's feminity. In earlier times, when my father

[445]Bhishma.
[446]Shatahrada.
[447]Krishna's name.
[448]Because they are protected by Krishna.

married Kali,[449] my father was satisfied and granted me the boon
that I would be invincible in battle, except when I decided to die
myself. I think the time has come for me to decide on my death.' On
learning that this was the decision of the infinitely energetic Bhishma,
the rishis and the Vasus, who were stationed in the sky, spoke these
words to Bhishma. 'O brave one! We are extremely delighted with
the decision you have taken. O great archer! Act in accordance with
your decision and withdraw from the battle.' When those words
were spoken, an auspicious and fragrant breeze began to blow. In
all the directions, it was moistened with drops of water that smelt
nice. The drums of the gods were sounded with a great roar. O king!
A shower of flowers fell down on Bhishma. O king! But the words
spoken were not heard by anyone there, with the exception of the
mighty-armed Bhishma and me, because of the energetic sage.[450]
O lord of the earth! There was great agitation among the thirty gods,
at the prospect of Bhishma, beloved of all the worlds, falling down
from his chariot.

"'Having heard the words of the masses of gods, the great-minded
one, Bhishma, Shantanu's son, dashed towards Bibhatsu, though he
had been pierced by sharp arrows that were capable of penetrating
every kind of armour. O great king! Shikhandi angrily struck the
grandfather of the Bharatas in the chest with nine sharp arrows. In
the battle, Bhishma, the grandfather of the Kurus, was wounded by
him. O great king! But he did not tremble and was like a mountain
during an earthquake. Bibhatsu laughed and drew back the Gandiva
bow. He pierced Gangeya with twenty-five kshurapras. Dhananjaya
was enraged and again swiftly struck him all over the body with one
hundred arrows that penetrated all his inner organs. In the great
battle, the others also wounded him severely. But these gold-tufted
arrows, sharpened on stone, did not cause him the slightest bit of
pain. Placing Shikhandi at the forefront, the wrathful Kiriti attacked

[449]This Kali is Satyavati. When Shantanu married Satyavati, Bhishma took
a vow that he would remain celibate and would not marry. That is the reason
Shantanu granted him a boon.

[450]Vyasadeva had conferred those powers on Sanjaya.

Bhishma and severed his bow once again.[451] He pierced him with ten arrows and sliced down his standard with one. He struck his charioteer with ten arrows and made him tremble. Gangeya took up another bow that was stronger still. In that great battle, in the twinkling of an eye and as soon as that other bow was taken up, Dhananjaya severed it into three with sharp and broad-headed arrows. In this fashion, he severed many bows.

'"At this, Bhishma, Shantanu's son, determined that he would not fight with Bibhatsu any more. However, he was pierced by twenty-five kshudrakas and thus pierced, the great archer spoke to Duhshasana. 'This maharatha Pandava Partha is enraged in the battle. In this encounter, he has shot many thousands of arrows towards me. No one is capable of vanquishing him in battle, not even the wielder of the vajra. No brave one is capable of defeating me, the gods, the danavas and the rakshasas, not to speak of extremely weak mortals.' While he was speaking thus, Phalguna placed Shikhandi in the forefront of the battle and pierced Bhishma with sharp arrows. Bhishma was severely pierced by the sharp arrows released by the wielder of Gandiva. He smiled and spoke to Duhshasana again. 'These are like vajra and thunder to the touch. They are sharp at the tip and have been released well. They have been shot in a continuous stream. These cannot be Shikhandi's arrows. They have penetrated my firm armour and have mangled my inner organs. They have struck me with the force of clubs. These cannot be Shikhandi's arrows. They are like Brahma's staff to the touch. They possess the force of the vajra and are impossible to resist. They are robbing me of my life. These cannot be Shikhandi's arrows. They are like angry serpents, full of virulent poison and with their tongues protruding. They are penetrating my inner organs. These cannot be Shikhandi's arrows. They are

---

[451]There is an anomaly here. The Critical edition excises some intervening shlokas, where Bhishma had counter-attacked. Since he had decided to die, the counter-attack is incongruous. However, without the counter-attack, there shouldn't have been a bow in Bhishma's hand. It had already been severed. The subsequent shlokas, with Bhishma taking up more bows, should also be excised.

destroying my life, like messengers sent by Yama. They are like clubs and maces to the touch. These cannot be Shikhandi's arrows. They are slicing through my body, like the month of Magha distresses cattle.[452] These are Arjuna's arrows. These cannot be Shikhandi's arrows. All the kings together cannot cause me any grief. The only exception is the brave Jishnu, the wielder of Gandiva and with the monkey on his banner.' O descendant of the Bharata lineage! Having spoken this, Shantanu's son hurled a javelin, as if he was going to burn up Pandava. It was flaming at the tip and had sparks throughout. O descendant of the Bharata lineage! While all the brave ones among the Kurus looked on, he[453] used sharp arrows to sever it into three and made the three parts fall down. At this, Gangeya grasped a shield that was made of gold and a sword. He was determined to obtain victory, or go to the world of the hereafter. But before he could get down from his chariot, the armoured one[454] shattered the shield into a hundred pieces and it was extraordinary.

'"He roared like a lion and incited his soldiers. 'Attack Gangeya. Do not have the slightest bit of fear.' With javelins, lances, masses of arrows from every direction, spears, swords, many other weapons, vatsadantas and broad-headed arrows, all of them attacked the one who was fighting single-handed. The Pandavas let out terrible roars, like lions. O king! Your sons wished to see that Bhishma was victorious. They surrounded him and roared like lions. O Indra among kings! On the tenth day, when Bhishma and Arjuna clashed, there was a dreadful battle between those on your side and those of the enemy. In a short while, there was a whirlpool, like when Ganga meets the ocean. The soldiers fought, wishing to kill each other. Because it was covered with blood, the earth became difficult to cross. It was impossible to distinguish the plain ground from the uneven. On the tenth day, stationed in that battle, though he was pierced in his vital organs, Bhishma killed ten thousand warriors. In a similar way, Partha Dhananjaya was stationed at the forefront of

[452]Magha spans January and February and is thus a wintry month.
[453]Arjuna.
[454]Arjuna.

the army and drove away the soldiers from the centre of the Kuru army. We were scared of Dhananjaya, Kunti's son, who was carried on white horses. We were oppressed by his sharp arrows and fled from the great battle. The Souviras, the Kitavas, those from the east, those from the west, those from the north, the Malavas, the Abhishahas, the Shurasenas, the Shibis, the Vasatayas, the Shalvas, the Shrayas, the Trigartas, the Ambashthas and the Kekayas—warriors from these twelve[455] countries were wounded and oppressed by the arrows, while Kiriti was fighting in that battle, wishing to kill Bhishma. The single one was surrounded by many from all directions. They defeated all the other Kurus and showered him with arrows. 'Bring down. Seize. Pierce. Tear.' O king! These and other tumultuous sounds were heard around Bhishma's chariot. Having slain hundreds and thousands with his shower of arrows, there wasn't even the span of a single finger on his body that was not mangled.

'"While your sons looked on, thus the lord, your father, was wounded with sharp-tipped arrows released by Phalguna and fell down from his chariot. There was a little bit of the day left. When Bhishma fell down from his chariot, great sounds of lamentation were heard from the gods in heaven and the kings in every direction. On seeing that the great-souled grandfather had fallen down, together with Bhishma, all our hearts also fell down. When the mighty-armed one fell down, the earth seemed to roar. The great archer fell down, like an uprooted pole that has been erected in Indra's honour. Because he was covered with a large number of arrows, he did not touch the ground. The great archer, bull among men, was supine on a bed of arrows. When he fell down from the chariot, a divine essence permeated him. The clouds showered rain and the earth trembled.

'"When he fell down, it was seen that the sun was diminished. O descendant of the Bharata lineage! The brave one did not allow his senses to depart, but thought about the right time.[456] He heard divine voices from everywhere in the sky. 'Why should the great-souled Gangeya, tiger among men and the supreme among those

---

[455]The east, the west and the north are not being counted.
[456]For his death.

who wield all weapons, decide on a time that is dakshinayana?'[457]
On hearing these words, Gangeya replied, 'I am still here.' Though
he had fallen down on the ground, he retained his life. Bhishma, the
grandfather of the Kurus, wished to wait till uttarayana. Knowing
his decision, Ganga, the daughter of the Himalayas, sent maharshis
to him, in the form of swans. Adopting the forms of swans from
Manasa,[458] they swifty arrived to see Bhishma, the grandfather of
the Kurus. The grandfather, the best of men, was lying down on his
bed of arrows. In the form of swans, the sages approached Bhishma.
They saw Bhishma, the grandfather of the Kurus, on his bed of
arrows. On seeing him, the great-souled ones circumambulated
Gangeya, the best of the Bharata lineage. The learned ones spoke to
each other. 'The sun is in the south now. Why should the great-souled
Bhishma depart during dakshinayana?' Having spoken in this way,
the swans started to leave for the southern direction. O descendant
of the Bharata lineage! On seeing this, the immensely intelligent one
began to think. Shantanu's son then said, 'I will never depart when
the sun remains in the south. This is my resolution. I will leave for
my earlier abode when the sun moves to the north. The swans have
spoken the truth. I will retain my life, wishing for uttarayana. I have
always had complete control about when I would give up my life.
Therefore, I will retain my life, wishing to die during the northern
course. This is the boon that my great-souled father granted me. His
boon was that I could determine my time of death and let that come
true. Since I possess control, I will retain my life.' Lying down on the
bed of arrows, he spoke these words to the swans.

'"When the immensely energetic Bhishma, the head of the Kurus,
fell down, the Pandavas and the Srinjayas roared like lions. O bull
among the Bharata lineage! When that great spirit among the Bharatas
was brought down, your son did not know what to do. There was
dreadful confusion among the Kurus then. With Duryodhana at the

[457]Dakshinayana is when the sun follows its southern course, from mid-July
to mid-January. Uttarayana is when the sun follows its northern course, from
mid-January to mid-July.

[458]Sacred lake near Mount Kailasa (Kailasha), in Tibet.

head, the kings sighed and wept. For a very long time, they were immersed in sorrow and were deprived of their senses. O great king! They were immobile and their minds were no longer on the fight. It was as if they had been grabbed by the thighs. They did not advance against the Pandavas. The immensely energetic Bhishma, Shantanu's son, who was incapable of being killed, had been brought down. O king! The great destruction of the Kurus seemed certain. The foremost among our brave ones had been brought down, mangled by sharp arrows. He had been vanquished by Savyasachi and we did not know what we should do. The Pandavas were victorious and obtained their supreme objective. All of those brave ones used arms like clubs to sound giant conch shells. O lord of men! The Somakas and the Panchalas were delighted. Those extremely powerful ones sounded thousands of tambourines. Bhimasena slapped his arms and roared dreadfully. When Gangeya had been brought down, the brave ones in both the armies laid down their weapons. Some lamented. Others ran around. And still others lost their senses. Others censured the life of kshatriyas and honoured Bhishma. The rishis and the ancestors praised the one who was great in his vows. The ancestors of the Bharatas also praised him. The valiant one resorted to the yoga described in the great Upanishads. The intelligent one meditated and remained there, wishing for the right time.'''

Chapter 975(115)

'Dhritarashtra said, "O Sanjaya! What was the state of the warriors without Bhishma? He was powerful and was like a god. He followed brahmacharya for the sake of his senior. When Bhishma did not strike Drupada's son because he despised him, I thought that the Kurus and the other kings had been killed. I cannot think of a greater misery. I am evil-minded and have heard about my father being brought down. O Sanjaya! My heart must certainly be made out of stone. On hearing that Bhishma has been brought down, it has not shattered into a hundred fragments. I cannot even think about Devavrata being brought down in the battle. In earlier times, he could not be slain by Jamadagni's son, despite his use of divine weapons. What did Bhishma, lion among men and the one who desired victory, do when he had been brought down? O Sanjaya! Tell me."

'Sanjaya replied, "He was brought down on the ground in the evening. On seeing the aged grandfather of the Kurus, the sons of Dhritarashtra were distressed and the Panchalas were delighted. He lay down on that bed of arrows, without touching the ground. A tumultuous sound of lamentation arose among all the beings. He was like a tree that stood at the boundary of the assembly of the Kurus and he was brought down. O king! O lord of the earth! On seeing Bhishma, Shantanu's son, with his armour and standard shattered, the kshatriyas in both the armies, those of the Kurus and the Pandavas, were overcome with fear. The sky was covered in darkness and the sun lost its splendor. On seeing that Bhishma, Shantanu's son, had been brought down, the earth seemed to be shrieking. This was the best among those who were learned about the brahman. This was the best among those who knew about the objective of the brahman. While the bull among the Bharata lineage lay down, this is what all the beings said. In earlier times, when Shantanu was overcome by desire, he followed his father's command. The bull among men held up his seed. As the middle one among the Bharata lineage[459] lay down on the bed of arrows, this is what the rishis, the siddhas and the charanas reflected. O descendant of the Bharata lineage! When Bhishma, Shantanu's son and the grandfather of the Kurus, was brought down, your sons did not know what to do. O descendant of the Bharata lineage! Their faces were pale and lost all their beauty. They were overcome with great shame and their heads hung down. Having obtained victory, the Pandavas were stationed at the heads of their ranks. All of them sounded great conch shells that were decorated with gold. O unblemished one! They loudly sounded

[459]Middle because Bhishma represented a bridge between the earlier generation of the Kurus and the current generation.

trumpets. O king! We saw the immensely strong Bhimasena in the field of battle. Kounteya was sporting, overcome with great delight. The extremely strong one had killed many enemies in battle. The Kurus were overcome by great confusion. Karna and Duryodhana sighed repeatedly. When Bhishma, the chief among the Kouravas, was brought down, a great lamentation of weakness arose amidst all of them.

'"On seeing that Bhishma had fallen, your son, Duhshasana, used great speed and proceeded towards Drona's army. The brave and armoured one, and his own soldiers, had been instructed by his brother.[460] Urging his own army on, that tiger among men now departed. O great king! On seeing Duhshasana, the Kurus surrounded him, wishing to hear what he had to say. Kourava informed Drona that Bhishma had been brought down. Hearing this unpleasant news, Drona suddenly fell down from his chariot. O venerable one! Having regained his senses, Bharadvaja's powerful son restrained his soldiers.[461] On seeing the Kurus withdraw, the Pandavas and their soldiers also retreated. They sent messengers on swift horses to instruct the respective soldiers everywhere to refrain from fighting. The kings removed their armour and went to the spot where Bhishma was. Hundreds and thousands of warriors withdrew from the battle. They went to the great-souled one, like the immortals before Prajapati. They approached the supine Bhishma, the bull among the Bharata lineage. The Kurus and the Pandavas showed him their obeisance and stood there. The Pandus and the Kurus bowed before him and stood there.

'"The great-souled Bhishma, Shantanu's son, spoke to them. 'O immensely fortunate ones! Welcome. O maharathas! Welcome. I am delighted to see you. You are the equals of the immortals.' With his head hanging down, he greeted them. 'My head is hanging down. Please give me a pillow.' The kings present there brought many soft and delicate pillows that were excellent. But the grandfather did not accept them. The tiger among men laughed and told those kings,

---

[460]To ensure Bhishma's protection.
[461]From continuing with the fight.

'O kings! These are not appropriate for a hero's bed.' The best of men then saw and addressed Pandava, the maharatha of all the worlds. 'O Dhananjaya! O long-armed one! My head is hanging down. Give me a pillow that you think to be appropriate.' He honoured the grandfather and grasped his giant bow. With his eyes full of tears, he spoke these words. 'O best of the Kurus! O supreme among those who wield all weapons! Command me. O invincible one! O grandfather! I am your servant. What can I do for you?' Shantanu's son replied, 'O son![462] My head is hanging down. O best of the Kuru lineage! O Phalguna! Give me a pillow. O brave one! Quickly grant me one that is appropriate for this bed. O Partha! O mighty-armed one! You are the best of all archers. You know about the dharma of kshatriyas. You possess intelligence and qualities.' Having been thus addressed, Phalguna quickly prepared to do as he had been instructed. He grasped Gandiva and arrows with drooping tufts. He took the permission of the great-souled one who was the middle one of the Bharata lineage. He shot three extremely forceful and sharp arrows and supported the head of his senior. Bhishma, the best of the Bharata lineage and learned about dharma and artha, was satisfied and praised Dhananjaya for having given him that pillow. Kunti's son was the best of warriors and brought delight to his well-wishers. He spoke to him. 'O Pandava! You have done well by giving me something that is appropriate for this bed. Had you done otherwise, I would have cursed you in rage. O mighty-armed one! This is the way in which kshatriyas should remain established in their dharma and sleep on a bed of arrows.' Having spoken thus to Bibhatsu, he spoke to all the kings and princes. 'See what Pandava has given me. I will sleep on this bed until the sun changes its path. Until it has traversed, the kings will be able to see me. When the sun goes beyond Vaishravana's direction[463] and the supremely energetic rays scorch the worlds from his chariot, I will give up my life, like a well-wisher who takes leave from a beloved one. O kings! Let a ditch be dug around the spot where I am. Pierced by a hundred arrows, I will worship

---

[462]The word used is tata.

[463]In this context, Vaishravana is Yama and Yama's direction is that of the south.

the sun. O kings! Abjure the enmity and give up this battle.' Many physicians came to him, those who were skilled in the knowledge of uprooting stakes. They possessed every kind of implement and were skilled and well-trained. On seeing them, Jahnavi's son spoke these words. 'Honour the physicians. Give them what needs to be given and let them go. I have been reduced to this state. What do I have to do with physicians? I have attained the supreme state that is praised by those who follow the dharma of kshatriyas. O lords of the earth! When I am lying on a bed of arrows, this should not be my dharma now.[464] O lords of men! I should be immolated with these arrows on my body.' Having heard these words, your son, Duryodhana, honoured the physicians in accordance with what they deserved and gave them permission to leave.

'"The lords of the different countries were overcome with great wonder. They beheld the supreme dharma on which the infinitely energetic Bhishma was established. O lord of men! Having given a pillow to your father, all the maharatha Pandavas and Kurus again approached the great-souled one, supine on that supreme bed. Having bowed before Bhishma, they circumambulated him. Having arranged for Bhishma's protection, all those brave ones went to their own camps in the evening and reflected in great misery. With bodies covered in blood, they retired. The maharatha Pandavas were delighted at Bhishma's downfall. At the appropriate time, Yadava approached the maharatha Pandavas and spoke to Yudhishthira, Dharma's son. 'O Kouravya! It is through good fortune that you have been victorious. It is through good fortune that Bhishma has been brought down. The maharatha was devoted to the truth and could not be slain by humans. He was skilled in the use of all weapons. O Partha! This was destiny. He could kill with his eyes. He could burn down with his terrible sight.' Thus addressed, Dharmaraja replied to Janardana, 'We have obtained victory through your favours. Your wrath is defeat. O Krishna! You are our refuge. You assure your devotees freedom from fear. O Keshava! It is not extraordinary that those whom you always protect in battle should be victorious. You

[464]Of being tended to by phyisicans and surgeons.

are always devoted to our welfare. We always seek refuge in you. It is my view that this is not extraordinary at all.' Having been thus addressed, Janardana smiled and said, 'O supreme among kings! The words that you have spoken can only come from someone like you.'"'

Chapter 976(116)

'Sanjaya said, "O great king! After night had passed, all the kings, the Pandavas and the sons of Dhritarashtra, approached the grandfather. The brave one, supreme among the Kurus, was lying down on a bed meant for heroes. The kshatriyas showed their obeisance to the bull among the kshatriyas. There were maidens everywhere, with powdered sandalwood, fried paddy and garlands. There were women, children and aged ones, and others who had gathered as spectators. They approached Shantanu's son, who was like the dispeller of darkness.[465] There were trumpets, courtesans, harlots, male dancers, female dancers and minor dancers. They approached the aged grandfather of the Kurus. The fighting ceased. The armour was cast aside. The Kurus and the Pandavas discarded their weapons. They approached the invincible Devavrata, the destroyer of enemies. They greeted each other affectionately, according to age, as they used to do in earlier times.[466] With the hundreds of kings assembled there, Bhishma looked resplendent. The descendant of the Bharata lineage was as radiant as a circle of gods in the firmament. The kings who honoured the grandfather were as brilliant as the gods worshipping the grandfather,[467] the lord of the gods.

'"O bull among the Bharata lineage! Bhishma bore his pain with fortitude. He was scorched by the arrows. But he spoke to the kings

[465]The sun.
[466]The Kurus and the Pandavas temporarily cast aside their enmity.
[467]Brahma.

with a cheerful mind and addressed them. 'My body is tormented with these arrows. I am losing my senses because of the arrows. I wish to have a drink.' O king! All the kshatriyas brought him excellent water pots filled with cold water.' On seeing that these had been brought, Bhishma, Shantanu's son, replied, 'O son![468] I am incapable of using objects of human pleasure now. I am lying on a bed of arrows, away from human enjoyment. I am established here, waiting for the moon and the sun to return along their paths.' Having spoken in this way, Shantanu's son rebuked all those kings. O descendant of the Bharata lineage! He addressed the mighty-armed Dhananjaya. The mighty-armed one approached and paid his respects to the grandfather. He stood there, hands joined in salutation, and asked, 'What will I do?' O king! On seeing Pandava Dhananjaya standing there in obeisance, Bhishma, with dharma in his soul, affectionately addressed him. 'My body is burning. I am covered with these great arrows. My inner organs are in pain and my mouth is dry. O Arjuna! You can use your bow to give me water for my body. O great archer! You alone are capable of giving me water in accordance with what is proper.' Having been thus addressed, the valiant Arjuna mounted his chariot. He grasped Gandiva with force and stretched the bow. The sound of the palm against the string of the bow was like the clap of thunder. On hearing this, all the beings and all the kings were frightened. On his chariot, the supreme of rathas circumambulated the supine one, who was the best of the Bharatas and supreme among those who wielded all weapons. The immensely illustrious one invoked and affixed a flaming arrow. While all the worlds looked on, he applied the *parjanya* weapon. Partha pierced the earth to Bhishma's right side. A clear and pure stream of water arose. It was cool and like amrita. It possessed a divine fragrance. With that cool stream of water, Partha satisfied Bhishma, the bull among the Kurus, whose valour and deeds were divine. Partha was like Shakra in his deeds. At this deed of his, all of the lords of the earth were struck with great wonder. On beholding Bibhatsu's superhuman and extraordinary

---

[468]The word used is tata, in the singular. The water was presumably brought by Duryodhana.

deed, all the Kurus trembled, like cows stricken by the cold. All the kings waved their upper garments in wonder. A tremendous sound of conch shells and the beating of drums was heard everywhere.

'"O king! In the presence of all the kings, Shantanu's son was satisfied. He honoured Bibhatsu and spoke to him. 'O mighty-armed one! O descendant of the Kuru lineage! You have done something wonderful. O infinitely radiant one! Narada spoke of you as an ancient rishi. With Vasudeva as your aide, you will perform great deeds that even Indra of the gods, with the other gods, will not attempt. O Partha! Those who are aware know that you will bring about the destruction of all the kshatriyas. Among all the brave men on earth, you alone are the one who can wield the bow. You are the best among men on earth, like Garuda among the birds, like the ocean is the best among all stores of water, like the cow is the best among all quadrupeds, like the sun is supreme among those with energy, Himalaya is foremost among all mountains, the brahmana is best among all classes and you are the foremost among all archers. Dhritarashtra's son paid no heed to the words repeatedly spoken by me and those uttered by Vidura, Drona, Rama,[469] Janardana and Sanjaya. He is beyond all intelligence. Duryodhana is like one who is bereft of his senses. He paid no attention to my words. He will soon be overwhelmed by Bhima's strength and weapons and will be killed.' On hearing these words, Duryodhana, the Indra among the Kouravas, became distressed.

'"Shantanu's son glanced at him and said, 'O king! Transcend your anger and listen to my words. O Duryodhana! You have seen how the intelligent Partha created a stream of water that is cool and bears the fragrance of amrita. There is no one else in this world capable of accomplishing this feat. Agneya, Varuna, Soumya, Vayavya, Vaishnava, Aindra, Pashupata, Brahma, Parameshtha, Prajapatya, Dhatu, Tvashtu, Savitu[470] and all the other divine weapons—among all the men on earth, Dhananjaya alone is the one who knows them. So does Krishna, Devaki's son. But no one else knows them.

---

[469]Parashurama.

[470]All of these are named after different gods.

O son![471] It is impossible to vanquish Pandava in battle. The deeds of the great-souled one are superhuman. He is spirited in battle. The brave one is the ornament of any battle. He is accomplished in battle. O king! O son! Make efforts towards peace. O son! As long as the mighty-armed Krishna controls himself in this assembly of Kurus, make efforts towards peace with the brave Parthas. O son! As long as your army is not destroyed through straight-tufted arrows shot by Arjuna, make efforts to bring about peace. O king! As long as your brothers and the remnants of these many kings remain stationed in battle, endeavour to bring about peace. O son! As long as your army is not consumed by the blazing anger in Yudhishthira's eyes, endeavour to bring about peace. O great king! O son! As long as Nakula, Sahadeva and Pandava Bhimasena do not destroy your entire army, it will please me if there is fraternal feeling between you and the Pandavas. O son! Let this feud end with my death. Have peace with the Pandavas. O unblemished one! Let these words spoken by me be acceptable to you. I think that this will be good for you and for the lineage. Abandon your anger and let there be peace with the Parthas. What Phalguna has already done is sufficient. Let Bhishma's death lead to affection. O king! Be pacified and let the remaining ones be alive. Give the Pandavas half of the kingdom. Let Dharmaraja go to Indraprastha. O Indra among the Kouravas! Do not kill your friends and be censured by the kings. Do not be famous for your evil deeds. With my end, let there be peace among the subjects. Let the kings depart cheerfully. O king! Let father and son, maternal uncle and nephew and brother and brother be happily united. If you do not accept my words, because you are overcome by delusion and because your intelligence is clouded, at the appropriate time, you will be destroyed and will remember all of Bhishma's words. I tell you truthfully that you will bear a great burden.' Having spoken these affectionate words to Bharata in the hearing of those kings, the son of the one who goes to the ocean became silent. His inner organs were in pain because of the stakes. Nevertheless, he overcame his pain and controlled his soul.'"

---

[471]The word used is tata.

Chapter 977(117)

'Sanjaya said, "O great king! After Bhishma, Shantanu's descendant had become silent, all the kings again returned to their own abodes. On hearing that Bhishma had been brought down, Radheya, bull among men, swiftly came to him, partly because he was terrified. He saw the great-souled one, lying down on his bed of arrows, like the lord, the god Kartikeya, lying down after his birth.[472] The brave one's eyes were closed. His voice choked with tears, Vrisha[473] worshipped the feet of the immensely radiant one who had fallen down. 'O best of the Kurus! I am Radheya. I have been in your sight, but you have always regarded me with hate.' He spoke these words. On hearing these words, the aged Kuru used his strength to slowly open his closed eyes and glanced at him. He spoke these affectionate words. He asked the guards to leave and once they were alone, glanced at him with benevolence.

'"Gangeya embraced him with one arm, like a father towards a son. 'Come. Come. You have always been my adversary and have always sought to rival me. If you had not come before me, there is no doubt that it would not have been good for you. You are a Kounteya. You are not Radheya. I have known this from Narada and from Krishna Dvaipayana[474] and Keshava. There is no doubt about this. O son![475] I do not hate you. I am telling you this truthfully. I have spoken harsh words towards you for the sake of reducing your energy. It is my view that you hated the Pandavas without any reason. O descendant of the sun! That is the reason I have spoken many harsh words to you. I know your valour in battle and that the enemy cannot withstand you. I know your devotion towards brahmanas, your valour and your supreme attachment to generosity. There is no man like you and you are like an immortal. I spoke harsh words towards you to prevent dissension in the lineage. In the use of

---

[472]Kartikeya was born in a clump of reeds.
[473]Karna's name.
[474]Vedavyasa.
[475]The word used is tata.

arrows, in aiming at a target, in dexterity and in the strength of your weapons, there is no one like you, with the exception of Phalguna and the great-souled Krishna. O Karna! You went to the king's capital and as a single archer, defeated all the kings in battle, for the sake of the king of the Kurus. The powerful King Jarasandha was invincible in an encounter and prided himself in battle. But even he wasn't your equal. You are devoted to brahmanas. You are truthful. You are like the sun in your energy and are superior to anyone else. You have been born from a god. You are invincible in battle. You are more than a man on earth. Today, I am giving up the anger I felt towards you earlier. Human endeavour is incapable of overturning destiny. O destroyer of enemies! The brave Pandavas are your brothers. O mighty-armed one! If you wish to please me, go to them. O son of the sun! With my end, let all the enmity be over. Let all the kings on earth be free from all danger.'

'"Karna replied, 'O immensely wise one! I know all this. There is no doubt about anything that you have said. O invincible one! I am a Kounteya and have not been born from a suta. But Kunti abandoned me and I was brought up by a suta. I have enjoyed Duryodhana's prosperity and have no interest in making that false now. My prosperity, body, life and fame are all for Duryodhana's sake. O one who is greatly generous! I am prepared to give all that up. I have depended on Suyodhana and have always angered the Pandavas. The outcome is inevitable and no one is capable of counteracting it. Who can overcome destiny through human enterprise? O grandfather! The omens indicate the destruction of the earth. These were noticed and spoken about in the assembly by you. I know everything about the Pandavas and Vasudeva being invincible to all other men. Nevertheless, I am interested in fighting. O father![476] You have always cheerfully given me permission to fight. O brave one! Since I have decided to fight, please give me permission. You should also forgive me any harsh and unpleasant words that I may have spoken against you, out of anger or folly, and any injurious acts that I may have performed.'

---

[476]The word used is tata.

'"Bhishma replied, 'O Karna! If you cannot discard the extremely terrible enmity that has been created, I grant you permission. Fight with a desire to attain heaven. Be free of anger and intolerance and perform the acts of the king to the best of your capacity and endeavour. Observe the conduct of the virtuous. I grant you the permission. May you obtain what you desire. There is no doubt that you will attain the worlds obtained through the practice of the dharma of kshatriyas. Resort to strength and valour and fight, without any vanity. There is nothing more desired by a kshatriya than a battle in accordance with dharma. I tried for a very long time to bring about peace. But I was not successful. Where there is dharma, victory will be there.'"

'Sanjaya said, "When Gangeya had spoken in this way, Radheya honoured him and obtained his favours. He then ascended his chariot and drove towards your son."'

This ends Bhishma Parva.

Drona Parva

Drona Parva continues with the account of the war. After Bhishma's death, Drona is instated as the commander of the Kourava army and some of the most ferocious fighting takes place in Drona Parva, when Drona is the commander for five days, days eleven to fifteen. The highlights of Drona Parva are the deaths of the sworn warriors, Abhimanyu, Jayadratha and Ghatotkacha. In the 18-parva classification, Drona Parva is the seventh. In the 100-parva classification, Drona Parva covers Sections 65 through 72. Drona Parva has 173 chapters. In the numbering of the chapters in Drona Parva, the first number is a consecutive one, starting with the beginning of the Mahabharata. And the second number, within brackets, is the numbering of the chapter within Drona Parva.

Dronabhisheka Parva

This parva has 634 shlokas and fifteen chapters.

Abhishekha *means instatement or consecration and the parva is named after Drona's consecration as the supreme commander. After the consecration, this section also describes the eleventh day of the battle. Drona promises to capture Yudhishthira alive. Despite a lot of fighting, nothing of great significance occurs on the eleventh day, though Drona kills some Panchala warriors.*

Chapter 978(1)

Janamejaya asked, 'Devavrata was unmatched in spirit, energy, strength, bravery and valour. On hearing that he had been killed[1] by Shikhandi of Panchala, what did King Dhritarashtra, with his senses overcome by sorrow, do? O brahmana rishi! His valiant father was slain. O illustrious one! His son wished to obtain the kingdom after vanquishing the great archers, the Pandavas, with rathas like Bhishma and Drona. O illustrious one! When the supreme among archers was killed, what did Kouravya[2] do? O supreme among brahmanas! Tell me all this.'

Vaishampayana replied, 'Hearing that his father had been killed, Dhritarashtra, the lord of men, could find no peace. Kouravya[3] was overcome by anxiety and sorrow. The king continually reflected on his misery. Gavalgana's son,[4] pure in soul, again came before him. It was night and Sanjaya had returned to the city of Nagasahrya from the camp. O great king! On hearing that Bhishma had been killed, Ambika's son was extremely distressed. Wishing for the victory of his sons, Dhritarashtra lamented in woe and asked . . .

'Dhritarashtra asked, "O son![5] The Kurus were driven by destiny. After conquering the misery as a consequence of Bhishma, whose valour was terrible, what did they do? The immensely energetic, brave and invincible one had been killed. The Kurus were immersed in an ocean of grief. What did they do? O Sanjaya! The great army of the great-souled Pandavas was capable of leading to the greatest fear in the three worlds. On Devavrata, the bull among the Kurus, having been killed, what did the kings do? O Sanjaya! Tell me."

'Sanjaya said, "O king! Listen, with a concentrated mind, to my words. I will tell you what your sons did when Devavrata was killed in battle. O king! Truth was Bhishma's valour. When he was killed, those on your side, and the Pandavas, thought about this separately. Having thought about the dharma of kshatriyas, they were both astounded and delighted. Having censured their own dharma, they bowed down before that great-souled one. They thought of

[1] We will use the words killed or slain, though Bhishma had not yet died.
[2] Duryodhana.
[3] Dhritarashtra.
[4] Sanjaya.
[5] The word used is tata.

the infinitely energetic Bhishma lying down on his bed of arrows. O tiger among men! His pillow was made out of straight-tufted arrows. Having made arrangements for Bhishma's protection, they conversed with each other. Having circumambulated Gangeya, they took his permission. Then they glanced towards each other, eyes red in anger. Driven by destiny, the kshatriyas emerged again to do battle. Trumpets and drums made a loud noise. Your soldiers, and those of the enemy, marched out. O Indra among kings! When Jahnavi's son fell down, the day had passed. Destiny had robbed them of their senses and they had been overcome by anger. They disregarded the beneficial words that the great-souled Gangeya had spoken. The best ones of the Bharata lineage marched out, armed with weapons. Because of your delusion and that of your sons, and because of the death of Shantanu's son, the Kouravas, together with the kings, seemed to have been summoned by death. They were like cattle without a herdsman, in a forest that was full of carnivores. Without Devavrata, they were extremely anxious in their minds. The best of the Bharata lineage had been brought down. The army of the Kurus looked like the firmament, devoid of stars, or the sky without any air, or the earth with crops destroyed, or words without refinement, or the ancient army of the asuras after Bali had been brought down, or a beautiful woman[6] who is a widow, or a descending river whose waters have dried, or a cow hemmed in by wolves in the forest when the leader of the herd has been killed, or a large mountainous cavern rendered impotent because the lion has been killed. O foremost among the Bharata lineage! After Jahnavi's son was brought down, the army of the Bharatas was like a feeble boat being tossed around on the great ocean by a tempest striking it from all directions. It was sorely afflicted by the brave and powerful Pandavas, who did not waver in their aim. With its horses, chariots and elephants, that army was extremely anxious. The men were seen to be distressed and dispirited. The kings and the soldiers were individually frightened. Without Devavrata, they were submerged in the nether regions.

[6]Specifically, a woman with beautiful hips.

'"The Kouravas then remembered Karna, who was like Devavrata himself. He was foremost among those who wielded all weapons and he was as resplendent as a guest. They resorted to him, like a person confronting a calamity turns to a friend. O descendant of the Bharata lineage! All the kings cried out, 'Karna. Karna. Radheya, the son of a suta, is prepared to lay down his life for our welfare. Together with his advisers and relatives, the immensely illustrious one has not fought for ten days. Summon him quickly.' While all the kshatriyas looked on, when Bhishma counted the rathas in accordance with their strength and valour, the mighty-armed one was counted as only half a ratha.[7] Karna, bull among men, is twice that.[8] Though he was thus enumerated among rathas and atirathas, he is foremost and is revered by all brave ones. He is keen to fight with Yama, Kubera, Varuna and the lord of the gods. O king! At that time, he angrily spoke to Gangeya. 'O Kouravya! As long as you are alive, I will never fight. O Kourava! But if you manage to kill the Pandaveyas in the great battle, I will take Duryodhana's permission and leave for the forest. O Bhishma! But if you are slain by the Pandavas and ascend to heaven, I will kill all those whom you think to be rathas on a single chariot.' O great king! Having thus spoken, the immensely illustrious Karna did not fight for ten days, with your son's permission. O king! Bhishma exhibited valour in the battle and in the encounter, bravely killed innumerable warriors on the side of the Pandaveyas. The greatly energetic and brave one, who never wavered in his aim, was then brought down. Like those wishing to cross with a boat, your sons thought of Karna. Together with all the kings, your sons exclaimed and said, 'Karna! This is the time for you to come.' He is unassailable in his manliness and he received instructions in weapons from Jamadagni's son.[9] Our minds turned towards Karna, as if towards a friend in times of hardship. O king! He is alone capable of saving us from this great fear, like Govinda always saves the thirty gods from extremely grave calamities."'

[7]This incident has been recounted in Section 59 (Volume 4).
[8]Twice a ratha.
[9]Parashurama.

Vaishampayana said, 'Thus did he[10] speak about Karna, supreme among warriors. Dhritarashtra sighed like a serpent and spoke these words to him. "Your minds then turned towards Vaikartana Karna. You saw that Radheya, the son of a suta, was ready to lay down his life. Did the warrior succeed in saving the distressed ones? Truth is his valour. They were depressed and frightened and sought safety with him, having honoured him. That warrior is foremost among all archers. But when Bhishma, the refuge of the Kouravas, was slain, did he succeed in filling the breach and did he fill the enemy with fear? Did he bring success to my sons, who were wishing for victory?"'

Chapter 979(2)

'Sanjaya said, "On learning that Bhishma had been slain, Adhiratha's son, the son of a suta, wished to save the Kurus, who were like a shattered boat in the fathomless ocean. He bore fraternal feelings towards the distressed ones. He wanted your son's army to cross over. On hearing that Shantanu's maharatha and undecaying son, Indra among men, had been brought down, Vrisha Karna,[11] the destroyer of enemies and supreme among those who wield bows, swiftly arrived. After Bhishma, supreme among rathas, was slain by the enemy, the Kurus were like a boat submerged in the ocean. He wished that your son's army might be able to cross over.

'"Karna said, 'He possessed fortitude, intelligence, valour, energy, self-control, truth, all the qualities of a hero and divine weapons. Humility, affection and pleasant speech existed in Bhishma. He was always grateful and killed those who hated brahmanas. These attributes were eternal in him, like Lakshmi in the moon. That destroyer of enemy heroes has now obtained peace and I think that all the other warriors have already been killed. Because everything in this world is assigned by action, there is nothing that is permanent. When

[10]Sanjaya.
[11]Vrisha is Karna's name.

the one who was great in his vows has been slain, who can certainly say today that the sun will rise tomorrow? He possessed the power of the Vasus. He was born from the energy of the Vasus. That lord of the earth has returned to the Vasus again. O Kurus! You should sorrow for your riches, your sons, the earth and the army.'"[12]

'Sanjaya said, "The granter of boons, the one who was great in his powers, was brought down. Shantanu's son was foremost in the world and was greatly energetic. The Bharatas were defeated and dispirited. O king! Karna began to console your sons and your soldiers and hearing this, the brave ones lamented and shed tears from their eyes, as copious as the words of woe. But urged by the kings, they returned again to the great battle and roared again. The bull among all maharathas then spoke these delightful words to the bulls among rathas.

"'Karna said, 'This transient world is always moving.[13] Noticing this, I think of everything as temporary. When all of you were present, how could that bull among the Kurus, who was like a mountain, be brought down in battle? Shantanu's maharatha son has been brought down, as if the sun has resorted to the ground. The kings are unable to withstand Dhananjaya, like trees against a storm that uproots mountains. With the foremost ones killed, they are dispirited and their bravery has been destroyed by the enemy. I will be their protector now and protect the army of the Kurus in battle, just as the great-souled one did. Such a burden now devolves on me. I notice that this world is transient. Since that skilled one has been brought down in the battle, why should I have any fear about the battle? I will roam around on the field of battle and use my straight-tufted arrows to convey the bulls among the Kurus[14] to Yama's abode. Knowing that fame is the supreme objective in this world, I will kill the enemy in battle, or lie down myself. Yudhishthira possesses steadfastness, intelligence, dharma and spirit. Vrikodara is the equal of one hundred elephants in valour. Arjuna has enterprise and is the son of the lord of the thirty gods. That army is not easy to defeat, even

---

[12]There is a pun that can't be captured in the English. Vasu means riches or prosperity and the earth is Vasundhara, the store of riches.

[13]Heading towards death.

[14]Meaning the Pandavas.

by the immortals. The twins are the equal of Yama in battle and that
army also has Satyaki and Devaki's son. It is like death with a gaping
mouth. A coward who approaches that army will not return. The
learned ones say that austerities have to be countered with austerities
and force with force. My mind is firmly fixed on resisting the enemy
and protecting my own. O charioteer! I will go and counter the power
of those intelligent ones and obtain victory today. I will accomplish
this deed of a virtuous man, or give up my life and follow Bhishma.
I will kill large numbers of the enemy in battle, or having been slain,
will go to the world of heroes. The women and children are crying
for help. The manliness of Dhritarashtra's son has been defeated. O
charioteer! I know my duty. Therefore, I will vanquish the enemies
of the son of Dhritarashtra. I will protect the Kurus and slaughter
the sons of Pandu, even if it means that I have to give up my life in
this dreadful fight. I will kill large numbers of the enemy in battle
and give the kingdom to Dhritarashtra's son. Fasten my beautiful,
golden and bright armour, radiant with jewels. Bring my helmet, like
the sun in brilliance, and my bow and arrows, like virulent snakes.
Fasten sixteen quivers and divine bows. Also bring swords, lances,
heavy clubs and the conch shell that is decorated with gold. Bring
my victorious and golden standard, with the complexion of a lotus
and bearing the marks of a victorious and healthy elephant. Have
it cleaned with an excellent garment and decorate it with colourful
garlands and nets. Bring swift and white horses that have the hue
of the clouds. They should be well-fed and bathed in water from
golden pots, and sanctified with mantras. They should possess
golden harnesses. O son of a charioteer! Quickly. Quickly. Bring an
excellent chariot with nets of gold, decorated with gems and with
the radiance of the moon and the sun. Let it be furnished with all
objects and weapons. Let it be yoked to swift horses. Bring colourful
and powerful bows with the supreme of bowstrings, so that they
are capable of striking. Let the large quivers be filled with arrows.
Let me be dressed with body-armour. Swiftly bring me everything
needed for departure. O brave one! Let golden and brass vessels be
filled with perfume. Bring garlands and adorn my body with them.
Let the drums quickly announce my victory. O charioteer! Take me

swiftly to the spot where Kiriti, Vrikodara, Dharma's son and the twins are. I will confront and kill them in battle. Or I will be slain by the enemy and follow Bhishma. That army has King Yudhishthira, who is firmly devoted to the truth, Bhima, Arjuna, Vasudeva, Satyaki and the Srinjayas. I think that it cannot be defeated by the kings. But even if Death, who robs everything, were to continually protect Kiriti in this encounter, I will confront him in battle and slay him. Or I will follow Bhishma's path to Yama. I am not saying that I will go there in the midst of these brave ones. Those who create dissension among friends and those who are weak in their devotion are evil-minded and are not my aides.'"[15]

'Sanjaya said, "He rode out on an excellent, supreme and firm chariot, which possessed a beautiful seat that was decorated with gold. It had a standard and was yoked to steeds that were as fleet as the wind. He rode out for victory. The bull among rathas, on white horses, was worshipped by the great-souled Kurus. The terrible archer left for the battle and went to where the bull among the Bharata lineage[16] was. The army was large and had standards. Karna's chariot was embellished with gold, pearls, jewels and diamonds. It was yoked to well-trained horses and roared like the sound of the clouds. It was as energetic as the sun. The archer was resplendent on his resplendent chariot. He was like the fire in his complexion and like the fire in his brilliance. Adhiratha's maharatha son was stationed on his chariot, like the king of the gods established on his own vimana."'

Chapter 980(3)

'Sanjaya said, "The great-souled and infinitely energetic one was lying down on his bed of arrows. He was like an ocean that had been dried up by a mighty wind. Savyasachi had used his divine

---

[15]Without specifically naming anyone, Karna is clearly casting aspersions on some on the Kourava side.

[16]Bhishma.

weapons to bring down the great archer and shattered the hopes
your sons entertained for victory and their armour and their peace.
He was like an island for those who wish to cross an ocean that
cannot be traversed. He was covered in a mass of arrows, like flows
in the river Yamuna. He was like the intolerable and giant Mount
Mainaka, brought down on the ground, like the sun which has been
dislodged from the firmament and has fallen down on earth. This was
as unthinkable as Shatakratu being vanquished by Vritra in earlier
times. All the soldiers were confounded at Bhishma having been
brought down in the battle. He was the bull among all the soldiers.
He was the objective of all archers. Your father, great in his vows,
was covered with Dhananjaya's arrows. The brave one, bull among
men, was lying down on a bed meant for heroes.

"'On seeing Bhishma, the middle one of the Bharata lineage,
Adhiratha's son descended from his chariot. He was tormented and
his voice was choked with tears. He joined his hands in salutation.
Having worshipped him, he spoke these words. 'O fortunate one! I
am Karna. O descendant of the Bharata lineage! Speak sacred and
auspicious words to me today. Open your eyes and look at me.
No man can ever enjoy the fruits of his good deeds on earth, since
you, aged and devoted to dharma, are lying down on the ground.
O supreme among the Kurus! In filling the treasury, in counsel, in
constructing vyuhas, in using weapons, I do not think I can see anyone
like you among the Kurus. You are united with intelligence and purity.
You have saved the Kurus from danger. Having deluged the warriors,
you are now proceeding to the world of the ancestors. O best of
the Bharata lineage! The Pandavas will now cause a destruction of
the Kurus, like enraged tigers destroying deer. The brave Kurus are
acquainted with Gandiva's roar and will be terrified by Savyasachi
now, like the asuras by the wielder of the vajra. In today's battle, the
Kurus and the other kings will be frightened by the sound released
from Gandiva, like the clap of thunder. The brave one[17] will be like
a fire before kindling and will be like a great conflagration that burns
down trees. Kiriti's arrows will destroy the sons of Dhritarashtra in

---

[17]Arjuna.

this way. O illustrious one! Wherever the wind and the fire advance
together in a forest, they burn down as they wish. There is no
doubt that Partha is like fire before kindling. O tiger among men!
There is no doubt that Krishna is like the wind. O descendant of
the Bharata lineage! On hearing Panchajanya's roar and Gandiva's
sound, all the soldiers will be overcome by terror. The destroyer of
enemies will advance on a chariot with a monkey on the banner. O
brave one! Without you, the kings will not be able to withstand that
sound. Other than you, who among the kings is capable of fighting
with Arjuna on the field of battle? The learned ones speak about
his celestial deeds. The encounter between the intelligent one and
Tryambaka[18] was superhuman. As a result of this, he obtained a
boon that is difficult for those with unclean souls to get. If you permit
me, I will fight with that excellent Pandava today. I am incapable of
tolerating him. He is like an extremely terrible and poisonous snake
which kills with its glances alone. I have placed death, or victory,
at the forefront.'"'

Chapter 981(4)

'Sanjaya said, "When he spoke in this way, the aged grandfather
of the Kurus heard him. His mind was delighted and he spoke
words that were appropriate to the time and the place. 'May you be
established amidst your well-wishers, like the ocean among rivers,
the sun among all stellar bodies, truth among the virtuous, fertile
ground among seeds and clouds among all beings. May your relatives
depend on you, like the immortals on the one with a thousand eyes.[19]
Through the strength of your own arms and your valour, you did
what brought pleasure to Dhritarashtra's son. O Karna! You went

[18]The one with three eyes, Mahadeva. This encounter has been described in
Section 31 (Volume 2).

[19]Indra has a thousand eyes.

to Rajapura and killed the Kambojas.[20] You went to Girivraja[21] and vanquished the kings, with Nagnajit at the forefront, and the Ambashthas, the Videhas and the Gandharas. O Karna! In earlier times, you brought those who dwelt in the Himalayas and Kiratas, who were harsh in battle, under Duryodhana's suzerainty. In every such place, you fought for Duryodhana's welfare. O brave one! O Karna! You conquered many greatly energetic ones. O son![22] Just as Duryodhana, with his relatives, his kin and his friends, is the refuge of the Kouravas, so are you. I am granting you an auspicious permission. Go and fight with the enemy. Lead the Kurus in battle and bring victory to Duryodhana. You are like my grandson, just as Duryodhana is. According to dharma, all of us are yours, just as we are his.[23] O best of men! Learned ones say that in this world, association with the virtuous is more important than a relationship resulting from birth. Do not make your relationship with the Kurus false. Protect Duryodhana's army, as if it were your own.' On hearing these words, Vaikartana Karna honoured his feet and quickly went to the spot where the warriors were. He saw that large and extensive mass of men. The broad-chested and well-armed soldiers were arranged in battle formation. On seeing the great archer, Karna, arrive for battle, the Kurus honoured him. They slapped their arms and roared like lions. They twanged their bows and made other kinds of sounds.'"

Chapter 982(5)

'Sanjaya said, "O king! On seeing Karna, tiger among men, stationed on his chariot, Duryodhana was delighted and spoke

[20]Rajapura was the capital of the Kamboja kingdom. On Duryodhana's behalf, Karna led an expedition there.

[21]Girivraja (Rajagriha or Rajgir) was the capital of Magadha and is now in Bihar.

[22]The word used is tata.

[23]This may be an allusion to Karna being Kunti's son.

these words. 'Now that it is protected by you, I think this army has found a protector. Now do what we are capable of, and what seems to be appropriate.'

'"Karna replied, 'O tiger among men! O king! You are the wisest. You tell us. Someone whose objective is at stake, sees things in a way that another person never can. O lord of men! All of us wish to hear your words. It is my view that you will never say anything that is inappropriate.'

'"Duryodhana said, 'Bhishma was our commander. He was senior and valiant. He was well-endowed with learning, possessed knowledge of weapons and had all the qualities. O Karna! He obtained great fame by slaying large numbers of the enemy. The great-souled one fought well for ten days and protected us. He performed extremely difficult deeds and is ascending to heaven. Who do you think should be our commander after him? Without a leader, the army cannot last for an instant in battle, like a boat in the water without a boatman. Just as a boatman steers a boat, a charioteer controls a chariot, a commander ensures that an army is not led astray. You are the best in battle. Look at all the great-souled ones among us and find a commander who can succeed Shantanu's son. O venerable one! Whoever you mention will be accepted by all us as our commander in this battle.'

'"Karna replied, 'All these supreme among men are great-souled. But we should not examine details about who should be our commander. All of them have been born in noble lineages. All of them know how to withstand onslaught. All of them possess strength, valour and intelligence. They are grateful and modest and do not retreat from battle. However, all of them cannot be the leader at the same time. There must be only one, who possesses special qualities. All these rival one another. If one is specially honoured, the others will be dispirited. O descendant of the Bharata lineage! It is clear that they will not fight. Among all us warriors, the preceptor is aged and is our senior. Drona, supreme among those who wield all weapons, should be made the commander. He is supreme among those who know the brahman. He is unassailable. If Drona is made the commander, who can stand against that? He is the equal of Shukra and Angiras in his learning.[24] O descendant of the Bharata lineage! When Drona advances into battle, there is not a single warrior among all these kings who will not follow him. He is foremost among all the leaders of soldiers and among those who wield weapons. He is foremost in intelligence. O king! He is also your preceptor. O Duryodhana! Quickly make the preceptor the commander, just as, wishing to defeat the asuras in battle, the immortals chose Kartikeya.'"

'Sanjaya said, "Drona was standing in the midst of the army. On hearing Karna's words, King Duryodhana spoke these words to him. 'Because of the superiority of your varna, the lineage in which you have been born, your learning, your age, your intelligence, your valour, your capacity, your invincibility, your knowledge of artha and law, your austerities, your gratitude and your superiority in all the qualities, I do not think there is anyone among all the kings who is your equal as a protector. Protect us, like Vasava among all the gods. O supreme among brahmanas! With you as our leader, we wish to vanquish the enemy. You are like Kapali among the Rudras, Pavaka among the Vasus, Kubera among the yakshas, Vasava among the Maruts, Vasishtha among the brahmanas, the sun among those with energy, Dharma among the ancestors, the king of the waters among the Adityas, the moon among stellar bodies and Ushanas among the sons of Diti.[25] You are the foremost among leaders of soldiers. Therefore, be our commander. O unblemished one! Let these eleven akshouhinis follow your instructions. Create a counter-vyuha against the enemy and kill them, like Indra against

---

[24]Respectively, Shukra (the preceptor of the demons) and Brihaspati (the preceptor of the gods, referred to as Angiras).

[25]In the singular, Rudra is used as a name for Shiva. In the plural, the Rudras are eleven in number. When the eleven Rudras are mentioned by name, Kapali is one of the names. However, Kapali is also one of Shiva's names. There are eight Vasus and Agni is mentioned as the first one. Pavaka is a name for Agni. Kubera is the lord of the yakshas and the Maruts are wind gods who follow Indra (Vasava). In the context of the ancestors, Dharma means Yama. While the Adityas are gods in general, their number is sometimes said to be seven or twelve and Varuna (king of the waters) figures prominently. The sons of Diti are daityas or demons and their preceptor is Shukra (Ushanas).

the danavas. Advance in front of us, like Pavaka's son ahead of
the gods.[26] We will follow you, like a herd of bulls following their
leader. You are terrible in wielding the bow. You are a great archer.
On seeing you stationed at our forefront, stretching your divine
bow, Arjuna will not strike. O tiger among men! If you become our
commander, it is certain that I will defeat Yudhishthira in battle,
together with his followers and relatives.' After he had spoken
in this way, all the kings exclaimed, 'Victory to Drona.' They
roared mightily like lions and delighted your son. The soldiers
were filled with joy and wished for the prosperity of that supreme
among brahmanas. With Duryodhana at their head, they desired
great fame.

'"Drona said, 'I know the Vedas and the six *angas*.[27] I know about
artha. I am conversant with human knowledge. I am acquainted
with the weapons of Tryambaka and with many other kinds of
weapons. You have described my qualities and I will try to exhibit
them, wishing to bring about your victory. I tell you truthfully that
I will fight with the Pandavas.'"

'Sanjaya said, "O king! Having thus obtained Drona's permission,
your son instated him as the commander, in accordance with the
prescribed rites. Drona was consecrated as the commander by the
kings, with Duryodhana leading the way, just as in ancient times
Skanda was instated by the gods, with Shakra at the forefront.
The men created a mighty sound, mixed with the noise of musical
instruments. Amidst this noise and joy, Drona became the
commander. There were sounds like those on auspicious occasions
and the pronouncement of benedictions. Minstrels, bards and
raconteurs chanted praise, to the sound of singing. The foremost
among brahmanas uttered benedictions for great fortune and victory.
They honoured Drona according to the rites and thought that the
Pandavas had already been defeated."'

[26]Pavaka is Agni and by Agni's son, one means Kartikeya.

[27]The six vedangas are shiksha (articulation and pronunciation), chhanda
(prosody), vyakarana (grammar), nirukta (etymology), jyotisha (astronomy)
and kalpa (rituals).

Chapter 983(6)

'Sanjaya said, "Bharadvaja's maharatha son became the commander. He arranged the soldiers in the form of a vyuha and set out to do battle, together with your sons. Saindhava, Kalinga and your son, Vikarna, were armoured and stationed themselves on the right flank. Shakuni supported them, with the best of horse-riders, and advanced with the warriors from Gandhara, wielding polished lances. Kripa, Kritavarma, Chitrasena and Vivimshati, with Duhshasana at the forefront, advanced and protected the left flank. They were supported by the Kambojas, with Sudakshina leading the way. They advanced on extremely swift horses, together with the Shakas and the Yavanas. The Madras, the Trigartas, the Ambashthas, the residents of the west and the north, the Shibis, the Shurasenas, the Shudras, the Maladas, the Souviras, the Kitavas and all those from the east and the south placed your son at the head, with the son of the suta at the rear. They delighted all the soldiers and added force to the army. Vaikartana Karna advanced at the head of all the archers. His blazing standard was giant in size and delighted his own army. That giant standard was resplendent with the sign of a healthy elephant and dazzled like the sun. On seeing Karna, no one thought about the calamity consequent to Bhishma's downfall. All the kings, together with the Kurus, were freed from their grief. In joy, the large number of warriors began to converse with one another. 'On seeing Karna in battle, the Pandavas will not be able to remain on the field of battle. Karna is capable of vanquishing the gods, together with Vasava, in battle. The sons of Pandu are inferior in bravery and valour. How can they remain in battle? The strong-armed Bhishma saved the Parthas in the battle. But there is no doubt that Karna will destroy them with his sharp arrows.' O lord of the earth! In delight, they spoke to each other in this way. They honoured and praised Radheya and advanced.

'"Drona instructed that our vyuha should be in the form of a cart.[28] O king! O descendant of the Bharata lineage! The vyuha of

---

[28]*Shakata*, meaning carriage or cart. The array was probably in the form of a wedge.

the enemy was in the form of a curlew.[29] Cheerfully, the great-souled Dharmaraja instructed this. Those bulls among men, Vishvaksena[30] and Dhananjaya, with the monkey on the standard, were at the front of their vyuha. This was the hump[31] of all the soldiers and the objective of all the archers. The infinitely energetic Partha's standard fluttered in the path of the sun. It illuminated the army of the great-souled Pandava, like the blazing sun on the earth at the end of a yuga. Arjuna is foremost among archers, Gandiva is supreme among bows, Vasudeva is supreme among beings and Sudarshana is supreme among chakras. These four kinds of energy[32] were borne by the chariot with white horses and it stationed itself in front of the hostile army, like the upraised wheel of time. Thus did the great-souled ones stand in front of those powerful armies—Karna before yours and Dhananjaya before that of the enemy. There was enmity between them and they wished to kill each other. In that battle, Karna and Pandava glanced towards each other.

'"Bharadvaja's maharatha son powerfully advanced. There was dreadful lamentation and the earth began to tremble. The wind raised a violent and terrible dust that was as tawny as silk. This covered the sky and the sun. Though there were no clouds in the sky, a shower of flesh, bones and blood fell down. O king! Thousands of vultures, hawks, wild crows, herons and crows repeatedly swooped down on the soldiers.[33] Jackals howled hideously and many fearful creatures swooped down on the left side of your army, desiring to eat the flesh and drink the blood.[34] Flaming and blazing meteors were seen to descend, covering the field of battle in every direction with their tails. They roared and caused a trembling. O king! When the commander of the army[35] advanced, the gigantic solar disc thundered and seemed to

[29]Krouncha, curlew or osprey.

[30]Krishna.

[31]*Kakuda*, which means hump. The suggestion is that this standard was the centre of the army.

[32]Krishna, Arjuna, Gandiva and Sudarshana.

[33]Meaning the Kourava soldiers.

[34]The left side is inauspicious.

[35]Drona.

emit lightning. There were many other fearful portents, inauspicious for the warring heroes and signifying a destruction of lives. Thus the battle between the Kuru and Pandava soldiers commenced, each side wishing to kill the other. The entire earth was full of that noise. The Pandavas and the Kouravas were extremely enraged. They grasped weapons and sought to kill each other with sharp arrows. The immensely radiant and great archer[36] rushed towards the Pandava soldiers with great force, showering hundreds of sharp arrows. O king! On seeing Drona advance, the Pandavas and the Srinjayas countered him, separately showering arrows. That great army was agitated and shattered by Drona. The Panchalas were destroyed, like a mountain by a storm. In a short instant, Drona unleashed many kinds of divine weapons in that battle and oppressed the Pandavas and the Srinjayas. With Dhrishtadyumna at the forefront, the Panchalas were slaughtered by Drona and trembled, like the danavas before Vasava. The brave maharatha, Yajnasena's son,[37] skilled in the use of divine weapons, used showers of arrows to penetrate Drona's army in many places. He repulsed Drona's shower of arrows with several showers of arrows. The powerful one killed the Kuru soldiers. In the battle, the mighty-armed Drona restrained his own soldiers and attacked Parshata. He released a great shower of arrows towards Parshata, like the angry Maghavan forcefully attacking the danavas. Drona's arrows made the Pandavas and the Srinjayas tremble. They were repeatedly routed, like deer by a lion. O king! The powerful Drona travelled through that army of the Pandvas like a circle of fire[38] and it was wonderful. His chariot was like a city in the sky, constructed by one conversant with sacred texts. The harnessed horses were controlled well. The standard fluttered in the wind. The pole of the standard was as bright as crystal and he tormented the enemy with his arrows. He was astride that supreme chariot and slaughtered the soldiers of the enemy."'

[36]Drona.

[37]Yajnasena is Drupada and by Drupada's son, one means Dhrishtadyumna here. Prishata is also one of Drupada's names and Dhrishtadyumna is Parshata.

[38]More accurately, a circle made out of firebrands.

Chapter 984(7)

'Sanjaya said, "On seeing Drona slaughter the horses, charioteers, rathas and elephants, the Pandavas were distressed and surrounded him. King Yudhishthira spoke to Dhrishtadyumna and Dhananjaya. 'Make endeavours to counter the one who was born from a pot and surround him.'[39] Arjuna and Parshata, with their followers, surrounded him, together with all the maharathas—the Kekayas, Bhimasena, Subhadra's son, Ghatotkacha, Yudhishthira, the twins, Matsya, Drupada's son, Droupadi's cheerful sons, Dhrishtaketu, Satyaki, the enraged Chekitana and maharatha Yuyutsu. O king! There were many other kings who followed the Pandavas. In accordance with their lineage and their valour, they performed many deeds. On seeing that the army of the Pandavas was thus protected in battle, Bharadvaja's son glanced at them, with anger in his eyes. He was stationed on his chariot, invincible in battle, and was overcome by terrible rage. He pierced the Pandava army, like the wind scattering clouds. He attacked the chariots, horses, men and elephants in every direction. Though he was old, Drona roamed around, like a mad young man. His horses were crimson in colour and were as fleet as the wind. They were covered in blood. O king! Those horses thus assumed a beautiful appearance. On seeing that angry one, rigid in his vows, descend like death, the Pandava warriors fled in every direction. Some fled in fright. Others returned. Some glanced at him and an extremely dreadful noise arose, causing delight among brave ones and leading to fright among those who were cowards. This completely filled the space between the sky and the earth. Yet again, Drona announced his name in the battle. He shot hundreds of arrows at the enemy and assumed a dreadful form. Though he was aged, the powerful Drona acted like one who was young. The intelligent one was like death amidst the Pandava soldiers. The fierce one sliced off the heads and the arms with their ornaments. The maharatha rendered the chariots empty and roared. O lord! Because of his roars of delight and because of the force of

[39]Drona was born from a pot.

his arrows, the warriors trembled in the field of battle, like cattle
because of the winter. As a result of the roar of Drona's chariot, the
stretching of his bowstring and the sound of his bow, a great sound
arose in the sky. Many thousands of arrows were released by him.
They covered all the directions and descended on the elephants,
the horses and the chariots. His extremely forceful bow was like
the fire, with arrows as its flames. The Panchalas and the Pandavas
attacked Drona. But he dispatched the rathas, elephants and horses
to Yama's abode. In a short while, Drona covered the earth with the
mud of blood. He showered supreme weapons and arrows in every
direction. Drona covered the directions with his net of arrows and
nothing could be seen. Foot soldiers, chariots, horses and elephants
were shrouded and his standard could be seen, roaming around, like
a cloud tinged with lightning.

'"With the bow and arrows in his hand, Drona used arrows to
penetrate the five brave ones from Kekaya and the king of Panchala
and then attacked Yudhishthira's army. Bhimasena, Dhananjaya,
Shini's grandson, Drupada's son, Shibi's son, the lord of Kashi and
Shibi were delighted. They roared and covered him with a large
number of arrows. They were assailed by arrows released from
Drona's bow. These were colourful and gold-tufted. They pierced the
bodies of elephants and young horses and penetrated the ground, the
tufts covered with blood. The earth was strewn with large numbers
of warriors, chariots, elephants and horses, mangled by the arrows.
They fell down on the ground and looked like dark clouds in the
sky. Desiring the prosperity of your sons, Drona crushed the armies
of Shinis's descendant, Bhima, Arjuna, Shibi, Abhimanyu, the king
of Kashi and many other brave ones in that battle. O Indra among
Kouravas! The great-souled one performed this, and many other
deeds, in the battle. O king! Having scorched the world, like the
sun at the time of destruction, Drona went to heaven. On his golden
chariot, the brave one killed hundreds and thousands of Pandava
warriors in the battle and was brought down by Parshata. He killed
more than two akshouhinis of brave ones who never retreated. After
that, the wise one attained the supreme objective. O king! The one
on the golden chariot performed extremely difficult deeds and was

then killed by the Pandavas and the Panchalas, the performers of inauspicious and cruel deeds. O king! When the preceptor was killed in the battle, there was a roar among the beings in the firmament and also among the soldiers. This resounded in heaven, the earth, the sky, the directions and the sub-directions. A great sound of 'shame' was heard among all the beings. The gods, the ancestors and all those who were his relatives saw that Bharadvaja's maharatha son was slain. Having obtained victory, the Pandavas roared like lions. The earth trembled because of that loud roar.'"

Chapter 985(8)

'Dhritarashtra asked, "How could the Pandavas and the Srinjayas kill Drona in battle? Among those who wielded all weapons, he was extremely skilled. Did his chariot break? When he was striking, did his bow shatter? Was Drona distracted and was that the reason for his death? O son![40] How could Parshata slay him? He was incapable of being oppressed by enemies. He showered large numbers of gold-tufted arrows. The foremost among brahmanas possessed dexterity of hand. He was accomplished and colourful in fighting. He could shoot from a great distance. He had self-control. He was skilled in war. The maharatha was undecaying and supreme. He was careful and performed terrible deeds in battle. It must be destiny that Panchala's son killed him. It is my view that it is manifest that destiny is superior to human endeavour. The brave Drona has been killed by the great-souled Parshata. The four types of weapons were established in the brave one.[41] The

[40]The word used is tata.

[41]Usually, five types of weapons are mentioned—mukta (those that are released from the hand, like a chakra), amukta (those that are never released, like a sword), muktamukta (those that can be released or not released, like a spear), yantramukta (those that are released from an implement, like an arrow) and mantramukta (magical weapons unleashed with incantations). These

preceptor Drona knew supreme weapons and has been slain. He
used to be on a golden chariot, covered with the skins of tigers and
decorated with pure gold. On hearing that he has been killed, I am
now overcome with sorrow. O Sanjaya! No one dies because of
the hardship that someone else faces. On hearing that Drona has
been slain, I am dead, though I am alive. My heart is made out of
hard stone. Despite learning that Drona has been killed, it has not
shattered into a hundred parts. He was worshipped by brahmanas
and princes who desired the qualities of knowledge of the brahman,
the Vedas and weapons. How could he have been taken away by
death? This is like the ocean drying up, Mount Meru moving, or the
sun falling down. I cannot tolerate Drona's downfall. He restrained
the proud and protected those who followed dharma. The scorcher
of enemies was prepared to give up his life to attain the objective of
my wicked and evil sons. Their victory depended on his valour. He
was the equal of Brihaspati and Ushanas in his intelligence. How
could he have been killed? His large Saindhava horses were crimson.
They were garlanded in gold. They were fleet as the wind and were
yoked to his chariot. They were beyond the reach of all sounds of
battle. They were powerful and neighed in joy. Those Saindhavas
were controlled and were trained in bearing.[42] They were firm in the
midst of battle and never suffered from distress or exhaustion. They
withstood the trumpeting of elephants in battle and the sound of
conch shells and drums. They tolerated the twanging of bowstrings
and the shower of arrows and weapons. They had conquered their
breathing and had conquered pain and they assured victory over the
enemy. Those fleet horses quickly bore the chariot of Bharadvaja's
son. How could they be overpowered? They were yoked to the golden
chariot and controlled by the foremost of men. O son! How could

---

are categories of weapons. Alternatively, especially for magical and celestial
weapons, there are the five techniques of employing, restraining, returning,
pacifying and counteracting. However, Dhanurveda (the art of war) is usually
described as having four parts. In the category-wise classification, this means
that mantramukta weapons are not included.

[42]Bearing the chariot.

they not cross that Pandava army? He was mounted on a supreme chariot, decorated with pure gold. What feats did Bharadvaja's brave son not accomplish in war? He made warriors weep. All the archers in the world depended on his knowledge. Drona was devoted to the truth. He was powerful. What did he accomplish in battle? He was foremost among all the great ones who wielded the bow, like Shakra in heaven. He was the performer of terrible deeds. Which rathas countered him in battle? On seeing the one on the golden chariot, did the Pandavas run away? Unleashing divine weapons, did he destroy that inexhaustible army? Or did Dharmaraja, together with his younger brothers and with Panchala as the harness, surround Drona from every direction with all the soldiers? Did Partha restrain the rathas with his arrows? Parshata, the performer of evil deeds, must have assailed Drona then. With the exception of Dhrishtadyumna, protected by the terrible Kiriti, I do not see anyone capable of killing the vigorous one. When the Kekayas, the Chedis, the Karushas and the other kings surrounded and agitated the brave preceptor, while he was performing a difficult deed, like ants against a serpent, the wicked Panchala must have killed him then. That is my view. He studied the four Vedas and the fifth one about the accounts.[43] He was the refuge of the brahmanas, like the ocean is of the rivers. How could that aged and powerful brahmana have been killed through a weapon? He was intolerant and proud, though he often suffered on my account. Though he did not deserve it, he reaped the fruits of his action through Kounteya. All the wielders of the bow on earth depended on his deeds for their livelihood. He was devoted to the truth. He performed good deeds. How could he have been killed by those who desire prosperity? He was foremost. He was great-spirited and extremely strong, like Shakra in heaven. How could he have been killed by the Parthas, like a whale by smaller fish? He was dexterous in the use of his hands. He was powerful. He was firm in wielding the bow. He was the destroyer of enemies. No one,

---

[43]*Itihasa–Purana*, the epics and the Purana literature, are referred to as the fifth Veda.

wishing to remain alive, faced him on the field and remained alive. As long as he was alive, two sounds never left him—the sound of the brahman by those who desired the Vedas and the sound of the bowstring by those who wielded the bow. I cannot tolerate Drona being killed in battle. He was like the lion and the elephant in his valour. O Sanjaya! He was invincible. The fame of his strength was never assailed. Who protected the great-souled one on the right flank and on the left? When he fought in the battle, which brave one was in front of him? Who were the brave ones who confronted him and gave up their lives, traversing the path of death? Who were the brave ones who faced Drona in battle and attained the supreme objective? O Sanjaya! Even if one faces a great hardship, one must do one's duty, in accordance with one's valour and one's capacity. All of this was established in him. My mind is distracted. O son! Let us stop for some time. O Sanjaya! I will ask you again, after I have regained my senses.'"

Chapter 986(9)

Vaishampayana said, 'Having asked the son of the suta in this way, he was afflicted by terrible sorrow. Dhritarashtra lost all hope about his sons being victorious and fell down on the ground. On seeing that he had lost his senses and had fallen down, the attendants sprinkled him with water. The water was extremely cold and was perfumed. They fanned him. O great king! On seeing that he had fallen down, the women of the Bharata lineage surrounded him from every direction and gently rubbed him with their hands. They gently raised the king up from the ground. With tears choking their throats, the beautiful women placed him on his seat. Having attained his seat, the king was still not conscious. He was immobile. They stood around him and fanned him. Having slowly regained his senses, the king trembled. He once again began to ask the suta, Gavalgana's son, about what exactly had happened.

'"He is like the rising sun.[44] He can dispel darkness through his own light. When Ajatashatru advanced, how did Drona counter him? He is like an elephant with shattered temples. He is angry and swift. He is resplendent and single-minded in purpose. He is incapable of being repulsed by a rival. When he advanced for victory, like one who desires intercourse with a female,[45] which brave warriors fought with that supreme of men in the field of battle? That mighty-armed one is capable of consuming Duryodhana's entire army with his terrible glance. He has intelligence and is devoted to the truth. The supreme archer can destroy with his sight, even if he is not protected, and he is fixed on victory. He is self-controlled and is revered by the entire world. Which brave ones surrounded him? That undecaying king is supreme among archers and is difficult to resist. When Kounteya, tiger among men, swiftly advanced and attacked Drona, who on my side countered him? Which brave ones surrounded the advancing Bhimasena? Bibhatsu is extremely valorous. He rides on a chariot that is like a dense cloud. He creates a tumultuous shower, like thunder. He showers arrows, like Maghavan showering rain. The one with the monkey on his banner envelopes the sky with his mass of arrows. All the directions resound with the clapping of his palms and the roar of his chariot wheels. The sound of his arrows makes him difficult to cross. His anger can thwart the clouds. His arrows are as swift as thought. His fierce arrows penetrate the inner organs. He floods the entire earth with blood, so that men find it difficult to traverse. In that battle, Duryodhana made endeavours and raised his terrible club. What did he do when Vijaya, the wielder of Gandiva, used arrows sharpened on stone and tufted with the feathers of vultures? When the intelligent one did this and destroyed the army with the sound of Gandiva, what was his[46] state of mind then? Arjuna performed terrible deeds and advanced fiercely. When Dhananjaya used his arrows to attack Drona, what did he do? He was like the

[44]Though not explicitly stated, this is Dhritarashtra speaking.
[45]That is, a female elephant. The imagery is of elephants fighting over a she-elephant.
[46]Duryodhana's.

wind scattering clouds, or like a tempest destroying reeds. Which
man can stand against the wielder of Gandiva in battle? Soldiers
trembled and brave ones were touched by fear. Who were those who
did not forsake Drona and who were the inferior ones who ran away?
Who were the ones who gave up their lives and advanced towards
death? Dhananjaya had vanquished superhuman combatants. Those
on my side are incapable of withstanding the force of his white
horses. Gandiva's noise is like the roll of thunder. Vishvaksena is the
charioteer and the warrior is Dhananjaya. It is my view that this
chariot cannot be vanquished, even by the gods and the asuras. The
brave Pandava is delicate, young, brave and handsome. He is
intelligent and skilled. He is wise in war and truth is his valour. When
Nakula emitted a loud roar, what did all the Kouravas do? When
the intelligent one advanced, which brave ones surrounded him?
Sahadeva is like an angry snake with virulent poison. He is invincible
in battle. When he advanced against the enemy, who countered him?
He is noble in his vows. He cannot be assailed. He is modest and
unvanquished. When he advanced against Drona, which brave ones
surrounded him? He[47] crushed the large army of the Souvira
kingdom. He obtained as his queen the desirable princess of Bhoja,
who was beautiful in all her limbs. Truthfulness, fortitude, valour
and brahmacharya are always completely vested in him. Yuyudhana
is a bull among men. He is strong. He is truthful in his deeds. He is
never distressed. He is unvanquished. He is Vasudeva's equal in battle
and is regarded as second to Vasudeva. Instructed by Dhananjaya,
he has become as brave as his preceptor in deeds. He is Partha's equal
in use of weapons. Who restrained him when he advanced against
Drona? He is supremely brave among the Vrishnis. He is valiant
among all archers. He is Rama's[48] equal in weapons, fame and valour.
He is supreme in truthfulness, fortitude, self-control, valour and
brahmacharya. All these are in Satvata,[49] just as the three worlds
are in Keshava. Vested with all these qualities, he is incapable of

[47]Satyaki.
[48]Parashurama's.
[49]Satyaki.

being resisted by the gods. When that great archer advanced, which brave ones surrounded him? The best of the Panchalas is loved by all those who have been born from noble lineages. Uttamouja always performs supreme deeds in battle. He is always engaged in Dhananjaya's welfare and in supreme injury towards me. He is the equal of Yama, Vaishravana, Aditya, the great Indra and Varuna. He is famous as a maharatha and fought against Drona in the battle. He was prepared to give up his life in that tumult? Which brave ones surrounded him? Dhrishtaketu was the only one among the Chedis who went to the Pandavas. When he advanced against Drona, who opposed him? The brave Ketuman slew Prince Sudarshana at the other end of the gate to the mountains.[50] When he advanced against Drona, who countered him? The tiger among men was a woman earlier and is conversant with his own good and bad qualities. Yajnasena's son, Shikhandi, is never distressed in battle. He was the reason behind the death of the great-souled Devavrata in battle. When he advanced towards Drona, which brave ones surrounded him? In all the qualities, the brave one surpasses Dhananjaya. His weapons are always truth and brahmacharya. He is Vasudeva's equal in valour and Dhananjaya's equal in strength. He is like the sun in his energy and like Brihaspati in his intelligence. The great-souled Abhimanyu is like death with a gaping mouth. When he advanced towards Drona, which brave ones surrounded him? Subhadra's son is the destroyer of enemy heroes. He is young, but is as celebrated as the ocean. When he advanced against Drona, what was the state of your mind then?[51] Droupadi's sons are tigers among men. They rushed towards Drona in that battle, like rivers towards the sea. Which brave ones repulsed them? Those children gave up all play for twelve years. They observed supreme vows and for the sake of weapons, served Bhishma. They were Kshatranjaya, Kshatradeva, Kshatradharma and Manina, the brave sons of Dhrishtadyumna. When they advanced against Drona, who opposed them? The Vrishnis look upon him as the equal of one hundred armoured ones

[50]The gate to the mountains may be a reference to Girivraja.
[51]Actually meaning the state of Duryodhana's mind.

in battle. When the great archer Chekitana advanced against Drona, who countered him? Anadhrishti was the son of Vriddhakshema and was never distressed in his soul. He once abducted the princess of Kalinga in a battle. Who restrained him when he advanced against Drona? The five brothers from Kekaya are devoted to dharma and truth is their valour. Their complexion is like fireflies. Their armour, weapons and standards are red. Those brave ones are the sons of the Pandavas's mother's sister and desire their victory.[52] When they attacked so as to kill Drona, which brave ones surrounded them? The angry kings fought against him for six months in Varanavata, wishing to kill him, but could not defeat him. He is the lord of battles. He is supreme among archers and is brave. He is extremely strong and is unwavering in his aim. When that tiger among men attacked Drona, who countered Yuyutsu? In Varanasi, wishing to obtain a wife, the maharatha used a broad-headed arrow in battle to bring down the son of the king of Kashi from his chariot.[53] Dhrishtadyumna, the great archer, is the counsellor of the Parthas. He was created for Drona's death and is engaged in causing injury to Duryodhana. In the battle, he consumed the warriors and shattered the ranks. When he advanced towards Drona, which brave ones restrained him? Shikhandi's son, Kshatradeva, was reared in Drupada's lap and is skilled in use of weapons. Who restrained his advance against Drona? Ushinara's maharatha son[54] covered the entire earth with the pole of his chariot, as if girding it with the hide of a calf. He is foremost among those who kill the enemy. He performed ten horse sacrifices, a substitute for all sacrifices, and provided an abundance of food, drink and *dakshina*. He protected his subjects as if they were his own sons. The brave one gave away as many cattle as dakshina as there are grains of sand in the waters of the Ganga. No man has accomplished such a deed earlier, nor will any man perform this feat

---

[52]The mother in question is Kunti. Kunti's sister was Shrutakirti and she was married to the Kekaya king, Dhrishtaketu.

[53]This is a reference to Dhrishtadyumna.

[54]Ushinara's son is Shibi. But son is being used in an extended sense here, meaning grandson. The person in question is Shaibya, Shibi's son and Ushinara's grandson.

in the future. The gods themselves exclaimed, 'This is an extremely difficult deed. In the three worlds, with their mobile and immobile objects, we do not see a second person like Ushinara's son, who has been born, or will be born.' Shaibya is brave. After death, he will go to places that are not attainable by men of this world. Who repulsed the grandson Shaibya, when he advanced towards Drona, like death with a gaping mouth? Virata of Matsya has an army of chariots and is the killer of enemies. When he advanced against Drona in battle, which brave ones surrounded him? Vrikodara's son grew up in a single day.[55] He is immensely strong and powerful. He is a terrible rakshasa and knows the use of maya. He causes great terror among those on my side. He desires the victory of the Parthas and is a thorn for my sons. Who restrained the mighty-armed Ghatotkacha's advance towards Drona? O Sanjaya! There are many others who have their objective in mind. They are prepared to give up their lives in battle. Who can they not vanquish? Their refuge is the tiger among men, the wielder of the Sharnga bow. He desires the welfare of the Parthas. How can they be defeated? He is infinite. He is the preceptor of the worlds. He is the eternal protector of the worlds. The divine Narayana is the protector in all battles. He is the lord with the celestial soul. The learned ones speak about his divine deeds. I will recount his deeds with devotion and thus obtain calmness in my own self.'"

Chapter 987(10)

'Dhritarashtra said, "O Sanjaya! Hear about Vasudeva's divine deeds. Govinda performed them and no other man can ever replicate them. O Sanjaya! When the great-souled one was brought up as a child in a family of cowherds, he made the strength of his arms known to the three worlds. When he dwelt in the forests along

---

[55]Ghatotkacha grew up in a single day.

the Yamuna, he killed the king of horses,[56] who was like the wind in speed and Uchchaishrava's equal in strength. There was a terrible danava in the form of a bull.[57] He arose among the cows, like death. Though still a child, he killed him with his arms. The one with lotus eyes also killed great asuras like Pralamba, Naraka, Jamba, Pitha and Muru, who was like a mountain. The immensely energetic Kamsa was protected by Jarasandha. But with his valour alone,[58] Krishna killed him and his followers in battle. The brave Sunama, the king of Shurasena, was the leader of an entire akshouhini. The valiant one was the second brother of Kamsa, the king of Bhoja. With Baladeva as his second, Krishna, the slayer of enemies, spiritedly consumed him in a battle, with all his soldiers. The brahmana rishi Durvasa was extremely prone to rage. He worshipped him with his wife and obtained a boon from him.[59] The lotus-eyed and brave one vanquished many kings at the svayamvara of the daughter of the king of Gandhara.[60] As if they were born horses, the intolerant kings were yoked to the wedding chariot and lacerated with whips. The mighty-armed Jarasandha was the leader of an entire akshouhini. Janardana thought of a way so that he might be killed by someone else.[61] The brave and powerful king of Chedi was the leader of kings. In the dispute over the arghya, he was killed like an animal.[62] Soubha,

[56]This is the demon Keshi, sent by Kamsa to kill Krishna. Keshi adopted the form of a horse. Having killed Keshi, Krishna came to be known as Keshava.

[57]Arishtasura, also sent by Kamsa to kill Krishna.

[58]That is, without using any weapons.

[59]The wife in question is Rukmini. There is a story about Durvasa visiting Krishna and Rukmini and their worshipping him with rice and milk. Durvasa asked Krishna to smear the remnants all over his body. Krishna did this, leaving out the feet. Durvasa granted Krishna the boon that he would not be killed through any part of the body that had been smeared with the remaining rice and milk.

[60]Satyabhama was the princess of Gandhara.

[61]Jarasandha was killed by Bhima, but Bhima was instigated by Krishna. The incident has been described in Section 22 (Volume 2).

[62]The king of Chedi is Shishupala. The incident has been described in Section 25 (Volume 2).

the city of the daityas, was established in the sky. It was protected by
Shalva and was invincible. Through his valour, Madhava brought it
down into the ocean.[63] He defeated in battle Anga, Vanga, Kalinga,
Magadha, Andhaka, Kasi, Kosala, Vatsa, Garga, Karusha and Pundra.
O Sanjaya! Avanti, the south, the mountains, Dasheraka, Kashmiraka,
Ourasaka, Pishacha, Samandara, Kamboja, Vatadhana, Chola,
Pandya, Trigarta, Malava and Darada were difficult to conquer.
Ashvas, Shakas and Yavanas and their followers arrived from different
directions. But Pundarikaksha vanquished them. In earlier times, he
penetrated the abode of makaras, inhabited by aquatic creatures. In
the midst of the waters, he vanquished Varuna in battle.[64] Hrishikesha
slew Panchajana, who resided in the nether regions of *patala* and
obtained the divine conch shell Panchajanya.[65] Together with Partha,
the immensely strong one satisfied Agni in Khandava and obtained the
invincible agneya weapon, the chakra.[66] He rode on Vinata's son and
caused terror in Amaravati.[67] The brave one brought *parijata* from the
great Indra's residence. Knowing his valour, Shakra tolerated this. We
have not heard of any king who has not been vanquished by Krishna.
O Sanjaya! Pundarikaksha performed an extremely wonderful deed
in my assembly hall.[68] Who else can do this? Because of that, I have
sought refuge with him in devotion. I look upon Krishna as the lord.
I know everything about it, having witnessed it myself. There is no
end to his valour, or to his intelligence. O Sanjaya! Nor can anyone
reach the limit of Hrishikesha's deeds.

'"Gada, Samba, Pradyumna, Viduratha, Agavaha, Aniruddha,
Charudeshna, Sarana, Ulmuka, Nishatha, Jhalli, the valiant Babhru,

[63]This has been described in Section 31 (Volume 2).

[64]Nanda (Krishna's foster-father) was abducted by Varuna's servants and
rescued by Krishna and Balarama.

[65]The sage Sandipani was Krishna's teacher and Sandipani's son was abducted
by the demon Panchajana. Krishna killed Panchajana the conch shell Panchajanya
was made out of Panchajana's bones.

[66]Sudarshana chakra.

[67]Vinata's son is Garuda and Amaravati is Indra's capital.

[68]This is a reference to Krishna manifesting his own self. The incident has
been described in Section 54 (Volume 4).

Prithu, Viprithu, Samika, Arimejaya—these and other powerful
Vrishni heroes are skilled in striking. They will station themselves
in battle, in the ranks of the Pandava army. They will be summoned
by the great-souled hero among the Vrishnis, Keshava. It is my view
that everything will then confront a great danger. Where Janardana
is, the brave Rama will be there.[69] He wields the plough and wears
a garland of wild flowers. His strength is like that of ten thousand
elephants. He is like the summit of Kailasa. The brahmanas describe
Vasudeva as the father of everything. O Sanjaya! Will he fight for
the cause of the sons of Pandu? O son![70] If Keshava dons his armour
for the sake of the Pandavas, there is no one in our army who can
withstand him. If all the Kurus manage to defeat all the Pandavas, for
their sake, Varshneya will take up his supreme weapons. That mighty-
armed tiger among men will kill all the kings and the Kouravas in
battle and give the earth to the sons of Kunti. Hrishikesha is the
charioteer and Dhananjaya is the warrior in that chariot. Where
is the ratha in our army who will confront them in battle? There
is no means whereby the Kurus can be seen to obtain victory. Tell
me everything about how the battle continued. Arjuna is Keshava's
soul and Krishna is Kiriti's soul. Arjuna is always victorious and
Krishna's deeds are eternal. All the qualities are vested in Keshava,
beyond measure. Because of his delusion, Duryodhana does not
know Krishna Madhava. Because of his delusion and because he is
driven by destiny, the noose of death is in front of him and he does
not know Dasharha Krishna and Pandava Arjuna. Earlier, those
great-souled ones were the gods Nara and Narayana. They were a
single soul and are seen by men on earth as divided into two. They are
famous and invincible. If they wish, they can destroy the army with
their minds. But because they are humans, they do not wish that.[71]
The destruction of the yuga is near and the people are deluded. O
son! That is the reason for the death of Bhishma and the great-souled

[69]Balarama. However, Balarama decided to remain neutral and went away
on a pilgrimage.

[70]The word used is tata.

[71]Having been born as men, they resort to human means alone.

Drona. Death can never be prevented through brahmacharya, the study of the Vedas, rites or weapons. Those brave ones were revered by the worlds. They were skilled in the use of weapons and were invincible in battle. O Sanjaya! On hearing that Bhishma and Drona have been slain, why should I remain alive? After learning about the death of Bhishma and Drona, we will now have to seek refuge with Yudhishthira, about whose prosperity we used to be jealous earlier. This destruction of the Kurus has come about because of my deeds. O suta! When one is ripe for slaughter, even a blade of grass is like the vajra. Yudhishthira will obtain unmatched prosperity in this world. It is because of his anger that the great archers, Bhishma and Drona, have been brought down. Dharma is naturally on his side, though humans typically have adharma. Destiny is cruel and it is time for everything to be destroyed. O son! Even learned men cannot think of means to counteract it. Everything progresses because of destiny. That is my view. Therefore, tell me everything, exactly as it happened, about that supreme hardship, without discarding anything. It cannot be crossed and leads to grievous reflection.'"

Chapter 988(11)

'Sanjaya said, "I will describe everything to you, exactly as I saw it, about how Drona was made to sit down and was brought down by the Pandus and the Srinjayas. Having been appointed the commander, in the midst of all the soldiers, Bharadvaja's maharatha son spoke these words to your son. 'O king! You have shown me great honour by appointing me the commander today, after that bull among the Kouravas, the son of the one who goes to the ocean. O king! You will obtain fruits that are commensurate with your action. What desire of yours can I satisfy today? Tell me what you desire.' At this, Duryodhana thought and consulted Karna, Duhshasana and the others. He told the invincible preceptor, foremost among victorious ones, 'If you wish, grant me the boon that you will capture

Yudhishthira, foremost among charioteers, alive and bring him before
me.' On hearing your son's words, the preceptor of the Kurus, spoke
these words, bringing delight to all the soldiers. 'The king, Kunti's
son, whom you wish to be captured, is fortunate. O extremely
invincible one! You have only asked for the boon that he should be
captured, not that he should be killed. O tiger among men! Why did
you not desire that he should be killed? O Duryodhana! There is no
doubt that you know about what should be done. It is wonderful
that Dharma's son should not have an enmity like that towards you.
O foremost among the Bharata lineage! If you wish to remain alive
and protect your own lineage, then after vanquishing the Pandavas in
battle, give them a share of the kingdom and act according to fraternal
relations. The king who is Kunti's son is fortunate. The intelligent
one has been born auspiciously. He is truly Ajatashatru.[72] Even you
are affectionate towards him.' O descendant of the Bharata lineage!
Thus addressed by Drona, your son suddenly displayed the sentiments
that always course through him. Even someone like Brihaspati is
incapable of controlling his countenance. O king! Therefore, your
son joyfully spoke these words. 'O preceptor! If Kunti's son is killed
by you, I will not be able to obtain victory. If Yudhishthira is slain,
there is no doubt that the Parthas will slaughter all of us. They are
incapable of being killed in battle, even by all the immortals. The
one among them who is left, will destroy us. But he[73] is truthful
in his pledges. When he is brought here, we will defeat him again
in a gambling match. The Kounteyas will follow him again to the
forest. Thus my victory will manifest itself for a long time to come.
That is the reason I do not desire Dharmaraja's death.' Drona was
intelligent and was knowledgeable about artha. Having ascertained
his crooked intention, he thought about this for some time and then
granted him the boon.

'"Drona replied, 'If Yudhishthira is not protected by the brave
Arjuna in battle, you can think that the eldest Pandava has already

[72]Ajatashatru is Yudhishthira's name and means someone who has no
enemies.
[73]Yudhishthira.

been brought under your control. O son![74] But Partha is incapable of being repulsed in battle, even by Indra and the gods and the asuras. That is the reason I cannot advance against him. In the knowledge of weapons, there is no doubt that he has been my disciple earlier. He is young and has accomplished many deeds. He is single-minded in purpose. He has obtained many weapons from Indra and Rudra. O king! You have also incensed him and I cannot advance against him. Let Partha be removed from the field of battle, by whatever means that are possible, and Dharmaraja will be vanquished. O bull among men! Once he has been captured, you think that victory will be yours. Think of means, so that his capture is beyond doubt. I will capture the king, who is devoted to truth and dharma. O king! There is no doubt that I will bring him under your control today, as long as he is stationed in the battle before me, even for an instant. But let Dhananjaya, Kunti's son and tiger among men, be removed. With Phalguna present, Partha Yudhishthira is incapable of being captured in battle, even by Indra and the gods and the asuras.'"

'Sanjaya said, "After Drona promised the king's capture, your extremely foolish sons thought that he had been already captured. Your son knew that Drona was partial towards the Pandavas. Therefore, to make him stick to the pledge, he made the counsel generally known. O destroyer of enemies! Duryodhana proclaimed among all the soldiers that Pandava would be captured."'

Chapter 989(12)

'Sanjaya said, "The soldiers heard that Yudhishthira would be captured. They roared like lions and this mingled with the sounds of their arrows and their conch shells. O descendant of the Bharata lineage! Dharmaraja got to know everything about this through his spies, and about what Bharadvaja's son desired to do.

[74]The word used is tata.

He summoned all his brothers and all the soldiers. Dharmaraja spoke these words to Dhananjaya. 'O tiger among men! You have heard about what Drona wishes to do today. Let all appropriate measures be taken accordingly. O destroyer of enemies! It is true that Drona has taken a pledge. But it is not infallible and everything depends on you. O mighty-armed one! Therefore, fight near me today, so that Duryodhana cannot obtain what he desires from Drona.'

'"Arjuna replied, 'O king! Just as I can never act so as to bring about the preceptor's death, I will never forsake you. O Pandava! I would rather give up my life than fight against my preceptor and kill him. O king! Dhritarashtra's son wishes to capture you in the battle. He will never accomplish his desire in the world of the living. As long as I am alive, Drona will never be able to capture you. Even if the wielder of the vajra himself, together with the gods and the daityas, were to try to capture you in battle, they will fail. O Indra among kings! As long as I am alive, you should not be frightened. Drona is foremost among wielders of weapons and among those who wield all weapons. I do not remember having ever uttered a falsehood. I do not remember ever having been vanquished. I do not remember having not fulfilled a pledge I have made, even partially.'"

'Sanjaya said, "O great king! Conch shells, drums, cymbals and tambourines were then sounded in the residence of the Pandavas. The great-souled Pandavas roared like lions. The fearful twang of bowstrings and the slapping of palms rose up into heaven. On hearing the conch shells sounded by the great-souled Pandavas, your army also caused musical instruments to be played. O descendant of the Bharata lineage! The arrays and divisions, on your side and theirs, slowly advanced towards each other, wishing to fight in the battle. A tumultuous battle commenced between the Pandavas and the Kurus and Drona and the Panchalas, and it made the body hair stand up. O king! Though they made every endeavour, the Srinjayas were unable to drive back Drona's army, because it was protected by Drona himself. The armed and mighty rathas of your son were unable to drive back the Pandava soldiers, because they were protected by Kiriti. Protected thus, the respective soldiers seemed to be subdued, like blossoms that are asleep in the forests in the night. O king! He[75] was on a golden chariot, as radiant as the sun. He shattered the divisions and roamed around, amidst the ranks. He was on a single chariot. But he acted so quickly in that battle, that the terrified Pandus and Srinjayas thought there were several of him. He released terrible arrows that travelled in every direction. O great king! There was fright in the army of the Pandaveyas. He seemed to be like the sun when it has attained midday, radiating a hundred rays and quickly drawing out sweat. That is what Drona looked like then. O venerable one! The Pandaveyas were incapable of glancing towards him in that battle, like the danavas towards the great Indra, when enraged. Bharadvaja's powerful son confounded the soldiers. He swiftly pierced Dhrishtadyumna's army with his sharp arrows. He seemed to cover and obstruct all the directions and the sky with his arrows. He crushed the army of the Pandus, even where Parshata was.'"

Chapter 990(13)

'Sanjaya said, "There was great confusion in the army of the Pandavas. Drona roamed amidst the Pandavas, like a fire consuming deadwood. He burnt those soldiers, as if Agni himself had arisen. On seeing him on the golden chariot in that battle, the Srinjayas trembled. He was swift in continuously stretching the bow. The twang of his bow could be heard, like the clap of thunder. Rathas, riders, elephants, horses and foot soldiers were mangled through the terrible arrows released by his hands. His arrows were like roaring clouds at the end of the summer, assisted by the wind. They were like a hailstorm and created terror among the enemy. O king! The lord roamed amidst the soldiers, agitating and terrifying them. He increased the fear that humans have for the foe. His bow,

[75]Drona.

decorated with gold, was like clouds tinged with lightning. It was repeatedly seen, as he roamed around on a chariot that was like dense clouds. The brave one was truthful, wise, always devoted to dharma and extremely terrible. He was like the controller at the end of a yuga, creating a terrible river. Its currents resulted from the power of his intolerance. It was full of large numbers of predators and overflowed with masses of soldiers. The heroes were trees along the banks, which were being eaten away. The blood was the water. The chariots were eddies. Elephants and horses were the banks. Armour constituted rafts, the flesh was the mud. The foam was formed out of fat, marrow, bones and excellent headdresses. The battle seemed to be completely covered by a cloud. It was infested with fish in the form of javelins. Men, elephants and horses flowed along, driven by the force of the arrows. The bodies were like the tops of trees, the arms were like snakes. The heads were like tender fruit. The swords were like fish. The chariots and elephants were like lakes and it was decorated with many ornaments. The maharathas were hundreds of whirlpools. The dust of the earth was like garlands. In that battle, it was possible for the greatly valiant ones to cross it. But cowards found it difficult to cross. Brave ones were strewn around like snakes. The ones who were alive were like aquatic birds. Torn umbrellas were like gigantic swans. The crowns were like smaller birds. The chakras were tortoises, the clubs were crocodiles, the arrows were smaller fish. It was populated by large numbers of terrible wild crows, vultures and jackals. In that battle, the powerful Drona killed beings with his arrows. O supreme among kings! Hundreds of them were conveyed to the world of the ancestors. Hundreds of bodies caused obstructions. The hair constituted moss and weeds. O king! Such was the terrible river that began to flow there and it increased one's fear. O descendant of the Bharata lineage! Thus was their army defeated by those on your side.

'"With Yudhishthira at the forefront, all of them attacked Drona from every direction. On seeing them advance, the brave ones on your side wielded firm bows and attacked them back on every side. The battle that commenced made the body hair stand up. Shakuni was conversant with a hundred different kinds of maya and attacked

Sahadeva, piercing his charioteer, standard and chariot with sharp
arrows. However, Madri's son wasn't greatly enraged. He pierced his
standard, bow, charioteer and horses with arrows and then pierced
his maternal uncle with sixty. At this, Soubala grasped a club and
jumped down from his supreme chariot. O king! With that club, he
brought down his[76] charioteer from his chariot. O king! Thus bereft
of his chariot, the immensely strong one grasped a club in his hands.
The brave ones began to sport in that battle, like two mountains
with peaks. Drona pierced the king of Panchala with ten arrows, was
himself pierced back in turn by many arrows and pierced back again
with more than a hundred arrows. Bhimasena pierced Vivimshati
with twenty sharp arrows. Though he was pierced, the brave one
did not tremble and it was extraordinary. O great king! Vivimshati
suddenly deprived Bhima of his horses, standard, bow and arrows
and all the soldiers honoured this feat. But the brave one[77] could not
tolerate the victory of the enemy in battle. With his club, he brought
down his charioteer and all his horses. The brave Shalya seemed to be
smiling. As if to anger him, he pierced Nakula, the beloved son of his
sister, with arrows. In the battle, the powerful Nakula brought down
his horses, umbrella, standard, charioteer and bow and blew on his
conch shell. Dhrishtaketu severed the many kinds of arrows Kripa
released towards him. He then pierced Kripa with seventy arrows and
then used three more to bring down the sign on his standard. Kripa
countered him with a great shower of arrows. In this fashion, in that
battle, the brahmana[78] countered Dhrishtaketu and fought with him.
Satyaki pierced Kritavarma between the breasts with an iron arrow.
Having pierced him, he smiled and pierced him with seventy arrows,
piercing him again with others. But Bhoja[79] pierced him with seventy-
seven sharp arrows. However, Shini's descendant did not waver, like
a mountain before a swift wind. Senapati quickly struck Susharma
in his inner organs and he[80] struck him back in the shoulder joint

[76]Sahadeva's.
[77]Bhima.
[78]Kripa.
[79]Kritavarma.
[80]Susharma.

with a lance. With the immensely valiant Matsyas, Virata attacked
Vaikartana in the battle and it was extraordinary. This was terrible
manliness on the part of the son of the suta. He countered the soldiers
with his straight-tufted arrows. Drupada himself confronted King
Bhagadatta. O great king! The battle between the two, skilled in the
use of weapons, was wonderful and created terror among beings. O
king! In the battle, the valiant Bhurishrava enveloped Yajnasena's
maharatha son[81] with a shower of arrows. O descendant of the
Bharata lineage! O lord of the earth! Shikhandi was enraged at this
and pierced Somadatta's son with ninety arrows, making him tremble.
The rakshasas, Hidimba's son and Alambusa, fought an extraordinary
battle against each other, wishing to kill each other. They proudly
created a hundred different kinds of maya and used maya against
each other. They disappeared as they wandered around, giving rise
to great wonder. Chekitana fought a terrible battle with Anuvinda,
like that between Bala and the immensely strong Shakra, when
the gods and the asuras fought. O king! Lakshmana fought fiercely
with Kshatradeva, like Vishnu in ancient times, when he fought
against Hiranyaksha.[82]

'"Pourava was on swift horses and his chariot was stocked
with every implement. O king! He roared and attacked Subhadra's
son. The immensely strong one swiftly attacked, desiring to fight.
Abhimanyu, the destroyer of enemies, fought a great battle with
him. Pourava enveloped Subhadra's son with a storm of arrows.
Arjuna's son brought down his standard, umbrella and bow on the
ground. Subhadra's son pierced Pourava with seven swift arrows.
He then pierced his horses and charioteer with five arrows. The
soldiers were delighted at this and he roared repeatedly like a lion.
Arjuna's son then quickly affixed an arrow that was certain to kill
Pourava. But Hardikya[83] used two arrows to slice down his bow and
arrow. Subhadra's son, the destroyer of enemy heroes, cast aside that
shattered bow. He grasped a sharp sword and a shield. He exhibited

[81]Shikhandi.

[82]Hiranyaksha was slain by Vishnu in his varaha (boar) incarnation and the
battle between the two lasted for one thousand years.

[83]Kritavarma.

his own valour and whirled it, as he moved around. He whirled it in front of him and brandished it in the air. He leapt up and shook it. O king! No difference could be distinguished between the sword and the shield. He leapt onto the shaft of Pourava's chariot and suddenly roared. Having ascended onto Pourava's chariot, he grasped him by the side of the hair. He killed the charioteer with a kick and sliced down the standard with his sword. He raised him up, like Tarkshya[84] agitating the water of the ocean and raising up a snake from it. All the kings saw him with his disheveled hair. He looked like an unconscious bull, when it has been brought down by a lion. Jayadratha could not tolerate the sight of Pourava having been brought down, afflicted and without a protector, and in the control of Arjuna's son. He grasped a shield marked with the giant wings of a peacock and decorated with a hundred bells, and a sword. He roared and jumped down from his chariot. On seeing Saindhava, Krishna's son[85] let go of Pourava. He swiftly leapt down from the chariot, like a hawk alighting. Spears, lances and swords were hurled towards him by the enemy. But Krishna's son sliced them down with his sword or countered them with his shield. He displayed the strength of his own arms to the soldiers. The strong one again raised his giant sword and shield. The brave one advanced against Vriddhakshatra's heir,[86] who was a sworn enemy of his father's. It was like a tiger advancing against an elephant. They cheerfully advanced and attacked each other, using swords as weapons, like a tiger and a lion using teeth and claws to fight. No one could distinguish any difference between those lions among men and the motions of the sword and the shield.[87] When they whirled their swords and brought them down, or when they fended off each other's blows, no special difference could be seen between the weapons. They roamed around in excellent motions, advancing and

---

[84]Garuda.

[85]Krishna means Arjuna in this context.

[86]Jayadratha.

[87]The text mentions three specific techniques of fighting with the sword— *sampata*, *abhipata* and *nipata*. Loosely, these can be translated as whirling, striking and descending.

retreating. The great-souled ones looked like mountains with wings. As he extended his sword to strike, Jayadratha struck the shield of Subhadra's illustrious son. The sword stuck in the radiant shield, which had plates made out of gold and the great sword snapped when the king of Sindhu tried to extract it forcefully. On seeing that the sword had been shattered, Jayadratha was instantly seen to retreat six steps and climb onto his chariot again. In the battle, Krishna's son resorted to his supreme chariot and all the kings surrounded him from every direction. Arjuna's immensely strong heir raised his shield and sword and roared, glancing towards Jayadratha. Subhadra's son, the destroyer of enemy heroes, then abandoned the king of Sindhu and tormented the soldiers, like the sun on the earth. In the encounter, Shalya hurled a terrible javelin at him. It was made completely out of iron and was decorated with gold. It was as radiant as the flames of a fire. As it descended, Krishna's son leapt up and caught it, like Vinata's son grasping a supreme serpent that has fallen from above. He then unsheathed his sword. On witnessing the dexterity and spirit of that infinitely energetic one, all the kings roared like lions. Subhadra's son, the destroyer of enemy heroes, then used the valour of his arms to hurl the javelin, radiant with lapis lazuli, back at Shalya. It was like a snake that had just cast off its skin. It reached Shalya's chariot and slew his charioteer and brought him down from the chariot. Virata, Drupada, Dhrishtaketu, Yudhishthira, Satyaki, the Kekayas, Bhima, Dhrishtadyumna, Shikhandi, the twins and Droupadi's sons uttered sounds of acclamation. There were many different kinds of sounds from arrows and diverse roars like lions. They arose and delighted Subhadra's son, who had not retreated. But your sons could not tolerate those signs of victory on the part of the enemy. O great king! They suddenly surrounded him and enveloped him with sharp arrows, like clouds pouring down on a mountain. Artayani,[88] the slayer of enemies, wished to do what would bring pleasure to your sons and was enraged because of the overthrow of his charioteer. He attacked Subhadra's son.'''

[88]Shalya.

Chapter 991(14)

'Dhritarashtra said, "O Sanjaya! You have described to me many wonderful duels. On hearing what you have said, I envy those who possess eyes. Men in the world will speak of this as wonderful, the fight between the Kurus and the Pandavas, like that between the gods and the asuras. I am never satisfied on hearing about this supreme battle. Therefore, tell me about the encounter between Artayani and Subhadra's son."

'Sanjaya said, "On seeing that his charioteer had been sent to the regulator,[89] Shalya grasped a club that was completely made out of iron. He leapt down from his supreme chariot and roared in anger. He looked like the flaming fire of destruction, or Death with a staff in his hand. Bhima grasped a mighty club and quickly rushed towards him. Subhadra's son also grasped a gigantic club that was like the vajra and summoned Shalya to a fight. But Bhima made efforts and restrained Subhadra's son. The powerful Bhimasena approached Shalya in that battle and stood immobile, like a mountain. The king of Madra saw the immensely strong Bhima and forcefully advanced towards him, like a tiger towards an elephant. Thousands of trumpets and conch shells were sounded. There were roars like those of lions and the mighty sounds of drums. On seeing those two, equal in spirit, rush towards each other, there were sounds of applause among hundreds of Pandavas and Kurus. O descendant of the Bharata lineage! Among all the kings, there is no one other than the lord of Madra who can withstand Bhimasena's force in battle. There is no warrior in this world, other than Vrikodara, who can withstand the force of the club of the great-souled lord of Madra. Bhima's mighty club was tied in hemp and decorated with gold. It caused great delight among the people. When wielded, it seemed to blaze. Shalya's beautiful club was also like a giant flash of lightning, when he roamed and whirled it around. They wandered around in circles and lowered their clubs. They roared like bulls, as if with horns lowered. They wielded their clubs and executed circular motions. In the encounter, there was no

---

[89]Yama.

difference between those lions among men. Struck by Bhimasena, Shalya's gigantic club emitted extremely terrible sparks of fire and the club was shattered. In similar fashion, when struck by the enemy, Bhimasena's club was as resplendent as a tree covered with fireflies during the evening of the monsoon. O descendant of the Bharata lineage! The king of Madra hurled a club in that battle.[90] It blazed through the sky and created many fires. Similarly, Bhimasena hurled a club at the enemy and tormented his soldiers, like a giant meteor that was falling down. The best of clubs struck each other. They sighed like the maidens of serpents and created fire. They were like giant tigers using claws, or giant elephants using tusks. They roamed around, striking each other with clubs. In a short while, struck by clubs, they were covered with blood and the great-souled ones looked like flowering kimshukas. The sounds of the clubs wielded by those lions among men could be heard in all the directions, like that of Shakra's vajra. The club of the king of Madra struck Bhima on the left and the right. But he did not waver, like a mountain that has been struck. Similarly, the immensely strong Bhima's club struck the lord of Madra. But he bore it with patience, like a mountain struck by the vajra. They raised their giant clubs and attacked each other with great force. They repeatedly roamed around, executing circular motions. They approached each other by eight steps and suddenly attacked each other like elephants wishing to kill each other, with clubs like iron rods. They were severely wounded from the force of each other's clubs. The brave ones simultaneously fell down, like shattered poles of Indra. Shalya was deprived of his senses, having been struck by the club, and sighed repeatedly. O great king! On seeing this, maharatha Kritavarma quickly approached him, as he was unconscious and immobile like a serpent, having been struck by the club. Maharatha Kritavarma swiftly lifted the lord of Madra up onto his own chariot and carried him away from the field of battle. The brave Bhima was unconscious, like someone who is drunk. However, the mighty-armed one raised himself in an instant and could be seen, with the club in his hand. Your sons saw that the lord

[90]Obviously, he had picked up another club.

of Madra had retreated. O venerable one! They trembled, with their
elephants, chariots, infantry and horses. Those on your side were
routed by the Pandavas, who desired victory. They were frightened
and fled in different directions, like clouds scattered by the wind.
The maharatha Pandaveyas defeated the sons of Dhritarashtra. O
king! The illustrious ones were radiant and roamed around on the
field of battle. They roared fiercely like lions and blew on their conch
shells in delight. Drums were sounded, together with kettledrums
and tambourines."'

Chapter 992(15)

'Sanjaya said, "Your great army was shattered in that battle by
the Pandus. On seeing this, Vrishasena exhibited the power of
his weapons and began to protect it single-handed. O venerable one!
Vrishasena released arrows in the ten directions. He roamed around
and pierced men, horses, chariots and elephants. The mighty-armed
one released thousands of mighty and flaming arrows. They were
like the rays of the sun during the summer. O great king! Rathas
and riders were oppressed by them and suddenly fell down on the
ground, like trees broken by the wind. O king! In that battle, masses
of horses, masses of chariots and masses of elephants were brought
down in every direction in hundreds and thousands. On seeing him
fearlessly roam around in that battle alone, all the kings[91] surrounded
him and attacked him together. Nakula's son, Shatanika, attacked
Vrishasena and pierced him with ten iron arrows that penetrated
the inner organs. At this, Karna's son severed his bow and brought
down his standard. Wishing to protect their brother, Droupadi's
other sons rushed towards him. They made Karna's son disappear
because of the shower of their arrows. Rathas, with Drona's son at
the forefront, advanced towards them. O great king! They quickly

[91]On the Pandava side.

enveloped Droupadi's maharatha sons with many types of arrows, like clouds on a mountain. Out of affection towards their sons, the Pandavas quickly countered them, together with warriors from the Panchalas, Kekayas, Matsyas and Srinjayas. The battle that raged between those on your side and the sons of Pandu was fearful and tumultuous and made the body hair stand up, like that between the gods and the danavas. The Kurus and the Pandavas fought well, excited by anger. They glanced towards each other, having earlier engendered the animosity towards each other. Because of that wrath, those infinitely energetic ones seemed to be like the supreme of birds[92] and the serpents, battling in the sky. With Bhima, Karna, Kripa, Drona, Drona's son, Parshata and Satyaki, the field of battle was resplendent, as if the sun of destruction had arisen. The immensely strong ones fiercely fought in that battle, seeking to kill each other, like Bali of the danavas against the gods. Yudhishthira's army let out a mighty roar and began to slaughter your soldiers, driving the maharathas away.

'"On seeing that the army was routed and sorely oppressed by the enemy, Drona said, 'O brave ones! Do not run away.' Drona possessed red horses. He was angry. He was like an elephant with four tusks. He penetrated the Pandava army and attacked Yudhishthira. Yudhishthira pierced him with sharp arrows tufted with heron feathers. But Drona severed his bow and quickly rushed against him. The illustrious Kumara from the Panchalas was protecting his[93] wheels and countered the advancing Drona, like the shoreline against the lord of the rivers. On seeing Drona, bull among the brahmanas, thus repulsed by Kumara, delighted leonine roars and sounds of applause were heard. In that great battle, Kumara angrily pierced Drona in the chest with an arrow and repeatedly roared, like a lion. But in that encounter, the immensely strong Drona repulsed Kumara. Having overcome all fatigue, he displayed the dexterity of his hands and released many thousands of arrows. The brave one, supreme among brahmanas, devoted to the conduct of aryas and well-versed in

[92]Garuda.
[93]Yudhishthira's.

the use of weapons, slew Kumara, the protector of the chariot wheels.
He penetrated the midst of the army and roamed around in all the
directions. Bharadvaja's son, bull among rathas, was the protector of
your soldiers. He pierced Shikhandi with twelve arrows, Uttamouja
with twenty, Nakula with five, Sahadeva with seven, Yudhishthira
with twelve, each of Droupadi's sons with three, Satyaki with five and
Matsya with ten. In that battle, he agitated the warriors and rushed
against them. With a desire to capture him, he advanced towards
Yudhishthira, Kunti's son. O king! Maharatha Yugandhara repulsed
Bharadvaja's son, who was enraged, like the ocean agitated by a
storm. Having pierced Yudhishthira with straight-tufted arrows, he[94]
brought Yugandhara down from the chariot with a broad-headed
arrow. Virata, Drupada, the Kekayas, Satyaki, Shibi, Vyaghradatta
from Panchala, the valiant Simhasena and many others sought to
protect Yudhishthira. They showered many arrows and obstructed
his path. O king! Vyaghradatta from Panchala pierced Drona with
fifty sharp arrows and the soldiers roared. Maharatha Simhasena
swiftly pierced Drona, rigid in his vows, and suddenly laughed out
in delight. Drona dilated his eyes and rubbed the string of his bow.
He slapped his palms loudly and attacked. The powerful one used
broad-headed arrows to sever the heads, adorned with earrings, of
Simhasena and Vyaghradatta from their bodies. He used a shower
of arrows to torment the maharatha Pandavas and approached
Yudhishthira, like death, the destroyer. O king! A loud sound arose
in Yudhishthira's army, among all the warriors, when the one who
was rigid in his vows approached him. On witnessing Drona's valour,
this is what the soldiers said. 'The king has been slain. The king who
is Dhritarashtra's son will be successful today. In this battle, he will
return to us and to Dhritarashtra's son.'[95] While your soldiers were
thus conversing, maharatha Kounteya swiftly arrived.

'"His chariot roared. He had created a terrible river. The water
was blood and the chariots were eddies. It was full of the bodies
and bones of brave ones and it conveyed beings to the world of the

[94]Drona.
[95]After having captured Yudhishthira.

dead. Masses of arrows were the giant foam and it was infested
with fish in the form of javelins. Having routed the Kurus, Pandava
quickly crossed that river. Kiriti suddenly attacked Drona's army and
shrouded and confounded it with a giant net of arrows. The illustrious
Kounteya quickly affixed arrows and shot them incessantly, so
that no one could distinguish a gap between these.[96] O great king!
The directions, the sky, the firmament and the earth disappeared,
covered by the arrows. O king! Nothing could be seen in the field
of battle then. The wielder of Gandiva created a great darkness
with his arrows. With the sun about to set, dust covered everything.
Enemy could no longer be distinguished from well-wisher. Drona,
Duryodhana and the others announced a withdrawal. Knowing that
the enemy was extremely terrified and no longer had its mind on
the fight, Bibhatsu slowly withdrew his own soldiers. The Pandus,
Srinjayas and Panchalas praised Partha with pleasant words, like
rishis praising the sun. Having vanquished the enemy, Dhananjaya
returned to his own camp, behind all the other soldiers. He was happy
and was with Keshava. Pandu's son was radiant on his colourful
chariot, which was decorated with excellent and expensive emeralds,
crystals, gold, diamonds and quartz. He was as radiant as the moon
in the sky, adorned with stars."'

[96]The two acts.

SECTION SIXTY-SIX

Samshaptaka Vadha Parva

This parva has 717 shlokas and sixteen chapters.

Samshaptakas are warriors who have taken an oath and these warriors (primarily the Trigartas) take an oath to die or kill Arjuna. This section is named after that oath. With Arjuna out of the way, the idea is that Drona will capture Yudhishthira. On the twelfth day of the battle, Arjuna kills several of the samshaptaka warriors. Drona kills many of the Panchalas, Matsyas and Kekayas. Bhima kills the king of Anga. Bhagadatta kills the king of Dasharna and Ruchiparva and unleashes the vaishnava weapon on Arjuna, which is countered by Krishna. Arjuna kills Bhagadatta. Arjuna kills Vrishaka and Achala, Shakuni's brothers. Ashvatthama kills Nila of Mahishmati. Arjuna kills three of Karna's brothers.

Chapter 993(16)

'Sanjaya said, "O lord of the earth! The soldiers returned to their own camps and retired, according to their respective ranks, arrays and divisions. Having asked the soldiers to withdraw, Drona was supremely distressed. He glanced towards Duryodhana, and in shame, spoke these words. 'I had told you earlier that if Dhananjaya is present, even the gods are incapable of capturing Yudhishthira in the battle. All of you endeavoured against Partha, but you were repulsed. Do not doubt my words that Krishna and Pandava are invincible. O king! But if the one with the white horses can be taken away, then Yudhishthira will come under your control today.[1] In the battle, let someone challenge him in a different part of the field and I will not return without vanquishing Kounteya.[2] O king! While Dhrishtadyumna looks on, I will use the void, while Arjuna is absent from the battle, to penetrate the army and capture Dharmaraja. Know that you will see me find ways to seize him. O king! If Pandava Yudhishthira, Dharma's son, stays before me even for an instant in the battle, there is no doubt that I will forcibly seize him today, with all his men and soldiers. This will be superior to an overall victory in the battle.' O king! On hearing Drona's words, the lord of Trigarta, together with his brothers, spoke these words. 'O king! The wielder of Gandiva has always treated us badly. O bull among the Bharata lineage! We have not caused him injury, but he has injured us. We remember those many instances of injury and are consumed by the fire of wrath. We can never sleep at night. The one with the divine weapons is now before our eyes. We will do everything that your heart desires and brings you pleasure and also brings us fame. We will draw him away from the field of battle and kill him. Let the earth be without Arjuna today, or without the Trigartas. We swear this before you and this pledge will not be falsified.' O descendant of the Bharata lineage! O great king! Satyaratha, Satyadharma,

---

[1]This is happening on the eve of the next day's battle.
[2]Yudhishthira.

Satyavarma, Satyeshu and Satyakarma—these five brothers arrived,[3] with ten thousand chariots, and spoke in this way. They took the pledge in that battle. The Malavas and the Tundirekas came with thirty thousand chariots. Susharma of Trigarta, tiger among men and the lord of Prasthala,[4] came with the Machellakas, Lalitthas and Madrakas, with ten thousand chariots and his brothers and took the oath. There were another ten thousand from many different countries. They arrived specially, for purposes of taking the oath.

'"They brought kindling so that each one could separately light a fire. They brought garments of kusha grass and colourful armour. They donned the armour, smeared themselves with clarified butter and clad themselves in the garments of kusha grass. The brave ones used bowstrings as girdles. They had given away hundreds and thousands of dakshina and had performed many sacrifices. They had sons. They had performed deeds to obtain worlds.[5] Having performed the deeds, they were ready to lay down their lives. They had devoted their souls to fame and victory. Through an excellent fight, they quickly aspired to obtain worlds that can be got through sacrifices at which a lot of dakshina is offered and rites, of which, brahmacharya and the study of the sacred texts are the foremost. Each of them separately satisfied the brahmanas by giving them gold coins, cows and garments. Then they addressed each other affectionately. They lit fires with black trails and took an oath for the battle. In front of the fires, firm in their resolution, they took the pledges. They took that oath for slaying Dhananjaya and loudly spoke these words, in the hearing of all beings. 'There are worlds for those who lie, those who kill brahmanas, drunkards, worlds for those who have intercourse with the preceptor's wife, those who rob the property of brahmanas, those who steal a king's grant,[6] those who forsake someone who seeks refuge, those who kill someone

---

[3]Before Duryodhana.

[4]Prasthala is the capital of Trigarta.

[5]In the hereafter.

[6]A royal grant is given in the expectation of a quid pro quo. Stealing means violating the conditions of the grant.

who seeks a favour, those who are arsonists, those who kill cows, those who are wicked, worlds for those who hate brahmanas, those who are overtaken by folly and do not have intercourse with their wives when it is the right season or have intercourse on the day of a shraddha, those who injure their own souls, those who misappropriate something left in trust, those who destroy learning, those who fight out of anger, those who follow inferior ones, worlds for those who are atheists, those who abandon their fires and their ancestors and there are worlds for those who are evil in conduct. If we return from the battle without killing Dhananjaya, or if we retreat because we are afflicted by his weapons, those[7] will be ours. If in this battle, we accomplish feats that are difficult to perform in this world, there is no doubt that we will obtain desirable worlds.' O king! Having spoken in this way, they advanced to do battle. The brave ones challenged Arjuna in the southern direction.[8]

'"Partha, tiger among men and the destroyer of enemy cities, was thus challenged and quickly spoke these words to Dharmaraja. 'I have a vow that I will not retreat if I am challenged. O king! The samshaptakas are repeatedly challenging me. Susharma, together with his brothers, is challenging me to a battle. You should give me permission to kill him, together with his followers. O bull among men! I am incapable of tolerating this challenge. Know that these enemies have already been killed in battle. I tell you this truthfully.' Yudhishthira replied, 'O son![9] You have heard what Drona desires to do. Act so that his intentions become false. Drona is brave and powerful. He is skilled in the use of weapons and has conquered fatigue. O maharatha! He has sworn to capture me.' Arjuna said, 'O king! This Satyajit will protect you in battle today. As long as this Panchala is alive, the preceptor's desire will not be fulfilled. If this lord Satyajit, tiger among men, is killed in the battle, you should never remain here, even if you are surrounded by everyone on our side.' At

[7]Those worlds.
[8]Literally translated, the text means the region inhabited by the ancestors. This is the southern direction.
[9]The word used is tata.

this, the king gave Phalguna the permission and embraced him. He glanced at him affectionately and pronounced many benedictions on him. Having made these arrangements, the powerful Partha advanced against the Trigartas. He was like a hungry lion, hunting a herd of deer to satisfy his hunger. Duryodhana's soldiers were filled with great delight. With Arjuna gone, they were extremely wrathful at the prospect of capturing Dharmaraja. With great energy, the soldiers rushed towards each other, like the powerful Ganga and Sarayu at the time of the monsoon, when they are overflowing with water.'"

Chapter 994(17)

'Sanjaya said, "O king! The samshaptakas were delighted. They stationed themselves and their chariots on level ground, arrayed in a vyuha in the shape of a half-moon. O venerable one! On seeing that Kiriti was advancing towards them, those tigers among men were delighted. They roared loudly. That noise resounded in the directions and the sub-directions and covered the sky. Because the ground was covered with only a few men, there were no echoes. On seeing that they were extremely delighted, Dhananjaya smiled a little and addressed these words to Krishna. 'O one who has Devaki as a mother! Behold. At a time when they should be weeping, the Trigarta brothers are delighted. They are about to be killed in the battle. Or perhaps, this is certainly a time for the Trigartas to rejoice. They will obtain excellent worlds that cannot be obtained by those who are cowards.' Having spoken these words to the mighty-armed Hrishikesha in the battle, Arjuna encountered the army of the Trigartas, arranged in a battle formation. Phalguna grasped the conch shell Devadatta, embellished with gold and blew it with great force, filling all the directions. The samshaptaka chariots were terrified at the sound. In that battle, they were motionless, as if they were made out of stone. Their mounts dilated their eyes, with the ears, heads and lips paralysed. Their feet did not move. They excreted urine and vomited blood.

'"When they regained consciousness, the army was arrayed again and simultaneously released arrows tufted with heron feathers towards Pandu's son. However, Arjuna used fifteen swift arrows to counter thousands of those. The valiant one was swift and severed the arrows before they could reach him. Each of them then pierced Arjuna with ten sharp arrows. But Partha pierced them back with three arrows each. O king! Each of them then pierced Partha with five arrows. But the valorous one pierced each of them back with two arrows. They became extremely angry and enveloped Arjuna and Keshava with sharp arrows, like rain showering down on a lake. Hundreds and thousands of arrows were released towards Arjuna, like hordes of bees descending on flowering trees in a forest. Subahu pierced and penetrated Savyasachi's diadem with thirty arrows that were as hard as rock. Those gold-tufted arrows stuck to Kiriti's diadem and he looked like a sacrificial post decorated with gold. In the encounter, Pandava used a broad-headed arrow to sever Subahu's arm-guard and enveloped him with a shower of arrows. Susharma, Suratha, Sudharma, Sudhanu and Subahu pierced Kiriti with ten arrows each. But the one with the monkey on his banner countered each of them separately with arrows. He pierced them back and severed their golden standards with broad-headed arrows. Having sliced down Sudhanu's bow, he killed his horses with arrows. Then he severed his helmeted head from his body. When that brave one was brought down, his followers were terrified. In fear, they fled towards Duryodhana's army. Vasava's son was extremely angry and slaughtered that large army with his net of arrows, like the sun's rays dispelling darkness. The army was shattered and fled in different directions. Savyasachi was overcome with great rage and the Trigartas were overcome with fear. They were slaughtered by Partha's straight-tufted arrows. They remained there, bereft of their senses, like a frightened herd of deer. The angry king of the Trigartas[10] spoke to the maharathas. 'O brave ones! Do not run away. You should not be overcome by fear. You pledged and took a terrible oath before all the soldiers. Having gone there, what will you tell the foremost ones

[10]Susharma.

among Duryodhana's soldiers? For this deed of ours in this battle, will we not be ridiculed in this world? All of us should unite and return to our respective divisions.' O king! Having been thus addressed, those brave ones repeatedly blew on their conch shells and gladdened each other. The masses of samshaptakas returned again, like the Narayana cowherds[11] that have returned to their death.""

Chapter 995(18)

'Sanjaya said, "On seeing the samshaptaka army return again, Arjuna spoke to the great-souled Vasudeva. 'O Hrishikesha! Drive the horses towards the army of the samshaptakas. They will not return alive from the battle. That is my view. Today, you will witness the terrible strength of my weapons and my arms. I will bring them down, like an angry Rudra against animals.' Hearing this, Krishna smiled and addressed him with auspicious words. The invincible one conveyed Arjuna to the spot where he desired to go. They were radiant on a chariot drawn by white horses and because of this, seemed to cause a loss of the senses, like a vimana that has risen in the sky. The chariot performed circular motions, it moved forwards and back. O king! It was like Shakra's chariot, in the battle between the gods and the asuras in ancient times. The angry Narayanas raised different kinds of weapons in their hands. They surrounded Dhananjaya and enveloped him with a storm of arrows. O bull among the Bharata lineage! In that battle, they made Dhananjaya, Kunti's son, invisible, together with Krishna. In that encounter, Phalguna became wrathful and showed double his valour. In that battle, he grasped the Gandiva and touched its string.

[11]This is a reference to the incidents recounted in Section 49 (Volume 4), when both Duryodhana and Arjuna had solicited Krishna's help. Arjuna had opted for the unarmed Krishna and Duryodhana for the cowherds known as Narayana soldiers. The Narayana soldiers are partly being equated with the samshaptakas.

There were frowns on his forehead, a sign of rage. Pandava blew on the great conch shell Devadatta. Arjuna resorted to the weapon known as *tvastra*, which was capable of destroying large numbers of the enemy at the same time. Many thousand of separate forms appeared.[12] Confused by these many different forms, they began to kill each other. Thinking each other to be Arjuna, they began to kill each other. 'This is Arjuna. This is Govinda. These are Yadava and Pandava.' They were confused and speaking in this way, they killed each other in that battle. They were confused by that supreme weapon and destroyed each other in this way. In that battle, the warriors were as beautiful as flowering kimshukas. The thousands of arrows released by those brave ones were reduced by that weapon to ashes and it conveyed them to Yama's abode.

'"Bibhatsu laughed and used his arrows to shatter the Lallittha, Malava, Machellaka and Trigarta warriors. Those brave kshatriyas were propelled by destiny. They were slaughtered and released many different showers of arrows towards Partha. Shrouded by that terrible shower of arrows, Arjuna, Keshava or the chariot could no longer be seen there. On seeing that the arrows had found their mark, they told each other in delight. 'Krishna and Arjuna have been killed.' They waved their garments in the air. The brave ones sounded thousands of drums, tambourines and conch shells. O venerable one! They emitted terrible roars, like lions. Krishna was covered in sweat and was exhausted. He told Arjuna, 'O Partha! Where are you? I cannot see you. O slayer of enemies! Are you alive?' He who knows all sentiments, thus adopted human sentiments. On discerning this, Pandava swiftly used the vayavya weapon and dispelled that shower of arrows. The illustrious Vayu[13] created a storm that blew away the samshaptakas, with their horses, elephants, chariots and weapons, as if they were heaps of dry leaves. O king! As they were borne away by the wind, they looked beautiful. O venerable one! They were like birds, flying

---

[12]That is, many different forms of Krishna and Arjuna appeared.
[13]Vayavya is a divine weapon named after Vayu, the wind god.

away from trees at the right time.[14] Having afflicted them in this way, Dhananjaya swiftly killed hundreds and thousands of them with his sharp arrows. He used broad-headed arrows to sever their heads and their arms, still grasping weapons. He used his arrows to bring down thighs that were like the trunks of elephants. Some were wounded on their backs. Others lost their legs, or their heads, eyes and fingers. Dhananjaya deprived their bodies of many limbs. Their many chariots looked like the cities of gandharvas. He shattered them, and the horses, chariots and elephants, with his arrows. With the standards brought down, some of those groups of chariots looked like forests of palm trees, with the heads lopped off. There were elephants with excellent weapons, standards, goads and warriors. They were brought down, like wooden mountains struck with Shakra's vajra. There were horses with tails like whisks and armoured riders. Wounded by Partha's arrows, they fell down on the ground, with their entrails and eyes plucked out. Foot soldiers held swords that looked like nails. But these dropped from their hand and their armour was shattered. Their inner organs were mangled. They were killed and whirled around. They fell and were falling down. Because of this, the field of battle looked terrible. A great cloud of dust had arisen and was now pacified by the shower of blood. Strewn with many headless torsos, the ground became difficult to cross. In that battle, Bibhatsu's chariot was fierce and radiant. He sported around like Rudra, slaughtering animals at the time of destruction. Killed by Partha, the horses, chariots and elephants became anxious. But they continued to rush at him, like guests visiting Shakra.[15] O foremost among the Bharata lineage! The ground was strewn with many slain maharathas. With all of them lying there, it looked like the world of dead spirits. While Savyasachi was thus furiously engaged, Drona and his battle formations attacked Yudhishthira. There were many armed ones in arrays and they swiftly attacked, so as to capture Yudhishthira. There was a great and tumultuous encounter.'''

[14]Such as at dawn.
[15]Implying that they were about to die.

Chapter 996(19)

'Sanjaya said, "O king! When the night had passed, Bharadvaja's maharatha son spoke to King Suyodhana. 'I have made arrangements for the masses of samshaptakas to be engaged with Partha.' When Partha had left to battle with the samshaptakas and kill them, Drona and his battle formation advanced against the great army of the Pandavas. O best of the Bharata lineage! He advanced, wishing to capture Dharmaraja. On seeing that Bharadvaja's son had arranged his vyuha in the form of a Garuda,[16] Yudhishthira created a counter-vyuha that was in the form of a half-circle. Bharadvaja's maharatha son was himself stationed in the mouth of the Suparna. King Duryodhana was at the head, with his brothers and followers. Kritavarma and the supremely radiant Goutama[17] were the eyes. Bhutavarma, Kshemasharma, the valiant Karakarsha, Kalingas, Simhalas, those from the east, brave Abhiras, Dasherakas, Shakas, Yavanas, Kambojas, Hamsapadas, Shurasenas, Daradas, Madras and Kekayas, with hundreds and thousands of elephants, horses, chariots and infantry, were stationed at the neck. Bhurishrava, Shala, Shalya, Somadatta and Bahlika—these brave ones were surrounded by one akshouhini and resorted to the right flank. Vinda and Anuvinda from Avanti and Sudakshina from Kamboja were stationed on the left flank, with Drona's son stationed at the forefront. Kalingas,[18] Ambashthas, Magadhas, Poundras, Madrakas, Gandharas, Shakunis, those from the eastern regions,[19] those from the mountainous regions and the Vastayas were at the rear. Vaikartana Karna, with his sons, kin and relatives, was at the tail, surrounded by a large army that raised many different kinds of standards. Jayadratha, Bhimaratha, Samyati, Triksabha, Jaya, Bhuminjaya, Vrisha, Kratha and the immensely strong Naishadha were surrounded by a large army and placed the world of Brahma as the objective.[20] O king! They were

---

[16]The text uses the word Suparna, which is the same as Garuda.

[17]Kripa.

[18]The Kalingas were divided into various segments.

[19]As with the Kalingas, there is repetition here too.

[20]That is, they were prepared to die.

skilled in war and placed themselves in the centre of the vyuha. The vyuha constructed by Drona had foot soldiers, horses, chariots and elephants. It was seen to be as turbulent as an ocean lashed by a storm. Those wishing to do battle emerged from its flanks and its sides. They were like clouds tinged with lightning, emerging in all the directions during summer. O king! Pragjyotisha[21] was resplendent in the midst, astride an elephant that had been properly prepared. He looked like the rising sun. The king was adorned with garlands and a white umbrella was above his head. He looked like the full moon, in conjunction with Krittika.[22] The elephant was blind with madness and was like a gigantic mountain, on which giant clouds were showering down. It looked like a mass of collyrium. He[23] was surrounded by many brave kings from the mountainous regions, adorned with diverse weapons, and was like Shakra, surrounded by masses of gods.

'"Yudhishthira saw that superhuman vyuha, incapable of being vanquished by enemies in battle. He spoke these words to Parshata. 'O lord! Your horses have the complexion of pigeons.[24] Determine a policy so that I am not captured today by the brahmana.' Dhrishtadyumna replied, 'O one who is excellent in vows! No matter how hard Drona tries, he will not be able to bring you under his control. I will check Drona today, together with his followers. O Kouravya! As long as I am alive, you should not be anxious. Drona will never be able to defeat me in battle.' Having said this, Drupada's powerful son, with horses that had the hue of pigeons, released arrows and himself attacked Drona. On seeing the evil omen of Dhrishtadyumna stationed before him,[25] Drona instantly became distressed. On seeing this, your son Durmukha, the destroyer of enemies, wished to do that which would bring pleasure to Drona and countered Dhrishtadyumna. O descendant of the Bharata lineage! A terrible battle raged between the brave Parshata

---

[21]Bhagadatta.

[22]The third of the twenty-seven nakshatras, Pleiades.

[23]Bhagadatta.

[24]They are white.

[25]Dhrishtadyumna was destined to kill Drona.

and Durmukha and they were each other's equal. Parshata swiftly enveloped Durmukha with a net of arrows and countered Bharadvaja's son with a great shower of arrows. On seeing that Drona had been sorely countered, your son confounded Parshata with a shower of many different kinds of arrows. While the one from Panchala and the foremost among the Kurus were thus engaged in battle, Drona killed many of Yudhishthira's soldiers with arrows. They were routed in diverse directions, like clouds by the wind. Partha's soldiers were thus scattered.

'"For a short while, the encounter seemed to be pleasant. O king! But it then became violent and no consideration was shown to anyone. O king! As they fought each other, they could not distinguish friend from foe. The battle raged on, on the basis of guessing and signs. The rays of the sun reflected on the gems on headdresses, necklaces, ornaments, swords and shields and they assumed the complexion of the sun. The chariots, elephants and horses streamed banners and seemed to assume the form of clouds, with flocks of cranes in them. Men killed men. Horses fiercely killed horses. Charioteers killed charioteers and elephants killed supreme elephants. In a short instant, there was a terrible and fierce encounter between elephants and other supreme elephants, all bedecked with pennants. As they rubbed their bodies against each other and clashed against each other with their tusks, flames tinged with smoke arose from the friction. Because of the fire generated from the tusks, the standards were brought down. They looked like masses of resplendent clouds in the sky, tinged with lightning. The earth was strewn with elephants that roared as they were brought down, like clouds shrouding the autumn sky. The elephants were slaughtered with showers of arrows and javelins and roared, like clouds during a deluge. Some supreme elephants were struck with arrows and javelins and were terrified. Others shrieked and fled, frightening all beings. Some elephants were wounded by the tusks of other elephants. They roared in tones of woe, like clouds at the time of a terrible calamity. Some elephants were driven back by other supreme elephants. But urged by excellent goads, they returned to the battle. Elephant-riders struck elephant-riders with arrows and javelins. With weapons and goads dislodged, they fell down from the backs of elephants to the ground. Many elephants were bereft of their riders and wandered in different directions. They fell down when they encountered each other, like scattered clouds. They bore slain drivers and the best of warriors. Those giant elephants wandered in all the directions, as if they were solitary.[26] Some elephants were attacked. Others were attacked with javelins, swords and battleaxes. They uttered roars of distress and fell down. Bodies that were like mountains fell down suddenly. The earth was suddenly struck and quaked, and seemed to be shrieking. The earth was strewn in every direction with warriors, elephant-riders, pennants and elephants and was beautiful, as if it was covered with hills. In that battle, elephant-riders on elephants were pierced in their hearts. Charioteers were brought down with broad-headed arrows and lances and goads were strewn around. Other elephants were wounded with iron arrows and shrieked like cranes. They fled in the ten directions, crushing foes and friends. O king! The earth was covered with masses of elephants, horses, charioteers and their bodies and the slush of flesh and blood. Chariots, with wheels and without wheels, and with the maharathas, were uprooted by elephants with the tips of their tusks. Chariots were bereft of charioteers and elephants were bereft of riders. With their riders slain, horses and elephants fled in different directions, afflicted by the arrows. The father killed the son and the son killed the father. In that tumultuous battle, nothing could be distinguished. In that slush of blood, men sank down, up to their ankles. They were as dazzling as giant trees in a conflagration. The garments, armour, umbrellas and standards were all seen to be drenched red in blood. Masses of horses, masses of chariots and masses of men were brought down. They were again crushed into many pieces by the wheels of chariots. The soldiers were like an ocean. The masses of elephants were the mighty currents. The slain men were the moss. The masses of chariots were eddies. Desiring victory and prosperity, warriors immersed themselves in that ocean, using their mounts as large

---

[26]The word used is *ekachara*. The elephants were solitary, as if they had lost their herds. Ekachara also means a rhinoceros. Therefore, an alternative translation is also possible. The elephants wandered around, like rhinos.

boats, and sought to confound the others.[27] Each of those warriors was covered with a shower of arrows, but did not deviate from the objective. Though they lost their signs,[28] they did not lose heart. In that terrible and fearful battle, Drona confounded the enemy and rushed towards Yudhishthira.”’

Chapter 997(20)

‘Sanjaya said, “On seeing that Drona was near him, Yudhishthira was not frightened, but received him with a mighty shower of arrows. Sounds of applause arose in Yudhishthira’s army, like that made by a herd of elephants when its leader is attacked by a lion. On seeing that Drona was advancing to capture Yudhishthira, the brave Satyajit, with truth as his valour, attacked the preceptor. The preceptor and Panchala fought against each other. They agitated each other’s soldiers, like Indra and Virochana’s son.[29] The preceptor swiftly pierced Satyajit with ten sharp arrows that penetrated the inner organs and severed his bow and arrows. The powerful one quickly grasped another bow and struck Drona with twenty arrows shafted with the feathers of herons. On learning that Satyajit had been grasped by Drona in the battle, Vrika from Panchala oppressed Drona with hundreds of sharp arrows. O king! On seeing that Drona was enveloped by the maharatha in the battle, the Pandavas roared and waved their garments around. O king! Extremely enraged, the powerful Vrika pierced Drona between the breasts with sixty arrows and it was extraordinary. Maharatha Drona dilated his eyes in rage. Using great force, he powerfully shrouded them with showers of arrows. Having severed the bows of Satyajit and Vrika, Drona killed Vrika, his charioteer and his horses with six arrows. Satyajit took up another bow that was more powerful and pierced Drona, his horses,

---

[27]The enemy.
[28]They lost their standards and the signs of belonging to specific divisions.
[29]Virochana’s son was Bali.

his charioteer and his standard with arrows. Drona could not tolerate this oppression by Panchala in that battle. He released arrows, so as to quickly destroy him. Drona shot thousands of showers of arrows to envelope his horses, his standards, the handle of his bow and his parshni charioteers. Despite his bow being repeatedly severed, Panchala, who knew about supreme weapons, continued to fight the one with the red horses.[30] On witnessing Satyajit's increasing energy in that great battle, the great-souled one sliced off his head with an arrow that was in the shape of a crescent. When the mighty warrior, the Panchala who was a bull among rathas, was slain, Yudhishthira became frightened of Drona and fled on swift horses.

'"On seeing Drona, the Panchalas, Kekayas, Matsyas, Chedis, Karushas and Kosalas wished to protect Yudhishthira and cheerfully attacked. The preceptor, the destroyer of large numbers of the enemy, wished to capture Yudhishthira. He slew those soldiers, like a fire consuming large masses of cotton. On witnessing that Drona was repeatedly consuming the soldiers, Shatanika, the younger brother of Matsya, attacked him. He severely pierced Drona, his charioteer and his horses with six arrows that were like the rays of the sun and had been polished by artisans, and roared. While he was thus roaring, Drona swiftly sliced off his head, adorned with earrings, from his body with a kshurapra. At this, the Matsyas fled. Having defeated the Matsyas, Bharadvaja's son repeatedly vanquished the Chedis, Karushas, Kekayas, Panchalas, Srinjayas and Pandus. On beholding the angry one on the golden chariot, consuming the soldiers in his rage, like a fire in a forest, the Srinjayas trembled. The one who was swift in his deeds drew his bowstring and the excellent sound of the twang was heard in all the directions, as he slaughtered the enemy. The terrible arrows released from his hands mangled elephants, horses, infantry, charioteers and elephant-riders. He was like a roaring cloud at the end of winter, mingled with the wind, pouring down a shower of hailstones and the enemy was frightened. The great archer, powerful and brave, the one who protected his enemies from fear, roamed around in all the directions, causing agitation and fright. The

[30]Drona.

infinitely energetic Drona's bow was decorated with gold and looked like lightning flashing in the clouds. It was seen in all the directions. Drona caused great carnage among the Pandava soldiers, like that caused by Vishnu, revered by gods and asuras, among the masses of daityas. He was brave and truthful in speech. He was wise and powerful. Truth was his valour. He was noble-minded. He created a terrible river, like the one at the time of destruction, terrifying to cowards. Armour was the waves. Standards were eddies. It flowed and carried away the mortals. Elephants and horses were the giant crocodiles. The swords were fish and it[31] was difficult to cross. The bones of brave ones were its terrible stones. Drums and tambourines were the turtles. Shields and armour were the terrible boats. The hair was moss and weeds. Masses of arrows and bows were the current. It was full of serpents in the form of arms.[32] It flowed fiercely through the field of battle and bore along the soldiers of the Kurus and the Srinjayas. The heads of men were the boulders. Javelins were the fish and clubs were rafts. The headdresses were the foam on the surface. The disemboweled entrails were the reptiles. It was fierce and bore brave ones away. The flesh and the blood was the mud. The elephants were the crocodiles. The standards were the trees.[33] Kshatriyas were submerged in it. It was terrible and congested with bodies. The riders were the sharks and it was difficult to cross. Drona created a river there and it flowed to the world of the dead. It was full of large numbers of carrion-eaters and had tens of thousands of dogs and jackals. In every direction, it was frequented by extremely fierce flesh-eaters.

'"On seeing that the great ratha was consuming the soldiers, like Death, they attacked Drona from all sides, with Kunti's son at the forefront. Those on your side, the kings and the princes, raised their weapons and surrounded the brave and great archer. Drona never deviated in his aim and was like an elephant with a shattered temple. He overcame that mass of chariots and brought down Dridhasena. He approached King Kshema, who was fighting fearlessly, and piercing

---

[31]The river.
[32]The severed arms of warriors.
[33]Along the banks of the river.

him with nine arrows, slew and felled him from his chariot. He
penetrated the midst of the soldiers and roaming around, repulsed
them in every direction. He protected all the others. But he himself
had no need for protection. He pierced Shikhandi with twelve and
Uttamouja with twenty arrows. With a broad-headed arrow, he sent
Vasudana to Yama's abode. He struck Kshatravarma with eighty
arrows and Sudakshina with twenty-six. With a broad-headed arrow,
he brought Kshatradeva down from the seat of his chariot. He pierced
Yudhamanyu with sixty-four arrows and Satyaki with thirty. The
one on the golden chariot then quickly approached Yudhishthira.
The deceitful[34] Yudhishthira, supreme among kings, swiftly fled
on fast horses. Panchala[35] attacked him. But Drona struck him, his
bow, his horses and his charioteer. Slain, he fell down on the ground
from his chariot, like a stellar body dropping down from the sky.
When that illustrious prince of Panchala was killed, there was a great
and tumultuous sound of 'Kill Drona! Kill Drona!' The Panchalas,
Matsyas and Kekayas were filled with great rage. However, the
powerful Drona crushed the Srinjayas and the Pandavas. Satyaki,
Chekitana, Dhrishtadyumna, Shikhandi, Vardhakshemi, Chitrasena,
Senabindu, Suvarchas—these and many other kings from many
different countries were all vanquished in that battle by Drona,
who was surrounded by the Kurus. O great king! Those on your
side obtained victory in that great battle. As the Pandavas fled in all
directions, they were slaughtered in that battle, like the danavas being
slaughtered by the great-souled Indra. O descendant of the Bharata
lineage! The Panchalas, Kekayas and Matsyas trembled.'''

Chapter 998(21)

'Dhritarashtra asked, "When the Pandavas were routed by
Bharadvaja's son in that great battle, did anyone among all the

---

[34]Because he did not stay to fight.
[35]This particular Panchala is not named.

Panchalas advance against him? Was there no noble one who wished
to earn fame, as befits a kshatriya, and set his mind on fighting? He
should not have been served by cowards. He should have been served
by bulls among men. It must have been a brave man and charioteer
who returned from that rout. On seeing that Drona was stationed,
was there no such man? He was like a tiger with a yawning mouth.
He was like an elephant with a shattered temple. He was prepared
to give up his life in battle. He was armoured and was wonderful
in fighting. He was a great archer. He was a tiger among men. He
increased fear among his enemies. He was grateful and devoted to
the truth. He was engaged in Duryodhana's welfare. O Sanjaya! On
seeing that Bharadvaja's brave son was stationed in that army, which
brave ones advanced against him? Tell me."

'Sanjaya replied, "On seeing that the Panchalas, Pandavas,
Matsyas, Srinjayas, Chedis and Kekayas were driven away from the
battle by Drona's arrows, the Kouravas roared like lions and sounded
many musical instruments. Large numbers of arrows were swiftly
released from Drona's bow and they[36] were like shattered boats
tossed around on the giant waves of the ocean. They surrounded the
chariots, elephants and men from all directions.[37] King Duryodhana
was stationed in the midst of his soldiers, surrounded by his relatives.
On seeing them, he laughed and spoke these words of joy to Karna.
'O Radheya! Behold! The Panchalas have been shattered by Drona's
arrows. They have been terrified by the wielder of the firm bow, like
wild deer by a lion. It is my view that they will never return to fight
again. They have been broken by Drona, like giant trees by a tempest.
They have been consumed by the gold-tufted arrows of the great-
souled one. They are fleeing through multiple routes and seemed to
be whirled around. They have been confined by the Kouravas and
the great-souled Drona. They are like elephants huddled together,
because of a fire. Because of Drona's sharp arrows, they are like a
cluster of bees. They are huddling together and are trying to run
away. Bhima is firm in his anger. But he has been abandoned by

[36]The Pandavas.
[37]The Kouravas surrounded the Pandavas.

the Pandavas and the Srinjayas. O Karna! Surrounded by those on my side, he seeks to threaten us. The evil-minded one now sees the entire world as if it is full of Drona. Pandava has now lost all hope of remaining alive and of regaining the kingdom.'

'"Karna said, 'As long as there is life left in him, this mighty-armed one will never give up the battle. O tiger among men! Nor will he tolerate these roars like lions. It is my view that the Pandavas have not been defeated in battle. They are brave and powerful. They are skilled in the use of weapons and are invincible in war. The Pandavas will remember the hardships from poisoning, arson, gambling and dwelling in the forest.[38] It is my view that they will not retreat from the battle. The mighty-armed and infinitely energetic Vrikodara has already returned. This Kounteya is supreme among the best and he will kill the best of our rathas. With a sword, bow, javelin, horses, elephants, men, chariots[39] and an iron staff, he will slay large numbers. Other rathas, Satyaki and the others, are also returning after him—the Panchalas, Kekayas and Matsyas, and particularly the Pandavas. Those maharathas are brave, powerful and valiant. They are enraged and are being specially urged by Bhima. The bulls among the Kurus[40] have surrounded Drona from all sides. Wishing to protect Vrikodara, they are like clouds around the sun. They are united in their purpose and will oppress the one who is rigid in his vows and is unprotected. They are like insects on the point of death, around a lamp. There is no doubt that they are skilled in the use of weapons and are capable of countering him. I think that the burden on Bharadvaja's son will be too much to bear. Let us quickly go to the spot where Drona is stationed. They are seeking to slay the one who is rigid in his vows, like wolves around a mighty elephant.'"

'Sanjaya said, "O king! On hearing Radheya's words, King Duryodhana left towards Drona's chariot, together with his brothers. A great uproar was created there by the Pandavas who

[38]Before the gambling match, Duryodhana had tried poisoning and arson.

[39]Bhima will also use horses, elephants, men and chariots as implements of war.

[40]Meaning the Pandavas.

had returned, wishing to kill Drona. They were on supreme horses with diverse hues.'"

Chapter 999(22)

'Dhritarashtra said, "O Sanjaya! Tell me about the signs on the chariots of those who angrily attacked Drona, with Bhima at the forefront."

'Sanjaya replied, "Vrikodara advanced into battle on horses that had the complexion of antelopes.[41] On seeing him, Shini's brave descendant[42] advanced on horses that were silvery. Nakula swiftly advanced against your army, borne on handsome horses from Kamboja that were decorated with the feathers of parrots. Sahadeva was borne on horses that were as dark as clouds. That tiger among men raised his weapons and advanced with great force, on horses that were as fleet as the wind. Yudhishthira advanced on horses that were as fleet as the wind and were caparisoned with the best of gold. All the other soldiers followed him. King Drupada of Panchala advanced after the king.[43] A golden umbrella was held aloft his head and he protected all his soldiers. The great archer Shantabhi advanced in the midst of all the kings. He was yoked to beautiful horses that were capable of withstanding every kind of noise in battle. Virata followed him, with all other brave maharathas. So did the Kekayas, Shikhandi and Dhrishtaketu, surrounded by their respective soldiers. All of them followed the king of Matsya.[44] Matsya, the slayer of enemies, was resplendent as he was borne by supreme horses, with the complexion of *patala* flowers.[45] The king of Virata's son[46] was

[41]The horses were dappled.
[42]Satyaki.
[43]Yudhishthira.
[44]Virata.
[45]Patala is a kind of rose or the trumpet-flower. The complexion is reddish pink.
[46]Uttara.

swiftly borne on swift horses that were yellow in complexion and were garlanded with gold. The five brothers from Kekaya were on horses that had the hue of fireflies. All of them dazzled like pure gold and possessed red standards. All those brave ones had golden garlands and were skilled in fighting. They were seen to be armoured and showered[47] like clouds. Shikhandi, the infinitely energetic one from Panchala was yoked to controlled steeds that were coppery red, like unbaked earthen vessels. Of the twelve thousand maharathas from Panchala, six thousand followed Shikhandi. O venerable one! Shishupala's son, Dhrishtaketu, was a lion among men. He was borne on playful horses that had the complexion of deer. That bull among the Chedis was powerful. He was invincible and he advanced on horses from Kamboja that were dappled. Vrihatkshatra from Kekaya was borne on excellent and delicate horses that were swift and from Sindhu. They had the hue of smoking straw. Shikhandi's son, the brave Kshatradeva, was borne on horses that had eyes like jasmines. They had the complexion of lotuses, were adorned and were born in Bahlika. The young and delicate son of the king of Kashi was a maharatha. He was borne into battle on supreme horses that had the complexion of cranes. O king! The prince Prativindhya was borne on white horses with black necks that were as swift as thought and were obedient to the driver.[48] Partha obtained his son Sutasoma through Dhoumya.[49] Horses that had the complexion of *masha* flowers bore him into battle.[50] He possessed the radiance of one thousand moons. He was born in the city of the Kurus named Udayendu. Having been born thus, in the midst of those of the lunar lineage, he came to be known as

[47]Showered arrows.

[48]Prativindhya was Yudhishthira's son, Sutasoma Bhima's, Shrutakarma Arjuna's, Shatanika Nakula's and Shrutasena Sahadeva's. All five were Droupadi's sons.

[49]This Partha is Bhima. Dhoumya was priest to the Pandavas. He encouraged them to participate in Droupadi's svayamvara and was also the priest when each of the five Pandavas were married to Droupadi. Having said this, there is no particular reason to single out Dhoumya for Sutasoma.

[50]Masha is wild bean and the colour of the flowers is whitish yellow.

Sutasoma.[51] Nakula's son, Shatanika, was borne on horses that had
the complexion of shala flowers. He was worthy of praise and was
like the rising sun in his radiance. Droupadi's son, Shrutakarma,
tiger among men, was borne on horses that had complexions like
the necks of peacocks and were caparisoned in gold. Droupadi's son,
Shrutakirti, was an ocean of learning.[52] He was the equal of Partha
in battle[53] and was on supreme horses. These horses possessed hues
like those on the feathers of blue jays. Horses with a tawny hue bore
the young Abhimanyu into battle. In his qualities of fighting, he was
regarded as one-and-a-half times superior to Krishna and Partha.
There was only a single one among the sons of Dhritarashtra who
had sided with the Pandavas in battle and large and gigantic horses
bore Yuyutsu into battle. The swift Vardhakhemi was carried into
that dreadful battle on cheerful horses that were adorned and had
the complexion of strands of straw. There were horses with black
feet, armoured with golden plates and obedient to the driver. These
bore the youthful Souchitti into battle. There were controlled horses
with the complexion of red silk. Their backs were covered with
golden plates and they were in golden harnesses. These bore
Shrenimana. The praiseworthy and brave king of Kashi was borne
on the best of horses. These possessed golden harnesses and the
complexion of gold and were ornamented. Satyadhriti was skilled
in weapons, the knowledge of fighting and in knowledge about the
brahman. He was borne on red steeds. Dhrishtadyumna, the
commander of the Panchalas, had been given Drona as his share.[54]
He was borne on horses that had the complexion of pigeons.
Satyadhriti and the invincible Souchitti followed him into battle and

[51]The text uses the word *somasa*. That is, Sutasoma was born in the midst
of the Somasas. Some non-critical versions say Somakas. We have interpreted
Somasas as those of the lunar lineage, since all the Bharatas were born in the lunar
dynasty. Sutasoma literally means the son of Soma (the moon) and Udayendu
means the rising moon. There is some problem with the text in this segment.

[52]Shrutakirti is the same as Shrutakarma. This should probably read Shrutasena.

[53]Depending on whether this is Shrutakarma or Shrutasena, the Partha in
question is Arjuna or Sahadeva.

[54]Dhrishtadyumna would kill Drona.

so did Shrenimana, Vasudana and Vibhu, the sons of the king of Kashi. They were yoked to supreme and swift horses from Kamboja, with golden harnesses. Each was equal to Yama or Vaishravana and could strike terror into enemy soldiers.[55] There were six thousand Prabhadrakas from Panchala, with raised weapons. They were on the best of horses, with many hues, and possessed golden and colourful standards on their chariots. They stretched their bows and released showers of arrows that confused the enemy. They were determined to die together and followed Dhrishtadyumna. There were supreme horses that were resplendent with a complexion like that of silk and possessed excellent golden harnesses. They cheerfully bore Chekitana. Savyasachi's maternal uncle, Purujit Kuntibhoja, was on excellent and obedient horses.[56] They possessed the complexion of Indra's weapon.[57] King Rochamana was borne into that battle on horses that had the colour of the firmament, decorated with stars. Jarasandha's son, Sahadeva, was borne on the best of horses, with speckled complexions and black feet. They were adorned in nets of gold. Sudama was borne on swift horses that were coloured like hawks and had complexions like those of lotus stalks. Simhasena from Panchala, the son of Gopati, was borne on horses that had the complexion of red antelopes, with white streaks on their bodies. The tiger among the Panchalas was known by the name of Janamejaya.[58] He was on supreme horses that had the colour of mustard flowers. There were large and swift horses that possessed the colour of straw. They had golden harnesses. Their backs were like curd and their mouths were like the moon. These bore Panchala.[59] There were brave

---

[55]The text is such that this can be translated as Vaishravana (Vishrava's son) Yama or Yama and Vaishravana (Kubera).

[56]Kuntibhoja was Kunti's father and Purujit was Kuntibhoja's son. By extension, Purujit is also being referred to as Kuntibhoja, since he was Kuntibhoja's son. As Kunti's brother, Purujit was Arjuna's maternal uncle.

[57]Meaning Indra's bow, that is, the rainbow.

[58]Not to be confused with the more famous Janamejaya who was Parikshit's son and to whom, the story of the Mahabharata is being told.

[59]It is by no means obvious that this Panchala means Drupada. Drupada has already been mentioned and this could be anyone from Panchala.

and gentle steeds that had the hue of reeds. These were as dazzling as the filaments of lotuses and they bore Dandadhara. There were horses that were resplendent in golden harnesses, with stomachs with the complexion of chakravaka birds. These bore Sukshatra, the son of the king of Kosala. There were giant, speckled and controlled horses, caparisoned in gold. These bore Satyadhriti, who was skilled in fighting. Shukla advanced, with everything of the same white colour—standard, armour, horses and bow. Samudrasena's son, Chandrasena, was terrible in his energy. He was borne on horses that were like the moon and had been bred along the coast of the ocean. Shaibya was wonderful in battle. He was borne on horses that possessed the complexion of blue lotuses. They were ornamented in gold and had colourful garlands. Rathasena was invincible in battle. He was borne on the best of horses, with a complexion like that of groundnut flowers, with white and red streaks on their bodies. The king who slew the Patacharas is known as the bravest among all men. He was borne on horses with the colour of parrots. Chitrayudha was adorned in colourful garlands. He possessed colourful armour, weapons and standards. He was borne on the best of horses, with a complexion like that of kimshuka flowers. King Nila advanced, with everything in an identical blue colour—standard, armour, bow, chariot and horses. Chitra advanced, adorned with gems and with colourful guards for his chariot, standard and bow. His horses, standards and pennants were colourful. Hemavarna, Rochamana's son, was on the best of horses, with complexions like that of lotus leaves. Dandaketu was borne on gentle horses that were controlled by staffs that were like the stalks of reeds. They possessed the complexion of the white eggs of hens. Horses with the complexion of *atarusha*[60] flowers bore one hundred and forty thousand foremost rathas who followed Pandya. The brave Ghatotkacha was borne by horses with many different colours and forms. Their mouths were of different types and he had the wheel of a chariot on his standard.

'"Yudhishthira was knowledgeable about dharma and the best of horses surrounded that best of kings from every direction and

---

[60]The medicinal herb *Ailanthus excelsa*.

followed him at the rear. They possessed golden complexions. There were Prabhadrakas on well-trained and divine horses, with many different kinds of colours. They possessed golden standards and made endeavours, together with Bhimasena. O Indra among kings! He was seen to be like Indra, with the residents of heaven. Dhrishtadyumna was delighted that all of them were advancing together. But Bharadvaja's son surpassed all those soldiers.'"

Chapter 1000(23)

'Dhritarashtra said, "Those rathas who returned to the battle, with Vrikodara at the forefront, were capable of afflicting even the soldiers of the gods. A man is certainly driven by destiny. That is the reason why different outcomes result from all action. That is the reason Yudhishthira had to spend a long time in the forest, wearing matted hair and antelope skin, and also had to remain undetected to people. He has now assembled a mighty army in this battle. What can befall my sons, other than what is determined by destiny? It is certain that a man's fortune is determined by destiny. He is compelled to do what he does not himself desire. Yudhishthira suffered hardship because of his addiction to gambling. It is again because of fortune that he has now obtained allies. 'I have obtained half of the Kekayas,[61] the Kashis and the Kosalas. The Chedis, the Vangas and others have sought refuge with me. O father! The entire earth is on my side and not on that of the Parthas.' This is what my evil-minded son, Duryodhana, told me then. Drona was protected well, in the midst of the soldiers. If he has been killed by Parshata's son, what can this be other than destiny? The mighty-armed one was in the midst of the kings and has always delighted in battle. He was skilled in the use of all weapons. How could death have approached Drona? I am confronting distress and have been overcome

[61]Some of the Kekayas were opposed to Duryodhana.

by supreme senselessness. On hearing that Bhishma and Drona have been slain, I have no interest in remaining alive any more. O son![62] On beholding my affection for my son, Kshatta[63] had spoken to me. O suta! Duryodhana and I are now confronted with all of that. Had I abandoned Duryodhana, it would have been supremely cruel. But my remaining sons would not have faced hardship and death. If a man gives up dharma and is addicted to artha, he confronts decay in this world and falls prey to inferior sentiments. O Sanjaya! With the bow and hump[64] of this kingdom destroyed, it has lost all enterprise. I see that nothing will be left. Those two forgiving bulls among men were always our refuge. When they have been destroyed, how can anything be left? Tell me details about how that battle raged. Who were the ones who fought? Who were the ones who attacked? Which inferior ones fled out of fear? Tell me what Dhananjaya, bull among rathas, did. We are scared of him and especially of his brother.[65] O Sanjaya! When the Pandavas returned, there must have been an extremely terrible confrontation between them and my remaining soldiers. Which brave ones on my side countered them there?"'

Chapter 1001(24)[66]

'Sanjaya said, "The Pandus returned and we were immersed in great terror. Drona was enveloped, like the sun by the clouds. They raised a terrible cloud of dust and covered your army. On seeing this and on our sight having been obstructed, we thought that Drona had been slain. Those brave and great archers desired to commit a cruel deed.[67]

[62]The word used is tata.

[63]Vidura.

[64]In the sense of a metaphor.

[65]Bhima.

[66]This entire chapter has inconsistencies and doesn't quite belong.

[67]The deed was cruel because Drona was a brahmana and killing a brahmana was cruel.

On seeing this, Duryodhana quickly urged all his soldiers. 'O lords of men! Use the utmost of your strengths, the utmost of your enterprise, the utmost of your spirits. Engage yourselves according to your tasks and restrain the Pandava formations.' Your son, Durmarshana, saw that Bhima was advancing. Wishing to save Drona's life, he covered him with a shower of arrows. Like death in that battle, he angrily assailed him with arrows. Bhima also attacked him with arrows and a great and fierce battle raged between them. Wise, brave and armed warriors were instructed by their lords. Outwardly giving up all fear of death, they attacked the enemy. O lord of the earth! Wishing to save Drona, Kritavarma, the ornament of any assembly, repulsed Shini's brave son.[68] As Shini's descendant angrily advanced, he wrathfully showered him with arrows. Kritavarma acted against Shini's descendant, like a mad elephant against another crazy one. Saindhava, fierce with the bow and a great archer, used a shower of arrows to fall upon Kshatradharma, when he endeavoured to attack Drona. Kshatradharma severed the standard and bow of the lord of Sindhu. He angrily used many iron arrows to pierce him in all his inner organs. Saindhava displayed the dexterity of his hands and grasped another bow. In that battle, he pierced Kshatradharma with arrows that were made completely out of iron. For the sake of the Pandavas, the brave maharatha Yuyutsu sought to attack Drona, but was countered by his brother, Subahu. Yuyutsu used two sharp and yellow arrows that were as sharp as razors to slice off the arms of his younger brother, Subahu. Those arms were like clubs and held a bow and arrows.[69] King Yudhishthira was the best of the Pandavas and had dharma in his soul. The king of Madra countered him, like the shoreline against a turbulent ocean. Dharmaraja pierced him with many arrows that could penetrate the inner organs and the lord of Madra severely wounded him with sixty-four arrows and roared. But while he was still roaring, the best of the Pandavas sliced down his standard and bow with two razor-sharp arrows and all

[68]Meaning Satyaki.

[69]This is inconsistent. All of Duryodhana's brothers were killed by Bhima. And Subahu has already been killed by Bhima in Section 64.

the people shouted in applause. King Bahlika, with his army, used arrows to counter King Drupada, with his army. Together with their soldiers, these two aged ones fought a terrible battle. This was like that between two gigantic leaders of herds of elephants, with shattered temples. Vinda and Anuvinda from Avanti countered Virata of Matsya, with his soldiers and his army, like Agni against Bali in ancient times.[70] That disorderly encounter between the Matsyas and the Kekayas was like that between the gods and the asuras. Horses, charioteers and elephants fought fearlessly.

'"In that battle, Bhutakarma, the lord of assemblies, used a net of arrows to prevent Nakula's son, Shatanika, from advancing against Drona. Nakula's heir used three extremely sharp and broad-headed arrows and in that battle, deprived Bhutakarma of his two arms and his head. The valiant Sutasoma was advancing towards Drona. But the brave Vivimshati repulsed him with a shower of arrows. However, Sutasoma was enraged and armoured. He pierced Vivimshati, his own paternal uncle, with straight-tufted arrows. Bhimaratha used six swift arrows that were completely made out of iron and dispatched Shalva, together with his horses and charioteer, to Yama's abode.[71] O great king! As your grandson, Shrutakarma, advanced on horses that looked like peacocks, Chitrasena's son countered him. Those two grandsons of yours were invincible and wished to kill each other to accomplish the objectives of their respective fathers and fought a supreme battle. On seeing that Prativindhya was stationed at the forefront of that battle, Drona's son desired to show honour to his father and obstructed him with arrows. Prativindhya was enraged at this and pierced the one who was stationed so as to protect his father, and bore the signs of a lion's tail on his standard,[72] with sharp arrows. O bull among men! Droupadi's son covered Drona's son

---

[70]The demon Bali was eventually vanquished by Vishnu in his dwarf (vamana) incarnation. Prior to that, Bali defeated the gods. However, there is no particular story connecting Agni with Bali.

[71]There is a problem with this. Bhimaratha is Duryodhana's brother and was killed by Bhima in Section 64. Shalva was killed much later, by Satyaki. Chitrasena is also Duryodhana's brother.

[72]References to Ashvatthama.

with a shower of arrows, like seeds being scattered at the time of sowing. O king! Both the armies regarded the slayer of the Patacharas as the best among brave ones and Lakshmana restrained him. O descendant of the Bharata lineage! But that radiant one blazed forth, showering a net of arrows on Lakshmana. Taking aim, he severed Lakshmana's bow and arrow. As Shikhandi, Yajnasena's youthful son, advanced into battle, the young and immensely wise Vikarna countered him. Yajnasena's son enveloped him with a net of arrows. But your powerful son repulsed that net of arrows and looked resplendent. In that battle, as the brave Uttamouja advanced in Drona's direction, Angada countered him with vatsadanta arrows. The encounter between those two lions among men was wonderful and it increased the delight of all the soldiers. As the brave Purujit Kuntibhoja advanced against Drona, the powerful and great archer Durmukha countered him. He struck Durmukha in the midst of his eyebrows with an iron arrow and his[73] face looked as beautiful as a lotus with a stalk.

'"The five brothers from Kekaya possessed red standards. As they advanced towards Drona, Karna countered them with showers of arrows. Countered by that storm of arrows, they became extremely enraged and enveloped him with arrows, becoming repeatedly shrouded by nets of arrows in return. Enveloped by those arrows, Karna and the five brothers could not be seen. The respective arrows covered their horses, charioteers, standards and chariots. Your sons, Durjaya, Jaya and Vijaya, countered Nila, Kashi and Jaya. Three were against three. The terrible encounter between them gladdened the spectators, like that between a lion, tiger and wolf on one side and a buffalo and a bull on the other. As the warrior Satvata[74] advanced against Drona, the brothers Kshemadhurti and Brihanta countered him and wounded him with their sharp arrows. The battle between them was extraordinary, like that between a lion and a foremost elephant, with shattered temples, in the forest. King Ambashtha found delight in battle. As he advanced singly

[73]Durmukha's.
[74]Meaning Satyaki.

against Drona, the king of Chedi angrily restrained him with arrows. Ambashtha pierced him with a stake that penetrated right up to the bones and he[75] gave up his bow and arrows and fell down from his chariot onto the ground. Sharadvata Kripa repulsed Varshneya Vardhakshemi with kshudraka arrows, as he angrily attacked Drona with arrows. Those who saw Kripa and Varshneya fight in that wonderful fashion became so engrossed in that encounter that they forgot about doing anything else. Somadatta's son wished to increase Drona's glory. As King Manimana vigilantly advanced, he countered him. Somadatta's son swiftly sliced down the string of his bow, the standard, the pennant, the charioteer and umbrella and made him fall down from his chariot. The one with the sacrificial stake on his standard, the destroyer of enemies,[76] then quickly descended from his chariot. He grasped a supreme sword and cut him down, together with his horses, charioteer, standard and chariot.[77] O king! He then climbed onto his own chariot again and grasping another bow and steering his horses himself,[78] began to slaughter the Pandava soldiers. Ghatotkacha wished to get at Drona and created terror among the soldiers. He used clubs, maces, chakras, catapults, battleaxes, dust, wind, fire, water, ashes, stones, grass and trees to strike and fight, showering these down and causing a rout. However, the rakshasa Alambusa became enraged and countered the other rakshasa with many different kinds of weapons and many diverse implements of war. The battle between the two foremost among the rakshasas was like that in ancient times, between Shambara and the king of the immortals.[79] O fortunate one! In this fashion, in that melee, there were hundreds of duels between rathas, elephants, horses and infantry, between those on your side and those of the enemy. A battle like this has not been witnessed earlier, nor heard of, like that between

---

[75]The king of Chedi.

[76]Descriptions of Somadatta's son, Bhurishrava.

[77]However, Manimana will later be killed by Drona.

[78]The implication is that Bhurishrava's charioteer was also slain.

[79]There were several demons named Shambara. One of them was killed by Indra.

those who wished to assault Drona and those who sought to protect him. O lord! In different parts of the field, many such encounters were seen—terrible, wonderful and fierce."'

Chapter 1002(25)

'Dhritarashtra asked, "When they[80] had returned and engaged in different divisions, how did the spirited ones on the side of the Parthas, and on mine, fight? How did Arjuna act towards the army of the samshaptakas? O Sanjaya! What did the samshaptakas do to Arjuna?"

'Sanjaya replied, "When they had returned and engaged themselves in different divisions, your son himself attacked Bhima with an army of elephants. It was like an elephant encountering an elephant, or a bull encountering a bull. He[81] was himself summoned and attacked by the king with that army of elephants. Partha was skilled in fighting and possessed the strength of his arms. O venerable one! He swiftly shattered that army of elephants. Those elephants were like mountains and exuded musth everywhere. They were mangled and forced to retreat by Bhimasena's iron arrows. It was like winds driving away a mass of clouds in every direction. That maddened army was thus slaughtered by Pavana's son. Bhima released arrows at those elephants and was as radiant as the rising sun in the sky, striking everything in the world with his rays. Hundreds of Bhima's arrows wounded the elephants and they were as beautiful as masses of clouds in the sky, streaked with the rays of the sun.[82] The son of the wind thus afflicted the elephants. Duryodhana was enraged at this and pierced him with sharp arrows. Bhima's eyes became red with rage and he wished to destroy the king in a short instant. So

[80]The Pandavas.
[81]Bhima.
[82]Because they were wounded, the elephants were streaked with blood.

he pierced him with arrows. With arrows wounding all his limbs, he became angry and smilingly, pierced Pandava Bhimasena back with iron arrows that were as bright as the sun's rays. The sign of a bejewelled elephant was on his[83] standard, embellished with gems. Pandava used broad-headed arrows to swiftly sever this, together with his bow. O venerable one! On seeing that Duryodhana was thus afflicted by Bhima, the lord of Anga arrived there on an elephant, wishing to attack him. On seeing that the elephant was advancing, with a roar like the rumbling of the clouds, Bhimasena used iron arrows to severely strike it between its two frontal lobes. It passed through the body and penetrated the ground. The elephant fell down, like a mountain struck by lightning. As the elephant fell, the lord of the mlecchas[84] also began to fall down. But the swift-acting Vrikodara sliced off his head with a broad-headed arrow. On seeing that the brave one had been brought down, his army fled. Horses, elephants and charioteers were terrified and crushed infantry as they fled.

'"As that army was scattered and routed in every direction, Pragjyotisha attacked Bhima, astride an elephant. It was like Maghavan astride an elephant, victorious against the daityas and the danavas. That supreme of elephants suddenly descended on Bhima. Its ears were drawn back. Its forelegs and trunk were contracted. Its eyes were dilated in rage and it seemed about to consume Pandava. O venerable one! All the soldiers let out a great roar. 'Alas! Bhima has been killed by the elephant.' O king! The Pandava soldiers were terrified by this roar and quickly ran away to the spot where Vrikodara was. King Yudhishthira thought that Vrikodara had been slain. With the Panchalas, he attacked and surrounded Bhagadatta. Having surrounded the best of rathas with chariots from every direction, he covered him with hundreds and thousands of sharp arrows. The lord of the mountains countered all these arrows with his goad and slaughtered the Pandus and Panchalas with his elephant. O lord of the earth! In that battle, we witnessed the aged Bhagadatta's extraordinary conduct, using his elephant. At this, the

---

[83]Duryodhana's.
[84]Meaning, the lord of Anga.

king of Dasharna attacked Pragjyotisha on a swift elephant that
advanced from the flank. Both elephants were terrible in form and
the battle between them was like that between two winged mountains
in ancient times, both covered with trees.[85] Pragjyotisha's elephant
circled around and struck the elephant of the king of Dasharna on
the side, bringing it down. Bhagadatta used seven javelins that were
as bright as the rays of the sun. As his enemy was dislodged from
his seat on the falling elephant, he slew him.

"'Yudhishthira attacked King Bhagadatta and surrounded him
from every direction with a great army of chariots. Astride his
elephant and surrounded by all these rathas in every direction, he
was resplendent, like a flaming fire on a mountain, in the midst of
the forest. He was astride his elephant, inside a circle formed in every
direction by fierce rathas who were archers and showered arrows at
him from every side. The king of Pragjyotisha urged his bull among
elephants and made it swiftly advance towards Yuyudhana's chariot.
The mighty elephant grasped the chariot of Shini's grandson and
used great force to fling it away. However, Yuyudhana escaped.
The charioteer abandoned the large Saindhava horses that were
yoked to the chariot and hurried to the spot where Satyaki was.
The elephant swiftly emerged from that circle of chariots. Having
emerged, it began to fling away all those kings. Those bulls among
men were frightened at its speed. In that battle, the kings thought
that a single elephant had multiplied into hundreds. At that time,
Bhagadatta on his elephant crushed the Pandavas, like the king of the
gods on Airavata, acting against the danavas. There was a terrible
roar as the Panchalas fled. A great noise was made by the elephants
and the horses. In that battle, Bhagadatta was like death before the
Pandus. Bhima became angry and attacked Pragjyotisha again. The
elephant sprinkled water from its trunk and frightened his horses,
which then bore Partha away from the field. Kriti's son, Ruchiparva,
swiftly attacked then. Stationed on his chariot, he showered arrows,
like death personified. The lord of the mountains used a well-crafted
arrow with drooping tufts to dispatch Ruchiparva to Vaivasvata's

---

[85]In ancient times, mountains are believed to have possessed wings.

eternal abode. When that brave one fell, Subhadra's son, Droupadi's sons, Chekitana, Dhrishtaketu and Yuyutsu attacked the elephant. They wished to kill it. Roaring, they showered down arrows on it. The skilled rider urged the elephant with heels, toes and goad. It swiftly advanced, with its trunk extended and its eyes and ears immobile. It killed Yuyutsu's horses and charioteer with its feet. At this time, your son angrily rushed against the chariot of Subhadra's son. Astride his elephant, the king[86] showered arrows on his enemies. He was as dazzling as a sun that has arisen, scattering rays on the world. Arjuna's son pierced him with twelve arrows and Yuyutsu with ten. Each of Droupadi's sons pierced him with three arrows and so did Dhrishtaketu. Those well-released arrows stuck to the body and the elephant looked resplendent, like a large cloud streaked with the rays of the sun. It was afflicted by arrows released by the enemy.

'"But the elephant was controlled by the skill and enterprise of the rider. It began to fling away enemies, to the left and to the right. Like a herd of animals controlled in the forest by a cowherd with a staff, the soldiers were repeatedly afflicted by Bhagadatta. A grievous sound of lamentation arose among the fleeing Pandaveyas, like the cawing of crows when they are quickly attacked by a hawk. O king! When goaded by the hook, the king of elephants looked like a winged mountain in ancient times. It afflicted the enemy with great fear, like a group of traders at the sight of a turbulent ocean. As they ran away in fright, the elephants, charioteers, horses and kings made a terrible noise. O king! In that battle, it filled the earth, the directions and the sub-directions. The king was astride that supreme of elephants and severely oppressed the army of the enemy. This was like Virochana against the army of the gods in ancient times, when it was well-protected in battle by the gods. The friend of the fire[87] began to blow violently and created dust. This covered the sky and the soldiers in a short instant. The people thought that a single elephant had become hundreds of elephants and began to run away in every direction."'

[86]Back to Bhagadatta.
[87]The wind is the friend of the fire.

Chapter 1003(26)

'Sanjaya said, "You have asked me about the deeds performed by Partha in that battle. O great king! Listen to what Partha accomplished in that battle. On seeing that a dust had arisen and on hearing the roar of the elephant, when Bhagadatta caused subjugation, Kounteya spoke to Krishna. 'O Madhusudana! It is certain that this tumult has been caused by the elephant of the king of Pragjyotisha, when he has swiftly attacked. He is not inferior to Indra in battle. He is skilled in steering an elephant. In my view, on this earth, he is the first or the second.[88] He possesses the best of elephants and there is no elephant which can withstand it in battle. It can tolerate all the sounds of battle. It is accomplished in deeds and has conquered exhaustion. O unblemished one! It can tolerate the downpour of all weapons and can even bear the touch of fire. It is evident that it will destroy the Pandava army today. With the exception of the two of us, there is no one who is capable of countering it. Therefore, swiftly go to the spot where the lord of Pragjyotisha is. He is Shakra's friend.[89] He is strong because of the elephant. He should be marvelled at, despite his age. I will dispatch him today, as a beloved guest, to the destroyer of Bala.' As soon as Savyasachi spoke these words, Krishna left and went to the spot where Bhagadatta was mauling the Pandava army. As he was going there, fourteen thousand maharatha samshaptakas summoned him from the back. O lord of men! Ten thousand of those were Trigartas and another four thousand were followers of Vasudeva.[90] O venerable one! On seeing that Bhagadatta was shattering the army and on also being challenged, he[91] was caught in two minds and thought, 'What is the best course of action for me? Should I return here, or

[88]In fighting with elephants. Effectively meaning that there is no one superior to Bhagadatta.

[89]Bhagadatta was Indra's friend.

[90]These were the followers of Krishna who participated on the Kourava side in the war.

[91]Arjuna.

should I go to Yudhishthira?' O extender of the Kuru lineage! Thus
did Arjuna reflect in his mind and decided that he should kill the
samshaptakas. The one with the foremost of monkeys on his banner
suddenly returned. Vasava's son wished to single-handedly kill
thousands of rathas in battle. This is what Duryodhana and Karna
had also plotted, when the two of them had thought about means of
killing Arjuna. That is the reason they had arranged for this divided
feeling in Pandava's mind. But he foiled them by deciding to take on
those foremost of rathas on his chariot.

'"O king! The maharatha samshaptakas shot hundreds and
thousands of arrows with drooping tufts towards Arjuna. O king!
Enveloped by those arrows, Partha, Kunti's son, Krishna Janardana,
the horses and the chariot could not be seen. Janardana was deprived
on his senses and began to sweat. At this, Partha used the vajra
weapon and killed most of them. Hundreds of arms, still holding
bowstrings and bows, were severed. Standards, horses, charioteers
and rathas fell down on the ground. Slain by Partha's arrows and
bereft of their riders, elephants fell down on the ground. They were
like mountain summits with trees and looked like well-crafted rain
clouds. Their seats and harnesses were shredded. Their temples
were shattered and they were destroyed. Wounded by Partha's
arrows, horses fell down, together with their riders. With their
arms severed, but still holding on to swords, shields, scimitars like
nails, clubs and battleaxes, men were brought down by Kiriti's
broad-headed arrows. O venerable one! There were youthful and
dazzling heads, as beautiful as the morning sun, the lotus, or the
moon. These were severed by Arjuna's arrows. The enemy soldiers
who were slaughtered by the enraged Phalguna, with arrows that fed
on lives, seemed to blaze in many different forms. The soldiers were
agitated, like lotuses by an elephant. Masses of beings applauded
and worshipped Dhananjaya. On witnessing Partha's deeds there,
like those of Vasava himself, Madhava was overcome by great
wonder and applauded him with his hands. Having killed most of
the samshaptakas who were stationed there, Partha urged Krishna
to take him to Bhagadatta."'

Chapter 1004(27)

'Sanjaya said, "According to Partha's wishes, Krishna urged the horses, which were as swift as thought, white and caparisoned in gold, and drove them towards Drona's army. While that best of the Kurus departed to save those on his side who were tormented by Drona, Susharma and his brothers followed him from the rear, wishing to do battle. The unvanquished Jaya, possessor of the white horses, spoke to Krishna. 'O Achyuta! Susharma and his brothers are challenging me. O destroyer of enemies! Our soldiers are being shattered towards the north. Because of the samshaptakas, I am again caught in two minds now. Should I kill the samshaptakas or should I protect our soldiers who are afflicted by the enemy? Know that this is what I am thinking of. What is more beneficial for me?' Having been thus addressed, Dasharha reversed the chariot and took Pandava to the spot where the lord of Trigarta was challenging him. Arjuna pierced Susharma with seven swift arrows and brought down his standard and bow with a razor-sharp arrow. Partha then used six iron arrows to swiftly send the brother of the lord of Trigarta, his horses and his charioteer to Yama's abode. At this, Susharma grasped an iron javelin that was like a serpent and hurled this towards him, also throwing a spear at Vasudeva. Arjuna used three arrows to shatter the javelin and another three to fragment the spear. He then confounded Susharma with his storm of arrows and forced him to retreat. O king! Like Vasava pouring down rain, he showered down many fierce arrows on your soldiers and there was no one who could oppose him. Dhananjaya advanced, slaying all the maharatha Kouravas with his arrows, like a fire consuming dry wood. Like beings who cannot bear the touch of fire, no one was capable of withstanding the force of Kunti's intelligent son.

'"O king! Pandava showered down arrows on the assembled army, and like Suparna[92] swooping down, approached Pragjyotisha. Jishnu held the bow which was like the granter of boons to virtuous Bharatas

---

[92]Garuda.

and was the bringer of tears to enemies in battle. O king! Because of your son's deceit in gambling with the dice, Arjuna grasped the bow that would destroy kshatriyas. O great king! Thus it was that your army was agitated by Partha, like a boat that is shattered when it strikes a mountain. Ten thousand archers advanced. Those angry and brave ones had made up their minds to do battle, regardless of victory or defeat. Their hearts were devoid of fear. Headed towards calamity, they obstructed the ratha's path. Partha was capable of handling a grave burden and could withstand all burdens in battle. He was like an enraged elephant with rent temples that is sixty years of age and is let loose on a forest of lotuses, destroying it. In that fashion, Partha shattered your army. When the soldiers were thus being crushed, King Bhagadatta suddenly attacked Dhananjaya on that elephant. The tiger among men remained on his chariot and received him. A tumultuous encounter commenced between the chariot and the elephant, when the two brave ones, Bhagadatta and Dhananjaya, fought each other. The elephant was like a cloud and Lord Bhagadatta, who was like Indra, showered down arrows on Dhananjaya. Vasava's son repulsed that shower of arrows released by the valiant Bhagadatta with his own shower of arrows and sliced them down before they could reach him. O descendant of the Bharata lineage! King Pragjyotisha also repulsed that shower of arrows and tried to kill the mighty-armed Partha and Krishna with his arrows. Those two were enveloped with a giant shower of arrows and he urged the elephant on, to kill Achyuta and Partha. On seeing that the elephant was descending, like angry Death, Janardana quickly wheeled the chariot, so that it[93] remained on the left. Dhananjaya thus got an opportunity to slay the mighty elephant and its rider. But remembering his dharma, he did not do this.[94] O venerable one! That elephant descended on elephants, chariots and horses and dispatched them to the world of the dead. At this, Dhananjaya was enraged."'

[93]The elephant.
[94]The rules of fair combat required one to fight from the front, not the sides or the rear.

Chapter 1005(28)

'Dhritarashtra asked, "Having been enraged, how did Pandava act against Bhagadatta? What did Pragjyotisha do to Partha? Tell me everything as it happened."

'Sanjaya replied, "When Dasharha and Pandava were thus engaged with Pragjyotisha, all the beings thought that they had reached the jaws of death. O lord! Stationed on the neck of the elephant, Bhagadatta incessantly showered down arrows on the two Krishnas,[95] as they were stationed on the chariot. He stretched his bow back to its full extent and pierced Devaki's son with black arrows that were completely made out of iron, gold-tufted and sharpened on stone. Released by Bhagadatta, they were sharp and their touch was like that of the fire. Those arrows pierced Devaki's son and penetrated the ground. At this, Partha severed his bow and his quiver and began to fight with King Bhagadatta, as if he was sporting with him. He[96] hurled fourteen javelins at Savyasachi. They were sharp and were as bright as the rays of the sun. But he sliced each of them down into three fragments. Then the son of Paka's destroyer[97] penetrated the elephant's armour with his net of arrows and it looked like a king of mountains, covered with clouds. Pragjyotisha hurled a javelin towards Vasudeva. It had a golden handle and was made completely out of iron. Arjuna severed it into two fragments. Arjuna used his arrows to slice down the king's umbrella and standard. He then smiled and swiftly pierced the lord of the mountains with ten arrows. He was thus pierced by Arjuna's arrows, which had excellent tufts and the feathers of herons. Bhagadatta became angry at the great-souled Pandava. He hurled javelins towards his head and roared. In that battle, these dislodged Arjuna's diadem. Phalguna adjusted the diadem back and spoke these words to the king. 'Look upon this world with delight.'[98] Having been thus addressed, he grasped

[95]Krishna is one of Arjuna's names.
[96]Bhagadatta.
[97]Indra is Paka's destroyer and Arjuna was Indra's son.
[98]Implying that Bhagadatta would not look upon the world for long.

a radiant bow and angrily showered down arrows on Pandava and Govinda. Partha severed his bow and destroyed his quiver and quickly struck him with seventy-two arrows that afflicted all his inner organs.

'"Having been thus pierced and pained, he angrily resorted to the vaishnava weapon. He invoked the mantra on his goad and hurled it towards Pandava's chest.[99] That weapon was capable of slaying everything and was released by Bhagadatta. Covering Partha, Keshava received it on his own chest. On Keshava's chest, that weapon became the *vaijayanti* garland.[100] Distressed in his mind, Arjuna spoke to Keshava. 'O Janardana! You are not supposed to fight. You are only supposed to steer my horses. O Pundarikaksha! This is what you said. But you did not keep your promise. If I am in distress, or if I am incapable of countering, it is only then that you should act in this way. You should not act in this way if I am standing. With my arrows and with my bow, I am capable of conquering all the worlds, with the gods, the asuras and humans. This is known to you.' Having been thus addressed by Arjuna, Vasudeva replied in these words. 'O Partha! O unblemished one! Listen to this ancient and secret account. I am engaged in saving the worlds and have four forms. For the sake of the welfare of the worlds, I divide myself into different parts. One of my forms is based on earth and is engaged in austerities. Another form beholds the virtuous and evil deeds in the universe. Another form resorts to the world of men and performs deeds. The fourth and final form lies down and sleeps for a thousand years. This form of mine awakes at the end of a thousand years and at that time, grants the best of boons to those who are deserving of boons. On one such occasion, the earth got to know and, for the sake of Naraka,[101] asked a boon from me. Listen to this. "Having

[99]Any divine weapon possessed the characteristic that with the appropriate mantra, any object could be invested with the power of the weapon. Thus, the vaishnava weapon was invoked on the goad.

[100]While vaijayanti literally means a garland that portends of victory, it is also the name of Vishnu's garland or necklace.

[101]The demon Naraka was the earth's son.

obtained the vaishnava weapon, let it be such that my son cannot be killed by gods and asuras. Grant me this boon." In ancient times, having heard of this boon, I gave the invincible vaishnava weapon to the earth's son and said, "O earth! Let this weapon be infallible in protecting Naraka. No one will be able to kill him. Protected by this weapon, your son will be able to crush the armies of all enemies. He will always be invincible in all the worlds." Having been thus addressed, the intelligent goddess departed, her wishes having been fulfilled. That is how Naraka, the scorcher of enemies, became invincible. O Partha! It was from him that Pragjyotisha obtained this weapon of mine.[102] O venerable one! There is no one in the worlds, not even Indra and Rudra, who cannot be killed by it. It is for your sake that I repulsed the weapon and violated my pledge. O Partha! The great asura has now lost his supreme weapon. Kill him, as I killed Naraka earlier, for the sake of welfare. The invincible Bhagadatta is your enemy in battle. He is an enemy of the gods.'[103] Thus addressed by the great-souled Keshava, Partha suddenly shrouded Bhagadatta with sharp arrows. Without any fear, the mighty-armed and high-minded Partha struck the elephant between its frontal lobes with an iron arrow. That arrow struck the elephant, like the vajra against a mountain. It penetrated right up to its tufts, like a snake entering a termite hill. With its limbs paralysed, it fell down and struck the ground with its tusks. The giant elephant roared in woe and gave up its life. Partha then used an arrow with a drooping tuft, with a head that was in the shape of the half-moon, and pierced King Bhagadatta in the heart with this. With his heart thus pierced by Kiriti, King Bhagadatta let go of his bow and arrows and lost his life. His head fell down and so did the beautiful goad, like a petal falling off a lotus, when the stalk of the lotus has been destroyed. Garlanded in gold, he fell down from the golden housing on the elephant that was like a mountain. He was like a blossoming karnikara,[104] dislodged

[102]Naraka was killed by Krishna, when he began to oppress women. Naraka ruled in Pragjyotisha and Bhagadatta was Naraka's son.

[103]Bhagadatta was actually Indra's friend.

[104]The Indian laburnum.

from the summit of a mountain by the violent force of the wind.
The king was like Indra in his valour. He was Indra's friend and was
killed by Indra's son in the battle. Desiring victory, the men then
began to shatter the ones on your side, like the strength of the wind
unleashed on trees.'"

Chapter 1006(29)

'Sanjaya said, "The infinitely energetic Pragjyotisha was Indra's
beloved friend. Having killed him, Arjuna circumambulated
him. The two sons of the king of Gandhara, the brothers Vrishaka
and Achala, the conquerors of enemy cities, began to afflict Arjuna
in the battle. Those two brave archers united and pierced Arjuna
severely from the front and the back, using extremely swift and
sharp arrows. In an instant, Partha used sharp arrows to pierce the
horses, charioteer, bow, umbrella, chariot and standard of Vrishaka,
Subala's son. Arjuna again used a storm of arrows and many other
weapons. He oppressed the Gandhara soldiers, with Subala's
son at the forefront. There were five hundred brave Gandhara
warriors, with their weapons raised. The enraged Dhananjaya
used arrows to send them to the world of the dead. With his horses
slain, the mighty-armed one[105] quickly descended from his chariot
and ascending onto his brother's chariot, grasped another bow.
Those two brothers, Vrishaka and Achala, were stationed on the
same chariot. They repeatedly pierced Bibhatsu with a shower of
arrows. Those two great-souled kings, Vrishaka and Achala, your
brothers-in-law, severely wounded Partha, like Indra against Vritra
and Bala. Those two from Gandhara were themselves not injured,
but successful in striking the target, again struck Pandava. It was
like the months of summer and monsoon, afflicting the world with

---

[105]Vrishaka.

sweat and rain.[106] Those two kings, tigers among men, Vrishaka
and Achala, were stationed on the same chariot. O king! They were
stationed next to each other and Arjuna slew them with a single
arrow. They were like lions, giant-armed and with red eyes. They
were brothers and possessed similar features. Those two brave
ones lost their lives and fell down from the chariot. Their bodies,
loved by their relatives, fell down from the chariot onto the ground.
They lay there, spreading their sacred fame in the ten directions. O
lord of the earth! On seeing that their maternal uncles, who never
retreated, had been slain in the battle, your sons fiercely showered
down weapons.

'"Shakuni was skilled in a hundred different kinds of maya. On
seeing that his brothers had been killed, he confused the two Krishnas
with his maya. Sticks, iron balls, shataghnis, javelins, clubs, maces,
swords, spears, bludgeons, spikes, kampanas, scimitars, nails, mallets,
battleaxes, razors, kshurapras, hollow arrows,[107] vatsadantas,
weapons with joints, chakras, tufted arrows, darts and many other
weapons showered down on Arjuna from all the directions. Asses,
camels, buffaloes, lions, tigers, small deer,[108] kites, bears, wolves,
vultures, monkeys, reptiles and many other kinds of flesh-eaters[109]
hungrily dashed towards Arjuna. Many diverse kinds of crows angrily
rushed towards him. Kunti's son, the brave Dhananjaya, was skilled
in the use of divine weapons. He suddenly unleashed a net of arrows
and attacked them. The arrows released by the brave one were firm
and excellent and they were slain by these. They let out a giant wail,
as all of them were slain and destroyed. Darkness then appeared

---

[106]The text should be translated as two months, not several months. An
alternative translation of two months of summer, excluding the monsoon, is
also possible.

[107]*Nalika*s. However, these can be any hollowed weapon.

[108]The word used is *srimara*. While this is a kind of small deer, in general
it also means an animal that frequents marshy places and has been identified
as nilgai.

[109]The word used is rakshasas. But in this context, the more general flesh-
eater is more appropriate.

and enveloped Arjuna's chariot.[110] From within that darkness, a cruel voice censured Arjuna. But Arjuna destroyed this with the mighty weapon known as jyotisha.[111] When that was destroyed, a terrible flood of water appeared. For destroying this, Arjuna used the weapon named aditya. Thanks to this weapon, the water was almost completely dried up. Subala's son repeatedly resorted to many different kinds of maya. But Arjuna laughed and used the strength of his weapons to destroy them all. When his maya was destroyed, Shakuni was injured by Arjuna's arrows. He fled on his swift horses, like an ordinary man.

'"Arjuna was the best among those who were skilled in the use of weapons and he showed his nature to the enemy. He showered down a flood of arrows on the Kourava army. The army of your son was slaughtered by Partha. O great king! It became divided into two, like the Ganga when it confronts a mountain. O king! Some maharathas sought shelter with Drona. Others were afflicted by Kiriti and went to Duryodhana. Since they were covered by darkness, we could not see the soldiers or him then. I heard the twang of Gandiva on my south.[112] There was the sound of conch shells and drums and the noise of musical instruments. Gandiva's roar could be heard above all of these. A fight then again commenced towards the south, between wonderful warriors and Arjuna. However, I followed Drona. O descendant of the Bharata lineage! At that time, the many different divisions in your son's army were slaughtered by Arjuna, like the wind scattering clouds in the sky. Like Vasava raining down copiously, the great archer and tiger among men showered down a flood of arrows and no one could counter the fierce one. Those on your side were killed by Partha and were severely afflicted. As they fled hither and thither, they killed many on their own side. The arrows shot by Arjuna were tufted with the feathers of herons and were capable of penetrating the body. They descended like locusts that covered the ten directions. O venerable one! Horses, charioteers, elephants were

[110]This was part of Shakuni's maya too.
[111]Jyotisha has several meanings. It can also be translated as light.
[112]Alternatively, my right.

pierced and the arrows then penetrated the ground, like snakes into a termite hill. He did not shoot a second arrow at any elephant, horse or man. Shot by a single arrow, they fell down, losing their lives. Men and horses were slain everywhere. Elephants were struck by arrows and brought down. At that time, dogs, jackals and wild crows howled and the field of battle looked wonderful. Oppressed by arrows, father abandoned son, well-wisher abandoned well-wisher and son abandoned father. Everyone sought to protect himself. Oppressed by Partha, they abandoned their mounts.'''

Chapter 1007(30)

'Dhritarashtra asked, "O Sanjaya! When those divisions were shattered by Pandu's son and fled quickly, what was the state of your mind then? When divisions are shattered and do not see a place where they can make a stand, it is very difficult to counter this. O Sanjaya! Tell me everything about this."

'Sanjaya replied, "O lord of the earth! Despite this, there were those who wished to bring pleasure to your son. To preserve their fame in this world, those brave ones followed Drona. They raised their weapons and approached Yudhishthira. They performed noble and terrible deeds and were truly fearless. O lord! They detected a weakness in the infinitely energetic Bhimasena, the brave Satyaki and Dhrishtadyumna. The Panchalas cruelly urged, 'Drona! Drona!' However, your sons urged all the Kurus, 'Not Drona!' One side said, 'Drona! Drona!' The other side said, 'Not Drona!' The Kurus and the Pandavas seemed to be gambling over Drona. Wherever Drona sought to attack the chariots of the Panchalas, Panchala Dhrishtadyumna stationed himself at those spots. There was a terrible battle where one did not follow the respective divisions. Brave ones clashed against brave ones and roared against the enemy. The enemy was incapable of making the Pandavas tremble there. But because they remembered their own hardships, they made the enemy divisions waver. Though they were modest, they were overcome by anger and driven by their spirit. They were prepared to give up their lives and sought to kill Drona in that great battle. There was a tumultuous battle, in which, those infinitely energetic ones offered their lives as stake. It was as if iron was clashing against rock. Even the aged could not remember a battle like this. O great king! Such had not been witnessed earlier, nor heard of. When those brave ones were slaughtered, the earth trembled, oppressed by the great burden of those two oceans of soldiers. As the armies whirled around, the firmament seemed to roar and stand still. Ajatashatru angrily advanced against your son. Drona roamed around in that battle. He approached the Pandu army and shattered it with thousands of sharp arrows. They were routed by Drona's extraordinary deeds. Then the commander[113] himself engaged with Drona and there was an extraordinary battle between Drona and Panchala. It is my view that there has never been anything that is equal to this.

"'Like a fire, Nila burnt down the Kuru army. The arrows were the sparks and he was like a fire burning down dry wood. When he was burning down the soldiers, Drona's powerful son, who had wished to have an encounter with him from earlier times,[114] smilingly addressed him. 'O Nila! What will you gain by burning down these warriors with the rays of your arrows? Fight with me and angrily strike me with your swift arrows.' Nila's eyes were like the petals of lotuses. He pierced the one whose face was as beautiful as a blooming lotus and whose body was like a collection of lotuses.[115] On being thus suddenly pierced, Drona's son used three sharp and broad-headed arrows to slice down the bow, standard and umbrella of the enemy. Nila swiftly jumped down from his chariot and grasped a shield and a supreme sword, wishing to sever, like a bird,[116] the head of Drona's son from his body. O unblemished one! But Drona's son smiled. He

---

[113]Dhrishtadyumna.

[114]Nila was the king of Mahishmati and there was an ancient enmity between him and Ashvatthama.

[115]Nila pierced Ashvatthama.

[116]The image is of a bird flying away with a prey in its talons.

used a broad-headed arrow to sever his head, with a beautiful nose and with earrings, from his body. The face was as radiant as the full moon. The eyes were like the petals of lotuses. The shoulders were elevated and he[117] was tall. He was slain and fell down on the ground. At this, the Pandava soldiers were distressed and became extremely anxious. Blazing in his energy, Nila was killed by the son of the preceptor. O venerable one! All the Pandava maharathas began to think, 'How will Vasava's son be able to save us from the enemy? The brave one is engaged in fighting with the soldiers in the southern direction, with the remaining soldiers in the samshaptaka and narayana army.'"'

Chapter 1008 (31)

'Sanjaya said, "Vrikodara could not tolerate the slaughter of the soldiers. He struck Bahlika with sixty and Karna with ten arrows. Drona wished to kill him and used sharp and iron arrows that were whetted at the tip and penetrated the inner organs to swiftly strike him, wishing to take away his life. Karna pierced him with twelve arrows, Ashvatthama with seven and King Duryodhana with six. But the immensely strong Bhimasena pierced all of them back in return. He struck Drona with fifty arrows, Karna with ten arrows, Duryodhana with twelve and Drona's son with eight swift arrows. Having engaged in that battle, he let out a loud roar. They fought, prepared to give up their lives, and death was easily achieved. Ajatashatru sent many warriors, instructing them to save Bhima. Those infinitely energetic ones approached near Bhimasena. There were Yuyudhana and the others and the two Pandavas who were Madri's sons. Those bulls among men were angry and united. They advanced, wishing to shatter Drona's army, which was protected by the supreme among great archers. Those immensely valorous ones,

[117]Nila.

Bhima and the other rathas, advanced and were fiercely received by
Drona and the best of rathas. Those brave and immensely strong
atirathas were the ornaments of any battle. Outwardly giving up all
fear of death, those on your side fought with the Pandavas. Riders
killed riders and rathas killed rathas. The battle commenced, lances
against lances, and with swords and battleaxes. There was a terrible
clash with swords and it led to a cruel carnage. Because of the clash
of elephants, the battle became extremely dreadful. Some fell down
from elephants. Others fell down from horses, their heads hanging
down. O venerable one! Other men fell down from chariots, pierced
by arrows. Others were crushed in that encounter and fell down,
shorn of their armour. Elephants attacked the chests and crushed
the heads. In other places, elephants crushed men who had fallen
down. Elephants struck the ground with their tusks and mangled
many rathas. Other men were crushed by elephants that were pierced
with weapons. Hundreds of elephants roamed around and crushed
hundreds of men. There were men with bronze armour on their
bodies and horses, chariots and elephants. They fell down and were
crushed by elephants, as if they were thick reeds. Kings lay down
to sleep on beds made out of the feathers of vultures.[118] They were
modest. But having been ripened by time, they lay down on beds of
great distress. Advancing on a chariot, the father killed the son. Out
of confusion and disregarding all honour, the son killed the father.
Wheels of chariots were shattered. Standards were torn. Umbrellas
were shredded and brought down. Dragging broken yokes, horses
ran away. Arms wielding swords were brought down. Heads sporting
earrings were severed. Powerful elephants threw down chariots and
crushed them down on the ground. Charioteers struck elephants
with iron arrows and brought them down. Severely wounded by
elephants, riders fell down from horses. A cruel and great battle
raged and it was extremely terrible. 'Alas, father! Alas, son! Friend,
where are you? Stay! Where are you going? Strike! Capture! Kill!'
These and other words mixed with the roars and sounds of laughter
and many other kinds of noise were spoken and heard. The blood

---

[118]That is, on beds made out of arrows.

of men, horses and elephants mingled together. The dust that arose from the ground was pacified.[119] Those who were cowards became distressed. They dragged each other by the hair. There were terrible fights with fists. Brave ones fought with nails and teeth, wishing to find refuge where no refuge could be found. Heroes raised swords in their arms, but those were severed. So were others holding bows, arrows or goads. Someone loudly challenged another. Someone else fled, running away. Others confronted others and severed the head from the body. Some attacked others with loud roars. Others were severely frightened at the sounds and fled. Some killed the enemy, or those on one's own side, with sharp arrows. Elephants that were like the peaks of mountains were brought down by iron arrows. They lay down, like islands in a river during the summer. There were elephants that exuded musth like mountainous streams. They crushed chariots down on the ground with their feet, together with the horses and the charioteers. There were brave ones who were skilled in the use of weapons. On seeing that they were covered with blood, but were still striking each other, those who were cowards and weak in heart lost their senses. Everyone was distressed and nothing could be distinguished. Despite the dust raised by the soldiers, the cruel battle raged on.

'"The commander[120] said, 'Make haste. This is the time.' He swiftly led the Pandavas, who were always full of enterprise. Having been thus instructed, the illustrious Pandaveyas advanced towards Drona's chariot, wishing to kill him, like swans descending on a lake. 'Seize! Do not flee! Do not be scared! Cut him down!' These and other sounds were heard in the vicinity of the invincible one's chariot. Drona, Kripa, Karna, Drona's son, King Jayadratha, Vinda and Anuvinda from Avanti and Shalya repulsed them. The Panchalas and the Pandavas were noble in their dharma. They were angry. They were difficult to counter and difficult to resist. Though oppressed by arrows, they did not withdraw from Drona. Drona became extremely enraged and released hundreds of arrows, causing a great carnage

[119]Because of the blood.
[120]Dhrishtadyumna.

among the Chedis, Panchalas and Pandavas. O venerable one! The twang of his bowstring and the slapping of his palms were heard in all the directions. They were like the sound of thunder and caused fright among many of the Pandavas.

'"At this time, having slain the powerful samshaptakas, Jishnu arrived at the spot where Drona was crushing the Pandus. He had crossed many whirlpools made out of arrows and giant lakes made out of blood. Having crossed them and having killed the samshaptakas, Phalguna showed himself. He was the accomplisher of deeds. He was like the sun in his energy. The one with the monkey on his banner was seen to be radiant in his energy. He had dried up the ocean of the samshaptakas with the rays of his weapons. Pandava now scorched the Kurus, like the sun at the destruction of a yuga. All the Kurus were burnt by the energy of Arjuna's weapons, like a comet that has arisen and destroys all beings at the end of a yuga.[121] Elephants, horses, rathas and warriors were struck by the thousands of arrows released by him and oppressed by these arrows, discarded their weapons and fell down on the ground. Some wailed in lamentation. Still others roared. Slain by Partha's arrows, some fell down, deprived of their lives. Remembering the vow of warriors, Arjuna did not kill the warriors who had fallen down, or were falling down, or were retreating. Most of the Kurus were shattered and, devoid of their chariots, were in retreat. They called upon Karna for protection. On discerning the lamentation and the cries for refuge, Adhiratha's son assured them that they need not be frightened and advanced in Arjuna's direction. He was foremost among all the Bharata rathas and was the one who brought delight to all the Bharatas. He was supreme among those who knew about weapons and he invoked the agneya weapon. A mass of blazing arrows was released by the one who wielded a blazing bow. But Dhananjaya repulsed that mass of arrows with his net of arrows. Weapon was countered by weapon and these arrows preserved life.

---

[121]The word used in the text is dhumaketu. While this means comet, it can also be translated as something that has smoke as its banner, that is, a fire.

'"Dhrishtadyumna, Bhima and maharatha Satyaki approached Karna and each pierced him with three swift arrows. Radheya countered Arjuna's weapon with his own shower of arrows. He then used three tufted arrows to sever the bows of those three. With their weapons gone, those brave ones were like snakes without venom. They hurled javelins from their chariots and roared like lions. Those javelins hurled from their arms were immensely forceful. Those mighty javelins were like snakes and blazed. They descended towards the chariot of Adhiratha's son. But Karna severed them with three swift arrows and powerfully shooting arrows at Partha, roared. Arjuna pierced Radheya with seven swift arrows. With three sharp arrows, he then killed Karna's younger brother. Partha killed Shatrunjaya with six arrows. As Vipatha stood on his chariot, he severed his head with a broad-headed arrow.[122] While the sons of Dhritarashtra looked on, Kiriti single-handedly killed the three, who were foremost among the brothers of the son of the suta. Bhima leapt down from his chariot, like Vinata's son.[123] With a supreme sword, he killed the fifteen who were guarding Karna's flank. He then again ascended his chariot and grasped another bow. He pierced Karna with ten arrows and his charioteer and horses with five. Dhrishtadyumna grasped a supreme sword and a lustrous shield. With these, he killed Chandravarma and Pourava Brihatkshatra. Panchala then ascended his chariot and grasped another bow. In that battle, he pierced Karna with seventy-three arrows and roared. Shini's descendant grasped another bow that was like Indra's weapon in its radiance. He pierced the suta's son with sixty-four arrows and roared like a lion. With two broad-headed arrows that were released well, he severed Karna's bow. He again pierced Karna in the arms and the chest with three arrows. Radheya was about to be submerged in the ocean that Satyaki represented. At this, Duryodhana, Drona and King Jayadratha rescued him. Dhrishtadyumna, Bhima, Subhadra's son, Arjuna himself, Nakula and Sahadeva began to protect Satyaki in that battle.

---

[122]Shatrunjaya and Vipatha are sometimes stated to have been Karna's sons, though they are described as brothers here.
[123]Garuda.

'"Thus the extremely terrible battle between those on your side and that of the enemy raged. It was destructive of all archers. They were prepared to give up their lives. Infantry, chariots, elephants and horses fought with elephants, horses, chariots and infantry. Chariots fought with elephants and infantry, chariots fought with infantry and chariots fought with elephants. Horses fought with horses, elephants with elephants and chariots with chariots. Infantry was seen to be engaged with infantry. Thus did that extremely fierce battle continue and it caused delight to flesh-eating creatures. Those great warriors were without fear and this extended Yama's kingdom. Many men, rathas, horses and elephants were killed there by elephants, rathas, horses and infantry. Elephants were killed by elephants, rathas by armed rathas, horses by horses and large numbers of infantry by infantry. Elephants were slain by rathas, giant horses by the best of elephants, men by horses and horses by the supreme of rathas. Tongues were lolling out. Teeth and eyes were gouged out. Armour and ornaments were shattered. Destroyed, they fell down on the ground. There were many others who were struck down by the best of warriors. They fell down on the ground with fearful visages. They were mangled and crushed by the feet of horses and elephants. They were severely hurt and wounded by the wheels of chariots and hooves. It brought delight to carnivorous beasts, birds and flesh-eaters. There was a terrible carnage of people there. Those extremely strong ones were angry. Using the utmost of their energy, they sought to kill each other. When the strength of both sides was severely diminished, they glanced towards each other, their bodies drenched with blood. The sun was stationed above the mountain on which it sets. O descendant of the Bharata lineage! The armies retreated to their respective camps."'

The sixth volume completes Drona Parva and features the deaths of Abhimanyu, Jayadratha, Ghatotkacha and Drona. The Narayana weapon is released at Arjuna, following which Bhagadatta is killed. Some of the most ferocious fighting in the Kurukshetra war takes place in Drona Parva, specifically, in this volume. At the close of this volume, the war is virtually over and Karna assumes the mantle of commander-in-chief after Drona's death.

About the Translator

Bibek Debroy is a member of NITI Aayog, the successor to the Planning Commission. He is an economist who has published popular articles, papers and books on economics. Before NITI Aayog, he has worked in academic institutes, industry chambers and for the government. Bibek Debroy also writes on Indology and Sanskrit. Penguin published his translation of the Bhagavad Gita in 2006 and *Sarama and Her Children: The Dog in Indian Myth* in 2008. The 10-volume unabridged translation of the Mahabharata was sequentially published between 2010 and 2014 and he is now translating the Hari Vamsha, to be published in 2016. Bibek Debroy was awarded the Padma Shri in 2015.